WORDSWORTH CLASSICS
OF WORLD LITERATURE

General Editor: Tom Griffith

LE MORTE DARTHUR

D0028277

Sir Thomas Malory
Le Morte Darthur

❖

With an Introduction by Helen Moore

WORDSWORTH CLASSICS
OF WORLD LITERATURE

For my husband
ANTHONY JOHN RANSON
with love from your wife, the publisher
Eternally grateful for your
unconditional love

Readers who are interested in other titles from
Wordsworth Editions are invited to visit our
website at www.wordsworth-editions.com

First printed and published by William Caxton 1485

This edition published 1996 by Wordsworth Editions Limited
8B East Street, Ware, Hertfordshire SG 12 9HJ

ISBN 978 1 85326 463 4

Wordsworth Editions is
the company founded in 1987 by
MICHAEL TRAYLER

Typeset in Great Britain by Antony Gray
Printed and bound by Clays Ltd, St Ives plc

INTRODUCTION

The Writer and his Times The precise identity of the Sir Thomas Malory who wrote *Le Morte Darthur* has always been shrouded in mystery, and has provoked much speculation. The work itself provides one piece of significant information. This comes at the end of the book, when the author reveals that he is a knight and that he completed his work in 'the ninth year of the reign of King Edward the Fourth' (p. 804), that is, sometime between 4 March 1469 and 3 March 1470. The leading candidate for identification as the author of *Le Morte Darthur* is Sir Thomas Malory of Newbold Revel in Warwickshire.[*] He was probably born between 1414 and 1418, and died on 12 or 14 March 1471.[†] The son of John and Philippa Malory, Thomas is first recorded in 1439, as witness to a legal settlement made by his cousin. The first reference to Thomas as a knight comes in 1441, so he must have been knighted at some point in the intervening years.[‡] Malory's wife was called Elizabeth (the date of their marriage is unknown) and they had at least two children: Robert, their heir, and Thomas, who probably died around 1457.[§]

Malory's later life overlapped with the period of English history sometimes called the 'Wars of the Roses', indicating the period

---

[*] P. J. C. Field, in *The Life and Times of Sir Thomas Malory* (Woodbridge, 1993), pp. 8–24, discusses and discounts the five other fifteenth-century men called Thomas Malory who are possible contenders. They are the Thomas Malorys of Holcot (Northamptonshire), Papworth St Agnes (Cambridgeshire), Tachbrook Mallory (Warwickshire), Long Whatton (Leicestershire) and Hutton Conyers (Yorkshire).
[†] *Ibid.,* pp. 64 and 34
[‡] *Ibid.,* pp. 83–4
[§] *Ibid.,* pp. 84 and 121

1455–85, during which the two noble families of Lancaster and York, with their respective allies, were in conflict for the monarchy. The surviving records show that Malory's personal life was just as turbulent as the times in which he lived. The period 1440–51 saw him elected as member of parliament for Warwickshire (in 1445), and it is possible that he experienced military service overseas in Gascony (now part of France). He was also the subject of a succession of criminal charges, including wounding, theft, burglary, rape and extortion, and was even accused of laying an ambush for the Duke of Buckingham and breaking into the Duke's deer park. On his arrest in July 1451, Malory apparently broke out of prison, swam the moat and robbed an abbey before being recaptured and appearing before the Justices.* In extenuation of his subject, Malory's biographer makes the point that

> A combination of crimes and membership of parliament makes a
> pattern all too familiar to Englishmen in the middle of the
> fifteenth century. Malory was not the only man who was
> sometimes law-abiding or even a legislator, but who at other
> times ignored the law to take what he wanted or what he felt was
> his due.†

Malory spent most of the years 1452–60 in prison on these charges, but never came to trial. He was probably freed in around 1460, but was excluded by name from a general pardon issued by King Edward IV in 1468. He was again excluded from another general royal pardon in 1470. These two exclusions suggest that, for unknown reasons, Malory was regarded as posing a significant threat to the authorities. The fact that *Le Morte Darthur* was finished in prison would suggest that Malory's second period of imprisonment lasted from about 1468 to 1470, when Edward IV fled into exile.

In 1485, the printer William Caxton published his version of Malory's *Le Morte Darthur*. Caxton is an important figure in English literary history because he was probably the first man to set up a printing press in England. Caxton's version of Malory was the only one known until 1934, when the 'Winchester Manuscript' was

---

* For these incidents, see Field, *Life and Times,* pp. 86–102
† *Ibid.,* p. 102

discovered, which differs in many respects from Caxton's text.* It is therefore thought that Caxton's text and the Winchester Manuscript are different versions of Malory's original, which either no longer survives or has yet to be discovered.

Le Morte Darthur was written by a man who had first-hand experience of the vagaries of war, and knew the dangers of a political life. To this practical experience Malory added an extensive knowledge of, and enthusiasm for, the ideology, rhetoric and practice of chivalry as depicted in the lengthy French prose romances of the thirteenth century. He made use of the French prose works *Suite du Merlin*, the *Tristan* and the *Lancelot*, and two English poems – the alliterative *Morte Arthure* and the stanzaic *Morte Arthur*. It is these stories which provided Malory with most of the raw material for his *Morte Darthur*. Malory's approach to his sources combines the techniques of translation, abridgement and re-writing. He does not specify which source he is using at any moment, but instead makes use of formulaic phrases such as 'the book saith' or 'as the French book maketh mention'. These phrases are not, in fact, primarily intended to draw attention to any particular source. Rather, they serve a variety of narrative purposes peculiar to Malory's own text. A phrase such as 'the book saith' can signal an appeal to literary authority (p. 112), introduce a change from one topic or incident to another (p. 361) or indicate an explanation (p. 368). It can also be used for purposes of narrative recapitulation (p. 531) and for glossing over passages omitted from the sources (p. 741). It can even be employed in an apologetic or regretful sense, as when Malory records that 'as the book saith, Sir Launcelot began to resort unto Queen Guenever again' (p. 675).

The Work   *Le Morte Darthur* is a chivalric romance, which was one of the most enduringly popular types of literature in the Middle Ages and Renaissance. A chivalric romance is essentially a story detailing the adventures and loves of a single knight or a group of knights. It usually has a foreign or fantastic setting, and may include magical events. Love is an important theme in romance, so women often play a central role in the story and exercise considerable influence over the course of events. The significance of the heroines of *Le Morte Darthur*

---

* This manuscript has been edited by Eugène Vinaver and revised by P. J. C. Field as Sir Thomas Malory, *The Works*, 3rd edition (Oxford, 1990).

is indisputable: Launcelot and Tristram undertake mighty deeds for the service of Guenever and Isoud respectively, and both heroes experience madness brought on by the trials of love. An interesting development on the theme of the romance heroine is to be found in the character of Elaine, the Maid of Astolat. She spurns the confined life of the traditional heroine and instead takes on the questing, active behaviour of the knight in her search for Launcelot. Elaine, like the magical female figures, Morgan le Fay and the Lady of the Lake, defies categorisation: she is skilled in the female virtue of healing, but is also well versed in the rhetoric of desire and conquest which is more usually voiced by men (pp. 699–700 and 706). Even in death, she continues to speak of her love for Launcelot, as she arranges for her body to sail in a ship to Westminster, bearing a letter to the king and queen. The sight of her body in the ship functions as an eloquent declaration of unrequited love (p. 708).

A chivalric romance is usually concerned with war as well as with love, and Le Morte Darthur is no exception. The romance contains three main types of military activity – the combat, the tournament, and the battle. Combats occur during the course of a knight's adventuring, and may be either spontaneous or pre-arranged. They consist of a joust between two knights, often followed by a sword fight on foot when one, or both, of the knights has been unhorsed. The combat is a ritualised form of behaviour, and it is usually accompanied by formulaic verbal expressions of challenge, insult and acceptance of the combat. The combat between Sir Gareth and the Red Knight provides a good example of this sequence of rhetoric followed by action (pp. 204–5). The second type of military encounter, the tournament, is made up of a succession of individual or simultaneous combats, in a formalised setting. A tournament is called by a king, usually for purposes of military display. It is the primary medium for the exhibition of the knightly virtue of 'prowess', that is, skill with lance and sword. Particularly lavish and lengthy tournaments are held at Surluse (p. 435–49) and Lonazep (pp. 481–508). Genuine warfare is also very much a part of the matter of Le Morte Darthur. Arthur's reign begins and ends with war: his succession to the throne is followed by a drawn-out period of conflict with the eleven northern kings who oppose his claim (pp. 17–28) and the 'wicked day of destiny' which ends his reign is the battle near Salisbury (pp. 784–89). Even though the contents of Malory's work may have been largely dictated by the demands of his sources, and by the genre of chivalric romance as a whole, his literary individuality is not constrained by this circumstance. The detailed description of the combat between King Ban and the King of the Hundred Knights (p. 24), and the haunting vision (expanded from the poem *Morte Arthur*) of pillagers robbing the bodies after the battle near Salisbury (p. 791), both demonstrate Malory's consummate skill as a storyteller.

The themes of love and war, two essential elements of chivalric romance, are skilfully woven together by Malory in his depiction of family ties. Marriage alliances are often described as though they were the private equivalent of public combat and conciliation. For example, after Sir Gareth delivers Dame Lionesse from her enemy, he then marries her (p. 236). The alliance is further cemented by the marriage of his brothers Gaheris and Agravaine to her sister Linet and niece Laurel respectively. Thus the public world of war and the private world of love are united in marriage. As well as linking love and war, the theme of family is also one of the means Malory employs to bind together the disparate elements of his story, drawn as it is from many different sources. All the knights, from whichever source they originate, are slotted into a world which catalogues them according to their descent as well as their chivalric honour, or 'worship'. Galahad, for example, is defined according to his noble descent (from Launcelot) as well as his superlative achievement in the Grail quest. Parentage is of vital importance to all the knights in Malory's romance: it is an index of strength and heroism, and it links knights together in bonds of family loyalty. The two most significant family groupings in the *Morte Darthur* are the Launcelot group (which includes Sir Galahad, Sir Bors and Sir Ector) and the Orkney knights Gawaine, Gaheris, Agravaine and Mordred. In the middle stands Sir Gareth, brother to the Orkney knights but linked by allegiance to Launcelot. During the early stages of the romance, family loyalties are subjugated to the ideal of communal action, which is embodied in the Round Table. As Malory unfolds his story, however, he shows this communal ideal giving way under the pressure of partisan feuding and revenge. Intimations of the ultimate fate of the Round Table ideal begin to appear as early as Book X, in the account of the escalating hatred between Sir Lamorak and the Orkney knights. This conflict demonstrates the way in which the instinct towards private vengeance struggles against the demands of a public code. Malory threads references to this hatred throughout his work, and in particular the story of Lamorak's death at the hands of Gawaine and his brothers is referred to again and again (pp. 459, 461, 475, 537, 678). After a while, the death of Lamorak begins to achieve the quality of a refrain to the text, or a commentary upon it: every time it is mentioned it highlights the tension between private hate and public good which lies at the heart of the romance.

Despite the immense scope of his romance, Malory also gives attention to the personal, private moments which occur amidst great events. Thus he records the young Arthur's grief when he realises that Ector is not his real father (p. 8), and Launcelot's unfortunate tendency to 'clatter in his sleep' which alerts Guenever to the fact that he is with Elaine (p. 533). The indignant 'hemming' with which Guenever greets this discovery provides one of the most memorable and humorous moments in the romance. It might well be that Malory 'has no time for dallying with sentiment', as one critic has claimed,* but that does not mean that the romance is lacking in detail when it comes to depicting the lives and loves of its characters.

Le Morte Darthur is concerned not only with the practicalities of warfare, tournaments and love affairs, but also with the interpretation of these events in the wider context of existence. The romance abounds in acts of interpretation, decoding and prophecy. In this, the reader's experience is very much like that of the questing knight errant: just as the knight sets out into an unknown landscape in search of unknown adventures, and has to puzzle out the meaning of events as he goes along, so the reader must embark on a reading quest with the aim of discovering not only *what* is going to happen, but *how* and *why*. This feature of the romance is most evident in the Tale of the Sangreal (Books XIII–XVII) which is concerned not simply with chivalric achievement, but with the spiritual significance which lies behind the knights' adventures. The Sangreal (now more usually 'Holy Grail' in English) was reputed to be the cup used by Christ at the Last Supper and was supposedly brought to Britain by Joseph of Arimathea. The legend held that it contained some of the blood shed by Christ at his crucifixion. The significance of the Grail in Le Morte Darthur therefore possesses both a physical and a spiritual

---

* Terence McCarthy, 'Malory and the Alliterative Tradition', in James W. Spisak (ed.), *Studies in Malory* (Kalamazoo, 1985), p. 76.

dimension. The cup – mystical, desired and yet supremely elusive – is a highly appropriate subject for a chivalric quest, since the knights' searching tests their 'prowess' to the limits. Yet the Grail, as well as being a physical cup, is also a spiritual ideal. This is demonstrated by the hermit Nacien in his explanation to Sir Gawaine, who fails the quest. The hermit reveals that the quest will only be achieved by one who can combine the qualities of earthly chivalry with those of spiritual holiness. Gawaine has failed, the hermit tells him, because the cup 'appeareth not to sinners' (p. 621). Attainment of the Grail therefore represents the achievement of a spiritual ideal as well as of a physical quest.

As Nacien's explanation shows, events do not usually occur in isolation in *Le Morte Darthur*, but tend to be linked to past or future circumstances. Malory employs three primary methods of linking the incidents which occur within his romance. First, there are the physical statements of meaning which are littered about the Arthurian landscape. The sword in the stone is one of these: it bears the message 'Whoso pulleth out this sword of this stone and anvil, is rightwise king born of all England' (p. 6). The sword in the stone is a symbol and a test, but it explains itself by means of the written word. One of the most obvious signposts in the romance is exactly that – a cross bearing writing which is discovered by Bagdemagus' squire. The writing communicates the fact that 'Bagdemagus should never return unto the court again, till he had won a knight's body of the Round Table, body for body' (p. 94). The cross is therefore both a prophecy and an instruction, linking the present moment with future endeavours by the subject, Sir Bagdemagus. Whilst the sword in the stone and this cross are self-explanatory, sometimes events or symbols need an interpreter. This is the second means by which Malory locates individual incidents in the wider context of the legend. When Balin succeeds in pulling the enchanted sword from its scabbard in Book II, for example, the damsel who brought it to the court interprets his success ('this is a passing good knight') but also prophesies that 'that sword shall be your destruction' (p. 44). However, an erroneous interpretation is provided by the knights who witness this deed: they hold that Balin achieved it 'by witchcraft' (p. 45). Erroneous interpretations can be malicious, as here, but they can also be accidental, and as such indicate the fallibility of human sign-reading. Sir Melias, for example, finds himself in all sorts of trouble because he chooses the left-hand path at a junction, in spite of the warning written on a cross at the division of the ways (p. 579). The spiritual significance of his mistake has to be pointed out to him by 'a good man' (p. 581).

As well as containing interpreters and self-speaking signs, *Le Morte Darthur* often employs the figure of the prophet to contextualise events, and to draw together the disparate elements of the romance. Merlin is the romance's pre-eminent prophet: he foretells Arthur's doom and his own death (p. 32), the Grail quest (p. 55), the strife between Launcelot and Gawaine (p. 66) and the love of Guenever and Launcelot (p.68). At times, Merlin's role as prophet means that he also acts as an internal narrator: he is a part of the romance but is also the agent whereby the plot is unravelled. For example, in warning Arthur not to kill King Pellinore, Merlin reveals that Pellinore will be a significant player later in the story. This suggests that the story has already been written (which, indeed, it has, in Malory's sources), and implies that Merlin has been charged with the responsibility of ensuring that the pre-existent story acts itself out in 'reality'. Merlin, therefore, is not only important in terms of his contribution to the theme of interpretation in the romance, but he is also one of the devices which provide narrative structure and coherence in the romance. In this, the function of Merlin is rather like that of the references to 'the French book': both provide the means whereby Malory weaves the threads of many stories into the fabric of his *Morte Darthur*.

Malory's *Le Morte Darthur* combines the narrative excitement of an adventure story with the relative sophistication of allegorical romance. Although constructed from various sources, and comprising numerous storylines, it can be read successfully as a single work. The fall of the Round Table can be comprehended only in the context of the ideals and achievements which brought it into being. As Launcelot points out, in a moment of striking dramatic irony, the tighter the bonds which bind the knights of Arthur's fellowship, the greater will be the chaos when those bonds are finally broken: 'there is hard battle thereas kin and friends do battle either against other, there may be no mercy but mortal war' (p. 702).

HELEN MOORE
Pembroke College, Oxford

SUGGESTIONS FOR FURTHER READING

P. J. C. Field, *The Life and Times of Sir Thomas Malory*, Woodbridge, 1993

Maurice Keen, *Chivalry*, New Haven, 1985

Beverly Kennedy, *Knighthood in the 'Morte Darthur'*, Woodbridge, 1985

R. S. Loomis (ed.), *Arthurian Literature in the Middle Ages*, Oxford, 1959

T. H. White, *The Sword in the Stone*, 1939

T. H. White, *The Once and Future King*, 1958

NOTE ON THE TEXT

The edition reprinted here is that prepared by A. W. Pollard and published by Macmillan in 1900. It is based upon H. Oskar Sommer's 1890 edition of Caxton's Malory. In the bibliographical note to his edition, Pollard stresses that 'the most anxious care has been taken to produce a text modernised as to spelling, but in other respects in accurate accordance with Caxton's text, as represented by Dr Sommer's reprint. Obvious misprints have been silently corrected, but in a few cases notes show where emendations have been introduced from Wynkyn de Worde [who reprinted Caxton's text in 1498 and 1529].'

PREFACE OF WILLIAM CAXTON

After that I had accomplished and finished divers histories, as well of contemplation as of other historial and worldly acts of great conquerors and princes, and also certain books of ensamples and doctrine, many noble and divers gentlemen of this realm of England came and demanded me many and oft times, wherefore that I have not do made and imprint the noble history of the Saint Greal, and of the most renowned Christian king, first and chief of the three best Christian, and worthy, King Arthur, which ought most to be remembered among us Englishmen to-fore all other Christian kings; for it is notoyrly known through the universal world, that there be nine worthy and the best that ever were, that is to wit, three Paynims, three Jews, and three Christian men. As for the Paynims, they were to-fore the Incarnation of Christ, which were named, the first Hector of Troy, of whom the history is comen both in ballad and in prose, the second Alexander the Great, and the third Julius Caesar, Emperor of Rome, of whom the histories be well known and had. And as for the three Jews, which also were to-fore the incarnation of our Lord, of whom the first was duke Joshua which brought the children of Israel into the land of behest, the second David king of Jerusalem, and the third Judas Machabeus, of these three the Bible rehearseth all their noble histories and acts. And since the said Incarnation have been three noble Christian men, stalled and admitted through the universal world into the number of the nine best and worthy. Of whom was first the noble Arthur, whose noble acts I purpose to write in this present book here following. The second was Charlemain, or Charles the Great, of whom the history is had in many places, both in French and in English. And the third and last was Godfrey of Boloine, of whose acts and life I made a book unto the excellent prince and king of noble memory, King Edward the Fourth.

The said noble gentlemen instantly required me to imprint the history of the said noble king and conqueror King Arthur, and of his knights, with the history of the Saint Greal, and of the death and ending of the said Arthur; affirming that I ought rather to imprint his acts and noble feats, than of Godfrey of Boloine, or any of the other eight, considering that he was a man born within this realm, and king and emperor of the same: and that there be in French divers and many noble volumes of his acts, and also of his knights. To whom I answered that divers men hold opinion that there was no such Arthur, and that all such books as been made of him be feigned and fables, because that some chronicles make of him no mention, nor remember him nothing, nor of his knights. Whereto they answered, and one in special said, that in him that should say or think that there was never such a king called Arthur might well be aretted great folly and blindness. For he said that there were many evidences of the contrary. First ye may see his sepulchre in the monastery of Glastonbury. And also in Policronicon, in the fifth book the sixth chapter, and in the seventh book the twenty-third chapter, where his body was buried, and after found, and translated into the said monastery. Ye shall see also in the history of Bochas, in his book *De Casu Principum*, part of his noble acts, and also of his fall. Also Galfridus in his British book recounteth his life: and in divers places of England many remembrances be yet of him, and shall remain perpetually, and also of his knights. First in the abbey of Westminster, at St Edward's shrine, remaineth the print of his seal in red wax closed in beryl, in which is written, *Patricius Arthurus Britannie, Gallie, Germanie, Dacie, Imperator*. Item in the castle of Dover ye may see Gawaine's skull, and Cradok's mantle: at Winchester the Round Table: in other places Launcelot's sword and many other things. Then all these things considered, there can no man reasonably gainsay but there was a king of this land named Arthur. For in all places, Christian and heathen, he is reputed and taken for one of the nine worthy, and the first of the three Christian men. And also, he is more spoken of beyond the sea, more books made of his noble acts, than there be in England, as well in Dutch, Italian, Spanish, and Greekish, as in French. And yet of record remain in witness of him in Wales, in the town of Camelot, the great stones and the marvellous works of iron lying under the ground, and royal vaults, which divers now living have seen. Wherefore it is a marvel why he is no more renowned in his own country, save only it accordeth to the Word of God, which saith that no man is accepted for a prophet in his own country.

Then all these things aforesaid alleged, I could not well deny but that there was such a noble king named Arthur, and reputed one of the nine worthy, and first and chief of the Christian men. And many noble volumes be made of him and of his noble knights in French, which I have seen and read beyond the sea, which be not had in our maternal tongue. But in Welsh be many and also in French, and some in English but nowhere nigh all. Wherefore, such as have late been drawn out briefly into English I have after the simple conning that God hath sent to me, under the favour and correction of all noble lords and gentlemen, enprised to imprint a book of the noble histories of the said King Arthur, and of certain of his knights, after a copy unto me delivered, which copy Sir Thomas Malorye did take out of certain books of French, and reduced it into English. And I, according to my copy, have done set it in imprint, to the intent that noble men may see and learn the noble acts of chivalry, the gentle and virtuous deeds that some knights used in those days, by which they came to honour, and how they that were vicious were punished and oft put to shame and rebuke; humbly beseeching all noble lords and ladies, with all other estates of what estate or degree they been of, that shall see and read in this said book and work, that they take the good and honest acts in their remembrance, and to follow the same. Wherein they shall find many joyous and pleasant histories, and noble and renowned acts of humanity, gentleness, and chivalry. For herein may be seen noble chivalry, courtesy, humanity, friendliness, hardiness, love, friendship, cowardice, murder, hate, virtue, and sin. Do after the good and leave the evil, and it shall bring you to good fame and renown. And for to pass the time this book shall be pleasant to read in, but for to give faith and belief that all is true that is contained herein, ye be at your liberty: but all is written for our doctrine, and for to beware that we fall not to vice nor sin, but to exercise and follow virtue, by which we may come and attain to good fame and renown in this life, and after this short and transitory life to come unto everlasting bliss in heaven; the which He grant us that reigneth in heaven, the blessed Trinity. Amen.

Then to proceed forth in this said book, which I direct unto all noble princes, lords and ladies, gentlemen or gentlewomen, that desire to read or hear read of the noble and joyous history of the great conqueror and excellent king, King Arthur, sometime king of this noble realm, then called Britain; I, William Caxton, simple person, present this book following, which I have enprised to imprint: and treateth of the noble acts, feats of arms of chivalry, prowess, hardiness, humanity, love, courtesy, and very gentleness, with many wonderful histories and adventures. And for to understand briefly the content of this volume, I have divided it into xxi books, and every book chaptered, as hereafter shall by God's grace follow. The First Book shall treat how Uther Pendragon gat the noble conqueror King Arthur, and containeth xxviii chapters. The Second Book treateth of Balin the noble knight, and containeth xix chapters. The Third Book treateth of the marriage of King Arthur to Queen Guenever, with other matters, and containeth xv chapters. The Fourth Book, how Merlin was assotted, and of war made to King Arthur, and containeth xxix chapters. The Fifth Book treateth of the conquest of Lucius the emperor, and containeth xii chapters. The Sixth Book treateth of Sir Launcelot and Sir Lionel, and marvellous adventures, and containeth xviii chapters. The Seventh Book treateth of a noble knight called Sir Gareth, and named by Sir Kay Beaumains, and containeth xxxvi chapters. The Eighth Book treateth of the birth of Sir Tristram the noble knight, and of his acts, and containeth xli chapters. The Ninth Book treateth of a knight named by Sir Kay Le Cote Male Taille, and also of Sir Tristram, and containeth xliv chapters. The Tenth Book treateth of Sir Tristram, and other marvellous adventures, and containeth lxxxviii chapters. The Eleventh Book treateth of Sir Launcelot and Sir Galahad, and containeth xiv chapters. The Twelfth Book treateth of Sir Launcelot and his madness, and containeth xiv chapters. The Thirteenth Book treateth how Galahad came first to King Arthur's court, and the quest how the Sangreal was begun, and containeth xx chapters. The Fourteenth Book treateth of the quest of the Sangreal, and containeth x chapters. The Fifteenth Book treateth of Sir Launcelot, and containeth vi chapters. The Sixteenth Book treateth of Sir Bors and Sir Lionel his brother, and containeth xvii chapters. The Seventeenth Book treateth of the Sangreal, and containeth xxiii chapters. The Eighteenth Book treateth of Sir Launcelot and the queen, and containeth xxv chapters. The Nine-teenth Book treateth of Queen Guenever and Launcelot, and containeth xiii chapters. The Twentieth Book treateth of the piteous death of Arthur, and containeth xxii chapters. The Twenty-first Book treateth of his last departing, and how Sir Launcelot came to revenge his death, and containeth xiii chapters. The sum is twenty-one books, which contain the sum of five hundred and seven chapters, as more plainly shall follow hereafter.

THE TABLE OR RUBRYSSHE OF THE CONTENT OF CHAPTERS

BOOK ONE

BOOK TWO

BOOK THREE

BOOK FOUR

BOOK FIVE

BOOK SIX

BOOK SEVEN

BOOK EIGHT

BOOK NINE

BOOK TEN

BOOK ELEVEN

BOOK TWELVE

BOOK FOURTEEN

BOOK FIFTEEN

BOOK SIXTEEN

BOOK SEVENTEEN

BOOK EIGHTEEN

BOOK NINETEEN

BOOK TWENTY

BOOK TWENTY-ONE

LE MORTE DARTHUR

BOOK ONE

CHAPTER I

*How Uther Pendragon sent for the duke of Cornwall and
Igraine his wife, and of their departing suddenly again.*

It befell in the days of Uther Pendragon, when he was king of all
England, and so reigned, that there was a mighty duke in Cornwall
that held war against him long time. And the duke was called the
Duke of Tintagil. And so by means King Uther sent for this duke,
charging him to bring his wife with him, for she was called a fair lady,
and a passing wise, and her name was called Igraine.

So when the duke and his wife were come unto the king, by the
means of great lords they were accorded both. The king liked and
loved this lady well, and he made them great cheer out of measure,
and desired to have lain by her. But she was a passing good woman,
and would not assent unto the king. And then she told the duke her
husband, and said, I suppose that we were sent for that I should be
dishonoured; wherefore, husband, I counsel you, that we depart from
hence suddenly, that we may ride all night unto our own castle. And
in like wise as she said so they departed, that neither the king nor
none of his council were ware of their departing. All so soon as King
Uther knew of their departing so suddenly, he was wonderly wroth.
Then he called to him his privy council, and told them of the sudden
departing of the duke and his wife.

Then they advised the king to send for the duke and his wife by a
great charge; and if he will not come at your summons, then may ye
do your best, then have ye cause to make mighty war upon him. So
that was done, and the messengers had their answers; and that was this
shortly, that neither he nor his wife would not come at him.

Then was the king wonderly wroth. And then the king sent him
plain word again, and bade him be ready and stuff him and garnish

him, for within forty days he would fetch him out of the biggest
castle that he hath.

When the duke had this warning, anon he went and furnished and
garnished two strong castles of his, of the which the one hight Tintagil,
and the other castle hight Terrabil. So his wife Dame Igraine he put in
the castle of Tintagil, and himself he put in the castle of Terrabil, the
which had many issues and posterns out. Then in all haste came Uther
with a great host, and laid a siege about the castle of Terrabil. And
there he pight many pavilions, and there was great war made on both
parties, and much people slain. Then for pure anger and for great love
of fair Igraine the king Uther fell sick. So came to the king Uther Sir
Ulfius, a noble knight, and asked the king why he was sick. I shall tell
thee, said the king, I am sick for anger and for love of fair Igraine, that
I may not be whole. Well, my lord, said Sir Ulfius, I shall seek Merlin,
and he shall do you remedy, that your heart shall be pleased. So Ulfius
departed, and by adventure he met Merlin in a beggar's array, and
there Merlin asked Ulfius whom he sought. And he said he had little
ado to tell him. Well, said Merlin, I know whom thou seekest, for
thou seekest Merlin, therefore seek no farther, for I am he; and if King
Uther will well reward me, and be sworn unto me to fulfil my desire,
that shall be his honour and profit more than mine; for I shall cause
him to have all his desire. All this will I undertake, said Ulfius, that
there shall be nothing reasonable but thou shalt have thy desire. Well,
said Merlin, he shall have his intent and desire. And therefore, said
Merlin, ride on your way, for I will not be long behind.

CHAPTER II

*How Uther Pendragon made war on the duke of Cornwall, and
how by the mean of Merlin he lay by the duchess and gat Arthur.*

Then Ulfius was glad, and rode on more than a pace till that he came
to King Uther Pendragon, and told him he had met with Merlin.
Where is he? said the king. Sir, said Ulfius, he will not dwell long.
Therewithal Ulfius was ware where Merlin stood at the porch of the
pavilion's door. And then Merlin was bound to come to the king.
When King Uther saw him, he said he was welcome. Sir, said

Merlin, I know all your heart every deal; so ye will be sworn unto me as ye be a true king anointed, to fulfil my desire, ye shall have your desire. Then the king was sworn upon the Four Evangelists. Sir, said Merlin, this is my desire: the first night that ye shall lie by Igraine ye shall get a child on her, and when that is born, that it shall be delivered to me for to nourish there as I will have it; for it shall be your worship, and the child's avail, as mickle as the child is worth. I will well, said the king, as thou wilt have it. Now make you ready, said Merlin, this night ye shall lie with Igraine in the castle of Tintagil; and ye shall be like the duke her husband, Ulfius shall be like Sir Brastias, a knight of the duke's, and I will be like a knight that hight Sir Jordanus, a knight of the duke's. But wait ye make not many questions with her nor her men, but say ye are diseased, and so hie you to bed, and rise not on the morn till I come to you, for the castle of Tintagil is but ten miles hence; so this was done as they devised. But the duke of Tintagil espied how the king rode from the siege of Terrabil, and therefore that night he issued out of the castle at a postern for to have distressed the king's host. And so, through his own issue, the duke himself was slain or ever the king came at the castle of Tintagil.

So after the death of the duke, King Uther lay with Igraine more than three hours after his death, and begat on her that night Arthur, and on day came Merlin to the king, and bade him make him ready, and so he kissed the lady Igraine and departed in all haste. But when the lady heard tell of the duke her husband, and by all record he was dead or ever King Uther came to her, then she marvelled who that might be that lay with her in likeness of her lord; so she mourned privily and held her peace. Then all the barons by one assent prayed the king of accord betwixt the lady Igraine and him; the king gave them leave, for fain would he have been accorded with her. So the king put all the trust in Ulfius to entreat between them, so by the entreaty at the last the king and she met together. Now will we do well, said Ulfius, our king is a lusty knight and wifeless, and my lady Igraine is a passing fair lady; it were great joy unto us all, an it might please the king to make her his queen. Unto that they all well accorded and moved it to the king. And anon, like a lusty knight, he assented thereto with good will, and so in all haste they were married in a morning with great mirth and joy.

And King Lot of Lothian and of Orkney then wedded Margawse

that was Gawaine's mother, and King Nentres of the land of Garlot wedded Elaine. All this was done at the request of King Uther. And the third sister Morgan le Fay was put to school in a nunnery, and there she learned so much that she was a great clerk of necromancy. And after she was wedded to King Uriens of the land of Gore, that was Sir Ewain's le Blanchemain's father.

CHAPTER III

Of the birth of King Arthur and of his nurture.

Then Queen Igraine waxed daily greater and greater, so it befell after within half a year, as King Uther lay by his queen, he asked her, by the faith she owed to him, whose was the child within her body; then she sore abashed to give answer. Dismay you not, said the king, but tell me the truth, and I shall love you the better, by the faith of my body. Sir, said she, I shall tell you the truth. The same night that my lord was dead, the hour of his death, as his knights record, there came into my castle of Tintagil a man like my lord in speech and in countenance, and two knights with him in likeness of his two knights Brastias and Jordanus, and so I went unto bed with him as I ought to do with my lord, and the same night, as I shall answer unto God, this child was begotten upon me. That is truth, said the king, as ye say; for it was I myself that came in the likeness, and therefore dismay you not, for I am father of the child; and there he told her all the cause, how it was by Merlin's counsel. Then the queen made great joy when she knew who was the father of her child.

Soon came Merlin unto the king, and said, Sir, ye must purvey you for the nourishing of your child. As thou wilt, said the king, be it. Well, said Merlin, I know a lord of yours in this land, that is a passing true man and a faithful, and he shall have the nourishing of your child, and his name is Sir Ector, and he is a lord of fair livelihood in many parts in England and Wales; and this lord, Sir Ector, let him be sent for, for to come and speak with you, and desire him yourself, as he loveth you, that he will put his own child to nourishing to another woman, and that his wife nourish yours. And when the child is born let it be delivered to me at yonder privy postern unchristened. So like as Merlin devised it was done. And when Sir Ector was come he made fiaunce to the king for to nourish the child like as the king desired; and there the king granted Sir Ector great rewards. Then when the lady was delivered, the king commanded two knights and two ladies to take the child, bound in a cloth of gold, and that ye deliver him to what poor man ye meet at the postern gate of the castle. So the child was delivered unto Merlin, and so he bare it forth unto Sir Ector, and made an holy man to christen him, and named him Arthur; and so Sir Ector's wife nourished him with her own pap.

CHAPTER IV

Of the death of King Uther Pendragon.

Then within two years King Uther fell sick of a great malady. And in the meanwhile his enemies usurped upon him, and did a great battle upon his men, and slew many of his people. Sir, said Merlin, ye may not lie so as ye do, for ye must to the field though ye ride on an horse-litter: for ye shall never have the better of your enemies but if your person be there, and then shall ye have the victory. So it was done as Merlin had devised, and they carried the king forth in an horse-litter with a great host towards his enemies. And at St Albans there met with the king a great host of the North. And that day Sir Ulfius and Sir Brastias did great deeds of arms, and King Uther's men overcame the Northern battle and slew many people, and put the remnant to flight. And then the king returned unto London, and made great joy of his victory. And then he fell passing sore sick, so that three days and three nights he was speechless: wherefore all the barons made great sorrow, and asked Merlin what counsel were best. There is none other remedy, said Merlin, but God will have his will. But look ye all barons be before King Uther to-morn, and God and I shall make him to speak. So on the morn all the barons with Merlin came to-fore the king; then Merlin said aloud unto King Uther, Sir, shall your son Arthur be king after your days, of this realm with all the appurtenance? Then Uther Pendragon turned him, and said in hearing of them all, I give him God's blessing and mine, and bid him pray for my soul, and righteously and worshipfully that he claim the

crown, upon forfeiture of my blessing; and therewith he yielded up
the ghost, and then was he interred as longed to a king. Wherefore
the queen, fair Igraine, made great sorrow, and all the barons.

CHAPTER V

*How Arthur was chosen king, and of wonders and marvels of
a sword taken out of a stone by the said Arthur.*

Then stood the realm in great jeopardy long while, for every lord that
was mighty of men made him strong, and many weened to have
been king. Then Merlin went to the Archbishop of Canterbury, and
counselled him for to send for all the lords of the realm, and all the
gentlemen of arms, that they should to London come by Christmas,
upon pain of cursing; and for this cause, that Jesus, that was born on
that night, that he would of his great mercy show some miracle, as he
was come to be king of mankind, for to show some miracle who
should be rightwise king of this realm. So the Archbishop, by the
advice of Merlin, sent for all the lords and gentlemen of arms that
they should come by Christmas even unto London. And many of
them made them clean of their life, that their prayer might be the
more acceptable unto God. So in the greatest church of London,
whether it were Paul's or not the French book maketh no mention,
all the estates were long or day in the church for to pray. And when
matins and the first mass was done, there was seen in the churchyard,
against the high altar, a great stone four square, like unto a marble
stone; and in midst thereof was like an anvil of steel a foot on high,
and therein stuck a fair sword naked by the point, and letters there
were written in gold about the sword that said thus: – Whoso pulleth
out this sword of this stone and anvil, is rightwise king born of all
England. Then the people marvelled, and told it to the Archbishop. I
command, said the Archbishop, that ye keep you within your church
and pray unto God still, that no man touch the sword till the high
mass be all done. So when all masses were done all the lords went to
behold the stone and the sword. And when they saw the scripture
some assayed, such as would have been king. But none might stir the
sword nor move it. He is not here, said the Archbishop, that shall

achieve the sword, but doubt not God will make him known. But this is my counsel, said the Archbishop, that we let purvey ten knights, men of good fame, and they to keep this sword. So it was ordained, and then there was made a cry, that every man should assay that would, for to win the sword. And upon New Year's Day the barons let make a jousts and a tournament, that all knights that would joust or tourney there might play, and all this was ordained for to keep the lords together and the commons, for the Archbishop trusted that God would make him known that should win the sword.

So upon New Year's Day, when the service was done, the barons rode unto the field, some to joust and some to tourney, and so it happened that Sir Ector, that had great livelihood about London, rode unto the jousts, and with him rode Sir Kay his son, and young Arthur that was his nourished brother; and Sir Kay was made knight at All Hallowmass afore. So as they rode to the jousts-ward, Sir Kay lost his sword, for he had left it at his father's lodging, and so he prayed young Arthur for to ride for his sword. I will well, said Arthur, and rode fast after the sword, and when he came home, the lady and all were out to see the jousting. Then was Arthur wroth, and said to himself, I will ride to the churchyard, and take the sword with me that sticketh in the stone, for my brother Sir Kay shall not be without a sword this day. So when he came to the churchyard, Sir Arthur alighted and tied his horse to the stile, and so he went to the tent, and found no knights there, for they were at the jousting. And so he handled the sword by the handles, and lightly and fiercely pulled it out of the stone, and took his horse and rode his way until he came to his brother Sir Kay, and delivered him the sword. And as soon as Sir Kay saw the sword, he wist well it was the sword of the stone, and so he rode to his father Sir Ector, and said: Sir, lo here is the sword of the stone, wherefore I must be king of this land. When Sir Ector beheld the sword, he returned again and came to the church, and there they alighted all three, and went into the church. And anon he made Sir Kay swear upon a book how he came to that sword. Sir, said Sir Kay, by my brother Arthur, for he brought it to me. How gat ye this sword? said Sir Ector to Arthur. Sir, I will tell you. When I came home for my brother's sword, I found nobody at home to deliver me his sword; and so I thought my brother Sir Kay should not be swordless, and so I came hither eagerly and pulled it out of the stone without any pain. Found ye any knights about this sword? said

Sir Ector. Nay, said Arthur. Now, said Sir Ector to Arthur, I
understand ye must be king of this land. Wherefore I, said Arthur,
and for what cause? Sir, said Ector, for God will have it so; for there
should never man have drawn out this sword, but he that shall be
rightwise king of this land. Now let me see whether ye can put the
sword there as it was, and pull it out again. That is no mastery, said
Arthur, and so he put it in the stone; wherewithal Sir Ector assayed to
pull out the sword and failed.

CHAPTER VI

How King Arthur pulled out the sword divers times.

Now assay, said Sir Ector unto Sir Kay. And anon he pulled at the
sword with all his might; but it would not be. Now shall ye assay, said
Sir Ector to Arthur. I will well, said Arthur, and pulled it out easily.
And therewithal Sir Ector knelt down to the earth, and Sir Kay. Alas,
said Arthur, my own dear father and brother, why kneel ye to me?
Nay, nay, my lord Arthur, it is not so; I was never your father nor of
your blood, but I wot well ye are of an higher blood than I weened
ye were. And then Sir Ector told him all, how he was betaken him
for to nourish him, and by whose commandment, and by Merlin's
deliverance.

Then Arthur made great dole when he understood that Sir Ector
was not his father. Sir, said Ector unto Arthur, will ye be my good
and gracious lord when ye are king? Else were I to blame, said
Arthur, for ye are the man in the world that I am most beholden to,
and my good lady and mother your wife, that as well as her own hath
fostered me and kept. And if ever it be God's will that I be king as ye
say, ye shall desire of me what I may do, and I shall not fail you; God
forbid I should fail you. Sir, said Sir Ector, I will ask no more of you,
but that ye will make my son, your foster brother, Sir Kay, seneschal
of all your lands. That shall be done, said Arthur, and more, by the
faith of my body, that never man shall have that office but he, while
he and I live. Therewithal they went unto the Archbishop, and told
him how the sword was achieved, and by whom; and on Twelfth-
day all the barons came thither, and to assay to take the sword, who

that would assay. But there afore them all, there might none take it out but Arthur; wherefore there were many lords wroth, and said it was great shame unto them all and the realm, to be overgoverned with a boy of no high blood born. And so they fell out at that time that it was put off till Candlemas, and then all the barons should meet there again; but always the ten knights were ordained to watch the sword day and night, and so they set a pavilion over the stone and the sword, and five always watched. So at Candlemas many more great lords came thither for to have won the sword, but there might none prevail. And right as Arthur did at Christmas, he did at Candlemas, and pulled out the sword easily, whereof the barons were sore aggrieved and put it off in delay till the high feast of Easter. And as Arthur sped before, so did he at Easter; yet there were some of the great lords had indignation that Arthur should be king, and put it off in a delay till the feast of Pentecost.

Then the Archbishop of Canterbury by Merlin's providence let purvey then of the best knights that they might get, and such knights as Uther Pendragon loved best and most trusted in his days. And such knights were put about Arthur as Sir Baudwin of Britain, Sir Kay, Sir Ulfius, Sir Brastias. All these, with many other, were always about Arthur, day and night, till the feast of Pentecost.

CHAPTER VII

How King Arthur was crowned and how he made officers.

And at the feast of Pentecost all manner of men assayed to pull at the sword that would assay; but none might prevail but Arthur, and pulled it out afore all the lords and commons that were there, wherefore all the commons cried at once, We will have Arthur unto our king, we will put him no more in delay, for we all see that it is God's will that he shall be our king, and who that holdeth against it, we will slay him. And therewithal they kneeled at once, both rich and poor, and cried Arthur mercy because they had delayed him so long, and Arthur forgave them, and took the sword between both his hands, and offered it upon the altar where the Archbishop was, and so was he made knight of the best man that was there. And so anon was the coronation made. And there was he sworn unto his lords and the commons for to be a true king, to stand with true justice from thenceforth the days of this life. Also then he made all lords that held of the crown to come in, and to do service as they ought to do. And many complaints were made unto Sir Arthur of great wrongs that were done since the death of King Uther, of many lands that were bereaved lords, knights, ladies, and gentlemen. Wherefore King Arthur made the lands to be given again unto them that owned them.

When this was done, that the king had stablished all the countries about London, then he let make Sir Kay seneschal of England; and Sir Baudwin of Britain was made constable; and Sir Ulfius was made chamberlain; and Sir Brastias was made warden to wait upon the north from Trent forwards, for it was that time the most party the king's enemies. But within few years after Arthur won all the north, Scotland, and all that were under their obeissance. Also Wales, a part of it, held against Arthur, but he overcame them all, as he did the remnant, through the noble prowess of himself and his knights of the Round Table.

CHAPTER VIII

How King Arthur held in Wales, at a Pentecost, a great feast, and what kings and lords came to his feast.

Then the king removed into Wales, and let cry a great feast that it should be holden at Pentecost after the incoronation of him at the city of Carlion. Unto the feast came King Lot of Lothian and of Orkney, with five hundred knights with him. Also there came to the feast King Uriens of Gore with four hundred knights with him. Also there came to that feast King Nentres of Garlot, with seven hundred knights with him. Also there came to the feast the king of Scotland with six hundred knights with him, and he was but a young man. Also there came to the feast a king that was called the King with the Hundred Knights, but he and his men were passing well beseen at all points. Also there came the king of Carados with five hundred knights. And King Arthur was glad of their coming, for he weened that all the kings and knights had come for great love, and to have done him worship at his feast; wherefore the king made great joy, and sent the kings and knights great presents. But the kings would none receive, but rebuked the messengers shamefully, and said they had no joy to receive no gifts of a beardless boy that was come of low blood, and sent him word they would none of his gifts, but that they were come to give him gifts with hard swords betwixt the neck and the shoulders: and therefore they came thither, so they told to the messengers plainly, for it was great shame to all them to see such a boy to have a rule of so noble a realm as this land was. With this answer the messengers departed and told to King Arthur this answer. Wherefore, by the advice of his barons, he took him to a strong tower with five hundred good men with him. And all the kings aforesaid in a manner laid a siege to-fore him, but King Arthur was well victualled. And within fifteen days there came Merlin among them into the city of Carlion. Then all the kings were passing glad of Merlin, and asked him, For what cause is that boy Arthur made your king? Sirs, said Merlin, I shall tell you the cause, for he is King Uther Pendragon's son, born in wedlock, gotten on Igraine, the duke's wife of Tintagil. Then is he a bastard, they said all. Nay, said Merlin, after the death of the duke, more than three hours, was Arthur begotten, and thirteen days after King Uther wedded Igraine; and therefore I prove him he is no bastard. And who saith nay, he shall be king and overcome all his enemies; and, or he die, he shall be long king of all England, and have under his obeissance Wales, Ireland, and Scotland, and more realms than I will now rehearse. Some of the kings had marvel of Merlin's words, and deemed well that it should be as he said; and some of them laughed him to scorn, as King Lot; and more other called him a witch. But then were they accorded with Merlin, that King Arthur should come out and speak with the kings, and to come safe and to go safe, such surance there was made. So Merlin went unto King Arthur, and told him how he had done, and bade him fear not, but come out boldly and speak with them, and spare them not, but answer them as their king and chieftain; for ye shall overcome them all, whether they will or nill.

CHAPTER IX

Of the first war that King Arthur had, and how he won the field.

Then King Arthur came out of his tower, and had under his gown a jesseraunt of double mail, and there went with him the Archbishop of Canterbury, and Sir Baudwin of Britain, and Sir Kay, and Sir Brastias: these were the men of most worship that were with him. And when they were met there was no meekness, but stout words on both sides; but always King Arthur answered them, and said he would make them to bow an he lived. Wherefore they departed with wrath, and King Arthur bade keep them well, and they bade the king keep him well. So the king returned him to the tower again and armed him and all his knights. What will ye do? said Merlin to the kings; ye were better for to stint, for ye shall not here prevail though ye were ten times so many. Be we well advised to be afeared of a dream-reader? said King Lot. With that Merlin vanished away, and came to King Arthur, and bade him set on them fiercely; and in the meanwhile there were three hundred good men, of the best that were with the kings, that went straight unto King Arthur, and that comforted him greatly. Sir, said Merlin to Arthur, fight not with the sword that ye had by miracle, till that ye see ye go unto the worse, then draw it out and do your best. So forthwithal King Arthur set upon them in their lodging. And Sir Baudwin, Sir Kay, and Sir Brastias slew on the right hand and on the left hand that it was marvel; and always King Arthur on horseback laid on with a sword, and did marvellous deeds of arms, that many of the kings had great joy of his deeds and hardiness.

Then King Lot brake out on the back side, and the King with the Hundred Knights, and King Carados, and set on Arthur fiercely behind him. With that Sir Arthur turned with his knights, and smote behind and before, and ever Sir Arthur was in the foremost press till his horse was slain underneath him. And therewith King Lot smote down King Arthur. With that his four knights received him and set him on horseback. Then he drew his sword Excalibur, but it was so bright in his enemies' eyes, that it gave light like thirty torches. And therewith he put them a-back, and slew much people. And then the commons of Carlion arose with clubs and staves and slew many knights; but all the kings held them together with their knights that were left alive, and so fled and departed. And Merlin came unto Arthur, and counselled him to follow them no further.

CHAPTER X

How Merlin counselled King Arthur to send for King Ban and King Bors, and of their counsel taken for the war.

So after the feast and journey, King Arthur drew him unto London, and so by the counsel of Merlin, the king let call his barons to council, for Merlin had told the king that the six kings that made war upon him would in all haste be awroke on him and on his lands. Wherefore the king asked counsel at them all. They could no counsel give, but said they were big enough. Ye say well, said Arthur; I thank you for your good courage, but will ye all that loveth me speak with Merlin? ye know well that he hath done much for me, and he knoweth many things, and when he is afore you, I would that ye prayed him heartily of his best advice. All the barons said they would pray him and desire him. So Merlin was sent for, and fair desired of all the barons to give them best counsel. I shall say you, said Merlin, I warn you all, your enemies are passing strong for you, and they are good men of arms as be alive, and by this time they have gotten to them four kings more, and a mighty duke; and unless that our king have more chivalry with him than he may make within the bounds of his own realm, an he fight with them in battle, he shall be overcome and slain. What were best to do in this cause? said all the barons. I shall tell you, said Merlin, mine advice; there are two brethren beyond the sea, and they be kings both, and marvellous good men of their hands; and that one hight King Ban of Benwick, and that other hight King Bors of Gaul, that is France. And on these two kings warreth a mighty man of men, the King Claudas, and striveth with them for a castle, and great war is betwixt them. But this Claudas is so mighty of goods whereof he getteth good knights, that he putteth these two kings most part to the worse; wherefore this is my counsel, that our king and sovereign lord send unto the kings Ban and Bors by two trusty knights with letters well devised, that an they will come and see King Arthur and his court, and so help him in his wars, that he will be sworn unto them to help them in their wars against King Claudas. Now, what say ye unto this counsel? said Merlin. This is well counselled, said the king and all the barons.

Right so in all haste there were ordained to go two knights on the message unto the two kings. So were there made letters in the pleasant wise according unto King Arthur's desire. Ulfius and Brastias were made the messengers, and so rode forth well horsed and well armed and as the guise was that time, and so passed the sea and rode toward the city of Benwick. And there besides were eight knights that espied them, and at a strait passage they met with Ulfius and Brastias, and would have taken them prisoners; so they prayed them that they might pass, for they were messengers unto King Ban and Bors sent from King Arthur. Therefore, said the eight knights, ye shall die or be prisoners, for we be knights of King Claudas. And therewith two of them dressed their spears, and Ulfius and Brastias dressed their spears, and ran together with great raundon. And Claudas' knights brake their spears, and theirs to-held and bare the two knights out of their saddles to the earth, and so left them lying, and rode their ways. And the other six knights rode afore to a passage to meet with them again, and so Ulfius and Brastias smote other two down, and so passed on their ways. And at the fourth passage there met two for two, and both were laid unto the earth; so there was none of the eight knights but he was sore hurt or bruised. And when they come to Benwick it fortuned there were both kings, Ban and Bors.

And when it was told the kings that there were come messengers, there were sent unto them two knights of worship, the one hight Lionses, lord of the country of Payarne, and Sir Phariance a worshipful knight. Anon they asked from whence they came, and they said from King Arthur, king of England; so they took them in their arms and made great joy each of other. But anon, as the two kings wist they were messengers of Arthur's, there was made no tarrying, but forthwith they spake with the knights, and welcomed them in the faithfullest wise, and said they were most welcome unto them before all the kings living; and therewith they kissed the letters and delivered them. And when Ban and Bors understood the letters, then they were more welcome than they were before. And after the haste of the letters they gave them this answer, that they would fulfil the desire of King Arthur's writing, and Ulfius and Brastias, tarry there as long as they would, they should have such cheer as might be made them in those marches. Then Ulfius and Brastias told the kings of the adventure at their passages of the eight knights. Ha! ah! said Ban and Bors, they were my good friends. I would I had wist of them; they should not have escaped so. So Ulfius and Brastias had good cheer and great gifts, as much as they might bear away; and had their answer by mouth and by writing, that those two kings would come unto Arthur in all the haste that they might. So the two knights rode on afore, and passed the sea, and came to their lord, and told him how they had sped, whereof King Arthur was passing glad. At what time suppose ye the two kings will be here? Sir, said they, afore All Hallowmass. Then the king let purvey for a great feast, and let cry a great jousts. And by All Hallowmass the two kings were come over the sea with three hundred knights well arrayed both for the peace and for the war. And King Arthur met with them ten mile out of London, and there was great joy as could be thought or made. And on All Hallowmass at the great feast, sat in the hall the three kings, and Sir Kay seneschal served in the hall, and Sir Lucas the butler, that was Duke Corneus' son, and Sir Griflet, that was the son of Cardol, these three knights had the rule of all the service that served the kings. And anon, as they had washen and risen, all knights that would joust made them ready; by then they were ready on horseback there were seven hundred knights. And Arthur, Ban, and Bors, with the Archbishop of Canterbury, and Sir Ector, Kay's father, they were in a place covered with cloth of gold like an hall, with ladies and gentlewomen, for to behold who did best, and thereon to give judgment.

CHAPTER XI

Of a great tourney made by King Arthur and the two kings Ban and Bors, and how they went over the sea.

And King Arthur and the two kings let depart the seven hundred knights in two parties. And there were three hundred knights of the realm of Benwick and of Gaul turned on the other side. Then they dressed their shields, and began to couch their spears many good knights. So Griflet was the first that met with a knight, one Ladinas, and they met so eagerly that all men had wonder; and they so fought that their shields fell to pieces, and horse and man fell to the earth; and both the French knight and the English knight lay so long that all men weened they had been dead. When Lucas the butler saw Griflet so lie, he horsed him again anon, and they two did marvellous deeds of arms with many bachelors. Also Sir Kay came out of an ambushment with five knights with him, and they six smote other six down. But Sir Kay did that day marvellous deeds of arms, that there was none did so well as he that day. Then there came Ladinas and Gracian, two knights of France, and did passing well, that all men praised them.

Then came there Sir Placidas, a good knight, and met with Sir Kay, and smote him down horse and man, wherefore Sir Griflet was wroth, and met with Sir Placidas so hard, that horse and man fell to the earth. But when the five knights wist that Sir Kay had a fall, they were wroth out of wit, and therewith each of them five bare down a knight. When King Arthur and the two kings saw them begin to wax wroth on both parties, they leapt on small hackneys, and let cry that all men should depart unto their lodging. And so they went home and unarmed them, and so to evensong and supper. And after, the three kings went into a garden, and gave the prize unto Sir Kay, and to Lucas the butler, and unto Sir Griflet. And then they went unto council, and with them Gwenbaus, the brother unto Sir Ban and Bors, a wise clerk, and thither went Ulfius and Brastias, and Merlin. And after they had been in council, they went unto bed. And on the morn they heard mass, and to dinner, and so to their council, and made many arguments what were best to do. At the last they were concluded, that Merlin should go with a token of King Ban, and that was a ring, unto his men and King Bors'; and Gracian and Placidas should go again and keep their castles and their countries, as for [dread of King Claudas] King Ban of Benwick, and King Bors of Gaul had ordained them, and so passed the sea and came to Benwick. And when the people saw King Ban's ring, and Gracian and Placidas, they were glad, and asked how the kings fared, and made great joy of their welfare and cording, and according unto the sovereign lords' desire, the men of war made them ready in all haste possible, so that they were fifteen thousand on horse and foot, and they had great plenty of victual with them, by Merlin's provision. But Gracian and Placidas were left to furnish and garnish the castles, for dread of King Claudas. Right so Merlin passed the sea, well victualled both by water and by land. And when he came to the sea he sent home the footmen again, and took no more with him but ten thousand men on horseback, the most part men of arms, and so shipped and passed the sea into England, and landed at Dover; and through the wit of Merlin, he had the host northward, the priviest way that could be thought, unto the forest of Bedegraine, and there in a valley he lodged them secretly.

Then rode Merlin unto Arthur and the two kings, and told them how he had sped; whereof they had great marvel, that man on earth might speed so soon, and go and come. So Merlin told them ten thousand were in the forest of Bedegraine, well armed at all points. Then was there no more to say, but to horseback went all the host as Arthur had afore purveyed. So with twenty thousand he passed by night and day, but there was made such an ordinance afore by Merlin, that there should no man of war ride nor go in no country on this side Trent water, but if he had a token from King Arthur, where through the king's enemies durst not ride as they did to-fore to espy.

CHAPTER XII

How eleven kings gathered a great host against King Arthur.

And so within a little space the three kings came unto the castle of Bedegraine, and found there a passing fair fellowship, and well beseen, whereof they had great joy, and victual they wanted none. This was the cause of the northern host: that they were reared for the despite and rebuke the six kings had at Carlion. And those six kings by their means, gat unto them five other kings; and thus they began to gather their people.

And now they sware that for weal nor woe, they should not leave other, till they had destroyed Arthur. And then they made an oath. The first that began the oath was the Duke of Cambenet, that he would bring with him five thousand men of arms, the which were

ready on horseback. Then sware King Brandegoris of Stranggore that
he would bring five thousand men of arms on horseback. Then sware
King Clariance of Northumberland he would bring three thousand
men of arms. Then sware the King of the Hundred Knights, that was
a passing good man and a young, that he would bring four thousand
men of arms on horseback. Then there swore King Lot, a passing
good knight, and Sir Gawain's father, that he would bring five
thousand men of arms on horseback. Also there swore King Urience,
that was Sir Uwain's father, of the land of Gore, and he would bring
six thousand men of arms on horseback. Also there swore King Idres
of Cornwall, that he would bring five thousand men of arms on
horseback. Also there swore King Cradelmas to bring five thousand
men on horseback. Also there swore King Agwisance of Ireland to
bring five thousand men of arms on horseback. Also there swore
King Nentres to bring five thousand men of arms on horseback. Also
there swore King Carados to bring five thousand men of arms on
horseback. So their whole host was of clean men of arms on
horseback fifty thousand, and a-foot ten thousand of good men's
bodies. Then were they soon ready, and mounted upon horse and
sent forth their fore-riders, for these eleven kings in their ways laid a
siege unto the castle of Bedegraine; and so they departed and drew
toward Arthur, and left few to abide at the siege, for the castle of
Bedegraine was holden of King Arthur, and the men that were
therein were Arthur's.

CHAPTER XIII

Of a dream of the King with the Hundred Knights.

So by Merlin's advice there were sent fore-riders to skim the country,
and they met with the fore-riders of the north, and made them to tell
which way the host came, and then they told it to Arthur, and by
King Ban and Bors' council they let burn and destroy all the country
afore them, there they should ride.

The King with the Hundred Knights met a wonder dream two
nights afore the battle, that there blew a great wind, and blew down
their castles and their towns, and after that came a water and bare it all

away. All that heard of the sweven said it was a token of great battle. Then by counsel of Merlin, when they wist which way the eleven kings would ride and lodge that night, at midnight they set upon them, as they were in their pavilions. But the scout-watch by their host cried, Lords! at arms! for here be your enemies at your hand!

CHAPTER XIV

How the eleven kings with their host fought against Arthur and his host, and many great feats of the war.

Then King Arthur and King Ban and King Bors, with their good and trusty knights, set on them so fiercely that they made them overthrow their pavilions on their heads, but the eleven kings, by manly prowess of arms, took a fair champaign, but there was slain that morrowtide ten thousand good men's bodies. And so they had afore them a strong passage, yet were they fifty thousand of hardy men. Then it drew toward day. Now shall ye do by mine advice, said Merlin unto the three kings: I would that King Ban and King Bors, with their fellowship of ten thousand men, were put in a wood here beside, in an ambushment, and keep them privy, and that they be laid or the light of the day come, and that they stir not till ye and your knights have fought with them long. And when it is daylight, dress your battle even afore them and the passage, that they may see all your host, for then will they be the more hardy, when they see you but about twenty thousand men, and cause them to be the gladder to suffer you and your host to come over the passage. All the three kings and the whole barons said that Merlin said passingly well, and it was done anon as Merlin had devised. So on the morn, when either host saw other, the host of the north was well comforted. Then to Ulfius and Brastias were delivered three thousand men of arms, and they set on them fiercely in the passage, and slew on the right hand and on the left hand that it was wonder to tell.

When that the eleven kings saw that there was so few a fellowship did such deeds of arms, they were ashamed and set on them again fiercely; and there was Sir Ulfius's horse slain under him, but he did marvellously well on foot. But the Duke Eustace of Cambenet and

King Clariance of Northumberland, were alway grievous on Ulfius. Then Brastias saw his fellow fared so withal he smote the duke with a spear, that horse and man fell down. That saw King Clariance and returned unto Brastias, and either smote other so that horse and man went to the earth, and so they lay long astonied, and their horses' knees brast to the hard bone. Then came Sir Kay the seneschal with six fellows with him, and did passing well. With that came the eleven kings, and there was Griflet put to the earth, horse and man, and Lucas the butler, horse and man, by King Brandegoris, and King Idres, and King Agwisance. Then waxed the medley passing hard on both parties. When Sir Kay saw Griflet on foot, he rode on King Nentres and smote him down, and led his horse unto Sir Griflet, and horsed him again. Also Sir Kay with the same spear smote down King Lot, and hurt him passing sore. That saw the King with the Hundred Knights, and ran unto Sir Kay and smote him down, and took his horse, and gave him King Lot, whereof he said gramercy. When Sir Griflet saw Sir Kay and Lucas the butler on foot, he took a sharp spear, great and square, and rode to Pinel, a good man of arms, and smote horse and man down, and then he took his horse, and gave him unto Sir Kay. Then King Lot saw King Nentres on foot, he ran unto Melot de la Roche, and smote him down, horse and man, and gave King Nentres the horse, and horsed him again. Also the King of the Hundred Knights saw King Idres on foot; then he ran unto Gwimiart de Bloi, and smote him down, horse and man, and gave King Idres the horse, and horsed him again; and King Lot smote down Clariance de la Forest Savage, and gave the horse unto Duke Eustace. And so when they had horsed the kings again they drew them, all eleven kings, together, and said they would be revenged of the damage that they had taken that day. The meanwhile came in Sir Ector with an eager countenance, and found Ulfius and Brastias on foot, in great peril of death, that were foul defoiled under horse-feet.

Then Arthur as a lion, ran unto King Cradelment of North Wales, and smote him through the left side, that the horse and the king fell down; and then he took the horse by the rein, and led him unto Ulfius, and said, Have this horse, mine old friend, for great need hast thou of horse. Gramercy, said Ulfius. Then Sir Arthur did so marvellously in arms, that all men had wonder. When the King with the Hundred Knights saw King Cradelment on foot, he ran unto Sir Ector, that was well horsed, Sir Kay's father, and smote horse and man

down, and gave the horse unto the king, and horsed him again. And
when King Arthur saw the king ride on Sir Ector's horse, he was
wroth and with his sword he smote the king on the helm, that a
quarter of the helm and shield fell down, and so the sword carved
down unto the horse's neck, and so the king and the horse fell down
to the ground. Then Sir Kay came unto Sir Morganore, seneschal with
the King of the Hundred Knights, and smote him down, horse and
man, and led the horse unto his father, Sir Ector; then Sir Ector ran
unto a knight, hight Lardans, and smote horse and man down, and led
the horse unto Sir Brastias, that great need had of an horse, and was
greatly defoiled. When Brastias beheld Lucas the butler, that lay like a
dead man under the horses' feet, and ever Sir Griflet did marvellously
for to rescue him, and there were always fourteen knights on Sir Lucas;
then Brastias smote one of them on the helm, that it went to the teeth,
and he rode to another and smote him, that the arm flew into the field.
Then he went to the third and smote him on the shoulder, that
shoulder and arm flew in the field. And when Griflet saw rescues, he
smote a knight on the temples, that head and helm went to the earth,
and Griflet took the horse of that knight, and led him unto Sir Lucas,
and bade him mount upon the horse and revenge his hurts. For
Brastias had slain a knight to-fore and horsed Griflet.

<h2 style="text-align:center">CHAPTER XV</h2>

Yet of the same battle.

Then Lucas saw King Agwisance, that late had slain Moris de la
Roche, and Lucas ran to him with a short spear that was great, that he
gave him such a fall, that the horse fell down to the earth. Also Lucas
found there on foot, Bloias de La Flandres, and Sir Gwinas, two
hardy knights, and in that woodness that Lucas was in, he slew two
bachelors and horsed them again. Then waxed the battle passing hard
on both parties, but Arthur was glad that his knights were horsed
again, and then they fought together, that the noise and sound rang
by the water and the wood. Wherefore King Ban and King Bors
made them ready, and dressed their shields and harness, and they
were so courageous that many knights shook and bevered for

eagerness. All this while Lucas, and Gwinas, and Briant, and Bellias of Flanders, held strong medley against six kings, that was King Lot, King Nentres, King Brandegoris, King Idres, King Uriens, and King Agwisance. So with the help of Sir Kay and of Sir Griflet they held these six kings hard, that unnethe they had any power to defend them. But when Sir Arthur saw the battle would not be ended by no manner, he fared wood as a lion, and steered his horse here and there, on the right hand, and on the left hand, that he stinted not till he had slain twenty knights. Also he wounded King Lot sore on the shoulder, and made him to leave that ground, for Sir Kay and Griflet did with King Arthur there great deeds of arms. Then Ulfius, and Brastias, and Sir Ector encountered against the Duke Eustace, and King Cradelment, and King Clariance of Northumberland, and King Carados, and against the King with the Hundred Knights. So these knights encountered with these kings, that they made them to avoid the ground. Then King Lot made great dole for his damages and his fellows, and said unto the ten kings, But if ye will do as I devise we shall be slain and destroyed; let me have the King with the Hundred Knights, and King Agwisance, and King Idres, and the Duke of Cambenet, and we five kings will have fifteen thousand men of arms with us, and we will go apart while ye six kings hold medley with twelve thousand; an we see that ye have foughten with them long, then will we come on fiercely, and else shall we never match them, said King Lot, but by this mean. So they departed as they here devised, and six kings made their party strong against Arthur, and made great war long.

In the meanwhile brake the ambushment of King Ban and King Bors, and Lionses and Phariance had the vanguard, and they two knights met with King Idres and his fellowship, and there began a great medley of breaking of spears, and smiting of swords, with slaying of men and horses, and King Idres was near at discomforture.

That saw Agwisance the king, and put Lionses and Phariance in point of death; for the Duke of Cambenet came on withal with a great fellowship. So these two knights were in great danger of their lives that they were fain to return, but always they rescued themselves and their fellowship marvellously. When King Bors saw those knights put aback, it grieved him sore; then he came on so fast that his fellowship seemed as black as Inde. When King Lot had espied King Bors, he knew him well, then he said, O Jesu, defend us from death and horrible maims! for I see well we be in great peril of death; for I see yonder a king, one of the most worshipfullest men and one of the best knights of the world, is inclined unto his fellowship. What is he? said the King with the Hundred Knights. It is, said King Lot, King Bors of Gaul; I marvel how they came into this country without witting of us all. It was by Merlin's advice, said the knight. As for him, said King Carados, I will encounter with King Bors, an ye will rescue me when myster is. Go on, said they all, we will do all that we may. Then King Carados and his host rode on a soft pace, till that they came as nigh King Bors as bow-draught; then either battle let their horse run as fast as they might. And Bleoberis, that was godson unto King Bors, he bare his chief standard, that was a passing good knight. Now shall we see, said King Bors, how these northern Britons can bear the arms: and King Bors encountered with a knight, and smote him throughout with a spear that he fell dead unto the earth; and after drew his sword and did marvellous deeds of arms, that all parties had great wonder thereof; and his knights failed not, but did their part, and King Carados was smitten to the earth. With that came the King with the Hundred Knights and rescued King Carados mightily by force of arms, for he was a passing good knight of a king, and but a young man.

CHAPTER XVI

Yet more of the same battle.

By then came into the field King Ban as fierce as a lion, with bands of green and thereupon gold. Ha! a! said King Lot, we must be discomfited, for yonder I see the most valiant knight of the world, and the man of the most renown, for such two brethren as is King Ban and King Bors are not living, wherefore we must needs void or die; and but if we avoid manly and wisely there is but death. When King Ban came into the battle, he came in so fiercely that the strokes redounded again from the wood and the water; wherefore King Lot wept for pity and dole that he saw so many good knights take their end. But through the great force of King Ban they made both the northern battles that were departed hurtled together for great dread;

and the three kings and their knights slew on ever, that it was pity on to behold that multitude of the people that fled. But King Lot, and King of the Hundred Knights, and King Morganore gathered the people together passing knightly, and did great prowess of arms, and held the battle all that day, like hard.

When the King of the Hundred Knights beheld the great damage that King Ban did, he thrust unto him with his horse, and smote him on high upon the helm, a great stroke, and astonied him sore. Then King Ban was wroth with him, and followed on him fiercely; the other saw that, and cast up his shield, and spurred his horse forward, but the stroke of King Ban fell down and carved a cantel off the shield, and the sword slid down by the hauberk behind his back, and cut through the trapping of steel and the horse even in two pieces, that the sword felt the earth. Then the King of the Hundred Knights voided the horse lightly, and with his sword he broached the horse of King Ban through and through. With that King Ban voided lightly from the dead horse, and then King Ban smote at the other so eagerly, and smote him on the helm that he fell to the earth. Also in that ire he felled King Morganore, and there was great slaughter of good knights and much people. By then came into the press King Arthur, and found King Ban standing among dead men and dead horses, fighting on foot as a wood lion, that there came none nigh him, as far as he might reach with his sword, but he caught a grievous buffet; whereof King Arthur had great pity. And Arthur was so bloody, that by his shield there might no man know him, for all was blood and brains on his sword. And as Arthur looked by him he saw a knight that was passingly well horsed, and therewith Sir Arthur ran to him, and smote him on the helm, that his sword went unto his teeth, and the knight sank down to the earth dead, and anon Arthur took the horse by the rein, and led him unto King Ban, and said, Fair brother, have this horse, for he have great myster thereof, and me repenteth sore of your great damage. It shall be soon revenged, said King Ban, for I trust in God mine ure is not such but some of them may sore repent this. I will well, said Arthur, for I see your deeds full actual; nevertheless, I might not come at you at that time.

But when King Ban was mounted on horseback, then there began new battle, the which was sore and hard, and passing great slaughter. And so through great force King Arthur, King Ban, and King Bors made their knights a little to withdraw them. But alway the eleven kings with their chivalry never turned back; and so withdrew them to a little wood, and so over a little river, and there they rested them, for on the night they might have no rest on the field. And then the eleven kings and knights put them on a heap all together, as men adread and out of all comfort. But there was no man might pass them, they held them so hard together both behind and before, that King Arthur had marvel of their deeds of arms, and was passing wroth. Ah, Sir Arthur, said King Ban and King Bors, blame them not, for they do as good men ought to do. For by my faith, said King Ban, they are the best fighting men, and knights of most prowess, that ever I saw or heard speak of, and those eleven kings are men of great worship; and if they were longing unto you there were no king under the heaven had such eleven knights, and of such worship. I may not love them, said Arthur, they would destroy me. That wot we well, said King Ban and King Bors, for they are your mortal enemies, and that hath been proved aforehand; and this day they have done their part, and that is great pity of their wilfulness.

Then all the eleven kings drew them together, and then said King Lot, Lords, ye must other ways than ye do, or else the great loss is behind; ye may see what people we have lost, and what good men we lose, because we wait always on these foot-men, and ever in saving of one of the foot-men we lose ten horsemen for him; therefore this is mine advice, let us put our foot-men from us, for it is near night, for the noble Arthur will not tarry on the footmen, for they may save themselves, the wood is near hand. And when we horsemen be together, look every each of you kings let make such ordinance that none break upon pain of death. And who that seeth any man dress him to flee, lightly that he be slain, for it is better that we slay a coward, than through a coward all we to be slain. How say ye? said King Lot, answer me all ye kings. It is well said, quoth King Nentres; so said the King of the Hundred Knights; the same said the King Carados, and King Uriens; so did King Idres and King Brandegoris; and so did King Cradelment, and the Duke of Cambenet; the same said King Clariance and King Agwisance, and sware they would never fail other, neither for life nor for death. And whoso that fled, but did as they did, should be slain. Then they amended their harness, and righted their shields, and took new spears and set them on their thighs, and stood still as it had been a plump of wood.

CHAPTER XVII

Yet more of the same battle, and how it was ended by Merlin.

When Sir Arthur and King Ban and Bors beheld them and all their knights, they praised them much for their noble cheer of chivalry, for the hardiest fighters that ever they heard or saw. With that, there dressed them a forty noble knights, and said unto the three kings, they would break their battle; these were their names: Lionses, Phariance, Ulfius, Brastias, Ector, Kay, Lucas the butler, Griflet le Fise de Dieu, Mariet de la Roche, Guinas de Bloi, Briant de la Forest Savage, Bellaus, Morians of the Castle [of] Maidens, Flannedrius of the Castle of Ladies, Annecians that was King Bors' godson, a noble knight, Ladinas de la Rouse, Emerause, Caulas, Graciens le Castlein, one Blois de la Case, and Sir Colgrevaunce de Gorre; all these knights rode on afore with spears on their thighs, and spurred their horses mightily as the horses might run. And the eleven kings with part of their knights rushed with their horses as fast as they might with their spears, and there they did on both parties marvellous deeds of arms. So came into the thick of the press, Arthur, Ban, and Bors, and slew down right on both hands, that their horses went in blood up to the fetlocks. But ever the eleven kings and their host was ever in the visage of Arthur. Wherefore Ban and Bors had great marvel, considering the great slaughter that there was, but at the last they were driven aback over a little river. With that came Merlin on a great black horse, and said unto Arthur, Thou hast never done! Hast thou not done enough? of three score thousand this day hast thou left alive but fifteen thousand, and it is time to say Ho! For God is wroth with thee, that thou wilt never have done; for yonder eleven kings at this time will not be overthrown, but an thou tarry on them any longer, thy fortune will turn and they shall increase. And therefore withdraw you unto your lodging, and rest you as soon as ye may, and reward your good knights with gold and with silver, for they have well deserved it; there may no riches be too dear for them, for of so few men as ye have, there were never men did more of prowess than they have done today, for ye have matched this day with the best fighters of the

world. That is truth, said King Ban and Bors. Also said Merlin,
withdraw you where ye list, for this three year I dare undertake they
shall not dere you; and by then ye shall hear new tidings. And then
Merlin said unto Arthur, These eleven kings have more on hand than
they are ware of, for the Saracens are landed in their countries, more
than forty thousand, that burn and slay, and have laid siege at the castle
Wandesborow, and make great destruction; therefore dread you not
this three year. Also, sir, all the goods that be gotten at this battle, let it
be searched, and when ye have it in your hands, let it be given freely
unto these two kings, Ban and Bors, that they may reward their
knights withal; and that shall cause strangers to be of better will to do
you service at need. Also you be able to reward your own knights of
your own goods whensomever it liketh you. It is well said, quoth
Arthur, and as thou hast devised, so shall it be done. When it was
delivered to Ban and Bors, they gave the goods as freely to their
knights as freely as it was given to them. Then Merlin took his leave
of Arthur and of the two kings, for to go and see his master Bleise, that
dwelt in Northumberland; and so he departed and came to his master,
that was passing glad of his coming; and there he told how Arthur and
the two kings had sped at the great battle, and how it was ended, and
told the names of every king and knight of worship that was there.
And so Bleise wrote the battle word by word, as Merlin told him,
how it began, and by whom, and in likewise how it was ended, and
who had the worse. All the battles that were done in Arthur's days
Merlin did his master Bleise do write; also he did do write all the
battles that every worthy knight did of Arthur's court.

After this Merlin departed from his master and came to King
Arthur, that was in the castle of Bedegraine, that was one of the
castles that stand in the forest of Sherwood. And Merlin was so
disguised that King Arthur knew him not, for he was all befurred in
black sheep-skins, and a great pair of boots, and a bow and arrows, in
a russet gown, and brought wild geese in his hand, and it was on the
morn after Candlemas day; but King Arthur knew him not. Sir, said
Merlin unto the king, will ye give me a gift? Wherefore, said King
Arthur, should I give thee a gift, churl? Sir, said Merlin, ye were
better to give me a gift that is not in your hand than to lose great
riches, for here in the same place where the great battle was, is great
treasure hid in the earth. Who told thee so, churl? said Arthur. Merlin
told me so, said he. Then Ulfius and Brastias knew him well enough,

and smiled. Sir, said these two knights, it is Merlin that so speaketh unto you. Then King Arthur was greatly abashed, and had marvel of Merlin, and so had King Ban and King Bors, and so they had great disport at him. So in the meanwhile there came a damosel that was an earl's daughter: his name was Sanam, and her name was Lionors, a passing fair damosel; and so she came thither for to do homage, as other lords did after the great battle. And King Arthur set his love greatly upon her, and so did she upon him, and the king had ado with her, and gat on her a child: his name was Borre, that was after a good knight, and of the Table Round. Then there came word that the King Rience of North Wales made great war on King Leodegrance of Cameliard, for the which thing Arthur was wroth, for he loved him well, and hated King Rience, for he was alway against him. So by ordinance of the three kings that were sent home unto Benwick, all they would depart for dread of King Claudas; and Phariance, and Antemes, and Gratian, and Lionses [of] Payarne, with the leaders of those that should keep the kings' lands.

CHAPTER XVIII

How King Arthur, King Ban, and King Bors rescued King Leodegrance, and other incidents.

And then King Arthur, and King Ban, and King Bors departed with their fellowship, a twenty thousand, and came within six days into the country of Cameliard, and there rescued King Leodegrance, and slew there much people of King Rience, unto the number of ten thousand men, and put him to flight. And then had these three kings great cheer of King Leodegrance, that thanked them of their great goodness, that they would revenge him of his enemies; and there had Arthur the first sight of Guenever, the king's daughter of Cameliard, and ever after he loved her. After they were wedded, as it telleth in the book. So, briefly to make an end, they took their leave to go into their own countries, for King Claudas did great destruction on their lands. Then said Arthur, I will go with you. Nay, said the kings, ye shall not at this time, for ye have much to do yet in these lands, therefore we will depart, and with the great goods that we have gotten in these lands by your gifts, we shall wage good knights and withstand the King Claudas' malice, for by the grace of God, an we have need we will send to you for your succour; and if ye have need, send for us, and we will not tarry, by the faith of our bodies. It shall not, said Merlin, need that these two kings come again in the way of war, but I know well King Arthur may not be long from you, for within a year or two ye shall have great need, and then shall he revenge you on your enemies, as ye have done on his. For these eleven kings shall die all in a day, by the great might and prowess of arms of two valiant knights (as it telleth after); their names be Balin le Savage, and Balan, his brother, that be marvellous good knights as be any living.

Now turn we to the eleven kings that returned unto a city that hight Sorhaute, the which city was within King Uriens', and there they refreshed them as well as they might, and made leeches search their wounds, and sorrowed greatly for the death of their people. With that there came a messenger and told how there was come into their lands people that were lawless as well as Saracens, a forty thousand, and have burnt and slain all the people that they may come by, without mercy, and have laid siege on the castle of Wandesborow. Alas, said the eleven kings, here is sorrow upon sorrow, and if we had not warred against Arthur as we have done, he would soon revenge us. As for King Leodegrance, he loveth Arthur better than us, and as for King Rience, he hath enough to do with Leodegrance, for he hath laid siege unto him. So they consented together to keep all the marches of Cornwall, of Wales, and of the North. So first, they put King Idres in the City of Nauntes in Britain, with four thousand men of arms, to watch both the water and the land. Also they put in the city of Windesan, King Nentres of Garlot, with four thousand knights to watch both on water and on land. Also they had of other men of war more than eight thousand, for to fortify all the fortresses in the marches of Cornwall. Also they put more knights in all the marches of Wales and Scotland, with many good men of arms, and so they kept them together the space of three year, and ever allied them with mighty kings and dukes and lords. And to them fell King Rience of North Wales, the which was a mighty man of men, and Nero that was a mighty man of men. And all this while they furnished them and garnished them of good men of arms, and victual, and of all manner of habiliment that pretendeth to the war, to avenge them for the battle of Bedegraine, as it telleth in the book of adventures following.

CHAPTER XIX

*How King Arthur rode to Carlion, and of his dream, and
how he saw the questing beast.*

Then after the departing of King Ban and of King Bors, King Arthur
rode into Carlion. And thither came to him, King Lot's wife, of
Orkney, in manner of a message, but she was sent thither to espy the
court of King Arthur; and she came richly beseen, with her four sons,
Gawaine, Gaheris, Agravine, and Gareth, with many other knights
and ladies. For she was a passing fair lady, therefore the king cast great
love unto her, and desired to lie by her; so they were agreed, and he
begat upon her Mordred, and she was his sister, on his mother's side,
Igraine. So there she rested her a month, and at the last departed.
Then the king dreamed a marvellous dream whereof he was sore
adread. But all this time King Arthur knew not that King Lot's wife
was his sister. Thus was the dream of Arthur: Him thought there was
come into this land griffins and serpents, and him thought they burnt
and slew all the people in the land, and then him thought he fought
with them, and they did him passing great harm, and wounded him
full sore, but at the last he slew them. When the king awaked, he was
passing heavy of his dream, and so to put it out of thoughts, he made
him ready with many knights to ride a-hunting. As soon as he was in
the forest the king saw a great hart afore him. This hart will I chase,
said King Arthur, and so he spurred the horse, and rode after long,
and so by fine force oft he was like to have smitten the hart; whereas
the king had chased the hart so long, that his horse lost his breath, and
fell down dead. Then a yeoman fetched the king another horse.

So the king saw the hart enbushed, and his horse dead, he set him
down by a fountain, and there he fell in great thoughts. And as he sat
so, him thought he heard a noise of hounds, to the sum of thirty. And
with that the king saw coming toward him the strangest beast that
ever he saw or heard of; so the beast went to the well and drank, and
the noise was in the beast's belly like unto the questing of thirty
couple hounds; but all the while the beast drank there was no noise in
the beast's belly: and therewith the beast departed with a great noise,

whereof the king had great marvel. And so he was in a great thought, and therewith he fell asleep. Right so there came a knight afoot unto Arthur and said, Knight full of thought and sleepy, tell me if thou sawest a strange beast pass this way. Such one saw I, said King Arthur, that is past two mile; what would ye with the beast? said Arthur. Sir, I have followed that beast long time, and killed mine horse, so would God I had another to follow my quest. Right so came one with the king's horse, and when the knight saw the horse, he prayed the king to give him the horse: for I have followed this quest this twelvemonth, and either I shall achieve him, or bleed of the best blood of my body. Pellinore, that time king, followed the Questing Beast, and after his death Sir Palomides followed it.

CHAPTER XX

How King Pellinore took Arthur's horse and followed the Questing Beast, and how Merlin met with Arthur.

Sir knight, said the king, leave that quest, and suffer me to have it, and I will follow it another twelvemonth. Ah, fool, said the knight unto Arthur, it is in vain thy desire, for it shall never be achieved but by me, or my next kin. Therewith he started unto the king's horse and mounted into the saddle, and said, Gramercy, this horse is my own. Well, said the king, thou mayst take my horse by force, but an I might prove thee whether thou were better on horseback or I. – Well, said the knight, seek me here when thou wilt, and here nigh this well thou shalt find me, and so passed on his way. Then the king sat in a study, and bade his men fetch his horse as fast as ever they might. Right so came by him Merlin like a child of fourteen year of age, and saluted the king, and asked him why he was so pensive. I may well be pensive, said the king, for I have seen the marvellest sight that ever I saw. That know I well, said Merlin, as well as thyself, and of all thy thoughts, but thou art but a fool to take thought, for it will not amend thee. Also I know what thou art, and who was thy father, and of whom thou wert begotten; King Uther Pendragon was thy father, and begat thee on Igraine. That is false, said King Arthur, how shouldest thou know it, for thou art not so old of years to know my father? Yes, said Merlin, I know it better than ye or any man living. I will not believe thee, said Arthur, and was wroth with the child. So departed Merlin, and came again in the likeness of an old man of fourscore year of age, whereof the king was right glad, for he seemed to be right wise.

Then said the old man, Why are ye so sad? I may well be heavy, said Arthur, for many things. Also here was a child, and told me many things that meseemeth he should not know, for he was not of age to know my father. Yes, said the old man, the child told you truth, and more would he have told you an ye would have suffered him. But ye have done a thing late that God is displeased with you, for ye have lain by your sister, and on her ye have gotten a child that shall destroy you and all the knights of your realm. What are ye, said Arthur, that tell me these tidings? I am Merlin, and I was he in the child's likeness. Ah, said King Arthur, ye are a marvellous man, but I marvel much of thy words that I must die in battle. Marvel not, said Merlin, for it is God's will your body to be punished for your foul deeds; but I may well be sorry, said Merlin, for I shall die a shameful death, to be put in the earth quick, and ye shall die a worshipful death. And as they talked this, came one with the king's horse, and so the king mounted on his horse, and Merlin on another, and so rode unto Carlion. And anon the king asked Ector and Ulfius how he was begotten, and they told him Uther Pendragon was his father and Queen Igraine his mother. Then he said to Merlin, I will that my mother be sent for, that I may speak with her; and if she say so herself, then will I believe it. In all haste, the queen was sent for, and she came and brought with her Morgan le Fay, her daughter, that was as fair a lady as any might be, and the king welcomed Igraine in the best manner.

CHAPTER XXI

*How Ulfius impeached Queen Igraine, Arthur's mother, of
treason; and how a knight came and desired to have the
death of his master revenged.*

Right so came Ulfius, and said openly, that the king and all might
hear that were feasted that day, Ye are the falsest lady of the world,
and the most traitress unto the king's person. Beware, said Arthur,
what thou sayest; thou speakest a great word. I am well ware, said
Ulfius, what I speak, and here is my glove to prove it upon any man
that will say the contrary, that this Queen Igraine is causer of your
great damage, and of your great war. For, an she would have uttered
it in the life of King Uther Pendragon, of the birth of you, and how
ye were begotten, ye had never had the mortal wars that ye have had;
for the most part of your barons of your realm knew never whose son
ye were, nor of whom ye were begotten; and she that bare you of her
body should have made it known openly in excusing of her worship
and yours, and in like wise to all the realm wherefore I prove her false
to God and to you and to all you realm, and who will say the
contrary I will prove it on his body.

Then spake Igraine and said, I am a woman and I may not fight,
but rather than I should be dishonoured, there would some good
man take my quarrel. More, she said, Merlin knoweth well, and ye
Sir Ulfius, how King Uther came to me in the Castle of Tintagil in
the likeness of my lord, that was dead three hours to-fore, and
thereby gat a child that night upon me. And after the thirteenth day
King Uther wedded me, and by his commandment when the child
was born it was delivered unto Merlin and nourished by him, and so
I saw the child never after, nor wot not what is his name, for I knew
him never yet. And there, Ulfius said to the queen, Merlin is more to
blame than ye. Well I wot, said the queen, I bare a child by my lord
King Uther, but I wot not where he is become. Then Merlin took
the king by the hand, saying, This is your mother. And therewith Sir
Ector bare witness how he nourished him by Uther's commandment.

And therewith King Arthur took his mother, Queen Igraine, in his arms and kissed her, and either wept upon other. And then the king let make a feast that lasted eight days.

Then on a day there came in the court a squire on horseback, leading a knight before him wounded to the death, and told him how there was a knight in the forest had reared up a pavilion by a well, and hath slain my master, a good knight, his name was Miles; wherefore I beseech you that my master may be buried, and that some knight may revenge my master's death. Then the noise was great of that knight's death in the court, and every man said his advice. Then came Griflet that was but a squire, and he was but young, of the age of the king Arthur, so he besought the king for all his service that he had done him to give the order of knighthood.

CHAPTER XXII

How Griflet was made knight, and jousted with a knight.

Thou art full young and tender of age, said Arthur, for to take so high an order on thee. Sir, said Griflet, I beseech you make me knight. Sir, said Merlin, it were great pity to lose Griflet for he will be a passing good man when he is of age, abiding with you the term of his life. And if he adventure his body with yonder knight at the fountain, it is in great peril if ever he come again, for he is one of the best knights of the world, and the strongest man of arms. Well, said Arthur. So at the desire of Griflet the king made him knight. Now, said Arthur unto Sir Griflet, sith I have made you knight thou must give me a gift. What ye will, said Griflet. Thou shalt promise me by the faith of thy body, when thou hast jousted with the knight at the fountain, whether it fall ye be on foot or on horseback, that right so ye shall come again unto me without making any more debate. I will promise you, said Griflet, as you desire. Then took Griflet his horse in great haste, and dressed his shield and took a spear in his hand, and so he rode a great wallop till he came to the fountain, and thereby he saw a rich pavilion, and thereby under a cloth stood a fair horse well saddled and bridled, and on a tree a shield of divers colours and a great spear. Then Griflet smote on the shield with the butt of his spear, that the shield fell down to the ground. With that the knight came out of the pavilion, and said, Fair knight, why smote ye down my shield? For I will joust with you, said Griflet. It is better ye do not, said the knight, for ye are but young, and late made knight, and your might is nothing to mine. As for that, said Griflet, I will joust with you. That is me loath, said the knight, but sith I must needs, I will dress me thereto. Of whence be ye? said the knight. Sir, I am of Arthur's court. So the two knights ran together that Griflet's spear all to-shivered; and therewithal he smote Griflet through the shield and the left side, and brake the spear that the truncheon stuck in his body, that horse and knight fell down.

CHAPTER XXIII

How twelve knights came from Rome and asked truage for this land of Arthur, and how Arthur fought with a knight.

When the knight saw him lie so on the ground, he alighted, and was passing heavy, for he weened he had slain him, and then he unlaced his helm and gat him wind, and so with the truncheon he set him on his horse, and so betook him to God, and said he had a mighty heart, and if he might live he would prove a passing good knight. And so Sir Griflet rode to the court, where great dole was made for him. But through good leeches he was healed and saved. Right so came into the court twelve knights, and were aged men, and they came from the Emperor of Rome, and they asked of Arthur truage for this realm, other else the emperor would destroy him and his land. Well, said King Arthur, ye are messengers, therefore ye may say what ye will, other else ye should die therefore. But this is mine answer: I owe the emperor no truage, nor none will I hold him, but on a fair field I shall give him my truage that shall be with a sharp spear, or else with a sharp sword, and that shall not be long, by my father's soul, Uther Pendragon. And therewith the messengers departed passingly wroth, and King Arthur as wroth, for in evil time came they then; for the king was passingly wroth for the hurt of Sir Griflet. And so he commanded a privy man of his chamber that or it be day his best horse and armour, with all that longeth unto his person, be without the city or to-morrow day. Right so or to-morrow day he met with his man and his horse, and so mounted up and dressed his shield and took his spear, and bade his chamberlain tarry there till he came again. And so Arthur rode a soft pace till it was day, and then was he ware of three churls chasing Merlin, and would have slain him. Then the king rode unto them, and bade them: Flee, churls! then were they afeard when they saw a knight, and fled. O Merlin, said Arthur, here hadst thou been slain for all thy crafts had I not been. Nay, said Merlin, not so, for I could save myself an I would; and thou art more near thy death than I am, for thou goest to the deathward, an God be not thy friend.

So as they went thus talking they came to the fountain, and the rich pavilion there by it. Then King Arthur was ware where sat a knight armed in a chair. Sir knight, said Arthur, for what cause abidest thou here, that there may no knight ride this way but if he joust with thee? said the king. I rede thee leave that custom, said Arthur. This custom, said the knight, have I used and will use maugre who saith nay, and who is grieved with my custom let him amend it that will. I will amend it, said Arthur. I shall defend thee, said the knight. Anon he took his horse and dressed his shield and took a spear, and they met so hard either in other's shields, that all to-shivered their spears. Therewith anon Arthur pulled out his sword. Nay, not so, said the knight; it is fairer, said the knight, that we twain run more together with sharp spears. I will well, said Arthur, an I had any more spears. I have enow, said the knight; so there came a squire and brought two good spears, and Arthur chose one and he another; so they spurred their horses and came together with all their mights, that either brake their spears to their hands. Then Arthur set hand on his sword. Nay, said the knight, ye shall do better, ye are a passing good jouster as ever I met withal, and once for the love of the high order of knighthood let us joust once again. I assent me, said Arthur. Anon there were brought two great spears, and every knight gat a spear, and therewith they ran together that Arthur's spear all to-shivered. But the other knight hit him so hard in midst of the shield, that horse and man fell to the earth, and therewith Arthur was eager, and pulled out his sword, and said, I will assay thee, sir knight, on foot, for I have lost the honour on horseback. I will be on horseback, said the knight. Then was Arthur wroth, and dressed his shield toward him with his sword drawn. When the knight saw that, he alighted, for him thought no

worship to have a knight at such avail, he to be on horseback and he
on foot, and so he alighted and dressed his shield unto Arthur. And
there began a strong battle with many great strokes, and so hewed
with their swords that the cantels flew in the fields, and much blood
they bled both, that all the place there as they fought was overbled
with blood, and thus they fought long and rested them, and then they
went to the battle again, and so hurtled together like two rams that
either fell to the earth. So at the last they smote together that both
their swords met even together. But the sword of the knight smote
King Arthur's sword in two pieces, wherefore he was heavy. Then
said the knight unto Arthur, Thou art in my daunger whether me list
to save thee or slay thee, and but thou yield thee as overcome and
recreant, thou shalt die. As for death, said King Arthur, welcome be it
when it cometh, but to yield me unto thee as recreant I had liefer die
than to be so shamed. And therewithal the king leapt unto Pellinore,
and took him by the middle and threw him down, and raced off his
helm. When the knight felt that he was adread, for he was a passing
big man of might, and anon he brought Arthur under him, and raced
off his helm and would have smitten off his head.

CHAPTER XXIV

How Merlin saved Arthur's life, and threw an enchantment
on King Pellinore and made him to sleep.

Therewithal came Merlin and said, Knight, hold thy hand, for an
thou slay that knight thou puttest this realm in the greatest damage
that ever was realm: for this knight is a man of more worship than
thou wottest of. Why, who is he? said the knight. It is King Arthur.
Then would he have slain him for dread of his wrath, and heaved up
his sword, and therewith Merlin cast an enchantment to the knight,
that he fell to the earth in a great sleep. Then Merlin took up King
Arthur, and rode forth on the knight's horse. Alas! said Arthur, what
hast thou done, Merlin? hast thou slain this good knight by thy crafts?
There liveth not so worshipful a knight as he was; I had liefer than
the stint of my land a year that he were alive. Care ye not, said
Merlin, for he is wholer than ye; for he is but asleep, and will awake

within three hours. I told you, said Merlin, what a knight he was; here had ye been slain had I not been. Also there liveth not a bigger knight than he is one, and he shall hereafter do you right good service; and his name is Pellinore, and he shall have two sons that shall be passing good men; save one they shall have no fellow of prowess and of good living, and their names shall be Percivale of Wales and Lamerake of Wales, and he shall tell you the name of your own son, begotten of your sister, that shall be the destruction of all this realm.

CHAPTER XXV

How Arthur by the mean of Merlin gat Excalibur his sword of the Lady of the Lake.

Right so the king and he departed, and went unto an hermit that was a good man and a great leech. So the hermit searched all his wounds and gave him good salves; so the king was there three days, and then were his wounds well amended that he might ride and go, and so departed. And as they rode, Arthur said, I have no sword. No force, said Merlin, hereby is a sword that shall be yours, an I may. So they rode till they came to a lake, the which was a fair water and broad, and in the midst of the lake Arthur was ware of an arm clothed in white samite, that held a fair sword in that hand. Lo! said Merlin, yonder is that sword that I spake of. With that they saw a damosel going upon the lake. What damosel is that? said Arthur. That is the Lady of the Lake, said Merlin; and within that lake is a rock, and therein is as fair a place as any on earth, and richly beseen; and this damosel will come to you anon, and then speak ye fair to her that she will give you that sword. Anon withal came the damosel unto Arthur, and saluted him, and he her again. Damosel, said Arthur, what sword is that, that yonder the arm holdeth above the water? I would it were mine, for I have no sword. Sir Arthur, king, said the damosel, that sword is mine, and if ye will give me a gift when I ask it you, ye shall have it. By my faith, said Arthur, I will give you what gift ye will ask. Well, said the damosel, go ye into yonder barge, and row yourself to the sword, and take it and the scabbard with you, and I will ask my gift when I see my time. So Sir Arthur and Merlin alighted and tied their horses to two trees, and so they went into the ship, and when they came to the sword that the hand held, Sir Arthur took it up by the handles, and took it with him, and the arm and the hand went under the water. And so [they] came unto the land and rode forth, and then Sir Arthur saw a rich pavilion. What signifieth yonder pavilion? It is the knight's pavilion, said Merlin, that ye fought with last, Sir Pellinore; but he is out, he is not there. He hath ado with a knight of yours that hight Egglame, and they have foughten together, but at the last Egglame fled, and else he had been dead, and he hath chased him even to Carlion, and we shall meet with him anon in the highway. That is well said, said Arthur, now have I a sword, now will I wage battle with him, and be avenged on him. Sir, you shall not so, said Merlin, for the knight is weary of fighting and chasing, so that ye shall have no worship to have ado with him; also he will not be lightly matched of one knight living, and therefore it is my counsel, let him pass, for he shall do you good service in short time, and his sons after his days. Also ye shall see that day in short space, you shall be right glad to give him your sister to wed. When I see him, I will do as ye advise, said Arthur.

Then Sir Arthur looked on the sword, and liked it passing well. Whether liketh you better, said Merlin, the sword or the scabbard? Me liketh better the sword, said Arthur. Ye are more unwise, said Merlin, for the scabbard is worth ten of the swords, for whiles ye have the scabbard upon you, ye shall never lose no blood, be ye never so sore wounded; therefore keep well the scabbard always with you. So they rode unto Carlion, and by the way they met with Sir Pellinore; but Merlin had done such a craft, that Pellinore saw not Arthur, and he passed by without any words. I marvel, said Arthur, that the knight would not speak. Sir, said Merlin, he saw you not, for an he had seen you, ye had not lightly departed. So they came unto Carlion, whereof his knights were passing glad. And when they heard of his adventures, they marvelled that he would jeopard his person so, alone. But all men of worship said it was merry to be under such a chieftain, that would put his person in adventure as other poor knights did.

CHAPTER XXVI

*How tidings came to Arthur that King Rience had overcome
eleven kings, and how he desired Arthur's beard to
trim his mantle.*

This meanwhile came a messenger from King Rience of North
Wales, and king he was of all Ireland, and of many isles. And this was
his message, greeting well King Arthur in this manner wise, saying
that King Rience had discomfited and overcome eleven kings, and
everych of them did him homage, and that was this, they gave him
their beards clean flayed off, as much as there was; wherefore the
messenger came for King Arthur's beard. For King Rience had
purfled a mantle with kings' beards, and there lacked one place of the
mantle; wherefore he sent for his beard, or else he would enter into
his lands, and burn and slay, and never leave till he have the head and
the beard. Well, said Arthur, thou hast said thy message, the which is
the most villainous and lewdest message that ever man heard sent
unto a king; also thou mayest see my beard is full young yet to make
a purfle of it. But tell thou thy king this: I owe him none homage,
nor none of mine elders; but or it be long to, he shall do me homage
on both his knees, or else he shall lose his head, by the faith of my
body, for this is the most shamefullest message that ever I heard speak
of. I have espied thy king met never yet with worshipful man, but tell
him, I will have his head without he do me homage. Then the
messenger departed.

Now is there any here, said Arthur, that knoweth King Rience?
Then answered a knight that hight Naram, Sir, I know the king well;
he is a passing good man of his body, as few be living, and a passing
proud man, and Sir, doubt ye not he will make war on you with a
mighty puissance. Well, said Arthur, I shall ordain for him in short
time.

CHAPTER XXVII

How all the children were sent for that were born on
May-day, and how Mordred was saved.

Then King Arthur let send for all the children born on May-day,
begotten of lords and born of ladies; for Merlin told King Arthur that
he that should destroy him should be born on May-day, wherefore
he sent for them all, upon pain of death; and so there were found
many lords' sons, and all were sent unto the king and so was Mordred
sent by King Lot's wife, and all were put in a ship to the sea, and
some were four weeks old, and some less. And so by fortune the ship
drave unto a castle, and was all to-riven, and destroyed the most part,
save that Mordred was cast up, and a good man found him, and
nourished him till he was fourteen year old, and then he brought him
to the court, as it rehearseth afterward, toward the end of the Death
of Arthur. So many lords and barons of this realm were displeased, for
their children were so lost, and many put the wite on Merlin more
than on Arthur; so what for dread and for love, they held their peace.
But when the messenger came to King Rience, then was he wood
out of measure, and purveyed him for a great host, as it rehearseth
after in the book of Balin le Savage, that followeth next after, how by
adventure Balin gat the sword.

Explicit liber primus. Incipit liber secundus.

BOOK TWO

CHAPTER I

Of a damosel which came girt with a sword for to find a man of such virtue to draw it out of the scabbard.

After the death of Uther Pendragon reigned Arthur his son, the which had great war in his days for to get all England into his hand. For there were many kings within the realm of England, and in Wales, Scotland, and Cornwall. So it befell on a time when King Arthur was at London, there came a knight and told the king tidings how that the King Rience of North Wales had reared a great number of people, and were entered into the land, and burnt and slew the king's true liege people. If this be true, said Arthur, it were great shame unto mine estate but that he were mightily withstood. It is truth, said the knight, for I saw the host myself. Well, said the king, let make a cry, that all the lords, knights, and gentlemen of arms, should draw unto a castle called Camelot in those days, and there the king would let make a council-general and a great jousts.

So when the king was come thither with all his baronage, and lodged as they seemed best, there was come a damosel the which was sent on message from the great lady Lile of Avelion. And when she came before King Arthur, she told from whom she came, and how she was sent on message unto him for these causes. Then she let her mantle fall that was richly furred; and then was she girt with a noble sword whereof the king had marvel, and said, Damosel, for what cause are ye girt with that sword? it beseemeth you not. Now shall I tell you, said the damosel; this sword that I am girt withal doth me great sorrow and cumbrance, for I may not be delivered of this sword but by a knight, but he must be a passing good man of his hands and of his deeds, and without villainy or treachery, and without treason. And if I may find such a knight that hath all these virtues, he may draw out this sword out of the sheath, for I have been at King Rience's, it was told me there were passing good knights, and he and all his knights have assayed it and none can speed. This is a great marvel, said Arthur, if this be sooth; I will myself assay to draw out the sword, not presuming upon myself that I am the best knight, but that I will begin to draw at your sword in giving example to all the barons that they shall assay everych one after other when I have assayed it. Then Arthur took the sword by the sheath and by the girdle and pulled at it eagerly, but the sword would not out.

Sir, said the damosel, you need not to pull half so hard, for he that shall pull it out shall do it with little might. Ye say well, said Arthur; now assay ye all my barons, but beware ye be not defiled with shame, treachery, nor guile. Then it will not avail, said the damosel, for he must be a clean knight without villainy, and of a gentle strain of father side and mother side. Most of all the barons of the Round Table that were there at that time assayed all by row, but there might none speed; wherefore the damosel made great sorrow out of measure, and said, Alas! I weened in this court had been the best knights without treachery or treason. By my faith, said Arthur, here are good knights, as I deem, as any be in the world, but their grace is not to help you, wherefore I am displeased.

CHAPTER II

How Balin, arrayed like a poor knight, pulled out the sword, which afterward was the cause of his death.

Then fell it so that time there was a poor knight with King Arthur, that had been prisoner with him half a year and more for slaying of a knight, the which was cousin unto King Arthur. The name of this knight was called Balin, and by good means of the barons he was delivered out of prison, for he was a good man named of his body, and he was born in Northumberland. And so he went privily into the court, and saw this adventure, whereof it raised his heart, and he would assay it as other knights did, but for he was poor and poorly arrayed he put him not far in press. But in his heart he was fully assured to do as well, if his grace happed him, as any knight that there was. And as the damosel took her leave of Arthur and of all the barons, so departing, this knight Balin called unto her, and said, Damosel, I pray you of your courtesy, suffer me as well to assay as these lords; though that I be so poorly clothed, in my heart meseemeth I am fully assured as some of these others, and meseemeth in my heart to speed right well. The damosel beheld the poor knight, and saw he was a likely man, but for his poor arrayment she thought he should be of no worship without villainy or treachery. And then she said unto the knight, Sir, it needeth not to put me to more pain or labour, for it seemeth not you to speed there as other have failed. Ah! fair damosel, said Balin, worthiness, and good tatches, and good deeds, are not only in arrayment, but manhood and worship is hid within man's person, and many a worshipful knight is not known unto all people, and therefore worship and hardiness is not in arrayment. By God, said the damosel, ye say sooth; therefore ye shall assay to do what ye may. Then Balin took the sword by the girdle and sheath, and drew it out easily; and when he looked on the sword it pleased him much. Then had the king and all the barons great marvel that Balin had done that adventure, and many knights had great despite of Balin. Certes, said the damosel, this is a passing good knight, and the best that ever I found, and most of worship without treason, treachery, or villainy, and many marvels shall he do. Now, gentle and courteous knight, give me the sword again. Nay, said Balin, for this sword will I keep, but it be taken from me with force. Well, said the damosel, ye are not wise to keep the sword from me, for ye shall slay with the sword the best friend that ye have, and the man that ye most love in the world, and the sword shall be your destruction. I shall take the adventure, said Balin, that God will ordain me, but the sword ye shall not have at this time, by the faith of my body. Ye shall repent it within short time, said the damosel, for I would have the sword more for your avail than for mine, for I am passing heavy for your sake; for ye will not believe that sword shall be your destruction, and that is great pity. With that the damosel departed, making great sorrow.

Anon after, Balin sent for his horse and armour, and so would depart from the court, and took his leave of King Arthur. Nay, said the king, I suppose ye will not depart so lightly from this fellowship, I suppose ye are displeased that I have showed you unkindness; blame me the less, for I was misinformed against you, but I weened ye had not been such a knight as ye are, of worship and prowess, and if ye will abide in this court among my fellowship, I shall so advance you as ye shall be pleased. God thank your highness, said Balin, your bounty and highness may no man praise half to the value; but at this time I must needs depart, beseeching you alway of your good grace. Truly, said the king, I am right wroth for your departing; I pray you, fair knight, that ye tarry not long, and ye shall be right welcome to me, and to my barons, and I shall amend all miss that I have done against you. God thank your great lordship, said Balin, and therewith made him ready to depart. Then the most part of the knights of the Round Table said that Balin did not this adventure all only by might, but by witchcraft.

CHAPTER III

How the Lady of the Lake demanded the knight's head that
had won the sword, or the maiden's head.

The meanwhile, that this knight was making him ready to depart, there came into the court a lady that hight the Lady of the Lake. And she came on horseback, richly beseen, and saluted King Arthur, and there asked him a gift that he promised her when she gave him the sword. That is sooth, said Arthur, a gift I promised you, but I have forgotten the name of my sword that ye gave me. The name of it, said the lady, is Excalibur, that is as much to say as Cut-steel. Ye say well, said the king; ask what ye will and ye shall have it, an it lie in my power to give it. Well, said the lady, I ask the head of the knight that hath won the sword, or else the damosel's head that brought it; I take no force though I have both their heads, for he slew my brother, a good knight and a true, and that gentlewoman was causer of my father's death. Truly, said King Arthur, I may not grant neither of their heads with my worship, therefore ask what ye will else, and I shall fulfil your desire. I will ask none other thing, said the lady. When Balin was ready to depart, he saw the Lady of the Lake, that by her means had slain Balin's mother, and he had sought her three years; and when it was told him that she asked his head of King Arthur, he went to her straight and said, Evil be you found; ye would have my head, and therefore ye shall lose yours, and with his sword lightly he smote off her head before King Arthur. Alas, for shame! said Arthur, why have ye done so? ye have shamed me and all my court, for this was a lady that I was beholden to, and hither she came under my safe-conduct; I shall never forgive you that trespass. Sir, said Balin, me forthinketh of your displeasure, for this same lady was the untruest lady living, and by enchantment and sorcery she hath been the destroyer of many good knights, and she was causer that my mother was burnt, through her falsehood and treachery. What cause soever ye had, said Arthur, ye should have forborne her in my presence; therefore, think not the contrary, ye shall repent it, for such another despite had I never in my court; therefore withdraw you out of my court in all haste ye may.

Then Balin took up the head of the lady, and bare it with him to his hostelry, and there he met with his squire, that was sorry he had displeased King Arthur, and so they rode forth out of the town. Now, said Balin, we must depart, take thou this head and bear it to my friends, and tell them how I have sped, and tell my friends in Northumberland that my most foe is dead. Also tell them how I am out of prison, and what adventure befell me at the getting of this sword. Alas! said the squire, ye are greatly to blame for to displease King Arthur. As for that, said Balin, I will hie me, in all the haste that I may, to meet with King Rience and destroy him, either else to die therefore; and if it may hap me to win him, then will King Arthur be my good and gracious lord. Where shall I meet with you? said the squire. In King Arthur's court, said Balin. So his squire and he departed at that time. Then King Arthur and all the court made great dole and had shame of the death of the Lady of the Lake. Then the king buried her richly.

CHAPTER IV

How Merlin told the adventure of this damosel.

At that time there was a knight, the which was the king's son of Ireland, and his name was Lanceor, the which was an orgulous knight, and counted himself one of the best of the court; and he had great despite at Balin for the achieving of the sword, that any should

be accounted more hardy, or more of prowess; and he asked King
Arthur if he would give him leave to ride after Balin and to revenge
the despite that he had done. Do your best, said Arthur, I am right
wroth with Balin; I would he were quit of the despite that he hath
done to me and to my court. Then this Lanceor went to his hostelry
to make him ready. In the meanwhile came Merlin unto the court of
King Arthur, and there was told him the adventure of the sword, and
the death of the Lady of the Lake. Now shall I say you, said Merlin;
this same damosel that here standeth, that brought the sword unto
your court, I shall tell you the cause of her coming: she was the falsest
damosel that liveth. Say not so, said they. She hath a brother, a
passing good knight of prowess and a full true man; and this damosel
loved another knight that held her to paramour, and this good knight
her brother met with the knight that held her to paramour, and slew
him by force of his hands. When this false damosel understood this,
she went to the Lady Lile of Avelion, and besought her of help, to be
avenged on her own brother.

CHAPTER V

How Balin was pursued by Sir Lanceor, knight of Ireland, and how he jousted and slew him.

And so this Lady Lile of Avelion took her this sword that she brought
with her, and told there should no man pull it out of the sheath but if
he be one of the best knights of this realm, and he should be hard and
full of prowess, and with that sword he should slay her brother. This
was the cause that the damosel came into this court. I know it as well
as ye. Would God she had not come into this court, but she came
never in fellowship of worship to do good, but always great harm;
and that knight that hath achieved the sword shall be destroyed by
that sword, for the which will be great damage, for there liveth not a
knight of more prowess than he is, and he shall do unto you, my
Lord Arthur, great honour and kindness; and it is great pity he shall
not endure but a while, for of his strength and hardiness I know not
his match living.

So the knight of Ireland armed him at all points, and dressed his shield on his shoulder, and mounted upon horseback, and took his spear in his hand, and rode after a great pace, as much as his horse might go; and within a little space on a mountain he had a sight of Balin, and with a loud voice he cried, Abide, knight, for ye shall abide whether ye will or nill, and the shield that is to-fore you shall not help. When Balin heard the noise, he turned his horse fiercely, and said, Fair knight, what will ye with me, will ye joust with me? Yea, said the Irish knight, therefore come I after you. Peradventure, said Balin, it had been better to have holden you at home, for many a man weeneth to put his enemy to a rebuke, and oft it falleth to himself. Of what court be ye sent from? said Balin. I am come from the court of King Arthur, said the knight of Ireland, that come hither for to revenge the despite ye did this day to King Arthur and to his court. Well, said Balin, I see well I must have ado with you, that me forthinketh for to grieve King Arthur, or any of his court; and your quarrel is full simple, said Balin, unto me, for the lady that is dead, did me great damage, and else would I have been loath as any knight that liveth for to slay a lady. Make you ready, said the knight Lanceor, and dress you unto me, for that one shall abide in the field. Then they took their spears, and came together as much as their horses might drive, and the Irish knight smote Balin on the shield, that all went shivers off his spear, and Balin hit him through the shield, and the hauberk perished, and so pierced through his body and the horse's croup, and anon turned his horse fiercely, and drew out his sword, and wist not that he had slain him; and then he saw him lie as a dead corpse.

CHAPTER VI

How a damosel, which was love to Lanceor, slew herself for love, and how Balin met with his brother Balan.

Then he looked by him, and was ware of a damosel that came riding full fast as the horse might ride, on a fair palfrey. And when she espied that Lanceor was slain, she made sorrow out of measure, and said, O Balin, two bodies thou hast slain and one heart, and two hearts in one body, and two souls thou hast lost. And therewith she took the sword from her love that lay dead, and fell to the ground in a swoon. And when she arose she made great dole out of measure, the which sorrow grieved Balin passingly sore, and he went unto her for to have taken the sword out of her hand, but she held it so fast he might not take it out of her hand unless he should have hurt her, and suddenly she set the pommel to the ground, and rove herself through the body. When Balin espied her deeds, he was passing heavy in his heart, and ashamed that so fair a damosel had destroyed herself for the love of his death. Alas, said Balin, me repenteth sore the death of this knight, for the love of this damosel, for there was much true love betwixt them both, and for sorrow might not longer behold him, but turned his horse and looked toward a great forest, and there he was ware, by the arms, of his brother Balan. And when they were met they put off their helms and kissed together, and wept for joy and pity. Then Balan said, I little weened to have met with you at this sudden adventure; I am right glad of your deliverance out of your dolorous prisonment, for a man told me, in the castle of Four Stones, that ye were delivered, and that man had seen you in the court of King Arthur, and therefore I came hither into this country, for here I supposed to find you. Anon the knight Balin told his brother of his adventure of the sword, and of the death of the Lady of the Lake, and how King Arthur was displeased with him. Wherefore he sent this knight after me, that lieth here dead, and the death of this damosel grieveth me sore. So doth it me, said Balan, but ye must take the adventure that God will ordain you. Truly, said Balin, I am right heavy that my Lord Arthur is displeased with me, for he is the most worshipful knight that reigneth now on earth, and his love will I get or else will I put my life in adventure. For the King Rience lieth at a siege at the Castle Terrabil, and thither will we draw in all haste, to prove our worship and prowess upon him. I will well, said Balan, that we do, and we will help each other as brethren ought to do.

CHAPTER VII

*How a dwarf reproved Balin for the death of Lanceor, and
how King Mark of Cornwall found them, and made
a tomb over them.*

Now go we hence, said Balin, and well be we met. The meanwhile
as they talked, there came a dwarf from the city of Camelot on
horseback, as much as he might, and found the dead bodies,
wherefore he made great dole, and pulled out his hair for sorrow, and
said, Which of you knights have done this deed? Whereby askest
thou it? said Balan. For I would wit it, said the dwarf. It was I, said
Balin, that slew this knight in my defence, for hither he came to chase
me, and either I must slay him or he me; and this damosel slew herself
for his love, which repenteth me, and for her sake I shall owe all
women the better love. Alas, said the dwarf, thou hast done great
damage unto thyself, for this knight that is here dead was one of the
most valiantest men that lived, and trust well, Balin, the kin of this
knight will chase you through the world till they have slain you. As
for that, said Balin, I fear not greatly, but I am right heavy that I have
displeased my lord King Arthur, for the death of this knight. So as
they talked together, there came a king of Cornwall riding, the which
hight King Mark. And when he saw these two bodies dead, and
understood how they were dead, by the two knights above said, then
made the king great sorrow for the true love that was betwixt them,
and said, I will not depart till I have on this earth made a tomb, and
there he pight his pavilions and sought through all the country to find
a tomb, and in a church they found one was fair and rich, and then
the king let put them both in the earth, and put the tomb upon them,
and wrote the names of them both on the tomb. How here lieth
Lanceor the king's son of Ireland, that at his own request was slain by
the hands of Balin; and how his lady, Colombe, and paramour, slew
herself with her love's sword for dole and sorrow.

CHAPTER VIII

How Merlin prophesied that the two best knights of the world should fight there, which were Sir Lancelot and Sir Tristram.

The meanwhile as this was a-doing, in came Merlin to King Mark, and seeing all his doing, said, Here shall be in this same place the greatest battle betwixt two knights that was or ever shall be, and the truest lovers, and yet none of them shall slay other. And there Merlin wrote their names upon the tomb with letters of gold that should fight in that place, whose names were Launcelot du Lake, and Tristram. Thou art a marvellous man, said King Mark unto Merlin, that speakest of such marvels, thou art a boistous man and an unlikely to tell of such deeds. What is thy name? said King Mark. At this time, said Merlin, I will not tell, but at that time when Sir Tristram is taken with his sovereign lady, then ye shall hear and know my name, and at that time ye shall hear tidings that shall not please you. Then said Merlin to Balin, Thou hast done thyself great hurt, because that thou savest not this lady that slew herself, that might have saved her an thou wouldest. By the faith of my body, said Balin, I might not save her, for she slew herself suddenly. Me repenteth, said Merlin; because of the death of that lady thou shalt strike a stroke most dolorous that ever man struck, except the stroke of our Lord, for thou shalt hurt the truest knight and the man of most worship that now liveth, and through that stroke three kingdoms shall be in great poverty, misery and wretchedness twelve years, and the knight shall not be whole of that wound for many years. Then Merlin took his leave of Balin. And Balin said, If I wist it were sooth that ye say I should do such a perilous deed as that, I would slay myself to make thee a liar. Therewith Merlin vanished away suddenly. And then Balan and his brother took their leave of King Mark. First, said the king, tell me your name. Sir, said Balan, ye may see he beareth two swords, thereby ye may call him the Knight with the Two Swords. And so departed King Mark unto Camelot to King Arthur, and Balin took the way toward King Rience; and as they rode together they met with Merlin disguised, but they knew him not. Whither ride you? said Merlin. We have little to do, said the two knights, to tell thee. But what is thy name? said Balin. At this time, said Merlin, I will not tell it thee. It is evil seen, said the knights, that thou art a true man that thou wilt not tell thy name. As for that, said Merlin, be it as it be may, I can tell you wherefore ye ride this way, for to meet King Rience; but it will not avail you without ye have my counsel. Ah! said Balin, ye are Merlin; we will be ruled by your counsel. Come on, said Merlin, ye shall have great worship, and look that ye do knightly, for ye shall have great need. As for that, said Balin, dread you not, we will do what we may.

<h2 style="text-align:center">CHAPTER IX</h2>

How Balin and his brother, by the counsel of Merlin, took King Rience and brought him to King Arthur.

Then Merlin lodged them in a wood among leaves beside the highway, and took off the bridles of their horses and put them to grass and laid them down to rest them till it was nigh midnight. Then Merlin bade them rise, and make them ready, for the king was nigh them, that was stolen away from his host with a three score horses of his best knights, and twenty of them rode to-fore to warn the Lady de Vance that the king was coming; for that night King Rience should have lain with her. Which is the king? said Balin. Abide, said Merlin, here in a strait way ye shall meet with him; and therewith he showed Balin and his brother where he rode.

Anon Balin and his brother met with the king, and smote him down, and wounded him fiercely, and laid him to the ground; and there they slew on the right hand and the left hand, and slew more than forty of his men, and the remnant fled. Then went they again to King Rience and would have slain him had he not yielded him unto their grace. Then said he thus: Knights full of prowess, slay me not, for by my life ye may win, and by my death ye shall win nothing. Then said these two knights, Ye say sooth and truth, and so laid him on a horse-litter. With that Merlin was vanished, and came to King Arthur aforehand, and told him how his most enemy was taken and discomfited. By whom? said King Arthur. By two knights, said Merlin, that would please your lordship, and to-morrow ye shall know what knights they are. Anon after came the Knight with the Two Swords and Balan his brother, and brought with them King Rience of North Wales, and there delivered him to the porters, and charged them with him; and so they two returned again in the dawning of the day. King Arthur came then to King Rience, and said, Sir king, ye are welcome: by what adventure come ye hither? Sir, said King Rience, I came hither by an hard adventure. Who won you? said King Arthur. Sir, said the king, the Knight with the Two Swords and his brother, which are two marvellous knights of prowess. I know them not, said Arthur, but much I am beholden to them. Ah, said Merlin, I shall tell you: it is Balin that achieved the sword, and his brother Balan, a good knight, there liveth not a better of prowess and of worthiness, and it shall be the greatest dole of him that ever I knew of knight, for he shall not long endure. Alas, said King Arthur, that is great pity; for I am much beholden unto him, and I have ill deserved it unto him for his kindness. Nay, said Merlin, he shall do much more for you, and that shall ye know in haste. But, sir, are ye purveyed, said Merlin, for to-morn the host of Nero, King Rience's brother, will set on you or noon with a great host, and therefore make you ready, for I will depart from you.

CHAPTER X

How King Arthur had a battle against Nero and King Lot of Orkney, and how King Lot was deceived by Merlin, and how twelve kings were slain.

Then King Arthur made ready his host in ten battles, and Nero was ready in the field afore the Castle Terrabil with a great host, and he had ten battles, with many more people than Arthur had. Then Nero had the vanguard with the most part of his people, and Merlin came to King Lot of the Isle of Orkney, and held him with a tale of prophecy, till Nero and his people were destroyed. And there Sir Kay the seneschal did passingly well, that the days of his life the worship went never from him; and Sir Hervis de Revel did marvellous deeds with King Arthur, and King Arthur slew that day twenty knights and maimed forty. At that time came in the Knight with the Two Swords and his brother Balan, but they two did so marvellously that the king and all the knights marvelled of them, and all they that beheld them said they were sent from heaven as angels, or devils from hell; and King Arthur said himself they were the best knights that ever he saw, for they gave such strokes that all men had wonder of them.

In the meanwhile came one to King Lot, and told him while he tarried there Nero was destroyed and slain with all his people. Alas, said King Lot, I am ashamed, for by my default there is many a worshipful man slain, for an we had been together there had been none host under the heaven that had been able for to have matched with us; this faiter with his prophecy hath mocked me. All that did Merlin, for he knew well that an King Lot had been with his body there at the first battle, King Arthur had been slain, and all his people destroyed; and well Merlin knew that one of the kings should be dead that day, and loath was Merlin that any of them both should be slain; but of the twain, he had liefer King Lot had been slain than King Arthur. Now what is best to do? said King Lot of Orkney; whether is me better to treat with King Arthur or to fight, for the greater part of our people are slain and destroyed? Sir, said a knight, set on Arthur for they are weary and forfoughten and we be fresh. As for me, said King Lot, I would every knight would do his part as I would do mine. And then they advanced banners and smote together and all to-shivered their spears; and Arthur's knights, with the help of the Knight with the Two Swords and his brother Balan, put King Lot and his host to the worse. But always King Lot held him in the foremost front, and did marvellous deeds of arms, for all his host was borne up by his hands, for he abode all knights. Alas he might not endure, the which was great pity, that so worthy a knight as he was one should be overmatched, that of late time afore had been a knight of King Arthur's, and wedded the sister of King Arthur; and for King Arthur lay by King Lot's wife, the which was Arthur's sister, and gat on her Mordred, therefore King Lot held against Arthur. So there was a knight that was called the Knight with the Strange Beast, and at that time his right name was called Pellinore, the which was a good man of prowess, and he smote a mighty stroke at King Lot as he fought with all his enemies, and he failed of his stroke, and smote the horse's neck, that he fell to the ground with King Lot. And therewith anon

Pellinore smote him a great stroke through the helm and head unto the brows. And then all the host of Orkney fled for the death of King Lot, and there were slain many mothers' sons. But King Pellinore bare the wite of the death of King Lot, wherefore Sir Gawaine revenged the death of his father the tenth year after he was made knight, and slew King Pellinore with his own hands. Also there were slain at that battle twelve kings on the side of King Lot with Nero, and all were buried in the Church of Saint Stephen's in Camelot, and the remnant of knights and of others were buried in a great rock.

CHAPTER XI

Of the interment of twelve kings, and of the prophecy of Merlin, and how Balin should give the dolorous stroke.

So at the interment came King Lot's wife Margawse with her four sons, Gawaine, Agravaine, Gaheris, and Gareth. Also there came thither King Uriens, Sir Ewaine's father, and Morgan le Fay his wife that was King Arthur's sister. All these came to the interment. But of all these twelve kings King Arthur let make the tomb of King Lot passing richly, and made his tomb by his own; and then Arthur let make twelve images of latten and copper, and over-gilt it with gold, in the sign of twelve kings, and each one of them held a taper of wax that burnt day and night; and King Arthur was made in sign of a figure standing above them with a sword drawn in his hand, and all the twelve figures had countenance like unto men that were overcome. All this made Merlin by his subtle craft, and there he told the king, When I am dead these tapers shall burn no longer, and soon after the adventures of the Sangreal shall come among you and be achieved. Also he told Arthur how Balin the worshipful knight shall give the dolorous stroke, whereof shall fall great vengeance. Oh, where is Balin and Balan and Pellinore? said King Arthur. As for Pellinore, said Merlin, he will meet with you soon; and as for Balin he will not be long from you; but the other brother will depart, ye shall see him no more. By my faith, said Arthur, they are two marvellous knights, and namely Balin passeth of prowess of any knight that ever I found, for much beholden am I unto him; would

God he would abide with me. Sir, said Merlin, look ye keep well the scabbard of Excalibur, for ye shall lose no blood while ye have the scabbard upon you, though ye have as many wounds upon you as ye may have. So after, for great trust, Arthur betook the scabbard to Morgan le Fay his sister, and she loved another knight better than her husband King Uriens or King Arthur, and she would have had Arthur her brother slain, and therefore she let make another scabbard like it by enchantment, and gave the scabbard Excalibur to her love; and the knight's name was called Accolon, that after had near slain King Arthur. After this Merlin told unto King Arthur of the prophecy that there should be a great battle beside Salisbury, and Mordred his own son should be against him. Also he told him that Basdemegus was his cousin, and germain unto King Uriens.

CHAPTER XII

How a sorrowful knight came before Arthur, and how Balin fetched him, and how that knight was slain by a knight invisible.

Within a day or two King Arthur was somewhat sick, and he let pitch his pavilion in a meadow, and there he laid him down on a pallet to sleep, but he might have no rest. Right so he heard a great noise of an horse, and therewith the king looked out at the porch of the pavilion, and saw a knight coming even by him, making great dole. Abide, fair sir, said Arthur, and tell me wherefore thou makest this sorrow. Ye may little amend me, said the knight, and so passed forth to the castle of Meliot. Anon after there came Balin, and when he saw King Arthur he alighted off his horse, and came to the king on foot, and saluted him. By my head, said Arthur, ye be welcome. Sir, right now came riding this way a knight making great mourn, for what cause I cannot tell; wherefore I would desire of you of your courtesy and of your gentleness to fetch again that knight either by force or else by his good will. I will do more for your lordship than that, said Balin; and so he rode more than a pace, and found the knight with a damosel in a forest, and said, Sir knight, ye must come with me unto King Arthur, for to tell him of your sorrow. That will I not, said the knight, for it will scathe me greatly, and do you none avail. Sir, said Balin, I pray you make you ready, for ye must go with me, or else I must fight with you and bring you by force, and that were me loath to do. Will ye be my warrant, said the knight, an I go with you? Yea, said Balin, or else I will die therefore. And so he made him ready to go with Balin, and left the damosel still. And as they were even afore King Arthur's pavilion, there came one invisible, and smote this knight that went with Balin throughout the body with a spear. Alas, said the knight, I am slain under your conduct with a knight called Garlon; therefore take my horse that is better than yours, and ride to the damosel, and follow the quest that I was in as she will lead you, and revenge my death when ye may. That shall I do, said Balin, and that I make vow unto knighthood; and so he departed from this knight with great sorrow. So King Arthur let bury this knight richly, and made a mention on his tomb, how there was slain Herlews le Berbeus, and by whom the treachery was done, the knight Garlon. But ever the damosel bare the truncheon of the spear with her that Sir Herlews was slain withal.

CHAPTER XIII

*How Balin and the damosel met with a knight which was in
likewise slain, and how the damosel bled for the
custom of a castle.*

So Balin and the damosel rode into a forest, and there met with a knight that had been a-hunting, and that knight asked Balin for what cause he made so great sorrow. Me list not to tell you, said Balin. Now, said the knight, an I were armed as ye be I would fight with you. That should little need, said Balin, I am not afeard to tell you, and told him all the cause how it was. Ah, said the knight, is this all? here I ensure you by the faith of my body never to depart from you while my life lasteth. And so they went to the hostelry and armed them, and so rode forth with Balin. And as they came by an hermitage even by a churchyard, there came the knight Garlon invisible, and smote this knight, Perin de Mountbeliard, through the body with a spear. Alas, said the knight, I am slain by this traitor

knight that rideth invisible. Alas, said Balin, it is not the first despite
he hath done me; and there the hermit and Balin buried the knight
under a rich stone and a tomb royal. And on the morn they found
letters of gold written, how Sir Gawaine shall revenge his father's
death, King Lot, on the King Pellinore. Anon after this Balin and the
damosel rode till they came to a castle, and there Balin alighted, and
he and the damosel went to go into the castle, and anon as Balin
came within the castle's gate the portcullis fell down at his back, and
there fell many men about the damosel, and would have slain her.
When Balin saw that, he was sore aggrieved, for he might not help
the damosel. Then he went up into the tower, and leapt over walls
into the ditch, and hurt him not; and anon he pulled out his sword
and would have foughten with them. And they all said nay, they
would not fight with him, for they did nothing but the old custom of
the castle; and told him how their lady was sick, and had lain many
years, and she might not be whole but if she had a dish of silver full of
blood of a clean maid and a king's daughter; and therefore the custom
of this castle is, there shall no damosel pass this way but she shall bleed
of her blood in a silver dish full. Well, said Balin, she shall bleed as
much as she may bleed, but I will not lose the life of her whiles my
life lasteth. And so Balin made her to bleed by her good will, but her
blood helped not the lady. And so he and she rested there all night,
and had there right good cheer, and on the morn they passed on their
ways. And as it telleth after in the Sangreal, that Sir Percivale's sister
helped that lady with her blood, whereof she was dead.

CHAPTER XIV

*How Balin met with that knight named Garlon at a feast,
and there he slew him, to have his blood to heal therewith the
son of his host.*

Then they rode three or four days and never met with adventure, and
by hap they were lodged with a gentle man that was a rich man and
well at ease. And as they sat at their supper Balin overheard one
complain grievously by him in a chair. What is this noise? said Balin.
Forsooth, said his host, I will tell you. I was but late at a jousting, and

there I jousted with a knight that is brother unto King Pellam, and twice smote I him down, and then he promised to quit me on my best friend; and so he wounded my son, that cannot be whole till I have of that knight's blood, and he rideth alway invisible; but I know not his name. Ah! said Balin, I know that knight, his name is Garlon, he hath slain two knights of mine in the same manner, therefore I had liefer meet with that knight than all the gold in this realm, for the despite he hath done me. Well, said his host, I shall tell you, King Pellam of Listeneise hath made do cry in all this country a great feast that shall be within these twenty days, and no knight may come there but if he bring his wife with him, or his paramour; and that knight, your enemy and mine, ye shall see that day. Then I behote you, said Balin, part of his blood to heal your son withal. We will be forward to-morn, said his host. So on the morn they rode all three toward Pellam and they had fifteen days' journey or they came thither; and that same day began the great feast. And so they alighted and stabled their horses, and went into the castle; but Balin's host might not be let in because he had no lady. Then Balin was well received and brought unto a chamber and unarmed him; and there were brought him robes to his pleasure, and would have had Balin leave his sword behind him. Nay, said Balin, that do I not, for it is the custom of my country a knight always to keep his weapon with him, and that custom will I keep, or else I will depart as I came. Then they gave him leave to wear his sword, and so he went unto the castle, and was set among knights of worship, and his lady afore him.

Soon Balin asked a knight, Is there not a knight in this court whose name is Garlon? Yonder he goeth, said a knight, he with the black face; he is the marvellest knight that is now living, for he destroyeth many good knights, for he goeth invisible. Ah well, said Balin, is that he? Then Balin advised him long: If I slay him here I shall not escape, and if I leave him now, peradventure I shall never meet with him again at such a steven, and much harm he will do an he live. Therewith this Garlon espied that this Balin beheld him, and then he came and smote Balin on the face with the back of his hand, and said, Knight, why beholdest me so? for shame therefore, eat thy meat and do that thou came for. Thou sayest sooth, said Balin, this is not the first despite that thou hast done me, and therefore I will do what I came for, and rose up fiercely and clave his head to the shoulders. Give me the truncheon, said Balin to his lady, wherewith he slew your knight. Anon she gave it him, for alway she bare the truncheon with her. And therewith Balin smote him through the body, and said openly, With that truncheon thou hast slain a good knight, and now it sticketh in thy body. And then Balin called unto him his host, saying, Now may ye fetch blood enough to heal your son withal.

CHAPTER XV

How Balin fought with King Pellam, and how his sword brake, and how he gat a spear wherewith he smote the dolorous stroke.

Anon all the knights arose from the table for to set on Balin, and King Pellam himself arose up fiercely, and said, Knight, hast thou slain my brother? thou shalt die therefore or thou depart. Well, said Balin, do it yourself. Yes, said King Pellam, there shall no man have ado with thee but myself, for the love of my brother. Then King Pellam caught in his hand a grim weapon and smote eagerly at Balin; but Balin put the sword betwixt his head and the stroke, and therewith his sword burst in sunder. And when Balin was weaponless he ran into a chamber for to seek some weapon, and so from chamber to chamber, and no weapon he could find, and always King Pellam after him. And at the last he entered into a chamber that was marvellously well dight and richly, and a bed arrayed with cloth of gold, the richest that might be thought, and one lying therein, and thereby stood a table of clean gold with four pillars of silver that bare up the table, and upon the table stood a marvellous spear strangely wrought. And when Balin saw that spear, he gat it in his hand and turned him to King Pellam, and smote him passingly sore with that spear, that King Pellam fell down in a swoon, and therewith the castle roof and walls brake and fell to the earth, and Balin fell down so that he might not stir foot nor hand. And so the most part of the castle, that was fallen down through that dolorous stroke, lay upon Pellam and Balin three days.

CHAPTER XVI

How Balin was delivered by Merlin, and saved a knight that would have slain himself for love.

Then Merlin came thither and took up Balin, and gat him a good horse, for his was dead, and bade him ride out of that country. I would have my damosel, said Balin. Lo, said Merlin, where she lieth dead. And King Pellam lay so, many years sore wounded, and might never be whole till Galahad the haut prince healed him in the quest of the Sangreal, for in that place was part of the blood of our Lord Jesus Christ, that Joseph of Arimathea brought into this land, and there himself lay in that rich bed. And that was the same spear that Longinus smote our Lord to the heart; and King Pellam was nigh of Joseph's kin, and that was the most worshipful man that lived in those days, and great pity it was of his hurt, for through that stroke, turned to great dole, tray and tene. Then departed Balin from Merlin, and said, In this world we meet never no more. So he rode forth through the fair countries and cities, and found the people dead, slain on every side. And all that were alive cried, O Balin, thou hast caused great damage in these countries; for the dolorous stroke thou gavest unto King Pellam three countries are destroyed, and doubt not but the vengeance will fall on thee at the last. When Balin was past those countries he was passing fain.

So he rode eight days or he met with adventure. And at the last he came into a fair forest in a valley, and was ware of a tower, and there beside he saw a great horse of war, tied to a tree, and there beside sat a fair knight on the ground and made great mourning, and he was a likely man, and a well made. Balin said, God save you, why be ye so heavy? tell me and I will amend it, an I may, to my power. Sir knight, said he again, thou dost me great grief, for I was in merry thoughts, and now thou puttest me to more pain. Balin went a little from him, and looked on his horse; then heard Balin him say thus: Ah, fair lady, why have ye broken thy promise, for thou promisest me to meet me here by noon, and I may curse thee that ever ye gave me this sword, for with this sword I slay myself, and pulled it out. And therewith Balin stert unto him and took him by the hand. Let go my hand, said the knight, or else I shall slay thee. That shall not need, said Balin, for I shall promise you my help to get you your lady, an ye will tell me where she is. What is your name? said the knight. My name is Balin le Savage. Ah, sir, I know you well enough, ye are the Knight with the Two Swords, and the man of most prowess of your hands living. What is your name? said Balin. My name is Garnish of the Mount, a poor man's son, but by my prowess and hardiness a duke hath made me knight, and gave me lands; his name is Duke Hermel, and his daughter is she that I love, and she me as I deemed. How far is she hence? said Balin. But six mile, said the knight. Now ride we hence, said these two knights. So they rode more than a pace, till that they came to a fair castle well walled and ditched. I will into the castle, said Balin, and look if she be there. So he went in and searched from chamber to chamber, and found her bed, but she was not there. Then Balin looked into a fair little garden, and under a laurel tree he saw her lie upon a quilt of green samite and a knight in her arms, fast halsing either other, and under their heads grass and herbs. When Balin saw her lie so with the foulest knight that ever he saw, and she a fair lady, then Balin went through all the chambers again, and told the knight how he found her as she had slept fast, and so brought him in the place there she lay fast sleeping.

CHAPTER XVII

How that knight slew his love and a knight lying by her, and after, how he slew himself with his own sword, and how Balin rode toward a castle where he lost his life.

And when Garnish beheld her so lying, for pure sorrow his mouth and nose burst out a-bleeding, and with his sword he smote off both their heads, and then he made sorrow out of measure, and said, O Balin, much sorrow hast thou brought unto me, for hadst thou not showed me that sight I should have passed my sorrow. Forsooth, said Balin, I did it to this intent that it should better thy courage, and that ye might see and know her falsehood, and to cause you to leave love of such a lady; God knoweth I did none other but as I would ye did to me. Alas, said Garnish, now is my sorrow double that I may not

endure, now have I slain that I most loved in all my life; and
therewith suddenly he rove himself on his own sword unto the hilts.
When Balin saw that, he dressed him thenceward, lest folk would say
he had slain them; and so he rode forth, and within three days he
came by a cross, and thereon were letters of gold written, that said, It
is not for no knight alone to ride toward this castle. Then saw he an
old hoar gentleman coming toward him, that said, Balin le Savage,
thou passest thy bounds to come this way, therefore turn again and it
will avail thee. And he vanished away anon; and so he heard an horn
blow as it had been the death of a beast. That blast, said Balin, is
blown for me, for I am the prize and yet am I not dead. Anon withal
he saw an hundred ladies and many knights, that welcomed him with
fair semblant, and made him passing good cheer unto his sight, and
led him into the castle, and there was dancing and minstrelsy and all
manner of joy. Then the chief lady of the castle said, Knight with the
Two Swords, ye must have ado and joust with a knight hereby that
keepeth an island, for there may no man pass this way but he must
joust or he pass. That is an unhappy custom, said Balin, that a knight
may not pass this way but if he joust. Ye shall not have ado but with
one knight, said the lady.

Well, said Balin, since I shall thereto I am ready, but travelling men
are oft weary and their horses too; but though my horse be weary my
heart is not weary, I would be fain there my death should be. Sir, said
a knight to Balin, methinketh your shield is not good, I will lend you
a bigger. Thereof I pray you. And so he took the shield that was
unknown and left his own, and so rode unto the island, and put him
and his horse in a great boat; and when he came on the other side he
met with a damosel, and she said, O knight Balin, why have ye left
your own shield? alas ye have put yourself in great danger, for by
your shield ye should have been known; it is great pity of you as ever
was of knight, for of thy prowess and hardiness thou hast no fellow
living. Me repenteth, said Balin, that ever I came within this country,
but I may not turn now again for shame, and what adventure shall fall
to me, be it life or death, I will take the adventure that shall come to
me. And then he looked on his armour, and understood he was well
armed, and therewith blessed him and mounted upon his horse.

CHAPTER XVIII

How Balin met with his brother Balan, and how each of them slew other unknown, till they were wounded to death.

Then afore him he saw come riding out of a castle a knight, and his horse trapped all red, and himself in the same colour. When this knight in the red beheld Balin, him thought it should be his brother Balin by cause of his two swords, but by cause he knew not his shield he deemed it was not he. And so they aventred their spears and came marvellously fast together, and they smote each other in the shields, but their spears and their course were so big that it bare down horse and man, that they lay both in a swoon. But Balin was bruised sore with the fall of his horse, for he was weary of travel. And Balan was the first that rose on foot and drew his sword, and went toward Balin, and he arose and went against him; but Balan smote Balin first, and he put up his shield and smote him through the shield and tamed his helm. Then Balin smote him again with that unhappy sword, and well-nigh had felled his brother Balan, and so they fought there together till their breaths failed. Then Balin looked up to the castle and saw the towers stand full of ladies. So they went unto battle again, and wounded everych other dolefully, and then they breathed ofttimes, and so went unto battle that all the place there as they fought was blood red. And at that time there was none of them both but they had either smitten other seven great wounds, so that the least of them might have been the death of the mightiest giant in this world.

Then they went to battle again so marvellously that doubt it was to hear of that battle for the great blood-shedding, and their hauberks unnailed that naked they were on every side. At last Balan the younger brother withdrew him a little and laid him down. Then said Balin le Savage, What knight art thou? for or now I found never no knight that matched me. My name is, said he, Balan, brother unto the good knight, Balin. Alas, said Balin, that ever I should see this day, and therewith he fell backward in a swoon. Then Balan yede on all four feet and hands, and put off the helm off his brother, and might not know him by the visage it was so ful hewn and bled; but when he awoke he said, O Balan, my brother, thou hast slain me and I thee, wherefore all the wide world shall speak of us both. Alas, said Balan, that ever I saw this day, that through mishap I might not know you, for I espied well your two swords, but by cause ye had another shield I deemed ye had been another knight. Alas, said Balin, all that made an unhappy knight in the castle, for he caused me to leave my own shield to our both's destruction, and if I might live I would destroy that castle for ill customs. That were well done, said Balan, for I had never grace to depart from them since that I came hither, for here it happed me to slay a knight that kept this island, and since might I never depart, and no more should ye, brother, an ye might have slain me as ye have, and escaped yourself with the life.

Right so came the lady of the tower with four knights and six ladies and six yeomen unto them, and there she heard how they made their moan either to other, and said, We came both out of one tomb, that is to say one mother's belly, and so shall we lie both in one pit. So Balan prayed the lady of her gentleness, for his true service, that she would bury them both in that same place there the battle was done. And she granted them, with weeping, it should be done richly in the best manner. Now, will ye send for a priest, that we may receive our sacrament, and receive the blessed body of our Lord Jesus Christ? Yea, said the lady, it shall be done; and so she sent for a priest and gave them their rights. Now, said Balin, when we are buried in one tomb, and the mention made over us how two brethren slew each other, there will never good knight, nor good man, see our tomb but they will pray for our souls. And so all the ladies and gentlewomen wept for pity. Then anon Balan died, but Balin died not till the midnight after, and so were they buried both, and the lady let make a mention of Balan how he was there slain by his brother's hands, but she knew not Balin's name.

CHAPTER XIX

How Merlin buried them both in one tomb, and of Balin's sword.

In the morn came Merlin and let write Balin's name on the tomb with letters of gold, that Here lieth Balin le Savage that was the Knight with the Two Swords, and he that smote the Dolorous Stroke. Also Merlin let make there a bed, that there should never man lie therein but he went out of his wit, yet Launcelot de Lake fordid that bed through his noblesse. And anon after Balin was dead, Merlin took his sword, and took off the pommel and set on another pommel. So Merlin bade a knight that stood afore him handle that sword, and he assayed, and he might not handle it. Then Merlin laughed. Why laugh ye? said the knight. This is the cause, said Merlin: there shall never man handle this sword but the best knight of the world, and that shall be Sir Launcelot or else Galahad his son, and Launcelot with this sword shall slay the man that in the world he loved best, that shall be Sir Gawaine. All this he let write in the pommel of the sword. Then Merlin let make a bridge of iron and of steel into that island, and it was but half a foot broad, and there shall never man pass that bridge, nor have hardiness to go over, but if he were a passing good man and a good knight without treachery or villainy. Also the scabbard of Balin's sword Merlin left it on this side the island, that Galahad should find it. Also Merlin let make by his subtilty that Balin's sword was put in a marble stone standing upright as great as a mill stone, and the stone hoved always above the water and did many years, and so by adventure it swam down the stream to the City of Camelot, that is in English Winchester. And that same day Galahad the haut prince came with King Arthur, and so Galahad brought with him the scabbard and achieved the sword that was there in the marble stone hoving upon the water. And on Whitsunday he achieved the sword as it is rehearsed in the book of Sangreal.

Soon after this was done Merlin came to King Arthur and told him of the dolorous stroke that Balin gave to King Pellam, and how Balin and Balan fought together the marvellest battle that ever was heard of, and how they were buried both in one tomb. Alas, said King Arthur, this is the greatest pity that ever I heard tell of two knights, for in the world I know not such two knights. Thus endeth the tale of Balin and of Balan, two brethren born in Northumberland, good knights.

Sequitur iii liber.

BOOK THREE

CHAPTER I

How King Arthur took a wife, and wedded Guenever, daughter to Leodegrance, King of the land of Cameliard, with whom he had the Round Table.

In the beginning of Arthur, after he was chosen king by adventure and by grace, for the most part of the barons knew not that he was Uther Pendragon's son, but as Merlin made it openly known. But yet many kings and lords held great war against him for that cause, but well Arthur overcame them all, for the most part the days of his life he was ruled much by the counsel of Merlin. So it fell on a time King Arthur said unto Merlin, My barons will let me have no rest, but needs I must take a wife, and I will none take but by thy counsel and by thine advice. It is well done, said Merlin, that ye take a wife, for a man of your bounty and noblesse should not be without a wife. Now is there any that ye love more than another? Yea, said King Arthur, I love Guenever the king's daughter, Leodegrance of the land of Cameliard, the which holdeth in his house the Table Round that ye told he had of my father Uther. And this damosel is the most valiant and fairest lady that I know living, or yet that ever I could find. Sir, said Merlin, as of her beauty and fairness she is one of the fairest alive, but, an ye loved her not so well as ye do, I should find you a damosel of beauty and of goodness that should like you and please you, an your heart were not set; but there as a man's heart is set, he will be loath to return. That is truth, said King Arthur. But Merlin warned the king covertly that Guenever was not wholesome for him to take to wife, for he warned him that Launcelot should love her, and she him again; and so he turned his tale to the adventures of Sangreal.

Then Merlin desired of the king for to have men with him that should enquire of Guenever, and so the king granted him, and Merlin went forth unto King Leodegrance of Cameliard, and told him of the desire of the king that he would have unto his wife Guenever his daughter. That is to me, said King Leodegrance, the best tidings that ever I heard, that so worthy a king of prowess and noblesse will wed my daughter. And as for my lands, I will give him, wist I it might please him, but he hath lands enow, him needeth none; but I shall send him a gift shall please him much more, for I shall give him the Table Round, the which Uther Pendragon gave me, and when it is full complete, there is an hundred knights and fifty. And as for an hundred good knights I have myself, but I faute fifty, for so many have been slain in my days. And so Leodegrance delivered his daughter Guenever unto Merlin, and the Table Round with the hundred knights, and so they rode freshly, with great royalty, what by water and what by land, till that they came nigh unto London.

CHAPTER II

How the Knights of the Round Table were ordained and their sieges blessed by the Bishop of Canterbury.

When King Arthur heard of the coming of Guenever and the hundred knights with the Table Round, then King Arthur made great joy for her coming, and that rich present, and said openly, This fair lady is passing welcome unto me, for I have loved her long, and therefore there is nothing so lief to me. And these knights with the Round Table please me more than right great riches. And in all haste the king let ordain for the marriage and the coronation in the most honourable wise that could be devised. Now, Merlin, said King Arthur, go thou and espy me in all this land fifty knights which be of most prowess and worship. Within short time Merlin had found such knights that should fulfil twenty and eight knights, but no more he could find. Then the Bishop of Canterbury was fetched, and he blessed the sieges with great royalty and devotion, and there set the eight and twenty knights in their sieges. And when this was done Merlin said, Fair sirs, ye must all arise and come to King Arthur for to do him homage; he will have the better will to maintain you. And so they arose and did their homage, and when they were gone Merlin

found in every sieges letters of gold that told the knights' names that
had sitten therein. But two sieges were void. And so anon came
young Gawaine and asked the king a gift. Ask, said the king, and I
shall grant it you. Sir, I ask that ye will make me knight that same day
ye shall wed fair Guenever. I will do it with a good will, said King
Arthur, and do unto you all the worship that I may, for I must by
reason ye are my nephew, my sister's son.

CHAPTER III

How a poor man riding upon a lean mare desired King Arthur to make his son knight.

Forthwithal there came a poor man into the court, and brought with
him a fair young man of eighteen years of age riding upon a lean
mare; and the poor man asked all men that he met, Where shall I find
King Arthur? Yonder he is, said the knights, wilt thou anything with
him? Yea, said the poor man, therefore I came hither. Anon as he
came before the king, he saluted him and said: O King Arthur, the
flower of all knights and kings, I beseech Jesu save thee. Sir, it was
told me that at this time of your marriage ye would give any man the
gift that he would ask, out except that were unreasonable. That is
truth, said the king, such cries I let make, and that will I hold, so it
apair not my realm nor mine estate. Ye say well and graciously, said
the poor man; Sir, I ask nothing else but that ye will make my son
here a knight. It is a great thing thou askest of me, said the king.
What is thy name? said the king to the poor man. Sir, my name is
Aries the cowherd. Whether cometh this of thee or of thy son? said
the king. Nay, sir, said Aries, this desire cometh of my son and not of
me, for I shall tell you I have thirteen sons, and all they will fall to
what labour I put them, and will be right glad to do labour, but this
child will not labour for me, for anything that my wife or I may do,
but always he will be shooting or casting darts, and glad for to see
battles and to behold knights, and always day and night he desireth of
me to be made a knight. What is thy name? said the king unto the
young man. Sir, my name is Tor. The king beheld him fast, and saw
he was passingly well-visaged and passingly well made of his years.

Well, said King Arthur unto Aries the cowherd, fetch all thy sons afore me that I may see them. And so the poor man did, and all were shaped much like the poor man. But Tor was not like none of them all in shape nor in countenance, for he was much more than any of them. Now, said King Arthur unto the cowherd, where is the sword he shall be made knight withal? It is here, said Tor. Take it out of the sheath, said the king, and require me to make you a knight.

Then Tor alighted off his mare and pulled out his sword, kneeling, and requiring the king that he would make him knight, and that he might be a knight of the Table Round. As for a knight I will make you, and therewith smote him in the neck with the sword, saying, Be ye a good knight, and so I pray to God so ye may be, and if ye be of prowess and of worthiness ye shall be a knight of the Table Round. Now Merlin, said Arthur, say whether this Tor shall be a good knight or no. Yea, sir, he ought to be a good knight, for he is come of as good a man as any is alive, and of kings' blood. How so, sir? said the king. I shall tell you, said Merlin: This poor man, Aries the cowherd, is not his father; he is nothing sib to him, for King Pellinore is his father. I suppose nay, said the cowherd. Fetch thy wife afore me, said Merlin, and she shall not say nay. Anon the wife was fetched, which was a fair housewife, and there she answered Merlin full womanly, and there she told the king and Merlin that when she was a maid, and went to milk kine, there met with her a stern knight, and half by force he had my maidenhead, and at that time he begat my son Tor, and he took away from me my greyhound that I had that time with me, and said that he would keep the greyhound for my love. Ah, said the cowherd, I weened not this, but I may believe it well, for he had never no tatches of me. Sir, said Tor unto Merlin, dishonour not my mother. Sir, said Merlin, it is more for your worship than hurt, for your father is a good man and a king, and he might well advance you and your mother, for ye were begotten or ever she was wedded. That is truth, said the wife. It is the less grief unto me, said the cowherd.

CHAPTER IV

How Sir Tor was known for son of King Pellinore, and how Gawaine was made knight.

So on the morn King Pellinore came to the court of King Arthur, which had great joy of him, and told him of Tor, how he was his son, and how he had made him knight at the request of the cowherd. When Pellinore beheld Tor, he pleased him much. So the king made Gawaine knight, but Tor was the first he made at the feast. What is the cause, said King Arthur, that there be two places void in the sieges? Sir, said Merlin, there shall no man sit in those places but they that shall be of most worship. But in the Siege Perilous there shall no man sit therein but one, and if there be any so hardy to do it he shall be destroyed, and he that shall sit there shall have no fellow. And therewith Merlin took King Pellinore by the hand, and in the one hand next the two sieges and the Siege Perilous he said, in open audience, This is your place and best ye are worthy to sit therein of any that is here. Thereat sat Sir Gawaine in great envy and told Gaheris his brother, yonder knight is put to great worship, the which grieveth me sore, for he slew our father King Lot, therefore I will slay him, said Gawaine, with a sword that was sent me that is passing trenchant. Ye shall not so, said Gaheris, at this time, for at this time I am but a squire, and when I am made knight I will be avenged on him, and therefore, brother, it is best ye suffer till another time, that we may have him out of the court, for an we did so we should trouble this high feast. I will well, said Gawaine, as ye will.

CHAPTER V

*How at feast of the wedding of King Arthur to Guenever, a
white hart came into the hall, and thirty couple hounds, and
how a brachet pinched the hart which was taken away.*

Then was the high feast made ready, and the king was wedded at
Camelot unto Dame Guenever in the church of Saint Stephen's, with
great solemnity. And as every man was set after his degree, Merlin
went to all the knights of the Round Table, and bade them sit still, that
none of them remove. For ye shall see a strange and a marvellous
adventure. Right so as they sat there came running in a white hart into
the hall, and a white brachet next him, and thirty couple of black
running hounds came after with a great cry, and the hart went about
the Table Round as he went by other boards. The white brachet bit
him by the buttock and pulled out a piece, wherethrough the hart
leapt a great leap and overthrew a knight that sat at the board side; and
therewith the knight arose and took up the brachet, and so went forth
out of the hall, and took his horse and rode his way with the brachet.
Right so anon came in a lady on a white palfrey, and cried aloud to
King Arthur, Sir, suffer me not to have this despite, for the brachet was
mine that the knight led away. I may not do therewith, said the king.

With this there came a knight riding all armed on a great horse, and
took the lady away with him with force, and ever she cried and made
great dole. When she was gone the king was glad, for she made such
a noise. Nay, said Merlin, ye may not leave these adventures so
lightly; for these adventures must be brought again or else it would be
disworship to you and to your feast. I will, said the king, that all be
done by your advice. Then, said Merlin, let call Sir Gawaine, for he
must bring again the white hart. Also, sir, ye must let call Sir Tor, for
he must bring again the brachet and the knight, or else slay him. Also
let call King Pellinore, for he must bring again the lady and the
knight, or else slay him. And these three knights shall do marvellous
adventures or they come again. Then were they called all three as it
rehearseth afore, and each of them took his charge, and armed them
surely. But Sir Gawaine had the first request, and therefore we will
begin at him.

CHAPTER VI

*How Sir Gawaine rode for to fetch again the hart, and how
two brethren fought each against other for the hart.*

Sir Gawaine rode more than a pace, and Gaheris his brother that rode
with him instead of a squire to do him service. So as they rode they
saw two knights fight on horseback passing sore; so Sir Gawaine and
his brother rode betwixt them, and asked them for what cause they
fought so. The one knight answered and said, We fight for a simple
matter, for we two be two brethren born and begotten of one man
and of one woman. Alas, said Sir Gawaine, why do ye so? Sir, said
the elder, there came a white hart this way this day, and many hounds
chased him, and a white brachet was alway next him, and we
understood it was adventure made for the high feast of King Arthur,
and therefore I would have gone after to have won me worship; and
here my younger brother said he would go after the hart, for he was
better knight than I: and for this cause we fell at debate, and so we
thought to prove which of us both was better knight. This is a simple
cause, said Sir Gawaine; uncouth men ye should debate withal, and
not brother with brother; therefore but if you will do by my counsel
I will have ado with you, that is ye shall yield you unto me, and that
ye go unto King Arthur and yield you unto his grace. Sir knight, said
the two brethren, we are forfoughten and much blood have we lost
through our wilfulness, and therefore we would be loath to have ado
with you. Then do as I will have you, said Sir Gawaine. We will
agree to fulfil your will; but by whom shall we say that we be thither
sent? Ye may say, By the knight that followeth the quest of the hart
that was white. Now what is your name? said Gawaine. Sorlouse of
the Forest, said the elder. And my name is, said the younger, Brian of
the Forest. And so they departed and went to the king's court, and Sir
Gawaine on his quest.

And as Gawaine followed the hart by the cry of the hounds, even
afore him there was a great river, and the hart swam over; and as Sir
Gawaine would follow after, there stood a knight over the other side,
and said, Sir knight, come not over after this hart but if thou wilt

joust with me. I will not fail as for that, said Sir Gawaine, to follow the quest that I am in, and so made his horse to swim over the water. And anon they gat their spears and ran together full hard; but Sir Gawaine smote him off his horse, and then he turned his horse and bade him yield him. Nay, said the knight, not so, though thou have the better of me on horseback. I pray thee, valiant knight, alight afoot, and match we together with swords. What is your name? said Sir Gawaine. Allardin of the Isles, said the other. Then either dressed their shields and smote together, but Sir Gawaine smote him so hard through the helm that it went to the brains, and the knight fell down dead. Ah! said Gaheris, that was a mighty stroke of a young knight.

CHAPTER VII

How the hart was chased into a castle and there slain, and how Sir Gawaine slew a lady.

Then Gawaine and Gaheris rode more than a pace after the white hart, and let slip at the hart three couple of greyhounds, and so they chased the hart into a castle, and in the chief place of the castle they slew the hart; Sir Gawaine and Gaheris followed after. Right so there came a knight out of a chamber with a sword drawn in his hand and slew two of the greyhounds, even in the sight of Sir Gawaine, and the remnant he chased them with his sword out of the castle. And when he came again, he said, O my white hart, me repenteth that thou art dead, for my sovereign lady gave thee to me, and evil have I kept thee, and thy death shall be dear bought an I live. And anon he went into his chamber and armed him, and came out fiercely, and there met he with Sir Gawaine. Why have ye slain my hounds? said Sir Gawaine, for they did but their kind, and liefer I had ye had wroken your anger upon me than upon a dumb beast. Thou sayest truth, said the knight, I have avenged me on thy hounds, and so I will on thee or thou go. Then Sir Gawaine alighted afoot and dressed his shield, and struck together mightily, and clave their shields, and stoned their helms, and brake their hauberks that the blood ran down to their feet.

At the last Sir Gawaine smote the knight so hard that he fell to the earth, and then he cried mercy, and yielded him, and besought him as he was a knight and gentleman, to save his life. Thou shalt die, said Sir Gawaine, for slaying of my hounds. I will make amends, said the knight, unto my power. Sir Gawaine would no mercy have, but unlaced his helm to have stricken off his head. Right so came his lady out of a chamber and fell over him, and so he smote off her head by misadventure. Alas, said Gaheris, that is foully and shamefully done, that shame shall never from you; also ye should give mercy unto them that ask mercy, for a knight without mercy is without worship. Sir Gawaine was so stonied of the death of this fair lady that he wist not what he did, and said unto the knight, Arise, I will give thee mercy. Nay, nay, said the knight, I take no force of mercy now, for thou hast slain my love and my lady that I loved best of all earthly things. Me sore repenteth it, said Sir Gawaine, for I thought to strike unto thee; but now thou shalt go unto King Arthur and tell him of thine adventures, and how thou art overcome by the knight that went in the quest of the white hart. I take no force, said the knight, whether I live or I die; but so for dread of death he swore to go unto King Arthur, and he made him to bear one greyhound before him on his horse, and another behind him. What is your name? said Sir Gawaine, or we depart. My name is, said the knight, Ablamar of the Marsh. So he departed toward Camelot.

CHAPTER VIII

How four knights fought against Gawaine and Gaheris, and
how they were overcome, and their lives saved
at request of four ladies.

And Sir Gawaine went into the castle, and made him ready to lie there all night, and would have unarmed him. What will ye do, said Gaheris, will ye unarm you in this country? Ye may think ye have many enemies here. They had not sooner said that word but there came four knights well armed, and assailed Sir Gawaine hard, and said unto him, Thou new-made knight, thou hast shamed thy knighthood, for a knight without mercy is dishonoured. Also thou hast slain a fair lady to thy great shame to the world's end, and doubt thou not thou shalt have great need of mercy or thou depart from us. And therewith one of them smote Sir Gawaine a great stroke that nigh he fell to the earth, and Gaheris smote him again sore, and so they were on the one side and on the other, that Sir Gawaine and Gaheris were in jeopardy of their lives; and one with a bow, an archer, smote Sir Gawaine through the arm that it grieved him wonderly sore. And as they should have been slain, there came four fair ladies, and besought the knights of grace for Sir Gawaine; and goodly at request of the ladies they gave Sir Gawaine and Gaheris their lives, and made them to yield them as prisoners. Then Gawaine and Gaheris made great dole. Alas! said Sir Gawaine, mine arm grieveth me sore, I am like to be maimed; and so made his complaint piteously.

Early on the morrow there came to Sir Gawaine one of the four ladies that had heard all his complaint, and said, Sir knight, what cheer? Not good, said he. It is your own default, said the lady, for ye have done a passing foul deed in the slaying of the lady, the which will be great villainy unto you. But be ye not of King Arthur's kin? said the lady. Yes truly, said Sir Gawaine. What is your name? said the lady, ye must tell it me or ye pass. My name is Gawaine, the King Lot of Orkney's son, and my mother is King Arthur's sister. Ah! then are ye nephew unto King Arthur, said the lady, and I shall so speak for you that ye shall have conduct to go to King Arthur for his love. And so she departed and told the four knights how their prisoner was King Arthur's nephew, and his name is Sir Gawaine, King Lot's son of Orkney. And they gave him the hart's head because it was in his quest. Then anon they delivered Sir Gawaine under this promise, that he should bear the dead lady with him in this manner; the head of her was hanged about his neck, and the whole body of her lay before him on his horse's mane. Right so rode he forth unto Camelot. And anon as he was come, Merlin desired of King Arthur that Sir Gawaine should be sworn to tell of all his adventures, and how he slew the lady, and how he would give no mercy unto the knight, wherethrough the lady was slain. Then the king and the queen were greatly displeased with Sir Gawaine for the slaying of the lady. And there by ordinance of the queen there was set a quest of ladies on Sir Gawaine, and they judged him for ever while he lived to be with all ladies, and to fight for their quarrels; and that ever he should be courteous, and never to refuse mercy to him that asketh mercy. Thus was Gawaine sworn upon the Four Evangelists that he should never be against lady nor gentlewoman, but if he fought for a lady and his adversary fought for another. And thus endeth the adventure of Sir Gawaine that he did at the marriage of King Arthur. Amen.

CHAPTER IX

How Sir Tor rode after the knight with the brachet, and of his adventure by the way.

When Sir Tor was ready, he mounted upon his horseback, and rode after the knight with the brachet. So as he rode he met with a dwarf suddenly that smote his horse on the head with a staff, that he went backward his spear length. Why dost thou so? said Sir Tor. For thou shalt not pass this way, but if thou joust with yonder knights of the pavilions. Then was Tor ware where two pavilions were, and great spears stood out, and two shields hung on trees by the pavilions. I may not tarry, said Sir Tor, for I am in a quest that I must needs follow. Thou shalt not pass, said the dwarf, and therewithal he blew his horn. Then there came one armed on horseback, and dressed his shield, and came fast toward Tor and he dressed him against him, and so ran together that Tor bare him from his horse. And anon the knight yielded him to his mercy. But, sir, I have a fellow in yonder pavilion that will have ado with you anon. He shall be welcome, said Sir Tor. Then was he ware of another knight coming with great raundon, and each of them dressed to other, that marvel it was to see; but the knight smote Sir Tor a great stroke in midst of the shield that his spear all to-shivered. And Sir Tor smote him through the shield below of the shield that it went through the cost of the knight, but the stroke slew him not. And therewith Sir Tor alighted and smote him on the helm a great stroke, and therewith the knight yielded him and besought him of mercy. I will well, said Sir Tor, but thou and thy fellow must go unto King Arthur, and yield you prisoners unto him. By whom shall we say are we thither sent? Ye shall say by the knight that went in the quest of the knight that went with the brachet. Now, what be your two names? said Sir Tor. My name is, said the one, Sir Felot of Langduk; and my name is, said the other, Sir Petipase of Winchelsea. Now go ye forth, said Sir Tor, and God

speed you and me. Then came the dwarf and said unto Sir Tor, I
pray you give me a gift. I will well, said Sir Tor, ask. I ask no more,
said the dwarf, but that ye will suffer me to do you service, for I will
serve no more recreant knights. Take an horse, said Sir Tor, and ride
on with me. I wot ye ride after the knight with the white brachet,
and I shall bring you where he is, said the dwarf. And so they rode
throughout a forest, and at the last they were ware of two pavilions,
even by a priory, with two shields, and the one shield was enewed
with white, and the other shield was red.

CHAPTER X

*How Sir Tor found the brachet with a lady, and how a
knight assailed him for the said brachet.*

Therewith Sir Tor alighted and took the dwarf his glaive, and so he
came to the white pavilion, and saw three damosels lie in it, on one
pallet, sleeping, and so he went to the other pavilion, and found a
lady lying sleeping therein, but there was the white brachet that
bayed at her fast, and therewith the lady yede out of the pavilion and
all her damosels. But anon as Sir Tor espied the white brachet, he
took her by force and took her to the dwarf. What, will ye so, said
the lady, take my brachet from me? Yea, said Sir Tor, this brachet
have I sought from King Arthur's court hither. Well, said the lady,
knight, ye shall not go far with her, but that ye shall be met and
grieved. I shall abide what adventure that cometh by the grace of
God, and so mounted upon his horse, and passed on his way toward
Camelot; but it was so near night he might not pass but little further.
Know ye any lodging? said Tor. I know none, said the dwarf, but
here beside is an hermitage, and there ye must take lodging as ye find.
And within a while they came to the hermitage and took lodging;
and was there grass, oats and bread for their horses; soon it was sped,
and full hard was their supper; but there they rested them all night till
on the morn, and heard a mass devoutly, and took their leave of the
hermit, and Sir Tor prayed the hermit to pray for him. He said he
would, and betook him to God. And so mounted upon horseback
and rode towards Camelot a long while.

With that they heard a knight call loud that came after them, and he said, Knight, abide and yield my brachet that thou took from my lady. Sir Tor returned again, and beheld him how he was a seemly knight and well horsed, and well armed at all points; then Sir Tor dressed his shield, and took his spear in his hands, and the other came fiercely upon him, and smote both horse and man to the earth. Anon they arose lightly and drew their swords as eagerly as lions, and put their shields afore them, and smote through the shields, that the cantels fell off both parties. Also they tamed their helms that the hot blood ran out, and the thick mails of their hauberks they carved and rove in sunder that the hot blood ran to the earth, and both they had many wounds and were passing weary. But Sir Tor espied that the other knight fainted, and then he sued fast upon him, and doubled his strokes, and gart him go to the earth on the one side. Then Sir Tor bade him yield him. That will I not, said Abelleus, while my life lasteth and the soul is within my body, unless that thou wilt give me the brachet. That will I not do, said Sir Tor, for it was my quest to bring again thy brachet, thee, or both.

CHAPTER XI

*How Sir Tor overcame the knight, and how he lost his head
at the request of a lady.*

With that came a damosel riding on a palfrey as fast as she might drive, and cried with a loud voice unto Sir Tor. What will ye with me? said Sir Tor. I beseech thee, said the damosel, for King Arthur's love, give me a gift; I require thee, gentle knight, as thou art a gentleman. Now, said Tor, ask a gift and I will give it you. Gramercy, said the damosel; now I ask the head of the false knight Abelleus, for he is the most outrageous knight that liveth, and the greatest murderer. I am loath, said Sir Tor, of that gift I have given you; let him make amends in that he hath trespassed unto you. Now, said the damosel, he may not, for he slew mine own brother before mine own eyes, that was a better knight than he, an he had had grace; and I kneeled half an hour afore him in the mire for to save my brother's life, that had done him no damage, but fought with him by adventure of arms, and so for all that I could do he struck off his head; wherefore I require thee, as thou art a true knight, to give me my gift, or else I shall shame thee in all the court of King Arthur; for he is the falsest knight living, and a great destroyer of good knights. Then when Abelleus heard this, he was more afeard, and yielded him and asked mercy. I may not now, said Sir Tor, but if I should be found false of my promise; for while I would have taken you to mercy ye would none ask, but if ye had the brachet again, that was my quest. And therewith he took off his helm, and he arose and fled, and Sir Tor after him, and smote off his head quite.

Now sir, said the damosel, it is near night; I pray you come and lodge with me here at my place, it is here fast by. I will well, said Sir Tor, for his horse and he had fared evil since they departed from Camelot, and so he rode with her, and had passing good cheer with her; and she had a passing fair old knight to her husband that made him passing good cheer, and well eased both his horse and him. And on the morn he heard his mass, and brake his fast, and took his leave of the knight and of the lady, that besought him to tell them his name. Truly, he said, my name is Sir Tor that was late made knight, and this was the first quest of arms that ever I did, to bring again that this knight Abelleus took away from King Arthur's court. O fair knight, said the lady and her husband, an ye come here in our marches, come and see our poor lodging, and it shall be always at your commandment. So Sir Tor departed and came to Camelot on the third day by noon, and the king and the queen and all the court was passing fain of his coming, and made great joy that he was come again; for he went from the court with little succour, but as King Pellinore his father gave him an old courser, and King Arthur gave him armour and a sword, and else had he none other succour, but rode so forth himself alone. And then the king and the queen by Merlin's advice made him to swear to tell of his adventures, and so he told and made proofs of his deeds as it is afore rehearsed, wherefore the king and the queen made great joy. Nay, nay, said Merlin, these be but japes to that he shall do; for he shall prove a noble knight of prowess, as good as any is living, and gentle and courteous, and of good tatches, and passing true of his promise, and never shall outrage. Wherethrough Merlin's words King Arthur gave him an earldom of lands that fell unto him. And here endeth the quest of Sir Tor, King Pellinore's son.

CHAPTER XII

How King Pellinore rode after the lady and the knight that
led her away, and how a lady desired help of him, and how he
fought with two knights for that lady, of whom he slew
the one at the first stroke.

Then King Pellinore armed him and mounted upon his horse, and
rode more than a pace after the lady that the knight led away. And as
he rode in a forest, he saw in a valley a damosel sit by a well, and a
wounded knight in her arms, and Pellinore saluted her. And when
she was ware of him, she cried overloud, Help me, knight; for
Christ's sake, King Pellinore. And he would not tarry, he was so
eager in his quest, and ever she cried an hundred times after help.
When she saw he would not abide, she prayed unto God to send him
as much need of help as she had, and that he might feel it or he died.
So, as the book telleth, the knight there died that there was wounded,
wherefore the lady for pure sorrow slew herself with his sword. As
King Pellinore rode in that valley he met with a poor man, a
labourer. Sawest thou not, said Pellinore, a knight riding and leading
away a lady? Yea, said the man, I saw that knight, and the lady that
made great dole; and yonder beneath in a valley there shall ye see two
pavilions, and one of the knights of the pavilions challenged that lady
of that knight, and said she was his cousin near, wherefore he should
lead her no farther. And so they waged battle in that quarrel, the one
said he would have her by force, and the other said he would have
the rule of her, by cause he was her kinsman, and would lead her to
her kin. For this quarrel he left them fighting. And if ye will ride a
pace ye shall find them fighting, and the lady was beleft with the two
squires in the pavilions. God thank thee, said King Pellinore.

Then he rode a wallop till he had a sight of the two pavilions, and
the two knights fighting. Anon he rode unto the pavilions, and saw
the lady that was his quest, and said, Fair lady, ye must go with me
unto the court of King Arthur. Sir knight, said the two squires that
were with her, yonder are two knights that fight for this lady, go

thither and depart them, and be agreed with them, and then may ye have her at your pleasure. Ye say well, said King Pellinore. And anon he rode betwixt them, and departed them, and asked them the causes why that they fought? Sir knight, said the one, I shall tell you, this lady is my kinswoman nigh, mine aunt's daughter, and when I heard her complain that she was with him maugre her head, I waged battle to fight with him. Sir knight, said the other, whose name was Hontzlake of Wentland, and this lady I gat by my prowess of arms this day at Arthur's court. That is untruly said, said King Pellinore, for ye came in suddenly there as we were at the high feast, and took away this lady or any man might make him ready; and therefore it was my quest to bring her again and you both, or else the one of us to abide in the field; therefore the lady shall go with me, or I will die for it, for I have promised it King Arthur. And therefore fight ye no more, for none of you shall have no part of her at this time; and if ye list to fight for her, fight with me, and I will defend her. Well, said the knights, make you ready, and we shall assail you with all our power. And as King Pellinore would have put his horse from them, Sir Hontzlake rove his horse through with a sword, and said: Now art thou on foot as well as we are. When King Pellinore espied that his horse was slain, lightly he leapt from his horse and pulled out his sword, and put his shield afore him, and said, Knight, keep well thy head, for thou shalt have a buffet for the slaying of my horse. So King Pellinore gave him such a stroke upon the helm that he clave the head down to the chin, that he fell to the earth dead.

CHAPTER XIII

How King Pellinore gat the lady and brought her to Camelot to the court of King Arthur.

And then he turned him to the other knight, that was sore wounded. But when he saw the other's buffet, he would not fight, but kneeled down and said, Take my cousin the lady with you at your request, and I require you, as ye be a true knight, put her to no shame nor villainy. What, said King Pellinore, will ye not fight for her? No, sir, said the knight, I will not fight with such a knight of prowess as ye be.

Well, said Pellinore, ye say well; I promise you she shall have no villainy by me, as I am true knight; but now me lacketh an horse, said Pellinore, but I will have Hontzlake's horse. Ye shall not need, said the knight, for I shall give you such an horse as shall please you, so that you will lodge with me, for it is near night. I will well, said King Pellinore, abide with you all night. And there he had with him right good cheer, and fared of the best with passing good wine, and had merry rest that night. And on the morn he heard a mass and dined; and then was brought him a fair bay courser, and King Pellinore's saddle set upon him. Now, what shall I call you? said the knight, inasmuch as ye have my cousin at your desire of your quest. Sir, I shall tell you, my name is King Pellinore of the Isles and knight of the Table Round. Now I am glad, said the knight, that such a noble man shall have the rule of my cousin. Now, what is your name? said Pellinore, I pray you tell me. Sir, my name is Sir Meliot of Logurs, and this lady my cousin hight Nimue, and the knight that was in the other pavilion is my sworn brother, a passing good knight, and his name is Brian of the Isles, and he is full loath to do wrong, and full loath to fight with any man, but if he be sore sought on, so that for shame he may not leave it. It is marvel, said Pellinore, that he will not have ado with me. Sir, he will not have ado with no man but if it be at his request. Bring him to the court, said Pellinore, one of these days. Sir, we will come together. And ye shall be welcome, said Pellinore, to the court of King Arthur, and greatly allowed for your coming. And so he departed with the lady, and brought her to Camelot.

So as they rode in a valley it was full of stones, and there the lady's horse stumbled and threw her down, that her arm was sore bruised and near she swooned for pain. Alas! sir, said the lady, mine arm is out of lithe, wherethrough I must needs rest me. Ye shall well, said King Pellinore. And so he alighted under a fair tree where was fair grass, and he put his horse thereto, and so laid him under the tree and slept till it was nigh night. And when he awoke he would have ridden. Sir, said the lady, it is so dark that ye may as well ride backward as forward. So they abode still and made there their lodging. Then Sir Pellinore put off his armour; then a little afore midnight they heard the trotting of an horse. Be ye still, said King Pellinore, for we shall hear of some adventure.

CHAPTER XIV

How on the way he heard two knights, as he lay by night in a valley, and of their adventures.

And therewith he armed him. So right even afore him there met two knights, the one came froward Camelot, and the other from the north, and either saluted other. What tidings at Camelot? said the one. By my head, said the other, there have I been and espied the court of King Arthur, and there is such a fellowship they may never be broken, and well-nigh all the world holdeth with Arthur, for there is the flower of chivalry. Now for this cause I am riding into the north, to tell our chieftains of the fellowship that is withholden with King Arthur. As for that, said the other knight, I have brought a remedy with me, that is the greatest poison that ever ye heard speak of, and to Camelot will I with it, for we have a friend right nigh King Arthur, and well cherished, that shall poison King Arthur; for so he hath promised our chieftains, and received great gifts for to do it. Beware, said the other knight, of Merlin, for he knoweth all things by the devil's craft. Therefore will I not let it, said the knight. And so they departed asunder. Anon after Pellinore made him ready, and his lady, [and] rode toward Camelot; and as they came by the well there as the wounded knight was and the lady, there he found the knight, and the lady eaten with lions or wild beasts, all save the head, wherefore he made great sorrow, and wept passing sore, and said, Alas! her life might I have saved; but I was so fierce in my quest, therefore I would not abide. Wherefore make ye such dole? said the lady. I wot not, said Pellinore, but my heart mourneth sore of the death of her, for she was a passing fair lady and a young. Now, will ye do by mine advice? said the lady, take this knight and let him be buried in an hermitage, and then take the lady's head and bear it with you unto Arthur. So King Pellinore took this dead knight on his shoulders, and brought him to the hermitage, and charged the hermit with the corpse, that service should be done for the soul; and take his harness for your pain. It shall be done, said the hermit, as I will answer unto God.

CHAPTER XV

*How when he was come to Camelot he was sworn upon a
book to tell the truth of his quest.*

And therewith they departed, and came there as the head of the lady
lay with a fair yellow hair that grieved King Pellinore passingly sore
when he looked on it, for much he cast his heart on the visage. And
so by noon they came to Camelot; and the king and the queen were
passing fain of his coming to the court. And there he was made to
swear upon the Four Evangelists, to tell the truth of his quest from
the one to the other. Ah! Sir Pellinore, said Queen Guenever, ye
were greatly to blame that ye saved not this lady's life. Madam, said
Pellinore, ye were greatly to blame an ye would not save your own
life an ye might, but, save your pleasure, I was so furious in my quest
that I would not abide, and that repenteth me, and shall the days of
my life. Truly, said Merlin, ye ought sore to repent it, for that lady
was your own daughter begotten on the lady of the Rule, and that
knight that was dead was her love, and should have wedded her, and
he was a right good knight of a young man, and would have proved a
good man, and to this court was he coming, and his name was Sir
Miles of the Launds, and a knight came behind him and slew him
with a spear, and his name is Loraine le Savage, a false knight and a
coward; and she for great sorrow and dole slew herself with his
sword, and her name was Eleine. And because ye would not abide
and help her, ye shall see your best friend fail you when ye be in the
greatest distress that ever ye were or shall be. And that penance God
hath ordained you for that deed, that he that ye shall most trust to of
any man alive, he shall leave you there ye shall be slain. Me
forthinketh, said King Pellinore, that this shall me betide, but God
may fordo well destiny.

Thus, when the quest was done of the white hart, the which
followed Sir Gawaine; and the quest of the brachet, followed of Sir
Tor, Pellinore's son; and the quest of the lady that the knight took
away, the which King Pellinore at that time followed; then the king
stablished all his knights, and them that were of lands not rich he gave

them lands, and charged them never to do outrageousity nor murder, and always to flee treason; also, by no means to be cruel, but to give mercy unto him that asketh mercy, upon pain of forfeiture of their worship and lordship of King Arthur for evermore; and always to do ladies, damosels, and gentlewomen succour, upon pain of death. Also, that no man take no battles in a wrongful quarrel for no law, nor for no world's goods. Unto this were all the knights sworn of the Table Round, both old and young. And every year were they sworn at the high feast of Pentecost.

Explicit the Wedding of King Arthur.
Sequitur quartus liber.

BOOK FOUR

CHAPTER I

How Merlin was assotted and doted on one of the ladies of the lake, and how he was shut in a rock under a stone and there died.

So after these quests of Sir Gawaine, Sir Tor, and King Pellinore, it fell so that Merlin fell in a dotage on the damosel that King Pellinore brought to court, and she was one of the damosels of the lake, that hight Nimue. But Merlin would let her have no rest, but always he would be with her. And ever she made Merlin good cheer till she had learned of him all manner thing that she desired; and he was assotted upon her, that he might not be from her. So on a time he told King Arthur that he should not dure long, but for all his crafts he should be put in the earth quick. And so he told the king many things that should befall, but always he warned the king to keep well his sword and the scabbard, for he told him how the sword and the scabbard should be stolen by a woman from him that he most trusted. Also he told King Arthur that he should miss him, − Yet had ye liefer than all your lands to have me again. Ah, said the king, since ye know of your adventure, purvey for it, and put away by your crafts that misadventure. Nay, said Merlin, it will not be; so he departed from the king. And within a while the Damosel of the Lake departed, and Merlin went with her evermore wheresomever she went. And ofttimes Merlin would have had her privily away by his subtle crafts; then she made him to swear that he should never do none enchantment upon her if he would have his will. And so he sware; so she and Merlin went over the sea unto the land of Benwick, whereas King Ban was king that had great war against King Claudas, and there Merlin spake with King Ban's wife, a fair lady and a good, and her name was Elaine, and there he saw young Launcelot. There the queen made great sorrow for the mortal war that King Claudas made on her lord and on her lands. Take none heaviness, said Merlin, for this same child within this twenty year shall revenge you on King Claudas, that all Christendom shall speak of it; and this same child shall be the most man of worship of the world, and his first name is Galahad, that know I well, said Merlin, and since ye have confirmed him Launcelot. That is truth, said the queen, his first name was Galahad. O Merlin, said the queen, shall I live to see my son such a man of prowess? Yea, lady, on my peril ye shall see it, and live many winters after.

And so, soon after, the lady and Merlin departed, and by the way Merlin showed her many wonders, and came into Cornwall. And always Merlin lay about the lady to have her maidenhood, and she was ever passing weary of him, and fain would have been delivered of him, for she was afeard of him because he was a devil's son, and she could not beskift him by no mean. And so on a time it happed that Merlin showed to her in a rock whereas was a great wonder, and wrought by enchantment, that went under a great stone. So by her subtle working she made Merlin to go under that stone to let her wit of the marvels there; but she wrought so there for him that he came never out for all the craft he could do. And so she departed and left Merlin.

CHAPTER II

How five kings came into this land to war against King Arthur, and what counsel Arthur had against them.

And as King Arthur rode to Camelot, and held there a great feast with mirth and joy, so soon after he returned unto Cardoile, and there came unto Arthur new tidings that the king of Denmark, and the king of Ireland that was his brother, and the king of the Vale, and the king of Soleise, and the king of the Isle of Longtains, all these five kings with a great host were entered into the land of King Arthur, and burnt and slew clean afore them, both cities and castles, that it was pity to hear. Alas, said Arthur, yet had I never rest one month since I was crowned king of this land. Now shall I never rest till I meet with those kings in a fair field, that I make mine avow; for my true liege people shall not be destroyed in my default, go with me who will, and abide who that will. Then the king let write unto King Pellinore, and prayed him in all haste to make him ready with such people as he might lightliest rear and hie him after in all haste. All the barons were privily wroth that the king would depart so suddenly; but the king by no mean would abide, but made writing unto them that were not there, and bade them hie after him, such as were not at that time in the court. Then the king came to Queen Guenever, and said, Lady, make you ready, for ye shall go with me, for I may not long miss you; ye shall cause me to be the more hardy, what adventure so befall me; I will not wit my lady to be in no jeopardy. Sir, said she, I am at your commandment, and shall be ready what time so ye be ready. So on the morn the king and the queen departed with such fellowship as they had, and came into the north, into a forest beside Humber, and there lodged them. When the word and tiding came unto the five kings above said, that Arthur was beside Humber in a forest, there was a knight, brother unto one of the five kings, that gave them this counsel: Ye know well that Sir Arthur hath the flower of chivalry of the world with him, as it is proved by the great battle he did with the eleven kings; and therefore hie unto him night and day till that we be nigh him, for the longer he tarrieth the bigger he is, and we ever the weaker; and he is so courageous of himself that he is come to the field with little people, and therefore let us set upon him or day and we shall slay down; of his knights there shall none escape.

CHAPTER III

How King Arthur had ado with them and overthrew them, and slew the five kings and made the remnant to flee.

Unto this counsel these five kings assented, and so they passed forth with their host through North Wales, and came upon Arthur by night, and set upon his host as the king and his knights were in their pavilions. King Arthur was unarmed, and had laid him to rest with his Queen Guenever. Sir, said Sir Kay, it is not good we be unarmed. We shall have no need, said Sir Gawaine and Sir Griflet, that lay in a little pavilion by the king. With that they heard a great noise, and many cried, Treason, treason! Alas, said King Arthur, we be betrayed! Unto arms, fellows, then he cried. So they were armed anon at all points. Then came there a wounded knight unto the king, and said, Sir, save yourself and my lady the queen, for our host is destroyed, and much people of ours slain. So anon the king and the queen and the three knights took their horses, and rode toward Humber to pass over it, and the water was so rough that they were afraid to pass over. Now may ye choose, said King Arthur, whether ye will abide and take the adventure on this side, for an ye be taken they will slay you. It were me liefer, said the queen, to die in the water than to fall in your enemies' hands and there be slain.

And as they stood so talking, Sir Kay saw the five kings coming on horseback by themselves alone, with their spears in their hands even toward them. Lo, said Sir Kay, yonder be the five kings; let us go to them and match them. That were folly, said Sir Gawaine, for we are but three and they be five. That is truth, said Sir Griflet. No force, said Sir Kay, I will undertake for two of them, and then may ye three undertake for the other three. And therewithal, Sir Kay let his horse run as fast as he might, and struck one of them through the shield and the body a fathom, that the king fell to the earth stark dead. That saw Sir Gawaine, and ran unto another king so hard that he smote him through the body. And therewithal King Arthur ran to another, and smote him through the body with a spear, that he fell to the earth dead. Then Sir Griflet ran unto the fourth king, and gave him such a fall that his neck brake. Anon Sir Kay ran unto the fifth king, and smote him so hard on the helm that the stroke clave the helm and the head to the earth. That was well stricken, said King Arthur, and worshipfully hast thou holden thy promise, therefore I shall honour thee while that I live. And therewithal they set the queen in a barge into Humber; but always Queen Guenever praised Sir Kay for his deeds, and said, What lady that ye love, and she love you not again she were greatly to blame; and among ladies, said the queen, I shall bear your noble fame, for ye spake a great word, and fulfilled it worshipfully. And therewith the queen departed.

Then the king and the three knights rode into the forest, for there they supposed to hear of them that were escaped; and there he found the most part of his people, and told them all how the five kings were dead. And therefore let us hold us together till it be day, and when

their host have espied that their chieftains be slain, they will make
such dole that they shall no more help themselves. And right so as the
king said, so it was; for when they found the five kings dead, they
make such dole that they fell from their horses. Therewithal came
King Arthur but with a few people, and slew on the left hand and on
the right hand, that well-nigh there escaped no man, but all were
slain to the number thirty thousand. And when the battle was all
ended, the king kneeled down and thanked God meekly. And then
he sent for the queen, and soon she was come, and she made great
joy of the overcoming of that battle.

CHAPTER IV

*How the battle was finished or he came, and how King
Arthur founded an abbey where the battle was.*

Therewithal came one to King Arthur, and told him that King
Pellinore was within three mile with a great host; and he said, Go
unto him, and let him understand how we have sped. So within a
while King Pellinore came with a great host, and saluted the people
and the king, and there was great joy made on every side. Then the
king let search how much people of his party there was slain; and
there were found but little past two hundred men slain and eight
knights of the Table Round in their pavilions. Then the king let rear
and devise in the same place whereat the battle was done a fair abbey,
and endowed it with great livelihood, and let it call the Abbey of La
Beale Adventure. But when some of them came into their countries,
whereof the five kings were kings, and told them how they were
slain, there was made great dole. And all King Arthur's enemies, as
the King of North Wales, and the kings of the North, [when they]
wist of the battle, they were passing heavy. And so the king returned
unto Camelot in haste.

And when he was come to Camelot he called King Pellinore unto
him, and said, Ye understand well that we have lost eight knights of
the best of the Table Round, and by your advice we will choose eight
again of the best we may find in this court. Sir, said Pellinore, I shall
counsel you after my conceit the best: there are in your court full

noble knights both of old and young; and therefore by mine advice ye shall choose half of the old and half of the young. Which be the old? said King Arthur. Sir, said King Pellinore, meseemeth that King Uriens that hath wedded your sister Morgan le Fay, and the King of the Lake, and Sir Hervise de Revel, a noble knight, and Sir Galagars, the fourth. This is well devised, said King Arthur, and right so shall it be. Now, which are the four young knights? said Arthur. Sir, said Pellinore, the first is Sir Gawaine, your nephew, that is as good a knight of his time as any is in this land; and the second as meseemeth best is Sir Griflet le Fise de Dieu, that is a good knight and full desirous in arms, and who may see him live he shall prove a good knight; and the third as meseemeth is well to be one of the knights of the Round Table, Sir Kay the Seneschal, for many times he hath done full worshipfully, and now at your last battle he did full honourably for to undertake to slay two kings. By my head, said Arthur, he is best worth to be a knight of the Round Table of any that ye have rehearsed, an he had done no more prowess in his life days.

CHAPTER V

How Sir Tor was made Knight of the Round Table, and how Bagdemagus was displeased.

Now, said King Pellinore, I shall put to you two knights, and ye shall choose which is most worthy, that is Sir Bagdemagus, and Sir Tor, my son. But because Sir Tor is my son I may not praise him, but else, an he were not my son, I durst say that of his age there is not in this land a better knight than he is, nor of better conditions and loath to do any wrong, and loath to take any wrong. By my head, said Arthur, he is a passing good knight as any ye spake of this day, that wot I well, said the king; for I have seen him proved, but he saith little and he doth much more, for I know none in all this court an he were as well born on his mother's side as he is on your side, that is like him of prowess and of might: and therefore I will have him at this time, and leave Sir Bagdemagus till another time. So when they were so chosen by the assent of all the barons, so were there found in their sieges every knights' names that here are rehearsed, and so were they set in their sieges; whereof Sir Bagdemagus was wonderly wroth, that Sir Tor was advanced afore him, and therefore suddenly he departed from the court, and took his squire with him, and rode long in a forest till they came to a cross, and there alighted and said his prayers devoutly. The meanwhile his squire found written upon the cross, that Bagdemagus should never return unto the court again, till he had won a knight's body of the Round Table, body for body. So, sir, said the squire, here I find writing of you, therefore I rede you return again to the court. That shall I never, said Bagdemagus, till men speak of me great worship, and that I be worthy to be a knight of the Round Table. And so he rode forth, and there by the way he found a branch of an holy herb that was the Sign of the Sangreal, and no knight found such tokens but he were a good liver.

So, as Sir Bagdemagus rode to see many adventures, it happed him to come to the rock whereas the Lady of the Lake had put Merlin under the stone, and there he heard him make great dole; whereof Sir Bagdemagus would have holpen him, and went unto the great stone, and it was so heavy that an hundred men might not lift it up. When Merlin wist he was there, he bade leave his labour, for all was in vain, for he might never be holpen but by her that put him there. And so Bagdemagus departed and did many adventures, and proved after a full good knight, and came again to the court and was made knight of the Round Table. So on the morn there fell new tidings and other adventures.

CHAPTER VI

*How King Arthur, King Uriens, and Sir Accolon of Gaul,
chased an hart, and of their marvellous adventures.*

Then it befell that Arthur and many of his knights rode a-hunting into a great forest, and it happed King Arthur, King Uriens, and Sir Accolon of Gaul, followed a great hart, for they three were well horsed, and so they chased so fast that within a while they three were then ten mile from their fellowship. And at the last they chased so sore that they slew their horses underneath them. Then were they all three on foot, and ever they saw the hart afore them passing weary and enbushed. What will we do? said King Arthur, we are hard bestead. Let us go on foot, said King Uriens, till we may meet with some lodging. Then were they ware of the hart that lay on a great water bank, and a brachet biting on his throat, and more other hounds came after. Then King Arthur blew the prise and dight the hart.

Then the king looked about the world, and saw afore him in a great water a little ship, all apparelled with silk down to the water, and the ship came right unto them and landed on the sands. Then Arthur went to the bank and looked in, and saw none earthly creature therein. Sirs, said the king, come thence, and let us see what is in this ship. So they went in all three, and found it richly behanged with cloth of silk. By then it was dark night, and there suddenly were about them an hundred torches set upon all the sides of the ship boards, and it gave great light; and therewithal there came out twelve fair damosels and saluted King Arthur on their knees, and called him by his name, and said he was right welcome, and such cheer as they had he should have of the best. The king thanked them fair. Therewithal they led the king and his two fellows into a fair chamber, and there was a cloth laid, richly beseen of all that longed unto a table, and there were they served of all wines and meats that they could think; of that the king had great marvel, for he fared never better in his life as for one supper. And so when they had supped at their leisure, King Arthur was led into a chamber, a richer beseen chamber saw he never none, and so was King Uriens served, and led into such another chamber, and Sir Accolon was led into the third chamber passing richly and well beseen; and so they were laid in their beds easily. And anon they fell asleep, and slept marvellously sore all the night. And on the morrow King Uriens was in Camelot abed in his wife's arms, Morgan le Fay. And when he awoke he had great marvel, how he came there, for on the even afore he was two days' journey from Camelot. And when King Arthur awoke he found himself in a dark prison, hearing about him many complaints of woful knights.

CHAPTER VII

*How Arthur took upon him to fight to be delivered out of
prison, and also for to deliver twenty knights
that were in prison.*

What are ye that so complain? said King Arthur. We be here twenty
knights, prisoners, said they, and some of us have lain here seven year,
and some more and some less. For what cause? said Arthur. We shall
tell you, said the knights; this lord of this castle, his name is Sir Damas,
and he is the falsest knight that liveth, and full of treason, and a very
coward as any liveth, and he hath a younger brother, a good knight
of prowess, his name is Sir Ontzlake; and this traitor Damas, the elder
brother will give him no part of his livelihood, but as Sir Ontzlake
keepeth thorough prowess of his hands, and so he keepeth from him
a full fair manor and a rich, and therein Sir Ontzlake dwelleth
worshipfully, and is well beloved of all people. And this Sir Damas
our master is as evil beloved, for he is without mercy, and he is a
coward, and great war hath been betwixt them both, but Ontzlake
hath ever the better, and ever he proffereth Sir Damas to fight for the
livelihood, body for body, but he will not do; other-else to find a
knight to fight for him. Unto that Sir Damas had granted to find a
knight, but he is so evil beloved and hated, that there is never a
knight will fight for him. And when Damas saw this, that there was
never a knight would fight for him, he hath daily lain await with
many knights with him, and taken all the knights in this country to
see and espy their adventures, he hath taken them by force and
brought them to his prison. And so he took us separately as we rode
on our adventures, and many good knights have died in this prison
for hunger, to the number of eighteen knights; and if any of us all that
here is, or hath been, would have foughten with his brother
Ontzlake, he would have delivered us, but for because this Damas is
so false and so full of treason we would never fight for him to die for
it. And we be so lean for hunger that unnethe we may stand on our
feet. God deliver you, for his mercy, said Arthur.

Anon, therewithal there came a damosel unto Arthur, and asked

him, What cheer? I cannot say, said he. Sir, said she, an ye will fight
for my lord, ye shall be delivered out of prison, and else ye escape
never the life. Now, said Arthur, that is hard, yet had I liefer to fight
with a knight than to die in prison; with this, said Arthur, I may be
delivered and all these prisoners, I will do the battle. Yes, said the
damosel. I am ready, said Arthur, an I had horse and armour. Ye shall
lack none, said the damosel. Meseemeth, damosel, I should have seen
you in the court of Arthur. Nay, said the damosel, I came never
there, I am the lord's daughter of this castle. Yet was she false, for she
was one of the damosels of Morgan le Fay.

Anon she went unto Sir Damas, and told him how he would do
battle for him, and so he sent for Arthur. And when he came he was
well coloured, and well made of his limbs, that all knights that saw
him said it were pity that such a knight should die in prison. So Sir
Damas and he were agreed that he should fight for him upon this
covenant, that all other knights should be delivered; and unto that
was Sir Damas sworn unto Arthur, and also to do the battle to the
uttermost. And with that all the twenty knights were brought out of
the dark prison into the hall, and delivered, and so they all abode to
see the battle.

CHAPTER VIII

How Accolon found himself by a well, and he took upon him
to do battle against Arthur.

Now turn we unto Accolon of Gaul, that when he awoke he found
himself by a deep well-side, within half a foot, in great peril of death.
And there came out of that fountain a pipe of silver, and out of that
pipe ran water all on high in a stone of marble. When Sir Accolon
saw this, he blessed him and said, Jesus save my lord King Arthur, and
King Uriens, for these damosels in this ship have betrayed us, they
were devils and no women; and if I may escape this misadventure, I
shall destroy all where I may find these false damosels that use
enchantments. Right with that there came a dwarf with a great
mouth and a flat nose, and saluted Sir Accolon, and said how he came
from Queen Morgan le Fay, and she greeteth you well, and biddeth

you be of strong heart, for ye shall fight tomorrow with a knight at the hour of prime, and therefore she hath sent you here Excalibur, Arthur's sword, and the scabbard, and she biddeth you as ye love her, that ye do the battle to the uttermost, without any mercy, like as ye had promised her when ye spake together in privity; and what damosel that bringeth her the knight's head, which ye shall fight withal, she will make her a queen. Now I understand you well, said Accolon, I shall hold that I have promised her now I have the sword: when saw ye my lady Queen Morgan le Fay? Right late, said the dwarf. Then Accolon took him in his arms and said, Recommend me unto my lady queen, and tell her all shall be done that I have promised her, and else I will die for it. Now I suppose, said Accolon, she hath made all these crafts and enchantments for this battle. Ye may well believe it, said the dwarf. Right so there came a knight and a lady with six squires, and saluted Accolon, and prayed him for to arise, and come and rest him at his manor. And so Accolon mounted upon a void horse, and went with the knight unto a fair manor by a priory, and there he had passing good cheer.

Then Sir Damas sent unto his brother Sir Ontzlake, and bade make him ready by to-morn at the hour of prime, and to be in the field to fight with a good knight, for he had found a good knight that was ready to do battle at all points. When this word came unto Sir Ontzlake he was passing heavy, for he was wounded a little to-fore through both his thighs with a spear, and made great dole; but as he was wounded, he would have taken the battle on hand. So it happed at that time, by the means of Morgan le Fay, Accolon was with Sir Ontzlake lodged; and when he heard of that battle, and how Ontzlake was wounded, he said that he would fight for him. Because Morgan le Fay had sent him Excalibur and the sheath for to fight with the knight on the morn: this was the cause Sir Accolon took the battle on hand. Then Sir Ontzlake was passing glad, and thanked Sir Accolon with all his heart that he would do so much for him. And therewithal Sir Ontzlake sent word unto his brother Sir Damas, that he had a knight that for him should be ready in the field by the hour of prime.

So on the morn Sir Arthur was armed and well horsed, and asked Sir Damas, When shall we to the field? Sir, said Sir Damas, ye shall hear mass. And so Arthur heard a mass, and when mass was done there came a squire on a great horse, and asked Sir Damas if his knight were ready, for our knight is ready in the field. Then Sir

Arthur mounted upon horseback, and there were all the knights and commons of that country; and so by all advices there were chosen twelve good men of the country for to wait upon the two knights. And right as Arthur was on horseback there came a damosel from Morgan le Fay, and brought unto Sir Arthur a sword like unto Excalibur, and the scabbard, and said unto Arthur, Morgan le Fay sendeth here your sword for great love. And he thanked her, and weened it had been so, but she was false, for the sword and the scabbard was counterfeit, and brittle, and false.

CHAPTER IX

Of the battle between King Arthur and Accolon.

And then they dressed them on both parties of the field, and let their horses run so fast that either smote other in the midst of the shield with their spear-heads, that both horse and man went to the earth; and then they started up both, and pulled out their swords. The meanwhile that they were thus at the battle, came the Damosel of the Lake into the field, that put Merlin under the stone; and she came thither for love of King Arthur, for she knew how Morgan le Fay had so ordained that King Arthur should have been slain that day, and therefore she came to save his life. And so they went eagerly to the battle, and gave many great strokes, but always Arthur's sword bit not like Accolon's sword; but for the most part, every stroke that Accolon gave he wounded sore Arthur, that it was marvel he stood, and always his blood fell from him fast.

When Arthur beheld the ground so sore be-bled he was dismayed, and then he deemed treason that his sword was changed; for his sword bit not steel as it was wont to do, therefore he dreaded him sore to be dead, for ever him seemed that the sword in Accolon's hand was Excalibur, for at every stroke that Accolon struck he drew blood on Arthur. Now, knight, said Accolon unto Arthur, keep thee well from me; but Arthur answered not again, and gave him such a buffet on the helm that it made him to stoop, nigh falling down to the earth. Then Sir Accolon withdrew him a little, and came on with Excalibur on high, and smote Sir Arthur such a buffet that he fell nigh to the earth. Then were they wroth both, and gave each other many sore strokes, but always Sir Arthur lost so much blood that it was marvel he stood on his feet, but he was so full of knighthood that knightly he endured the pain. And Sir Accolon lost not a deal of blood, therefore he waxed passing light, and Sir Arthur was passing feeble, and weened verily to have died; but for all that he made countenance as though he might endure, and held Accolon as short as he might. But Accolon was so bold because of Excalibur that he waxed passing hardy. But all men that beheld him said they saw never knight fight so well as Arthur did considering the blood that he bled. So was all the people sorry for him, but the two brethren would not accord. Then always they fought together as fierce knights, and Sir Arthur withdrew him a little for to rest him, and Sir Accolon called him to battle and said, It is no time for me to suffer thee to rest. And therewith he came fiercely upon Arthur, and Sir Arthur was wroth for the blood that he had lost, and smote Accolon on high upon the helm, so mightily, that he made him nigh to fall to the earth; and therewith Arthur's sword brast at the cross, and fell in the grass among the blood, and the pommel and the sure handles he held in his hands. When Sir Arthur saw that, he was in great fear to die, but always he held up his shield and lost no ground, nor bated no cheer.

CHAPTER X

How King Arthur's sword that he fought with brake, and how he recovered of Accolon his own sword Excalibur, and overcame his enemy.

Then Sir Accolon began with words of treason, and said, Knight, thou art overcome and mayst not endure, and also thou art weaponless, and thou hast lost much of thy blood, and I am full loath to slay thee, therefore yield thee to me as recreant. Nay, said Sir Arthur, I may not so, for I have promised to do the battle to the uttermost, by the faith of my body, while me lasteth the life, and therefore I had liefer to die with honour than to live with shame; and if it were possible for me to die an hundred times, I had liefer to die so oft than yield me to thee; for though I lack weapon, I shall lack no worship, and if thou slay me weaponless that shall be thy shame. Well, said Accolon, as for the shame I will not spare, now keep thee from me, for thou art but a dead man. And therewith Accolon gave him such a stroke that he fell nigh to the earth, and would have had Arthur to have cried him mercy. But Sir Arthur pressed unto Accolon with his shield, and gave him with the pommel in his hand such a buffet that he went three strides aback.

When the Damosel of the Lake beheld Arthur, how full of prowess his body was, and the false treason that was wrought for him to have had him slain, she had great pity that so good a knight and such a man of worship should so be destroyed. And at the next stroke Sir Accolon struck him such a stroke that by the damosel's enchantment the sword Excalibur fell out of Accolon's hand to the earth. And therewithal Sir Arthur lightly leapt to it, and gat it in his hand, and forthwithal he knew that it was his sword Excalibur, and said, Thou hast been from me all too long, and much damage hast thou done me; and therewith he espied the scabbard hanging by his side, and suddenly he sterte to him and pulled the scabbard from him, and threw it from him as far as he might throw it. O knight, said Arthur, this day hast thou done me great damage with this sword; now are ye come unto your death, for I shall not warrant you but ye shall as well be rewarded with this sword, or ever we depart, as thou hast rewarded me; for much pain have ye made me to endure, and much blood have I lost. And therewith Sir Arthur rushed on him with all his might and pulled him to the earth, and then rushed off his helm, and gave him such a buffet on the head that the blood came out at his ears, his nose, and his mouth. Now will I slay thee, said Arthur. Slay me ye may well, said Accolon, an it please you, for ye are the best knight that ever I found, and I see well that God is with you. But for I promised to do this battle, said Accolon, to the uttermost, and never to be recreant while I lived, therefore shall I never yield me with my mouth, but God do with my body what he will. Then Sir Arthur remembered him, and thought he should have seen this knight. Now tell me, said Arthur, or I will slay thee, of what country art thou, and of what court? Sir Knight, said Sir Accolon, I am of the court of King Arthur, and my name is Accolon of Gaul. Then was Arthur more dismayed than he was beforehand; for then he remembered him of his sister Morgan le Fay, and of the enchantment of the ship. O sir knight, said he, I pray you tell me who gave you this sword, and by whom ye had it.

CHAPTER XI

*How Accolon confessed the treason of Morgan le Fay, King
Arthur's sister, and how she would have done slay him.*

Then Sir Accolon bethought him, and said, Woe worth this sword,
for by it have I got my death. It may well be, said the king. Now, sir,
said Accolon, I will tell you; this sword hath been in my keeping the
most part of this twelvemonth; and Morgan le Fay, King Uriens' wife,
sent it me yesterday by a dwarf, to this intent, that I should slay King
Arthur, her brother. For ye shall understand King Arthur is the man in
the world that she most hateth, because he is most of worship and of
prowess of any of her blood; also she loveth me out of measure as
paramour, and I her again; and if she might bring about to slay Arthur
by her crafts, she would slay her husband King Uriens lightly, and
then had she me devised to be king in this land, and so to reign, and
she to be my queen; but that is now done, said Accolon, for I am sure
of my death. Well, said Sir Arthur, I feel by you ye would have been
king in this land. It had been great damage to have destroyed your
lord, said Arthur. It is truth, said Accolon, but now I have told you
truth, wherefore I pray you tell me of whence ye are, and of what
court? O Accolon, said King Arthur, now I let thee wit that I am
King Arthur, to whom thou hast done great damage. When Accolon
heard that he cried aloud, Fair, sweet lord, have mercy on me, for I
knew not you. O Sir Accolon, said King Arthur, mercy shalt thou
have, because I feel by thy words at this time thou knewest not my
person; but I understand well by thy words that thou hast agreed to
the death of my person, and therefore thou art a traitor; but I wite
thee the less, for my sister Morgan le Fay by her false crafts made thee
to agree and consent to her false lusts, but I shall be sore avenged upon
her an I live, that all Christendom shall speak of it; God knoweth I
have honoured her and worshipped her more than all my kin, and
more have I trusted her than mine own wife and all my kin after.

Then Sir Arthur called the keepers of the field, and said, Sirs, come
hither, for here are we two knights that have fought unto a great
damage unto us both, and like each one of us to have slain other, if it

had happed so; and had any of us known other, here had been no
battle, nor stroke stricken. Then all aloud cried Accolon unto all the
knights and men that were then there gathered together, and said to
them in this manner, O lords, this noble knight that I have fought
withal, the which me sore repenteth, is the most man of prowess, of
manhood, and of worship in the world, for it is himself King Arthur,
our alther liege lord, and with mishap and with misadventure have I
done this battle with the king and lord that I am holden withal.

CHAPTER XII

*How Arthur accorded the two brethren, and delivered the
twenty knights, and how Sir Accolon died.*

Then all the people fell down on their knees and cried King Arthur
mercy. Mercy shall ye have, said Arthur: here may ye see what
adventures befall ofttime of errant knights, how that I have fought
with a knight of mine own unto my great damage and his both. But,
sirs, because I am sore hurt, and he both, and I had great need of a
little rest, ye shall understand the opinion betwixt you two brethren:
As to thee, Sir Damas, for whom I have been champion and won the
field of this knight, yet will I judge because ye, Sir Damas, are called
an orgulous knight, and full of villainy, and not worth of prowess
your deeds, therefore I will that ye give unto your brother all the
whole manor with the appurtenance, under this form, that Sir
Ontzlake hold the manor of you, and yearly to give you a palfrey to
ride upon, for that will become you better to ride on than upon a
courser. Also I charge thee, Sir Damas, upon pain of death, that thou
never distress no knights errant that ride on their adventure. And also
that thou restore these twenty knights that thou hast long kept
prisoners, of all their harness, that they be content for; and if any of
them come to my court and complain of thee, by my head thou shalt
die therefore. Also, Sir Ontzlake, as to you, because ye are named a
good knight, and full of prowess, and true and gentle in all your
deeds, this shall be your charge I will give you, that in all goodly haste
ye come unto me and my court, and ye shall be a knight of mine, and
if your deeds be thereafter I shall so prefer you, by the grace of God,

that ye shall in short time be in ease for to live as worshipfully as your brother Sir Damas. God thank your largeness of your goodness and of your bounty, I shall be from henceforward at all times at your commandment; for, sir, said Sir Ontzlake, as God would, as I was hurt but late with an adventurous knight through both my thighs, that grieved me sore, and else had I done this battle with you. God would, said Arthur, it had been so, for then had not I been hurt as I am. I shall tell you the cause why: for I had not been hurt as I am, had it not been mine own sword, that was stolen from me by treason; and this battle was ordained aforehand to have slain me, and so it was brought to the purpose by false treason, and by false enchantment. Alas, said Sir Ontzlake, that is great pity that ever so noble a man as ye are of your deeds and prowess, that any man or woman might find in their hearts to work any treason against you. I shall reward them, said Arthur, in short time, by the grace of God. Now, tell me, said Arthur, how far am I from Camelot? Sir, ye are two days' journey therefrom. I would fain be at some place of worship, said Sir Arthur, that I might rest me. Sir, said Sir Ontzlake, hereby is a rich abbey of your elders' foundation, of nuns, but three miles hence. So the king took his leave of all the people, and mounted upon horseback, and Sir Accolon with him. And when they were come to the abbey, he let fetch leeches and search his wounds and Accolon's both; but Sir Accolon died within four days, for he had bled so much blood that he might not live, but King Arthur was well recovered. So when Accolon was dead he let send him on an horse-bier with six knights unto Camelot, and said: Bear him to my sister Morgan le Fay, and say that I send her him to a present, and tell her I have my sword Excalibur and the scabbard; so they departed with the body.

CHAPTER XIII

How Morgan would have slain Sir Uriens her husband, and how Sir Uwaine her son saved him.

The meanwhile Morgan le Fay had weened King Arthur had been dead. So on a day she espied King Uriens lay in his bed sleeping. Then she called unto her a maiden of her counsel, and said, Go fetch me my lord's sword, for I saw never better time to slay him than now. O madam, said the damosel, an ye slay my lord ye can never escape. Care not you, said Morgan le Fay, for now I see my time in the which it is best to do it, and therefore hie thee fast and fetch me the sword. Then the damosel departed, and found Sir Uwaine sleeping upon a bed in another chamber, so she went unto Sir Uwaine, and awaked him, and bade him, Arise, and wait on my lady your mother, for she will slay the king your father sleeping in his bed, for I go to fetch his sword. Well, said Sir Uwaine, go on your way, and let me deal. Anon the damosel brought Morgan the sword with quaking hands, and she lightly took the sword, and pulled it out, and went boldly unto the bed's side, and awaited how and where she might slay him best. And as she lifted up the sword to smite, Sir Uwaine leapt unto his mother, and caught her by the hand, and said, Ah, fiend, what wilt thou do? An thou wert not my mother, with this sword I should smite off thy head. Ah, said Sir Uwaine, men saith that Merlin was begotten of a devil, but I may say an earthly devil bare me. O fair son, Uwaine, have mercy upon me, I was tempted with a devil, wherefore I cry thee mercy; I will never more do so; and save my worship and discover me not. On this covenant, said Sir Uwaine, I will forgive it you, so ye will never be about to do such deeds. Nay, son, said she, and that I make you assurance.

CHAPTER XIV

How Queen Morgan le Fay made great sorrow for the death of Accolon, and how she stole away the scabbard from Arthur.

Then came tidings unto Morgan le Fay that Accolon was dead, and his body brought unto the church, and how King Arthur had his sword again. But when Queen Morgan wist that Accolon was dead, she was so sorrowful that near her heart to-brast. But because she would not it were known, outward she kept her countenance, and made no semblant of sorrow. But well she wist an she abode till her brother Arthur came thither, there should no gold go for her life.

Then she went unto Queen Guenever, and asked her leave to ride into the country. Ye may abide, said Queen Guenever, till your brother the king come home. I may not, said Morgan le Fay, for I have such hasty tidings, that I may not tarry. Well, said Guenever, ye may depart when ye will. So early on the morn, or it was day, she took her horse and rode all that day and most part of the night, and on the morn by noon she came to the same abbey of nuns whereas lay King Arthur; and she knowing he was there, she asked where he was. And they answered how he had laid him in his bed to sleep, for he had had but little rest these three nights. Well, said she, I charge you that none of you awake him till I do, and then she alighted off her horse, and thought for to steal away Excalibur his sword, and so she went straight unto his chamber, and no man durst disobey her commandment, and there she found Arthur asleep in his bed, and Excalibur in his right hand naked. When she saw that she was passing heavy that she might not come by the sword without she had awaked him, and then she wist well she had been dead. Then she took the scabbard and went her way on horseback. When the king awoke and missed his scabbard, he was wroth, and he asked who had been there, and they said his sister, Queen Morgan had been there, and had put the scabbard under her mantle and was gone. Alas, said Arthur, falsely ye have watched me. Sir, said they all, we durst not disobey your sister's commandment. Ah, said the king, let fetch the best horse may be found, and bid Sir Ontzlake arm him in all haste, and take another good horse and ride with me. So anon the king and Ontzlake were well armed, and rode after this lady, and so they came by a cross and found a cowherd, and they asked the poor man if there came any lady riding that way. Sir, said this poor man, right late came a lady riding with a forty horses, and to yonder forest she rode. Then they spurred their horses, and followed fast, and within a while Arthur had a sight of Morgan le Fay; then he chased as fast as he might. When she espied him following her, she rode a greater pace through the forest till she came to a plain, and when she saw she might not escape, she rode unto a lake thereby, and said, Whatsoever come of me, my brother shall not have this scabbard. And then she let throw the scabbard in the deepest of the water so it sank, for it was heavy of gold and precious stones.

Then she rode into a valley where many great stones were, and when she saw she must be overtaken, she shaped herself, horse and man, by enchantment unto a great marble stone. Anon withal came Sir Arthur and Sir Ontzlake whereas the king might know his sister and her men, and one knight from another. Ah, said the king, here may ye see the vengeance of God, and now am I sorry that this misadventure is befallen. And then he looked for the scabbard, but it would not be found, so he returned to the abbey where he came from. So when Arthur was gone she turned all into the likeliness as she and they were before, and said, Sirs, now may we go where we will.

CHAPTER XV

How Morgan le Fay saved a knight that should have been drowned, and how King Arthur returned home again.

Then said Morgan, Saw ye Arthur, my brother? Yea, said her knights, right well, and that ye should have found an we might have stirred from one stead, for by his armyvestal countenance he would have caused us to have fled. I believe you, said Morgan. Anon after as she rode she met a knight leading another knight on his horse before him, bound hand and foot, blindfold, to have drowned him in a fountain. When she saw this knight so bound, she asked him, What will ye do with that knight? Lady, said he, I will drown him. For what cause? she asked. For I found him with my wife, and she shall have the same death anon. That were pity, said Morgan le Fay. Now, what say ye, knight, is it truth that he saith of you? she said to the knight that should be drowned. Nay truly, madam, he saith not right on me. Of whence be ye, said Morgan le Fay, and of what country? I am of the court of King Arthur, and my name is Manassen, cousin unto Accolon of Gaul. Ye say well, said she, and for the love of him ye shall be delivered, and ye shall have your adversary in the same case ye be in. So Manassen was loosed and the other knight bound. And anon Manassen unarmed him, and armed himself in his harness, and so mounted on horseback, and the knight afore him, and so threw him into the fountain and drowned him. And then he rode unto Morgan again, and asked if she would anything unto King Arthur. Tell him that I rescued thee, not for the love of him but for the love of Accolon, and tell him I fear him not while I can make me and them that be with me in likeness of stones; and let him wit I can do much more when I see my time. And so she departed into the country of

Gore, and there was she richly received, and made her castles and towns passing strong, for always she dreaded much King Arthur.

When the king had well rested him at the abbey, he rode unto Camelot, and found his queen and his barons right glad of his coming. And when they heard of his strange adventures as is afore rehearsed, then all had marvel of the falsehood of Morgan le Fay; many knights wished her burnt. Then came Manassen to court and told the king of his adventure. Well, said the king, she is a kind sister; I shall so be avenged on her an I live, that all Christendom shall speak of it. So on the morn there came a damosel from Morgan to the king, and she brought with her the richest mantle that ever was seen in that court, for it was set as full of precious stones as one might stand by another, and there were the richest stones that ever the king saw. And the damosel said, Your sister sendeth you this mantle, and desireth that ye should take this gift of her; and in what thing she hath offended you, she will amend it at your own pleasure. When the king beheld this mantle it pleased him much, but he said but little.

CHAPTER XVI

How the Damosel of the Lake saved King Arthur from a mantle that should have burnt him.

With that came the Damosel of the Lake unto the king, and said, Sir, I must speak with you in privity. Say on, said the king, what ye will. Sir, said the damosel, put not on you this mantle till ye have seen more, and in no wise let it not come on you, nor on no knight of yours, till ye command the bringer thereof to put it upon her. Well, said King Arthur, it shall be done as ye counsel me. And then he said unto the damosel that came from his sister, Damosel, this mantle that ye have brought me, I will see it upon you. Sir, she said, it will not beseem me to wear a king's garment. By my head, said Arthur, ye shall wear it or it come on my back, or any man's that here is. And so the king made it to be put upon her, and forthwithal she fell down dead, and never more spake word after and burnt to coals. Then was the king wonderly wroth, more than he was to-forehand, and said unto King Uriens, My sister, your wife, is alway about to betray me, and well I wot either ye, or my nephew, your son, is of counsel with her to have me destroyed; but as for you, said the king to King Uriens, I deem not greatly that ye be of her counsel, for Accolon confessed to me by his own mouth, that she would have destroyed you as well as me, therefore I hold you excused; but as for your son, Sir Uwaine, I hold him suspect, therefore I charge you put him out of my court. So Sir Uwaine was discharged. And when Sir Gawaine wist that, he made him ready to go with him; and said, whoso banisheth my cousin-germain shall banish me. So they two departed, and rode into a great forest, and so they came to an abbey of monks, and there were well lodged. But when the king wist that Sir Gawaine was departed from the court, there was made great sorrow among all the estates. Now, said Gaheris, Gawaine's brother, we have lost two good knights for the love of one. So on the morn they heard their masses in the abbey, and so they rode forth till that they came to a great forest. Then was Sir Gawaine ware in a valley by a turret [of] twelve fair damosels, and two knights armed on great horses, and the damosels went to and fro by a tree. And then was Sir Gawaine ware how there hung a white shield on that tree, and ever as the damosels came by it they spit upon it, and some threw mire upon the shield.

CHAPTER XVII

How Sir Gawaine and Sir Uwaine met with twelve fair damosels, and how they complained on Sir Marhaus.

Then Sir Gawaine and Sir Uwaine went and saluted them, and asked why they did that despite to the shield. Sir, said the damosels, we shall tell you. There is a knight in this country that owneth this white shield, and he is a passing good man of his hands, but he hateth all ladies and gentlewomen, and therefore we do all this despite to the shield. I shall say you, said Sir Gawaine, it beseemeth evil a good knight to despise all ladies and gentlewomen, and peradventure though he hate you he hath some certain cause, and peradventure he loveth in some other places ladies and gentlewomen, and to be loved again, an he be such a man of prowess as ye speak of. Now, what is his name? Sir, said they, his name is Marhaus, the king's son of

Ireland. I know him well, said Sir Uwaine, he is a passing good knight as any is alive, for I saw him once proved at a jousts where many knights were gathered, and that time there might no man withstand him. Ah! said Sir Gawaine, damosels, methinketh ye are to blame, for it is to suppose, he that hung that shield there, he will not be long therefrom, and then may those knights match him on horseback, and that is more your worship than thus; for I will abide no longer to see a knight's shield dishonoured. And therewith Sir Uwaine and Gawaine departed a little from them, and then were they ware where Sir Marhaus came riding on a great horse straight toward them. And when the twelve damosels saw Sir Marhaus they fled into the turret as they were wild, so that some of them fell by the way. Then the one of the knights of the tower dressed his shield, and said on high, Sir Marhaus, defend thee. And so they ran together that the knight brake his spear on Marhaus, and Marhaus smote him so hard that he brake his neck and the horse's back. That saw the other knight of the turret, and dressed him toward Marhaus, and they met so eagerly together that the knight of the turret was soon smitten down, horse and man, stark dead.

CHAPTER XVIII

How Sir Marhaus jousted with Sir Gawaine and Sir Uwaine, and overthrew them both.

And then Sir Marhaus rode unto his shield, and saw how it was defouled, and said, Of this despite I am a part avenged, but for her love that gave me this white shield I shall wear thee, and hang mine where thou wast; and so he hanged it about his neck. Then he rode straight unto Sir Gawaine and to Sir Uwaine, and asked them what they did there? They answered him that they came from King Arthur's court to see adventures. Well, said Sir Marhaus, here am I ready, an adventurous knight that will fulfil any adventure that ye will desire; and so departed from them, to fetch his range. Let him go, said Sir Uwaine unto Sir Gawaine, for he is a passing good knight as any is living; I would not by my will that any of us were matched with him. Nay, said Sir Gawaine, not so, it were shame to us were he not assayed, were he never so good a knight. Well, said Sir Uwaine, I will assay him afore you, for I am more weaker than ye, and if he smite me down then may ye revenge me. So these two knights came together with great raundon, that Sir Uwaine smote Sir Marhaus that his spear brast in pieces on the shield, and Sir Marhaus smote him so sore that horse and man he bare to the earth, and hurt Sir Uwaine on the left side.

Then Sir Marhaus turned his horse and rode toward Gawaine with his spear, and when Sir Gawaine saw that he dressed his shield, and they aventred their spears, and they came together with all the might of their horses, that either knight smote other so hard in midst of their shields, but Sir Gawaine's spear brake, but Sir Marhaus' spear held; and therewith Sir Gawaine and his horse rushed down to the earth. And lightly Sir Gawaine rose on his feet, and pulled out his sword, and dressed him toward Sir Marhaus on foot, and Sir Marhaus saw that, and pulled out his sword and began to come to Sir Gawaine on horseback. Sir knight, said Sir Gawaine, alight on foot, or else I will slay thy horse. Gramercy, said Sir Marhaus, of your gentleness ye teach me courtesy, for it is not for one knight to be on foot, and the other on horseback. And therewith Sir Marhaus set his spear against a tree and alighted and tied his horse to a tree, and dressed his shield, and either came unto other eagerly, and smote together with their swords that their shields flew in cantels, and they bruised their helms and their hauberks, and wounded either other. But Sir Gawaine from it passed nine of the clock waxed ever stronger and stronger, for then it came to the hour of noon, and thrice his might was increased. All this espied Sir Marhaus and had great wonder how his might increased, and so they wounded other passing sore. And then when it was past noon, and when it drew toward evensong, Sir Gawaine's strength feebled, and waxed passing faint that unnethes he might dure any longer, and Sir Marhaus was then bigger and bigger. Sir knight, said Sir Marhaus, I have well felt that ye are a passing good knight and a marvellous man of might as ever I felt any, while it lasteth, and our quarrels are not great, and therefore it were pity to do you hurt, for I feel ye are passing feeble. Ah, said Sir Gawaine, gentle knight, ye say the word that I should say. And therewith they took off their helms, and either kissed other, and there they swore together either to love other as brethren. And Sir Marhaus prayed Sir Gawaine to lodge with him that night. And so they took their horses, and rode toward Sir

Marhaus' house. And as they rode by the way, Sir knight, said Sir Gawaine, I have marvel that so valiant a man as ye be love no ladies nor damosels. Sir, said Sir Marhaus, they name me wrongfully those that give me that name, but well I wot it be the damosels of the turret that so name me, and other such as they be. Now shall I tell you for what cause I hate them: for they be sorceresses and enchanters many of them, and be a knight never so good of his body and full of prowess as man may be, they will make him a stark coward to have the better of him, and this is the principal cause that I hate them; and to all good ladies and gentlewomen I owe my service as a knight ought to do.

As the book rehearseth in French, there were many knights that overmatched Sir Gawaine, for all the thrice might that he had: Sir Launcelot de Lake, Sir Tristram, Sir Bors de Ganis, Sir Percivale, Sir Pelleas, and Sir Marhaus, these six knights had the better of Sir Gawaine. Then within a little while they came to Sir Marhaus' place, which was in a little priory, and there they alighted, and ladies and damosels unarmed them, and hastily looked to their hurts, for they were all three hurt. And so they had all three good lodging with Sir Marhaus, and good cheer; for when he wist that they were King Arthur's sister's sons he made them all the cheer that lay in his power, and so they sojourned there a sennight, and were well eased of their wounds, and at the last departed. Now, said Sir Marhaus, we will not depart so lightly, for I will bring you through the forest; and rode day by day well a seven days or they found any adventure. At the last they came into a great forest, that was named the country and forest of Arroy, and the country of strange adventures. In this country, said Sir Marhaus, came never knight since it was christened but he found strange adventures; and so they rode, and came into a deep valley full of stones, and thereby they saw a fair stream of water; above thereby was the head of the stream a fair fountain, and three damosels sitting thereby. And then they rode to them, and either saluted other, and the eldest had a garland of gold about her head, and she was three score winter of age or more, and her hair was white under the garland. The second damosel was of thirty winter of age, with a circlet of gold about her head. The third damosel was but fifteen year of age, and a garland of flowers about her head. When these knights had so beheld them, they asked them the cause why they sat at that fountain? We be here, said the damosels, for this cause: if we may see any errant knights, to teach them unto strange adventures; and ye be three knights that seek adventures, and we be three damosels, and therefore each one of you must choose one of us; and when ye have done so we will lead you unto three highways, and there each of you shall choose a way and his damosel with him. And this day twelvemonth ye must meet here again, and God send you your lives, and thereto ye must plight your troth. This is well said, said Sir Marhaus.

CHAPTER XIX*

*How Sir Marhaus, Sir Gawaine, and Sir Uwaine met three
damosels and each of them took one.*

Now shall everych of us choose a damosel. I shall tell you, said Sir Uwaine, I am the youngest and most weakest of you both, therefore I will have the eldest damosel, for she hath seen much, and can best help me when I have need, for I have most need of help of you both. Now, said Sir Marhaus, I will have the damosel of thirty winter age, for she falleth best to me. Well, said Sir Gawaine, I thank you, for ye have left me the youngest and the fairest, and she is most liefest to me. Then every damosel took her knight by the reins of his bridle, and brought him to the three ways, and there was their oath made to meet at the fountain that day twelvemonth an they were living, and so they kissed and departed, and each knight set his lady behind him. And Sir Uwaine took the way that lay west, and Sir Marhaus took the way that lay south, and Sir Gawaine took the way that lay north. Now will we begin at Sir Gawaine, that held that way till that he came unto a fair manor, where dwelled an old knight and a good householder, and there Sir Gawaine asked the knight if he knew any adventures in that country. I shall show you some to-morn, said the old knight, and that marvellous. So, on the morn they rode into the forest of adventures to a laund, and thereby they found a cross, and as they stood and hoved there came by them the fairest knight and the seemliest man that ever they saw, making the greatest dole that ever

* Misnumbered xx by William Caxton

man made. And then he was ware of Sir Gawaine, and saluted him, and prayed God to send him much worship. As to that, said Sir Gawaine, gramercy; also I pray to God that he send you honour and worship. Ah, said the knight, I may lay that aside, for sorrow and shame cometh to me after worship.

CHAPTER XX

How a knight and a dwarf strove for a lady.

And therewith he passed unto the one side of the laund; and on the other side saw Sir Gawaine ten knights that hoved still and made them ready with their shields and spears against that one knight that came by Sir Gawaine.

Then this one knight aventred a great spear, and one of the ten knights encountered with him, but this woful knight smote him so hard that he fell over his horse's tail. So this same dolorous knight served them all, that at the leastway he smote down horse and man, and all he did with one spear; and so when they were all ten on foot, they went to that one knight, and he stood stone still, and suffered them to pull him down off his horse, and bound him hand and foot, and tied him under the horse's belly, and so led him with them. O Jesu! said Sir Gawaine, this is a doleful sight, to see the yonder knight so to be entreated, and it seemeth by the knight that he suffereth them to bind him so, for he maketh no resistance. No, said his host, that is truth, for an he would they all were too weak so to do him. Sir, said the damosel unto Sir Gawaine, meseemeth it were your worship to help that dolorous knight, for methinketh he is one of the best knights that ever I saw. I would do for him, said Sir Gawaine, but it seemeth he will have no help. Then, said the damosel, methinketh ye have no lust to help him.

Thus as they talked they saw a knight on the other side of the laund all armed save the head. And on the other side there came a dwarf on horseback all armed save the head, with a great mouth and a short nose; and when the dwarf came nigh he said, Where is the lady should meet us here? and therewithal she came forth out of the wood. And then they began to strive for the lady; for the knight said he would have her, and the dwarf said he would have her. Will we do well? said the dwarf; yonder is a knight at the cross, let us put it both upon him, and as he deemeth so shall it be. I will well, said the knight, and so they went all three unto Sir Gawaine and told him wherefore they strove. Well, sirs, said he, will ye put the matter in my hand? Yea, they said both. Now damosel, said Sir Gawaine, ye shall stand betwixt them both, and whether ye list better to go to, he shall have you. And when she was set between them both, she left the knight and went to the dwarf, and the dwarf took her and went his way singing, and the knight went his way with great mourning.

Then came there two knights all armed, and cried on high, Sir Gawaine! knight of King Arthur's, make thee ready in all haste and joust with me. So they ran together, that either fell down, and then on foot they drew their swords, and did full actually. The meanwhile the other knight went to the damosel, and asked her why she abode with that knight, and if ye would abide with me, I will be your faithful knight. And with you will I be, said the damosel, for with Sir Gawaine I may not find in mine heart to be with him; for now here was one knight discomfited ten knights, and at the last he was cowardly led away; and therefore let us two go whilst they fight. And Sir Gawaine fought with that other knight long, but at the last they accorded both. And then the knight prayed Sir Gawaine to lodge with him that night. So as Sir Gawaine went with this knight he asked him, What knight is he in this country that smote down the ten knights? For when he had done so manfully he suffered them to bind him hand and foot, and so led him away. Ah, said the knight, that is the best knight I trow in the world, and the most man of prowess, and he hath been served so as he was even more than ten times, and his name hight Sir Pelleas, and he loveth a great lady in this country and her name is Ettard. And so when he loved her there was cried in this country a great jousts three days, and all the knights of this country were there and gentlewomen, and who that proved him the best knight should have a passing good sword and a circlet of gold, and the circlet the knight should give it to the fairest lady that was at the jousts. And this knight Sir Pelleas was the best knight that was there, and there were five hundred knights, but there was never man that ever Sir Pelleas met withal but he struck him down, or else from his horse; and every day of three days he struck down twenty knights, therefore they gave him the prize, and forthwithal he went thereas

the Lady Ettard was, and gave her the circlet, and said openly she was
the fairest lady that there was, and that would he prove upon any
knight that would say nay.

CHAPTER XXI

*How King Pelleas suffered himself to be taken prisoner
because he would have a sight of his lady, and how Sir
Gawaine promised him to get to him the love of his lady.*

And so he chose her for his sovereign lady, and never to love other
but her, but she was so proud that she had scorn of him, and said that
she would never love him though he would die for her. Wherefore
all ladies and gentlewomen had scorn of her that she was so proud, for
there were fairer than she, and there was none that was there but an
Sir Pelleas would have proffered them love, they would have loved
him for his noble prowess. And so this knight promised the Lady
Ettard to follow her into this country, and never to leave her till she
loved him. And thus he is here the most part nigh her, and lodged by
a priory, and every week she sendeth knights to fight with him. And
when he hath put them to the worse, then will he suffer them
wilfully to take him prisoner, because he would have a sight of this
lady. And always she doth him great despite, for sometime she
maketh her knights to tie him to his horse's tail, and some to bind
him under the horse's belly; thus in the most shamefullest ways that
she can think he is brought to her. And all she doth it for to cause
him to leave this country, and to leave his loving; but all this cannot
make him to leave, for an he would have fought on foot he might
have had the better of the ten knights as well on foot as on horseback.
Alas, said Sir Gawaine, it is great pity of him; and after this night I will
seek him to-morrow, in this forest, to do him all the help I can. So on
the morn Sir Gawaine took his leave of his host Sir Carados, and rode
into the forest; and at the last he met with Sir Pelleas, making great
moan out of measure, so each of them saluted other, and asked him
why he made such sorrow. And as it is above rehearsed, Sir Pelleas
told Sir Gawaine: But always I suffer her knights to fare so with me as
ye saw yesterday, in trust at the last to win her love, for she knoweth

well all her knights should not lightly win me, an me list to fight with them to the uttermost. Wherefore an I loved her not so sore, I had liefer die an hundred times, an I might die so oft, rather than I would suffer that despite; but I trust she will have pity upon me at the last, for love causeth many a good knight to suffer to have his entent, but alas I am unfortunate. And therewith he made so great dole and sorrow that unnethe he might hold him on horseback.

Now, said Sir Gawaine, leave your mourning and I shall promise you by the faith of my body to do all that lieth in my power to get you the love of your lady, and thereto I will plight you my troth. Ah, said Sir Pelleas, of what court are ye? tell me, I pray you, my good friend. And then Sir Gawaine said, I am of the court of King Arthur, and his sister's son, and King Lot of Orkney was my father, and my name is Sir Gawaine. And then he said, My name is Sir Pelleas, born in the Isles, and of many isles I am lord, and never have I loved lady nor damosel till now in an unhappy time; and, sir knight, since ye are so nigh cousin unto King Arthur, and a king's son, therefore betray me not but help me, for I may never come by her but by some good knight, for she is in a strong castle here, fast by within this four mile, and over all this country she is lady of. And so I may never come to her presence, but as I suffer her knights to take me, and but if I did so that I might have a sight of her, I had been dead long or this time; and yet fair word had I never of her, but when I am brought to-fore her she rebuketh me in the foulest manner. And then they take my horse and harness and put me out of the gates, and she will not suffer me to eat nor drink; and always I offer me to be her prisoner, but that she will not suffer me, for I would desire no more, what pains so ever I had, so that I might have a sight of her daily. Well, said Sir Gawaine, all this shall I amend an ye will do as I shall devise; I will have your horse and your armour, and so will I ride unto her castle and tell her that I have slain you, and so shall I come within her to cause her to cherish me, and then shall I do my true part that ye shall not fail to have the love of her.

CHAPTER XXII

*How Sir Gawaine came to the Lady Ettard,
and how Sir Pelleas found them sleeping.*

And therewith Sir Gawaine plight his troth unto Sir Pelleas to be true
and faithful unto him; so each one plight their troth to other, and so
they changed horses and harness, and Sir Gawaine departed, and came
to the castle whereas stood the pavilions of this lady without the gate.
And as soon as Ettard had espied Sir Gawaine she fled in toward the
castle. Sir Gawaine spake on high, and bade her abide, for he was not
Sir Pelleas; I am another knight that have slain Sir Pelleas. Do off your
helm, said the Lady Ettard, that I may see your visage. And so when
she saw that it was not Sir Pelleas, she bade him alight and led him
unto her castle, and asked him faithfully whether he had slain Sir
Pelleas. And he said her yea, and told her his name was Sir Gawaine of
the court of King Arthur, and his sister's son. Truly, said she, that is
great pity, for he was a passing good knight of his body, but of all men
alive I hated him most, for I could never be quit of him; and for ye
have slain him I shall be your woman, and to do anything that might
please you. So she made Sir Gawaine good cheer. Then Sir Gawaine
said that he loved a lady and by no means she would love him. She is
to blame, said Ettard, an she will not love you, for ye that be so well
born a man, and such a man of prowess, there is no lady in the world
too good for you. Will ye, said Sir Gawaine, promise me to do all that
ye may, by the faith of your body, to get me the love of my lady? Yea,
sir, said she, and that I promise you by the faith of my body. Now,
said Sir Gawaine, it is yourself that I love so well, therefore I pray you
hold your promise. I may not choose, said the Lady Ettard, but if I
should be forsworn; and so she granted him to fulfil all his desire.

So it was then in the month of May that she and Sir Gawaine went
out of the castle and supped in a pavilion, and there was made a bed,
and there Sir Gawaine and the Lady Ettard went to bed together, and
in another pavilion she laid her damosels, and in the third pavilion she
laid part of her knights, for then she had no dread of Sir Pelleas. And
there Sir Gawaine lay with her in that pavilion two days and two

nights. And on the third day, in the morning early, Sir Pelleas armed
him, for he had never slept since Sir Gawaine departed from him; for
Sir Gawaine had promised him by the faith of his body, to come to
him unto his pavilion by that priory within the space of a day and a
night.

Then Sir Pelleas mounted upon horseback, and came to the
pavilions that stood without the castle, and found in the first pavilion
three knights in three beds, and three squires lying at their feet. Then
went he to the second pavilion and found four gentlewomen lying in
four beds. And then he yede to the third pavilion and found Sir
Gawaine lying in bed with his Lady Ettard, and either clipping other
in arms, and when he saw that his heart well-nigh brast for sorrow,
and said: Alas! that ever a knight should be found so false; and then he
took his horse and might not abide no longer for pure sorrow. And
when he had ridden nigh half a mile he turned again and thought to
slay them both; and when he saw them both so lie sleeping fast,
unnethe he might hold him on horseback for sorrow, and said thus to
himself, Though this knight be never so false, I will never slay him
sleeping, for I will never destroy the high order of knighthood; and
therewith he departed again. And or he had ridden half a mile he
returned again, and thought then to slay them both, making the
greatest sorrow that ever man made. And when he came to the
pavilions, he tied his horse unto a tree, and pulled out his sword naked
in his hand, and went to them thereas they lay, and yet he thought it
were shame to slay them sleeping, and laid the naked sword
overthwart both their throats, and so took his horse and rode his way.

And when Sir Pelleas came to his pavilions he told his knights and
his squires how he had sped, and said thus to them, For your true and
good service ye have done me I shall give you all my goods, for I will
go unto my bed and never arise until I am dead. And when that I am
dead I charge you that ye take the heart out of my body and bear it
her betwixt two silver dishes, and tell her how I saw her lie with the
false knight Sir Gawaine. Right so Sir Pelleas unarmed himself, and
went unto his bed making marvellous dole and sorrow.

When Sir Gawaine and Ettard awoke of their sleep, and found the
naked sword overthwart their throats, then she knew well it was Sir
Pelleas' sword. Alas! said she to Sir Gawaine, ye have betrayed me
and Sir Pelleas both, for ye told me ye had slain him, and now I know
well it is not so, he is alive. And if Sir Pelleas had been as uncourteous

to you as ye have been to him ye had been a dead knight; but ye have deceived me and betrayed me falsely, that all ladies and damosels may beware by you and me. And therewith Sir Gawaine made him ready, and went into the forest. So it happed then that the Damosel of the Lake, Nimue, met with a knight of Sir Pelleas, that went on his foot in the forest making great dole, and she asked him the cause. And so the woful knight told her how his master and lord was betrayed through a knight and lady, and how he will never arise out of his bed till he be dead. Bring me to him, said she anon, and I will warrant his life he shall not die for love, and she that hath caused him so to love, she shall be in as evil plight as he is or it be long to, for it is no joy of such a proud lady that will have no mercy of such a valiant knight. Anon that knight brought her unto him, and when she saw him lie in his bed, she thought she saw never so likely a knight; and therewith she threw an enchantment upon him, and he fell asleep. And therewhile she rode unto the Lady Ettard, and charged no man to awake him till she came again. So within two hours she brought the Lady Ettard thither, and both ladies found him asleep: Lo, said the Damosel of the Lake, ye ought to be ashamed for to murder such a knight. And therewith she threw such an enchantment upon her that she loved him sore, that well-nigh she was out of her mind. O Lord Jesu, said the Lady Ettard, how is it befallen unto me that I love now him that I have most hated of any man alive? That is the righteous judgment of God, said the damosel. And then anon Sir Pelleas awaked and looked upon Ettard; and when he saw her he knew her, and then he hated her more than any woman alive, and said: Away, traitress, come never in my sight. And when she heard him say so, she wept and made great sorrow out of measure.

CHAPTER XXIII

How Sir Pelleas loved no more Ettard by means of the Damosel of the Lake, whom he loved ever after.

Sir Knight Pelleas, said the Damosel of the Lake, take your horse and come forth with me out of this country, and ye shall love a lady that shall love you. I will well, said Sir Pelleas, for this Lady Ettard hath done me great despite and shame, and there he told her the beginning and ending, and how he had purposed never to have arisen till that he had been dead. And now such grace God hath sent me, that I hate her as much as ever I loved her, thanked be our Lord Jesus! Thank me, said the Damosel of the Lake. Anon Sir Pelleas armed him, and took his horse, and commanded his men to bring after his pavilions and his stuff where the Damosel of the Lake would assign. So the Lady Ettard died for sorrow, and the Damosel of the Lake rejoiced Sir Pelleas, and loved together during their life days.

CHAPTER XXIV

How Sir Marhaus rode with the damosel, and how he came to the Duke of the South Marches.

Now turn we unto Sir Marhaus, that rode with the damosel of thirty winter of age, southward. And so they came into a deep forest, and by fortune they were nighted, and rode long in a deep way, and at the last they came unto a courtelage, and there they asked harbour. But the man of the courtelage would not lodge them for no treatise that they could treat, but thus much the good man said, An ye will take the adventure of your lodging, I shall bring you where ye shall be lodged. What adventure is that that I shall have for my lodging? said Sir Marhaus. Ye shall wit when ye come there, said the good man. Sir, what adventure so it be, bring me thither I pray thee, said Sir Marhaus; for I am weary, my damosel, and my horse. So the good man went and opened the gate, and within an hour he brought him unto a fair castle, and then the poor man called the porter, and anon he was let into the castle, and so he told the lord how he brought him a knight errant and a damosel that would be lodged with him. Let him in, said the lord, it may happen he shall repent that they took their lodging here.

So Sir Marhaus was let in with torchlight, and there was a goodly sight of young men that welcomed him. And then his horse was led into the stable, and he and the damosel were brought into the hall, and there stood a mighty duke and many goodly men about him. Then this lord asked him what he hight, and from whence he came, and with whom he dwelt. Sir, he said, I am a knight of King Arthur's and knight of the Table Round, and my name is Sir Marhaus, and born I am in Ireland. And then said the duke to him, That me sore repenteth: the cause is this, for I love not thy lord nor none of thy fellows of the Table Round; and therefore ease thyself this night as well as thou mayest, for as to-morn I and my six sons shall match with you. Is there no remedy but that I must have ado with you and your six sons at once? said Sir Marhaus. No, said the duke, for this cause I made mine avow, for Sir Gawaine slew my seven sons in a recounter, therefore I made mine avow, there should never knight of King Arthur's court lodge with me, or come thereas I might have ado with him, but that I would have a revenging of my sons' death. What is your name? said Sir Marhaus; I require you tell me, an it please you. Wit thou well I am the Duke of South Marches. Ah, said Sir Marhaus, I have heard say that ye have been long time a great foe unto my lord Arthur and to his knights. That shall ye feel to-morn, said the duke. Shall I have ado with you? said Sir Marhaus. Yea, said the duke, thereof shalt thou not choose, and therefore take you to your chamber, and ye shall have all that to you longeth. So Sir Marhaus departed and was led to a chamber, and his damosel was led unto her chamber. And on the morn the duke sent unto Sir Marhaus and bade make him ready. And so Sir Marhaus arose and armed him, and then there was a mass sung afore him, and brake his fast, and so mounted on horseback in the court of the castle where they should do the battle. So there was the duke all ready on horseback, clean armed, and his six sons by him, and everych had a spear in his hand, and so they encountered, whereas the duke and his two sons brake their spears upon him, but Sir Marhaus held up his spear and touched none of them.

CHAPTER XXV

How Sir Marhaus fought with the duke and his four sons
and made them to yield them.

Then came the four sons by couple, and two of them brake their spears, and so did the other two. And all this while Sir Marhaus touched them not. Then Sir Marhaus ran to the duke, and smote him

with his spear that horse and man fell to the earth, and so he served
his sons; and then Sir Marhaus alighted down and bade the duke yield
him or else he would slay him. And then some of his sons recovered,
and would have set upon Sir Marhaus; then Sir Marhaus said to the
duke, Cease thy sons, or else I will do the uttermost to you all. Then
the duke saw he might not escape the death, he cried to his sons, and
charged them to yield them to Sir Marhaus; and they kneeled all
down and put the pommels of their swords to the knight, and so he
received them. And then they helped up their father, and so by their
cominal assent promised to Sir Marhaus never to be foes unto King
Arthur, and thereupon at Whitsuntide after to come, he and his sons,
and put them in the king's grace.

Then Sir Marhaus departed, and within two days his damosel
brought him whereas was a great tournament that the Lady de Vawse
had cried. And who that did best should have a rich circlet of gold
worth a thousand besants. And there Sir Marhaus did so nobly that he
was renowned, and had sometime down forty knights, and so the
circlet of gold was rewarded him. Then he departed from them with
great worship; and so within seven nights his damosel brought him to
an earl's place, his name was the Earl Fergus, that after was Sir
Tristram's knight; and this earl was but a young man, and late come
into his lands, and there was a giant fast by him that hight Taulurd,
and he had another brother in Cornwall that hight Taulas, that Sir
Tristram slew when he was out of his mind. So this earl made his
complaint unto Sir Marhaus, that there was a giant by him that
destroyed all his lands, and how he durst nowhere ride nor go for
him. Sir, said the knight, whether useth he to fight on horseback or
on foot? Nay, said the earl, there may no horse bear him. Well, said
Sir Marhaus, then will I fight with him on foot; so on the morn Sir
Marhaus prayed the earl that one of his men might bring him
whereas the giant was; and so he was, for he saw him sit under a tree
of holly, and many clubs of iron and gisarms about him. So this
knight dressed him to the giant, putting his shield afore him, and the
giant took an iron club in his hand, and at the first stroke he clave Sir
Marhaus' shield in two pieces. And there he was in great peril, for the
giant was a wily fighter, but at last Sir Marhaus smote off his right arm
above the elbow.

Then the giant fled and the knight after him, and so he drove him
into a water, but the giant was so high that he might not wade after

him. And then Sir Marhaus made the Earl Fergus' man to fetch him stones, and with those stones the knight gave the giant many sore knocks, till at the last he made him fall down into the water, and so was he there dead. Then Sir Marhaus went unto the giant's castle, and there he delivered twenty-four ladies and twelve knights out of the giant's prison, and there he had great riches without number, so that the days of his life he was never poor man. Then he returned to the Earl Fergus, the which thanked him greatly, and would have given him half his lands, but he would none take. So Sir Marhaus dwelled with the earl nigh half a year, for he was sore bruised with the giant, and at the last he took his leave. And as he rode by the way, he met with Sir Gawaine and Sir Uwaine, and so by adventure he met with four knights of Arthur's court, the first was Sir Sagramore le Desirous, Sir Osanna, Sir Dodinas le Savage, and Sir Felot of Listinoise; and there Sir Marhaus with one spear smote down these four knights, and hurt them sore. So he departed to meet at his day aforeset.

CHAPTER XXVI

How Sir Uwaine rode with the damosel of sixty year of age, and how he gat the prize at tourneying.

Now turn we unto Sir Uwaine, that rode westward with his damosel of three score winter of age, and she brought him thereas was a tournament nigh the march of Wales. And at that tournament Sir Uwaine smote down thirty knights, therefore was given him the prize, and that was a gerfalcon, and a white steed trapped with cloth of gold. So then Sir Uwaine did many strange adventures by the means of the old damosel, and so she brought him to a lady that was called the Lady of the Rock, the which was much courteous. So there were in the country two knights that were brethren, and they were called two perilous knights, the one knight hight Sir Edward of the Red Castle, and the other Sir Hue of the Red Castle; and these two brethren had disherited the Lady of the Rock of a barony of lands by their extortion. And as this knight was lodged with this lady she made her complaint to him of these two knights.

Madam, said Sir Uwaine, they are to blame, for they do against the high order of knighthood, and the oath that they made; and if it like you I will speak with them, because I am a knight of King Arthur's, and I will entreat them with fairness; and if they will not, I shall do battle with them, and in the defence of your right. Gramercy, said the lady, and thereas I may not acquit you, God shall. So on the morn the two knights were sent for, that they should come thither to speak with the Lady of the Rock, and wit ye well they failed not, for they came with an hundred horse. But when this lady saw them in this manner so big, she would not suffer Sir Uwaine to go out to them upon no surety nor for no fair language, but she made him speak with them over a tower, but finally these two brethren would not be entreated, and answered that they would keep that they had. Well, said Sir Uwaine, then will I fight with one of you, and prove that ye do this lady wrong. That will we not, said they, for an we do battle, we two will fight with one knight at once, and therefore if ye will fight so, we will be ready at what hour ye will assign. And if ye win us in battle the lady shall have her lands again. Ye say well, said Sir Uwaine, therefore make you ready so that ye be here to-morn in the defence of the lady's right.

CHAPTER XXVII

How Sir Uwaine fought with two knights and overcame them.

So was there sikerness made on both parties that no treason should be wrought on neither party; so then the knights departed and made them ready, and that night Sir Uwaine had great cheer. And on the morn he arose early and heard mass, and brake his fast, and so he rode unto the plain without the gates, where hoved the two brethren abiding him. So they rode together passing sore, that Sir Edward and Sir Hue brake their spears upon Sir Uwaine. And Sir Uwaine smote Sir Edward that he fell over his horse and yet his spear brast not. And then he spurred his horse and came upon Sir Hue and overthrew him, but they soon recovered and dressed their shields and drew their swords and bade Sir Uwaine alight and do his battle to the uttermost. Then Sir Uwaine devoided his horse suddenly, and put his shield

afore him and drew his sword, and so they dressed together, and
either gave other such strokes, and there these two brethren
wounded Sir Uwaine passing grievously that the Lady of the Rock
weened he should have died. And thus they fought together five
hours as men raged out of reason. And at the last Sir Uwaine smote
Sir Edward upon the helm such a stroke that his sword carved unto
his canel bone, and then Sir Hue abated his courage, but Sir Uwaine
pressed fast to have slain him. That saw Sir Hue: he kneeled down
and yielded him to Sir Uwaine. And he of his gentleness received his
sword, and took him by the hand, and went into the castle together.
Then the Lady of the Rock was passing glad, and the other brother
made great sorrow for his brother's death. Then the lady was restored
of all her lands, and Sir Hue was commanded to be at the court of
King Arthur at the next feast of Pentecost. So Sir Uwaine dwelt with
the lady nigh half a year, for it was long or he might be whole of his
great hurts. And so when it drew nigh the term-day that Sir Gawaine,
Sir Marhaus, and Sir Uwaine should meet at the cross-way, then
every knight drew him thither to hold his promise that they had
made; and Sir Marhaus and Sir Uwaine brought their damosels with
them, but Sir Gawaine had lost his damosel, as it is afore rehearsed.

CHAPTER XXVIII

*How at the year's end all three knights with their three
damosels met at the fountain.*

Right so at the twelvemonths' end they met all three knights at the
fountain and their damosels, but the damosel that Sir Gawaine had
could say but little worship of him; so they departed from the
damosels and rode through a great forest, and there they met with a
messenger that came from King Arthur, that had sought them well-
nigh a twelvemonth throughout all England, Wales, and Scotland,
and charged if ever he might find Sir Gawaine and Sir Uwaine to
bring them to the court again. And then were they all glad, and so
prayed they Sir Marhaus to ride with them to the king's court. And
so within twelve days they came to Camelot, and the king was
passing glad of their coming, and so was all the court. Then the king

made them to swear upon a book to tell him all their adventures that had befallen them that twelvemonth, and so they did. And there was Sir Marhaus well known, for there were knights that he had matched aforetime, and he was named one of the best knights living.

Against the feast of Pentecost came the Damosel of the Lake and brought with her Sir Pelleas; and at that high feast there was great jousting of knights, and of all knights that were at that jousts, Sir Pelleas had the prize, and Sir Marhaus was named the next; but Sir Pelleas was so strong there might but few knights sit him a buffet with a spear. And at that next feast Sir Pelleas and Sir Marhaus were made knights of the Table Round, for there were two sieges void, for two knights were slain that twelvemonth, and great joy had King Arthur of Sir Pelleas and of Sir Marhaus. But Pelleas loved never after Sir Gawaine, but as he spared him for the love of King Arthur; but ofttimes at jousts and tournaments Sir Pelleas quit Sir Gawaine, for so it rehearseth in the book of French. So Sir Tristram many days after fought with Sir Marhaus in an island, and there they did a great battle, but at the last Sir Tristram slew him, so Sir Tristram was wounded that unnethe he might recover, and lay at a nunnery half a year. And Sir Pelleas was a worshipful knight, and was one of the four that achieved the Sangreal, and the Damosel of the Lake made by her means that never he had ado with Sir Launcelot de Lake, for where Sir Launcelot was at any jousts or any tournament, she would not suffer him be there that day, but if it were on the side of Sir Launcelot.

Explicit liber quartus. Incipit liber quintus.

BOOK FIVE

CHAPTER I

How twelve aged ambassadors of Rome came to King Arthur to demand truage for Britain.

When King Arthur had after long war rested, and held a royal feast and Table Round with his allies of kings, princes, and noble knights all of the Round Table, there came into his hall, he sitting in his throne royal, twelve ancient men, bearing each of them a branch of olive, in token that they came as ambassadors and messengers from the Emperor Lucius, which was called at that time, Dictator or Procuror of the Public Weal of Rome. Which said messengers, after their entering and coming into the presence of King Arthur, did to him their obeisance in making to him reverence, and said to him in this wise: The high and mighty Emperor Lucius sendeth to the King of Britain greeting, commanding thee to acknowledge him for thy lord, and to send him the truage due of this realm unto the Empire, which thy father and other to-fore thy precessors have paid as is of record, and thou as rebel, not knowing him as thy sovereign, withholdest and retainest contrary to the statutes and decrees made by the noble and worthy Julius Caesar, conqueror of this realm, and first Emperor of Rome. And if thou refuse his demand and command-ment, know thou for certain that he shall make strong war against thee, thy realms and lands, and shall chastise thee and thy subjects, that it shall be ensample perpetual unto all kings and princes, for to deny their truage unto that noble empire which domineth upon the universal world. Then when they had showed the effect of their message, the king commanded them to withdraw them, and said he should take advice of council and give to them an answer. Then some of the young knights, hearing this their message, would have run on them to have slain them, saying that it was a rebuke to all the knights there being present to suffer them to say so to the king. And anon the king commanded that none of them, upon pain of death, to missay them nor do them any harm, and commanded a knight to bring them to their lodging, and see that they have all that is necessary and requisite for them, with the best cheer, and that no dainty be spared, for the Romans be great lords, and though their message please me not nor my court, yet I must remember mine honour.

After this the king let call all his lords and knights of the Round Table to counsel upon this matter, and desired them to say their advice. Then Sir Cador of Cornwall spake first and said, Sir, this message liketh me well, for we have many days rested us and have been idle, and now I hope ye shall make sharp war on the Romans, where I doubt not we shall get honour. I believe well, said Arthur, that this matter pleaseth thee well, but these answers may not be answered, for the demand grieveth me sore, for truly I will never pay truage to Rome, wherefore I pray you to counsel me. I have understood that Belinus and Brenius, kings of Britain, have had the empire in their hands many days, and also Constantine the son of Heleine, which is an open evidence that we owe no tribute to Rome, but of right we that be descended of them have right to claim the title of the empire.

CHAPTER II

How the kings and lords promised to King Arthur aid and help against the Romans.

Then answered King Anguish of Scotland, Sir, ye ought of right to be above all other kings, for unto you is none like nor pareil in Christendom, of knighthood nor of dignity, and I counsel you never to obey the Romans, for when they reigned on us they distressed our elders, and put this land to great extortions and tallies, wherefore I make here mine avow to avenge me on them; and for to strengthen your quarrel I shall furnish twenty thousand good men of war, and wage them on my costs, which shall await on you with myself when it shall please you. And the king of Little Britain granted him to the same thirty thousand; wherefore King Arthur thanked them. And then every man agreed to make war, and to aid after their power; that is to wit, the lord of West Wales promised to bring thirty thousand men, and Sir Uwaine, Sir Ider his son, with their cousins, promised to bring thirty thousand. Then Sir Launcelot with all other promised in likewise every man a great multitude.

And when King Arthur understood their courages and good wills he thanked them heartily, and after let call the ambassadors to hear their answer. And in presence of all his lords and knights he said to them in this wise: I will that ye return unto your lord and Procuror of the Common Weal for the Romans, and say ye to him, Of his demand and commandment I set nothing, and that I know of no truage nor tribute that I owe to him, nor to none earthly prince, Christian nor heathen; but I pretend to have and occupy the sovereignty of the empire, wherein I am entitled by the right of my predecessors, sometime kings of this land; and say to him that I am delibered and fully concluded, to go with mine army with strength and power unto Rome, by the grace of God, to take possession in the empire and subdue them that be rebel. Wherefore I command him and all them of Rome, that incontinent they make to me their homage, and to acknowledge me for their Emperor and Governor, upon pain that shall ensue. And then he commanded his treasurer to give to them great and large gifts, and to pay all their dispenses, and assigned Sir Cador to convey them out of the land. And so they took their leave and departed, and took their shipping at Sandwich, and passed forth by Flanders, Almaine, the mountains, and all Italy, until they came unto Lucius. And after the reverence made, they made relation of their answer, like as ye to-fore have heard.

When the Emperor Lucius had well understood their credence, he was sore moved as he had been all araged, and said, I had supposed that Arthur would have obeyed to my commandment, and have served you himself, as him well beseemed or any other king to do. O Sir, said one of the senators, let be such vain words, for we let you wit that I and my fellows were full sore afeard to behold his countenance; I fear me ye have made a rod for yourself, for he intendeth to be lord of this empire, which sore is to be doubted if he come, for he is all another man than ye ween, and holdeth the most noble court of the world, all other kings nor princes may not compare unto his noble maintenance. On New Year's Day we saw him in his estate, which was the royalest that ever we saw, for he was served at his table with nine kings, and the noblest fellowship of other princes, lords, and knights that be in the world, and every knight approved and like a lord, and holdeth Table Round: and in his person the most manly man that liveth, and is like to conquer all the world, for unto his courage it is too little: wherefore I advise you to keep well your marches and straits in the mountains; for certainly he is a lord to be doubted. Well, said Lucius, before Easter I suppose to pass the mountains, and so forth into France, and there bereave him his lands with Genoese and other mighty warriors of Tuscany and Lombardy. And I shall send for them all that be subjects and allied to the empire of Rome to come to mine aid. And forthwith sent old wise knights unto these countries following: first to Ambage and Arrage, to Alexandria, to India, to Armenia, whereas the river of Euphrates runneth into Asia, to Africa, and Europe the Large, to Ertayne and Elamye, to Araby, Egypt, and to Damascus, to Damietta and Cayer, to Cappadocia, to Tarsus, Turkey, Pontus and Pamphylia, to Syria and Galatia. And all these were subject to Rome and many more, as Greece, Cyprus, Macedonia, Calabria, Cateland, Portugal, with many thousands of Spaniards. Thus all these kings, dukes, and admirals, assembled about Rome, with sixteen kings at once, with great multitude of people. When the emperor understood their coming he made ready his Romans and all the people between him and Flanders.

Also he had gotten with him fifty giants which had been engendered of fiends; and they were ordained to guard his person, and to break the front of the battle of King Arthur. And thus departed from Rome, and came down the mountains for to destroy the lands that Arthur had conquered, and came unto Cologne, and besieged a castle thereby, and won it soon, and stuffed it with two hundred Saracens or Infidels, and after destroyed many fair countries which Arthur had won of King Claudas. And thus Lucius came with all his host, which were disperplyd sixty mile in breadth, and commanded them to meet with him in Burgoyne, for he purposed to destroy the realm of Little Britain.

CHAPTER III

*How King Arthur held a parliament at York, and how he
ordained the realm should be governed in his absence.*

Now leave we of Lucius the Emperor and speak we of King Arthur,
that commanded all them of his retinue to be ready at the utas of
Hilary for to hold a parliament at York. And at that parliament was
concluded to arrest all the navy of the land, and to be ready within
fifteen days at Sandwich, and there he showed to his army how he
purposed to conquer the empire which he ought to have of right.
And there he ordained two governors of this realm, that is to say, Sir
Baudwin of Britain, for to counsel to the best, and Sir Constantine,
son to Sir Cador of Cornwall, which after the death of Arthur was
king of this realm. And in the presence of all his lords he resigned the
rule of the realm and Guenever his queen to them, wherefore Sir
Launcelot was wroth, for he left Sir Tristram with King Mark for the
love of Beale Isould. Then the Queen Guenever made great sorrow
for the departing of her lord and other, and swooned in such wise
that the ladies bare her into her chamber. Thus the king with his great
army departed, leaving the queen and realm in the governance of Sir
Baudwin and Constantine. And when he was on his horse he said
with an high voice, If I die in this journey I will that Sir Constantine
be mine heir and king crowned of this realm as next of my blood.
And after departed and entered into the sea at Sandwich with all his
army, with a great multitude of ships, galleys, cogs, and dromounds,
sailing on the sea.

CHAPTER IV

How King Arthur being shipped and lying in his cabin had a marvellous dream and of the exposition thereof.

And as the king lay in his cabin in the ship, he fell in a slumbering and dreamed a marvellous dream: him seemed that a dreadful dragon did drown much of his people, and he came flying out of the west, and his head was enamelled with azure, and his shoulders shone as gold, his belly like mails of a marvellous hue, his tail full of tatters, his feet full of fine sable, and his claws like fine gold; and an hideous flame of fire flew out of his mouth, like as the land and water had flamed all of fire. After, him seemed there came out of the orient, a grimly boar all black in a cloud, and his paws as big as a post; he was rugged looking roughly, he was the foulest beast that ever man saw, he roared and romed so hideously that it were marvel to hear. Then the dreadful dragon advanced him and came in the wind like a falcon giving great strokes on the boar, and the boar hit him again with his grizzly tusks that his breast was all bloody, and that the hot blood made all the sea red of his blood. Then the dragon flew away all on an height, and came down with such a swough, and smote the boar on the ridge, which was ten foot large from the head to the tail, and smote the boar all to powder both flesh and bones, that it flittered all abroad on the sea.

And therewith the king awoke anon, and was sore abashed of this dream, and sent anon for a wise philosopher, commanding to tell him the signification of his dream. Sir, said the philosopher, the dragon that thou dreamedst of betokeneth thine own person that sailest here, and the colours of his wings be thy realms that thou hast won, and his tail which is all to-tattered signifieth the noble knights of the Round Table; and the boar that the dragon slew coming from the clouds betokeneth some tyrant that tormenteth the people, or else thou art like to fight with some giant thyself, being horrible and abominable, whose peer ye saw never in your days, wherefore of this dreadful dream doubt thee nothing, but as a conqueror come forth thyself.

Then after this soon they had sight of land, and sailed till they arrived at Barflete in Flanders, and when they were there he found many of his great lords ready, as they had been commanded to wait upon him.

CHAPTER V

How a man of the country told to him of a marvellous giant,
and how he fought and conquered him.

Then came to him an husbandman of the country, and told him how there was in the country of Constantine, beside Brittany, a great giant which had slain, murdered, and devoured much people of the country, and had been sustained seven year with the children of the commons of that land, insomuch that all the children be all slain and destroyed; and now late he hath taken the Duchess of Brittany as she rode with her meiny, and hath led her to his lodging which is in a mountain, for to ravish and lie by her to her life's end, and many people followed her, more than five hundred, but all they might not rescue her, but they left her shrieking and crying lamentably, wherefore I suppose that he hath slain her in fulfilling his foul lust of lechery. She was wife unto thy cousin Sir Howell, whom we call full nigh of thy blood. Now, as thou art a rightful king, have pity on this lady, and revenge us all as thou art a noble conqueror. Alas, said King Arthur, this is a great mischief, I had liefer than the best realm that I have that I had been a furlong way to-fore him for to have rescued that lady. Now, fellow, said King Arthur, canst thou bring me thereas this giant haunteth? Yea, Sir, said the good man, look yonder whereas thou seest those two great fires, there shalt thou find him, and more treasure than I suppose is in all France. When the king had understood this piteous case, he returned into his tent.

Then he called to him Sir Kay and Sir Bedivere, and commanded them secretly to make ready horse and harness for himself and them twain; for after evensong he would ride on pilgrimage with them two only unto Saint Michael's mount. And then anon he made him ready, and armed him at all points, and took his horse and his shield. And so they three departed thence and rode forth as fast as ever they might till that they came to the foreland of that mount. And there they alighted, and the king commanded them to tarry there, for he would himself go up into that mount. And so he ascended up into that hill till he came to a great fire, and there he found a careful widow wringing her hands and making great sorrow, sitting by a grave new made. And then King Arthur saluted her, and demanded of her wherefore she made such lamentation, to whom she answered and said, Sir knight, speak soft, for yonder is a devil, if he hear thee speak he will come and destroy thee; I hold thee unhappy; what dost thou here in this mountain? for if ye were such fifty as ye be, ye were not able to make resistance against this devil: here lieth a duchess dead, the which was the fairest of all the world, wife to Sir Howell, Duke of Brittany, he hath murdered her in forcing her, and hath slit her unto the navel.

Dame, said the king, I come from the noble conqueror King Arthur, for to treat with that tyrant for his liege people. Fie on such treaties, said she, he setteth not by the king nor by no man else; but an if thou have brought Arthur's wife, dame Guenever, he shall be gladder than thou hadst given to him half France. Beware, approach him not too nigh, for he hath vanquished fifteen kings, and hath made him a coat full of precious stones embroidered with their beards, which they sent him to have his love for salvation of their people at this last Christmas. And if thou wilt, speak with him at yonder great fire at supper. Well, said Arthur, I will accomplish my message for all your fearful words; and went forth by the crest of that hill, and saw where he sat at supper gnawing on a limb of a man, baking his broad limbs by the fire, and breechless, and three fair damosels turning three broaches whereon were broached twelve young children late born, like young birds.

When King Arthur beheld that piteous sight he had great compassion on them, so that his heart bled for sorrow, and hailed him, saying in this wise: He that all the world wieldeth give thee short life and shameful death and the devil have thy soul; why hast thou murdered these young innocent children, and murdered this duchess? Therefore, arise and dress thee, thou glutton, for this day shalt thou die of my hand. Then the glutton anon started up, and took a great club in his hand, and smote at the king that his coronal fell to the earth. And the king hit him again that he carved his belly and cut off his genitours, that his guts and his entrails fell down to the ground. Then the giant threw away his club, and caught the king in his arms that he crushed his ribs. Then the three maidens kneeled down and called to Christ for help and comfort of Arthur. And then Arthur weltered and wrung, that he was other while under and another time above. And so weltering and wallowing they rolled down the hill till they came to the sea mark, and ever as they so weltered Arthur smote him with his dagger.

And it fortuned they came to the place whereas the two knights were and kept Arthur's horse; then when they saw the king fast in the giant's arms they came and loosed him. And then the king commanded Sir Kay to smite off the giant's head, and to set it upon a truncheon of a spear, and bear it to Sir Howell, and tell him that his enemy was slain; and after let this head be bound to a barbican that all the people may see and behold it; and go ye two up to the mountain, and fetch me my shield, my sword, and the club of iron; and as for the treasure, take ye it, for ye shall find there goods out of number; so I have the kirtle and the club I desire no more. This was the fiercest giant that ever I met with, save one in the mount of Araby, which I overcame, but this was greater and fiercer. Then the knights fetched the club and the kirtle, and some of the treasure they took to themselves, and returned again to the host. And anon this was known through all the country, wherefore the people came and thanked the king. And he said again, Give the thanks to God, and depart the goods among you.

And after that King Arthur said and commanded his cousin Howell, that he should ordain for a church to be builded on the same hill in the worship of Saint Michael. And on the morn the king removed with his great battle, and came into Champayne and in a valley, and there they pight their tents; and the king being set at his dinner, there came in two messengers, of whom that one was Marshal of France, and said to the king that the emperor was entered into France, and had destroyed a great part, and was in Burgoyne, and had destroyed and made great slaughter of people, and burnt towns and boroughs; wherefore, if thou come not hastily, they must yield up their bodies and goods.

CHAPTER VI

How King Arthur sent Sir Gawaine and other to Lucius,
and how they were assailed and escaped with worship.

Then the king did do call Sir Gawaine, Sir Bors, Sir Lionel, and Sir
Bedivere, and commanded them to go straight to Sir Lucius, and say
ye to him that hastily he remove out of my land; and if he will not,
bid him make him ready to battle and not distress the poor people.
Then anon these noble knights dressed them to horseback, and when
they came to the green wood, they saw many pavilions set in a
meadow, of silk of divers colours, beside a river, and the emperor's
pavilion was in the middle with an eagle displayed above. To the
which tent our knights rode toward, and ordained Sir Gawaine and
Sir Bors to do the message, and left in a bushment Sir Lionel and Sir
Bedivere. And then Sir Gawaine and Sir Bors did their message, and
commanded Lucius, in Arthur's name to avoid his land, or shortly to
address him to battle. To whom Lucius answered and said, Ye shall
return to your lord, and say ye to him that I shall subdue him and all
his lands. Then Sir Gawaine was wroth and said, I had liefer than all
France fight against thee; and so had I, said Sir Bors, liefer than all
Brittany or Burgoyne.

Then a knight named Sir Gainus, nigh cousin to the emperor, said,
Lo, how these Britons be full of pride and boast, and they brag as
though they bare up all the world. Then Sir Gawaine was sore
grieved with these words, and pulled out his sword and smote off his
head. And therewith turned their horses and rode over waters and
through woods till they came to their bushment, whereas Sir Lionel
and Sir Bedivere were hoving. The Romans followed fast after, on
horseback and on foot, over a champaign unto a wood; then Sir Bors
turned his horse and saw a knight come fast on, whom he smote
through the body with a spear that he fell dead down to the earth;
then came Caliburn one of the strongest of Pavie, and smote down
many of Arthur's knights. And when Sir Bors saw him do so much
harm, he addressed toward him, and smote him through the breast,
that he fell down dead to the earth. Then Sir Feldenak thought to

revenge the death of Gainus upon Sir Gawaine, but Sir Gawaine was ware thereof, and smote him on the head, which stroke stinted not till it came to his breast. And then he returned and came to his fellows in the bushment. And there was a recounter, for the bushment brake on the Romans, and slew and hew down the Romans, and forced the Romans to flee and return, whom the noble knights chased unto their tents.

Then the Romans gathered more people, and also footmen came on, and there was a new battle, and so much people that Sir Bors and Sir Berel were taken. But when Sir Gawaine saw that, he took with him Sir Idrus the good knight, and said he would never see King Arthur but if he rescued them, and pulled out Galatine his good sword, and followed them that led those two knights away; and he smote him that led Sir Bors, and took Sir Bors from him and delivered him to his fellows. And Sir Idrus in likewise rescued Sir Berel. Then began the battle to be great, that our knights were in great jeopardy, wherefore Sir Gawaine sent to King Arthur for succour, and that he hie him, for I am sore wounded, and that our prisoners may pay goods out of number. And the messenger came to the king and told him his message. And anon the king did do assemble his army, but anon, or he departed the prisoners were come, and Sir Gawaine and his fellows gat the field and put the Romans to flight, and after returned and came with their fellowship in such wise that no man of worship was lost of them, save that Sir Gawaine was sore hurt. Then the king did do ransack his wounds and comforted him. And thus was the beginning of the first journey of the Britons and Romans, and there were slain of the Romans more than ten thousand, and great joy and mirth was made that night in the host of King Arthur. And on the morn he sent all the prisoners into Paris under the guard of Sir Launcelot, with many knights, and of Sir Cador.

CHAPTER VII

How Lucius sent certain spies in a bushment for to have taken his knights being prisoners, and how they were letted.

Now turn we to the Emperor of Rome, which espied that these prisoners should be sent to Paris, and anon he sent to lie in a bushment certain knights and princes with sixty thousand men, for to rescue his knights and lords that were prisoners. And so on the morn as Launcelot and Sir Cador, chieftains and governors of all them that conveyed the prisoners, as they should pass through a wood, Sir Launcelot sent certain knights to espy if any were in the woods to let them. And when the said knights came into the wood, anon they espied and saw the great embushment, and returned and told Sir Launcelot that there lay in await for them three score thousand Romans. And then Sir Launcelot with such knights as he had, and men of war to the number of ten thousand, put them in array, and met with them and fought with them manly, and slew and detrenched many of the Romans, and slew many knights and admirals of the party of the Romans and Saracens; there was slain the king of Lyly and three great lords, Aladuke, Herawd, and Heringdale. But Sir Launcelot fought so nobly that no man might endure a stroke of his hand, but where he came he showed his prowess and might, for he slew down right on every side; and the Romans and Saracens fled from him as the sheep from the wolf or from the lion, and put them, all that abode alive, to flight.

And so long they fought that tidings came to King Arthur, and anon he graithed him and came to the battle, and saw his knights how they had vanquished the battle, he embraced them knight by knight in his arms, and said, Ye be worthy to wield all your honour and worship; there was never king save myself that had so noble knights. Sir, said Cador, there was none of us failed other, but of the prowess and manhood of Sir Launcelot were more than wonder to tell, and also of his cousins which did that day many noble feats of war. And also Sir Cador told who of his knights were slain, as Sir Berel, and other Sir Moris and Sir Maurel, two good knights. Then the king wept, and dried his eyes with a kerchief, and said, Your courage had near-hand destroyed you, for though ye had returned again, ye had lost no worship; for I call it folly, knights to abide when they be overmatched. Nay, said Launcelot and the other, for once shamed may never be recovered.

CHAPTER VIII

How a senator told to Lucius of their discomfiture, and also of the great battle between Arthur and Lucius.

Now leave we King Arthur and his noble knights which had won the field, and had brought their prisoners to Paris, and speak we of a senator which escaped from the battle, and came to Lucius the emperor, and said to him, Sir emperor, I advise thee for to withdraw thee; what dost thou here? thou shalt win nothing in these marches but great strokes out of all measure, for this day one of Arthur's knights was worth in the battle an hundred of ours. Fie on thee, said Lucius, thou speakest cowardly; for thy words grieve me more than all the loss that I had this day. And anon he sent forth a king, which hight Sir Leomie, with a great army, and bade him hie him fast to-fore, and he would follow hastily after. King Arthur was warned privily, and sent his people to Sessoine, and took up the towns and castles from the Romans. Then the king commanded Sir Cador to take the rearward, and to take with him certain knights of the Round Table, and Sir Launcelot, Sir Bors, Sir Kay, Sir Marrok, with Sir Marhaus, shall await on our person. Thus the King Arthur disperpled his host in divers parties, to the end that his enemies should not escape.

When the emperor was entered into the vale of Sessoine, he might see where King Arthur was embattled and his banner displayed; and he was beset round about with his enemies, that needs he must fight or yield him, for he might not flee, but said openly unto the Romans, Sirs, I admonish you that this day ye fight and acquit you as men, and remember how Rome domineth and is chief and head over all the earth and universal world, and suffer not these Britons this day to abide against us; and therewith he did command his trumpets to blow the bloody sounds, in such wise that the ground trembled and dindled.

Then the battles approached and shoved and shouted on both sides, and great strokes were smitten on both sides, many men overthrown, hurt, and slain; and great valiances, prowesses and appertices of war were that day showed, which were over long to recount the noble feats of every man, for they should contain an whole volume. But in especial, King Arthur rode in the battle exhorting his knights to do well, and himself did as nobly with his hands as was possible a man to do; he drew out Excalibur his sword, and awaited ever whereas the Romans were thickest and most grieved his people, and anon he addressed him on that part, and hew and slew down right, and rescued his people; and he slew a great giant named Galapas, which was a man of an huge quantity and height, he shorted him and smote off both his legs by the knees, saying, Now art thou better of a size to deal with than thou were, and after smote off his head. There Sir Gawaine fought nobly and slew three admirals in that battle. And so did all the knights of the Round Table. Thus the battle between King Arthur and Lucius the Emperor endured long. Lucius had on his side many Saracens which were slain. And thus the battle was great, and oftsides that one party was at a fordeal and anon at an afterdeal, which endured so long till at the last King Arthur espied where Lucius the Emperor fought, and did wonder with his own hands. And anon he rode to him. And either smote other fiercely, and at last Lucius smote Arthur thwart the visage, and gave him a large wound. And when King Arthur felt himself hurt, anon he smote him again with Excalibur that it cleft his head, from the summit of his head, and stinted not till it came to his breast. And then the emperor fell down dead and there ended his life.

And when it was known that the emperor was slain, anon all the Romans with all their host put them to flight, and King Arthur with all his knights followed the chase, and slew down right all them that they might attain. And thus was the victory given to King Arthur, and the triumph; and there were slain on the part of Lucius more than an hundred thousand. And after King Arthur did do ransack the dead bodies, and did do bury them that were slain of his retinue, every man according to the estate and degree that he was of. And them that were hurt he let the surgeons do search their hurts and wounds, and commanded to spare no salves nor medicines till they were whole.

Then the king rode straight to the place where the Emperor Lucius lay dead, and with him he found slain the Soudan of Syria, the King of Egypt and of Ethiopia, which were two noble kings, with seventeen other kings of divers regions, and also sixty senators of Rome, all noble men, whom the king did do balm and gum with many good gums aromatic, and after did do cere them in sixty fold of cered cloth of sendal, and laid them in chests of lead, because they should not chafe nor savour, and upon all these bodies their shields with their arms and banners were set, to the end they should be known of what country they were. And after he found three senators which were alive, to whom he said, For to save your lives I will that ye take these dead bodies, and carry them with you unto great Rome, and present them to the Potestate on my behalf, showing him my letters, and tell them that I in my person shall hastily be at Rome. And I suppose the Romans shall beware how they shall demand any tribute of me. And I command you to say when ye shall come to Rome, to the Potestate and all the Council and Senate, that I send to them these dead bodies for the tribute that they have demanded. And if they be not content with these, I shall pay more at my coming, for other tribute owe I none, nor none other will I pay. And methinketh this sufficeth for Britain, Ireland and all Almaine with Germany. And furthermore, I charge you to say to them, that l command them upon pain of their heads never to demand tribute nor tax of me nor of my lands. Then with this charge and commandment, the three senators aforesaid departed with all the said dead bodies, laying the body of Lucius in a car covered with the arms of the Empire all alone; and after alway two bodies of kings in a chariot, and then the bodies of the senators after them, and so went toward Rome, and showed their legation and message to the Potestate and Senate, recounting the battle done in France, and how the field was lost and much people and innumerable slain. Wherefore they advised them in no wise to move no more war against that noble conqueror Arthur, for his might and prowess is most to be doubted, seen the noble kings and great multitude of knights of the Round Table, to whom none earthly prince may compare.

CHAPTER IX

*How Arthur, after he had achieved the battle against the
Romans, entered into Almaine, and so into Italy.*

Now turn we unto King Arthur and his noble knights, which, after
the great battle achieved against the Romans, entered into Lorraine,
Brabant and Flanders, and sithen returned into Haut Almaine, and so
over the mountains into Lombardy, and after, into Tuscany wherein
was a city which in no wise would yield themself nor obey,
wherefore King Arthur besieged it, and lay long about it, and gave
many assaults to the city; and they within defended them valiantly.
Then, on a time, the king called Sir Florence, a knight, and said to
him they lacked victual, And not far from hence be great forests and
woods, wherein be many of mine enemies with much bestial: I will
that thou make thee ready and go thither in foraying, and take with
thee Sir Gawaine my nephew, Sir Wisshard, Sir Clegis, Sir Cleremond,
and the Captain of Cardiff with other, and bring with you all the
beasts that ye there can get.

And anon these knights made them ready, and rode over holts and
hills, through forests and woods, till they came into a fair meadow full
of fair flowers and grass; and there they rested them and their horses
all that night. And in the springing of the day in the next morn, Sir
Gawaine took his horse and stole away from his fellowship, to seek
some adventures. And anon he was ware of a man armed, walking his
horse easily by a wood's side, and his shield laced to his shoulder,
sitting on a strong courser, without any man saving a page bearing a
mighty spear. The knight bare in his shield three griffins of gold, in
sable carbuncle, the chief of silver. When Sir Gawaine espied this gay
knight, he feutred his spear, and rode straight to him, and demanded
of him from whence that he was. That other answered and said he
was of Tuscany, and demanded of Sir Gawaine, What, profferest
thou, proud knight, thee so boldly? here gettest thou no prey, thou
mayest prove what thou wilt, for thou shalt be my prisoner or thou
depart. Then said Gawaine, thou avauntest thee greatly and speakest

proud words, I counsel thee for all thy boast that thou make thee ready, and take thy gear to thee, to-fore greater grame fall to thee.

CHAPTER X

Of a battle done by Sir Gawaine against a Saracen, which after was yielden and became Christian.

Then they took their spears and ran each at other with all the might they had, and smote each other through their shields into their shoulders, wherefore anon they pulled out their swords, and smote great strokes that the fire sprang out of their helms. Then Sir Gawaine was all abashed, and with Galatine his good sword he smote through shield and thick hauberk made of thick mails, and all to-rushed and break the precious stones, and made him a large wound, that men might see both liver and lung. Then groaned that knight, and addressed him to Sir Gawaine, and with an awk stroke gave him a great wound and cut a vein, which grieved Gawaine sore, and he bled sore. Then the knight said to Sir Gawaine, bind thy wound or thy blee[ding] change, for thou be-bleedest all thy horse and thy fair arms, for all the barbers of Brittany shall not con staunch thy blood, for whosomever is hurt with this blade he shall never be staunched of bleeding. Then answered Gawaine, it grieveth me but little, thy great words shall not fear me nor lessen my courage, but thou shalt suffer teen and sorrow or we depart, but tell me in haste who may staunch my bleeding. That may I do, said the knight, if I will, and so will I if thou wilt succour and aid me, that I may be christened and believe on God, and thereof I require thee of thy manhood, and it shall be great merit for thy soul. I grant, said Gawaine, so God help me, to accomplish all thy desire, but first tell me what thou soughtest here thus alone, and of what land and liegiance thou art of. Sir, he said, my name is Priamus, and a great prince is my father, and he hath been rebel unto Rome and overridden many of their lands. My father is lineally descended of Alexander and of Hector by right line. And Duke Joshua and Maccabæus were of our lineage. I am right inheritor of Alexandria and Africa, and all the out isles, yet will I believe on thy Lord that thou believest on; and for thy labour I shall give thee treasure enough. I was so elate and hauteyn in my heart that I thought no man my peer, nor to me semblable. I was sent into this war with seven score knights, and now I have encountered with thee, which hast given to me of fighting my fill, wherefore sir knight, I pray thee to tell me what thou art. I am no knight, said Gawaine, I have been brought up in the guardrobe with the noble King Arthur many years, for to take heed to his armour and his other array, and to point his paltocks that long to himself. At Yule last he made me yeoman, and gave to me horse and harness, and an hundred pound in money; and if fortune be my friend, I doubt not but to be well advanced and holpen by my liege lord. Ah, said Priamus, if his knaves be so keen and fierce, his knights be passing good: now for the King's love of Heaven, whether thou be a knave or a knight, tell thou me thy name. By God, said Sir Gawaine, now I will say thee sooth, my name is Sir Gawaine, and known I am in his court and in his chamber, and one of the knights of the Round Table, he dubbed me a duke with his own hand. Therefore grudge not if this grace is to me fortuned, it is the goodness of God that lent to me my strength. Now am I better pleased, said Priamus, than thou hadst given to me all the Provence and Paris the rich. I had liefer to have been torn with wild horses, than any varlet had won such loos, or any page or priker should have had prize on me. But now sir knight I warn thee that hereby is a Duke of Lorraine with his army, and the noblest men of Dolphiny, and lords of Lombardy, with the garrison of Godard, and Saracens of Southland, y-numbered sixty thousand of good men of arms; wherefore but if we hie us hence, it will harm us both, for we be sore hurt, never like to recover; but take heed to my page, that he no horn blow, for if he do, there be hoving here fast by an hundred knights awaiting on my person, and if they take thee, there shall no ransom of gold nor silver acquit thee.

Then Sir Gawaine rode over a water for to save him, and the knight followed him, and so rode forth till they came to his fellows which were in the meadow, where they had been all the night. Anon as Sir Wisshard was ware of Sir Gawaine and saw that he was hurt, he ran to him sorrowfully weeping, and demanded of him who had so hurt him; and Gawaine told how he had foughten with that man, and each of them had hurt other, and how he had salves to heal them; but I can tell you other tidings, that soon we shall have ado with many enemies.

Then Sir Priamus and Sir Gawaine alighted, and let their horses graze in the meadow, and unarmed them, and then the blood ran freshly from their wounds. And Priamus took from his page a vial full of the four waters that came out of Paradise, and with certain balm anointed their wounds, and washed them with that water, and within an hour after they were both as whole as ever they were. And then with a trumpet were they all assembled to council, and there Priamus told unto them what lords and knights had sworn to rescue him, and that without fail they should be assailed with many thousands, wherefore he counselled them to withdraw them. Then Sir Gawaine said, it were great shame to them to avoid without any strokes; Wherefore I advise to take our arms and to make us ready to meet with these Saracens and misbelieving men, and with the help of God we shall overthrow them and have a fair day on them. And Sir Florence shall abide still in this field to keep the stale as a noble knight, and we shall not forsake yonder fellows. Now, said Priamus, cease your words, for I warn you ye shall find in yonder woods many perilous knights; they will put forth beasts to call you on, they be out of number, and ye are not past seven hundred, which be over few to fight with so many. Nevertheless, said Sir Gawaine, we shall once encounter them, and see what they can do, and the best shall have the victory.

CHAPTER XI

*How the Saracens came out of a wood for to rescue their
beasts, and of a great battle.*

Then Sir Florence called to him Sir Floridas, with an hundred knights, and drove forth the herd of beasts. Then followed him seven hundred men of arms; and Sir Ferant of Spain on a fair steed came springing out of the woods, and came to Sir Florence and asked him why he fled. Then Sir Florence took his spear and rode against him, and smote him in the forehead and brake his neck bone. Then all the other were moved, and thought to avenge the death of Sir Ferant, and smote in among them, and there was great fight, and many slain and laid down to ground, and Sir Florence with his hundred knights alway kept the stale, and fought manly.

Then when Priamus the good knight perceived the great fight, he went to Sir Gawaine, and bade him that he should go and succour his fellowship, which were sore bestead with their enemies. Sir, grieve you not, said Sir Gawaine, for their gree shall be theirs. I shall not once move my horse to them ward, but if I see more than there be; for they be strong enough to match them.

And with that he saw an earl called Sir Ethelwold and the duke of Dutchmen, came leaping out of a wood with many thousands, and Priamus' knights, and came straight unto the battle. Then Sir Gawaine comforted his knights, and bade them not to be abashed, for all shall be ours. Then they began to wallop and met with their enemies, there were men slain and overthrown on every side. Then thrust in among them the knights of the Table Round, and smote down to the earth all them that withstood them, in so much that they made them to recoil and flee. By God, said Sir Gawaine, this gladdeth my heart, for now be they less in number by twenty thousand. Then entered into the battle Jubance a giant, and fought and slew down right, and distressed many of our knights, among whom was slain Sir Gherard, a knight of Wales. Then our knights took heart to them, and slew many Saracens. And then came in Sir Priamus with his pennon, and rode with the knights of the Round Table, and fought so manfully that many of their enemies lost their lives. And there Sir Priamus slew the Marquis of Moises land, and Sir Gawaine with his fellows so quit them that they had the field, but in that stour was Sir Chestelaine, a child and ward of Sir Gawaine slain, wherefore was much sorrow made, and his death was soon avenged. Thus was the battle ended, and many lords of Lombardy and Saracens left dead in the field.

Then Sir Florence and Sir Gawaine harboured surely their people, and took great plenty of bestial, of gold and silver, and great treasure and riches, and returned unto King Arthur, which lay still at the siege. And when they came to the king they presented their prisoners and recounted their adventures, and how they had vanquished their enemies.

CHAPTER XII

How Sir Gawaine returned to King Arthur with his prisoners, and how the King won a city, and how he was crowned Emperor.

Now thanked be God, said the noble King Arthur. But what manner man is he that standeth by himself, him seemeth no prisoner. Sir, said Gawaine, this is a good man of arms, he hath matched me, but he is yielden unto God, and to me, for to become Christian; had not he have been we should never have returned, wherefore I pray you that he may be baptised, for there liveth not a nobler man nor better knight of his hands. Then the king let him anon be christened, and did do call him his first name Priamus, and made him a duke and knight of the Table Round. And then anon the king let do cry assault to the city, and there was rearing of ladders, breaking of walls, and the ditch filled, that men with little pain might enter into the city. Then came out a duchess, and Clarisin the countess, with many ladies and damosels, and kneeling before King Arthur, required him for the love of God to receive the city, and not to take it by assault, for then should many guiltless be slain. Then the king avaled his visor with a meek and noble countenance, and said, Madam, there shall none of my subjects misdo you nor your maidens, nor to none that to you belong, but the duke shall abide my judgment. Then anon the king commanded to leave the assault, and anon the duke's oldest son brought out the keys, and kneeling delivered them to the king, and besought him of grace; and the king seized the town by assent of his lords, and took the duke and sent him to Dover, there for to abide prisoner term of his life, and assigned certain rents for the dower of the duchess and for her children.

Then he made lords to rule those lands, and laws as a lord ought to do in his own country; and after he took his journey toward Rome, and sent Sir Floris and Sir Floridas to-fore, with five hundred men of arms, and they came to the city of Urbino and laid there a bushment, thereas them seemed most best for them, and rode to-fore the town, where anon issued out much people and skirmished with the fore-riders. Then brake out the bushment and won the bridge, and after the town, and set upon the walls the king's banner. Then came the king upon an hill, and saw the city and his banner on the walls, by which he knew that the city was won. And anon he sent and commanded that none of his liege men should defoul nor lie by no lady, wife nor maid; and when he came into the city, he passed to the castle, and comforted them that were in sorrow, and ordained there a captain, a knight of his own country.

And when they of Milan heard that thilk city was won, they sent to King Arthur great sums of money, and besought him as their lord to have pity on them, promising to be his subjects for ever, and yield to him homage and fealty for the lands of Pleasance and Pavia, Petersaint, and the Port of Tremble, and to give him yearly a million of gold all his lifetime. Then he rideth into Tuscany, and winneth towns and castles, and wasted all in his way that to him will not obey, and so to Spolute and Viterbe, and from thence he rode into the Vale of Vicecount among the vines. And from thence he sent to the senators, to wit whether they would know him for their lord. But soon after on a Saturday came unto King Arthur all the senators that were left alive, and the noblest cardinals that then dwelt in Rome, and prayed him of peace, and proffered him full large, and besought him as governor to give licence for six weeks for to assemble all the Romans, and then to crown him emperor with cream as it belongeth to so high estate. I assent, said the king, like as ye have devised, and at Christmas there to be crowned, and to hold my Round Table with my knights as me liketh. And then the senators made ready for his enthronization. And at the day appointed, as the romance telleth, he came into Rome, and was crowned emperor by the pope's hand, with all the royalty that could be made, and sojourned there a time, and established all his lands from Rome into France, and gave lands and realms unto his servants and knights, to everych after his desert, in such wise that none complained, rich nor poor. And he gave to Sir Priamus the duchy of Lorraine; and he thanked him, and said he would serve him the days of his life; and after made dukes and earls, and made every man rich.

Then after this all his knights and lords assembled them afore him, and said: Blessed be God, your war is finished and your conquest achieved, in so much that we know none so great nor mighty that dare make war against you: wherefore we beseech you to return homeward, and give us licence to go home to our wives, from whom we have been long, and to rest us, for your journey is finished with honour and worship. Then said the king, Ye say truth, and for to tempt God it is no wisdom, and therefore make you ready and return we into England. Then there was trussing of harness and baggage and great carriage. And after licence given, he returned and commanded that no man in pain of death should not rob nor take victual, nor other thing by the way but that he should pay therefore. And thus he came over the sea and landed at Sandwich, against whom Queen Guenever his wife came and met him, and he was nobly received of all his commons in every city and burgh, and great gifts presented to him at his home-coming to welcome him with.

Thus endeth the fifth book of the conquest that King Arthur had against Lucius the Emperor of Rome, and here followeth the sixth book, which is of Sir Launcelot du Lake.

BOOK SIX

CHAPTER I

*How Sir Launcelot and Sir Lionel departed from the court,
and how Sir Lionel left him sleeping and was taken.*

Soon after that King Arthur was come from Rome into England,
then all the knights of the Table Round resorted unto the king, and
made many jousts and tournaments, and some there were that were
but knights, which increased so in arms and worship that they passed
all their fellows in prowess and noble deeds, and that was well proved
on many; but in especial it was proved on Sir Launcelot du Lake, for
in all tournaments and jousts and deeds of arms, both for life and
death, he passed all other knights, and at no time he was never
overcome but if it were by treason or enchantment; so Sir Launcelot
increased so marvellously in worship, and in honour, therefore is he
the first knight that the French book maketh mention of after King
Arthur came from Rome. Wherefore Queen Guenever had him in
great favour above all other knights, and in certain he loved the
queen again above all other ladies and damosels of his life, and for her
he did many deeds of arms, and saved her from the fire through his
noble chivalry.

Thus Sir Launcelot rested him long with play and game. And when
he thought himself to prove himself in strange adventures, then he
bade his nephew, Sir Lionel, for to make him ready; for we two will
seek adventures. So they mounted on their horses, armed at all rights,
and rode into a deep forest and so into a deep plain. And then the
weather was hot about noon, and Sir Launcelot had great lust to
sleep. Then Sir Lionel espied a great apple-tree that stood by an
hedge, and said, Brother, yonder is a fair shadow, there may we rest
us [and] our horses. It is well said, fair brother, said Sir Launcelot, for
this eight year I was not so sleepy as I am now; and so they there

alighted and tied their horses unto sundry trees, and so Sir Launcelot laid him down under an apple-tree, and his helm he laid under his head. And Sir Lionel waked while he slept. So Sir Launcelot was asleep passing fast.

And in the meanwhile there came three knights riding, as fast fleeing as ever they might ride. And there followed them three but one knight. And when Sir Lionel saw him, him thought he saw never so great a knight, nor so well faring a man, neither so well apparelled unto all rights. So within a while this strong knight had overtaken one of these knights, and there he smote him to the cold earth that he lay still. And then he rode unto the second knight, and smote him so that man and horse fell down. And then straight to the third knight he rode, and smote him behind his horse's arse a spear length. And then he alighted down and reined his horse on the bridle, and bound all the three knights fast with the reins of their own bridles. When Sir Lionel saw him do thus, he thought to assay him, and made him ready, and stilly and privily he took his horse, and thought not for to awake Sir Launcelot. And when he was mounted upon his horse, he overtook this strong knight, and bade him turn, and the other smote Sir Lionel so hard that horse and man he bare to the earth, and so he alighted down and bound him fast, and threw him overthwart his own horse, and so he served them all four, and rode with them away to his own castle. And when he came there he gart unarm them, and beat them with thorns all naked, and after put them in a deep prison where were many more knights, that made great dolour.

CHAPTER II

How Sir Ector followed for to seek Sir Launcelot,
and how he was taken by Sir Turquine.

When Sir Ector de Maris wist that Sir Launcelot was passed out of the court to seek adventures, he was wroth with himself, and made him ready to seek Sir Launcelot, and as he had ridden long in a great forest he met with a man was like a forester. Fair fellow, said Sir Ector, knowest thou in this country any adventures that be here nigh hand? Sir, said the forester, this country know I well, and hereby, within this mile, is a strong manor, and well dyked, and by that manor, on the left hand, there is a fair ford for horses to drink of, and over that ford there groweth a fair tree, and thereon hang many fair shields that wielded sometime good knights, and at the hole of the tree hangeth a basin of copper and latten, and strike upon that basin with the butt of thy spear thrice, and soon after thou shalt hear new tidings, and else hast thou the fairest grace that many a year had ever knight that passed through this forest. Gramercy, said Sir Ector, and departed and came to the tree, and saw many fair shields. And among them he saw his brother's shield, Sir Lionel, and many more that he knew that were his fellows of the Round Table, the which grieved his heart, and promised to revenge his brother.

Then anon Sir Ector beat on the basin as he were wood, and then he gave his horse drink at the ford, and there came a knight behind him and bade him come out of the water and make him ready; and Sir Ector anon turned him shortly, and in feuter cast his spear, and smote the other knight a great buffet that his horse turned twice about. This was well done, said the strong knight, and knightly thou hast stricken me; and therewith he rushed his horse on Sir Ector, and cleight him under his right arm, and bare him clean out of the saddle, and rode with him away into his own hall, and threw him down in midst of the floor. The name of this knight was Sir Turquine. Then he said unto Sir Ector, For thou hast done this day more unto me than any knight did these twelve years, now will I grant thee thy life, so thou wilt be sworn to be my prisoner all thy life days. Nay, said Sir Ector, that will I never promise thee, but that I will do mine advantage. That me repenteth, said Sir Turquine. And then he gart to unarm him, and beat him with thorns all naked, and sithen put him down in a deep dungeon, where he knew many of his fellows. But when Sir Ector saw Sir Lionel, then made he great sorrow. Alas, brother, said Sir Ector, where is my brother Sir Launcelot? Fair brother, I left him asleep when that I from him yode, under an apple-tree, and what is become of him I cannot tell you. Alas, said the knights, but Sir Launcelot help us we may never be delivered, for we know now no knight that is able to match our master Turquine.

CHAPTER III

*How four queens found Launcelot sleeping, and how by
enchantment he was taken and led into a castle.*

Now leave we these knights prisoners, and speak we of Sir Launcelot
du Lake that lieth under the apple-tree sleeping. Even about the
noon there came by him four queens of great estate; and, for the heat
should not annoy them, there rode four knights about them, and bare
a cloth of green silk on four spears, betwixt them and the sun, and the
queens rode on four white mules. Thus as they rode they heard by
them a great horse grimly neigh, then were they ware of a sleeping
knight, that lay all armed under an apple-tree; anon as these queens
looked on his face, they knew it was Sir Launcelot. Then they began
for to strive for that knight, everych one said they would have him to
her love. We shall not strive, said Morgan le Fay, that was King
Arthur's sister, I shall put an enchantment upon him that he shall not
awake in six hours, and then I will lead him away unto my castle, and
when he is surely within my hold, I shall take the enchantment from
him, and then let him choose which of us he will have unto
paramour.

So this enchantment was cast upon Sir Launcelot, and then they
laid him upon his shield, and bare him so on horseback betwixt two
knights, and brought him unto the castle Chariot, and there they laid
him in a chamber cold, and at night they sent unto him a fair damosel
with his supper ready dight. By that the enchantment was past, and
when she came she saluted him, and asked him what cheer. I cannot
say, fair damosel, said Sir Launcelot, for I wot not how I came into
this castle but it be by an enchantment. Sir, said she, ye must make
good cheer, and if ye be such a knight as it is said ye be, I shall tell you
more to-morn by prime of the day. Gramercy, fair damosel, said Sir
Launcelot, of your good will I require you. And so she departed. And
there he lay all that night without comfort of anybody. And on the
morn early came these four queens, passingly well beseen, all they
bidding him good morn, and he them again.

Sir knight, the four queens said, thou must understand thou art our prisoner, and we here know thee well that thou art Sir Launcelot du Lake, King Ban's son, and because we understand your worthiness, that thou art the noblest knight living, and as we know well there can no lady have thy love but one, and that is Queen Guenever, and now thou shalt lose her for ever, and she thee, and therefore thee behoveth now to choose one of us four. I am the Queen Morgan le Fay, queen of the land of Gore, and here is the queen of Northgalis, and the queen of Eastland, and the queen of the Out Isles; now choose one of us which thou wilt have to thy paramour, for thou mayest not choose or else in this prison to die. This is an hard case, said Sir Launcelot, that either I must die or else choose one of you, yet had I liefer to die in this prison with worship, than to have one of you to my paramour maugre my head. And therefore ye be answered, I will none of you, for ye be false enchantresses, and as for my lady, Dame Guenever, were I at my liberty as I was, I would prove it on you or on yours, that she is the truest lady unto her lord living. Well, said the queens, is this your answer, that ye will refuse us. Yea, on my life, said Sir Launcelot, refused ye be of me. So they departed and left him there alone that made great sorrow.

CHAPTER IV

How Sir Launcelot was delivered by the mean of a damosel.

Right so at the noon came the damosel unto him with his dinner, and asked him what cheer. Truly, fair damosel, said Sir Launcelot, in my life days never so ill. Sir, she said, that me repenteth, but an ye will be ruled by me, I shall help you out of this distress, and ye shall have no shame nor villainy, so that ye hold me a promise. Fair damosel, I will grant you, and sore I am of these queen-sorceresses afeard, for they have destroyed many a good knight. Sir, said she, that is sooth, and for the renown and bounty that they hear of you they would have your love, and Sir, they say, your name is Sir Launcelot du Lake, the flower of knights, and they be passing wroth with you that ye have refused them. But Sir, an ye would promise me to help my father on Tuesday next coming, that hath made a tournament betwixt him and the King of Northgalis – for the last Tuesday past my father lost the field through three knights of Arthur's court – an ye will be there on Tuesday next coming, and help my father, to-morn or prime, by the grace of God, I shall deliver you clean. Fair maiden, said Sir Launcelot, tell me what is your father's name, and then shall I give you an answer. Sir knight, she said, my father is King Bagdemagus, that was foul rebuked at the last tournament. I know your father well, said Sir Launcelot, for a noble king and a good knight, and by the faith of my body, ye shall have my body ready to do your father and you service at that day. Sir, she said, gramercy, and to-morn await ye be ready betimes, and I shall be she that shall deliver you and take you your armour and your horse, shield and spear, and hereby, within this ten mile, is an abbey of white monks, there I pray you that ye me abide, and thither shall I bring my father unto you. All this shall be done, said Sir Launcelot, as I am true knight.

And so she departed, and came on the morn early, and found him ready; then she brought him out of twelve locks, and brought him unto his armour, and when he was clean armed, she brought him until his own horse, and lightly he saddled him and took a great spear in his hand, and so rode forth, and said, Fair damosel, I shall not fail you, by the grace of God. And so he rode into a great forest all that day, and never could find no highway, and so the night fell on him, and then was he ware in a slade, of a pavilion of red sendal. By my faith, said Sir Launcelot, in that pavilion will I lodge all this night, and so there he alighted down, and tied his horse to the pavilion, and there he unarmed him, and there he found a bed, and laid him therein and fell asleep sadly.

CHAPTER V

*How a knight found Sir Launcelot lying in his leman's bed,
and how Sir Launcelot fought with the knight.*

Then within an hour there came the knight to whom the pavilion ought, and he weened that his leman had lain in that bed, and so he laid him down beside Sir Launcelot, and took him in his arms and began to kiss him. And when Sir Launcelot felt a rough beard kissing him, he started out of the bed lightly, and the other knight after him, and either of them gat their swords in their hands, and out at the pavilion door went the knight of the pavilion, and Sir Launcelot followed him, and there by a little slake Sir Launcelot wounded him sore, nigh unto the death. And then he yielded him unto Sir Launcelot, and so he granted him, so that he would tell him why he came into the bed. Sir, said the knight, the pavilion is mine own, and there this night I had assigned my lady to have slept with me, and now I am likely to die of this wound. That me repenteth, said Launcelot, of your hurt, but I was adread of treason, for I was late beguiled, and therefore come on your way into your pavilion and take your rest, and as I suppose I shall staunch your blood. And so they went both into the pavilion, and anon Sir Launcelot staunched his blood.

Therewithal came the knight's lady, that was a passing fair lady, and when she espied that her lord Belleus was sore wounded, she cried out on Sir Launcelot, and made great dole out of measure. Peace, my lady and my love, said Belleus, for this knight is a good man, and a knight adventurous, and there he told her all the cause how he was wounded; And when that I yielded me unto him, he left me goodly and hath staunched my blood. Sir, said the lady, I require thee tell me what knight ye be, and what is your name? Fair lady, he said, my name is Sir Launcelot du Lake. So me thought ever by your speech, said the lady, for I have seen you oft or this, and I know you better than ye ween. But now an ye would promise me of your courtesy, for the harms that ye have done to me and my Lord Belleus, that when he cometh unto Arthur's court for to cause him to be made knight of the Round Table, for he is a passing good man of arms, and a mighty lord of lands of many out isles.

Fair lady, said Sir Launcelot, let him come unto the court the next high feast, and look that ye come with him, and I shall do my power, an ye prove you doughty of your hands, that ye shall have your desire. So thus within a while, as they thus talked, the night passed, and the day shone, and then Sir Launcelot armed him, and took his horse, and they taught him to the Abbey, and thither he rode within the space of two hours.

CHAPTER VI

*How Sir Launcelot was received of King Bagdemagus'
daughter, and how he made his complaint to her father.*

And soon as Sir Launcelot came within the abbey yard, the daughter
of King Bagdemagus heard a great horse go on the pavement. And
she then arose and yede unto a window, and there she saw Sir
Launcelot, and anon she made men fast to take his horse from him
and let lead him into a stable, and himself was led into a fair chamber,
and unarmed him, and the lady sent him a long gown, and anon she
came herself. And then she made Launcelot passing good cheer, and
she said he was the knight in the world was most welcome to her.
Then in all haste she sent for her father Bagdemagus that was within
twelve mile of that Abbey, and afore even he came, with a fair
fellowship of knights with him. And when the king was alighted off
his horse he yode straight unto Sir Launcelot's chamber and there he
found his daughter, and then the king embraced Sir Launcelot in his
arms, and either made other good cheer.

Anon Sir Launcelot made his complaint unto the king how he was
betrayed, and how his brother Sir Lionel was departed from him he
wist not where, and how his daughter had delivered him out of
prison; Therefore while I live I shall do her service and all her kindred.
Then am I sure of your help, said the king, on Tuesday next coming.
Yea, sir, said Sir Launcelot, I shall not fail you, for so I have promised
my lady your daughter. But, sir, what knights be they of my lord
Arthur's that were with the King of Northgalis? And the king said it
was Sir Mador de la Porte, and Sir Mordred and Sir Gahalantine that
all for-fared my knights, for against them three I nor my knights might
bear no strength. Sir, said Sir Launcelot, as I hear say that the
tournament shall be here within this three mile of this abbey, ye shall
send unto me three knights of yours, such as ye trust, and look that the
three knights have all white shields, and I also, and no painture on the
shields, and we four will come out of a little wood in midst of both
parties, and we shall fall in the front of our enemies and grieve them
that we may; and thus shall I not be known what knight I am.

So they took their rest that night, and this was on the Sunday, and
so the king departed, and sent unto Sir Launcelot three knights with
the four white shields. And on the Tuesday they lodged them in a
little leaved wood beside there the tournament should be. And there
were scaffolds and holes that lords and ladies might behold and to give
the prize. Then came into the field the King of Northgalis with eight
score helms. And then the three knights of Arthur's stood by
themselves. Then came into the field King Bagdemagus with four
score of helms. And then they feutred their spears, and came together
with a great dash, and there were slain of knights at the first recounter
twelve of King Bagdemagus' party, and six of the King of Northgalis'
party, and King Bagdemagus' party was far set aback.

CHAPTER VII

*How Sir Launcelot behaved him in a tournament, and how
he met with Sir Turquine leading Sir Gaheris.*

With that came Sir Launcelot du Lake, and he thrust in with his spear
in the thickest of the press, and there he smote down with one spear
five knights, and of four of them he brake their backs. And in that
throng he smote down the King of Northgalis, and brake his thigh in
that fall. All this doing of Sir Launcelot saw the three knights of
Arthur's. Yonder is a shrewd guest, said Sir Mador de la Porte,
therefore have here once at him. So they encountered, and Sir
Launcelot bare him down horse and man, so that his shoulder went
out of lith. Now befalleth it to me to joust, said Mordred, for Sir
Mador hath a sore fall. Sir Launcelot was ware of him, and gat a great
spear in his hand, and met him, and Sir Mordred brake a spear upon
him, and Sir Launcelot gave him such a buffet that the arson of his
saddle brake, and so he flew over his horse's tail, that his helm butted
into the earth a foot and more, that nigh his neck was broken, and
there he lay long in a swoon.

Then came in Sir Gahalantine with a great spear and Launcelot
against him, with all their strength that they might drive, that both
their spears to-brast even to their hands, and then they flang out with
their swords and gave many a grim stroke. Then was Sir Launcelot

wroth out of measure, and then he smote Sir Gahalantine on the helm that his nose brast out on blood, and ears and mouth both, and therewith his head hung low. And therewith his horse ran away with him, and he fell down to the earth. Anon therewithal Sir Launcelot gat a great spear in his hand, and or ever that great spear brake, he bare down to the earth sixteen knights, some horse and man, and some the man and not the horse, and there was none but that he hit surely, he bare none arms that day. And then he gat another great spear, and smote down twelve knights, and the most part of them never throve after. And then the knights of the King of Northgalis would joust no more. And there the gree was given to King Bagdemagus.

So either party departed unto his own place, and Sir Launcelot rode forth with King Bagdemagus unto his castle, and there he had passing good cheer both with the king and with his daughter, and they proffered him great gifts. And on the morn he took his leave, and told the king that he would go and seek his brother Sir Lionel, that went from him when that he slept, so he took his horse, and betaught them all to God. And there he said unto the king's daughter, If ye have need any time of my service I pray you let me have knowledge, and I shall not fail you as I am true knight. And so Sir Launcelot departed, and by adventure he came into the same forest there he was taken sleeping. And in the midst of a highway he met a damosel riding on a white palfrey, and there either saluted other. Fair damosel, said Sir Launcelot, know ye in this country any adventures? Sir knight, said that damosel, here are adventures near hand, an thou durst prove them. Why should I not prove adventures? said Sir Launcelot, for that cause come I hither. Well, said she, thou seemest well to be a good knight, and if thou dare meet with a good knight, I shall bring thee where is the best knight, and the mightiest that ever thou found, so thou wilt tell me what is thy name, and what knight thou art. Damosel, as for to tell thee my name I take no great force; truly my name is Sir Launcelot du Lake. Sir, thou beseemest well, here be adventures by that fall for thee, for hereby dwelleth a knight that will not be overmatched for no man I know but ye overmatch him, and his name is Sir Turquine. And, as I understand, he hath in his prison, of Arthur's court, good knights three score and four, that he hath won with his own hands. But when ye have done that journey ye shall promise me as ye are a true knight for to go with me, and to help me and other damosels that are distressed daily with a false knight. All your intent, damosel, and desire I will fulfil, so ye will bring me unto this knight. Now, fair knight, come on your way; and so she brought him unto the ford and the tree where hung the basin.

So Sir Launcelot let his horse drink, and then he beat on the basin with the butt of his spear so hard with all his might till the bottom fell out, and long he did so, but he saw nothing. Then he rode endlong the gates of that manor nigh half-an-hour. And then was he ware of a great knight that drove an horse afore him, and overthwart the horse there lay an armed knight bound. And ever as they came near and near, Sir Launcelot thought he should know him. Then Sir Launcelot was ware that it was Sir Gaheris, Gawaine's brother, a knight of the Table Round. Now, fair damosel, said Sir Launcelot, I see yonder cometh a knight fast bounden that is a fellow of mine, and brother he is unto Sir Gawaine. And at the first beginning I promise you, by the leave of God, to rescue that knight; but if his master sit better in the saddle I shall deliver all the prisoners that he hath out of danger, for I am sure he hath two brethren of mine prisoners with him. By that time that either had seen other, they gripped their spears unto them. Now, fair knight, said Sir Launcelot, put that wounded knight off the horse, and let him rest awhile, and let us two prove our strengths; for as it is informed me, thou doest and hast done great despite and shame unto knights of the Round Table, and therefore now defend thee. An thou be of the Table Round, said Turquine, I defy thee and all thy fellowship. That is overmuch said, said Sir Launcelot.

CHAPTER VIII

How Sir Launcelot and Sir Turquine fought together.

And then they put their spears in the rests, and came together with their horses as fast as they might run, and either smote other in midst of their shields, that both their horses' backs brast under them, and the knights were both stonied. And as soon as they might avoid their horses, they took their shields afore them, and drew out their swords, and came together eagerly, and either gave other many strong strokes, for there might neither shields nor harness hold their strokes. And so within a while they had both grimly wounds, and bled passing grievously. Thus they fared two hours or more trasing and rasing either other, where they might hit any bare place.

Then at the last they were breathless both, and stood leaning on their swords. Now fellow, said Sir Turquine, hold thy hand a while, and tell me what I shall ask thee. Say on. Then Turquine said, Thou art the biggest man that ever I met withal, and the best breathed, and like one knight that I hate above all other knights; so be it that thou be not he I will lightly accord with thee, and for thy love I will deliver all the prisoners that I have, that is three score and four, so thou wilt tell me thy name. And thou and I we will be fellows together, and never to fail thee while that I live. It is well said, said Sir Launcelot, but sithen it is so that I may have thy friendship, what knight is he that thou so hatest above all other? Faithfully, said Sir Turquine, his name is Sir Launcelot du Lake, for he slew my brother, Sir Carados, at the dolorous tower, that was one of the best knights alive; and therefore him I except of all knights, for may I once meet with him, the one of us shall make an end of other, I make mine avow. And for Sir Launcelot's sake I have slain an hundred good knights, and as many I have maimed all utterly that they might never after help themselves, and many have died in prison, and yet have I three score and four, and all shall be delivered so thou wilt tell me thy name, so be it that thou be not Sir Launcelot.

Now, see I well, said Sir Launcelot, that such a man I might be, I might have peace, and such a man I might be, that there should be war mortal betwixt us. And now, sir knight, at thy request I will that thou wit and know that I am Launcelot du Lake, King Ban's son of Benwick, and very knight of the Table Round. And now I defy thee, and do thy best. Ah, said Turquine, Launcelot, thou art unto me most welcome that ever was knight, for we shall never depart till the one of us be dead. Then they hurtled together as two wild bulls rushing and lashing with their shields and swords, that sometime they fell both over their noses. Thus they fought still two hours and more, and never would have rest, and Sir Turquine gave Sir Launcelot many wounds that all the ground thereas they fought was all bespeckled with blood.

CHAPTER IX

*How Sir Turquine was slain, and how Sir Launcelot bade
Sir Gaheris deliver all the prisoners.*

Then at the last Sir Turquine waxed faint, and gave somewhat aback,
and bare his shield low for weariness. That espied Sir Launcelot, and
leapt upon him fiercely and gat him by the beaver of his helmet, and
plucked him down on his knees, and anon he raced off his helm, and
smote his neck in sunder. And when Sir Launcelot had done this, he
yode unto the damosel and said, Damosel, I am ready to go with you
where ye will have me, but I have no horse. Fair sir, said she, take this
wounded knight's horse and send him into this manor, and command him to deliver all the prisoners. So Sir Launcelot went unto
Gaheris, and prayed him not to be aggrieved for to lend him his
horse. Nay, fair lord, said Gaheris, I will that ye take my horse at your
own commandment, for ye have both saved me and my horse, and
this day I say ye are the best knight in the world, for ye have slain this
day in my sight the mightiest man and the best knight except you that
ever I saw, and, fair sir, said Gaheris, I pray you tell me your name.
Sir, my name is Sir Launcelot du Lake, that ought to help you of right
for King Arthur's sake, and in especial for my lord Sir Gawaine's sake,
your own dear brother; and when that ye come within yonder
manor, I am sure ye shall find there many knights of the Round
Table, for I have seen many of their shields that I know on yonder
tree. There is Kay's shield, and Sir Brandel's shield, and Sir Marhaus'
shield, and Sir Galind's shield, and Sir Brian de Listnois' shield, and
Sir Aliduke's shield, with many more that I am not now advised of,
and also my two brethren's shields, Sir Ector de Maris and Sir Lionel;
wherefore I pray you greet them all from me, and say that I bid them
take such stuff there as they find, and that in any wise my brethren go
unto the court and abide me there till that I come, for by the feast of
Pentecost I cast me to be there, for as at this time I must ride with this
damosel for to save my promise.

And so he departed from Gaheris, and Gaheris yede in to the
manor, and there he found a yeoman porter keeping there many

keys. Anon withal Sir Gaheris threw the porter unto the ground and took the keys from him, and hastily he opened the prison door, and there he let out all the prisoners, and every man loosed other of their bonds. And when they saw Sir Gaheris, all they thanked him, for they weened that he was wounded. Not so, said Gaheris, it was Launcelot that slew him worshipfully with his own hands. I saw it with mine own eyes. And he greeteth you all well, and prayeth you to haste you to the court; and as unto Sir Lionel and Ector de Maris he prayeth you to abide him at the court. That shall we not do, says his brethren, we will find him an we may live. So shall I, said Sir Kay, find him or I come at the court, as I am true knight.

Then all those knights sought the house thereas the armour was, and then they armed them, and every knight found his own horse, and all that ever longed unto him. And when this was done, there came a forester with four horses laden with fat venison. Anon, Sir Kay said, Here is good meat for us for one meal, for we had not many a day no good repast. And so that venison was roasted, baken, and sodden, and so after supper some abode there all night, but Sir Lionel and Ector de Maris and Sir Kay rode after Sir Launcelot to find him if they might.

CHAPTER X

How Sir Launcelot rode with a damosel and slew a knight
that distressed all ladies and also a villain that kept a bridge.

Now turn we unto Sir Launcelot, that rode with the damosel in a fair highway. Sir, said the damosel, here by this way haunteth a knight that distressed all ladies and gentlewomen, and at the least he robbeth them or lieth by them. What, said Sir Launcelot, is he a thief and a knight and a ravisher of women? he doth shame unto the order of knighthood, and contrary unto his oath; it is pity that he liveth. But, fair damosel, ye shall ride on afore, yourself, and I will keep myself in covert, and if that he trouble you or distress you I shall be your rescue and learn him to be ruled as a knight.

So the maid rode on by the way a soft ambling pace, and within a while came out that knight on horseback out of the wood, and his page with him, and there he put the damosel from her horse, and then she cried. With that came Launcelot as fast as he might till he came to that knight, saying, O thou false knight and traitor unto knighthood, who did learn thee to distress ladies and gentlewomen? When the knight saw Sir Launcelot thus rebuking him he answered not, but drew his sword and rode unto Sir Launcelot, and Sir Launcelot threw his spear from him, and drew out his sword, and struck him such a buffet on the helmet that he clave his head and neck unto the throat. Now hast thou thy payment that long thou hast deserved! That is truth, said the damosel, for like as Sir Turquine watched to destroy knights, so did this knight attend to destroy and distress ladies, damosels, and gentlewomen, and his name was Sir Peris de Forest Savage. Now, damosel, said Sir Launcelot, will ye any more service of me? Nay, sir, she said, at this time, but almighty Jesu preserve you wheresomever ye ride or go, for the curteist knight thou art, and meekest unto all ladies and gentlewomen, that now liveth. But one thing, sir knight, methinketh ye lack, ye that are a knight wifeless, that he will not love some maiden or gentlewoman, for I could never hear say that ever ye loved any of no manner degree, and that is great pity; but it is noised that ye love Queen Guenever, and that she hath ordained by enchantment that ye shall never love none other but her, nor none other damosel nor lady shall rejoice you; wherefore many in this land, of high estate and low, make great sorrow.

Fair damosel, said Sir Launcelot, I may not warn people to speak of me what it pleaseth them; but for to be a wedded man, I think it not; for then I must couch with her, and leave arms and tournaments, battles, and adventures; and as for to say for to take my pleasaunce with paramours, that will I refuse in principal for dread of God; for knights that be adventurous or lecherous shall not be happy nor fortunate unto the wars, for other they shall be overcome with a simpler knight than they be themselves, other else they shall by unhap and their cursedness slay better men than they be themselves. And so who that useth paramours shall be unhappy, and all thing is unhappy that is about them.

And so Sir Launcelot and she departed. And then he rode in a deep forest two days and more, and had strait lodging. So on the third day he rode over a long bridge, and there stert upon him suddenly a passing foul churl, and he smote his horse on the nose that he turned about, and asked him why he rode over that bridge without his licence. Why should I not ride this way? said Sir Launcelot, I may not ride beside. Thou shalt not choose, said the churl, and lashed at him with a great club shod with iron. Then Sir Launcelot drew his sword and put the stroke aback, and clave his head unto the paps. At the end of the bridge was a fair village, and all the people, men and women, cried on Sir Launcelot, and said, A worse deed didst thou never for thyself, for thou hast slain the chief porter of our castle. Sir Launcelot let them say what they would, and straight he went into the castle; and when he came into the castle he alighted, and tied his horse to a ring on the wall and there he saw a fair green court, and thither he dressed him, for there him thought was a fair place to fight in. So he looked about, and saw much people in doors and windows that said, Fair knight, thou art unhappy.

CHAPTER XI

How Sir Launcelot slew two giants, and made a castle free.

Anon withal came there upon him two great giants, well armed all save the heads, with two horrible clubs in their hands. Sir Launcelot put his shield afore him and put the stroke away of the one giant, and with his sword he clave his head asunder. When his fellow saw that, he ran away as he were wood, for fear of the horrible strokes, and Launcelot after him with all his might, and smote him on the shoulder, and clave him to the navel. Then Sir Launcelot went into the hall, and there came afore him three score ladies and damosels, and all kneeled unto him, and thanked God and him of their deliverance; For sir, said they, the most party of us have been here this seven year their prisoners, and we have worked all manner of silk works for our meat, and we are all great gentlewomen born; and blessed be the time, knight, that ever thou be born, for thou hast done the most worship that ever did knight in this world, that will we bear record, and we all pray you to tell us your name, that we may tell our friends who delivered us out of prison. Fair damosel, he said, my name is Sir Launcelot du Lake. Ah, sir, said they all, well mayest thou be he, for else save yourself, as we deemed, there might never knight have the better of these two giants; for many fair knights have

assayed it, and here have ended, and many times have we wished after
you, and these two giants dread never knight but you. Now may ye
say, said Sir Launcelot, unto your friends how and who hath
delivered you, and greet them all from me, and if that I come in any
of your marches, show me such cheer as ye have cause, and what
treasure that there in this castle is I give it you for a reward for your
grievance, and the lord that is owner of this castle I would he
received it as is right. Fair sir, said they, the name of this castle is
Tintagil, and a duke ought it sometime that had wedded fair Igraine,
and after wedded her Uther Pendragon, and gat on her Arthur. Well,
said Sir Launcelot, I understand to whom this castle longeth; and so
he departed from them, and betaught them unto God.

And then he mounted upon his horse, and rode into many strange
and wild countries, and through many waters and valleys, and evil
was he lodged. And at the last by fortune him happened, against a
night, to come to a fair courtelage, and therein he found an old
gentlewoman that lodged him with good will, and there he had good
cheer for him and his horse. And when time was, his host brought
him into a fair garret, over the gate, to his bed. There Sir Launcelot
unarmed him, and set his harness by him, and went to bed, and anon
he fell asleep. So, soon after, there came one on horseback, and
knocked at the gate in great haste, and when Sir Launcelot heard this,
he arose up and looked out at the window, and saw by the moonlight
three knights came riding after that one man, and all three lashed on
him at once with swords, and that one knight turned on them
knightly again, and defended him. Truly, said Sir Launcelot, yonder
one knight shall I help, for it were shame for me to see three knights
on one, and if he be slain I am partner of his death; and therewith he
took his harness, and went out at a window by a sheet down to the
four knights, and then Sir Launcelot said on high, Turn you knights
unto me, and leave your fighting with that knight. And then they all
three left Sir Kay, and turned unto Sir Launcelot, and there began
great battle, for they alighted all three, and struck many great strokes
at Sir Launcelot, and assailed him on every side. Then Sir Kay dressed
him for to have holpen Sir Launcelot. Nay, sir, said he, I will none of
your help; therefore as ye will have my help, let me alone with them.
Sir Kay, for the pleasure of the knight, suffered him for to do his will,
and so stood aside. And then anon within six strokes, Sir Launcelot
had stricken them to the earth.

And then they all three cried: Sir knight, we yield us unto you as a man of might makeless. As to that, said Sir Launcelot, I will not take your yielding unto me. But so that ye will yield you unto Sir Kay the Seneschal, on that covenant I will save your lives, and else not. Fair knight, said they, that were we loath to do; for as for Sir Kay, we chased him hither, and had overcome him had not ye been, therefore to yield us unto him it were no reason. Well, as to that, said Launcelot, advise you well, for ye may choose whether ye will die or live, for an ye be yolden it shall be unto Sir Kay. Fair knight, then they said, in saving of our lives we will do as thou commandest us. Then shall ye, said Sir Launcelot, on Whitsunday next coming, go unto the court of King Arthur, and there shall ye yield you unto Queen Guenever, and put you all three in her grace and mercy, and say that Sir Kay sent you thither to be her prisoners. Sir, they said, it shall be done by the faith of our bodies, an we be living, and there they swore every knight upon his sword. And so Sir Launcelot suffered them so to depart. And then Sir Launcelot knocked at the gate with the pommel of his sword, and with that came his host, and in they entered Sir Kay and he. Sir, said his host, I weened ye had been in your bed. So I was, said Sir Launcelot, but I rose and leapt out at my window for to help an old fellow of mine. And so when they came nigh the light, Sir Kay knew well that it was Sir Launcelot, and therewith he kneeled down and thanked him of all his kindness that he had holpen him twice from the death. Sir, he said, I have nothing done but that me ought for to do, and ye are welcome, and here shall ye repose you and take your rest.

So when Sir Kay was unarmed, he asked after meat; so there was meat fetched him, and he ate strongly. And when he had supped they went to their beds and were lodged together in one bed. On the morn Sir Launcelot arose early, and left Sir Kay sleeping, and Sir Launcelot took Sir Kay's armour and his shield, and armed him, and so he went to the stable, and took his horse, and took his leave of his host, and so he departed. Then soon after arose Sir Kay and missed Sir Launcelot. And then he espied that he had his armour and his horse. Now by my faith I know well that he will grieve some of the court of King Arthur; for on him knights will be bold, and deem that it is I, and that will beguile them. And because of his armour and shield I am sure I shall ride in peace. And then soon after departed Sir Kay and thanked his host.

CHAPTER XII

How Sir Launcelot rode disguised in Sir Kay's harness, and how he smote down a knight.

Now turn we unto Sir Launcelot that had ridden long in a great forest, and at the last he came into a low country, full of fair rivers and meadows. And afore him he saw a long bridge, and three pavilions stood thereon, of silk and sendal of divers hue. And without the pavilions hung three white shields on truncheons of spears, and great long spears stood upright by the pavilions, and at every pavilion's door stood three fresh squires, and so Sir Launcelot passed by them and spake no word. When he was passed the three knights said them that it was the proud Kay; He weeneth no knight so good as he, and the contrary is ofttime proved. By my faith, said one of the knights, his name was Sir Gaunter, I will ride after him and assay him for all his pride, and ye may behold how that I speed. So this knight, Sir Gaunter, armed him, and hung his shield upon his shoulder, and mounted upon a great horse, and gat his spear in his hand, and walloped after Sir Launcelot. And when he came nigh him, he cried, Abide, thou proud knight Sir Kay, for thou shalt not pass quit. So Sir Launcelot turned him, and either feutred their spears, and came together with all their mights, and Sir Gaunter's spear brake, but Sir Launcelot smote him down horse and man. And when Sir Gaunter was at the earth his brethren said each one to other, Yonder knight is not Sir Kay, for he is bigger than he. I dare lay my head, said Sir Gilmere, yonder knight hath slain Sir Kay and hath taken his horse and his harness. Whether it be so or no, said Sir Raynold, the third brother, let us now go mount upon our horses and rescue our brother Sir Gaunter, upon pain of death. We all shall have work enough to match that knight, for ever meseemeth by his person it is Sir Launcelot, or Sir Tristram, or Sir Pelleas, the good knight.

Then anon they took their horses and overtook Sir Launcelot, and Sir Gilmere put forth his spear, and ran to Sir Launcelot, and Sir Launcelot smote him down that he lay in a swoon. Sir knight, said Sir Raynold, thou art a strong man, and as I suppose thou hast slain my two brethren, for the which raseth my heart sore against thee, and if I might with my worship I would not have ado with you, but needs I must take part as they do, and therefore, knight, he said, keep thyself. And so they hurtled together with all their mights, and all to-shivered both their spears. And then they drew their swords and lashed together eagerly. Anon therewith arose Sir Gaunter, and came unto his brother Sir Gilmere, and bade him, Arise, and help we our brother Sir Raynold, that yonder marvellously matched yonder good knight. Therewithal, they leapt on their horses and hurtled unto Sir Launcelot.

And when he saw them come he smote a sore stroke unto Sir Raynold, that he fell off his horse to the ground, and then he struck to the other two brethren, and at two strokes he struck them down to the earth. With that Sir Raynold began to start up with his head all bloody, and came straight unto Sir Launcelot. Now let be, said Sir Launcelot, I was not far from thee when thou wert made knight, Sir Raynold, and also I know thou art a good knight, and loath I were to slay thee. Gramercy, said Sir Raynold, as for your goodness; and I dare say as for me and my brethren, we will not be loath to yield us unto you, with that we knew your name, for well we know ye are not Sir Kay. As for that be it as it be may, for ye shall yield you unto dame Guenever, and look that ye be with her on Whitsunday, and yield you unto her as prisoners, and say that Sir Kay sent you unto her. Then they swore it should be done, and so passed forth Sir Launcelot, and each one of the brethren holp other as well as they might.

CHAPTER XIII

How Sir Launcelot jousted against four knights of the Round Table and overthrew them.

So Sir Launcelot rode into a deep forest, and thereby in a slade, he saw four knights hoving under an oak, and they were of Arthur's court, one was Sir Sagramour le Desirous, and Ector de Maris, and Sir Gawaine, and Sir Uwaine. Anon as these four knights had espied Sir Launcelot, they weened by his arms it had been Sir Kay. Now by my faith, said Sir Sagramour, I will prove Sir Kay's might, and gat his spear in his hand, and came toward Sir Launcelot. Therewith Sir Launcelot was ware and knew him well, and feutred his spear against him, and smote Sir Sagramour so sore that horse and man fell both to the earth. Lo, my fellows, said he, yonder ye may see what a buffet he hath; that knight is much bigger than ever was Sir Kay. Now shall ye see what I may do to him. So Sir Ector gat his spear in his hand and walloped toward Sir Launcelot, and Sir Launcelot smote him through the shield and shoulder, that man and horse went to the earth, and ever his spear held.

By my faith, said Sir Uwaine, yonder is a strong knight, and I am sure he hath slain Sir Kay; and I see by his great strength it will be hard to match him. And therewithal, Sir Uwaine gat his spear in his hand and rode toward Sir Launcelot, and Sir Launcelot knew him well, and so he met him on the plain, and gave him such a buffet that he was astonied, that long he wist not where he was. Now see I well, said Sir Gawaine, I must encounter with that knight. Then he dressed his shield and gat a good spear in his hand, and Sir Launcelot knew him well; and then they let run their horses with all their mights, and either knight smote other in midst of the shield. But Sir Gawaine's spear to-brast, and Sir Launcelot charged so sore upon him that his horse reversed up-so-down. And much sorrow had Sir Gawaine to avoid his horse, and so Sir Launcelot passed on a pace and smiled, and said, God give him joy that this spear made, for there came never a better in my hand.

Then the four knights went each one to other and comforted each other. What say ye by this guest? said Sir Gawaine, that one spear hath felled us all four. We commend him unto the devil, they said all, for he is a man of great might. Ye may well say it, said Sir Gawaine, that he is a man of might, for I dare lay my head it is Sir Launcelot, I know it by his riding. Let him go, said Sir Gawaine, for when we come to the court then shall we wit; and then had they much sorrow to get their horses again.

CHAPTER XIV

*How Sir Launcelot followed a brachet into a castle, where he
found a dead knight, and how he after was required of a
damosel to heal her brother.*

Now leave we there and speak of Sir Launcelot that rode a great
while in a deep forest, where he saw a black brachet, seeking in
manner as it had been in the feute of an hurt deer. And therewith he
rode after the brachet, and he saw lie on the ground a large feute of
blood. And then Sir Launcelot rode after. And ever the brachet
looked behind her, and so she went through a great marsh, and ever
Sir Launcelot followed. And then was he ware of an old manor, and
thither ran the brachet, and so over the bridge. So Sir Launcelot rode
over that bridge that was old and feeble; and when he came in midst
of a great hall, there he saw lie a dead knight that was a seemly man,
and that brachet licked his wounds. And therewithal came out a lady
weeping and wringing her hands; and then she said, O knight, too
much sorrow hast thou brought me. Why say ye so? said Sir
Launcelot, I did never this knight no harm, for hither by feute of
blood this brachet brought me; and therefore, fair lady, be not
displeased with me, for I am full sore aggrieved of your grievance.
Truly, sir, she said, I trow it be not ye that hath slain my husband, for
he that did that deed is sore wounded, and he is never likely to
recover, that shall I ensure him. What was your husband's name? said
Sir Launcelot. Sir, said she, his name was called Sir Gilbert the
Bastard, one of the best knights of the world, and he that hath slain
him I know not his name. Now God send you better comfort, said
Sir Launcelot; and so he departed and went into the forest again, and
there he met with a damosel, the which knew him well, and she said
aloud, Well be ye found, my lord; and now I require thee, on thy
knighthood, help my brother that is sore wounded, and never
stinteth bleeding; for this day he fought with Sir Gilbert the Bastard
and slew him in plain battle, and there was my brother sore
wounded, and there is a lady a sorceress that dwelleth in a castle here
beside, and this day she told me my brother's wounds should never

be whole till I could find a knight that would go into the Chapel
Perilous, and there he should find a sword and a bloody cloth that the
wounded knight was lapped in, and a piece of that cloth and sword
should heal my brother's wounds, so that his wounds were searched
with the sword and the cloth. This is a marvellous thing, said Sir
Launcelot, but what is your brother's name? Sir, she said, his name
was Sir Meliot de Logres. That me repenteth, said Sir Launcelot, for
he is a fellow of the Table Round, and to his help I will do my
power. Then, sir, said she, follow even this highway, and it will bring
you unto the Chapel Perilous; and here I shall abide till God send you
here again, and, but you speed, I know no knight living that may
achieve that adventure.

CHAPTER XV

*How Sir Launcelot came into the Chapel Perilous and gat
there of a dead corpse a piece of the cloth and a sword.*

Right so Sir Launcelot departed, and when he came unto the Chapel
Perilous he alighted down, and tied his horse unto a little gate. And as
soon as he was within the churchyard he saw on the front of the
chapel many fair rich shields turned up-so-down, and many of the
shields Sir Launcelot had seen knights bear beforehand. With that he
saw by him there stand a thirty great knights, more by a yard than any
man that ever he had seen, and all those grinned and gnashed at Sir
Launcelot. And when he saw their countenance he dreaded him sore,
and so put his shield afore him, and took his sword ready in his hand
ready unto battle, and they were all armed in black harness ready with
their shields and their swords drawn. And when Sir Launcelot would
have gone throughout them, they scattered on every side of him, and
gave him the way, and therewith he waxed all bold, and entered into
the chapel, and then he saw no light but a dim lamp burning, and
then was he ware of a corpse hilled with a cloth of silk. Then Sir
Launcelot stooped down, and cut a piece away of that cloth, and then
it fared under him as the earth had quaked a little; therewithal he
feared. And then he saw a fair sword lie by the dead knight, and that
he gat in his hand and hied him out of the chapel.

Anon as ever he was in the chapel yard all the knights spake to him with a grimly voice, and said, Knight, Sir Launcelot, lay that sword from thee or else thou shalt die. Whether that I live or die, said Sir Launcelot, with no great word get ye it again, therefore fight for it an ye list. Then right so he passed throughout them, and beyond the chapel yard there met him a fair damosel, and said, Sir Launcelot, leave that sword behind thee, or thou wilt die for it. I leave it not, said Sir Launcelot, for no treaties. No, said she, an thou didst leave that sword, Queen Guenever should thou never see. Then were I a fool an I would leave this sword, said Launcelot. Now, gentle knight, said the damosel, I require thee to kiss me but once. Nay, said Sir Launcelot, that God me forbid. Well, sir, said she, an thou hadst kissed me thy life days had been done, but now, alas, she said, I have lost all my labour, for I ordained this chapel for thy sake, and for Sir Gawaine. And once I had Sir Gawaine within me, and at that time he fought with that knight that lieth there dead in yonder chapel, Sir Gilbert the Bastard; and at that time he smote the left hand off of Sir Gilbert the Bastard. And, Sir Launcelot, now I tell thee, I have loved thee this seven year, but there may no woman have thy love but Queen Guenever. But sithen I may not rejoice thee to have thy body alive, I had kept no more joy in this world but to have thy body dead. Then would I have balmed it and served it, and so have kept it my life days, and daily I should have clipped thee, and kissed thee, in despite of Queen Guenever. Ye say well, said Sir Launcelot, Jesu preserve me from your subtle crafts. And therewithal he took his horse and so departed from her. And as the book saith, when Sir Launcelot was departed she took such sorrow that she died within a fourteen night, and her name was Hellawes the sorceress, Lady of the Castle Nigramous.

Anon Sir Launcelot met with the damosel, Sir Meliot's sister. And when she saw him she clapped her hands, and wept for joy. And then they rode unto a castle thereby where lay Sir Meliot. And anon as Sir Launcelot saw him he knew him, but he was passing pale, as the earth, for bleeding. When Sir Meliot saw Sir Launcelot he kneeled upon his knees and cried on high: O lord Sir Launcelot, help me! Anon Sir Launcelot leapt unto him and touched his wounds with Sir Gilbert's sword. And then he wiped his wounds with a part of the bloody cloth that Sir Gilbert was wrapped in, and anon an wholer man in his life was he never. And then there was great joy between them, and they made Sir Launcelot all the cheer that they might, and so on the morn Sir Launcelot took his leave, and bade Sir Meliot hie him to the court of my lord Arthur, for it draweth nigh to the Feast of Pentecost, and there by the grace of God ye shall find me. And therewith they departed.

CHAPTER XVI

How Sir Launcelot at the request of a lady recovered a falcon, by which he was deceived.

And so Sir Launcelot rode through many strange countries, over marshes and valleys, till by fortune he came to a fair castle, and as he passed beyond the castle him thought he heard two bells ring. And then was he ware of a falcon came flying over his head toward an high elm, and long lunes about her feet, and as she flew unto the elm to take her perch the lunes over-cast about a bough. And when she would have taken her flight she hung by the legs fast; and Sir Launcelot saw how she hung, and beheld the fair falcon perigot, and he was sorry for her.

The meanwhile came a lady out of the castle and cried on high: O Launcelot, Launcelot, as thou art flower of all knights, help me to get my hawk, for an my hawk be lost my lord will destroy me; for I kept the hawk and she slipped from me, and if my lord my husband wit it he is so hasty that he will slay me. What is your lord's name? said Sir Launcelot. Sir, she said, his name is Sir Phelot, a knight that longeth unto the King of Northgalis. Well, fair lady, since that ye know my name, and require me of knighthood to help you, I will do what I may to get your hawk, and yet God knoweth I am an ill climber, and the tree is passing high, and few boughs to help me withal. And therewith Sir Launcelot alighted, and tied his horse to the same tree, and prayed the lady to unarm him. And so when he was unarmed, he put off all his clothes unto his shirt and breech, and with might and force he clomb up to the falcon, and tied the lunes to a great rotten boyshe, and threw the hawk down and it withal.

Anon the lady gat the hawk in her hand; and therewithal came out Sir Phelot out of the groves suddenly, that was her husband, all armed and with his naked sword in his hand, and said: O knight Launcelot, now have I found thee as I would, and stood at the bole of the tree to slay him. Ah, lady, said Sir Launcelot, why have ye betrayed me? She hath done, said Sir Phelot, but as I commanded her, and therefore there nis none other boot but thine hour is come that thou must die. That were shame unto thee, said Sir Launcelot, thou an armed knight to slay a naked man by treason. Thou gettest none other grace, said Sir Phelot, and therefore help thyself an thou canst. Truly, said Sir Launcelot, that shall be thy shame, but since thou wilt do none other, take mine harness with thee, and hang my sword upon a bough that I may get it, and then do thy best to slay me an thou canst. Nay, nay, said Sir Phelot, for I know thee better than thou weenest, therefore thou gettest no weapon, an I may keep you therefrom. Alas, said Sir Launcelot, that ever a knight should die weaponless. And therewith he waited above him and under him, and over his head he saw a rownsepyk, a big bough leafless, and therewith he brake it off by the body. And then he came lower and awaited how his own horse stood, and suddenly he leapt on the further side of the horse, froward the knight. And then Sir Phelot lashed at him eagerly, weening to have slain him. But Sir Launcelot put away the stroke with the rownsepyk, and therewith he smote him on the one side of the head, that he fell down in a swoon to the ground. So then Sir Launcelot took his sword out of his hand, and struck his neck from the body. Then cried the lady, Alas! why hast thou slain my husband? I am not causer, said Sir Launcelot, for with falsehood ye would have had slain me with treason, and now it is fallen on you both. And then she swooned as though she would die. And therewithal Sir Launcelot gat all his armour as well as he might, and put it upon him for dread of more resort, for he dreaded that the knight's castle was so nigh. And so, as soon as he might, he took his horse and departed, and thanked God that he had escaped that adventure.

CHAPTER XVII

How Sir Launcelot overtook a knight which chased his wife
to have slain her, and how he said to him.

So Sir Launcelot rode many wild ways, throughout marches and
many wild ways. And as he rode in a valley he saw a knight chasing a
lady, with a naked sword, to have slain her. And by fortune as this
knight should have slain this lady, she cried on Sir Launcelot and
prayed him to rescue her. When Sir Launcelot saw that mischief, he
took his horse and rode between them, saying, Knight, fie for shame,
why wilt thou slay this lady? thou dost shame unto thee and all
knights. What hast thou to do betwixt me and my wife? said the
knight. I will slay her maugre thy head. That shall ye not, said Sir
Launcelot, for rather we two will have ado together. Sir Launcelot,
said the knight, thou dost not thy part, for this lady hath betrayed me.
It is not so, said the lady, truly he saith wrong on me. And for because
I love and cherish my cousin germain, he is jealous betwixt him and
me; and as I shall answer to God there was never sin betwixt us. But,
sir, said the lady, as thou art called the worshipfullest knight of the
world, I require thee of true knighthood, keep me and save me. For
whatsomever ye say he will slay me, for he is without mercy. Have ye
no doubt, said Launcelot, it shall not lie in his power. Sir, said the
knight, in your sight I will be ruled as ye will have me. And so Sir
Launcelot rode on the one side and she on the other: he had not
ridden but a while, but the knight bade Sir Launcelot turn him and
look behind him, and said, Sir, yonder come men of arms after us
riding. And so Sir Launcelot turned him and thought no treason, and
therewith was the knight and the lady on one side, and suddenly he
swapped off his lady's head.

And when Sir Launcelot had espied him what he had done, he
said, and called him, Traitor, thou hast shamed me for ever. And
suddenly Sir Launcelot alighted off his horse, and pulled out his
sword to slay him, and therewithal he fell flat to the earth, and
gripped Sir Launcelot by the thighs, and cried mercy. Fie on thee,
said Sir Launcelot, thou shameful knight, thou mayest have no

mercy, and therefore arise and fight with me. Nay, said the knight, I will never arise till ye grant me mercy. Now will I proffer thee fair, said Launcelot, I will unarm me unto my shirt, and I will have nothing upon me but my shirt, and my sword and my hand. And if thou canst slay me, quit be thou for ever. Nay, sir, said Pedivere, that will I never. Well, said Sir Launcelot, take this lady and the head, and bear it upon thee, and here shalt thou swear upon my sword, to bear it always upon thy back, and never to rest till thou come to Queen Guenever. Sir, said he, that will I do, by the faith of my body. Now, said Launcelot, tell me what is your name? Sir, my name is Pedivere. In a shameful hour wert thou born, said Launcelot.

So Pedivere departed with the dead lady and the head, and found the queen with King Arthur at Winchester, and there he told all the truth. Sir knight, said the queen, this is an horrible deed and a shameful, and a great rebuke unto Sir Launcelot; but notwithstanding his worship is not known in many divers countries; but this shall I give you in penance, make ye as good shift as ye can, ye shall bear this lady with you on horseback unto the Pope of Rome, and of him receive your penance for your foul deeds; and ye shall never rest one night whereas ye do another; an ye go to any bed the dead body shall lie with you. This oath there he made, and so departed. And as it telleth in the French book, when he came to Rome, the Pope bade him go again unto Queen Guenever, and in Rome was his lady buried by the Pope's commandment. And after this Sir Pedivere fell to great goodness, and was an holy man and an hermit.

CHAPTER XVIII

How Sir Launcelot came to King Arthur's court, and how there were recounted all his noble feats and acts.

Now turn we unto Sir Launcelot du Lake, that came home two days afore the Feast of Pentecost; and the king and all the court were passing fain of his coming. And when Sir Gawaine, Sir Uwaine, Sir Sagramore, Sir Ector de Maris, saw Sir Launcelot in Kay's armour, then they wist well it was he that smote them down all with one spear. Then there was laughing and smiling among them. And ever now and now came all the knights home that Sir Turquine had prisoners, and they all honoured and worshipped Sir Launcelot.

When Sir Gaheris heard them speak, he said, I saw all the battle from the beginning to the ending, and there he told King Arthur all how it was, and how Sir Turquine was the strongest knight that ever he saw except Sir Launcelot: there were many knights bare him record, nigh three score. Then Sir Kay told the king how Sir Launcelot had rescued him when he should have been slain, and how he made the knights yield them to me, and not to him. And there they were all three, and bare record. And by Jesu, said Sir Kay, because Sir Launcelot took my harness and left me his I rode in good peace, and no man would have ado with me.

Anon therewithal there came the three knights that fought with Sir Launcelot at the long bridge. And there they yielded them unto Sir Kay, and Sir Kay forsook them and said he fought never with them. But I shall ease your heart, said Sir Kay, yonder is Sir Launcelot that overcame you. When they wist that they were glad. And then Sir Meliot de Logres came home, and told the king how Sir Launcelot had saved him from the death. And all his deeds were known, how four queens, sorceresses, had him in prison, and how he was delivered by King Bagdemagus' daughter. Also there were told all the great deeds of arms that Sir Launcelot did betwixt the two kings, that is for to say the King of Northgalis and King Bagdemagus. All the truth Sir Gahalantine did tell, and Sir Mador de la Porte and Sir Mordred, for they were at that same tournament. Then came in the lady that knew Sir Launcelot when that he wounded Sir Belleus at the pavilion. And there, at request of Sir Launcelot, Sir Belleus was made knight of the Round Table. And so at that time Sir Launcelot had the greatest name of any knight of the world, and most he was honoured of high and low.

Explicit the noble tale of Sir Launcelot du Lake, which is the sixth book. Here followeth the tale of Sir Gareth of Orkney that was called Beaumains by Sir Kay, and is the seventh book.

BOOK SEVEN

CHAPTER I

How Beaumains came to King Arthur's court and demanded three petitions of King Arthur.

When Arthur held his Round Table most plenour, it fortuned that he commanded that the high feast of Pentecost should be holden at a city and a castle, the which in those days was called Kynke Kenadonne, upon the sands that marched nigh Wales. So ever the king had a custom that at the feast of Pentecost in especial, afore other feasts in the year, he would not go that day to meat until he had heard or seen of a great marvel. And for that custom all manner of strange adventures came before Arthur as at that feast before all other feasts. And so Sir Gawaine, a little to-fore noon of the day of Pentecost, espied at a window three men upon horseback, and a dwarf on foot, and so the three men alighted, and the dwarf kept their horses, and one of the three men was higher than the other twain by a foot and an half. Then Sir Gawaine went unto the king and said, Sir, go to your meat, for here at the hand come strange adventures. So Arthur went unto his meat with many other kings. And there were all the knights of the Round Table, [save] only those that were prisoners or slain at a recounter. Then at the high feast evermore they should be fulfilled the whole number of an hundred and fifty, for then was the Round Table fully complished.

Right so came into the hall two men well beseen and richly, and upon their shoulders there leaned the goodliest young man and the fairest that ever they all saw, and he was large and long, and broad in the shoulders, and well visaged, and the fairest and the largest handed that ever man saw, but he fared as though he might not go nor bear himself but if he leaned upon their shoulders. Anon as Arthur saw him there was made peace and room, and right so they yede with him unto the high dais, without saying of any words. Then this much young man pulled him aback, and easily stretched up straight, saying, King Arthur, God you bless and all your fair fellowship, and in especial the fellowship of the Table Round. And for this cause I am come hither, to pray you and require you to give me three gifts, and they shall not be unreasonably asked, but that ye may worshipfully and honourably grant them me, and to you no great hurt nor loss. And the first don and gift I will ask now, and the other two gifts I will ask this day twelvemonth, wheresomever ye hold your high feast. Now ask, said Arthur, and ye shall have your asking.

Now, sir, this is my petition for this feast, that ye will give me meat and drink sufficiently for this twelvemonth, and at that day I will ask mine other two gifts.

My fair son, said Arthur, ask better, I counsel thee, for this is but a simple asking; for my heart giveth me to thee greatly, that thou art come of men of worship, and greatly my conceit faileth me but thou shalt prove a man of right great worship. Sir, he said, thereof be as it be may, I have asked that I will ask. Well, said the king, ye shall have meat and drink enough; I never defended that none, neither my friend nor my foe. But what is thy name I would wit? I cannot tell you, said he. That is marvel, said the king, that thou knowest not thy name, and thou art the goodliest young man that ever I saw. Then the king betook him to Sir Kay the steward, and charged him that he should give him of all manner of meats and drinks of the best, and also that he had all manner of finding as though he were a lord's son. That shall little need, said Sir Kay, to do such cost upon him; for I dare undertake he is a villain born, and never will make man, for an he had come of gentlemen he would have asked of you horse and armour, but such as he is, so he asketh. And sithen he hath no name, I shall give him a name that shall be Beaumains, that is Fair-hands, and into the kitchen I shall bring him, and there he shall have fat brose every day, that he shall be as fat by the twelvemonths' end as a pork hog. Right so the two men departed and beleft him to Sir Kay, that scorned him and mocked him.

CHAPTER II

How Sir Launcelot and Sir Gawaine were wroth because Sir Kay mocked Beaumains, and of a damosel which desired a knight to fight for a lady.

Thereat was Sir Gawaine wroth, and in especial Sir Launcelot bade Sir Kay leave his mocking, for I dare lay my head he shall prove a man of great worship. Let be, said Sir Kay, it may not be by no reason, for as he is, so he hath asked. Beware, said Sir Launcelot, so ye gave the good knight Brewnor, Sir Dinadan's brother, a name, and ye called him La Cote Male Taile, and that turned you to anger afterward. As for that, said Sir Kay, this shall never prove none such. For Sir Brewnor desired ever worship, and this desireth bread and drink and broth; upon pain of my life he was fostered up in some abbey, and, howsomever it was, they failed meat and drink, and so hither he is come for his sustenance.

And so Sir Kay bade get him a place, and sit down to meat; so Beaumains went to the hall door, and set him down among boys and lads, and there he ate sadly. And then Sir Launcelot after meat bade him come to his chamber, and there he should have meat and drink enough. And so did Sir Gawaine: but he refused them all; he would do none other but as Sir Kay commanded him, for no proffer. But as touching Sir Gawaine, he had reason to proffer him lodging, meat, and drink, for that proffer came of his blood, for he was nearer kin to him than he wist. But that as Sir Launcelot did was of his great gentleness and courtesy.

So thus he was put into the kitchen, and lay nightly as the boys of the kitchen did. And so he endured all that twelvemonth, and never displeased man nor child, but always he was meek and mild. But ever when that he saw any jousting of knights, that would he see an he might. And ever Sir Launcelot would give him gold to spend, and clothes, and so did Sir Gawaine, and where there were any masteries done, thereat would he be, and there might none cast bar nor stone to him by two yards. Then would Sir Kay say, How liketh you my boy of the kitchen? So it passed on till the feast of Whitsuntide. And at that time the king held it at Carlion in the most royallest wise that might be, like as he did yearly. But the king would no meat eat upon the Whitsunday, until he heard some adventures. Then came there a squire to the king and said, Sir, ye may go to your meat, for here cometh a damosel with some strange adventures. Then was the king glad and sat him down.

Right so there came a damosel into the hall and saluted the king, and prayed him of succour. For whom? said the king, what is the adventure?

Sir, she said, I have a lady of great worship and renown, and she is besieged with a tyrant, so that she may not out of her castle; and because here are called the noblest knights of the world, I come to you to pray you of succour. What hight your lady, and where dwelleth she, and who is she, and what is his name that hath besieged her? Sir king, she said, as for my lady's name that shall not ye know for me as at this time, but I let you wit she is a lady of great worship and of great lands; and as for the tyrant that besiegeth her and destroyeth her lands, he is called the Red Knight of the Red Launds. I know him not, said the king. Sir, said Sir Gawaine, I know him well, for he is one of the perilloust knights of the world; men say that he hath seven men's strength, and from him I escaped once full hard with my life. Fair damosel, said the king, there be knights here would do their power for to rescue your lady, but because you will not tell her name, nor where she dwelleth, therefore none of my knights that here be now shall go with you by my will. Then must I speak further, said the damosel.

CHAPTER III

How Beaumains desired the battle, and how it was granted to him, and how he desired to be made knight of Sir Launcelot.

With these words came before the king Beaumains, while the damosel was there, and thus he said, Sir king, God thank you, I have been this twelvemonth in your kitchen, and have had my full sustenance, and now I will ask my two gifts that be behind. Ask, upon my peril, said the king. Sir, this shall be my two gifts, first that ye will grant me to have this adventure of the damosel, for it belongeth unto me. Thou shalt have it, said the king, I grant it thee. Then, sir, this is the other gift, that ye shall bid Launcelot du Lake to make me knight, for of him I will be made knight and else of none. And when I am passed I pray you let him ride after me, and make me knight when I require him. All this shall be done, said the king. Fie on thee, said the damosel, shall I have none but one that is your kitchen page? Then was she wroth, and took her horse and departed. And with that there came one to Beaumains and told him his horse and armour was come for him; and there was the dwarf come with all thing that him needed, in the richest manner; thereat all the court had much marvel from whence came all that gear. So when he was armed there was none but few so goodly a man as he was; and right so as he came into the hall and took his leave of King Arthur, and Sir Gawaine, and Sir Launcelot, and prayed that he would hie after him, and so departed and rode after the damosel.

CHAPTER IV

How Beaumains departed, and how he gat of Sir Kay a spear and a shield, and how he jousted with Sir Launcelot.

But there went many after to behold how well he was horsed and trapped in cloth of gold, but he had neither shield nor spear. Then Sir Kay said all open in the hall, I will ride after my boy in the kitchen, to wit whether he will know me for his better. Said Sir Launcelot and Sir Gawaine, Yet abide at home. So Sir Kay made him ready and took his horse and his spear, and rode after him. And right as Beaumains overtook the damosel, right so came Sir Kay and said, Beaumains, what, sir, know ye not me? Then he turned his horse, and knew it was Sir Kay, that had done him all the despite as ye have heard afore. Yea, said Beaumains, I know you for an ungentle knight of the court, and therefore beware of me. Therewith Sir Kay put his spear in the rest, and ran straight upon him; and Beaumains came as fast upon him with his sword in his hand, and so he put away his spear with his sword, and with a foin thrust him through the side, that Sir Kay fell down as he had been dead; and he alighted down and took Sir Kay's shield and his spear, and stert upon his own horse and rode his way.

All that saw Sir Launcelot, and so did the damosel. And then he bade his dwarf stert upon Sir Kay's horse, and so he did. By that Sir Launcelot was come, then he proffered Sir Launcelot to joust; and either made them ready, and they came together so fiercely that either bare down other to the earth, and sore were they bruised. Then Sir Launcelot arose and helped him from his horse. And then Beaumains threw his shield from him, and proffered to fight with Sir Launcelot on foot; and so they rushed together like boars, tracing, rasing, and foining to the mountenance of an hour; and Sir Launcelot felt him so big that he marvelled of his strength, for he fought more liker a giant than a knight, and that his fighting was durable and passing perilous. For Sir Launcelot had so much ado with him that he dreaded himself to be shamed, and said, Beaumains, fight not so sore, your quarrel and mine is not so great but we may leave off. Truly that is truth, said Beaumains, but it doth me good to feel your might, and yet, my lord, I showed not the utterance.

CHAPTER V

How Beaumains told to Sir Launcelot his name, and how he was dubbed knight of Sir Launcelot, and after overtook the damosel.

In God's name, said Sir Launcelot, for I promise you, by the faith of my body, I had as much to do as I might to save myself from you unshamed, and therefore have ye no doubt of none earthly knight. Hope ye so that I may any while stand a proved knight? said Beaumains. Yea, said Launcelot, do as ye have done, and I shall be your warrant. Then, I pray you, said Beaumains, give me the order of knighthood. Then must ye tell me your name, said Launcelot, and of what kin ye be born. Sir, so that ye will not discover me I shall, said Beaumains. Nay, said Sir Launcelot, and that I promise you by the faith of my body, until it be openly known. Then, sir, he said, my name is Gareth, and brother unto Sir Gawaine of father and mother. Ah, sir, said Sir Launcelot, I am more gladder of you than I was; for ever me thought ye should be of great blood, and that ye came not to the court neither for meat nor for drink. And then Sir Launcelot gave him the order of knighthood, and then Sir Gareth prayed him for to depart and let him go.

So Sir Launcelot departed from him and came to Sir Kay, and made him to be borne home upon his shield, and so he was healed hard with the life; and all men scorned Sir Kay, and in especial Sir Gawaine and Sir Launcelot said it was not his part to rebuke no young man, for full little knew he of what birth he is come, and for what cause he came to this court; and so we leave Sir Kay and turn we unto Beaumains.

When he had overtaken the damosel, anon she said, What dost thou here? thou stinkest all of the kitchen, thy clothes be bawdy of the grease and tallow that thou gainest in King Arthur's kitchen; weenest thou, said she, that I allow thee, for yonder knight that thou killest. Nay truly, for thou slewest him unhappily and cowardly; therefore turn again, bawdy kitchen page, I know thee well, for Sir Kay named thee Beaumains. What art thou but a lusk and a turner of broaches and a ladle-washer? Damosel, said Beaumains, say to me what ye will, I will not go from you whatsomever ye say, for I have undertaken to King Arthur for to achieve your adventure, and so shall I finish it to the end, either I shall die therefore. Fie on thee, kitchen knave, wilt thou finish mine adventure? thou shalt anon be met withal, that thou wouldest not for all the broth that ever thou suppest once look him in the face. I shall assay, said Beaumains.

So thus as they rode in the wood, there came a man flying all that ever he might. Whither wilt thou? said Beaumains. O lord, he said, help me, for here by in a slade are six thieves that have taken my lord and bound him, so I am afeard lest they will slay him. Bring me thither, said Beaumains. And so they rode together until they came thereas was the knight bounden; and then he rode unto them, and struck one unto the death, and then another, and at the third stroke he slew the third thief, and then the other three fled. And he rode after them, and he overtook them; and then those three thieves turned again and assailed Beaumains hard, but at the last he slew them, and returned and unbound the knight. And the knight thanked him, and prayed him to ride with him to his castle there a little beside, and he should worshipfully reward him for his good deeds. Sir, said Beaumains, I will no reward have: I was this day made knight of noble Sir Launcelot, and therefore I will no reward have, but God reward me. And also I must follow this damosel.

And when he came nigh her she bade him ride from her, For thou smellest all of the kitchen: weenest thou that I have joy of thee, for all this deed that thou hast done is but mishapped thee: but thou shalt see a sight shall make thee turn again, and that lightly. Then the same knight which was rescued of the thieves rode after that damosel, and prayed her to lodge with him all that night. And because it was near night the damosel rode with him to his castle, and there they had great cheer, and at supper the knight sat Sir Beaumains afore the damosel. Fie, fie, said she, Sir knight, ye are uncourteous to set a kitchen page afore me; him beseemeth better to stick a swine than to sit afore a damosel of high parage. Then the knight was ashamed at her words, and took him up, and set him at a sideboard, and set himself afore him, and so all that night they had good cheer and merry rest.

CHAPTER VI

How Beaumains fought and slew two knights at a passage.

And on the morn the damosel and he took their leave and thanked the knight, and so departed, and rode on their way until they came to a great forest. And there was a great river and but one passage, and there were ready two knights on the farther side to let them the passage. What sayest thou, said the damosel, wilt thou match yonder knights or turn again? Nay, said Sir Beaumains, I will not turn again an they were six more. And therewithal he rushed into the water, and in midst of the water either brake their spears upon other to their hands, and then they drew their swords, and smote eagerly at other. And at the last Sir Beaumains smote the other upon the helm that his head stonied, and therewithal he fell down in the water, and there was he drowned. And then he spurred his horse upon the land, where the other knight fell upon him, and brake his spear, and so they drew their swords and fought long together. At the last Sir Beaumains clave his helm and his head down to the shoulders; and so he rode unto the damosel and bade her ride forth on her way.

Alas, she said, that ever a kitchen page should have that fortune to destroy such two doughty knights: thou weenest thou hast done doughtily, that is not so; for the first knight his horse stumbled, and there he was drowned in the water, and never it was by thy force, nor by thy might. And the last knight by mishap thou camest behind him and mishappily thou slew him.

Damosel, said Beaumains, ye may say what ye will, but with whomsomever I have ado withal, I trust to God to serve him or he depart. And therefore I reck not what ye say, so that I may win your lady. Fie, fie, foul kitchen knave, thou shalt see knights that shall abate thy boast. Fair damosel, give me goodly language, and then my care is past, for what knights somever they be, I care not, nor I doubt them not. Also, said she, I say it for thine avail, yet mayest thou turn again with thy worship; for an thou follow me, thou art but slain, for I see all that ever thou dost is but by misadventure, and not by prowess of thy hands. Well, damosel, ye may say what ye will, but wheresomever ye go I will follow you. So this Beaumains rode with that lady till evensong time, and ever she chid him, and would not rest. And they came to a black laund; and there was a black hawthorn, and thereon hung a black banner, and on the other side there hung a black shield, and by it stood a black spear great and long, and a great black horse covered with silk, and a black stone fast by.

CHAPTER VII

How Beaumains fought with the Knight of the Black Launds, and fought with him till he fell down and died.

There sat a knight all armed in black harness, and his name was the Knight of the Black Laund. Then the damosel, when she saw that knight, she bade him flee down that valley, for his horse was not saddled. Gramercy, said Beaumains, for always ye would have me a coward. With that the Black Knight, when she came nigh him, spake and said, Damosel, have ye brought this knight of King Arthur to be your champion? Nay, fair knight, said she, this is but a kitchen knave that was fed in King Arthur's kitchen for alms. Why cometh he, said the knight, in such array? it is shame that he beareth you company.

Sir, I cannot be delivered of him, said she, for with me he rideth maugre mine head: God would that ye should put him from me, other to slay him an ye may, for he is an unhappy knave, and unhappily he hath done this day: through mishap I saw him slay two knights at the passage of the water; and other deeds he did before right marvellous and through unhappiness. That marvelleth me, said the Black Knight, that any man that is of worship will have ado with him. They know him not, said the damosel, and for because he rideth with me, they ween that he be some man of worship born. That may be, said the Black Knight; howbeit as ye say that he be no man of worship, he is a full likely person, and full like to be a strong man: but thus much shall I grant you, said the Black Knight; I shall put him down upon one foot, and his horse and his harness he shall leave with me, for it were shame to me to do him any more harm.

When Sir Beaumains heard him say thus, he said, Sir knight, thou art full large of my horse and my harness; I let thee wit it cost thee nought, and whether it liketh thee or not, this laund will I pass maugre thine head. And horse nor harness gettest thou none of mine, but if thou win them with thy hands; and therefore let see what thou canst do. Sayest thou that? said the Black Knight, now yield thy lady from thee, for it beseemeth never a kitchen page to ride with such a lady. Thou liest, said Beaumains, I am a gentleman born, and of more high lineage than thou, and that will I prove on thy body.

Then in great wrath they departed with their horses, and came together as it had been the thunder, and the Black Knight's spear brake, and Beaumains thrust him through both his sides, and therewith his spear brake, and the truncheon left still in his side. But nevertheless the Black Knight drew his sword, and smote many eager strokes, and of great might, and hurt Beaumains full sore. But at the last the Black Knight, within an hour and an half, he fell down off his horse in swoon, and there he died. And when Beaumains saw him so well horsed and armed, then he alighted down and armed him in his armour, and so took his horse and rode after the damosel.

When she saw him come nigh, she said, Away, kitchen knave, out of the wind, for the smell of thy bawdy clothes grieveth me. Alas, she said, that ever such a knave should by mishap slay so good a knight as thou hast done, but all this is thine unhappiness. But here by is one shall pay thee all thy payment, and therefore yet I counsel thee, flee. It may happen me, said Beaumains, to be beaten or slain, but I warn you, fair damosel, I will not flee away, nor leave your company, for all that ye can say; for ever ye say that they will kill me or beat me, but howsomever it happeneth I escape, and they lie on the ground. And therefore it were as good for you to hold you still thus all day rebuking me, for away will I not till I see the uttermost of this journey, or else I will be slain, other truly beaten; therefore ride on your way, for follow you I will whatsomever happen.

CHAPTER VIII

How the brother of the knight that was slain met with Beaumains, and fought with Beaumains till he was yielden.

Thus as they rode together, they saw a knight come driving by them all in green, both his horse and his harness; and when he came nigh the damosel, he asked her, Is that my brother the Black Knight that ye have brought with you? Nay, nay, she said, this unhappy kitchen knave hath slain your brother through unhappiness. Alas, said the Green Knight, that is great pity, that so noble a knight as he was should so unhappily be slain, and namely of a knave's hand, as ye say that he is. Ah! traitor, said the Green Knight, thou shalt die for slaying of my brother; he was a full noble knight, and his name was Sir Percard. I defy thee, said Beaumains, for I let thee wit I slew him knightly and not shamefully.

Therewithal the Green Knight rode unto an horn that was green, and it hung upon a thorn, and there he blew three deadly motes, and there came two damosels and armed him lightly. And then he took a great horse, and a green shield and a green spear. And then they ran together with all their mights, and brake their spears unto their hands. And then they drew their swords, and gave many sad strokes, and either of them wounded other full ill. And at the last, at an overthwart, Beaumains with his horse struck the Green Knight's horse upon the side, that he fell to the earth. And then the Green Knight avoided his horse lightly, and dressed him upon foot. That saw Beaumains, and therewithal he alighted, and they rushed together like two mighty kemps a long while, and sore they bled both. With that came the damosel, and said, My lord the Green

Knight, why for shame stand ye so long fighting with the kitchen knave? Alas, it is shame that ever ye were made knight, to see such a lad to match such a knight, as the weed overgrew the corn. Therewith the Green Knight was ashamed, and therewithal he gave a great stroke of might, and clave his shield through. When Beaumains saw his shield cloven asunder he was a little ashamed of that stroke and of her language; and then he gave him such a buffet upon the helm that he fell on his knees. And so suddenly Beaumains pulled him upon the ground grovelling. And then the Green Knight cried him mercy, and yielded him unto Sir Beaumains, and prayed him to slay him not. All is in vain, said Beaumains, for thou shalt die but if this damosel that came with me pray me to save thy life. And therewithal he unlaced his helm like as he would slay him. Fie upon thee, false kitchen page, I will never pray thee to save his life, for I will never be so much in thy danger. Then shall he die, said Beaumains. Not so hardy, thou bawdy knave, said the damosel, that thou slay him. Alas, said the Green Knight, suffer me not to die for a fair word may save me. Fair knight, said the Green Knight, save my life, and I will forgive thee the death of my brother, and for ever to become thy man, and thirty knights that hold of me for ever shall do you service. In the devil's name, said the damosel, that such a bawdy kitchen knave should have thee and thirty knights' service.

Sir knight, said Beaumains, all this availeth thee not, but if my damosel speak with me for thy life. And therewithal he made a semblant to slay him. Let be, said the damosel, thou bawdy knave; slay him not, for an thou do thou shalt repent it. Damosel, said Beaumains, your charge is to me a pleasure, and at your commandment his life shall be saved, and else not. Then he said, Sir knight with the green arms, I release thee quit at this damosel's request, for I will not make her wroth, I will fulfil all that she chargeth me. And then the Green Knight kneeled down, and did him homage with his sword. Then said the damosel, Me repenteth, Green Knight, of your damage, and of your brother's death, the Black Knight, for of your help I had great mister, for I dread me sore to pass this forest. Nay, dread you not, said the Green Knight, for ye shall lodge with me this night, and to-morn I shall help you through this forest. So they took their horses and rode to his manor, which was fast there beside.

CHAPTER IX

*How the damosel again rebuked Beaumains, and would not
suffer him to sit at her table, but called him kitchen boy.*

And ever she rebuked Beaumains, and would not suffer him to sit at
her table, but as the Green Knight took him and sat him at a side
table. Marvel methinketh, said the Green Knight to the damosel,
why ye rebuke this noble knight as ye do, for I warn you, damosel,
he is a full noble knight, and I know no knight is able to match him;
therefore ye do great wrong to rebuke him, for he shall do you right
good service, for whatsomever he maketh himself, ye shall prove at
the end that he is come of a noble blood and of king's lineage. Fie,
fie, said the damosel, it is shame for you to say of him such worship.
Truly, said the Green Knight, it were shame for me to say of him any
disworship, for he hath proved himself a better knight than I am, yet
have I met with many knights in my days, and never or this time
have I found no knight his match. And so that night they yede unto
rest, and all that night the Green Knight commanded thirty knights
privily to watch Beaumains, for to keep him from all treason.

And so on the morn they all arose, and heard their mass and brake
their fast; and then they took their horses and rode on their way, and
the Green Knight conveyed them through the forest; and there the
Green Knight said, My lord Beaumains, I and these thirty knights
shall be always at your summons, both early and late, at your calling
and whither that ever ye will send us. It is well said, said Beaumains;
when that I call upon you ye must yield you unto King Arthur, and
all your knights. If that ye so command us, we shall be ready at all
times, said the Green Knight. Fie, fie upon thee, in the devil's name,
said the damosel, that any good knights should be obedient unto a
kitchen knave. So then departed the Green Knight and the damosel.
And then she said unto Beaumains, Why followest thou me, thou
kitchen boy? Cast away thy shield and thy spear, and flee away; yet I
counsel thee betimes or thou shalt say right soon, alas; for wert thou
as wight as ever was Wade or Launcelot, Tristram, or the good
knight Sir Lamorak, thou shalt not pass a pass here that is called the

Pass Perilous. Damosel, said Beaumains, who is afeard let him flee, for it were shame to turn again sithen I have ridden so long with you. Well, said the damosel, ye shall soon, whether ye will or not.

CHAPTER X

How the third brother, called the Red Knight, jousted and fought against Beaumains, and how Beaumains overcame him.

So within a while they saw a tower as white as any snow, well matchecold all about, and double dyked. And over the tower gate there hung a fifty shields of divers colours, and under that tower there was a fair meadow. And therein were many knights and squires to behold, scaffolds and pavilions; for there upon the morn should be a great tournament: and the lord of the tower was in his castle and looked out at a window, and saw a damosel, a dwarf, and a knight armed at all points. So God me help, said the lord, with that knight will I joust, for I see that he is a knight-errant. And so he armed him and horsed him hastily. And when he was on horseback with his shield and his spear, it was all red, both his horse and his harness, and all that to him longeth. And when that he came nigh him he weened it had been his brother the Black Knight; and then he cried aloud, Brother, what do ye in these marches? Nay, nay, said the damosel, it is not he; this is but a kitchen knave that was brought up for alms in King Arthur's court. Nevertheless, said the Red Knight, I will speak with him or he depart. Ah, said the damosel, this knave hath killed thy brother, and Sir Kay named him Beaumains, and this horse and this harness was thy brother's, the Black Knight. Also I saw thy brother the Green Knight overcome of his hands. Now may ye be revenged upon him, for I may never be quit of him.

With this either knights departed in sunder, and they came together with all their might, and either of their horses fell to the earth, and they avoided their horses, and put their shields afore them and drew their swords, and either gave other sad strokes, now here, now there, rasing, tracing, foining, and hurling like two boars, the space of two hours. And then she cried on high to the Red Knight, Alas, thou noble Red Knight, think what worship hath followed thee, let never a kitchen knave endure thee so long as he doth. Then the Red Knight waxed wroth and doubled his strokes, and hurt Beaumains wonderly sore, that the blood ran down to the ground, that it was wonder to see that strong battle. Yet at the last Sir Beaumains struck him to the earth, and as he would have slain the Red Knight, he cried mercy, saying, Noble knight, slay me not, and I shall yield me to thee with fifty knights with me that be at my commandment. And I forgive thee all the despite that thou hast done to me, and the death of my brother the Black Knight. All this availeth not, said Beaumains, but if my damosel pray me to save thy life. And therewith he made semblant to strike off his head. Let be, thou Beaumains, slay him not, for he is a noble knight, and not so hardy, upon thine head, but thou save him.

Then Beaumains bade the Red Knight, Stand up, and thank the damosel now of thy life. Then the Red Knight prayed him to see his castle, and to be there all night. So the damosel then granted him, and there they had merry cheer. But always the damosel spake many foul words unto Beaumains, whereof the Red Knight had great marvel; and all that night the Red Knight made three score knights to watch Beaumains, that he should have no shame nor villainy. And upon the morn they heard mass and dined, and the Red Knight came before Beaumains with his three score knights, and there he proffered him his homage and fealty at all times, he and his knights to do him service. I thank you, said Beaumains, but this ye shall grant me: when I call upon you, to come afore my lord King Arthur, and yield you unto him to be his knights. Sir, said the Red Knight, I will be ready, and my fellowship, at your summons. So Sir Beaumains departed and the damosel, and ever she rode chiding him in the foulest manner.

CHAPTER XI

*How Sir Beaumains suffered great rebukes of the damosel,
and he suffered it patiently.*

Damosel, said Beaumains, ye are uncourteous so to rebuke me as ye do, for meseemeth I have done you good service, and ever ye threaten me I shall be beaten with knights that we meet, but ever for all your boast they lie in the dust or in the mire, and therefore I pray you rebuke me no more; and when ye see me beaten or yielden as recreant, then may ye bid me go from you shamefully; but first I let you wit I will not depart from you, for I were worse than a fool an I would depart from you all the while that I win worship. Well, said she, right soon there shall meet a knight shall pay thee all thy wages, for he is the most man of worship of the world, except King Arthur. I will well, said Beaumains, the more he is of worship, the more shall be my worship to have ado with him.

Then anon they were ware where was afore them a city rich and fair. And betwixt them and the city a mile and an half there was a fair meadow that seemed new mown, and therein were many pavilions fair to behold. Lo, said the damosel, yonder is a lord that owneth yonder city, and his custom is, when the weather is fair, to lie in this meadow to joust and tourney. And ever there be about him five hundred knights and gentlemen of arms, and there be all manner of games that any gentleman can devise. That goodly lord, said Beaumains, would I fain see. Thou shalt see him time enough, said the damosel, and so as she rode near she espied the pavilion where he was. Lo, said she, seest thou yonder pavilion that is all of the colour of Inde, and all manner of thing that there is about, men and women, and horses trapped, shields and spears were all of the colour of Inde, and his name is Sir Persant of Inde, the most lordliest knight that ever thou lookedst on. It may well be, said Beaumains, but be he never so stout a knight, in this field I shall abide till that I see him under his shield. Ah, fool, said she, thou wert better flee betimes. Why, said Beaumains, an he be such a knight as ye make him, he will not set upon me with all his men, or with his five hundred knights. For an there come no more but one at once, I shall him not fail whilst my life lasteth. Fie, fie, said the damosel, that ever such a stinking knave should blow such a boast. Damosel, he said, ye are to blame so to rebuke me, for I had liefer do five battles than so to be rebuked, let him come and then let him do his worst.

Sir, she said, I marvel what thou art and of what kin thou art come; boldly thou speakest, and boldly thou hast done, that have I seen; therefore I pray thee save thyself an thou mayest, for thy horse and thou have had great travail, and I dread we dwell over long from the siege, for it is but hence seven mile, and all perilous passages we are passed save all only this passage; and here I dread me sore lest ye shall catch some hurt, therefore I would ye were hence, that ye were not bruised nor hurt with this strong knight. But I let you wit that Sir Persant of Inde is nothing of might nor strength unto the knight that laid the siege about my lady. As for that, said Sir Beaumains, be it as it be may. For sithen I am come so nigh this knight I will prove his might or I depart from him, and else I shall be shamed an I now withdraw me from him. And therefore, damosel, have ye no doubt by the grace of God I shall so deal with this knight that within two hours after noon I shall deliver him. And then shall we come to the siege by daylight. O Jesu, marvel have I, said the damosel, what manner a man ye be, for it may never be otherwise but that ye be come of a noble blood, for so foul nor shamefully did never woman rule a knight as I have done you, and ever courteously ye have suffered me, and that came never but of a gentle blood.

Damosel, said Beaumains, a knight may little do that may not suffer a damosel, for whatsomever ye said unto me I took none heed to your words, for the more ye said the more ye angered me, and my wrath I wreaked upon them that I had ado withal. And therefore all the missaying that ye missaid me furthered me in my battle, and caused me to think to show and prove myself at the end what I was; for peradventure though I had meat in King Arthur's kitchen, yet I might have had meat enough in other places, but all that I did it for to prove and assay my friends, and that shall be known another day; and whether that I be a gentleman born or none, I let you wit, fair damosel, I have done you gentleman's service, and peradventure better service yet will I do or I depart from you. Alas, she said, fair Beaumains, forgive me all that I have missaid or done against thee. With all my heart, said he, I forgive it you, for ye did nothing but as

ye should do, for all your evil words pleased me; and damosel, said
Beaumains, since it liketh you to say thus fair unto me, wit ye well it
gladdeth my heart greatly, and now meseemeth there is no knight
living but I am able enough for him.

CHAPTER XII

*How Beaumains fought with Sir Persant of Inde, and made
him to be yielden.*

With this Sir Persant of Inde had espied them as they hoved in the
field, and knightly he sent to them whether he came in war or in
peace. Say to thy lord, said Beaumains, I take no force, but whether
as him list himself. So the messenger went again unto Sir Persant and
told him all his answer. Well then will I have ado with him to the
utterance, and so he purveyed him and rode against him. And
Beaumains saw him and made him ready, and there they met with all
that ever their horses might run, and brast their spears either in three
pieces, and their horses rushed so together that both their horses fell
dead to the earth; and lightly they avoided their horses and put their
shields afore them, and drew their swords, and gave many great
strokes that sometime they hurtled together that they fell grovelling
on the ground. Thus they fought two hours and more, that their
shields and their hauberks were all forhewen, and in many steads they
were wounded. So at the last Sir Beaumains smote him through the
cost of the body, and then he retrayed him here and there, and
knightly maintained his battle long time. And at the last, though him
loath were, Beaumains smote Sir Persant above upon the helm, that
he fell grovelling to the earth; and then he leapt upon him overthwart
and unlaced his helm to have slain him.

Then Sir Persant yielded him and asked him mercy. With that
came the damosel and prayed to save his life. I will well, for it were
pity this noble knight should die. Gramercy, said Persant, gentle
knight and damosel. For certainly now I wot well it was ye that slew
my brother the Black Knight at the black thorn; he was a full noble
knight, his name was Sir Percard. Also I am sure that ye are he that
won mine other brother the Green Knight, his name was Sir

Pertolepe. Also ye won my brother the Red Knight, Sir Perimones. And now since ye have won these, this shall I do for to please you: ye shall have homage and fealty of me, and an hundred knights to be always at your commandment, to go and ride where ye will command us. And so they went unto Sir Persant's pavilion and drank the wine, and ate spices, and afterward Sir Persant made him to rest upon a bed until supper time, and after supper to bed again. When Beaumains was abed, Sir Persant had a lady, a fair daughter of eighteen year of age, and there he called her unto him, and charged her and commanded her upon his blessing to go unto the knight's bed, and lie down by his side, and make him no strange cheer, but good cheer, and take him in thine arms and kiss him, and look that this be done, I charge you, as ye will have my love and my good will. So Sir Persant's daughter did as her father bade her, and so she went unto Sir Beaumains' bed, and privily she dispoiled her, and laid her down by him, and then he awoke and saw her, and asked her what she was. Sir, she said, I am Sir Persant's daughter, that by the commandment of my father am come hither. Be ye a maid or a wife? said he. Sir, she said, I am a clean maiden. God defend, said he, that I should defoil you to do Sir Persant such a shame; therefore, fair damosel, arise out of this bed or else I will. Sir, she said, I came not to you by mine own will, but as I was commanded. Alas, said Sir Beaumains, I were a shameful knight an I would do your father any disworship; and so he kissed her, and so she departed and came unto Sir Persant her father, and told him all how she had sped. Truly, said Sir Persant, whatsomever he be, he is come of a noble blood. And so we leave them there till on the morn.

CHAPTER XIII

*Of the goodly communication between Sir Persant
and Beaumains, and how he told him that his name
was Sir Gareth.*

And so on the morn the damosel and Sir Beaumains heard mass and
brake their fast, and so took their leave. Fair damosel, said Persant,
whitherward are ye way-leading this knight? Sir, she said, this knight
is going to the siege that besiegeth my sister in the Castle Dangerous.
Ah, ah, said Persant, that is the Knight of the Red Laund, the which
is the most perilous knight that I know now living, and a man that is
without mercy, and men say that he hath seven men's strength. God
save you, said he to Beaumains, from that knight, for he doth great
wrong to that lady, and that is great pity, for she is one of the fairest
ladies of the world, and meseemeth that your damosel is her sister: is
not your name Linet? said he. Yea, sir, said she, and my lady my
sister's name is Dame Lionesse. Now shall I tell you, said Sir Persant,
this Red Knight of the Red Laund hath lain long at the siege, well-
nigh this two years, and many times he might have had her an he had
would, but he prolongeth the time to this intent, for to have Sir
Launcelot du Lake to do battle with him, or Sir Tristram, or Sir
Lamorak de Galis, or Sir Gawaine, and this is his tarrying so long at
the siege.

Now my lord Sir Persant of Inde, said the damosel Linet, I require
you that ye will make this gentleman knight or ever he fight with the
Red Knight. I will with all my heart, said Sir Persant, an it please him
to take the order of knighthood of so simple a man as I am. Sir, said
Beaumains, I thank you for your good will, for I am better sped, for
certainly the noble knight Sir Launcelot made me knight. Ah, said Sir
Persant, of a more renowned knight might ye not be made knight;
for of all knights he may be called chief of knighthood; and so all the
world saith, that betwixt three knights is departed clearly knighthood,
that is Launcelot du Lake, Sir Tristram de Liones, and Sir Lamorak de
Galis: these bear now the renown. There be many other knights, as
Sir Palomides the Saracen and Sir Safere his brother; also Sir Bleoberis

and Sir Blamore de Ganis his brother; also Sir Bors de Ganis and Sir Ector de Maris and Sir Percivale de Galis; these and many more be noble knights, but there be none that pass the three above said; therefore God speed you well, said Sir Persant, for an ye may match the Red Knight ye shall be called the fourth of the world.

Sir, said Beaumains, I would fain be of good fame and of knighthood. And I let you wit I came of good men, for I dare say my father was a noble man, and so that ye will keep it in close, and this damosel, I will tell you of what kin I am. We will not discover you, said they both, till ye command us, by the faith we owe unto God. Truly then, said he, my name is Gareth of Orkney, and King Lot was my father, and my mother is King Arthur's sister, her name is Dame Morgawse, and Sir Gawaine is my brother, and Sir Agravaine and Sir Gaheris, and I am the youngest of them all. And yet wot not King Arthur nor Sir Gawaine what I am.

CHAPTER XIV

How the lady that was besieged had word from her sister how she had brought a knight to fight for her, and what battles he had achieved.

So the book saith that the lady that was besieged had word of her sister's coming by the dwarf, and a knight with her, and how he had passed all the perilous passages. What manner a man is he? said the lady. He is a noble knight, truly, madam, said the dwarf, and but a young man, but he is as likely a man as ever ye saw any. What is he? said the damosel, and of what kin is he come, and of whom was he made knight? Madam, said the dwarf, he is the king's son of Orkney, but his name I will not tell you as at this time; but wit ye well, of Sir Launcelot was he made knight, for of none other would he be made knight, and Sir Kay named him Beaumains. How escaped he, said the lady, from the brethren of Persant? Madam, he said, as a noble knight should. First, he slew two brethren at a passage of a water. Ah! said she, they were good knights, but they were murderers, the one hight Gherard le Breuse, and the other knight hight Sir Arnold le Breuse. Then, madam, he recountered with the Black Knight, and slew him in plain battle, and so he took his horse and his armour and fought with the Green Knight and won him in plain battle, and in like wise he served the Red Knight, and after in the same wise he served the Blue Knight and won him in plain battle. Then, said the lady, he hath overcome Sir Persant of Inde, one of the noblest knights of the world, and the dwarf said, He hath won all the four brethren and slain the Black Knight, and yet he did more to-fore: he overthrew Sir Kay and left him nigh dead upon the ground; also he did a great battle with Sir Launcelot, and there they departed on even hands: and then Sir Launcelot made him knight.

Dwarf, said the lady, I am glad of these tidings, therefore go thou in an hermitage of mine hereby, and there shalt thou bear with thee of my wine in two flagons of silver, they are of two gallons, and also two cast of bread with fat venison baked, and dainty fowls; and a cup of gold here I deliver thee, that is rich and precious; and bear all this to mine hermitage, and put it in the hermit's hands. And sithen go thou unto my sister and greet her well, and commend me unto that gentle knight, and pray him to eat and to drink and make him strong, and say ye him I thank him of his courtesy and goodness, that he would take upon him such labour for me that never did him bounty nor courtesy. Also pray him that he be of good heart and courage, for he shall meet with a full noble knight, but he is neither of bounty, courtesy, nor gentleness; for he attendeth unto nothing but to murder, and that is the cause I cannot praise him nor love him.

So this dwarf departed, and came to Sir Persant, where he found the damosel Linet and Sir Beaumains, and there he told them all as ye have heard; and then they took their leave, but Sir Persant took an ambling hackney and conveyed them on their ways, and then beleft them to God; and so within a little while they came to that hermitage, and there they drank the wine, and ate the venison and the fowls baken. And so when they had repasted them well, the dwarf returned again with his vessel unto the castle again; and there met with him the Red Knight of the Red Launds, and asked him from whence that he came, and where he had been. Sir, said the dwarf, I have been with my lady's sister of this castle, and she hath been at King Arthur's court, and brought a knight with her. Then I account her travail but lost; for though she had brought with her Sir Launcelot, Sir Tristram, Sir Lamorak, or Sir Gawaine, I would think myself good enough for them all.

It may well be, said the dwarf, but this knight hath passed all the perilous passages, and slain the Black Knight and other two more, and won the Green Knight, the Red Knight, and the Blue Knight. Then is he one of these four that I have afore rehearsed. He is none of those, said the dwarf, but he is a king's son. What is his name? said the Red Knight of the Red Launds. That will I not tell you, said the dwarf, but Sir Kay upon scorn named him Beaumains. I care not, said the knight, what knight so ever he be, for I shall soon deliver him. And if I ever match him he shall have a shameful death as many other have had. That were pity, said the dwarf, and it is marvel that ye make such shameful war upon noble knights.

CHAPTER XV

How the damosel and Beaumains came to the siege, and came to a sycamore tree, and there Beaumains blew a horn, and then the Knight of the Red Launds came to fight with him.

Now leave we the knight and the dwarf, and speak we of Beaumains, that all night lay in the hermitage; and upon the morn he and the damosel Linet heard their mass and brake their fast. And then they took their horses and rode throughout a fair forest; and then they came to a plain, and saw where were many pavilions and tents, and a fair castle, and there was much smoke and great noise; and when they came near the siege Sir Beaumains espied upon great trees, as he rode, how there hung full goodly armed knights by the neck, and their shields about their necks with their swords, and gilt spurs upon their heels, and so there hung nigh a forty knights shamefully with full rich arms.

Then Sir Beaumains abated his countenance and said, What meaneth this? Fair sir, said the damosel, abate not your cheer for all this sight, for ye must courage yourself, or else ye be all shent, for all these knights came hither to this siege to rescue my sister Dame Lionesse, and when the Red Knight of the Red Launds had overcome them, he put them to this shameful death without mercy and pity. And in the same wise he will serve you but if you quit you the better.

Now Jesu defend me, said Beaumains, from such a villainous death and shenship of arms. For rather than I should so be faren withal, I would rather be slain manly in plain battle. So were ye better, said the damosel; for trust not, in him is no courtesy, but all goeth to the death or shameful murder, and that is pity, for he is a full likely man, well made of body, and a full noble knight of prowess, and a lord of great lands and possessions. Truly, said Beaumains, he may well be a good knight, but he useth shameful customs, and it is marvel that he endureth so long that none of the noble knights of my lord Arthur's have not dealt with him.

And then they rode to the dykes, and saw them double dyked with full warlike walls; and there were lodged many great lords nigh the walls; and there was great noise of minstrelsy; and the sea beat upon the one side of the walls, where were many ships and mariners' noise with 'hale and how'. And also there was fast by a sycamore tree, and there hung an horn, the greatest that ever they saw, of an elephant's bone; and this Knight of the Red Launds had hanged it up there, that if there came any errant-knight, he must blow that horn, and then will he make him ready and come to him to do battle. But, sir, I pray you, said the damosel Linet, blow ye not the horn till it be high noon, for now it is about prime, and now increaseth his might, that as men say he hath seven men's strength. Ah, fie for shame, fair damosel, say ye never so more to me; for, an he were as good a knight as ever was, I shall never fail him in his most might, for either I will win worship worshipfully, or die knightly in the field. And therewith he spurred his horse straight to the sycamore tree, and blew so the horn eagerly that all the siege and the castle rang thereof. And then there leapt out knights out of their tents and pavilions, and they within the castle looked over the walls and out at windows.

Then the Red Knight of the Red Launds armed him hastily, and two barons set on his spurs upon his heels, and all was blood red, his armour, spear and shield. And an earl buckled his helm upon his head, and then they brought him a red spear and a red steed, and so he rode into a little vale under the castle, that all that were in the castle and at the siege might behold the battle.

CHAPTER XVI

How the two knights met together, and of their talking,
and how they began their battle.

Sir, said the damosel Linet unto Sir Beaumains, look ye be glad and
light, for yonder is your deadly enemy, and at yonder window is my
lady, my sister, Dame Lionesse. Where? said Beaumains. Yonder, said
the damosel, and pointed with her finger. That is truth, said
Beaumains. She beseemeth afar the fairest lady that ever I looked
upon; and truly, he said, I ask no better quarrel than now for to do
battle, for truly she shall be my lady, and for her I will fight. And ever
he looked up to the window with glad countenance, and the Lady
Lionesse made curtsey to him down to the earth, with holding up
both their hands.

With that the Red Knight of the Red Launds called to Sir
Beaumains, Leave, sir knight, thy looking, and behold me, I counsel
thee; for I warn thee well she is my lady, and for her I have done
many strong battles. If thou have so done, said Beaumains, meseemeth
it was but waste labour, for she loveth none of thy fellowship, and
thou to love that loveth not thee is but great folly. For an I
understood that she were not glad of my coming, I would be advised
or I did battle for her. But I understand by the besieging of this castle
she may forbear thy fellowship. And therefore wit thou well, thou
Red Knight of the Red Launds, I love her, and will rescue her, or
else to die. Sayst thou that? said the Red Knight, meseemeth thou
ought of reason to be ware by yonder knights that thou sawest hang
upon yonder trees. Fie for shame, said Beaumains, that ever thou
shouldest say or do so evil, for in that thou shamest thyself and
knighthood, and thou mayst be sure there will no lady love thee that
knoweth thy wicked customs. And now thou weenest that the sight
of these hanged knights should fear me. Nay truly, not so; that
shameful sight causeth me to have courage and hardiness against thee,
more than I would have had against thee an thou wert a well-ruled
knight. Make thee ready, said the Red Knight of the Red Launds,
and talk no longer with me.

Then Sir Beaumains bade the damosel go from him; and then they put their spears in their rests, and came together with all their might that they had both, and either smote other in midst of their shields that the paitrelles, surcingles, and cruppers brast, and fell to the earth both, and the reins of their bridles in their hands; and so they lay a great while sore astonied, that all that were in the castle and in the siege weened their necks had been broken; and then many a stranger and other said the strange knight was a big man, and a noble jouster, for or now we saw never no knight match the Red Knight of the Red Launds: thus they said, both within the castle and without. Then lightly they avoided their horses and put their shields afore them, and drew their swords and ran together like two fierce lions, and either gave other such buffets upon their helms that they reeled backward both two strides; and then they recovered both, and hewed great pieces off their harness and their shields that a great part fell into the fields.

CHAPTER XVII

How after long fighting Beaumains overcame the knight and would have slain him, but at the request of the lords he saved his life, and made him to yield him to the lady.

And then thus they fought till it was past noon, and never would stint, till at the last they lacked wind both; and then they stood wagging and scattering, panting, blowing and bleeding, that all that beheld them for the most part wept for pity. So when they had rested them a while they yede to battle again, tracing, racing, foining as two boars. And at some time they took their run as it had been two rams, and hurtled together that sometime they fell grovelling to the earth: and at some time they were so amazed that either took other's sword instead of his own.

Thus they endured till evensong time, that there was none that beheld them might know whether was like to win the battle; and their armour was so forhewn that men might see their naked sides; and in other places they were naked, but ever the naked places they did defend. And the Red Knight was a wily knight of war, and his wily fighting taught Sir Beaumains to be wise; but he abought it full sore or he did espy his fighting.

And thus by assent of them both they granted either other to rest; and so they set them down upon two molehills there beside the fighting place, and either of them unlaced his helm, and took the cold wind; for either of their pages was fast by them, to come when they called to unlace their harness and to set them on again at their commandment. And then when Sir Beaumains' helm was off, he looked up to the window, and there he saw the fair lady Dame Lionesse, and she made him such countenance that his heart waxed light and jolly; and therewith he bade the Red Knight of the Red Launds make him ready, and let us do the battle to the utterance. I will well, said the knight, and then they laced up their helms, and their pages avoided, and they stepped together and fought freshly; but the Red Knight of the Red Launds awaited him, and at an overthwart smote him within the hand, that his sword fell out of his hand; and yet he gave him another buffet upon the helm that he fell grovelling to the earth, and the Red Knight fell over him, for to hold him down.

Then cried the maiden Linet on high: O Sir Beaumains, where is thy courage become? Alas, my lady my sister beholdeth thee, and she sobbeth and weepeth, that maketh mine heart heavy. When Sir Beaumains heard her say so, he abraid up with a great might and gat him upon his feet, and lightly he leapt to his sword and gripped it in his hand, and doubled his pace unto the Red Knight, and there they fought a new battle together. But Sir Beaumains then doubled his strokes, and smote so thick that he smote the sword out of his hand, and then he smote him upon the helm that he fell to the earth, and Sir Beaumains fell upon him, and unlaced his helm to have slain him; and then he yielded him and asked mercy, and said with a loud voice: O noble knight, I yield me to thy mercy.

Then Sir Beaumains bethought him upon the knights that he had made to be hanged shamefully, and then he said: I may not with my worship save thy life, for the shameful deaths that thou hast caused many full good knights to die. Sir, said the Red Knight of the Red Launds, hold your hand and ye shall know the causes why I put them to so shameful a death. Say on, said Sir Beaumains. Sir, I loved once a lady, a fair damosel, and she had her brother slain; and she said it was Sir Launcelot du Lake, or else Sir Gawaine; and she prayed me as that

I loved her heartily, that I would make her a promise by the faith of my knighthood, for to labour daily in arms unto I met with one of them; and all that I might overcome I should put them unto a villainous death; and this is the cause that I have put all these knights to death, and so I ensured her to do all the villainy unto King Arthur's knights, and that I should take vengeance upon all these knights. And, sir, now I will thee tell that every day my strength increaseth till noon, and all this time have I seven men's strength.

CHAPTER XVIII

How the knight yielded him, and how Beaumains made him to go unto King Arthur's court, and to cry Sir Launcelot mercy.

Then came there many earls, and barons, and noble knights, and prayed that knight to save his life, and take him to your prisoner. And all they fell upon their knees, and prayed him of mercy, and that he would save his life; and, Sir, they all said, it were fairer of him to take homage and fealty, and let him hold his lands of you than for to slay him; by his death ye shall have none advantage, and his misdeeds that be done may not be undone; and therefore he shall make amends to all parties, and we all will become your men and do you homage and fealty. Fair lords, said Beaumains, wit you well I am full loath to slay this knight, nevertheless he hath done passing ill and shamefully; but insomuch all that he did was at a lady's request I blame him the less; and so for your sake I will release him that he shall have his life upon this covenant, that he go within the castle, and yield him there to the lady, and if she will forgive and quit him, I will well; with this he make her amends of all the trespass he hath done against her and her lands. And also, when that is done, that ye go unto the court of King Arthur, and there that ye ask Sir Launcelot mercy, and Sir Gawaine, for the evil will ye have had against them. Sir, said the Red Knight of the Red Launds, all this will I do as ye command, and siker assurance and borrows ye shall have. And so then when the assurance was made, he made his homage and fealty, and all those earls and barons with him.

And then the maiden Linet came to Sir Beaumains, and unarmed him and searched his wounds, and stinted his blood, and in likewise she did to the Red Knight of the Red Launds. And there they sojourned ten days in their tents; and the Red Knight made his lords and servants to do all the pleasure that they might unto Sir Beaumains. And so within a while the Red Knight of the Red Launds yede unto the castle, and put him in her grace. And so she received him upon sufficient surety, so all her hurts were well restored of all that she could complain. And then he departed unto the court of King Arthur, and there openly the Red Knight of the Red Launds put him in the mercy of Sir Launcelot and Sir Gawaine, and there he told openly how he was overcome and by whom, and also he told all the battles from the beginning unto the ending. Jesu mercy, said King Arthur and Sir Gawaine, we marvel much of what blood he is come, for he is a noble knight. Have ye no marvel, said Sir Launcelot, for ye shall right well wit that he is come of a full noble blood; and as for his might and hardiness, there be but few now living that is so mighty as he is, and so noble of prowess. It seemeth by you, said King Arthur, that ye know his name, and from whence he is come, and of what blood he is. I suppose I do so, said Launcelot, or else I would not have given him the order of knighthood; but he gave me such charge at that time that I should never discover him until he required me, or else it be known openly by some other.

CHAPTER XIX

How Beaumains came to the lady, and when he came to the castle the gates were closed against him, and of the words that the lady said to him.

Now turn we unto Sir Beaumains that desired of Linet that he might see her sister, his lady. Sir, she said, I would fain ye saw her. Then Sir Beaumains all armed him, and took his horse and his spear, and rode straight unto the castle. And when he came to the gate he found there many men armed, and pulled up the drawbridge and drew the port close.

Then marvelled he why they would not suffer him to enter. And then he looked up to the window; and there he saw the fair Lionesse that said on high: Go thy way, Sir Beaumains, for as yet thou shalt not have wholly my love, unto the time that thou be called one of the number of the worthy knights. And therefore go labour in worship this twelvemonth, and then thou shalt hear new tidings. Alas, fair lady, said Beaumains, I have not deserved that ye should show me this strangeness, and I had weened that I should have right good cheer with you, and unto my power I have deserved thank, and well I am sure I have bought your love with part of the best blood within my body. Fair courteous knight, said Dame Lionesse, be not displeased nor over-hasty; for wit you well your great travail nor good love shall not be lost, for I consider your great travail and labour, your bounty and your goodness as me ought to do. And therefore go on your way, and look that ye be of good comfort, for all shall be for your worship and for the best, and perdy a twelvemonth will soon be done, and trust me, fair knight, I shall be true to you, and never to betray you, but to my death I shall love you and none other. And therewithal she turned her from the window, and Sir Beaumains rode awayward from the castle, making great dole, and so he rode here and there and wist not where he rode, till it was dark night. And then it happened him to come to a poor man's house, and there he was harboured all that night.

But Sir Beaumains had no rest, but wallowed and writhed for the love of the lady of the castle. And so upon the morrow he took his horse and rode until underne, and then he came to a broad water, and thereby was a great lodge, and there he alighted to sleep and laid his head upon the shield, and betook his horse to the dwarf, and commanded him to watch all night.

Now turn we to the lady of the same castle, that thought much upon Beaumains, and then she called unto her Sir Gringamore her brother, and prayed him in all manner, as he loved her heartily, that he would ride after Sir Beaumains: And ever have ye wait upon him till ye may find him sleeping, for I am sure in his heaviness he will alight down in some place, and lie him down to sleep; and therefore have ye your wait upon him, and in the priviest manner ye can, take his dwarf, and go ye your way with him as fast as ever ye may or Sir Beaumains awake. For my sister Linet telleth me that he can tell of what kindred he is come, and what is his right name. And the meanwhile I and my sister will ride unto your castle to await when ye bring with you the dwarf. And then when ye have brought him unto your castle, I will have him in examination myself. Unto the time that I know what is his right name, and of what kindred he is come, shall I never be merry at my heart. Sister, said Sir Gringamore, all this shall be done after your intent.

And so he rode all the other day and the night till that he found Sir Beaumains lying by a water, and his head upon his shield, for to sleep. And then when he saw Sir Beaumains fast asleep, he came stilly stalking behind the dwarf, and plucked him fast under his arm, and so he rode away with him as fast as ever he might unto his own castle. And this Sir Gringamore's arms were all black, and that to him longeth. But ever as he rode with the dwarf toward his castle, he cried unto his lord and prayed him of help. And therewith awoke Sir Beaumains, and up he leapt lightly, and saw where Sir Gringamore rode his way with the dwarf, and so Sir Gringamore rode out of his sight.

CHAPTER XX

How Sir Beaumains rode after to rescue his dwarf, and came into the castle where he was.

Then Sir Beaumains put on his helm anon, and buckled his shield, and took his horse, and rode after him all that ever he might ride through marshes, and fields, and great dales, that many times his horse and he plunged over the head in deep mires, for he knew not the way, but took the gainest way in that woodness, that many times he was like to perish. And at the last him happened to come to a fair green way, and there he met with a poor man of the country, whom he saluted and asked him whether he met not with a knight upon a black horse and all black harness, a little dwarf sitting behind him with heavy cheer. Sir, said the poor man, here by me came Sir Gringamore the knight, with such a dwarf mourning as ye say; and therefore I rede you not follow him, for he is one of the periloust knights of the world, and his castle is here nigh hand but two mile; therefore we advise you ride not after Sir Gringamore, but if ye owe him good will.

So leave we Sir Beaumains riding toward the castle, and speak we of Sir Gringamore and the dwarf. Anon as the dwarf was come to the castle, Dame Lionesse and Dame Linet her sister, asked the dwarf where was his master born, and of what lineage he was come. And but if thou tell me, said Dame Lionesse, thou shalt never escape this castle, but ever here to be prisoner. As for that, said the dwarf, I fear not greatly to tell his name and of what kin he is come. Wit you well he is a king's son, and his mother is sister to King Arthur, and he is brother to the good knight Sir Gawaine, and his name is Sir Gareth of Orkney. And now I have told you his right name, I pray you, fair lady, let me go to my lord again, for he will never out of this country until that he have me again. And if he be angry he will do much harm or that he be stint, and work you wrack in this country. As for that threatening, said Sir Gringamore, be it as it be may, we will go to dinner. And so they washed and went to meat, and made them merry and well at ease, and because the Lady Lionesse of the castle was there, they made great joy. Truly, madam, said Linet unto her sister, well may he be a king's son, for he hath many good tatches on him, for he is courteous and mild, and the most suffering man that ever I met withal. For I dare say there was never gentlewoman reviled man in so foul a manner as I have rebuked him; and at all times he gave me goodly and meek answers again.

And as they sat thus talking, there came Sir Gareth in at the gate with an angry countenance, and his sword drawn in his hand, and cried aloud that all the castle might hear it, saying: Thou traitor, Sir Gringamore, deliver me my dwarf again, or by the faith that I owe to the order of knighthood, I shall do thee all the harm that I can. Then Sir Gringamore looked out at a window and said, Sir Gareth of Orkney, leave thy boasting words, for thou gettest not thy dwarf again. Thou coward knight, said Sir Gareth, bring him with thee, and come and do battle with me, and win him and take him. So will I do, said Sir Gringamore, an me list, but for all thy great words thou gettest him not. Ah! fair brother, said Dame Lionesse, I would he had his dwarf again, for I would he were not wroth, for now he hath told me all my desire I keep no more of the dwarf. And also, brother, he hath done much for me, and delivered me from the Red Knight of the Red Launds, and therefore, brother, I owe him my service afore all knights living. And wit ye well that I love him before all other, and full fain I would speak with him. But in nowise I would that he wist what I were, but that I were another strange lady.

Well, said Sir Gringamore, sithen I know now your will, I will obey now unto him. And right therewithal he went down unto Sir Gareth, and said: Sir, I cry you mercy, and all that I have misdone I will amend it at your will. And therefore I pray you that ye would alight, and take such cheer as I can make you in this castle. Shall I have my dwarf? said Sir Gareth. Yea, sir, and all the pleasaunce that I can make you, for as soon as your dwarf told me what ye were and of what blood ye are come, and what noble deeds ye have done in these marches, then I repented of my deeds. And then Sir Gareth alighted, and there came his dwarf and took his horse. O my fellow, said Sir Gareth, I have had many adventures for thy sake. And so Sir Gringamore took him by the hand and led him into the hall where his own wife was.

CHAPTER XXI

How Sir Gareth, otherwise called Beaumains, came to the
presence of his lady, and how they took acquaintance,
and of their love.

And then came forth Dame Lionesse arrayed like a princess, and there she made him passing good cheer, and he her again; and they had goodly language and lovely countenance together. And Sir Gareth thought many times, Jesu, would that the lady of the Castle Perilous were so fair as she was. There were all manner of games and plays, of dancing and singing. And ever the more Sir Gareth beheld that lady, the more he loved her; and so he burned in love that he was past himself in his reason; and forth toward night they yede unto supper, and Sir Gareth might not eat, for his love was so hot that he wist not where he was.

All these looks espied Sir Gringamore, and then at-after supper he called his sister Dame Lionesse into a chamber, and said: Fair sister, I have well espied your countenance betwixt you and this knight, and I will, sister, that ye wit he is a full noble knight, and if ye can make him to abide here I will do him all the pleasure that I can, for an ye were better than ye are, ye were well bywaryd upon him. Fair brother, said Dame Lionesse, I understand well that the knight is good, and come he is of a noble house. Notwithstanding, I will assay him better, howbeit I am most beholden to him of any earthly man; for he hath had great labour for my love, and passed many a dangerous passage.

Right so Sir Gringamore went unto Sir Gareth, and said, Sir, make ye good cheer, for ye shall have none other cause, for this lady, my sister, is yours at all times, her worship saved, for wit ye well she loveth you as well as ye do her, and better if better may be. An I wist that, said Sir Gareth, there lived not a gladder man than I would be. Upon my worship, said Sir Gringamore, trust unto my promise; and as long as it liketh you ye shall sojourn with me, and this lady shall be with us daily and nightly to make you all the cheer that she can. I will well, said Sir Gareth, for I have promised to be nigh this country this twelvemonth. And well I am sure King Arthur and other noble knights will find me where that I am within this twelvemonth. For I shall be sought and found, if that I be alive. And then the noble knight Sir Gareth went unto the Dame Lionesse, which he then much loved, and kissed her many times, and either made great joy of other. And there she promised him her love certainly, to love him and none other the days of her life. Then this lady, Dame Lionesse, by the assent of her brother, told Sir Gareth all the truth what she was, and how she was the same lady that he did battle for, and how she was lady of the Castle Perilous, and there she told him how she caused her brother to take away his dwarf,* for this cause, to know the certainty what was your name, and of what kin ye were come.

CHAPTER XXII

How at night came an armed knight, and fought with Sir Gareth, and he, sore hurt in the thigh, smote off the knight's head.

And then she let fetch to-fore him Linet, the damosel that had ridden with him many wildsome ways. Then was Sir Gareth more gladder than he was to-fore. And then they troth-plight each other to love, and never to fail whiles their life lasteth. And so they burnt both in

---

* Printed by Caxton as part of chapter xxii.

love, that they were accorded to abate their lusts secretly. And there Dame Lionesse counselled Sir Gareth to sleep in none other place but in the hall. And there she promised him to come to his bed a little afore midnight.

This counsel was not so privily kept but it was understood; for they were but young both, and tender of age, and had not used none such crafts to-fore. Wherefore the damosel Linet was a little displeased, and she thought her sister Dame Lionesse was a little over-hasty, that she might not abide the time of her marriage; and for saving their worship, she thought to abate their hot lusts. And so she let ordain by her subtle crafts that they had not their intents neither with other, as in their delights, until they were married. And so it passed on. At-after supper was made clean avoidance, that every lord and lady should go unto his rest. But Sir Gareth said plainly he would go no farther than the hall, for in such places, he said, was convenient for an errant-knight to take his rest in; and so there were ordained great couches, and thereon feather beds, and there laid him down to sleep; and within a while came Dame Lionesse, wrapped in a mantle furred with ermine, and laid her down beside Sir Gareth. And therewithal he began to kiss her. And then he looked afore him, and there he apperceived and saw come an armed knight, with many lights about him; and this knight had a long gisarm in his hand, and made grim countenance to smite him. When Sir Gareth saw him come in that wise, he leapt out of his bed, and gat in his hand his sword, and leapt straight toward that knight. And when the knight saw Sir Gareth come so fiercely upon him, he smote him with a foin through the thick of the thigh that the wound was a shaftmon broad and had cut a-two many veins and sinews. And therewithal Sir Gareth smote him upon the helm such a buffet that he fell grovelling; and then he leapt over him and unlaced his helm, and smote off his head from the body. And then he bled so fast that he might not stand, but so he laid him down upon his bed, and there he swooned and lay as he had been dead.

Then Dame Lionesse cried aloud, that her brother Sir Gringamore heard, and came down. And when he saw Sir Gareth so shamefully wounded he was sore displeased, and said: I am shamed that this noble knight is thus honoured. Sir, said Sir Gringamore, how may this be, that ye be here, and this noble knight wounded? Brother, she said, I can not tell you, for it was not done by me, nor by mine assent. For he is my lord and I am his, and he must be mine husband;

therefore, my brother, I will that ye wit I shame me not to be with him, nor to do him all the pleasure that I can. Sister, said Sir Gringamore, and I will that ye wit it, and Sir Gareth both, that it was never done by me, nor by my assent that this unhappy deed was done. And there they staunched his bleeding as well as they might, and great sorrow made Sir Gringamore and Dame Lionesse.

And forthwithal came Dame Linet, and took up the head in the sight of them all, and anointed it with an ointment thereas it was smitten off; and in the same wise she did to the other part thereas the head stuck, and then she set it together, and it stuck as fast as ever it did. And the knight arose lightly up, and the damosel Linet put him in her chamber. All this saw Sir Gringamore and Dame Lionesse, and so did Sir Gareth; and well he espied that it was the damosel Linet, that rode with him through the perilous passages. Ah well, damosel, said Sir Gareth, I weened ye would not have done as ye have done. My lord Gareth, said Linet, all that I have done I will avow, and all that I have done shall be for your honour and worship, and to us all. And so within a while Sir Gareth was nigh whole, and waxed light and jocund, and sang, danced, and gamed; and he and Dame Lionesse were so hot in burning love that they made their covenant at the tenth night after, that she should come to his bed. And because he was wounded afore, he laid his armour and his sword nigh his bed's side.

CHAPTER XXIII

How the said knight came again the next night and was beheaded again, and how at the feast of Pentecost all the knights that Sir Gareth had overcome came and yielded them to King Arthur.

Right as she promised she came; and she was not so soon in his bed but she espied an armed knight coming toward the bed: therewithal she warned Sir Gareth, and lightly through the good help of Dame Lionesse he was armed; and they hurtled together with great ire and malice all about the hall; and there was great light as it had been the number of twenty torches both before and behind, so that Sir Gareth strained him, so that his old wound brast again a-bleeding; but he was hot and courageous and took no keep, but with his great force he struck down that knight, and voided his helm, and struck off his head. Then he hewed the head in an hundred pieces. And when he had done so he took up all those pieces, and threw them out at a window into the ditches of the castle; and by this done he was so faint that unnethes he might stand for bleeding. And by when he was almost unarmed he fell in a deadly swoon on the floor; and then Dame Lionesse cried so that Sir Gringamore heard; and when he came and found Sir Gareth in that plight he made great sorrow; and there he awaked Sir Gareth, and gave him a drink that relieved him wonderly well; but the sorrow that Dame Lionesse made there may no tongue tell, for she so fared with herself as she would have died.

Right so came this damosel Linet before them all, and she had fetched all the gobbets of the head that Sir Gareth had thrown out at a window, and there she anointed them as she had done to-fore, and set them together again. Well, damosel Linet, said Sir Gareth, I have not deserved all this despite that ye do unto me. Sir knight, she said, I have nothing done but I will avow, and all that I have done shall be to your worship, and to us all. And then was Sir Gareth staunched of his bleeding. But the leeches said that there was no man that bare the life should heal him throughout of his wound but if they healed him that caused that stroke by enchantment.

So leave we Sir Gareth there with Sir Gringamore and his sisters, and turn we unto King Arthur, that at the next feast of Pentecost held his feast; and there came the Green Knight with fifty knights, and yielded them all unto King Arthur. And so there came the Red Knight his brother, and yielded him to King Arthur, and three score knights with him. Also there came the Blue Knight, brother to them, with an hundred knights, and yielded them unto King Arthur; and the Green Knight's name was Pertolepe, and the Red Knight's name was Perimones, and the Blue Knight's name was Sir Persant of Inde. These three brethren told King Arthur how they were overcome by a knight that a damosel had with her, and called him Beaumains. Jesu, said the king, I marvel what knight he is, and of what lineage he is come. He was with me a twelvemonth, and poorly and shamefully he was fostered, and Sir Kay in scorn named him Beaumains. So right as the king stood so talking with these three brethren, there came Sir Launcelot du Lake, and told the king that there was come a goodly lord with six hundred knights with him.

Then the king went out of Carlion, for there was the feast, and
there came to him this lord, and saluted the king in a goodly manner.
What will ye, said King Arthur, and what is your errand? Sir, he said,
my name is the Red Knight of the Red Launds, but my name is Sir
Ironside; and sir, wit ye well, here I am sent to you of a knight that is
called Beaumains, for he won me in plain battle hand for hand, and so
did never no knight but he, that ever had the better of me this thirty
winter; the which commanded to yield me to you at your will. Ye
are welcome, said the king, for ye have been long a great foe to me
and my court, and now I trust to God I shall so entreat you that ye
shall be my friend. Sir, both I and these five hundred knights shall
always be at your summons to do you service as may lie in our
powers. Jesu mercy, said King Arthur, I am much beholden unto that
knight that hath put so his body in devoir to worship me and my
court. And as to thee, Ironside, that art called the Red Knight of the
Red Launds, thou art called a perilous knight; and if thou wilt hold of
me I shall worship thee and make thee knight of the Table Round;
but then thou must be no more a murderer. Sir, as to that, I have
promised unto Sir Beaumains never more to use such customs, for all
the shameful customs that I used I did at the request of a lady that I
loved; and therefore I must go unto Sir Launcelot, and unto Sir
Gawaine, and ask them forgiveness of the evil will I had unto them;
for all that I put to death was all only for the love of Sir Launcelot and
of Sir Gawaine. They be here now, said the king, afore thee, now
may ye say to them what ye will. And then he kneeled down unto Sir
Launcelot, and to Sir Gawaine, and prayed them of forgiveness of his
enmity that ever he had against them.

CHAPTER XXIV

How King Arthur pardoned them, and demanded of them where Sir Gareth was.

Then goodly they said all at once, God forgive you, and we do, and
pray you that ye will tell us where we may find Sir Beaumains. Fair
lords, said Sir Ironside, I cannot tell you, for it is full hard to find him;
for such young knights as he is one, when they be in their adventures

be never abiding in no place. But to say the worship that the Red Knight of the Red Launds, and Sir Persant and his brother said of Beaumains, it was marvel to hear. Well, my fair lords, said King Arthur, wit you well I shall do you honour for the love of Sir Beaumains, and as soon as ever I meet with him I shall make you all upon one day knights of the Table Round. And as to thee, Sir Persant of Inde, thou hast been ever called a full noble knight, and so have ever been thy three brethren called. But I marvel, said the king, that I hear not of the Black Knight your brother, he was a full noble knight. Sir, said Pertolepe, the Green Knight, Sir Beaumains slew him in a recounter with his spear, his name was Sir Percard. That was great pity, said the king, and so said many knights. For these four brethren were full well known in the court of King Arthur for noble knights, for long time they had holden war against the knights of the Round Table. Then said Pertolepe, the Green Knight, to the king: At a passage of the water of Mortaise there encountered Sir Beaumains with two brethren that ever for the most part kept that passage, and they were two deadly knights, and there he slew the eldest brother in the water, and smote him upon the head such a buffet that he fell down in the water, and there he was drowned, and his name was Sir Gherard le Breusse; and after he slew the other brother upon the land, his name was Sir Arnold le Breusse.

CHAPTER XXV*

How the Queen of Orkney came to this feast of Pentecost, and Sir Gawaine and his brethren came to ask her blessing.

So then the king and they went to meat, and were served in the best manner. And as they sat at the meat, there came in the Queen of Orkney, with ladies and knights a great number. And then Sir Gawaine, Sir Agravaine, and Gaheris arose, and went to her and saluted her upon their knees, and asked her blessing; for in fifteen year they had not seen her. Then she spake on high to her brother King

* In Caxton's edition this chapter is misnumbered xxvi, setting the numeration wrong to the end of the book.

Arthur: Where have ye done my young son Sir Gareth? He was here amongst you a twelvemonth, and ye made a kitchen knave of him, the which is shame to you all. Alas, where have ye done my dear son that was my joy and bliss? O dear mother, said Sir Gawaine, I knew him not. Nor I, said the king, that now me repenteth, but thanked be God he is proved a worshipful knight as any is now living of his years, and I shall never be glad till I may find him.

Ah, brother, said the Queen unto King Arthur, and unto Sir Gawaine, and to all her sons, ye did yourself great shame when ye amongst you kept my son in the kitchen and fed him like a poor hog. Fair sister, said King Arthur, ye shall right well wit I knew him not, nor no more did Sir Gawaine, nor his brethren; but sithen it is so, said the king, that he is thus gone from us all, we must shape a remedy to find him. Also, sister, meseemeth ye might have done me to wit of his coming, and then an I had not done well to him ye might have blamed me. For when he came to this court he came leaning upon two men's shoulders, as though he might not have gone. And then he asked me three gifts; and one he asked the same day, that was that I would give him meat enough that twelvemonth; and the other two gifts he asked that day a twelvemonth, and that was that he might have the adventure of the damosel Linet, and the third was that Sir Launcelot should make him knight when he desired him. And so I granted him all his desire, and many in this court marvelled that he desired his sustenance for a twelvemonth. And thereby, we deemed, many of us, that he was not come of a noble house.

Sir, said the Queen of Orkney unto King Arthur her brother, wit ye well that I sent him unto you right well armed and horsed, and worshipfully beseen of his body, and gold and silver plenty to spend. It may be, said the King, but thereof saw we none, save that same day as he departed from us, knights told me that there came a dwarf hither suddenly, and brought him armour and a good horse full well and richly beseen; and thereat we all had marvel from whence that riches came, that we deemed all that he was come of men of worship. Brother, said the queen, all that ye say I believe, for ever sithen he was grown he was marvellously witted, and ever he was faithful and true of his promise. But I marvel, said she, that Sir Kay did mock him and scorn him, and gave him that name Beaumains; yet, Sir Kay, said the queen, named him more righteously than he weened; for I dare say an he be alive, he is as fair an handed man and well disposed as any is living. Sir, said Arthur, let this language be still, and by the grace of God he shall be found an he be within this seven realms, and let all this pass and be merry, for he is proved to be a man of worship, and that is my joy.

CHAPTER XXVI

How King Arthur sent for the Lady Lionesse, and how she let cry a tourney at her castle, whereas came many knights.

Then said Sir Gawaine and his brethren unto Arthur, Sir, an ye will give us leave, we will go and seek our brother. Nay, said Sir Launcelot, that shall ye not need; and so said Sir Baudwin of Britain: for as by our advice the king shall send unto Dame Lionesse a messenger, and pray her that she will come to the court in all the haste that she may, and doubt ye not she will come; and then she may give you best counsel where ye shall find him. This is well said of you, said the king. So then goodly letters were made, and the messenger sent forth, that night and day he went till he came unto the Castle Perilous. And then the lady Dame Lionesse was sent for, thereas she was with Sir Gringamore her brother and Sir Gareth. And when she understood this message, she bade him ride on his way unto King Arthur, and she would come after in all goodly haste. Then when she came to Sir Gringamore and to Sir Gareth, she told them all how King Arthur had sent for her. That is because of me, said Sir Gareth. Now advise me, said Dame Lionesse, what shall I say, and in what manner I shall rule me. My lady and my love, said Sir Gareth, I pray you in no wise be ye aknowen where I am; but well I wot my mother is there and all my brethren, and they will take upon them to seek me, I wot well that they do. But this, madam, I would ye said and advised the king when he questioned with you of me. Then may ye say, this is your advice that, an it like his good grace, ye will do make a cry against the feast of the Assumption of our Lady, that what knight there proveth him best he shall wield you and all your land. And if so be that he be a wedded man, that his wife shall have the degree, and a coronal of gold beset with stones of virtue to the value of a thousand pound, and a white gerfalcon.

So Dame Lionesse departed and came to King Arthur, where she was nobly received, and there she was sore questioned of the king and of the Queen of Orkney. And she answered, where Sir Gareth was she could not tell. But thus much she said unto Arthur: Sir, I will let cry a tournament that shall be done before my castle at the Assumption of our Lady, and the cry shall be this: that you, my lord Arthur, shall be there, and your knights, and I will purvey that my knights shall be against yours; and then I am sure ye shall hear of Sir Gareth. This is well advised, said King Arthur; and so she departed. And the king and she made great provision to that tournament.

When Dame Lionesse was come to the Isle of Avilion, that was the same isle thereas her brother Sir Gringamore dwelt, then she told them all how she had done, and what promise she had made to King Arthur. Alas, said Sir Gareth, I have been so wounded with unhappiness sithen I came into this castle that I shall not be able to do at that tournament like a knight; for I was never thoroughly whole since I was hurt. Be ye of good cheer, said the damosel Linet, for I undertake within these fifteen days to make ye whole, and as lusty as ever ye were. And then she laid an ointment and a salve to him as it pleased to her, that he was never so fresh nor so lusty. Then said the damosel Linet: Send you unto Sir Persant of Inde, and assummon him and his knights to be here with you as they have promised. Also, that ye send unto Sir Ironside, that is the Red Knight of the Red Launds, and charge him that he be ready with you with his whole sum of knights, and then shall ye be able to match with King Arthur and his knights. So this was done, and all knights were sent for unto the Castle Perilous; and then the Red Knight answered and said unto Dame Lionesse, and to Sir Gareth, Madam, and my lord Sir Gareth, ye shall understand that I have been at the court of King Arthur, and Sir Persant of Inde and his brethren, and there we have done our homage as ye commanded us. Also Sir Ironside said, I have taken upon me with Sir Persant of Inde and his brethren to hold part against my lord Sir Launcelot and the knights of that court. And this have I done for the love of my lady Dame Lionesse, and you my lord Sir Gareth. Ye have well done, said Sir Gareth; but wit you well ye shall be full sore matched with the most noble knights of the world; therefore we must purvey us of good knights, where we may get them. That is well said, said Sir Persant, and worshipfully.

And so the cry was made in England, Wales, and Scotland, Ireland,

Cornwall, and in all the Out Isles, and in Brittany and in many countries; that at the feast of our Lady the Assumption next coming, men should come to the Castle Perilous beside the Isle of Avilion; and there all the knights that there came should have the choice whether them list to be on the one party with the knights of the castle, or on the other party with King Arthur. And two months was to the day that the tournament should be. And so there came many good knights that were at their large, and held them for the most part against King Arthur and his knights of the Round Table, and came in the side of them of the castle. For Sir Epinogrus was the first, and he was the king's son of Northumberland, and Sir Palomides the Saracen was another, and Sir Safere his brother, and Sir Segwarides his brother, but they were christened, and Sir Malegrine another, and Sir Brian de les Isles, a noble knight, and Sir Grummore Grummursum, a good knight of Scotland, and Sir Carados of the dolorous tower, a noble knight, and Sir Turquine his brother, and Sir Arnold and Sir Gauter, two brethren, good knights of Cornwall. There came Sir Tristram de Liones, and with him Sir Dinas, the Seneschal, and Sir Sadok; but this Sir Tristram was not at that time knight of the Table Round, but he was one of the best knights of the world. And so all these noble knights accompanied them with the lady of the castle, and with the Red Knight of the Red Launds; but as for Sir Gareth, he would not take upon him more but as other mean knights.

CHAPTER XXVII

How King Arthur went to the tournament with his knights, and how the lady received him worshipfully, and how the knights encountered.

And then there came with King Arthur Sir Gawaine, Agravaine, Gaheris, his brethren. And then his nephews Sir Uwaine le Blanchemains, and Sir Aglovale, Sir Tor, Sir Percivale de Galis, and Sir Lamorak de Galis. Then came Sir Launcelot du Lake with his brethren, nephews, and cousins, as Sir Lionel, Sir Ector de Maris, Sir Bors de Ganis, and Sir Galihodin, Sir Galihud, and many more of Sir Launcelot's blood, and Sir Dinadan, Sir La Cote Male Taile, his brother, a good knight, and Sir Sagramore, a good knight; and all the most part of the Round Table. Also there came with King Arthur these knights, the King of Ireland, King Agwisance, and the King of Scotland, King Carados and King Uriens of the land of Gore, and King Bagdemagus and his son Sir Meliaganus, and Sir Galahault the noble prince. All these kings, princes, and earls, barons, and other noble knights, as Sir Brandiles, Sir Uwaine les Avoutres, and Sir Kay, Sir Bedivere, Sir Meliot de Logres, Sir Petipase of Winchelsea, Sir Godelake: all these came with King Arthur, and more that cannot be rehearsed.

Now leave we of these kings and knights, and let us speak of the great array that was made within the castle and about the castle for both parties. The Lady Dame Lionesse ordained great array upon her part for her noble knights, for all manner of lodging and victual that came by land and by water, that there lacked nothing for her party, nor for the other, but there was plenty to be had for gold and silver for King Arthur and his knights. And then there came the harbingers from King Arthur for to harbour him, and his kings, dukes, earls, barons, and knights. And then Sir Gareth prayed Dame Lionesse and the Red Knight of the Red Launds, and Sir Persant and his brother, and Sir Gringamore, that in no wise there should none of them tell not his name, and make no more of him than of the least knight that there was. For, he said, I will not be known of neither more nor less, neither at the beginning neither at the ending. Then Dame Lionesse said unto Sir Gareth: Sir, I will lend you a ring, but I would pray you as you love me heartily let me have it again when the tournament is done, for that ring increaseth my beauty much more than it is of himself. And the virtue of my ring is that, that is green it will turn to red, and that is red it will turn in likeness to green, and that is blue it will turn to likeness of white, and that is white it will turn in likeness to blue, and so it will do of all manner of colours. Also who that beareth my ring shall lose no blood, and for great love I will give you this ring. Gramercy, said Sir Gareth, mine own lady, for this ring is passing meet for me, for it will turn all manner of likeness that I am in, and that shall cause me that I shall not be known. Then Sir Gringamore gave Sir Gareth a bay courser that was a passing good horse; also he gave him good armour and sure, and a noble sword that sometime Sir Gringamore's father won upon an heathen tyrant. And so thus every knight made him ready to that tournament. And

King Arthur was come two days to-fore the Assumption of our Lady. And there was all manner of royalty of all minstrelsy that might be found. Also there came Queen Guenever and the Queen of Orkney, Sir Gareth's mother.

And upon the Assumption Day, when mass and matins were done, there were heralds with trumpets commanded to blow to the field. And so there came out Sir Epinogrus, the king's son of Northumberland, from the castle, and there encountered with him Sir Sagramore le Desirous, and either of them brake their spears to their hands. And then came in Sir Palomides out of the castle, and there encountered with him Gawaine, and either of them smote other so hard that both the good knights and their horses fell to the earth. And then knights of either party rescued their knights. And then came in Sir Safere and Sir Segwarides, brethren to Sir Palomides; and there encountered Sir Agravaine with Sir Safere and Sir Gaheris encountered with Sir Segwarides. So Sir Safere smote down Agravaine, Sir Gawaine's brother; and Sir Segwarides, Sir Safere's brother. And Sir Malegrine, a knight of the castle, encountered with Sir Uwaine le Blanchemains, and there Sir Uwaine gave Sir Malegrine a fall, that he had almost broke his neck.

CHAPTER XXVIII

How the knights bare them in the battle.

Then Sir Brian de les Isles and Grummore Grummursum, knights of the castle, encountered with Sir Aglovale, and Sir Tor smote down Sir Grummore Grummursum to the earth. Then came in Sir Carados of the dolorous tower, and Sir Turquine, knights of the castle; and there encountered with them Sir Percivale de Galis and Sir Lamorak de Galis, that were two brethren. And there encountered Sir Percivale with Sir Carados, and either brake their spears unto their hands, and then Sir Turquine with Sir Lamorak, and either of them smote down other's horse and all to the earth, and either parties rescued other, and horsed them again. And Sir Arnold and Sir Gauter, knights of the castle, encountered with Sir Brandiles and Sir Kay, and these four knights encountered mightily, and brake their spears to their hands. Then came in Sir Tristram, Sir Sadok, and Sir Dinas, knights of the castle, and there encountered Sir Tristram with Sir Bedivere, and there Sir Bedivere was smitten to the earth both horse and man. And Sir Sadok encountered with Sir Petipase, and there Sir Sadok was overthrown. And there Uwaine les Avoutres smote down Sir Dinas, the Seneschal. Then came in Sir Persant of Inde, a knight of the castle, and there encountered with him Sir Launcelot du Lake, and there he smote Sir Persant, horse and man, to the earth. Then came Sir Pertolepe from the castle, and there encountered with him Sir Lionel, and there Sir Pertolepe, the Green Knight, smote down Sir Lionel, brother to Sir Launcelot. All this was marked by noble heralds, who bare him best, and their names.

And then came into the field Sir Perimones, the Red Knight, Sir Persant's brother, that was a knight of the castle, and he encountered with Sir Ector de Maris, and either smote other so hard that both their horses and they fell to the earth. And then came in the Red Knight of the Red Launds, and Sir Gareth, from the castle, and there encountered with them Sir Bors de Ganis and Sir Bleoberis, and there the Red Knight and Sir Bors [either] smote other so hard that their spears brast, and their horses fell grovelling to the earth. Then Sir Bleoberis brake his spear upon Sir Gareth, but of that stroke Sir Bleoberis fell to the earth. When Sir Galihodin saw that he bade Sir Gareth keep him, and Sir Gareth smote him to the earth. Then Sir Galihud gat a spear to avenge his brother, and in the same wise Sir Gareth served him, and Sir Dinadan and his brother, La Cote Male Taile, and Sir Sagramore le Desirous, and Sir Dodinas le Savage. All these he bare down with one spear.

When King Agwisance of Ireland saw Sir Gareth fare so, he marvelled what he might be that one time seemed green, and another time, at his again coming, he seemed blue. And thus at every course that he rode to and fro he changed his colour, so that there might neither king nor knight have ready cognisance of him. Then Sir Agwisance, the King of Ireland, encountered with Sir Gareth, and there Sir Gareth smote him from his horse, saddle and all. And then came King Carados of Scotland, and Sir Gareth smote him down horse and man. And in the same wise he served King Uriens of the land of Gore. And then came in Sir Bagdemagus, and Sir Gareth smote him down, horse and man, to the earth. And Bagdemagus' son, Meliganus, brake a spear upon Sir Gareth mightily and knightly.

And then Sir Galahault, the noble prince, cried on high: Knight with the many colours, well hast thou jousted; now make thee ready that I may joust with thee. Sir Gareth heard him, and he gat a great spear, and so they encountered together, and there the prince brake his spear; but Sir Gareth smote him upon the left side of the helm that he reeled here and there, and he had fallen down had not his men recovered him.

So God me help, said King Arthur, that same knight with the many colours is a good knight. Wherefore the king called unto him Sir Launcelot, and prayed him to encounter with that knight. Sir, said Launcelot, I may well find in my heart for to forbear him as at this time, for he hath had travail enough this day; and when a good knight doth so well upon some day, it is no good knight's part to let him of his worship, and namely, when he seeth a knight hath done so great labour; for peradventure, said Sir Launcelot, his quarrel is here this day, and peradventure he is best beloved with this lady of all that be here; for I see well he paineth him and enforceth him to do great deeds, and therefore, said Sir Launcelot, as for me, this day he shall have the honour; though it lay in my power to put him from it I would not.

CHAPTER XXIX

Yet of the said tournament.

Then when this was done there was drawing of swords, and then there began a sore tournament. And there did Sir Lamorak marvellous deeds of arms; and betwixt Sir Lamorak and Sir Ironside, that was the Red Knight of the Red Launds, there was strong battle; and betwixt Sir Palomides and Bleoberis there was a strong battle; and Sir Gawaine and Sir Tristram met, and there Sir Gawaine had the worse, for he pulled Sir Gawaine from his horse, and there he was long upon foot, and defouled. Then came in Sir Launcelot, and he smote Sir Turquine, and he him; and then came Sir Carados his brother, and both at once they assailed him, and he as the most noblest knight of the world worshipfully fought with them both, that all men wondered of the noblesse of Sir Launcelot. And then came in Sir

Gareth, and knew that it was Sir Launcelot that fought with the two perilous knights. And then Sir Gareth came with his good horse and hurtled them in-sunder, and no stroke would he smite to Sir Launcelot. That espied Sir Launcelot, and deemed it should be the good knight Sir Gareth: and then Sir Gareth rode here and there, and smote on the right hand and on the left hand, and all the folk might well espy where that he rode. And by fortune he met with his brother Sir Gawaine, and there he put Sir Gawaine to the worse, for he put off his helm, and so he served five or six knights of the Round Table, that all men said he put him in the most pain, and best he did his devoir. For when Sir Tristram beheld him how he first jousted and after fought so well with a sword, then he rode unto Sir Ironside and to Sir Persant of Inde, and asked them, by their faith, What manner a knight is yonder knight that seemeth in so many divers colours? Truly, meseemeth, said Tristram, that he putteth himself in great pain, for he never ceaseth. Wot ye not what he is? said Sir Ironside. No, said Sir Tristram. Then shall ye know that this is he that loveth the lady of the castle, and she him again; and this is he that won me when I besieged the lady of this castle, and this is he that won Sir Persant of Inde, and his three brethren. What is his name, said Sir Tristram, and of what blood is he come? He was called in the court of King Arthur, Beaumains, but his right name is Sir Gareth of Orkney, brother to Sir Gawaine. By my head, said Sir Tristram, he is a good knight, and a big man of arms, and if he be young he shall prove a full noble knight. He is but a child, they all said, and of Sir Launcelot he was made knight. Therefore he is mickle the better, said Tristram. And then Sir Tristram, Sir Ironside, Sir Persant, and his brother, rode together for to help Sir Gareth; and then there were given many strong strokes.

And then Sir Gareth rode out on the one side to amend his helm; and then said his dwarf: Take me your ring, that ye lose it not while that ye drink. And so when he had drunk he gat on his helm, and eagerly took his horse and rode into the field, and left his ring with his dwarf; and the dwarf was glad the ring was from him, for then he wist well he should be known. And then when Sir Gareth was in the field all folks saw him well and plainly that he was in yellow colours; and there he rased off helms and pulled down knights, that King Arthur had marvel what knight he was, for the king saw by his hair that it was the same knight.

CHAPTER XXX

*How Sir Gareth was espied by the heralds, and how he
escaped out of the field.*

But before he was in so many colours, and now he is but in one
colour; that is yellow. Now go, said King Arthur unto divers heralds,
and ride about him, and espy what manner knight he is, for I have
spered of many knights this day that be upon his party, and all say
they know him not. And so an herald rode nigh Gareth as he could;
and there he saw written about his helm in gold, This helm is Sir
Gareth of Orkney. Then the herald cried as he were wood, and
many heralds with him: – This is Sir Gareth of Orkney in the yellow
arms; wherby* all kings and knights of Arthur's beheld him and
awaited; and then they pressed all to behold him, and ever the heralds
cried: This is Sir Gareth of Orkney, King Lot's son. And when Sir
Gareth espied that he was discovered, then he doubled his strokes,
and smote down Sir Sagramore, and his brother Sir Gawaine. O
brother, said Sir Gawaine, I weened ye would not have stricken me.

So when he heard him say so he thrang here and there, and so with
great pain he gat out of the press, and there he met with his dwarf. O
boy, said Sir Gareth, thou hast beguiled me foul this day that thou
kept my ring; give it me anon again, that I may hide my body withal;
and so he took it him. And then they all wist not where he was
become; and Sir Gawaine had in manner espied where Sir Gareth
rode, and then he rode after with all his might. That espied Sir
Gareth, and rode lightly into the forest, that Sir Gawaine wist not
where he was become. And when Sir Gareth wist that Sir Gawaine
was passed, he asked the dwarf of best counsel. Sir, said the dwarf,
meseemeth it were best, now that ye are escaped from spying, that ye
send my lady Dame Lionesse her ring. It is well advised, said Sir
Gareth; now have it here and bear it to her, and say that I
recommend me unto her good grace, and say her I will come when I
may, and I pray her to be true and faithful to me as I will be to her.

* So Wynkyn de Worde; Caxton 'that by'.

Sir, said the dwarf, it shall be done as ye command: and so he rode his way, and did his errand unto the lady. Then she said, Where is my knight, Sir Gareth? Madam, said the dwarf, he bade me say that he would not be long from you. And so lightly the dwarf came again unto Sir Gareth, that would full fain have had a lodging, for he had need to be reposed. And then fell there a thunder and a rain, as heaven and earth should go together. And Sir Gareth was not a little weary, for of all that day he had but little rest; neither his horse nor he. So this Sir Gareth rode so long in that forest until the night came. And ever it lightened and thundered, as it had been wood. At the last by fortune he came to a castle, and there he heard the waits upon the walls.

CHAPTER XXXI

How Sir Gareth came to a castle where he was well lodged,
and he jousted with a knight and slew him.

Then Sir Gareth rode unto the barbican of the castle, and prayed the porter fair to let him into the castle. The porter answered ungoodly again, and said, Thou gettest no lodging here. Fair sir, say not so, for I am a knight of King Arthur's, and pray the lord or the lady of this castle to give me harbour for the love of King Arthur. Then the porter went unto the duchess, and told her how there was a knight of King Arthur's would have harbour. Let him in, said the duchess, for I will see that knight, and for King Arthur's sake he shall not be harbourless. Then she yode up into a tower over the gate, with great torch-light.

When Sir Gareth saw that torch-light he cried on high: Whether thou be lord or lady, giant or champion, I take no force so that I may have harbour this night; and if it so be that I must needs fight, spare me not to-morn when I have rested me, for both I and mine horse be weary. Sir knight, said the lady, thou speakest knightly and boldly; but wit thou well the lord of this castle loveth not King Arthur, nor none of his court, for my lord hath ever been against him; and therefore thou were better not to come within this castle; for an thou come in this night, thou must come in under such form, that wheresomever thou meet my lord, by stigh or by street, thou must yield thee to him as prisoner. Madam, said Sir Gareth, what is your lord, and what is his name? Sir, my lord's name is the Duke de la Rowse. Well madam, said Sir Gareth, I shall promise you in what place I meet your lord I shall yield me unto him and to his good grace; with that I understand he will do me no harm: and if I understand that he will, I will release myself an I can with my spear and my sword. Ye say well, said the duchess; and then she let the drawbridge down, and so he rode into the hall, and there he alighted, and his horse was led into a stable; and in the hall he unarmed him and said, Madam, I will not out of this hall this night; and when it is daylight, let see who will have ado with me, he shall find me ready. Then was he set unto supper, and had many good dishes. Then Sir Gareth list well to eat, and knightly he ate his meat, and eagerly; there was many a fair lady by him, and some said they never saw a goodlier man nor so well of eating. Then they made him passing good cheer, and shortly when he had supped his bed was made there; so he rested him all night.

And on the morn he heard mass, and brake his fast and took his leave at the duchess, and at them all; and thanked her goodly of her lodging, and of his good cheer; and then she asked him his name. Madam, he said, truly my name is Gareth of Orkney, and some men call me Beaumains. Then knew she well it was the same knight that fought for Dame Lionesse. So Sir Gareth departed and rode up into a mountain, and there met him a knight, his name was Sir Bendelaine, and said to Sir Gareth: Thou shalt not pass this way, for either thou shalt joust with me, or else be my prisoner. Then will I joust, said Sir Gareth. And so they let their horses run, and there Sir Gareth smote him throughout the body; and Sir Bendelaine rode forth to his castle there beside, and there died. So Sir Gareth would have rested him, and he came riding to Bendelaine's castle. Then his knights and servants espied that it was he that had slain their lord. Then they armed twenty good men, and came out and assailed Sir Gareth; and so he had no spear, but his sword, and put his shield afore him; and there they brake their spears upon him, and they assailed him passingly sore. But ever Sir Gareth defended him as a knight.

CHAPTER XXXII

*How Sir Gareth fought with a knight that held within his
castle thirty ladies, and how he slew him.*

So when they saw that they might not overcome him, they rode
from him, and took their counsel to slay his horse; and so they came
in upon Sir Gareth, and with spears they slew his horse, and then they
assailed him hard. But when he was on foot, there was none that he
fought but he gave him such a buffet that he did never recover. So he
slew them by one and one till they were but four, and there they fled;
and Sir Gareth took a good horse that was one of theirs, and rode his
way.

Then he rode a great pace till that he came to a castle, and there he
heard much mourning of ladies and gentlewomen. So there came by
him a page. What noise is this, said Sir Gareth, that I hear within this
castle? Sir knight, said the page, here be within this castle thirty ladies,
and all they be widows; for here is a knight that waiteth daily upon
this castle, and his name is the Brown Knight without Pity, and he is
the periloust knight that now liveth; and therefore sir, said the page, I
rede you flee. Nay, said Sir Gareth, I will not flee though thou be
afeard of him. And then the page saw where came the Brown
Knight: Lo, said the page, yonder he cometh. Let me deal with him,
said Sir Gareth. And when either of other had a sight they let their
horses run, and the Brown Knight brake his spear, and Sir Gareth
smote him throughout the body, that he overthrew him to the
ground stark dead. So Sir Gareth rode into the castle, and prayed the
ladies that he might repose him. Alas, said the ladies, ye may not be
lodged here. Make him good cheer, said the page, for this knight
hath slain your enemy. Then they all made him good cheer as lay in
their power. But wit ye well they made him good cheer, for they
might none otherwise do, for they were but poor.

And so on the morn he went to mass, and there he saw the thirty
ladies kneel, and lay grovelling upon divers tombs, making great dole
and sorrow. Then Sir Gareth wist well that in the tombs lay their
lords. Fair ladies, said Sir Gareth, ye must at the next feast of

Pentecost be at the court of King Arthur, and say that I, Sir Gareth, sent you thither. We shall do this, said the ladies. So he departed, and by fortune he came to a mountain, and there he found a goodly knight that bade him, Abide sir knight, and joust with me. What are ye? said Sir Gareth. My name is, said he, the Duke de la Rowse. Ah sir, ye are the same knight that I lodged once in your castle; and there I made promise unto your lady that I should yield me unto you. Ah, said the duke, art thou that proud knight that profferest to fight with my knights; therefore make thee ready, for I will have ado with you. So they let their horses run, and there Sir Gareth smote the duke down from his horse. But the duke lightly avoided his horse, and dressed his shield and drew his sword, and bade Sir Gareth alight and fight with him. So he did alight, and they did great battle together more than an hour, and either hurt other full sore. At the last Sir Gareth gat the duke to the earth, and would have slain him, and then he yield him to him. Then must ye go, said Sir Gareth, unto Sir Arthur my lord at the next feast, and say that I, Sir Gareth of Orkney, sent you unto him. It shall be done, said the duke, and I will do to you homage and fealty with an hundred knights with me; and all the days of my life to do you service where ye will command me.

CHAPTER XXXIII

How Sir Gareth and Sir Gawaine fought each against other, and how they knew each other by the damosel Linet.

So the duke departed, and Sir Gareth stood there alone; and there he saw an armed knight coming toward him. Then Sir Gareth took the duke's shield, and mounted upon horseback, and so without biding they ran together as it had been the thunder. And there that knight hurt Sir Gareth under the side with his spear. And then they alighted and drew their swords, and gave great strokes that the blood trailed to the ground. And so they fought two hours.

At the last there came the damosel Linet, that some men called the damosel Savage, and she came riding upon an ambling mule; and there she cried all on high, Sir Gawaine, Sir Gawaine, leave thy fighting with thy brother Sir Gareth. And when he heard her say so he threw away his shield and his sword, and ran to Sir Gareth, and took him in his arms, and sithen kneeled down and asked him mercy. What are ye, said Sir Gareth, that right now were so strong and so mighty, and now so suddenly yield you to me? O Gareth, I am your brother Sir Gawaine, that for your sake have had great sorrow and labour. Then Sir Gareth unlaced his helm, and kneeled down to him, and asked him mercy. Then they rose both, and embraced either other in their arms, and wept a great while or they might speak, and either of them gave other the prize of the battle. And there were many kind words between them. Alas, my fair brother, said Sir Gawaine, perdy I owe of right to worship you an ye were not my brother, for ye have worshipped King Arthur and all his court, for ye have sent him* more worshipful knights this twelvemonth than six the best of the Round Table have done, except Sir Launcelot.

Then came the damosel Savage that was the Lady Linet, that rode with Sir Gareth so long, and there she did staunch Sir Gareth's wounds and Sir Gawaine's. Now what will ye do? said the damosel Savage; meseemeth that it were well done that Arthur had witting of you both, for your horses are so bruised that they may not bear. Now, fair damosel, said Sir Gawaine, I pray you ride unto my lord mine uncle, King Arthur, and tell him what adventure is to me betid here, and I suppose he will not tarry long. Then she took her mule, and lightly she came to King Arthur that was but two mile thence. And when she had told him tidings the king bade get him a palfrey. And when he was upon his back he bade the lords and ladies come after, who that would; and there was saddling and bridling of queens' horses and princes' horses, and well was him that soonest might be ready.

So when the king came thereas they were, he saw Sir Gawaine and Sir Gareth sit upon a little hill-side, and then the king avoided his horse. And when he came nigh Sir Gareth he would have spoken but he might not; and therewith he sank down in a swoon for gladness. And so they stert unto their uncle, and required him of his good grace to be of good comfort. Wit ye well the king made great joy, and many a piteous complaint he made to Sir Gareth, and ever he wept as he had been a child. With that came his mother, the Queen of Orkney, Dame Morgawse, and when she saw Sir Gareth readily in

* So Wynkyn de Worde; Caxton 'me'.

the visage she might not weep, but suddenly fell down in a swoon, and lay there a great while like as she had been dead. And then Sir Gareth recomforted his mother in such wise that she recovered and made good cheer. Then the king commanded that all manner of knights that were under his obeissance should make their lodging right there for the love of his nephews. And so it was done, and all manner of purveyance purveyed, that there lacked nothing that might be gotten of tame nor wild for gold or silver. And then by the means of the damosel Savage Sir Gawaine and Sir Gareth were healed of their wounds; and there they sojourned eight days.

Then said King Arthur unto the damosel Savage: I marvel that your sister, Dame Lionesse, cometh not here to me, and in especial that she cometh not to visit her knight, my nephew Sir Gareth, that hath had so much travail for her love. My lord, said the damosel Linet, ye must of your good grace hold her excused, for she knoweth not that my lord, Sir Gareth, is here. Go then for her, said King Arthur, that we may be appointed what is best to be done, according to the pleasure of my nephew. Sir, said the damosel, that shall be done, and so she rode unto her sister. And as lightly as she might she made her ready; and she came on the morn with her brother Sir Gringamore, and with her forty knights. And so when she was come she had all the cheer that might be done, both of the king, and of many other kings and queens.

CHAPTER XXXIV

How Sir Gareth acknowledged that they loved each other to King Arthur, and of the appointment of their wedding.

And among all these ladies she was named the fairest, and peerless. Then when Sir Gawaine saw her there was many a goodly look and goodly words, that all men of worship had joy to behold them. Then came King Arthur and many other kings, and Dame Guenever, and the Queen of Orkney. And there the king asked his nephew, Sir Gareth, whether he would have that lady as paramour, or to have her to his wife. My lord, wit you well that I love her above all ladies living. Now, fair lady, said King Arthur, what say ye? Most noble

King, said Dame Lionesse, wit you well that my lord, Sir Gareth, is to me more liefer to have and wield as my husband, than any king or prince that is christened; and if I may not have him I promise you I will never have none. For, my lord Arthur, said Dame Lionesse, wit ye well he is my first love, and he shall be the last; and if ye will suffer him to have his will and free choice I dare say he will have me. That is truth, said Sir Gareth; an I have not you and wield not you as my wife, there shall never lady nor gentlewoman rejoice me. What, nephew, said the king, is the wind in that door? for wit ye well I would not for the stint of my crown to be causer to withdraw your hearts; and wit ye well ye cannot love so well but I shall rather increase it than distress it. And also ye shall have my love and my lordship in the uttermost wise that may lie in my power. And in the same wise said Sir Gareth's mother.

Then there was made a provision for the day of marriage; and by the king's advice it was provided that it should be at Michaelmas following, at Kink Kenadon by the seaside, for there is a plentiful country. And so it was cried in all the places through the realm. And then Sir Gareth sent his summons to all these knights and ladies that he had won in battle to-fore, that they should be at his day of marriage at Kink Kenadon by the sands. And then Dame Lionesse, and the damosel Linet with Sir Gringamore, rode to their castle; and a goodly and a rich ring she gave to Sir Gareth, and he gave her another. And King Arthur gave her a rich pair of beads* of gold; and so she departed; and King Arthur and his fellowship rode toward Kink Kenadon, and Sir Gareth brought his lady on the way, and so came to the king again and rode with him. Lord! the great cheer that Sir Launcelot made of Sir Gareth and he of him, for there was never no knight that Sir Gareth loved so well as he did Sir Launcelot; and ever for the most part he would be in Sir Launcelot's company; for after Sir Gareth had espied Sir Gawaine's conditions, he withdrew himself from his brother, Sir Gawaine's, fellowship, for he was vengeable, and where he hated he would be avenged with murder, and that hated Sir Gareth.

---

* So Wynkyn de Worde; Caxton 'bee'.

CHAPTER XXXV

Of the Great Royalty, and what officers were made at the
feast of the wedding, and of the jousts at the feast.

So it drew fast to Michaelmas; and thither came Dame Lionesse, the
lady of the Castle Perilous, and her sister, Dame Linet, with Sir
Gringamore, her brother, with them, for he had the conduct of these
ladies. And there they were lodged at the device of King Arthur. And
upon Michaelmas Day the Bishop of Canterbury made the wedding
betwixt Sir Gareth and the Lady Lionesse with great solemnity. And
King Arthur made Gaheris to wed the Damosel Savage, that was
Dame Linet; and King Arthur made Sir Agravaine to wed Dame
Lionesse's niece, a fair lady, her name was Dame Laurel.

And so when this solemnization was done, then came in the Green
Knight, Sir Pertolepe, with thirty knights, and there he did homage
and fealty to Sir Gareth, and these knights to hold of him for
evermore. Also Sir Pertolepe said: I pray you that at this feast I may
be your chamberlain. With a good will, said Sir Gareth, sith it liketh
you to take so simple an office. Then came in the Red Knight, with
three score knights with him, and did to Sir Gareth homage and
fealty, and all those knights to hold of him for evermore. And then
this Sir Perimones prayed Sir Gareth to grant him to be his chief
butler at that high feast. I will well, said Sir Gareth, that ye have this
office, and it were better. Then came in Sir Persant of Inde, with an
hundred knights with him, and there he did homage and fealty, and
all his knights should do him service, and hold their lands of him for
ever; and there he prayed Sir Gareth to make him his sewer-chief at
the feast. I will well, said Sir Gareth, that ye have it, and it were
better. Then came the Duke de la Rowse, with an hundred knights
with him, and there he did homage and fealty to Sir Gareth, and so to
hold their lands of him for ever. And he required Sir Gareth that he
might serve him of the wine that day of that feast. I will well, said Sir
Gareth, and it were better. Then came in the Red Knight of the Red
Launds, that was Sir Ironside, and he brought with him three
hundred knights, and there he did homage and fealty, and all these

knights to hold their lands of him for ever. And then he asked Sir Gareth to be his carver. I will well, said Sir Gareth, an it please you.

Then came into the court thirty ladies, and all they seemed widows, and those thirty ladies brought with them many fair gentlewomen. And all they kneeled down at once unto King Arthur and unto Sir Gareth, and there all those ladies told the king how Sir Gareth delivered them from the dolorous tower, and slew the Brown Knight without Pity: And therefore we, and our heirs for evermore, will do homage unto Sir Gareth of Orkney. So then the kings and queens, princes and earls, barons and many bold knights, went unto meat; and well may ye wit there were all manner of meat plenteously, all manner revels and games, with all manner of minstrelsy that was used in those days. Also there was great jousts three days. But the king would not suffer Sir Gareth to joust, because of his new bride; for, as the French book saith, that Dame Lionesse desired of the king that none that were wedded should joust at that feast.

So the first day there jousted Sir Lamorak de Galis, for he overthrew thirty knights, and did passing marvellously deeds of arms; and then King Arthur made Sir Persant and his two brethren Knights of the Round Table to their lives' end, and gave them great lands. Also the second day there jousted Tristram best, and he overthrew forty knights, and did there marvellous deeds of arms. And there King Arthur made Ironside, that was the Red Knight of the Red Launds, a Knight of the Table Round to his life's end, and gave him great lands. The third day there jousted Sir Launcelot du Lake, and he overthrew fifty knights, and did many marvellous deeds of arms, that all men wondered on him. And there King Arthur made the Duke de la Rowse a Knight of the Round Table to his life's end, and gave him great lands to spend. But when these jousts were done, Sir Lamorak and Sir Tristram departed suddenly, and would not be known, for the which King Arthur and all the court were sore displeased. And so they held the court forty days with great solemnity. And this Sir Gareth was a noble knight, and a well-ruled, and fair-languaged.

Thus endeth this tale of Sir Gareth of Orkney that wedded Dame Lioness of the Castle Perilous. And also Sir Gaheris wedded her sister, Dame Linet, that was called the Damosel Savage. And Sir Agravaine wedded Dame Laurel, a fair lady and great, and mighty lands with great riches gave with them King Arthur, that royally they might live till their lives' end.

Here followeth the eighth book, the which is the first book of Sir Tristram de Liones, and who was his father and mother, and how he was born and fostered, and how he was made knight.

BOOK EIGHT

CHAPTER I

*How Sir Tristram de Liones was born, and how his mother
died at his birth, wherefore she named him Tristram.*

It was a king that hight Meliodas, and he was lord and king of the
country of Liones, and this Meliodas was a likely knight as any was
that time living. And by fortune he wedded King Mark's sister of
Cornwall, and she was called Elizabeth, that was called both good and
fair. And at that time King Arthur reigned, and he was whole king of
England, Wales, and Scotland, and of many other realms: howbeit
there were many kings that were lords of many countries, but all they
held their lands of King Arthur; for in Wales were two kings, and in
the north were many kings; and in Cornwall and in the west were
two kings; also in Ireland were two or three kings, and all were under
the obeissance of King Arthur. So was the King of France, and the
King of Brittany, and all the lordships unto Rome.

So when this King Meliodas had been with his wife, within a while
she waxed great with child, and she was a full meek lady, and well she
loved her lord, and he her again, so there was great joy betwixt them.
Then there was a lady in that country that had loved King Meliodas
long, and by no mean she never could get his love; therefore she let
ordain upon a day, as King Meliodas rode a-hunting, for he was a
great chaser, and there by an enchantment she made him chase an
hart by himself alone till that he came to an old castle, and there anon
he was taken prisoner by the lady that him loved. When Elizabeth,
King Meliodas' wife, missed her lord, and she was nigh out of her
wit, and also as great with child as she was, she took a gentlewoman
with her, and ran into the forest to seek her lord. And when she was
far in the forest she might no farther, for she began to travail fast of
her child. And she had many grimly throes; her gentlewoman helped

her all that she might, and so by miracle of Our Lady of Heaven she was delivered with great pains. But she had taken such cold for the default of help that deep draughts of death took her, that needs she must die and depart out of this world; there was none other bote.

And when this Queen Elizabeth saw that there was none other bote, then she made great dole, and said unto her gentlewoman: When ye see my lord, King Meliodas, recommend me unto him, and tell him what pains I endure here for his love, and how I must die here for his sake for default of good help; and let him wit that I am full sorry to depart out of this world from him, therefore pray him to be friend to my soul. Now let me see my little child for whom I have had all this sorrow. And when she saw him she said thus: Ah, my little son, thou hast murdered thy mother, and therefore I suppose, thou that art a murderer so young, thou art full likely to be a manly man in thine age. And because I shall die of the birth of thee, I charge thee, gentlewoman, that thou pray my lord, King Meliodas, that when he is christened let call him Tristram, that is as much to say as a sorrowful birth. And therewith this queen gave up the ghost and died. Then the gentlewoman laid her under an umbre of a great tree, and then she lapped the child as well as she might for cold. Right so there came the barons, following after the queen, and when they saw that she was dead, and understood none other but the king was destroyed,* then certain of them would have slain the child, because they would have been lords of the country of Liones.

CHAPTER II

How the stepmother of Sir Tristram had ordained poison for to have poisoned Sir Tristram.

But then through the fair speech of the gentlewoman, and by the means that she made, the most part of the barons would not assent thereto. And then they let carry home the dead queen, and much dole was made for her.

Then this meanwhile Merlin delivered King Meliodas out of prison

* Printed by Caxton as part of chapter ii.

on the morn after his queen was dead. And so when the king was come home the most part of the barons made great joy. But the sorrow that the king made for his queen that might no tongue tell. So then the king let inter her richly, and after he let christen his child as his wife had commanded afore her death. And then he let call him Tristram, the sorrowful born child. Then the King Meliodas endured seven years without a wife, and all this time Tristram was nourished well. Then it befell that King Meliodas wedded King Howell's daughter of Brittany, and anon she had children of King Meliodas: then was she heavy and wroth that her children should not rejoice the country of Liones, wherefore this queen ordained for to poison young Tristram. So she let poison be put in a piece of silver in the chamber whereas Tristram and her children were together, unto that intent that when Tristram were thirsty he should drink that drink. And so it fell upon a day, the queen's son, as he was in that chamber, espied the piece with poison, and he weened it had been good drink, and because the child was thirsty he took the piece with poison and drank freely; and therewithal suddenly the child brast and was dead.

When the queen of Meliodas wist of the death of her son, wit ye well that she was heavy. But yet the king understood nothing of her treason. Notwithstanding the queen would not leave this, but eft she let ordain more poison, and put it in a piece. And by fortune King Meliodas, her husband, found the piece with wine where was the poison, and he that was much thirsty took the piece for to drink thereout. And as he would have drunken thereof the queen espied him, and then she ran unto him, and pulled the piece from him suddenly. The king marvelled why she did so, and remembered him how her son was suddenly slain with poison. And then he took her by the hand, and said: Thou false traitress, thou shalt tell me what manner of drink this is, or else I shall slay thee. And therewith he pulled out his sword, and sware a great oath that he should slay her but if she told him truth. Ah! mercy, my lord, said she, and I shall tell you all. And then she told him why she would have slain Tristram, because her children should rejoice his land. Well, said King Meliodas, and therefore shall ye have the law. And so she was condemned by the assent of the barons to be burnt; and then was there made a great fire, and right as she was at the fire to take her execution, young Tristram kneeled afore King Meliodas, and besought him to give him a boon. I will well, said the king again. Then said young Tristram, Give me the life of thy queen, my stepmother. That is unrightfully asked, said King Meliodas, for thou ought of right to hate her, for she would have slain thee with that poison an she might have had her will; and for thy sake most is my cause that she should die.

Sir, said Tristram, as for that, I beseech you of your mercy that you will forgive it her, and as for my part, God forgive it her, and I do; and so much it liked your highness to grant me my boon, for God's love I require you hold your promise. Sithen it is so, said the king, I will that ye have her life. Then, said the king, I give her to you, and go ye to the fire and take her, and do with her what ye will. So Sir Tristram went to the fire, and by the commandment of the king delivered her from the death. But after that King Meliodas would never have ado with her, as at bed and board. But by the good means of young Tristram he made the king and her accorded. But then the king would not suffer young Tristram to abide no longer in his court.

CHAPTER III

How Sir Tristram was sent into France, and had one to govern him named Gouvernail, and how he learned to harp, hawk, and hunt.

And then he let ordain a gentleman that was well learned and taught, his name was Gouvernail; and then he sent young Tristram with Gouvernail into France to learn the language, and nurture, and deeds of arms. And there was Tristram more than seven years. And then when he well could speak the language, and had learned all that he might learn in that country, then he came home to his father, King Meliodas, again. And so Tristram learned to be an harper passing all other, that there was none such called in no country, and so on harping and on instruments of music he applied him in his youth for to learn.

And after, as he grew in might and strength, he laboured ever in hunting and in hawking, so that never gentleman more, that ever we heard read of. And as the book saith, he began good measures of blowing of beasts of venery, and beasts of chase, and all manner of vermin, and all these terms we have yet of hawking and hunting. And therefore the book of venery, of hawking, and hunting, is called the book of Sir Tristram. Wherefore, as meseemeth, all gentlemen that bear old arms ought of right to honour Sir Tristram for the goodly terms that gentlemen have and use, and shall to the day of doom, that thereby in a manner all men of worship may dissever a gentleman from a yeoman, and from a yeoman a villein. For he that gentle is will draw him unto gentle tatches, and to follow the customs of noble gentlemen.

Thus Sir Tristram endured in Cornwall until he was big and strong, of the age of eighteen years. And then the King Meliodas had great joy of Sir Tristram, and so had the queen, his wife. For ever after in her life, because Sir Tristram saved her from the fire, she did never hate him more after, but loved him ever after, and gave Tristram many great gifts; for every estate loved him, where that he went.

CHAPTER IV

How Sir Marhaus came out of Ireland for to ask truage of Cornwall, or else he would fight therefore.

Then it befell that King Anguish of Ireland sent unto King Mark of Cornwall for his truage, that Cornwall had paid many winters. And all that time King Mark was behind of the truage for seven years. And King Mark and his barons gave unto the messenger of Ireland these words and answer, that they would none pay; and bade the messenger go unto his King Anguish, and tell him we will pay him no truage, but tell your lord, an he will always have truage of us of Cornwall, bid him send a trusty knight of his land, that will fight for his right, and we shall find another for to defend our right. With this answer the messengers departed into Ireland. And when King Anguish understood the answer of the messengers he was wonderly wroth. And then he called unto him Sir Marhaus, the good knight, that was nobly proved, and a Knight of the Table Round. And this Marhaus was brother unto the queen of Ireland. Then the king said thus: Fair brother, Sir Marhaus, I pray you go into Cornwall for my sake, and do battle for our truage that of right we ought to have; and whatsomever ye spend ye shall have sufficiently, more than ye shall need. Sir, said Marhaus, wit ye well that I shall not be loath to do battle in the right of you and your land with the best knight of the Table Round; for I know them, for the most part, what be their deeds; and for to advance my deeds and to increase my worship I will right gladly go unto this journey for our right.

So in all haste there was made purveyance for Sir Marhaus, and he had all things that to him needed; and so he departed out of Ireland, and arrived up in Cornwall even fast by the Castle of Tintagil. And when King Mark understood that he was there arrived to fight for Ireland, then made King Mark great sorrow when he understood that the good and noble knight Sir Marhaus was come. For they knew no knight that durst have ado with him. For at that time Sir Marhaus was called one of the famousest and renowned knights of the world. And thus Sir Marhaus abode in the sea, and every day he sent unto King Mark for to pay the truage that was behind of seven year, other else to find a knight to fight with him for the truage. This manner of message Sir Marhaus sent daily unto King Mark.

Then they of Cornwall let make cries in every place, that what knight would fight for to save the truage of Cornwall, he should be rewarded so that he should fare the better, term of his life. Then some of the barons said to King Mark, and counselled him to send to the court of King Arthur for to seek Sir Launcelot du Lake, that was that time named for the marvelloust knight of all the world. Then there were some other barons that counselled the king not to do so, and said that it was labour in vain, because Sir Marhaus was a knight of the Round Table, therefore any of them will be loath to have ado with other, but if it were any knight at his own request would fight disguised and unknown. So the king and all his barons assented that it was no bote to seek any knight of the Round Table. This mean while came the language and the noise unto King Meliodas, how that Sir Marhaus abode battle fast by Tintagil, and how King Mark could find no manner knight to fight for him. When young Tristram heard of this he was wroth, and sore ashamed that there durst no knight in Cornwall have ado with Sir Marhaus of Ireland.

CHAPTER V

How Tristram enterprized the battle to fight for the truage
of Cornwall, and how he was made knight.

Therewithal Tristram went unto his father, King Meliodas, and asked
him counsel what was best to do for to recover Cornwall from
truage. For, as meseemeth, said Sir Tristram, it were shame that Sir
Marhaus, the queen's brother of Ireland, should go away unless that
he were foughten withal. As for that, said King Meliodas, wit you
well, son Tristram, that Sir Marhaus is called one of the best knights
of the world, and Knight of the Table Round; and therefore I know
no knight in this country that is able to match with him. Alas, said Sir
Tristram, that I am not made knight; and if Sir Marhaus should thus
depart into Ireland, God let me never have worship: an I were made
knight I should match him. And sir, said Tristram, I pray you give me
leave to ride to King Mark; and, so ye be not displeased, of King
Mark will I be made knight. I will well, said King Meliodas, that ye
be ruled as your courage will rule you. Then Sir Tristram thanked his
father much. And then he made him ready to ride into Cornwall.

In the meanwhile there came a messenger with letters of love from
King Faramon of France's daughter unto Sir Tristram, that were full
piteous letters, and in them were written many complaints of love;
but Sir Tristram had no joy of her letters nor regard unto her. Also
she sent him a little brachet that was passing fair. But when the king's
daughter understood that Sir Tristram would not love her, as the
book saith, she died for sorrow. And then the same squire that
brought the letter and the brachet came again unto Sir Tristram, as
after ye shall hear in the tale.

So this young Sir Tristram rode unto his eme, King Mark of
Cornwall. And when he came there he heard say that there would no
knight fight with Sir Marhaus. Then yede Sir Tristram unto his eme
and said: Sir, if ye will give me the order of knighthood, I will do
battle with Sir Marhaus. What are ye, said the king, and from whence
be ye come? Sir, said Tristram, I come from King Meliodas that
wedded your sister, and a gentleman wit ye well I am. King Mark

beheld Sir Tristram and saw that he was but a young man of age, but he was passingly well made and big. Fair sir, said the king, what is your name, and where were ye born? Sir, said he again, my name is Tristram, and in the country of Liones was I born. Ye say well, said the king; and if ye will do this battle I shall make you knight. Therefore I come to you, said Sir Tristram, and for none other cause. But then King Mark made him knight. And therewithal, anon as he had made him knight, he sent a messenger unto Sir Marhaus with letters that said that he had found a young knight ready for to take the battle to the uttermost. It may well be, said Sir Marhaus; but tell King Mark I will not fight with no knight but he be of blood royal, that is to say, other king's son, other queen's son, born of a prince or princess.

When King Mark understood that, he sent for Sir Tristram de Liones and told him what was the answer of Sir Marhaus. Then said Sir Tristram: Sithen that he saith so, let him wit that I am come of father side and mother side of as noble blood as he is: for, sir, now shall ye know that I am King Meliodas' son, born of your own sister, Dame Elizabeth, that died in the forest in the birth of me. O Jesu, said King Mark, ye are welcome fair nephew to me. Then in all the haste the king let horse Sir Tristram, and armed him in the best manner that might be had or gotten for gold or silver. And then King Mark sent unto Sir Marhaus, and did him to wit that a better born man than he was himself should fight with him, and his name is Sir Tristram de Liones, gotten of King Meliodas, and born of King Mark's sister. Then was Sir Marhaus glad and blithe that he should fight with such a gentleman. And so by the assent of King Mark and of Sir Marhaus they let ordain that they should fight within an island nigh Sir Marhaus' ships; and so was Sir Tristram put into a vessel both his horse and he, and all that to him longed both for his body and for his horse. Sir Tristram lacked nothing. And when King Mark and his barons of Cornwall beheld how young Sir Tristram departed with such a carriage to fight for the right of Cornwall, there was neither man nor woman of worship but they wept to see and understand so young a knight to jeopardy himself for their right.

CHAPTER VI

*How Sir Tristram arrived into the Island for to furnish the
battle with Sir Marhaus.*

So to shorten this tale, when Sir Tristram was arrived within the
island he looked to the farther side, and there he saw at an anchor six
ships nigh to the land; and under the shadow of the ships upon the
land, there hoved the noble knight, Sir Marhaus of Ireland. Then Sir
Tristram commanded his servant Gouvernail to bring his horse to the
land, and dress his harness at all manner of rights. And then when he
had so done he mounted upon his horse; and when he was in his
saddle well apparelled, and his shield dressed upon his shoulder,
Tristram asked Gouvernail, Where is this knight that I shall have ado
withal? Sir, said Gouvernail, see ye him not? I weened ye had seen
him; yonder he hoveth under the umbre of his ships on horseback,
with his spear in his hand and his shield upon his shoulder. That is
truth, said the noble knight, Sir Tristram, now I see him well enough.

Then he commanded his servant Gouvernail to go to his vessel
again: And commend me unto mine eme King Mark, and pray him,
if that I be slain in this battle, for to inter my body as him seemed
best; and as for me, let him wit that I will never yield me for
cowardice; and if I be slain and flee not, then they have lost no truage
for me; and if so be that I flee or yield me as recreant, bid mine eme
never bury me in Christian burials. And upon thy life, said Sir
Tristram to Gouvernail, come thou not nigh this island till that thou
see me overcome or slain, or else that I win yonder knight. So either
departed from other sore weeping.

CHAPTER VII

*How Sir Tristram fought against Sir Marhaus and
achieved his battle, and how Sir Marhaus fled to his ship.*

And then Sir Marhaus avised Sir Tristram, and said thus: Young
knight, Sir Tristram, what dost thou here? me sore repenteth of thy
courage, for wit thou well I have been assayed, and the best knights
of this land have been assayed of my hand; and also I have matched
with the best knights of the world, and therefore by my counsel
return again unto thy vessel. And fair knight, and well-proved knight,
said Sir Tristram, thou shalt well wit I may not forsake thee in this
quarrel, for I am for thy sake made knight. And thou shalt well wit
that I am a king's son born, and gotten upon a queen; and such
promise I have made at my uncle's request and mine own seeking,
that I shall fight with thee unto the uttermost, and deliver Cornwall
from the old truage. And also wit thou well, Sir Marhaus, that this is
the greatest cause that thou couragest me to have ado with thee, for
thou art called one of the most renowned knights of the world, and
because of that noise and fame that thou hast thou givest me courage
to have ado with thee, for never yet was I proved with good knight;
and sithen I took the order of knighthood this day, I am well pleased
that I may have ado with so good a knight as thou art. And now wit
thou well, Sir Marhaus, that I cast me to get worship on thy body;
and if that I be not proved, I trust to God that I shall be worshipfully
proved upon thy body, and to deliver the country of Cornwall for
ever from all manner of truage from Ireland for ever.

When Sir Marhaus had heard him say what he would, he said then
thus again: Fair knight, sithen it is so that thou castest to win worship
of me, I let thee wit worship may thou none lose by me if thou
mayest stand me three strokes; for I let thee wit for my noble deeds,
proved and seen, King Arthur made me Knight of the Table Round.

Then they began to feutre their spears, and they met so fiercely
together that they smote either other down, both horse and all. But
Sir Marhaus smote Sir Tristram a great wound in the side with his
spear, and then they avoided their horses, and pulled out their swords,

and threw their shields afore them. And then they lashed together as men that were wild and courageous. And when they had stricken so together long, then they left their strokes, and foined at their breaths and visors; and when they saw that that might not prevail them, then they hurtled together like rams to bear either other down. Thus they fought still more than half a day, and either were wounded passing sore, that the blood ran down freshly from them upon the ground. By then Sir Tristram waxed more fresher than Sir Marhaus, and better winded and bigger; and with a mighty stroke he smote Sir Marhaus upon the helm such a buffet that it went through his helm, and through the coif of steel, and through the brain-pan, and the sword stuck so fast in the helm and in his brain-pan that Sir Tristram pulled thrice at his sword or ever he might pull it out from his head; and there Marhaus fell down on his knees, the edge of Tristram's sword left in his brain-pan. And suddenly Sir Marhaus rose grovelling, and threw his sword and his shield from him, and so ran to his ships and fled his way, and Sir Tristram had ever his shield and his sword.

And when Sir Tristram saw Sir Marhaus withdraw him, he said: Ah! Sir Knight of the Round Table, why withdrawest thou thee? thou dost thyself and thy kin great shame, for I am but a young knight, or now I was never proved, and rather than I should withdraw me from thee, I had rather be hewn in an hundred pieces. Sir Marhaus answered no word but yede his way sore groaning. Well, Sir Knight, said Sir Tristram, I promise thee thy sword and thy shield shall be mine; and thy shield shall I wear in all places where I ride on mine adventures, and in the sight of King Arthur and all the Round Table.

CHAPTER VIII

How Sir Marhaus after that he was arrived in Ireland died of the stroke that Sir Tristram had given him, and how Tristram was hurt.

Anon Sir Marhaus and his fellowship departed into Ireland. And as soon as he came to the king, his brother, he let search his wounds. And when his head was searched a piece of Sir Tristram's sword was found therein, and might never be had out of his head for no surgeons, and so he died of Sir Tristram's sword; and that piece of the sword the queen, his sister, kept it for ever with her, for she thought to be revenged an she might.

Now turn we again unto Sir Tristram, that was sore wounded, and full sore bled that he might not within a little while, when he had taken cold, unnethe stir him of his limbs. And then he set him down softly upon a little hill, and bled fast. Then anon came Gouvernail, his man, with his vessel; and the king and his barons came with procession against him. And when he was come unto the land, King Mark took him in his arms, and the king and Sir Dinas, the seneschal, led Sir Tristram into the castle of Tintagil. And then was he searched in the best manner, and laid in his bed. And when King Mark saw his wounds he wept heartily, and so did all his lords. So God me help, said King Mark, I would not for all my lands that my nephew died. So Sir Tristram lay there a month and more, and ever he was like to die of that stroke that Sir Marhaus smote him first with the spear. For, as the French book saith, the spear's head was envenomed, that Sir Tristram might not be whole. Then was King Mark and all his barons passing heavy, for they deemed none other but that Sir Tristram should not recover. Then the king let send after all manner of leeches and surgeons, both unto men and women, and there was none that would behote him the life. Then came there a lady that was a right wise lady, and she said plainly unto King Mark, and to Sir Tristram, and to all his barons, that he should never be whole but if Sir Tristram went in the same country that the venom came from, and in that country should he be holpen or else never. Thus said the lady unto the king.

When King Mark understood that, he let purvey for Sir Tristram a fair vessel, well victualled, and therein was put Sir Tristram, and Gouvernail with him, and Sir Tristram took his harp with him, and so he was put into the sea to sail into Ireland; and so by good fortune he arrived up in Ireland, even fast by a castle where the king and the queen was; and at his arrival he sat and harped in his bed a merry lay, such one heard they never none in Ireland before that time.

And when it was told the king and the queen of such a knight that was such an harper, anon the king sent for him, and let search his wounds, and then asked him his name. Then he answered, I am of the country of Liones, and my name is Tramtrist, that thus was wounded in a battle as I fought for a lady's right. So God me help, said King Anguish, ye shall have all the help in this land that ye may have here; but I let you wit, in Cornwall I had a great loss as ever had king, for there I lost the best knight of the world; his name was Marhaus, a full noble knight, and Knight of the Table Round; and there he told Sir Tristram wherefore Sir Marhaus was slain. Sir Tristram made semblant as he had been sorry, and better knew he how it was than the king.

CHAPTER IX

How Sir Tristram was put to the keeping of La Beale Isoud first for to be healed of his wound.

Then the king for great favour made Tramtrist to be put in his daughter's ward and keeping, because she was a noble surgeon. And when she had searched him she found in the bottom of his wound that therein was poison, and so she healed him within a while; and therefore Tramtrist cast great love to La Beale Isoud, for she was at that time the fairest maid and lady of the world. And there Tramtrist learned her to harp, and she began to have a great fantasy unto him. And at that time Sir Palomides, the Saracen, was in that country, and well cherished with the king and the queen. And every day Sir Palomides drew unto La Beale Isoud and proffered her many gifts, for he loved her passingly well. All that espied Tramtrist, and full well knew he Sir Palomides for a noble knight and a mighty man. And wit you well Sir Tramtrist had great despite at Sir Palomides, for La Beale Isoud told Tramtrist that Palomides was in will to be christened for her sake. Thus was there great envy betwixt Tramtrist and Sir Palomides.

Then it befell that King Anguish let cry a great jousts and a great tournament for a lady that was called the Lady of the Launds, and she was nigh cousin unto the king. And what man won her, three days after he should wed her and have all her lands. This cry was made in England, Wales, Scotland, and also in France and in Brittany. It befell upon a day La Beale Isoud came unto Sir Tramtrist, and told him of this tournament. He answered and said: Fair lady, I am but a feeble knight, and but late I had been dead had not your good ladyship been. Now, fair lady, what would ye I should do in this matter? well ye wot, my lady, that I may not joust. Ah, Tramtrist, said La Beale Isoud, why will ye not have ado at that tournament? well I wot Sir Palomides shall be there, and to do what he may; and therefore Tramtrist, I pray you for to be there, for else Sir Palomides is like to win the degree. Madam, said Tramtrist, as for that, it may be so, for he is a proved knight, and I am but a young knight and late made; and the first battle that I did it mishapped me to be sore wounded as ye see. But an I wist ye would be my better lady, at that tournament I will be, so that ye will keep my counsel and let no creature have knowledge that I shall joust but yourself, and such as ye will to keep your counsel, my poor person shall I jeopard there for your sake, that, peradventure, Sir Palomides shall know when that I come. Thereto, said La Beale Isoud, do your best, and as I can, said La Beale Isoud, I shall purvey horse and armour for you at my device. As ye will so be it, said Sir Tramtrist, I will be at your commandment.

So at the day of jousts there came Sir Palomides with a black shield, and he overthrew many knights, that all the people had marvel of him. For he put to the worse Sir Gawaine, Gaheris, Agravaine, Bagdemagus, Kay, Dodinas le Savage, Sagramore le Desirous, Gumret le Petit, and Griflet le Fise de Dieu. All these the first day Sir Palomides struck down to the earth. And then all manner of knights were adread of Sir Palomides, and many called him the Knight with the Black Shield. So that day Sir Palomides had great worship.

Then came King Anguish unto Tramtrist, and asked him why he would not joust. Sir, he said, I was but late hurt, and as yet I dare not adventure me. Then came there the same squire that was sent from the king's daughter of France unto Sir Tristram. And when he had espied Sir Tristram he fell flat to his feet. All that espied La Beale Isoud, what courtesy the squire made unto Sir Tristram. And therewithal suddenly Sir Tristram ran unto his squire, whose name was Hebes le Renoumes, and prayed him heartily in no wise to tell his name. Sir, said Hebes, I will not discover your name but if ye command me.

CHAPTER X

*How Sir Tristram won the degree at a tournament in
Ireland, and there made Palomides to bear no more
harness in a year.*

Then Sir Tristram asked him what he did in those countries. Sir, he
said, I came hither with Sir Gawaine for to be made knight, and if it
please you, of your hands that I may be made knight. Await upon me
as to-morn secretly, and in the field I shall make you a knight.

Then had La Beale Isoud great suspicion unto Tramtrist, that he
was some man of worship proved, and therewith she comforted
herself, and cast more love unto him than she had done to-fore. And
so on the morn Sir Palomides made him ready to come into the field
as he did the first day. And there he smote down the King with the
Hundred Knights, and the King of Scots. Then had La Beale Isoud
ordained and well arrayed Sir Tristram in white horse and harness.
And right so she let put him out at a privy postern, and so he came
into the field as it had been a bright angel. And anon Sir Palomides
espied him, and therewith he feutred a spear unto Sir Tramtrist, and
he again unto him. And there Sir Tristram smote down Sir Palomides
unto the earth. And then there was a great noise of people: some said
Sir Palomides had a fall, some said the Knight with the Black Shield
had a fall. And wit you well La Beale Isoud was passing glad. And
then Sir Gawaine and his fellows nine had marvel what knight it
might be that had smitten down Sir Palomides. Then would there
none joust with Tramtrist, but all that there were forsook him, most
and least. Then Sir Tristram made Hebes a knight, and caused him to
put himself forth, and did right well that day. So after Sir Hebes held
him with Sir Tristram.

And when Sir Palomides had received this fall, wit ye well that he
was sore ashamed, and as privily as he might he withdrew him out of
the field. All that espied Sir Tristram, and lightly he rode after Sir
Palomides and overtook him, and bade him turn, for better he would
assay him or ever he departed. Then Sir Palomides turned him, and
either lashed at other with their swords. But at the first stroke Sir

Tristram smote down Palomides, and gave him such a stroke upon the head that he fell to the earth. So then Tristram bade yield him, and do his commandment, or else he would slay him. When Sir Palomides beheld his countenance, he dread his buffets so, that he granted all his askings. Well said, said Sir Tristram, this shall be your charge. First, upon pain of your life that ye forsake my lady La Beale Isoud, and in no manner wise that ye draw not to her. Also this twelvemonth and a day that ye bear none armour nor none harness of war. Now promise me this, or here shalt thou die. Alas, said Palomides, for ever am I ashamed. Then he sware as Sir Tristram had commanded him. Then for despite and anger Sir Palomides cut off his harness, and threw them away.

And so Sir Tristram turned again to the castle where was La Beale Isoud; and by the way he met with a damosel that asked after Sir Launcelot, that won the Dolorous Guard worshipfully; and this damosel asked Sir Tristram what he was. For it was told her that it was he that smote down Sir Palomides, by whom the ten knights of King Arthur's were smitten down. Then the damosel prayed Sir Tristram to tell her what he was, and whether that he were Sir Launcelot du Lake, for she deemed that there was no knight in the world might do such deeds of arms but if it were Launcelot. Fair damosel, said Sir Tristram, wit ye well that I am not Sir Launcelot, for I was never of such prowess, but in God is all that he may make me as good a knight as the good knight Sir Launcelot. Now, gentle knight, said she, put up thy visor; and when she beheld his visage she thought she saw never a better man's visage, nor a better faring knight. And then when the damosel knew certainly that he was not Sir Launcelot, then she took her leave, and departed from him. And then Sir Tristram rode privily unto the postern, where kept him La Beale Isoud, and there she made him good cheer, and thanked God of his good speed. So anon, within a while the king and the queen understood that it was Tramtrist that smote down Sir Palomides; then was he much made of, more than he was before.

CHAPTER XI

How the queen espied that Sir Tristram had slain her
brother Sir Marhaus by his sword, and in what
jeopardy he was.

Thus was Sir Tramtrist long there well cherished with the king and the queen, and namely with La Beale Isoud. So upon a day the queen and La Beale Isoud made a bain for Sir Tramtrist. And when he was in his bain the queen and Isoud, her daughter, roamed up and down in the chamber; and therewhiles Gouvernail and Hebes attended upon Tramtrist, and the queen beheld his sword thereas it lay upon his bed. And then by unhap the queen drew out his sword and beheld it a long while, and both they thought it a passing fair sword; but within a foot and an half of the point there was a great piece thereof out-broken of the edge. And when the queen espied that gap in the sword, she remembered her of a piece of a sword that was found in the brain-pan of Sir Marhaus, the good knight that was her brother. Alas then, said she unto her daughter, La Beale Isoud, this is the same traitor knight that slew my brother, thine eme. When Isoud heard her say so she was passing sore abashed, for passing well she loved Tramtrist, and full well she knew the cruelness of her mother the queen.

Anon therewithal the queen went unto her own chamber, and sought her coffer, and there she took out the piece of the sword that was pulled out of Sir Marhaus' head after that he was dead. And then she ran with that piece of iron to the sword that lay upon the bed. And when she put that piece of steel and iron unto the sword, it was as meet as it might be when it was new broken. And then the queen gripped that sword in her hand fiercely, and with all her might she ran straight upon Tramtrist where he sat in his bain, and there she had rived him through had not Sir Hebes gotten her in his arms, and pulled the sword from her, and else she had thrust him through.

Then when she was let of her evil will she ran to the King Anguish, her husband, and said on her knees: O my lord, here have ye in your house that traitor knight that slew my brother and your servant, that noble knight, Sir Marhaus. Who is that, said King Anguish, and where is he? Sir, she said, it is Sir Tramtrist, the same knight that my daughter healed. Alas, said the king, therefore am I right heavy, for he is a full noble knight as ever I saw in field. But I charge you, said the king to the queen, that ye have not ado with that knight, but let me deal with him.

Then the king went into the chamber unto Sir Tramtrist, and then was he gone unto his chamber, and the king found him all ready armed to mount upon his horse. When the king saw him all ready armed to go unto horseback, the king said: Nay, Tramtrist, it will not avail to compare thee against me; but thus much I shall do for my worship and for thy love; in so much as thou art within my court it were no worship for me to slay thee: therefore upon this condition I will give thee leave for to depart from this court in safety, so thou wilt tell me who was thy father, and what is thy name, and if thou slew Sir Marhaus, my brother.

CHAPTER XII

How Sir Tristram departed from the king and La Beale Isoud out of Ireland for to come into Cornwall.

Sir, said Tristram, now I shall tell you all the truth: my father's name is Sir Meliodas, King of Liones, and my mother hight Elizabeth, that was sister unto King Mark of Cornwall; and my mother died of me in the forest, and because thereof she commanded, or she died, that when I were christened they should christen me Tristram; and because I would not be known in this country I turned my name and let me call Tramtrist; and for the truage of Cornwall I fought for my eme's sake, and for the right of Cornwall that ye had posseded many years. And wit ye well, said Tristram unto the king, I did the battle for the love of mine uncle, King Mark, and for the love of the country of Cornwall, and for to increase mine honour; for that same day that I fought with Sir Marhaus I was made knight, and never or then did I battle with no knight, and from me he went alive, and left his shield and his sword behind.

So God me help, said the king, I may not say but ye did as a knight

should, and it was your part to do for your quarrel, and to increase
your worship as a knight should; howbeit I may not maintain you in
this country with my worship, unless that I should displease my
barons, and my wife and her kin. Sir, said Tristram, I thank you of
your good lordship that I have had with you here, and the great
goodness my lady, your daughter, hath showed me, and therefore,
said Sir Tristram, it may so happen that ye shall win more by my life
than by my death, for in the parts of England it may happen I may do
you service at some season, that ye shall be glad that ever ye showed
me your good lordship. With more I promise you as I am true
knight, that in all places I shall be my lady your daughter's servant and
knight in right and in wrong, and I shall never fail her, to do as much
as a knight may do. Also I beseech your good grace that I may take
my leave at my lady, your daughter, and at all the barons and knights.
I will well, said the king.

Then Sir Tristram went unto La Beale Isoud and took his leave of
her. And then he told her all, what he was, and how he had changed
his name because he would not be known, and how a lady told him
that he should never be whole till he came into this country where
the poison was made, wherethrough I was near my death had not
your ladyship been. O gentle knight, said La Beale Isoud, full woe am
I of thy departing, for I saw never man that I owed so good will to.
And therewithal she wept heartily. Madam, said Sir Tristram, ye shall
understand that my name is Sir Tristram de Liones, gotten of King
Meliodas, and born of his queen. And I promise you faithfully that I
shall be all the days of my life your knight. Gramercy, said La Beale
Isoud, and I promise you there-against that I shall not be married this
seven years but by your assent; and to whom that ye will I shall be
married to him will I have, and he will have me if ye will consent.

And then Sir Tristram gave her a ring, and she gave him another;
and therewith he departed from her, leaving her making great dole
and lamentation; and he straight went unto the court among all the
barons, and there he took his leave at most and least, and openly he
said among them all: Fair lords, now it is so that I must depart: if there
be any man here that I have offended unto, or that any man be with
me grieved, let complain him here afore me or that ever I depart, and
I shall amend it unto my power. And if there be any that will proffer
me wrong, or say of me wrong or shame behind my back, say it now
or never, and here is my body to make it good, body against body.

And all they stood still, there was not one that would say one word; yet were there some knights that were of the queen's blood, and of Sir Marhaus' blood, but they would not meddle with him.

CHAPTER XIII

How Sir Tristram and King Mark hurted each other for the love of a knight's wife.

So Sir Tristram departed, and took the sea, and with good wind he arrived up at Tintagil in Cornwall; and when King Mark was whole in his prosperity there came tidings that Sir Tristram was arrived, and whole of his wounds: thereof was King Mark passing glad, and so were all the barons; and when he saw his time he rode unto his father, King Meliodas, and there he had all the cheer that the king and the queen could make him. And then largely King Meliodas and his queen departed of their lands and goods to Sir Tristram.

Then by the license of King Meliodas, his father, he returned again unto the court of King Mark, and there he lived in great joy long time, until at the last there befell a jealousy and an unkindness betwixt King Mark and Sir Tristram, for they loved both one lady. And she was an earl's wife that hight Sir Segwarides. And this lady loved Sir Tristram passingly well. And he loved her again, for she was a passing fair lady, and that espied Sir Tristram well. Then King Mark understood that and was jealous, for King Mark loved her passingly well.

So it fell upon a day this lady sent a dwarf unto Sir Tristram, and bade him, as he loved her, that he would be with her the night next following. Also she charged you that ye come not to her but if ye be well armed, for her lover was called a good knight. Sir Tristram answered to the dwarf: Recommend me unto my lady, and tell her I will not fail but I will be with her the term that she hath set me. And with this answer the dwarf departed. And King Mark espied that the dwarf was with Sir Tristram upon message from Segwarides' wife; then King Mark sent for the dwarf, and when he was come he made the dwarf by force to tell him all, why and wherefore that he came on message from Sir Tristram. Now, said King Mark, go where thou wilt, and upon pain of death that thou say no word that thou spakest with me; so the dwarf departed from the king.

And that same night that the steven was set betwixt Segwarides' wife and Sir Tristram, King Mark armed him, and made him ready, and took two knights of his counsel with him; and so he rode afore for to abide by the way, for to wait upon Sir Tristram. And as Sir Tristram came riding upon his way with his spear in his hand, King Mark came hurtling upon him with his two knights suddenly. And all three smote him with their spears, and King Mark hurt Sir Tristram on the breast right sore. And then Sir Tristram feutred his spear, and smote his uncle, King Mark, so sore, that he rashed him to the earth, and bruised him that he lay still in a swoon, and long it was or ever he might wield himself. And then he ran to the one knight, and eft to the other, and smote them to the cold earth, that they lay still. And therewithal Sir Tristram rode forth sore wounded to the lady, and found her abiding him at a postern.

CHAPTER XIV

How Sir Tristram lay with the lady, and how her husband fought with Sir Tristram.

And there she welcomed him fair, and either halsed other in arms, and so she let put up his horse in the best wise, and then she unarmed him. And so they supped lightly, and went to bed with great joy and pleasaunce; and so in his raging he took no keep of his green wound that King Mark had given him. And so Sir Tristram be-bled both the over sheet and the nether, and pillows, and head sheet. And within a while there came one afore, that warned her that her lord was near-hand within a bow-draught. So she made Sir Tristram to arise, and so he armed him, and took his horse, and so departed. By then was come Segwarides, her lord, and when he found her bed troubled and broken, and went near and beheld it by candle light, then he saw that there had lain a wounded knight. Ah, false traitress, then he said, why hast thou betrayed me? And therewithal he swang out a sword, and said: But if thou tell me who hath been here, here thou shalt die. Ah, my lord, mercy, said the lady, and held up her hands, saying: Slay me not, and I shall tell you all who hath been here. Tell anon, said Segwarides, to me all the truth. Anon for dread she said: Here was Sir Tristram with me, and by the way as he came to me ward, he was sore wounded. Ah, false traitress, said Segwarides, where is he become? Sir, she said, he is armed, and departed on horseback, not yet hence half a mile. Ye say well, said Segwarides.

Then he armed him lightly, and gat his horse, and rode after Sir Tristram that rode straightway unto Tintagil. And within a while he overtook Sir Tristram, and then he bade him, Turn, false traitor knight. And Sir Tristram anon turned him against him. And therewithal Segwarides smote Sir Tristram with a spear that it all to-brast; and then he swang out his sword and smote fast at Sir Tristram. Sir knight, said Sir Tristram, I counsel you that ye smite no more, howbeit for the wrongs that I have done you I will forbear you as long as I may. Nay, said Segwarides, that shall not be, for either thou shalt die or I.

Then Sir Tristram drew out his sword, and hurtled his horse unto him fiercely, and through the waist of the body he smote Sir Segwarides that he fell to the earth in a swoon. And so Sir Tristram departed and left him there. And so he rode unto Tintagil and took his lodging secretly, for he would not be known that he was hurt. Also Sir Segwarides' men rode after their master, whom they found lying in the field sore wounded, and brought him home on his shield, and there he lay long or that he were whole, but at the last he recovered. Also King Mark would not be aknown of that Sir Tristram and he had met that night. And as for Sir Tristram, he knew not that King Mark had met with him. And so the king askance came to Sir Tristram, to comfort him as he lay sick in his bed. But as long as King Mark lived he loved never Sir Tristram after that; though there was fair speech, love was there none. And thus it passed many weeks and days, and all was forgiven and forgotten; for Sir Segwarides durst not have ado with Sir Tristram, because of his noble prowess, and also because he was nephew unto King Mark; therefore he let it overslip: for he that hath a privy hurt is loath to have a shame outward.

CHAPTER XV

How Sir Bleoberis demanded the fairest lady in King Mark's court, whom he took away, and how he was fought with.

Then it befell upon a day that the good knight Bleoberis de Ganis, brother to Blamore de Ganis, and nigh cousin unto the good knight Sir Launcelot du Lake, this Bleoberis came unto the court of King Mark, and there he asked of King Mark a boon, to give him what gift that he would ask in his court. When the king heard him ask so, he marvelled of his asking, but because he was a knight of the Round Table, and of a great renown, King Mark granted him his whole asking. Then, said Sir Bleoberis, I will have the fairest lady in your court that me list to choose. I may not say nay, said King Mark; now choose at your adventure. And so Sir Bleoberis did choose Sir Segwarides' wife, and took her by the hand, and so went his way with her; and so he took his horse and gart set her behind his squire, and rode upon his way.

When Sir Segwarides heard tell that his lady was gone with a knight of King Arthur's court, then he armed him and rode after that knight for to rescue his lady. So when Bleoberis was gone with this lady, King Mark and all the court was wroth that she was away. Then were there certain ladies that knew that there were great love between Sir Tristram and her, and also that lady loved Sir Tristram above all other knights. Then there was one lady that rebuked Sir Tristram in the horriblest wise, and called him coward knight, that he would for shame of his knighthood see a lady so shamefully be taken away from his uncle's court. But she meant that either of them had loved other with entire heart. But Sir Tristram answered her thus: Fair lady, it is not my part to have ado in such matters while her lord and husband is present here; and if it had been that her lord had not been here in this court, then for the worship of this court peradventure I would have been her champion, and if so be Sir Segwarides speed not well, it may happen that I will speak with that good knight or ever he pass from this country.

Then within a while came one of Sir Segwarides' squires, and told in the court that Sir Segwarides was beaten sore and wounded to the point of death; as he would have rescued his lady Sir Bleoberis overthrew him and sore hath wounded him. Then was King Mark heavy thereof, and all the court. When Sir Tristram heard of this he was ashamed and sore grieved; and then was he soon armed and on horseback, and Gouvernail, his servant, bare his shield and spear. And so as Sir Tristram rode fast he met with Sir Andred his cousin, that by the commandment of King Mark was sent to bring forth, an ever it lay in his power, two knights of Arthur's court, that rode by the country to seek their adventures. When Sir Tristram saw Sir Andred he asked him what tidings. So God me help, said Sir Andred, there was never worse with me, for here by the commandment of King Mark I was sent to fetch two knights of King Arthur's court, and that one beat me and wounded me, and set nought by my message. Fair cousin, said Sir Tristram, ride on your way, and if I may meet them it may happen I shall revenge you. So Sir Andred rode into Cornwall, and Sir Tristram rode after the two knights, the which one hight Sagramore le Desirous, and the other hight Dodinas le Savage.

CHAPTER XVI

How Sir Tristram fought with two knights of the Round Table.

Then within a while Sir Tristram saw them afore him, two likely knights. Sir, said Gouvernail unto his master, Sir, I would counsel you not to have ado with them, for they be two proved knights of Arthur's court. As for that, said Sir Tristram, have ye no doubt but I will have ado with them to increase my worship, for it is many day sithen I did any deeds of arms. Do as ye list, said Gouvernail. And therewithal anon Sir Tristram asked them from whence they came, and whither they would, and what they did in those marches. Sir Sagramore looked upon Sir Tristram, and had scorn of his words, and asked him again, Fair knight, be ye a knight of Cornwall? Whereby ask ye it? said Sir Tristram. For it is seldom seen, said Sir Sagramore, that ye Cornish knights be valiant men of arms; for within these two hours there met us one of your Cornish knights, and great words he spake, and anon with little might he was laid to the earth. And, as I trow, said Sir Sagramore, ye shall have the same handsel that he had. Fair lords, said Sir Tristram, it may so happen that I may better withstand than he did, and whether ye will or nill I will have ado with you, because he was my cousin that ye beat. And therefore here do your best, and wit ye well but if ye quit you the better here upon this ground, one knight of Cornwall shall beat you both.

When Sir Dodinas le Savage heard him say so he gat a spear in his hand, and said, Sir knight, keep well thyself. And then they departed and came together as it had been thunder. And Sir Dodinas' spear brast in-sunder, but Sir Tristram smote him with a more might, that he smote him clean over the horse-croup, that nigh he had broken his neck. When Sir Sagramore saw his fellow have such a fall he marvelled what knight he might be. And he dressed his spear with all his might, and Sir Tristram against him, and they came together as the thunder, and there Sir Tristram smote Sir Sagramore a strong buffet, that he bare his horse and him to the earth, and in the falling he brake his thigh.

When this was done Sir Tristram asked them: Fair knights, will ye any more? Be there no bigger knights in the court of King Arthur? it is to you shame to say of us knights of Cornwall dishonour, for it may happen a Cornish knight may match you. That is truth, said Sir Sagramore, that have we well proved; but I require thee, said Sir Sagramore, tell us your right name, by the faith and troth that ye owe to the high order of knighthood. Ye charge me with a great thing, said Sir Tristram, and sithen ye list to wit it, ye shall know and understand that my name is Sir Tristram de Liones, King Meliodas' son, and nephew unto King Mark. Then were they two knights fain that they had met with Tristram, and so they prayed him to abide in their fellowship. Nay, said Sir Tristram, for I must have ado with one of your fellows, his name is Sir Bleoberis de Ganis. God speed you well, said Sir Sagramore and Dodinas. Sir Tristram departed and rode onward on his way. And then was he ware before him in a valley where rode Sir Bleoberis, with Sir Segwarides' lady, that rode behind his squire upon a palfrey.

CHAPTER XVII

*How Sir Tristram fought with Sir Bleoberis for a lady, and
how the lady was put to choice to whom she would go.*

Then Sir Tristram rode more than a pace until that he had overtaken
him. Then spake Sir Tristram: Abide, he said, Knight of Arthur's
court, bring again that lady, or deliver her to me. I will do neither,
said Bleoberis, for I dread no Cornish knight so sore that me list to
deliver her. Why, said Sir Tristram, may not a Cornish knight do as
well as another knight? this same day two knights of your court
within this three mile met with me, and or ever we departed they
found a Cornish knight good enough for them both. What were
their names? said Bleoberis. They told me, said Sir Tristram, that the
one of them hight Sir Sagramore le Desirous, and the other hight
Dodinas le Savage. Ah, said Sir Bleoberis, have ye met with them? so
God me help, they were two good knights and men of great worship,
and if ye have beat them both ye must needs be a good knight; but if
it so be ye have beat them both, yet shall ye not fear me, but ye shall
beat me or ever ye have this lady. Then defend you, said Sir Tristram.
So they departed and came together like thunder, and either bare
other down, horse and all, to the earth.

Then they avoided their horses, and lashed together eagerly with
swords, and mightily, now tracing and traversing on the right hand
and on the left hand more than two hours. And sometime they
rushed together with such a might that they lay both grovelling on
the ground. Then Sir Bleoberis de Ganis stert aback, and said thus:
Now, gentle good knight, a while hold your hands, and let us speak
together. Say what ye will, said Tristram, and I will answer you. Sir,
said Bleoberis, I would wit of whence ye be, and of whom ye be
come, and what is your name? So God me help, said Sir Tristram, I
fear not to tell you my name. Wit ye well I am King Meliodas' son,
and my mother is King Mark's sister, and my name is Sir Tristram de
Liones, and King Mark is mine uncle. Truly, said Bleoberis, I am
right glad of you, for ye are he that slew Marhaus the knight, hand for
hand in an island, for the truage of Cornwall; also ye overcame Sir

Palomides the good knight, at a tournament in an island, where ye beat Sir Gawaine and his nine fellows. So God me help, said Sir Tristram, wit ye well that I am the same knight; now I have told you my name, tell me yours with good will. Wit ye well that my name is Sir Bleoberis de Ganis, and my brother hight Sir Blamore de Ganis, that is called a good knight, and we be sister's children unto my lord Sir Launcelot du Lake, that we call one of the best knights of the world. That is truth, said Sir Tristram, Sir Launcelot is called peerless of courtesy and of knighthood; and for his sake, said Sir Tristram, I will not with my good will fight no more with you, for the great love I have to Sir Launcelot du Lake. In good faith, said Bleoberis, as for me I will be loath to fight with you; but sithen ye follow me here to have this lady, I shall proffer you kindness, courtesy, and gentleness right here upon this ground. This lady shall be betwixt us both, and to whom that she will go, let him have her in peace. I will well, said Tristram, for, as I deem, she will leave you and come to me. Ye shall prove it anon, said Bleoberis.

CHAPTER XVIII

How the lady forsook Sir Tristram and abode with Sir Bleoberis, and how she desired to go to her husband.

So when she was set betwixt them both she said these words unto Sir Tristram: Wit ye well, Sir Tristram de Liones, that but late thou wast the man in the world that I most loved and trusted, and I weened thou hadst loved me again above all ladies; but when thou sawest this knight lead me away thou madest no cheer to rescue me, but suffered my lord Segwarides ride after me; but until that time I weened thou haddest loved me, and therefore now I will leave thee, and never love thee more. And therewithal she went unto Sir Bleoberis.

When Sir Tristram saw her do so he was wonderly wroth with that lady, and ashamed to come to the court. Sir Tristram, said Sir Bleoberis, ye are in the default, for I hear by this lady's words she before this day trusted you above all earthly knights, and, as she saith, ye have deceived her, therefore wit ye well, there may no man hold that will away; and rather than ye should be heartily displeased with me I would ye had her, an she would abide with you. Nay, said the lady, so God me help I will never go with him; for he that I loved most I weened he had loved me. And therefore, Sir Tristram, she said, ride as thou came, for though thou haddest overcome this knight, as ye was likely, with thee never would I have gone. And I shall pray this knight so fair of his knighthood, that or ever he pass this country, that he will lead me to the abbey where my lord Sir Segwarides lieth. So God me help, said Bleoberis, I let you wit, good knight Sir Tristram, because King Mark gave me the choice of a gift in this court, and so this lady liked me best – notwithstanding, she is wedded and hath a lord, and I have fulfilled my quest, she shall be sent unto her husband again, and in especial most for your sake, Sir Tristram; and if she would go with you I would ye had her. I thank you, said Sir Tristram, but for her love I shall beware what manner a lady I shall love or trust; for had her lord, Sir Segwarides, been away from the court, I should have been the first that should have followed you; but sithen that ye have refused me, as I am true knight I shall her know passingly well that I shall love or trust. And so they took their leave one from the other and departed.

And so Sir Tristram rode unto Tintagil, and Sir Bleoberis rode unto the abbey where Sir Segwarides lay sore wounded, and there he delivered his lady, and departed as a noble knight; and when Sir Segwarides saw his lady, he was greatly comforted; and then she told him that Sir Tristram had done great battle with Sir Bleoberis, and caused him to bring her again. These words pleased Sir Segwarides right well, that Sir Tristram would do so much; and so that lady told all the battle unto King Mark betwixt Sir Tristram and Sir Bleoberis.

CHAPTER XIX

How King Mark sent Sir Tristram for La Beale Isoud toward Ireland, and how by fortune he arrived into England.

Then when this was done King Mark cast always in his heart how he might destroy Sir Tristram. And then he imagined in himself to send Sir Tristram into Ireland for La Beale Isoud. For Sir Tristram had so praised her beauty and her goodness that King Mark said that he would wed her, whereupon he prayed Sir Tristram to take his way into Ireland for him on message. And all this was done to the intent to slay Sir Tristram. Notwithstanding, Sir Tristram would not refuse the message for no danger nor peril that might fall, for the pleasure of his uncle, but to go he made him ready in the most goodliest wise that might be devised. For Sir Tristram took with him the most goodliest knights that he might find in the court; and they were arrayed, after the guise that was then used, in the goodliest manner. So Sir Tristram departed and took the sea with all his fellowship. And anon, as he was in the broad sea a tempest took him and his fellowship, and drove them back into the coast of England; and there they arrived fast by Camelot, and full fain they were to take the land.

And when they were landed Sir Tristram set up his pavilion upon the land of Camelot, and there he let hang his shield upon the pavilion. And that same day came two knights of King Arthur's, that one was Sir Ector de Maris, and Sir Morganor. And they touched the shield, and bade him come out of the pavilion for to joust, an he would joust. Ye shall be answered, said Sir Tristram, an ye will tarry a little while. So he made him ready, and first he smote down Sir Ector de Maris, and after he smote down Sir Morganor, all with one spear, and sore bruised them. And when they lay upon the earth they asked Sir Tristram what he was, and of what country he was knight. Fair lords, said Sir Tristram, wit ye well that I am of Cornwall. Alas, said Sir Ector, now am I ashamed that ever any Cornish knight should overcome me. And then for despite Sir Ector put off his armour from him, and went on foot, and would not ride.

CHAPTER XX

How King Anguish of Ireland was summoned to come to King Arthur's court for treason.

Then it fell that Sir Bleoberis and Sir Blamore de Ganis, that were brethren, they had summoned the King Anguish of Ireland for to come to Arthur's court upon pain of forfeiture of King Arthur's good grace. And if the King of Ireland came not in, at the day assigned and set, the king should lose his lands. So it happened that at the day assigned, King Arthur neither Sir Launcelot might not be there for to give the judgment, for King Arthur was with Sir Launcelot at the Castle Joyous Garde. And so King Arthur assigned King Carados and the King of Scots to be there that day as judges. So when the kings were at Camelot King Anguish of Ireland was come to know his accusers. Then was there Sir Blamore de Ganis, and appealed the King of Ireland of treason, that he had slain a cousin of his in his court in Ireland by treason. The king was sore abashed of his accusation, forwhy he was come at the summons of King Arthur, and or he came at Camelot he wist not wherefore he was sent after. And when the king heard Sir Blamore say his will, he understood well there was none other remedy but for to answer him knightly; for the custom was such in those days, that an any man were appealed of any treason or murder he should fight body for body, or else to find another knight for him. And all manner of murders in those days were called treason.

So when King Anguish understood his accusing he was passing heavy, for he knew Sir Blamore de Ganis that he was a noble knight, and of noble knights come. Then the King of Ireland was simply purveyed of his answer; therefore the judges gave him respite by the third day to give his answer. So the king departed unto his lodging. The meanwhile there came a lady by Sir Tristram's pavilion making great dole. What aileth you, said Sir Tristram, that ye make such dole? Ah, fair knight, said the lady, I am ashamed unless that some good knight help me; for a great lady of worship sent by me a fair child and a rich, unto Sir Launcelot du Lake, and hereby there met with me a knight, and threw me down from my palfrey, and took away the child from me. Well, my lady, said Sir Tristram, and for my lord Sir Launcelot's sake I shall get you that child again, or else I shall be beaten for it. And so Sir Tristram took his horse, and asked the lady which way the knight rode; and then she told him. And he rode after him, and within a while he overtook that knight. And then Sir Tristram bade him turn and give again the child.

CHAPTER XXI

How Sir Tristram rescued a child from a knight, and how
Gouvernail told him of King Anguish.

The knight turned his horse and made him ready to fight. And then
Sir Tristram smote him with a sword such a buffet that he tumbled to
the earth. And then he yielded him unto Sir Tristram. Then come
thy way, said Sir Tristram, and bring the child to the lady again. So he
took his horse meekly and rode with Sir Tristram; and then by the
way Sir Tristram asked him his name. Then he said, My name is
Breuse Saunce Pité. So when he had delivered that child to the lady,
he said: Sir, as in this the child is well remedied. Then Sir Tristram let
him go again that sore repented him after, for he was a great foe unto
many good knights of King Arthur's court.

Then when Sir Tristram was in his pavilion Gouvernail, his man,
came and told him how that King Anguish of Ireland was come
thither, and he was put in great distress; and there Gouvernail told Sir
Tristram how King Anguish was summoned and appealed of
murder. So God me help, said Sir Tristram, these be the best tidings
that ever came to me this seven years, for now shall the King of
Ireland have need of my help; for I daresay there is no knight in this
country that is not of Arthur's court dare do battle with Sir Blamore
de Ganis; and for to win the love of the King of Ireland I will take
the battle upon me; and therefore Gouvernail bring me, I charge
thee, to the king.

Then Gouvernail went unto King Anguish of Ireland, and saluted
him fair. The king welcomed him and asked him what he would. Sir,
said Gouvernail, here is a knight near hand that desireth to speak with
you: he bade me say he would do you service. What knight is he?
said the king. Sir, said he, it is Sir Tristram de Liones, that for your
good grace that ye showed him in your lands will reward you in this
country. Come on, fellow, said the king, with me anon and show me
unto Sir Tristram. So the king took a little hackney and but few
fellowship with him, until he came unto Sir Tristram's pavilion. And
when Sir Tristram saw the king he ran unto him and would have

holden his stirrup. But the king leapt from his horse lightly, and either halsed other in their arms. My gracious lord, said Sir Tristram, gramercy of your great goodnesses showed unto me in your marches and lands: and at that time I promised you to do you service an ever it lay in my power. And, gentle knight, said the king unto Sir Tristram, now have I great need of you, never had I so great need of no knight's help. How so, my good lord? said Sir Tristram. I shall tell you, said the king: I am summoned and appealed from my country for the death of a knight that was kin unto the good knight Sir Launcelot; wherefore Sir Blamore de Ganis, brother to Sir Bleoberis hath appealed me to fight with him, outher to find a knight in my stead. And well I wot, said the king, these that are come of King Ban's blood, as Sir Launcelot and these other, are passing good knights, and hard men for to win in battle as any that I know now living. Sir, said Sir Tristram, for the good lordship ye showed me in Ireland, and for my lady your daughter's sake, La Beale Isoud, I will take the battle for you upon this condition that ye shall grant me two things: that one is that ye shall swear to me that ye are in the right, that ye were never consenting to the knight's death; Sir, then said Sir Tristram, when that I have done this battle, if God give me grace that I speed, that ye shall give me a reward, what thing reasonable that I will ask of you. So God me help, said the king, ye shall have whatsomever ye will ask. It is well said, said Sir Tristram.

CHAPTER XXII

How Sir Tristram fought for Sir Anguish and overcame his adversary, and how his adversary would never yield him.

Now make your answer that your champion is ready, for I shall die in your quarrel rather than to be recreant. I have no doubt of you, said the king, that, an ye should have ado with Sir Launcelot du Lake – Sir, said Sir Tristram, as for Sir Launcelot, he is called the noblest knight of the world, and wit ye well that the knights of his blood are noble men, and dread shame; and as for Bleoberis, brother unto Sir Blamore, I have done battle with him, therefore upon my head it is no shame to call him a good knight. It is noised, said the king, that Blamore is the hardier knight. Sir, as for that let him be, he shall never be refused, an as he were the best knight that now beareth shield or spear.

So King Anguish departed unto King Carados and the kings that were that time as judges, and told them that he had found his champion ready. Then by the commandment of the kings Sir Blamore de Ganis and Sir Tristram were sent for to hear the charge. And when they were come before the judges there were many kings and knights beheld Sir Tristram, and much speech they had of him because that he slew Sir Marhaus, the good knight, and because he for-jousted Sir Palomides the good knight. So when they had taken their charge they withdrew them to make them ready to do battle.

Then said Sir Bleoberis unto his brother, Sir Blamore: Fair dear brother, remember of what kin we be come of, and what a man is Sir Launcelot du Lake, neither farther nor nearer but brother's children, and there was never none of our kin that ever was shamed in battle; and rather suffer death, brother, than to be shamed. Brother, said Blamore, have ye no doubt of me, for I shall never shame none of my blood; howbeit I am sure that yonder knight is called a passing good knight as of his time one of the world, yet shall I never yield me, nor say the loath word: well may he happen to smite me down with his great might of chivalry, but rather shall he slay me than I shall yield me as recreant. God speed you well, said Sir Bleoberis, for ye shall find him the mightiest knight that ever ye had ado withal, for I know him, for I have had ado with him. God me speed, said Sir Blamore de Ganis; and therewith he took his horse at the one end of the lists, and Sir Tristram at the other end of the lists, and so they feutred their spears and came together as it had been thunder; and there Sir Tristram through great might smote down Sir Blamore and his horse to the earth. Then anon Sir Blamore avoided his horse and pulled out his sword and threw his shield afore him, and bade Sir Tristram alight: For though an horse hath failed me, I trust to God the earth will not fail me. And then Sir Tristram alighted, and dressed him unto battle; and there they lashed together strongly as racing and tracing, foining and dashing, many sad strokes, that the kings and knights had great wonder that they might stand; for ever they fought like wood men, so that there was never knights seen fight more fiercely than they did; for Sir Blamore was so hasty that he would have no rest, that all men wondered that they had breath to stand on their feet; and all the place was bloody that they fought in. And at the last, Sir

Tristram smote Sir Blamore such a buffet upon the helm that he there fell down upon his side, and Sir Tristram stood and beheld him.

CHAPTER XXIII

How Sir Blamore desired Tristram to slay him, and how Sir Tristram spared him, and how they took appointment.

Then when Sir Blamore might speak, he said thus: Sir Tristram de Liones, I require thee, as thou art a noble knight, and the best knight that ever I found, that thou wilt slay me out, for I would not live to be made lord of all the earth, for I have liefer die with worship than live with shame; and needs, Sir Tristram, thou must slay me, or else thou shalt never win the field, for I will never say the loath word. And therefore if thou dare slay me, slay me, I require thee. When Sir Tristram heard him say so knightly, he wist not what to do with him; he remembering him of both parties, of what blood he was come, and for Sir Launcelot's sake he would be loath to slay him; and in the other party in no wise he might not choose, but that he must make him to say the loath word, or else to slay him.

Then Sir Tristram stert aback, and went to the kings that were judges, and there he kneeled down to-fore them, and besought them for their worships, and for King Arthur's and Sir Launcelot's sake, that they would take this matter in their hands. For, my fair lords, said Sir Tristram, it were shame and pity that this noble knight that yonder lieth should be slain; for ye hear well, shamed will he not be, and I pray to God that he never be slain nor shamed for me. And as for the king for whom I fight for, I shall require him, as I am his true champion and true knight in this field, that he will have mercy upon this good knight. So God me help, said King Anguish, I will for your sake, Sir Tristram, be ruled as ye will have me, for I know you for my true knight; and therefore I will heartily pray the kings that be here as judges to take it in their hands. And the kings that were judges called Sir Bleoberis to them, and asked him his advice. My lords, said Bleoberis, though my brother be beaten, and hath the worse through might of arms, I dare say, though Sir Tristram hath beaten his body he hath not beaten his heart, and I thank God he is not shamed this day; and rather than he should be shamed I require you, said Bleoberis, let Sir Tristram slay him out. It shall not be so, said the kings, for his part adversary, both the king and the champion, have pity of Sir Blamore's knighthood. My lords, said Bleoberis, I will right well as ye will.

Then the kings called the King of Ireland, and found him goodly and treatable. And then, by all their advices, Sir Tristram and Sir Bleoberis took up Sir Blamore, and the two brethren were accorded with King Anguish, and kissed and made friends for ever. And then Sir Blamore and Sir Tristram kissed together, and there they made their oaths that they would never none of them two brethren fight with Sir Tristram, and Sir Tristram made the same oath. And for that gentle battle all the blood of Sir Launcelot loved Sir Tristram for ever.

Then King Anguish and Sir Tristram took their leave, and sailed into Ireland with great noblesse and joy. So when they were in Ireland the king let make it known throughout all the land how and in what manner Sir Tristram had done for him. Then the queen and all that there were made the most of him that they might. But the joy that La Beale Isoud made of Sir Tristram there might no tongue tell, for of all men earthly she loved him most.

CHAPTER XXIV

How Sir Tristram demanded La Beale Isoud for
King Mark, and how Sir Tristram and Isoud
drank the love drink.

Then upon a day King Anguish asked Sir Tristram why he asked not his boon, for whatsomever he had promised him he should have it without fail. Sir, said Sir Tristram, now is it time; this is all that I will desire, that ye will give me La Beale Isoud, your daughter, not for myself, but for mine uncle, King Mark, that shall have her to wife, for so have I promised him. Alas, said the king, I had liefer than all the land that I have ye would wed her yourself. Sir, an I did then I were shamed for ever in this world, and false of my promise. Therefore, said Sir Tristram, I pray you hold your promise that ye promised me; for this is my desire, that ye will give me La Beale Isoud to go with me into Cornwall for to be wedded to King Mark, mine uncle. As for that, said King Anguish, ye shall have her with you to do with her what it please you; that is for to say if that ye list to wed her yourself, that is me liefest, and if ye will give her unto King Mark, your uncle, that is in your choice. So, to make short conclusion, La Beale Isoud was made ready to go with Sir Tristram, and Dame Bragwaine went with her for her chief gentlewoman, with many other.

Then the queen, Isoud's mother, gave to her and Dame Bragwaine, her daughter's gentlewoman, and unto Gouvernail, a drink, and charged them that what day King Mark should wed, that same day they should give him that drink, so that King Mark should drink to La Beale Isoud, and then, said the queen, I undertake either shall love other the days of their life. So this drink was given unto Dame Bragwaine, and unto Gouvernail. And then anon Sir Tristram took the sea, and La Beale Isoud; and when they were in their cabin, it happed so that they were thirsty, and they saw a little flasket of gold stand by them, and it seemed by the colour and the taste that it was noble wine. Then Sir Tristram took the flasket in his hand, and said, Madam Isoud, here is the best drink that ever ye drank, that Dame Bragwaine, your maiden, and Gouvernail, my servant, have kept for themselves. Then they laughed and made good cheer, and either drank to other freely, and they thought never drink that ever they drank to other was so sweet nor so good. But by that their drink was in their bodies, they loved either other so well that never their love departed for weal neither for woe. And thus it happed the love first betwixt Sir Tristram and La Beale Isoud, the which love never departed the days of their life.

So then they sailed till by fortune they came nigh a castle that hight Pluere, and thereby arrived for to repose them, weening to them to have had good harbourage. But anon as Sir Tristram was within the castle they were taken prisoners; for the custom of the castle was such; who that rode by that castle and brought any lady, he must needs fight with the lord, that hight Breunor. And if it were so that Breunor won the field, then should the knight stranger and his lady be put to death, what that ever they were; and if it were so that the strange knight won the field of Sir Breunor, then should he die and his lady both. This custom was used many winters, for it was called the Castle Pluere, that is to say the Weeping Castle.

CHAPTER XXV

How Sir Tristram and Isoud were in prison, and how he fought for her beauty, and smote off another lady's head.

Thus as Sir Tristram and La Beale Isoud were in prison, it happed a knight and a lady came unto them where they were, to cheer them. I have marvel, said Tristram unto the knight and the lady, what is the cause the lord of this castle holdeth us in prison: it was never the custom of no place of worship that ever I came in, when a knight and a lady asked harbour, and they to receive them, and after to destroy them that be his guests. Sir, said the knight, this is the old custom of this castle, that when a knight cometh here he must needs fight with our lord, and he that is weaker must lose his head. And when that is done, if his lady that he bringeth be fouler than our lord's wife, she must lose her head: and if she be fairer proved than is our lady, then shall the lady of this castle lose her head. So God me help, said Sir Tristram, this is a foul custom and a shameful. But one advantage have I, said Sir Tristram, I have a lady is fair enough, fairer saw I never in all my life-days, and I doubt not for lack of beauty she shall not lose her head; and rather than I should lose my head I will fight for it on a fair field. Wherefore, sir knight, I pray you tell your lord that I will be ready as to-morn with my lady, and myself to do battle, if it be so I may have my horse and mine armour. Sir, said that knight, I undertake that your desire shall be sped right well. And then he said: Take your rest, and look that ye be up betimes and make you ready and your lady, for ye shall want no thing that you behoveth. And therewith he departed, and on the morn betimes that same knight came to Sir Tristram, and fetched him out and his lady, and brought him horse and armour that was his own, and bade him make him ready to the field, for all the estates and commons of that lordship were there ready to behold that battle and judgment.

Then came Sir Breunor, the lord of that castle, with his lady in his hand, muffled, and asked Sir Tristram where was his lady: For an thy lady be fairer than mine, with thy sword smite off my lady's head; and if my lady be fairer than thine, with my sword I must strike off her head. And if I may win thee, yet shall thy lady be mine, and thou shalt lose thy head. Sir, said Tristram, this is a foul custom and horrible; and rather than my lady should lose her head, yet had I liefer lose my head. Nay, nay, said Sir Breunor, the ladies shall be first showed together, and the one shall have her judgment. Nay, I will not so, said Sir Tristram, for here is none that will give righteous judgment. But I doubt not, said Sir Tristram, my lady is fairer than thine, and that will I prove and make good with my hand. And whosomever he be that will say the contrary I will prove it on his head. And therewith Sir Tristram showed La Beale Isoud, and turned her thrice about with his naked sword in his hand. And when Sir Breunor saw that, he did the same wise turn his lady. But when Sir Breunor beheld La Beale Isoud, him thought he saw never a fairer lady, and then he dread his lady's head should be off. And so all the people that were there present gave judgment that La Beale Isoud was the fairer lady and the better made. How now, said Sir Tristram, meseemeth it were pity that thy lady should lose her head, but because thou and she of long time have used this wicked custom, and by you both have many good knights and ladies been destroyed, for that cause it were no loss to destroy you both. So God me help, said Sir Breunor, for to say the sooth, thy lady is fairer than mine, and that me sore repenteth. And so I hear the people privily say, for of all women I saw none so fair; and therefore, an thou wilt slay my lady, I doubt not but I shall slay thee and have thy lady. Thou shalt win her, said Sir Tristram, as dear as ever knight won lady. And because of thine own judgment, as thou wouldst have done to my lady if that she had been fouler, and because of the evil custom, give me thy lady, said Sir Tristram. And therewithal Sir Tristram strode unto him and took his lady from him, and with an awk stroke he smote off her head clean. Well, knight, said Sir Breunor, now hast thou done me a despite;* now take thine horse: sithen I am ladyless I will win thy lady an I may.

---

* Printed by Caxton as part of chapter xxvi

CHAPTER XXVI

*How Sir Tristram fought with Sir Breunor, and at the last
smote off his head.*

Then they took their horses and came together as it had been the
thunder; and Sir Tristram smote Sir Breunor clean from his horse,
and lightly he rose up; and as Sir Tristram came again by him he
thrust his horse throughout both the shoulders, that his horse hurled
here and there and fell dead to the ground. And ever Sir Breunor ran
after to have slain Sir Tristram, but Sir Tristram was light and nimble,
and voided his horse lightly. And or ever Sir Tristram might dress his
shield and his sword the other gave him three or four sad strokes.
Then they rushed together like two boars, tracing and traversing
mightily and wisely as two noble knights. For this Sir Breunor was a
proved knight, and had been or then the death of many good
knights, that it was pity that he had so long endured.

Thus they fought, hurling here and there nigh two hours, and
either were wounded sore. Then at the last Sir Breunor rashed upon
Sir Tristram and took him in his arms, for he trusted much in his
strength. Then was Sir Tristram called the strongest and the highest
knight of the world; for he was called bigger than Sir Launcelot, but
Sir Launcelot was better breathed. So anon Sir Tristram thrust Sir
Breunor down grovelling, and then he unlaced his helm and struck
off his head. And then all they that longed to the castle came to him,
and did him homage and fealty, praying him that he would abide
there still a little while to fordo that foul custom. Sir Tristram granted
thereto. The meanwhile one of the knights of the castle rode unto Sir
Galahad, the haut prince, the which was Sir Breunor's son, which
was a noble knight, and told him what misadventure his father had
and his mother.

CHAPTER XXVII

How Sir Galahad fought with Sir Tristram, and how Sir
Tristram yielded him and promised to fellowship with
Launcelot.

Then came Sir Galahad, and the King with the Hundred Knights
with him; and this Sir Galahad proffered to fight with Sir Tristram
hand for hand. And so they made them ready to go unto battle on
horseback with great courage. Then Sir Galahad and Sir Tristram met
together so hard that either bare other down, horse and all, to the
earth. And then they avoided their horses as noble knights, and
dressed their shields, and drew their swords with ire and rancour, and
they lashed together many sad strokes, and one while striking,
another while foining, tracing and traversing as noble knights; thus
they fought long, near half a day, and either were sore wounded. At
the last Sir Tristram waxed light and big, and doubled his strokes, and
drove Sir Galahad aback on the one side and on the other, so that he
was like to have been slain.

With that came the King with the Hundred Knights, and all that
fellowship went fiercely upon Sir Tristram. When Sir Tristram saw
them coming upon him, then he wist well he might not endure.
Then as a wise knight of war, he said to Sir Galahad, the haut prince:
Sir, ye show to me no knighthood, for to suffer all your men to have
ado with me all at once; and as meseemeth ye be a noble knight of
your hands it is great shame to you. So God me help, said Sir
Galahad, there is none other way but thou must yield thee to me,
other else to die, said Sir Galahad to Sir Tristram. I will rather yield
me to you than die, for that is more for the might of your men than
of your hands. And therewithal Sir Tristram took his own sword by
the point, and put the pommel in the hand of Sir Galahad.

Therewithal came the King with the Hundred Knights, and hard
began to assail Sir Tristram. Let be, said Sir Galahad, be ye not so
hardy to touch him, for I have given this knight his life. That is your
shame, said the King with the Hundred Knights; hath he not slain
your father and your mother? As for that, said Sir Galahad, I may not

wite him greatly, for my father had him in prison, and enforced him
to do battle with him; and my father had such a custom that was a
shameful custom, that what knight came there to ask harbour his lady
must needs die but if she were fairer than my mother; and if my father
overcame that knight he must needs die. This was a shameful custom
and usage, a knight for his harbour-asking to have such harbourage.
And for this custom I would never draw about him. So God me help,
said the King, this was a shameful custom. Truly, said Sir Galahad, so
seemed me; and meseemed it had been great pity that this knight
should have been slain, for I dare say he is the noblest man that
beareth life, but if it were Sir Launcelot du Lake. Now, fair knight,
said Sir Galahad, I require thee tell me thy name, and of whence thou
art, and whither thou wilt. Sir, he said, my name is Sir Tristram de
Liones, and from King Mark of Cornwall I was sent on message unto
King Anguish of Ireland, for to fetch his daughter to be his wife, and
here she is ready to go with me into Cornwall, and her name is La
Beale Isoud. And, Sir Tristram, said Sir Galahad, the haut prince, well
be ye found in these marches, and so ye will promise me to go unto
Sir Launcelot du Lake, and accompany with him, ye shall go where ye
will, and your fair lady with you; and I shall promise you never in all
my days shall such customs be used in this castle as have been used.
Sir, said Sir Tristram, now I let you wit, so God me help, I weened ye
had been Sir Launcelot du Lake when I saw you first, and therefore I
dread you the more; and sir, I promise you, said Sir Tristram, as soon
as I may I will see Sir Launcelot and infellowship me with him; for of
all the knights of the world I most desire his fellowship.

CHAPTER XXVIII

*How Sir Launcelot met with Sir Carados bearing away
Sir Gawaine, and of the rescue of Sir Gawaine.*

And then Sir Tristram took his leave when he saw his time, and took
the sea. And in the meanwhile word came unto Sir Launcelot and to
Sir Tristram that Sir Carados, the mighty king, that was made like a
giant, fought with Sir Gawaine, and gave him such strokes that he
swooned in his saddle, and after that he took him by the collar and

pulled him out of his saddle, and fast bound him to the saddle-bow, and so rode his way with him toward his castle. And as he rode, by fortune Sir Launcelot met with Sir Carados, and anon he knew Sir Gawaine that lay bound after him. Ah, said Sir Launcelot unto Sir Gawaine, how stands it with you? Never so hard, said Sir Gawaine, unless that ye help me, for so God me help, without ye rescue me I know no knight that may, but outher you or Sir Tristram. Wherefore Sir Launcelot was heavy of Sir Gawaine's words. And then Sir Launcelot bade Sir Carados: Lay down that knight and fight with me. Thou art but a fool, said Sir Carados, for I will serve you in the same wise. As for that, said Sir Launcelot, spare me not, for I warn thee I will not spare thee. And then he bound Sir Gawaine hand and foot, and so threw him to the ground. And then he gat his spear of his squire, and departed from Sir Launcelot to fetch his course. And so either met with other, and brake their spears to their hands; and then they pulled out swords, and hurtled together on horseback more than an hour. And at the last Sir Launcelot smote Sir Carados such a buffet upon the helm that it pierced his brain-pan. So then Sir Launcelot took Sir Carados by the collar and pulled him under his horse's feet, and then he alighted and pulled off his helm and struck off his head. And then Sir Launcelot unbound Sir Gawaine. So this same tale was told to Sir Galahad and to Sir Tristram: – here may ye hear the nobleness that followeth Sir Launcelot. Alas, said Sir Tristram, an I had not this message in hand with this fair lady, truly I would never stint or I had found Sir Launcelot. Then Sir Tristram and La Beale Isoud went to the sea and came into Cornwall, and there all the barons met them.

CHAPTER XXIX

Of the wedding of King Mark to La Beale Isoud, and of Bragwaine her maid, and of Palomides.

And anon they were richly wedded with great noblesse. But ever, as the French book saith, Sir Tristram and La Beale Isoud loved ever together. Then was there great jousts and great tourneying, and many lords and ladies were at that feast, and Sir Tristram was most praised of all other. Thus dured the feast long, and after the feast was done, within a little while after, by the assent of two ladies that were with Queen Isoud, they ordained for hate and envy for to destroy Dame Bragwaine, that was maiden and lady unto La Beale Isoud; and she was sent into the forest for to fetch herbs, and there she was met, and bound feet and hand to a tree, and so she was bounden three days. And by fortune, Sir Palomides found Dame Bragwaine, and there he delivered her from the death, and brought her to a nunnery there beside, for to be recovered. When Isoud the queen missed her maiden, wit ye well she was right heavy as ever was any queen, for of all earthly women she loved her best: the cause was for she came with her out of her country. And so upon a day Queen Isoud walked into the forest to put away her thoughts, and there she went herself unto a well and made great moan. And suddenly there came Palomides to her, and had heard all her complaint, and said: Madam Isoud, an ye will grant me my boon, I shall bring to you Dame Bragwaine safe and sound. And the queen was so glad of his proffer that suddenly unadvised she granted all his asking. Well, Madam, said Palomides, I trust to your promise, and if ye will abide here half an hour I shall bring her to you. I shall abide you, said La Beale Isoud. And Sir Palomides rode forth his way to that nunnery, and lightly he came again with Dame Bragwaine; but by her good will she would not have come again, because for love of the queen she stood in adventure of her life. Notwithstanding, half against her will, she went with Sir Palomides unto the queen. And when the queen saw her she was passing glad. Now, Madam, said Palomides, remember upon your promise, for I have fulfilled my promise. Sir Palomides, said the queen, I wot not what is your desire, but I will that ye wit, howbeit I promised you largely, I thought none evil, nor I warn you none evil will I do. Madam, said Sir Palomides, as at this time, ye shall not know my desire, but before my lord your husband there shall ye know that I will have my desire that ye have promised me. And therewith the queen departed, and rode home to the king, and Sir Palomides rode after her. And when Sir Palomides came before the king, he said: Sir King, I require you as ye be a righteous king, that ye will judge me the right. Tell me your cause, said the king, and ye shall have right.

CHAPTER XXX

How Palomides demanded Queen Isoud, and how Lambegus
rode after to rescue her, and of the escape of Isoud.

Sir, said Palomides, I promised your Queen Isoud to bring again
Dame Bragwaine that she had lost, upon this covenant, that she
should grant me a boon that I would ask, and without grudging,
outher advisement, she granted me. What say ye, my lady? said the
king. It is as he saith, so God me help, said the queen; to say thee
sooth I promised him his asking for love and joy that I had to see her.
Well, Madam, said the king, and if ye were hasty to grant him what
boon he would ask, I will well that ye perform your promise. Then,
said Palomides, I will that ye wit that I will have your queen to lead
her and govern her whereas me list. Therewith the king stood still,
and bethought him of Sir Tristram, and deemed that he would rescue
her. And then hastily the king answered: Take her with the
adventures that shall fall of it, for as I suppose thou wilt not enjoy her
no while. As for that, said Palomides, I dare right well abide the
adventure. And so, to make short tale, Sir Palomides took her by the
hand and said: Madam, grudge not to go with me, for I desire
nothing but your own promise. As for that, said the queen, I fear not
greatly to go with thee, howbeit thou hast me at advantage upon my
promise, for I doubt not I shall be worshipfully rescued from thee. As
for that, said Sir Palomides, be it as it be may. So Queen Isoud was set
behind Palomides, and rode his way.

Anon the king sent after Sir Tristram, but in no wise he could be
found, for he was in the forest a-hunting; for that was always his
custom, but if he used arms, to chase and to hunt in the forests. Alas,
said the king, now I am shamed for ever, that by mine own assent my
lady and my queen shall be devoured. Then came forth a knight, his
name was Lambegus, and he was a knight of Sir Tristram. My lord,
said this knight, sith ye have trust in my lord, Sir Tristram, wit ye well
for his sake I will ride after your queen and rescue her, or else I shall
be beaten. Gramercy, said the king, as I live, Sir Lambegus, I shall
deserve it. And then Sir Lambegus armed him, and rode after as fast as

he might. And then within a while he overtook Sir Palomides. And then Sir Palomides left the queen. What art thou, said Palomides, art thou Tristram? Nay, he said, I am his servant, and my name is Sir Lambegus. That me repenteth, said Palomides. I had liefer thou hadst been Sir Tristram. I believe you well, said Lambegus, but when thou meetest with Sir Tristram thou shalt have thy hands full. And then they hurtled together and all to-brast their spears, and then they pulled out their swords, and hewed on helms and hauberks. At the last Sir Palomides gave Sir Lambegus such a wound that he fell down like a dead knight to the earth.

Then he looked after La Beale Isoud, and then she was gone he nist where. Wit ye well Sir Palomides was never so heavy. So the queen ran into the forest, and there she found a well, and therein she had thought to have drowned herself. And as good fortune would, there came a knight to her that had a castle thereby, his name was Sir Adtherp. And when he found the queen in that mischief he rescued her, and brought her to his castle. And when he wist what she was he armed him, and took his horse, and said he would be avenged upon Palomides; and so he rode on till he met with him, and there Sir Palomides wounded him sore, and by force he made him to tell him the cause why he did battle with him, and how he had led the queen unto his castle. Now bring me there, said Palomides, or thou shalt die of my hands. Sir, said Sir Adtherp, I am so wounded I may not follow, but ride you this way and it shall bring you into my castle, and there within is the queen. Then Sir Palomides rode still till he came to the castle. And at a window La Beale Isoud saw Sir Palomides; then she made the gates to be shut strongly. And when he saw he might not come within the castle, he put off his bridle and his saddle, and put his horse to pasture, and set himself down at the gate like a man that was out of his wit that recked not of himself.

CHAPTER XXXI

How Sir Tristram rode after Palomides, and how he found him and fought with him, and by the means of Isoud the battle ceased.

Now turn we unto Sir Tristram, that when he was come home and wist La Beale Isoud was gone with Sir Palomides, wit ye well he was wroth out of measure. Alas, said Sir Tristram, I am this day shamed. Then he cried to Gouvernail his man: Haste thee that I were armed and on horseback, for well I wot Lambegus hath no might nor strength to withstand Sir Palomides: alas that I have not been in his stead! So anon as he was armed and horsed Sir Tristram and Gouvernail rode after into the forest, and within a while he found his knight Lambegus almost wounded to the death; and Sir Tristram bare him to a forester, and charged him to keep him well. And then he rode forth, and there he found Sir Adtherp sore wounded, and he told him how the queen would have drowned herself had he not been, and how for her sake and love he had taken upon him to do battle with Sir Palomides. Where is my lady? said Sir Tristram. Sir, said the knight, she is sure enough within my castle, an she can hold her within it. Gramercy, said Sir Tristram, of thy great goodness. And so he rode till he came nigh to that castle; and then Sir Tristram saw where Sir Palomides sat at the gate sleeping, and his horse pastured fast afore him. Now go thou, Gouvernail, said Sir Tristram, and bid him awake, and make him ready. So Gouvernail rode unto him and said: Sir Palomides, arise, and take to thee thine harness. But he was in such a study he heard not what Gouvernail said. So Gouvernail came again and told Sir Tristram he slept, or else he was mad. Go thou again, said Sir Tristram, and bid him arise, and tell him that I am here, his mortal foe. So Gouvernail rode again and put upon him the butt of his spear, and said: Sir Palomides, make thee ready, for wit ye well Sir Tristram hoveth yonder, and sendeth thee word he is thy mortal foe.

And therewithal Sir Palomides arose stilly, without words, and gat his horse, and saddled him and bridled him, and lightly he leapt upon, and gat his spear in his hand, and either feutred their spears and hurtled fast together; and there Tristram smote down Sir Palomides over his horse's tail. Then lightly Sir Palomides put his shield afore him and drew his sword. And there began strong battle on both parts, for both they fought for the love of one lady, and ever she lay on the walls and beheld them how they fought out of measure, and either were wounded passing sore, but Palomides was much sorer wounded. Thus they fought tracing and traversing more than two hours, that well-nigh for dole and sorrow La Beale Isoud swooned. Alas, she said, that one I loved and yet do, and the other I love not, yet it were great pity that I should see Sir Palomides slain; for well I know by that time the end be done Sir Palomides is but a dead knight: because he is not christened I would be loath that he should die a Saracen. And therewithal she came down and besought Sir Tristram to fight no more. Ah, madam, said he, what mean you, will ye have me shamed? Well ye know I will be ruled by you. I will not your dishonour, said La Beale Isoud, but I would that ye would for my sake spare this unhappy Saracen Palomides. Madam, said Sir Tristram, I will leave fighting at this time for your sake. Then she said to Sir Palomides: This shall be your charge, that thou shalt go out of this country while I am therein. I will obey your commandment, said Sir Palomides, the which is sore against my will. Then take thy way, said La Beale Isoud, unto the court of King Arthur, and there recommend me unto Queen Guenever, and tell her that I send her word that there be within this land but four lovers, that is, Sir Launcelot du Lake and Queen Guenever, and Sir Tristram de Liones and Queen Isoud.

CHAPTER XXXII

How Sir Tristram brought Queen Isoud home, and of the debate of King Mark and Sir Tristram.

And so Sir Palomides departed with great heaviness. And Sir Tristram took the queen and brought her again to King Mark, and then was there made great joy of her home-coming. Who was cherished but Sir Tristram! Then Sir Tristram let fetch Sir Lambegus, his knight, from the forester's house, and it was long or he was whole, but at the last he was well recovered. Thus they lived with joy and play a long while. But ever Sir Andred, that was nigh cousin to Sir Tristram, lay in a watch to wait betwixt Sir Tristram and La Beale Isoud, for to take them and slander them. So upon a day Sir Tristram talked with La Beale Isoud in a window, and that espied Sir Andred, and told it to the King. Then King Mark took a sword in his hand and came to Sir Tristram, and called him false traitor, and would have stricken him. But Sir Tristram was nigh him, and ran under his sword, and took it out of his hand. And then the King cried: Where are my knights and my men? I charge you slay this traitor. But at that time there was not one would move for his words. When Sir Tristram saw that there was not one would be against him, he shook the sword to the king, and made countenance as though he would have stricken him. And then King Mark fled, and Sir Tristram followed him, and smote upon him five or six strokes flatling on the neck, that he made him to fall upon the nose. And then Sir Tristram yede his way and armed him, and took his horse and his man, and so he rode into that forest.

And there upon a day Sir Tristram met with two brethren that were knights with King Mark, and there he struck off the head of the one, and wounded the other to the death; and he made him to bear his brother's head in his helm unto the king, and thirty more there he wounded. And when that knight came before the king to say his message, he there died afore the king and the queen. Then King Mark called his council unto him, and asked advice of his barons what was best to do with Sir Tristram. Sir, said the barons, in especial Sir Dinas, the Seneschal, Sir, we will give you counsel for to send for Sir Tristram, for we will that ye wit many men will hold with Sir Tristram an he were hard bestead. And sir, said Sir Dinas, ye shall understand that Sir Tristram is called peerless and makeless of any Christian knight, and of his might and hardiness we knew none so good a knight, but if it be Sir Launcelot du Lake. And if he depart from your court and go to King Arthur's court, wit ye well he will get him such friends there that he will not set by your malice. And therefore, sir, I counsel you to take him to your grace. I will well, said the king, that he be sent for, that we may be friends. Then the barons sent for Sir Tristram under a safe conduct. And so when Sir Tristram came to the king he was welcome, and no rehearsal was made, and there was game and play. And then the king and the queen went a-hunting, and Sir Tristram.

CHAPTER XXXIII

How Sir Lamorak jousted with thirty knights, and Sir
Tristram at the request of King Mark smote his horse down.

The king and the queen made their pavilions and their tents in that
forest beside a river, and there was daily hunting and jousting, for
there were ever thirty knights ready to joust unto all them that came
in at that time. And there by fortune came Sir Lamorak de Galis and
Sir Driant; and there Sir Driant jousted right well, but at the last he
had a fall. Then Sir Lamorak proffered to joust. And when he began
he fared so with the thirty knights that there was not one of them but
that he gave him a fall, and some of them were sore hurt. I marvel,
said King Mark, what knight he is that doth such deeds of arms. Sir,
said Sir Tristram, I know him well for a noble knight as few now be
living, and his name is Sir Lamorak de Galis. It were great shame, said
the king, that he should go thus away, unless that some of you meet
with him better. Sir, said Sir Tristram, meseemeth it were no worship
for a noble man to have ado with him: and for because at this time he
hath done over much for any mean knight living, therefore, as
meseemeth, it were great shame and villainy to tempt him any more
at this time, insomuch as he and his horse are weary both; for the
deeds of arms that he hath done this day, an they be well considered,
it were enough for Sir Launcelot du Lake. As for that, said King
Mark, I require you, as ye love me and my lady the queen, La Beale
Isoud, take your arms and joust with Sir Lamorak de Galis. Sir, said
Sir Tristram, ye bid me do a thing that is against knighthood, and
well I can deem that I shall give him a fall, for it is no mastery, for my
horse and I be fresh both, and so is not his horse and he; and wit ye
well that he will take it for great unkindness, for ever one good
knight is loath to take another at disadvantage; but because I will not
displease you, as ye require me so will I do, and obey your
commandment.

And so Sir Tristram armed him and took his horse, and put him
forth, and there Sir Lamorak met him mightily, and what with the
might of his own spear, and of Sir Tristram's spear, Sir Lamorak's

horse fell to the earth, and he sitting in the saddle. Then anon as lightly as he might he avoided the saddle and his horse, and put his shield afore him and drew his sword. And then he bade Sir Tristram: Alight, thou knight, an thou durst. Nay, said Sir Tristram, I will no more have ado with thee, for I have done to thee over much unto my dishonour and to thy worship. As for that, said Sir Lamorak, I can thee no thank; since thou hast forjousted me on horseback I require thee and I beseech thee, an thou be Sir Tristram, fight with me on foot. I will not so, said Sir Tristram; and wit ye well my name is Sir Tristram de Liones, and well I know ye be Sir Lamorak de Galis, and this that I have done to you was against my will, but I was required thereto; but to say that I will do at your request as at this time, I will have no more ado with you, for me shameth of that I have done. As for the shame, said Sir Lamorak, on thy part or on mine, bear thou it an thou wilt, for though a mare's son hath failed me, now a queen's son shall not fail thee; and therefore, an thou be such a knight as men call thee, I require thee, alight, and fight with me. Sir Lamorak, said Sir Tristram, I understand your heart is great, and cause why ye have, to say thee sooth; for it would grieve me an any knight should keep him fresh and then to strike down a weary knight, for that knight nor horse was never formed that alway might stand or endure. And therefore, said Sir Tristram, I will not have ado with you, for me forthinketh of that I have done. As for that, said Sir Lamorak, I shall quit you, an ever I see my time.

CHAPTER XXXIV

How Sir Lamorak sent an horn to King Mark in despite of Sir Tristram, and how Sir Tristram was driven into a chapel.

So he departed from him with Sir Driant, and by the way they met with a knight that was sent from Morgan le Fay unto King Arthur; and this knight had a fair horn harnessed with gold, and the horn had such a virtue that there might no lady nor gentlewoman drink of that horn but if she were true to her husband, and if she were false she should spill all the drink, and if she were true to her lord she might drink peaceable. And because of the Queen Guenever, and in the despite of Sir Launcelot, this horn was sent unto King Arthur; and by force Sir Lamorak made that knight to tell all the cause why he bare that horn. Now shalt thou bear this horn, said Lamorak, unto King Mark, or else choose thou to die for it; for I tell thee plainly, in despite and reproof of Sir Tristram thou shalt bear that horn unto King Mark, his uncle, and say thou to him that I sent it him for to assay his lady, and if she be true to him he shall prove her. So the knight went his way unto King Mark, and brought him that rich horn, and said that Sir Lamorak sent it him, and thereto he told him the virtue of that horn. Then the king made Queen Isoud to drink thereof, and an hundred ladies, and there were but four ladies of all those that drank clean. Alas, said King Mark, this is a great despite, and sware a great oath that she should be burnt and the other ladies.

Then the barons gathered them together, and said plainly they would not have those ladies burnt for an horn made by sorcery, that came from as false a sorceress and witch as then was living. For that horn did never good, but caused strife and debate, and always in her days she had been an enemy to all true lovers. So there were many knights made their avow, an ever they met with Morgan le Fay, that they would show her short courtesy. Also Sir Tristram was passing wroth that Sir Lamorak sent that horn unto King Mark, for well he knew that it was done in the despite of him. And therefore he thought to quite Sir Lamorak.

Then Sir Tristram used daily and nightly to go to Queen Isoud when he might, and ever Sir Andred his cousin watched him night and day for to take him with La Beale Isoud. And so upon a night Sir Andred espied the hour and the time when Sir Tristram went to his lady. Then Sir Andred gat unto him twelve knights, and at midnight he set upon Sir Tristram secretly and suddenly, and there Sir Tristram was taken naked abed with La Beale Isoud, and then was he bound hand and foot, and so was he kept until day. And then by the assent of King Mark, and of Sir Andred, and of some of the barons, Sir Tristram was led unto a chapel that stood upon the sea rocks, there for to take his judgment: and so he was led bounden with forty knights. And when Sir Tristram saw that there was none other boot but needs that he must die, then said he: Fair lords, remember what I have done for the country of Cornwall, and in what jeopardy I have been in for the weal of you all; for when I fought for the truage of Cornwall with Sir Marhaus, the good knight, I was promised for to be better rewarded, when ye all refused to take the battle; therefore, as ye be good gentle knights, see me not thus shamefully to die, for it is shame to all knighthood thus to see me die; for I dare say, said Sir Tristram, that I never met with no knight but I was as good as he, or better. Fie upon thee, said Sir Andred, false traitor that thou art, with thine avaunting; for all thy boast thou shalt die this day. O Andred, Andred, said Sir Tristram, thou shouldst be my kinsman, and now thou art to me full unfriendly, but an there were no more but thou and I, thou wouldst not put me to death. No! said Sir Andred, and therewith he drew his sword, and would have slain him.

When Sir Tristram saw him make such countenance he looked upon both his hands that were fast bounden unto two knights, and suddenly he pulled them both to him, and unwrast his hands, and then he leapt unto his cousin, Sir Andred, and wrested his sword out of his hands; then he smote Sir Andred that he fell to the earth, and so Sir Tristram fought till that he had killed ten knights. So then Sir Tristram gat the chapel and kept it mightily. Then the cry was great, and the people drew fast unto Sir Andred, mo than an hundred. When Sir Tristram saw the people draw unto him, he remembered he was naked, and sperd fast the chapel door, and brake the bars of a window, and so he leapt out and fell upon the crags in the sea. And so at that time Sir Andred nor none of his fellows might get to him, at that time.

CHAPTER XXXV

How Sir Tristram was holpen by his men, and of Queen Isoud which was put in a lazar-cote, and how Tristram was hurt.

So when they were departed, Gouvernail, and Sir Lambegus, and Sir Sentraille de Lushon, that were Sir Tristram's men, sought their master. When they heard he was escaped then they were passing glad; and on the rocks they found him, and with towels they pulled him up. And then Sir Tristram asked them where was La Beale Isoud, for he weened she had been had away of Andred's people. Sir, said Gouvernail, she is put in a lazar-cote. Alas, said Sir Tristram, this is a full ungoodly place for such a fair lady, and if I may she shall not be

long there. And so he took his men and went thereas was La Beale
Isoud, and fetched her away, and brought her into a forest to a fair
manor, and Sir Tristram there abode with her. So the good knight
bade his men go from him: For at this time I may not help you. So
they departed all save Gouvernail. And so upon a day Sir Tristram
yede into the forest for to disport him, and then it happened that
there he fell asleep; and there came a man that Sir Tristram aforehand
had slain his brother, and when this man had found him he shot him
through the shoulder with an arrow, and Sir Tristram leapt up and
killed that man. And in the meantime it was told King Mark how Sir
Tristram and La Beale Isoud were in that same manor, and as soon as
ever he might thither he came with many knights to slay Sir Tristram.
And when he came there he found him gone; and there he took La
Beale Isoud home with him, and kept her strait that by no means
never she might wit nor send unto Tristram, nor he unto her. And
then when Sir Tristram came toward the old manor he found the
track of many horses, and thereby he wist his lady was gone. And
then Sir Tristram took great sorrow, and endured with great pain
long time, for the arrow that he was hurt withal was envenomed.

Then by the mean of La Beale Isoud she told a lady that was cousin
unto Dame Bragwaine, and she came to Sir Tristram, and told him
that he might not be whole by no means. For thy lady, La Beale
Isoud, may not help thee, therefore she biddeth you haste into
Brittany to King Howel, and there ye shall find his daughter, Isoud la
Blanche Mains, and she shall help thee. Then Sir Tristram and
Gouvernail gat them shipping, and so sailed into Brittany. And when
King Howel wist that it was Sir Tristram he was full glad of him. Sir,
he said, I am come into this country to have help of your daughter,
for it is told me that there is none other may heal me but she; and so
within a while she healed him.

CHAPTER XXXVI

How Sir Tristram served in war King Howel of Brittany,
and slew his adversary in the field.

There was an earl that hight Grip, and this earl made great war upon
the king, and put the king to the worse, and besieged him. And on a
time Sir Kehydius, that was son to King Howel, as he issued out he
was sore wounded, nigh to the death. Then Gouvernail went to the
king and said: Sir, I counsel you to desire my lord, Sir Tristram, as in
your need to help you. I will do by your counsel, said the king. And
so he yede unto Sir Tristram, and prayed him in his wars to help him:
For my son, Sir Kehydius, may not go into the field. Sir, said Sir
Tristram, I will go to the field and do what I may. Then Sir Tristram
issued out of the town with such fellowship as he might make, and
did such deeds that all Brittany spake of him. And then, at the last, by
great might and force, he slew the Earl Grip with his own hands, and
more than an hundred knights he slew that day. And then Sir
Tristram was received worshipfully with procession. Then King
Howel embraced him in his arms, and said: Sir Tristram, all my
kingdom I will resign to thee. God defend, said Sir Tristram, for I am
beholden unto you for your daughter's sake to do for you.

Then by the great means of King Howel and Kehydius his son, by
great proffers, there grew great love betwixt Isoud and Sir Tristram, for
that lady was both good and fair, and a woman of noble blood and
fame. And for because Sir Tristram had such cheer and riches, and all
other pleasaunce that he had, almost he had forsaken La Beale Isoud.
And so upon a time Sir Tristram agreed to wed Isoud la Blanche
Mains. And at the last they were wedded, and solemnly held their
marriage. And so when they were abed both Sir Tristram remembered
him of his old lady La Beale Isoud. And then he took such a thought
suddenly that he was all dismayed, and other cheer made he none but
with clipping and kissing; as for other fleshly lusts Sir Tristram never
thought nor had ado with her: such mention maketh the French book;
also it maketh mention that the lady weened there had been no
pleasure but kissing and clipping. And in the meantime there was a

knight in Brittany, his name was Suppinabiles, and he came over the sea into England, and then he came into the court of King Arthur, and there he met with Sir Launcelot du Lake, and told him of the marriage of Sir Tristram. Then said Sir Launcelot: Fie upon him, untrue knight to his lady, that so noble a knight as Sir Tristram is should be found to his first lady false, La Beale Isoud, Queen of Cornwall; but say ye him this, said Sir Launcelot, that of all knights in the world I loved him most, and had most joy of him, and all was for his noble deeds; and let him wit the love between him and me is done for ever, and that I give him warning from this day forth as his mortal enemy.

CHAPTER XXXVII

How Sir Suppinabiles told Sir Tristram how he was defamed in the court of King Arthur, and of Sir Lamorak.

Then departed Sir Suppinabiles unto Brittany again, and there he found Sir Tristram, and told him that he had been in King Arthur's court. Then said Sir Tristram: Heard ye anything of me? So God me help, said Sir Suppinabiles, there I heard Sir Launcelot speak of you great shame, and that ye be a false knight to your lady, and he bade me do you to wit that he will be your mortal enemy in every place where he may meet you. That me repenteth, said Tristram, for of all knights I loved to be in his fellowship. So Sir Tristram made great moan and was ashamed that noble knights should defame him for the sake of his lady. And in this meanwhile La Beale Isoud made a letter unto Queen Guenever, complaining her of the untruth of Sir Tristram, and how he had wedded the king's daughter of Brittany. Queen Guenever sent her another letter, and bade her be of good cheer, for she should have joy after sorrow, for Sir Tristram was so noble a knight called, that by crafts of sorcery ladies would make such noble men to wed them. But in the end, Queen Guenever said, it shall be thus, that he shall hate her, and love you better than ever he did to-fore.

So leave we Sir Tristram in Brittany, and speak we of Sir Lamorak de Galis, that as he sailed his ship fell on a rock and perished all, save Sir Lamorak and his squire; and there he swam mightily, and fishers of the Isle of Servage took him up, and his squire was drowned, and the shipmen had great labour to save Sir Lamorak's life, for all the comfort that they could do.

And the lord of that isle hight Sir Nabon le Noire, a great mighty giant. And this Sir Nabon hated all the knights of King Arthur's, and in no wise he would do them favour. And these fishers told Sir Lamorak all the guise of Sir Nabon; how there came never knight of King Arthur's but he destroyed him. And at the last battle that he did was slain Sir Nanowne le Petite, the which he put to a shameful death in despite of King Arthur, for he was drawn limb-meal. That forthinketh me, said Sir Lamorak, for that knight's death, for he was my cousin; and if I were at mine ease as well as ever I was, I would revenge his death. Peace, said the fishers, and make here no words, for or ever ye depart from hence Sir Nabon must know that ye have been here, or else we should die for your sake. So that I be whole, said Lamorak, of my disease that I have taken in the sea, I will that ye tell him that I am a knight of King Arthur's, for I was never afeard to reneye my lord.

CHAPTER XXXVIII

How Sir Tristram and his wife arrived in Wales, and how he met there with Sir Lamorak.

Now turn we unto Sir Tristram, that upon a day he took a little barget, and his wife Isoud la Blanche Mains, with Sir Kehydius her brother, to play them in the coasts. And when they were from the land, there was a wind drove them in to the coast of Wales upon this Isle of Servage, whereas was Sir Lamorak, and there the barget all to-rove; and there Dame Isoud was hurt; and as well as they might they gat into the forest, and there by a well he saw Segwarides and a damosel. And then either saluted other. Sir, said Segwarides, I know you for Sir Tristram de Liones, the man in the world that I have most cause to hate, because ye departed the love between me and my wife; but as for that, said Sir Segwarides, I will never hate a noble knight for a light lady; and therefore, I pray you, be my friend, and I will be yours unto my power; for wit ye well ye are hard bestead in this valley, and we shall have enough to do either of us to succour other. And then Sir Segwarides brought Sir Tristram to a lady thereby that was born in Cornwall, and she told him all the perils of that valley, and how there came never knight there but he were taken prisoner or slain. Wit you well, fair lady, said Sir Tristram, that I slew Sir Marhaus and delivered Cornwall from the truage of Ireland, and I am he that delivered the King of Ireland from Sir Blamore de Ganis, and I am he that beat Sir Palomides; and wit ye well I am Sir Tristram de Liones, that by the grace of God shall deliver this woful Isle of Servage. So Sir Tristram was well eased.

Then one told him there was a knight of King Arthur's that was wrecked on the rocks. What is his name? said Sir Tristram. We wot not, said the fishers, but he keepeth it no counsel but that he is a knight of King Arthur's, and by the mighty lord of this isle he setteth nought. I pray you, said Sir Tristram, an ye may, bring him hither that I may see him, and if he be any of the knights of Arthur's I shall know him. Then the lady prayed the fishers to bring him to her place. So on the morrow they brought him thither in a fisher's raiment; and as soon as Sir Tristram saw him he smiled upon him and knew him well, but he knew not Sir Tristram. Fair sir, said Sir Tristram, meseemeth by your cheer ye have been diseased but late, and also methinketh I should know you heretofore. I will well, said Sir Lamorak, that ye have seen me and met with me. Fair sir, said Sir Tristram, tell me your name. Upon a covenant I will tell you, said Sir Lamorak, that is, that ye will tell me whether ye be lord of this island or no, that is called Nabon le Noire. Forsooth, said Sir Tristram, I am not he, nor I hold not of him; I am his foe as well as ye be, and so shall I be found or I depart out of this isle. Well, said Sir Lamorak, since ye have said so largely unto me, my name is Sir Lamorak de Galis, son unto King Pellinore. Forsooth, I trow well, said Sir Tristram, for an ye said other I know the contrary. What are ye, said Sir Lamorak, that knoweth me? I am Sir Tristram de Liones. Ah, sir, remember ye not of the fall ye did give me once, and after ye refused me to fight on foot. That was not for fear I had of you, said Sir Tristram, but me shamed at that time to have more ado with you, for meseemed ye had enough; but, Sir Lamorak, for my kindness many ladies ye put to a reproof when ye sent the horn from Morgan le Fay to King Mark, whereas ye did this in despite of me. Well, said he, an it were to do again, so would I do, for I had liefer strife and debate fell in King Mark's court rather than

Arthur's court, for the honour of both courts be not alike. As to that, said Sir Tristram, I know well; but that that was done it was for despite of me, but all your malice, I thank God, hurt not greatly. Therefore, said Sir Tristram, ye shall leave all your malice, and so will I, and let us assay how we may win worship between you and me upon this giant Sir Nabon le Noire that is lord of this island, to destroy him. Sir, said Sir Lamorak, now I understand your knighthood, it may not be false that all men say, for of your bounty, noblesse, and worship, of all knights ye are peerless, and for your courtesy and gentleness I showed you ungentleness, and that now me repenteth.

CHAPTER XXXIX

How Sir Tristram fought with Sir Nabon, and overcame him, and made Sir Segwarides lord of the isle.

In the meantime there came word that Sir Nabon had made a cry that all the people of that isle should be at his castle the fifth day after. And the same day the son of Nabon should be made knight, and all the knights of that valley and thereabout should be there to joust, and all those of the realm of Logris should be there to joust with them of North Wales: and thither came five hundred knights, and they of the country brought thither Sir Lamorak, and Sir Tristram, and Sir Kehydius, and Sir Segwarides, for they durst none otherwise do; and then Sir Nabon lent Sir Lamorak horse and armour at Sir Lamorak's desire, and Sir Lamorak jousted and did such deeds of arms that Nabon and all the people said there was never knight that ever they saw do such deeds of arms; for, as the French book saith, he forjousted all that were there, for the most part of five hundred knights, that none abode him in his saddle.

Then Sir Nabon proffered to play with him his play: For I saw never no knight do so much upon a day. I will well, said Sir Lamorak, play as I may, but I am weary and sore bruised. And there either gat a spear, but Nabon would not encounter with Sir Lamorak, but smote his horse in the forehead, and so slew him; and then Sir Lamorak yede on foot, and turned his shield and drew his sword, and there began strong battle on foot. But Sir Lamorak was so sore bruised and short breathed, that he traced and traversed somewhat aback. Fair fellow, said Sir Nabon, hold thy hand and I shall show thee more courtesy than ever I showed knight, because I have seen this day thy noble knighthood, and therefore stand thou by, and I will wit whether any of thy fellows will have ado with me. Then when Sir Tristram heard that, he stepped forth and said: Nabon, lend me horse and sure armour, and I will have ado with thee. Well, fellow, said Sir Nabon, go thou to yonder pavilion, and arm thee of the best thou findest there, and I shall play a marvellous play with thee. Then said Sir Tristram: Look ye play well, or else peradventure I shall learn you a new play. That is well said, fellow, said Sir Nabon. So when Sir Tristram was armed as him liked best, and well shielded and sworded, he dressed to him on foot; for well he knew that Sir Nabon would not abide a stroke with a spear, therefore he would slay all knights' horses. Now, fair fellow, Sir Nabon, let us play. So then they fought long on foot, tracing and traversing, smiting and foining long without any rest. At the last Sir Nabon prayed him to tell him his name. Sir Nabon, I tell thee my name is Sir Tristram de Liones, a knight of Cornwall under King Mark. Thou art welcome, said Sir Nabon, for of all knights I have most desired to fight with thee or with Sir Launcelot.

So then they went eagerly together, and Sir Tristram slew Sir Nabon, and so forthwith he leapt to his son, and struck off his head; and then all the country said they would hold of Sir Tristram. Nay, said Sir Tristram, I will not so; here is a worshipful knight, Sir Lamorak de Galis, that for me he shall be lord of this country, for he hath done here great deeds of arms. Nay, said Sir Lamorak, I will not be lord of this country, for I have not deserved it as well as ye, therefore give ye it where ye will, for I will none have. Well, said Sir Tristram, since ye nor I will not have it, let us give it to him that hath not so well deserved it. Do as ye list, said Segwarides, for the gift is yours, for I will none have an I had deserved it. So was it given to Segwarides, whereof he thanked them; and so was he lord, and worshipfully he did govern it. And then Sir Segwarides delivered all prisoners, and set good governance in that valley; and so he returned into Cornwall, and told King Mark and La Beale Isoud how Sir Tristram had advanced him to the Isle of Servage, and there he proclaimed in all Cornwall of all the adventures of these two knights, so was it openly known. But full woe was La Beale Isoud when she heard tell that Sir Tristram was wedded to Isoud la Blanche Mains.

CHAPTER XL

*How Sir Lamorak departed from Sir Tristram, and how he
met with Sir Frol, and after with Sir Launcelot.*

So turn we unto Sir Lamorak, that rode toward Arthur's court, and
Sir Tristram's wife and Kehydius took a vessel and sailed into
Brittany, unto King Howel, where he was welcome. And when he
heard of these adventures they marvelled of his noble deeds. Now
turn we unto Sir Lamorak, that when he was departed from Sir
Tristram he rode out of the forest, till he came to an hermitage.
When the hermit saw him, he asked him from whence he came. Sir,
said Sir Lamorak, I come from this valley. Sir, said the hermit: thereof
I marvel. For this twenty winter I saw never no knight pass this
country but he was either slain or villainously wounded, or pass as a
poor prisoner. Those ill customs, said Sir Lamorak, are fordone, for
Sir Tristram slew your lord, Sir Nabon, and his son. Then was the
hermit glad, and all his brethren, for he said there was never such a
tyrant among Christian men. And therefore, said the hermit, this
valley and franchise we will hold of Sir Tristram.

So on the morrow Sir Lamorak departed; and as he rode he saw
four knights fight against one, and that one knight defended him well
but at the last the four knights had him down. And then Sir Lamorak
went betwixt them, and asked them why they would slay that one
knight, and said it was shame, four against one. Thou shalt well wit,
said the four knights, that he is false. That is your tale, said Sir
Lamorak, and when I hear him also speak, I will say as ye say. Then
said Lamorak: Ah, knight, can ye not excuse you, but that ye are a
false knight. Sir, said he, yet can I excuse me both with my word and
with my hands, that I will make good upon one of the best of them,
my body to his body. Then spake they all at once: We will not
jeopardy our bodies as for thee. But wit thou well, they said, an King
Arthur were here himself, it should not lie in his power to save his
life. That is too much said, said Sir Lamorak, but many speak behind
a man more than they will say to his face; and because of your words
ye shall understand that I am one of the simplest of King Arthur's

court; in the worship of my lord now do your best, and in despite of you I shall rescue him. And then they lashed all at once to Sir Lamorak, but anon at two strokes Sir Lamorak had slain two of them, and then the other two fled. So then Sir Lamorak turned again to that knight, and asked him his name. Sir, he said, my name is Sir Frol of the Out Isles. Then he rode with Sir Lamorak and bare him company.

And as they rode by the way they saw a seemly knight riding against them, and all in white. Ah, said Frol, yonder knight jousted late with me and smote me down, therefore I will joust with him. Ye shall not do so, said Sir Lamorak, by my counsel, an ye will tell me your quarrel, whether ye jousted at his request, or he at yours. Nay, said Sir Frol, I jousted with him at my request. Sir, said Lamorak, then will I counsel you deal no more with him, for meseemeth by his countenance he should be a noble knight, and no japer; for methinketh he should be of the Table Round. Therefore I will not spare, said Sir Frol. And then he cried and said: Sir knight, make thee ready to joust. That needeth not, said the White Knight, for I have no lust to joust with thee; but yet they feutred their spears, and the White Knight overthrew Sir Frol, and then he rode his way a soft pace. Then Sir Lamorak rode after him, and prayed him to tell him his name: For meseemeth ye should be of the fellowship of the Round Table. Upon a covenant, said he, I will tell you my name, so that ye will not discover my name, and also that ye will tell me yours. Then, said he, my name is Sir Lamorak de Galis. And my name is Sir Launcelot du Lake. Then they put up their swords, and kissed heartily together, and either made great joy of other. Sir, said Sir Lamorak, an it please you I will do you service. God defend, said Launcelot, that any of so noble a blood as ye be should do me service. Then he said: More, I am in a quest that I must do myself alone. Now God speed you, said Sir Lamorak, and so they departed. Then Sir Lamorak came to Sir Frol and horsed him again. What knight is that? said Sir Frol. Sir, he said, it is not for you to know, nor it is no point of my charge. Ye are the more uncourteous, said Sir Frol, and therefore I will depart from you. Ye may do as ye list, said Sir Lamorak, and yet by my company ye have saved the fairest flower of your garland; so they departed.

CHAPTER XLI

*How Sir Lamorak slew Sir Frol, and of the courteous
fighting with Sir Belliance his brother.*

Then within two or three days Sir Lamorak found a knight at a well
sleeping, and his lady sat with him and waked. Right so came Sir
Gawaine and took the knight's lady, and set her up behind his squire.
So Sir Lamorak rode after Sir Gawaine, and said: Sir Gawaine, turn
again. And then said Sir Gawaine: What will ye do with me? for I am
nephew unto King Arthur. Sir, said he, for that cause I will spare you,
else that lady should abide with me, or else ye should joust with me.
Then Sir Gawaine turned him and ran to him that ought the lady,
with his spear, but the knight with pure might smote down Sir
Gawaine, and took his lady with him. All this Sir Lamorak saw, and
said to himself: But I revenge my fellow he will say of me dishonour
in King Arthur's court. Then Sir Lamorak returned and proffered
that knight to joust. Sir, said he, I am ready. And there they came
together with all their might, and there Sir Lamorak smote the knight
through both sides that he fell to the earth dead.

Then that lady rode to that knight's brother that hight Belliance le
Orgulus, that dwelt fast thereby, and then she told him how his
brother was slain. Alas, said he, I will be revenged. And so he horsed
him, and armed him, and within a while he overtook Sir Lamorak,
and bade him: Turn and leave that lady, for thou and I must play a
new play; for thou hast slain my brother Sir Frol, that was a better
knight than ever wert thou. It might well be, said Sir Lamorak, but
this day in the field I was found the better. So they rode together, and
unhorsed other, and turned their shields, and drew their swords, and
fought mightily as noble knights proved, by the space of two hours.
So then Sir Belliance prayed him to tell him his name. Sir, said he,
my name is Sir Lamorak de Galis. Ah, said Sir Belliance, thou art the
man in the world that I most hate, for I slew my sons for thy sake,
where I saved thy life, and now thou hast slain my brother Sir Frol.
Alas, how should I be accorded with thee; therefore defend thee, for
thou shalt die, there is none other remedy. Alas, said Sir Lamorak, full

well me ought to know you, for ye are the man that most have done for me. And therewithal Sir Lamorak kneeled down, and besought him of grace. Arise, said Sir Belliance, or else thereas thou kneelest I shall slay thee. That shall not need, said Sir Lamorak, for I will yield me unto you, not for fear of you, nor for your strength, but your goodness maketh me full loath to have ado with you; wherefore I require you for God's sake, and for the honour of knighthood, forgive me all that I have offended unto you. Alas, said Belliance, leave thy kneeling, or else I shall slay thee without mercy.

Then they yede again unto battle, and either wounded other, that all the ground was bloody thereas they fought. And at the last Belliance withdrew him aback and set him down softly upon a little hill, for he was so faint for bleeding that he might not stand. Then Sir Lamorak threw his shield upon his back, and asked him what cheer. Well, said Sir Belliance. Ah, Sir, yet shall I show you favour in your mal-ease. Ah, Knight Sir Belliance, said Sir Lamorak, thou art a fool, for an I had had thee at such advantage as thou hast done me, I should slay thee; but thy gentleness is so good and so large, that I must needs forgive thee mine evil will. And then Sir Lamorak kneeled down, and unlaced first his umberere, and then his own, and then either kissed other with weeping tears. Then Sir Lamorak led Sir Belliance to an abbey fast by, and there Sir Lamorak would not depart from Belliance till he was whole. And then they sware together that none of them should never fight against other. So Sir Lamorak departed and went to the court of King Arthur.

Here leave we of Sir Lamorak and of Sir Tristram. And here beginneth the history of La Cote Male Taile.

BOOK NINE

CHAPTER I

How a young man came into the court of King Arthur, and how Sir Kay called him in scorn La Cote Male Taile.

At the court of King Arthur there came a young man and bigly made, and he was richly beseen: and he desired to be made knight of the king, but his over-garment sat over-thwartly, howbeit it was rich cloth of gold. What is your name? said King Arthur. Sir, said he, my name is Breunor le Noire, and within short space ye shall know that I am of good kin. It may well be, said Sir Kay, the Seneschal, but in mockage ye shall be called La Cote Male Taile, that is as much to say, the evil-shapen coat. It is a great thing that thou askest, said the king; and for what cause wearest thou that rich coat? tell me, for I can well think for some cause it is. Sir, he answered, I had a father, a noble knight, and as he rode a-hunting, upon a day it happed him to lay him down to sleep; and there came a knight that had been long his enemy, and when he saw he was fast asleep he all to-hew him; and this same coat had my father on the same time; and that maketh this coat to sit so evil upon me, for the strokes be on it as I found it, and never shall be amended for me. Thus to have my father's death in remembrance I wear this coat till I be revenged; and because ye are called the most noblest king of the world I come to you that ye should make me knight. Sir, said Sir Lamorak and Sir Gaheris, it were well done to make him knight; for him beseemeth well of person and of countenance, that he shall prove a good man, and a good knight, and a mighty; for, Sir, an ye be remembered, even such one was Sir Launcelot du Lake when he came first into this court, and full few of us knew from whence he came; and now is he proved the man of most worship in the world; and all your court and all your Round Table is by Sir Launcelot worshipped and amended more than by any knight now living. That is truth, said the king, and to-morrow at your request I shall make him knight.

So on the morrow there was an hart found, and thither rode King Arthur with a company of his knights to slay the hart. And this young man that Sir Kay named La Cote Male Taile was there left behind with Queen Guenever; and by sudden adventure there was an horrible lion kept in a strong tower of stone, and it happened that he at that time brake loose, and came hurling afore the queen and her knights. And when the queen saw the lion she cried and fled, and prayed her knights to rescue her. And there was none of them all but twelve that abode, and all the other fled. Then said La Cote Male Taile: Now I see well that all coward knights be not dead; and therewithal he drew his sword and dressed him afore the lion. And that lion gaped wide and came upon him ramping to have slain him. And he then smote him in the midst of the head such a mighty stroke that it clave his head in sunder, and dashed to the earth. Then was it told the queen how the young man that Sir Kay named by scorn La Cote Male Taile had slain the lion. With that the king came home. And when the queen told him of that adventure, he was well pleased, and said: Upon pain of mine head he shall prove a noble man and a faithful knight, and true of his promise: then the king forthwithal made him knight. Now Sir, said this young knight, I require you and all the knights of your court, that ye call me by none other name but La Cote Male Taile: in so much as Sir Kay hath so named me so will I be called. I assent me well thereto, said the king.

CHAPTER II

How a damosel came into the court and desired a knight to take on him an enquest, which La Cote Male Taile emprised.

Then that same day there came a damosel into the court, and she brought with her a great black shield, with a white hand in the midst holding a sword. Other picture was there none in that shield. When King Arthur saw her he asked her from whence she came and what she would. Sir, she said, I have ridden long and many a day with this shield many ways, and for this cause I am come to your court: there was a good knight that ought this shield, and this knight had undertaken a great deed of arms to enchieve it; and so it misfortuned him another strong knight met with him by sudden adventure, and there they fought long, and either wounded other passing sore; and they were so weary that they left that battle even hand. So this knight that ought this shield saw none other way but he must die; and then he commanded me to bear this shield to the court of King Arthur, he requiring and praying some good knight to take this shield, and that he would fulfil the quest that he was in. Now what say ye to this quest? said King Arthur; is there any of you here that will take upon him to wield this shield? Then was there not one that would speak one word. Then Sir Kay took the shield in his hands. Sir knight, said the damosel, what is your name? Wit ye well, said he, my name is Sir Kay, the Seneschal, that wide-where is known. Sir, said that damosel, lay down that shield, for wit ye well it falleth not for you, for he must be a better knight than ye that shall wield this shield. Damosel, said Sir Kay, wit ye well I took this shield in my hands by your leave for to behold it, not to that intent; but go wheresomever thou wilt, for I will not go with you.

Then the damosel stood still a great while and beheld many of those knights. Then spake the knight, La Cote Male Taile: Fair damosel, I will take the shield and that adventure upon me, so I wist I should know whitherward my journey might be; for because I was this day made knight I would take this adventure upon me. What is your name, fair young man? said the damosel. My name is, said he, La Cote Male Taile. Well mayest thou be called so, said the damosel, the knight with the evil-shapen coat; but an thou be so hardy to take upon thee to bear that shield and to follow me, wit thou well thy skin shall be as well hewn as thy coat. As for that, said La Cote Male Taile, when I am so hewn I will ask you no salve to heal me withal. And forthwithal there came into the court two squires and brought him great horses, and his armour, and his spears, and anon he was armed and took his leave. I would not by my will, said the king, that ye took upon you that hard adventure. Sir, said he, this adventure is mine, and the first that ever I took upon me, and that will I follow whatsomever come of me. Then that damosel departed, and La Cote Male Taile fast followed after. And within a while he overtook the damosel, and anon she missaid him in the foulest manner.

CHAPTER III

How La Cote Male Taile overthrew Sir Dagonet the king's fool, and of the rebuke that he had of the damosel.

Then Sir Kay ordained Sir Dagonet, King Arthur's fool, to follow after La Cote Male Taile; and there Sir Kay ordained that Sir Dagonet was horsed and armed, and bade him follow La Cote Male Taile and proffer him to joust, and so he did; and when he saw La Cote Male Taile, he cried and bade him make him ready to joust. So Sir La Cote Male Taile smote Sir Dagonet over his horse's croup. Then the damosel mocked La Cote Male Taile, and said: Fie for shame! now art thou shamed in Arthur's court, when they send a fool to have ado with thee, and specially at thy first jousts; thus she rode long, and chid. And within a while there came Sir Bleoberis, the good knight, and there he jousted with La Cote Male Taile, and there Sir Bleobēris smote him so sore, that horse and all fell to the earth. Then La Cote Male Taile arose up lightly, and dressed his shield, and drew his sword, and would have done battle to the utterance, for he was wood wroth. Not so, said Sir Bleoberis de Ganis, as at this time I will not fight upon foot. Then the damosel Maledisant rebuked him in the foulest manner, and bade him: Turn again, coward. Ah, damosel, he said, I pray you of mercy to missay me no more, my grief is enough though ye give me no more; I call myself never the worse knight when a mare's son faileth me, and also I count me never the worse knight for a fall of Sir Bleoberis.

So thus he rode with her two days; and by fortune there came Sir Palomides and encountered with him, and he in the same wise served him as did Bleoberis to-forehand. What dost thou here in my fellowship? said the damosel Maledisant, thou canst not sit no knight, nor withstand him one buffet, but if it were Sir Dagonet. Ah, fair damosel, I am not the worse to take a fall of Sir Palomides, and yet great disworship have I none, for neither Bleoberis nor yet Palomides would not fight with me on foot. As for that, said the damosel, wit thou well they have disdain and scorn to light off their horses to fight with such a lewd knight as thou art. So in the meanwhile there came

Sir Mordred, Sir Gawaine's brother, and so he fell in the fellowship with the damosel Maledisant. And then they came afore the Castle Orgulous, and there was such a custom that there might no knight come by that castle but either he must joust or be prisoner, or at the least to lose his horse and his harness. And there came out two knights against them, and Sir Mordred jousted with the foremost, and that knight of the castle smote Sir Mordred down off his horse. And then La Cote Male Taile jousted with that other, and either of them smote other down, horse and all, to the earth. And when they avoided their horses, then either of them took other's horses. And then La Cote Male Taile rode unto that knight that smote down Sir Mordred, and jousted with him. And there Sir La Cote Male Taile hurt and wounded him passing sore, and put him from his horse as he had been dead. So he turned unto him that met him afore, and he took the flight towards the castle, and Sir La Cote Male Taile rode after him into the Castle Orgulous, and there La Cote Male Taile slew him.

CHAPTER IV

How La Cote Male Taile fought against an hundred knights, and how he escaped by the mean of a lady.

And anon there came an hundred knights about him and assailed him; and when he saw his horse should be slain he alighted and voided his horse, and put the bridle under his feet, and so put him out of the gate. And when he had so done he hurled in among them, and dressed his back unto a lady's chamber-wall, thinking himself that he had liefer die there with worship than to abide the rebukes of the damosel Maledisant. And in the meantime as he stood and fought, that lady whose was the chamber went out slily at her postern, and without the gates she found La Cote Male Taile's horse, and lightly she gat him by the bridle, and tied him to the postern. And then she went unto her chamber slily again for to behold how that one knight fought against an hundred knights. And when she had beheld him long she went to a window behind his back, and said: Thou knight, thou fightest wonderly well, but for all that at the last thou must needs die, but, an thou canst through thy mighty prowess, win unto yonder postern, for there have I fastened thy horse to abide thee: but wit thou well thou must think on thy worship, and think not to die, for thou mayst not win unto that postern without thou do nobly and mightily. When La Cote Male Taile heard her say so he gripped his sword in his hands, and put his shield fair afore him, and through the thickest press he thrulled through them. And when he came to the postern he found there ready four knights, and at two the first strokes he slew two of the knights, and the other fled; and so he won his horse and rode from them. And all as it was it was rehearsed in King Arthur's court, how he slew twelve knights within the Castle Orgulous; and so he rode on his way.

And in the meanwhile the damosel said to Sir Mordred: I ween my foolish knight be either slain or taken prisoner: then were they ware where he came riding. And when he was come unto them he told all how he had sped and escaped in despite of them all: And some of the best of them will tell no tales. Thou liest falsely, said the damosel, that dare I make good, but as a fool and a dastard to all knighthood they have let thee pass. That may ye prove, said La Cote Male Taile. With that she sent a courier of hers, that rode alway with her, for to know the truth of this deed; and so he rode thither lightly, and asked how and in what manner that La Cote Male Taile was escaped out of the castle. Then all the knights cursed him, and said that he was a fiend and no man: For he hath slain here twelve of our best knights, and we weened unto this day that it had been too much for Sir Launcelot du Lake or for Sir Tristram de Liones. And in despite of us all he is departed from us and maugre our heads.

With this answer the courier departed and came to Maledisant his lady, and told her all how Sir La Cote Male Taile had sped at the Castle Orgulous. Then she smote down her head, and said little. By my head, said Sir Mordred to the damosel, ye are greatly to blame so to rebuke him, for I warn you plainly he is a good knight, and I doubt not but he shall prove a noble knight; but as yet he may not yet sit sure on horseback, for he that shall be a good horseman it must come of usage and exercise. But when he cometh to the strokes of his sword he is then noble and mighty, and that saw Sir Bleoberis and Sir Palomides, for wit ye well they are wily men of arms, and anon they know when they see a young knight by his riding, how they are sure to give him a fall from his horse or a great buffet. But for the most part they will not light on foot with young knights, for they are wight and strongly armed. For in likewise Sir Launcelot du Lake, when he was first made knight, he was often put to the worse upon horseback, but ever upon foot he recovered his renown, and slew and defoiled many knights of the Round Table. And therefore the rebukes that Sir Launcelot did unto many knights causeth them that be men of prowess to beware; for often I have seen the old proved knights rebuked and slain by them that were but young beginners. Thus they rode sure talking by the way together.

CHAPTER V

How Sir Launcelot came to the court and heard of La Cote Male Taile, and how he followed after him, and how La Cote Male Taile was prisoner.

Here leave we off a while of this tale, and speak we of Sir Launcelot du Lake,* that when he was come to the court of King Arthur, then heard he tell of the young knight La Cote Male Taile, how he slew the lion, and how he took upon him the adventure of the black shield, the which was named at that time the hardiest adventure of the world. So God me save, said Sir Launcelot unto many of his fellows, it was shame to all the noble knights to suffer such a young knight to take such adventure upon him for his destruction; for I will that ye wit, said Sir Launcelot, that that damosel Maledisant hath borne that shield many a day for to seek the most proved knights, and that was she that Breuse Saunce Pité took that shield from her, and after Tristram de Liones rescued that shield from him and gave it to the damosel again, a little afore that time that Sir Tristram fought with my nephew Sir Blamore de Ganis, for a quarrel that was betwixt the King of Ireland and him. Then many knights were sorry that Sir La Cote Male Taile was gone forth to that adventure. Truly, said Sir Launcelot, I cast me to ride after him. And within seven days Sir Launcelot overtook La Cote Male Taile, and then he saluted him and the damosel Maledisant. And when Sir Mordred saw Sir Launcelot,

---

* Printed by Caxton as part of chapter iv.

then he left their fellowship; and so Sir Launcelot rode with them all a day, and ever that damosel rebuked La Cote Male Taile; and then Sir Launcelot answered for him, then she left off, and rebuked Sir Launcelot.

So this meantime Sir Tristram sent by a damosel a letter unto Sir Launcelot, excusing him of the wedding of Isoud la Blanche Mains; and said in the letter, as he was a true knight he had never ado fleshly with Isoud la Blanche Mains; and passing courteously and gently Sir Tristram wrote unto Sir Launcelot, ever beseeching him to be his good friend and unto La Beale Isoud of Cornwall, and that Sir Launcelot would excuse him if that ever he saw her. And within short time by the grace of God, said Sir Tristram, that he would speak with La Beale Isoud, and with him right hastily. Then Sir Launcelot departed from the damosel and from Sir La Cote Male Taile, for to oversee that letter, and to write another letter unto Sir Tristram de Liones.

And in the meanwhile La Cote Male Taile rode with the damosel until they came to a castle that hight Pendragon; and there were six knights stood afore him, and one of them proffered to joust with La Cote Male Taile. And there La Cote Male Taile smote him over his horse's croup. And then the five knights set upon him all at once with their spears, and there they smote La Cote Male Taile down, horse and man. And then they alighted suddenly, and set their hands upon him all at once, and took him prisoner, and so led him unto the castle and kept him as prisoner.

And on the morn Sir Launcelot arose, and delivered the damosel with letters unto Sir Tristram, and then he took his way after La Cote Male Taile; and by the way upon a bridge there was a knight proffered Sir Launcelot to joust, and Sir Launcelot smote him down, and then they fought upon foot a noble battle together, and a mighty; and at the last Sir Launcelot smote him down grovelling upon his hands and his knees. And then that knight yielded him, and Sir Launcelot received him fair. Sir, said the knight, I require thee tell me your name, for much my heart giveth unto you. Nay, said Sir Launcelot, as at this time I will not tell you my name, unless then that ye tell me your name. Certainly, said the knight, my name is Sir Nerovens, that was made knight of my lord Sir Launcelot du Lake. Ah, Nerovens de Lile, said Sir Launcelot, I am right glad that ye are proved a good knight, for now wit ye well my name is Sir Launcelot du Lake. Alas, said Sir Nerovens de Lile, what have I done ! And therewithal flatling he fell to his feet, and would have kissed them, but Sir Launcelot would not let him; and then either made great joy of other. And then Sir Nerovens told Sir Launcelot that he should not go by the Castle of Pendragon: For there is a lord, a mighty knight, and many knights with him, and this night I heard say that they took a knight prisoner yesterday that rode with a damosel, and they say he is a Knight of the Round Table.

CHAPTER VI

How Sir Launcelot fought with six knights, and after with Sir Brian, and how he delivered the prisoners.

Ah, said Sir Launcelot, that knight is my fellow, and him shall I rescue or else I shall lose my life therefore. And therewithal he rode fast till he came before the Castle of Pendragon; and anon therewithal there came six knights, and all made them ready to set upon Sir Launcelot at once; then Sir Launcelot feutred his spear, and smote the foremost that he brake his back in-sunder, and three of them hit and three failed. And then Sir Launcelot passed through them, and lightly he turned in again, and smote another knight through the breast and throughout the back more than an ell, and therewithal his spear brake. So then all the remnant of the four knights drew their swords and lashed at Sir Launcelot. And at every stroke Sir Launcelot bestowed so his strokes that at four strokes sundry they avoided their saddles, passing sore wounded; and forthwithal he rode hurling into that castle.

And anon the lord of the castle, that was that time cleped Sir Brian de les Isles, the which was a noble man and a great enemy unto King Arthur, within a while he was armed and upon horseback. And then they feutred their spears and hurled together so strongly that both their horses rashed to the earth. And then they avoided their saddles, and dressed their shields, and drew their swords, and flang together as wood men, and there were many strokes given in a while. At the last Sir Launcelot gave to Sir Brian such a buffet that he kneeled upon his knees, and then Sir Launcelot rashed upon him, and with great force he pulled off his helm; and when Sir Brian saw that he should be slain he yielded him, and put him in his mercy and in his grace. Then Sir Launcelot made him to deliver all his prisoners that he had within his castle, and therein Sir Launcelot found of Arthur's knights thirty, and forty ladies, and so he delivered them; and then he rode his way. And anon as La Cote Male Taile was delivered he gat his horse, and his harness, and his damosel Maledisant.

The meanwhile Sir Nerovens, that Sir Launcelot had foughten withal afore at the bridge, he sent a damosel after Sir Launcelot to wit how he sped at the Castle of Pendragon. And then they within the castle marvelled what knight he was, when Sir Brian and his knights delivered all those prisoners. Have ye no marvel, said the damosel, for the best knight in this world was here, and did this journey, and wit ye well, she said, it was Sir Launcelot. Then was Sir Brian full glad, and so was his lady, and all his knights, that such a man should win them. And when the damosel and La Cote Male Taile understood that it was Sir Launcelot du Lake that had ridden with them in fellowship, and that she remembered her how she had rebuked him and called him coward, then was she passing heavy.

CHAPTER VII

How Sir Launcelot met with the damosel named
Maledisant, and named her the Damosel Bienpensant.

So then they took their horses and rode forth a pace after Sir Launcelot. And within two mile they overtook him and saluted him, and thanked him, and the damosel cried Sir Launcelot mercy of her evil deed and saying: For now I know the flower of all knighthood is departed even between Sir Tristram and you. For God knoweth, said the damosel, that I have sought you my lord, Sir Launcelot, and Sir Tristram long, and now I thank God I have met with you; and once at Camelot I met with Sir Tristram, and there he rescued this black shield with the white hand holding a naked sword that Sir Breuse Saunce Pité had taken from me. Now, fair damosel, said Sir Launcelot, who told you my name? Sir, said she, there came a damosel from a knight that ye fought withal at the bridge, and she told me your name was Sir Launcelot du Lake. Blame have she then, said Sir Launcelot, but her lord, Sir Nerovens, hath told her. But, damosel, said Sir Launcelot, upon this covenant I will ride with you, so that ye will not rebuke this knight Sir La Cote Male Taile no more; for he is a good knight, and I doubt not he shall prove a noble knight, and for his sake and pity that he should not be destroyed I followed him to succour him in this great need. Ah, Jesu thank you, said the damosel, for now I will say unto you and to him both, I rebuked him never for no hate that I hated him, but for great love that I had to him. For ever I supposed that he had been too young and too tender to take upon him these adventures. And therefore by my will I would have driven him away for jealousy that I had of his life, for it may be no young knight's deed that shall enchieve this adventure to the end. Pardieu, said Sir Launcelot, it is well said, and where ye are called the Damosel Maledisant I will call you the Damosel Bienpensant.

And so they rode forth a great while unto they came to the border of the country of Surluse, and there they found a fair village with a strong bridge like a fortress. And when Sir Launcelot and they were at the bridge there stert forth afore them of gentlemen and yeomen many, that said: Fair lords, ye may not pass this bridge and this fortress because of that black shield that I see one of you bear, and therefore there shall not pass but one of you at once; therefore choose you which of you shall enter within this bridge first. Then Sir Launcelot proffered himself first to enter within this bridge. Sir, said La Cote Male Taile, I beseech you let me enter within this fortress, and if I may speed well I will send for you, and if it happened that I be slain, there it goeth. And if so be that I am a prisoner taken, then may ye rescue me. I am loath, said Sir Launcelot, to let you pass this passage. Sir, said La Cote Male Taile, I pray you let me put my body in this adventure. Now go your way, said Sir Launcelot, and Jesu be your speed.

So he entered, and anon there met with him two brethren, the one hight Sir Plaine de Force, and the other hight Sir Plaine de Amours. And anon they met with Sir La Cote Male Taile; and first La Cote Male Taile smote down Plaine de Force, and after he smote down Plaine de Amours; and then they dressed them to their shields and swords, and bade La Cote Male Taile alight, and so he did; and there was dashing and foining with swords, and so they began to assail full hard La Cote Male Taile, and many great wounds they gave him upon his head, and upon his breast, and upon his shoulders. And as he might ever among he gave sad strokes again. And then the two brethren traced and traversed for to be of both hands of Sir La Cote Male Taile, but he by fine force and knightly prowess gat them afore him. And then when he felt himself so wounded, then he doubled his strokes, and gave them so many wounds that he felled them to the earth, and would have slain them had they not yielded them. And right so Sir La Cote Male Taile took the best horse that there was of them three, and so rode forth his way to the other fortress and bridge; and there he met with the third brother whose name was Sir Plenorius, a full noble knight, and there they jousted together, and either smote other down, horse and man, to the earth. And then they avoided their horses, and dressed their shields, and drew their swords, and gave many sad strokes, and one while the one knight was afore on the bridge, and another while the other. And thus they fought two hours and more, and never rested. And ever Sir Launcelot and the damosel beheld them. Alas, said the damosel, my knight fighteth passing sore and over long. Now may ye see, said Sir Launcelot, that he is a noble knight, for to consider his first battle, and his grievous wounds; and even forthwithal so wounded as he is, it is marvel that he may endure this long battle with that good knight.

CHAPTER VIII

How La Cote Male Taile was taken prisoner,
and after rescued by Sir Launcelot,
and how Sir Launcelot overcame four brethren.

This meanwhile Sir La Cote Male Taile sank right down upon the earth, what for-wounded and what for-bled he might not stand. Then the other knight had pity of him, and said: Fair young knight, dismay you not, for had ye been fresh when ye met with me, as I was, I wot well that I should not have endured so long as ye have done; and therefore for your noble deeds of arms I shall show to you kindness and gentleness in all that I may. And forthwithal this noble knight, Sir Plenorius, took him up in his arms, and led him into his tower. And then he commanded him the wine, and made to search him and to stop his bleeding wounds. Sir, said La Cote Male Taile, withdraw you from me, and hie you to yonder bridge again, for there will meet with you another manner knight than ever was I. Why, said Plenorius, is there another manner knight behind of your fellowship? Yea, said La Cote Male Taile, there is a much better knight than I am. What is his name? said Plenorius. Ye shall not know for me, said La Cote Male Taile. Well, said the knight, he shall be encountered withal whatsomever he be.

Then Sir Plenorius heard a knight call that said: Sir Plenorius, where art thou? either thou must deliver me the prisoner that thou hast led unto thy tower, or else come and do battle with me. Then Plenorius gat his horse, and came with a spear in his hand walloping toward Sir Launcelot; and then they began to feutre their spears, and came together as thunder, and smote either other so mightily that their horses fell down under them. And then they avoided their horses, and pulled out their swords, and like two bulls they lashed together with great strokes and foins; but ever Sir Launcelot recovered ground upon him, and Sir Plenorius traced to have gone about him. But Sir Launcelot would not suffer that, but bare him backer and backer, till he came nigh his tower gate. And then said Sir Launcelot: I know thee well for a good knight, but wit thou well thy life and death is in my hand, and therefore yield thee to me, and thy prisoner. The other answered no word, but struck mightily upon Sir Launcelot's helm, that the fire sprang out of his eyes. Then Sir Launcelot doubled his strokes so thick, and smote at him so mightily, that he made him kneel upon his knees. And therewith Sir Launcelot leapt upon him, and pulled him grovelling down. Then Sir Plenorius yielded him, and his tower, and all his prisoners at his will.

Then Sir Launcelot received him and took his troth; and then he rode to the other bridge, and there Sir Launcelot jousted with other three of his brethren, the one hight Pillounes, and the other hight Pellogris, and the third Sir Pellandris. And first upon horseback Sir Launcelot smote them down, and afterward he beat them on foot, and made them to yield them unto him; and then he returned unto Sir Plenorius, and there he found in his prison King Carados of Scotland, and many other knights, and all they were delivered. And then Sir La Cote Male Taile came to Sir Launcelot, and then Sir Launcelot would have given him all these fortresses and these bridges.

Nay, said La Cote Male Taile, I will not have Sir Plenorius' livelihood; with that he will grant you, my lord Sir Launcelot, to come unto King Arthur's court, and to be his knight, and all his brethren, I will pray you, my lord, to let him have his livelihood. I will well, said Sir Launcelot, with this that he will come to the court of King Arthur and become his man, and his brethren five. And as for you, Sir Plenorius, I will undertake, said Sir Launcelot, at the next feast, so there be a place voided, that ye shall be Knight of the Round Table. Sir, said Plenorius, at the next feast of Pentecost I will be at Arthur's court, and at that time I will be guided and ruled as King Arthur and ye will have me. Then Sir Launcelot and Sir La Cote Male Taile reposed them there, unto the time that Sir La Cote Male Taile was whole of his wounds, and there they had merry cheer, and good rest, and many good games, and there were many fair ladies.

CHAPTER IX

How Sir Launcelot made La Cote Male Taile lord of the Castle of Pendragon, and after was made knight of the Round Table.

And in the meanwhile came Sir Kay, the Seneschal, and Sir Brandiles, and anon they fellowshipped with them. And then within ten days, then departed those knights of Arthur's court from these fortresses. And as Sir Launcelot came by the Castle of Pendragon there he put Sir Brian de les Isles from his lands, for cause he would never be withhold with King Arthur; and all that Castle of Pendragon and all the lands thereof he gave to Sir La Cote Male Taile. And then Sir Launcelot sent for Nerovens that he made once knight, and he made him to have all the rule of that castle and of that country, under La Cote Male Taile; and so they rode to Arthur's court all wholly together. And at Pentecost next following there was Sir Plenorius and Sir La Cote Male Taile, called otherwise by right Sir Breunor le Noire, both made Knights of the Table Round; and great lands King Arthur gave them, and there Breunor le Noire wedded that damosel Maledisant. And after she was called Beauvivante, but ever after for the more part he was called La Cote Male Taile; and he proved a

passing noble knight, and mighty; and many worshipful deeds he did
after in his life; and Sir Plenorius proved a noble knight and full of
prowess, and all the days of their life for the most part they awaited
upon Sir Launcelot; and Sir Plenorius' brethren were ever knights of
King Arthur. And also, as the French book maketh mention, Sir La
Cote Male Taile avenged his father's death.

CHAPTER X

*How La Beale Isoud sent letters to Sir Tristram by her maid
Bragwaine, and of divers adventures of Sir Tristram.*

Now leave we here Sir La Cote Male Taile, and turn we unto Sir
Tristram de Liones that was in Brittany. When La Beale Isoud
understood that he was wedded she sent to him by her maiden
Bragwaine as piteous letters as could be thought and made, and her
conclusion was that, an it pleased Sir Tristram, that he would come to
her court, and bring with him Isoud la Blanche Mains, and they
should be kept as well as she herself. Then Sir Tristram called unto
him Sir Kehydius, and asked him whether he would go with him
into Cornwall secretly. He answered him that he was ready at all
times. And then he let ordain privily a little vessel, and therein they
went, Sir Tristram, Kehydius, Dame Bragwaine, and Gouvernail, Sir
Tristram's squire. So when they were in the sea a contrarious wind
blew them on the coasts of North Wales, nigh the Castle Perilous.
Then said Sir Tristram: Here shall ye abide me these ten days, and
Gouvernail, my squire, with you. And if so be I come not again by
that day take the next way into Cornwall; for in this forest are many
strange adventures, as I have heard say, and some of them I cast me to
prove or I depart. And when I may I shall hie me after you.

Then Sir Tristram and Kehydius took their horses and departed
from their fellowship. And so they rode within that forest a mile and
more; and at the last Sir Tristram saw afore him a likely knight,
armed, sitting by a well, and a strong mighty horse passing nigh him
tied to an oak, and a man hoving and riding by him leading an horse
laden with spears. And this knight that sat at the well seemed by his
countenance to be passing heavy. Then Sir Tristram rode near him

and said: Fair knight, why sit ye so drooping? ye seem to be a knight-errant by your arms and harness, and therefore dress you to joust with one of us, or with both. Therewithal that knight made no words, but took his shield and buckled it about his neck, and lightly he took his horse and leapt upon him. And then he took a great spear of his squire, and departed his way a furlong. Sir Kehydius asked leave of Sir Tristram to joust first. Do your best, said Sir Tristram. So they met together, and there Sir Kehydius had a fall, and was sore wounded on high above the paps. Then Sir Tristram said: Knight, that is well jousted, now make you ready unto me. I am ready, said the knight. And then that knight took a greater spear in his hand, and encountered with Sir Tristram, and there by great force that knight smote down Sir Tristram from his horse and had a great fall. Then Sir Tristram was sore ashamed, and lightly he avoided his horse, and put his shield afore his shoulder, and drew his sword And then Sir Tristram required that knight of his knighthood to alight upon foot and fight with him. I will well, said the knight; and so he alighted upon foot, and avoided his horse, and cast his shield upon his shoulder, and drew his sword, and there they fought a long battle together full nigh two hours. Then Sir Tristram said: Fair knight, hold thine hand; and tell me of whence thou art, and what is thy name. As for that, said the knight, I will be avised; but an thou wilt tell me thy name peradventure I will tell thee mine.

CHAPTER XI

*How Sir Tristram met with Sir Lamorak de Galis, and how
they fought, and after accorded never to fight together.*

Now fair knight, he said, my name is Sir Tristram de Liones. Sir, said the other knight, and my name is Sir Lamorak de Galis. Ah, Sir Lamorak, said Sir Tristram, well be we met, and bethink thee now of the despite thou didst me of the sending of the horn unto King Mark's court, to the intent to have slain or dishonoured my lady the Queen, La Beale Isoud; and therefore wit thou well, said Sir Tristram, the one of us shall die or we depart. Sir, said Sir Lamorak, remember that we were together in the Isle of Servage, and at that time ye promised me great friendship. Then Sir Tristram would make no longer delays, but lashed at Sir Lamorak; and thus they fought long till either were weary of other. Then Sir Tristram said to Sir Lamorak: In all my life met I never with such a knight that was so big and well breathed as ye be, therefore, said Sir Tristram, it were pity that any of us both should here be mischieved. Sir, said Sir Lamorak, for your renown and name I will that ye have the worship of this battle, and therefore I will yield me unto you. And therewith he took the point of his sword to yield him. Nay, said Sir Tristram, ye shall not do so, for well I know your proffers, and more of your gentleness than for any fear or dread ye have of me. And therewithal Sir Tristram proffered him his sword and said: Sir Lamorak, as an overcome knight I yield me unto you as to a man of the most noble prowess that ever I met withal. Nay, said Sir Lamorak, I will do you gentleness; I require you let us be sworn together that never none of us shall after this day have ado with other. And therewithal Sir Tristram and Sir Lamorak sware that never none of them should fight against other, nor for weal nor for woe.

CHAPTER XII

How Sir Palomides followed the Questing Beast, and smote down Sir Tristram and Sir Lamorak with one spear.

And this meanwhile there came Sir Palomides, the good knight, following the Questing Beast that had in shape a head like a serpent's head, and a body like a leopard, buttocks like a lion, and footed like an hart; and in his body there was such a noise as it had been the noise of thirty couple of hounds questing, and such a noise that beast made wheresomever he went; and this beast evermore Sir Palomides followed, for it was called his quest. And right so as he followed this beast it came by Sir Tristram, and soon after came Palomides. And to brief this matter he smote down Sir Tristram and Sir Lamorak both with one spear; and so he departed after the beast Galtisant, that was called the Questing Beast; wherefore these two knights were passing wroth that Sir Palomides would not fight on foot with them. Here men may understand that be of worship, that he was never formed that all times might stand, but sometime he was put to the worse by mal-fortune; and at sometime the worse knight put the better knight to a rebuke.

Then Sir Tristram and Sir Lamorak gat Sir Kehydius upon a shield betwixt them both, and led him to a forester's lodge, and there they gave him in charge to keep him well, and with him they abode three days. Then the two knights took their horses and at the cross they departed. And then said Sir Tristram to Sir Lamorak: I require you if ye hap to meet with Sir Palomides, say him that he shall find me at the same well where I met him, and there I, Sir Tristram, shall prove whether he be better knight than I. And so either departed from other a sundry way, and Sir Tristram rode nigh thereas was Sir Kehydius; and Sir Lamorak rode until he came to a chapel, and there he put his horse unto pasture. And anon there came Sir Meliagaunce, that was King Bagdemagus' son, and he there put his horse to pasture, and was not ware of Sir Lamorak; and then this knight Sir Meliagaunce made his moan of the love that he had to Queen Guenever, and there he made a woful complaint. All this heard Sir Lamorak, and on the morn Sir Lamorak took his horse and rode unto the forest, and there he met with two knights hoving under the wood shaw. Fair knights, said Sir Lamorak, what do ye hoving here and watching? and if ye be knights-errant that will joust, lo I am ready. Nay, sir knight, they said, not so, we abide not here to joust with you, but we lie here in await of a knight that slew our brother. What knight was that, said Sir Lamorak, that you would fain meet withal? Sir, they said, it is Sir Launcelot that slew our brother, and if ever we may meet with him he shall not escape, but we shall slay him. Ye take upon you a great charge, said Sir Lamorak, for Sir Launcelot is a noble proved knight. As for that we doubt not, for there nis none of us but we are good enough for him. I will not believe that, said Sir Lamorak, for I heard never yet of no knight the days of my life but Sir Launcelot was too big for him.

CHAPTER XIII

How Sir Lamorak met with Sir Meliagaunce, and fought together for the beauty of Dame Guenever.

Right so as they stood talking thus Sir Lamorak was ware how Sir Launcelot came riding straight toward them; then Sir Lamorak saluted him, and he him again. And then Sir Lamorak asked Sir Launcelot if there were anything that he might do for him in these marches. Nay, said Sir Launcelot, not at this time I thank you. Then either departed from other, and Sir Lamorak rode again thereas he left the two knights, and then he found them hid in the leaved wood. Fie on you, said Sir Lamorak, false cowards, pity and shame it is that any of you should take the high order of knighthood.

So Sir Lamorak departed from them, and within a while he met with Sir Meliagaunce. And then Sir Lamorak asked him why he loved Queen Guenever as he did: For I was not far from you when ye made your complaint by the chapel. Did ye so? said Sir Meliagaunce, then will I abide by it: I love Queen Guenever, what will ye with it? I will prove and make good that she is the fairest lady and most of beauty in the world. As to that, said Sir Lamorak, I say nay thereto, for Queen Morgawse of Orkney, mother to Sir Gawaine, and his mother is the fairest queen and lady that beareth the life. That is not so, said Sir Meliagaunce, and that will I prove with my hands upon thy body. Will ye so? said Sir Lamorak, and in a better quarrel keep I not to fight. Then they departed either from other in great wrath. And then they came riding together as it had been thunder, and either smote other so sore that their horses fell backward to the earth. And then they avoided their horses, and dressed their shields, and drew their swords. And then they hurtled together as wild boars, and thus they fought a great while. For Meliagaunce was a good man and of great might, but Sir Lamorak was hard big for him, and put him always aback, but either had wounded other sore.

And as they stood thus fighting, by fortune came Sir Launcelot and Sir Bleoberis riding. And then Sir Launcelot rode betwixt them, and asked them for what cause they fought so together: And ye are both knights of King Arthur!

CHAPTER XIV

How Sir Meliagaunce told for what cause they fought, and how Sir Lamorak jousted with King Arthur.

Sir, said Meliagaunce, I shall tell you for what cause we do this battle. I praised my lady, Queen Guenever, and said she was the fairest lady of the world, and Sir Lamorak said nay thereto, for he said Queen Morgawse of Orkney was fairer than she and more of beauty. Ah, Sir Lamorak, why sayest thou so? it is not thy part to dispraise thy princess that thou art under her obeissance, and we all. And therewith he alighted on foot, and said: For this quarrel, make thee ready, for I will prove upon thee that Queen Guenever is the fairest lady and most of bounty in the world. Sir, said Sir Lamorak, I am loath to have ado with you in this quarrel, for every man thinketh his own lady fairest; and though I praise the lady that I love most ye should not be wroth; for though my lady, Queen Guenever, be fairest in your eye, wit ye well Queen Morgawse of Orkney is fairest in mine eye, and so every knight thinketh his own lady fairest; and wit ye well, sir, ye are the man in the world except Sir Tristram that I am most loathest to have ado withal, but, an ye will needs fight with me I shall endure you as long as I may. Then spake Sir Bleoberis and said: My lord Sir Launcelot, I wist you never so misadvised as ye are now, for Sir Lamorak sayeth you but reason and knightly; for I warn you I have a lady, and methinketh that she is the fairest lady of the world. Were this a great reason that ye should be wroth with me for such language? And well ye wot, that Sir Lamorak is as noble a knight as I know, and he hath ought you and us ever good will, and therefore I pray you be good friends. Then Sir Launcelot said unto Sir Lamorak: I pray you forgive me mine evil will, and if I was misadvised I will amend it. Sir, said Sir Lamorak, the amends is soon made betwixt you and me. And so Sir Launcelot and Sir Bleoberis departed, and Sir Meliagaunce and Sir Lamorak took their horses, and either departed from other.

And within a while came King Arthur, and met with Sir Lamorak, and jousted with him; and there he smote down Sir Lamorak, and wounded him sore with a spear, and so he rode from him; wherefore Sir Lamorak was wroth that he would not fight with him on foot, howbeit that Sir Lamorak knew not King Arthur.

CHAPTER XV

How Sir Kay met with Sir Tristram, and after of the shame spoken of the knights of Cornwall, and how they jousted.

Now leave we of this tale, and speak we of Sir Tristram, that as he rode he met with Sir Kay, the Seneschal; and there Sir Kay asked Sir Tristram of what country he was. He answered that he was of the country of Cornwall. It may well be, said Sir Kay, for yet heard I never that ever good knight came out of Cornwall. That is evil spoken, said Sir Tristram, but an it please you to tell me your name I require you. Sir, wit ye well, said Sir Kay, that my name is Sir Kay, the Seneschal. Is that your name? said Sir Tristram, now wit ye well that ye are named the shamefullest knight of your tongue that now is living; howbeit ye are called a good knight, but ye are called unfortunate, and passing overthwart of your tongue. And thus they rode together till they came to a bridge. And there was a knight would not let them pass till one of them jousted with him; and so that knight jousted with Sir Kay, and there that knight gave Sir Kay a fall: his name was Sir Tor, Sir Lamorak's half-brother. And then they two rode to their lodging, and there they found Sir Brandiles, and Sir Tor came thither anon after. And as they sat at supper these four knights, three of them spake all shame by Cornish knights. Sir Tristram heard all that they said and he said but little, but he thought the more, but at that time he discovered not his name.

Upon the morn Sir Tristram took his horse and abode them upon their way. And there Sir Brandiles proffered to joust with Sir Tristram, and Sir Tristram smote him down, horse and all, to the earth. Then Sir Tor le Fise de Vayshoure encountered with Sir Tristram, and there Sir Tristram smote him down, and then he rode his way, and Sir Kay followed him, but he would not of his fellowship. Then Sir Brandiles came to Sir Kay and said: I would wit fain what is that knight's name. Come on with me, said Sir Kay, and we shall pray him to tell us his name. So they rode together till they came nigh him, and then they were ware where he sat by a well, and had put off his helm to drink at the well. And when he saw them come he laced on his helm lightly, and took his horse, and proffered them to joust. Nay, said Sir Brandiles, we jousted late enough with you, we come not in that intent. But for this we come to require you of knighthood to tell us your name. My fair knights, sithen that is your desire, and to please you, ye shall wit that my name is Sir Tristram de Liones, nephew unto King Mark of Cornwall. In good time, said Sir Brandiles, and well be ye found, and wit ye well that we be right glad that we have found you, and we be of a fellowship that would be right glad of your company. For ye are the knight in the world that the noble fellowship of the Round Table most desireth to have the company of. God thank them, said Sir Tristram, of their great goodness, but as yet I feel well that I am unable to be of their fellowship, for I was never yet of such deeds of worthiness to be in the company of such a fellowship. Ah, said Sir Kay, an ye be Sir Tristram de Liones, ye are the man called now most of prowess except Sir Launcelot du Lake; for he beareth not the life, Christian nor heathen, that can find such another knight, to speak of his prowess, and of his hands, and of his truth withal. For yet could there never creature say of him dishonour and make it good. Thus they talked a great while, and then they departed either from other such ways as them seemed best.

CHAPTER XVI

How King Arthur was brought into the Forest Perilous, and how Sir Tristram saved his life.

Now shall ye hear what was the cause that King Arthur came into the Forest Perilous, that was in North Wales, by the means of a lady. Her name was Annowre, and this lady came to King Arthur at Cardiff; and she by fair promise and fair behests made King Arthur to ride with her into that Forest Perilous; and she was a great sorceress; and many days she had loved King Arthur, and because she would have him to lie by her she came into that country. So when the king was gone with her many of his knights followed after King Arthur when they missed him, as Sir Launcelot, Brandiles, and many other; and when she had brought him to her tower she desired him to lie by her; and then the king remembered him of his lady, and would not lie by her for no craft that she could do. Then every day she would make him ride into that forest with his own knights, to the intent to have had King Arthur slain. For when this Lady Annowre saw that she might not have him at her will, then she laboured by false means to have destroyed King Arthur, and slain.

Then the Lady of the Lake that was alway friendly to King Arthur, she understood by her subtle crafts that King Arthur was like to be destroyed. And therefore this Lady of the Lake, that hight Nimue, came into that forest to seek after Sir Launcelot du Lake or Sir Tristram for to help King Arthur; foras that same day this Lady of the Lake knew well that King Arthur should be slain, unless that he had help of one of these two knights. And thus she rode up and down till she met with Sir Tristram, and anon as she saw him she knew him. O my lord Sir Tristram, she said, well be ye met, and blessed be the time that I have met with you; for this same day, and within these two hours, shall be done the foulest deed that ever was done in this land. O fair damosel, said Sir Tristram, may I amend it. Come on with me, she said, and that in all the haste ye may, for ye shall see the most worshipfullest knight of the world hard bestead. Then said Sir Tristram: I am ready to help such a noble man. He is neither better nor worse, said the Lady of the Lake, but the noble King Arthur himself. God defend, said Sir Tristram, that ever he should be in such distress. Then they rode together a great pace, until they came to a little turret or castle; and underneath that castle they saw a knight standing upon foot fighting with two knights; and so Sir Tristram beheld them, and at the last the two knights smote down the one knight, and that one of them unlaced his helm to have slain him. And the Lady Annowre gat King Arthur's sword in her hand to have stricken off his head. And therewithal came Sir Tristram with all his might, crying: Traitress, traitress, leave that. And anon there Sir Tristram smote the one of the knights through the body that he fell dead; and then he rashed to the other and smote his back asunder; and in the meanwhile the Lady of the Lake cried to King Arthur: Let not that false lady escape. Then King Arthur overtook her, and with the same sword he smote off her head, and the Lady of the Lake took up her head and hung it up by the hair of her saddle-bow. And then Sir Tristram horsed King Arthur and rode forth with him, but he charged the Lady of the Lake not to discover his name as at that time.

When the king was horsed he thanked heartily Sir Tristram, and desired to wit his name; but he would not tell him, but that he was a poor knight adventurous; and so he bare King Arthur fellowship till he met with some of his knights. And within a while he met with Sir Ector de Maris, and he knew not King Arthur nor Sir Tristram, and he desired to joust with one of them. Then Sir Tristram rode unto Sir Ector, and smote him from his horse. And when he had done so he came again to the king and said: My lord, yonder is one of your knights, he may bear you fellowship, and another day that deed that I have done for you I trust to God ye shall understand that I would do you service. Alas, said King Arthur, let me wit what ye are? Not at this time, said Sir Tristram. So he departed and left King Arthur and Sir Ector together.

CHAPTER XVII

How Sir Tristram came to La Beale Isoud, and how Kehydius began to love Beale Isoud, and of a letter that Tristram found.

And then at a day set Sir Tristram and Sir Lamorak met at the well; and then they took Kehydius at the forester's house, and so they rode with him to the ship where they left Dame Bragwaine and Gouvernail, and so they sailed into Cornwall all wholly together. And by assent and information of Dame Bragwaine when they were landed they rode unto Sir Dinas, the Seneschal, a trusty friend of Sir Tristram's. And so Dame Bragwaine and Sir Dinas rode to the court of King Mark, and told the queen, La Beale Isoud, that Sir Tristram was nigh her in that country. Then for very pure joy La Beale Isoud swooned; and when she might speak she said: Gentle knight Seneschal, help that I might speak with him, outher my heart will brast. Then Sir Dinas and Dame Bragwaine brought Sir Tristram and Kehydius privily unto

the court, unto a chamber whereas La Beale Isoud had assigned it; and
to tell the joys that were betwixt La Beale Isoud and Sir Tristram,
there is no tongue can tell it, nor heart think it, nor pen write it. And
as the French book maketh mention, at the first time that ever Sir
Kehydius saw La Beale Isoud he was so enamoured upon her that for
very pure love he might never withdraw it. And at the last, as ye shall
hear or the book be ended, Sir Kehydius died for the love of La Beale
Isoud. And then privily he wrote unto her letters and ballads of the
most goodliest that were used in those days. And when La Beale Isoud
understood his letters she had pity of his complaint, and unavised she
wrote another letter to comfort him withal.

And Sir Tristram was all this while in a turret at the commandment
of La Beale Isoud, and when she might she came unto Sir Tristram.
So on a day King Mark played at the chess under a chamber window;
and at that time Sir Tristram and Sir Kehydius were within the
chamber over King Mark, and as it mishapped Sir Tristram found the
letter that Kehydius sent unto La Beale Isoud, also he had found the
letter that she wrote unto Kehydius, and at that same time La Beale
Isoud was in the same chamber. Then Sir Tristram came unto La
Beale Isoud and said: Madam, here is a letter that was sent unto you,
and here is the letter that ye sent unto him that sent you that letter.
Alas, Madam, the good love that I have loved you; and many lands
and riches have I forsaken for your love, and now ye are a traitress to
me, the which doth me great pain. But as for thee, Sir Kehydius, I
brought thee out of Brittany into this country, and thy father, King
Howel, I won his lands, howbeit I wedded thy sister Isoud la Blanche
Mains for the goodness she did unto me. And yet, as I am true
knight, she is a clean maiden for me; but wit thou well, Sir Kehydius,
for this falsehood and treason thou hast done me, I will revenge it
upon thee. And therewithal Sir Tristram drew out his sword and said:
Sir Kehydius, keep thee, and then La Beale Isoud swooned to the
earth. And when Sir Kehydius saw Sir Tristram come upon him he
saw none other boot, but leapt out at a bay-window even over the
head where sat King Mark playing at the chess. And when the king
saw one come hurling over his head he said: Fellow, what art thou,
and what is the cause thou leapest out at that window? My lord the
king, said Kehydius, it fortuned me that I was asleep in the window
above your head, and as I slept I slumbered, and so I fell down. And
thus Sir Kehydius excused him.

CHAPTER XVIII

How Sir Tristram departed from Tintagil,
and how he sorrowed and was so long in a forest
till he was out of his mind.

Then Sir Tristram dread sore lest he were discovered unto the king that he was there; wherefore he drew him to the strength of the Tower, and armed him in such armour as he had for to fight with them that would withstand him. And so when Sir Tristram saw there was no resistance against him he sent Gouvernail for his horse and his spear, and knightly he rode forth out of the castle openly, that was called the Castle of Tintagil. And even at gate he met with Gingalin, Sir Gawaine's son. And anon Sir Gingalin put his spear in his rest, and ran upon Sir Tristram and brake his spear; and Sir Tristram at that time had but a sword, and gave him such a buffet upon the helm that he fell down from his saddle, and his sword slid adown, and carved asunder his horse's neck. And so Sir Tristram rode his way into the forest, and all this doing saw King Mark. And then he sent a squire unto the hurt knight, and commanded him to come to him, and so he did. And when King Mark wist that it was Sir Gingalin he welcomed him and gave him an horse, and asked him what knight it was that had encountered with him. Sir, said Gingalin, I wot not what knight he was, but well I wot that he sigheth and maketh great dole.

Then Sir Tristram within a while met with a knight of his own, that hight Sir Fergus. And when he had met with him he made great sorrow, insomuch that he fell down off his horse in a swoon, and in such sorrow he was in three days and three nights. Then at the last Sir Tristram sent unto the court by Sir Fergus, for to spere what tidings. And so as he rode by the way he met with a damosel that came from Sir Palomides, to know and seek how Sir Tristram did. Then Sir Fergus told her how he was almost out of his mind. Alas, said the damosel, where shall I find him? In such a place, said Sir Fergus. Then Sir Fergus found Queen Isoud sick in her bed, making the greatest dole that ever any earthly woman made. And when the damosel found Sir Tristram she made great dole because she might not amend him, for the more she made of him the more was his pain. And at the last Sir Tristram took his horse and rode away from her. And then was it three days or that she could find him, and then she brought him meat and drink, but he would none; and then another time Sir Tristram escaped away from the damosel, and it happed him to ride by the same castle where Sir Palomides and Sir Tristram did battle when La Beale Isoud departed them. And there by fortune the damosel met with Sir Tristram again, making the greatest dole that ever earthly creature made; and she yede to the lady of that castle and told her of the misadventure of Sir Tristram. Alas, said the lady of that castle, where is my lord, Sir Tristram? Right here by your castle, said the damosel. In good time, said the lady, is he so nigh me; he shall have meat and drink of the best; and an harp I have of his whereupon he taught me, for of goodly harping he beareth the prize in the world. So this lady and damosel brought him meat and drink, but he ate little thereof. Then upon a night he put his horse from him, and then he unlaced his armour, and then Sir Tristram would go into the wilderness, and brast down the trees and boughs; and otherwhile when he found the harp that the lady sent him, then would he harp, and play thereupon and weep together. And sometime when Sir Tristram was in the wood that the lady wist not where he was, then would she sit her down and play upon that harp: then would Sir Tristram come to that harp, and hearken thereto, and sometime he would harp himself. Thus he there endured a quarter of a year. Then at the last he ran his way, and she wist not where he was become. And then was he naked and waxed lean and poor of flesh; and so he fell in the fellowship of herdmen and shepherds, and daily they would give him some of their meat and drink. And when he did any shrewd deed they would beat him with rods, and so they clipped him with shears and made him like a fool.

CHAPTER XIX

How Sir Tristram soused Dagonet in a well, and how
Palomides sent a damosel to seek Tristram, and how
Palomides met with King Mark.

And upon a day Dagonet, King Arthur's fool, came into Cornwall with two squires with him; and as they rode through that forest they came by a fair well where Sir Tristram was wont to be; and the weather was hot, and they alighted to drink of that well, and in the meanwhile their horses brake loose. Right so Sir Tristram came unto them, and first he soused Sir Dagonet in that well, and after his squires, and thereat laughed the shepherds; and forthwithal he ran after their horses and brought them again one by one, and right so, wet as they were, he made them leap up and ride their ways. Thus Sir Tristram endured there an half year naked, and would never come in town nor village. The meanwhile the damosel that Sir Palomides sent to seek Sir Tristram, she yede unto Sir Palomides and told him all the mischief that Sir Tristram endured. Alas, said Sir Palomides, it is great pity that ever so noble a knight should be so mischieved for the love of a lady; but nevertheless, I will go and seek him, and comfort him an I may. Then a little before that time La Beale Isoud had commanded Sir Kehydius out of the country of Cornwall. So Sir Kehydius departed with a dolorous heart, and by adventure he met with Sir Palomides, and they enfellowshipped together; and either complained to other of their hot love that they loved La Beale Isoud. Now let us, said Sir Palomides, seek Sir Tristram, that loved her as well as we, and let us prove whether we may recover him. So they rode into that forest, and three days and three nights they would never take their lodging, but ever sought Sir Tristram.

And upon a time, by adventure, they met with King Mark that was ridden from his men all alone. When they saw him Sir Palomides knew him, but Sir Kehydius knew him not. Ah, false king, said Sir Palomides, it is pity thou hast thy life, for thou art a destroyer of all worshipful knights, and by thy mischief and thy vengeance thou hast destroyed that most noble knight, Sir Tristram de Liones. And therefore defend thee, said Sir Palomides, for thou shalt die this day. That were shame, said King Mark, for ye two are armed and I am unarmed. As for that, said Sir Palomides, I shall find a remedy therefore; here is a knight with me, and thou shalt have his harness. Nay, said King Mark, I will not have ado with you, for cause have ye none to me; for all the misease that Sir Tristram hath was for a letter that he found; for as to me I did to him no displeasure, and God knoweth I am full sorry for his disease and malady. So when the king had thus excused him they were friends, and King Mark would have had them unto Tintagil; but Sir Palomides would not, but turned unto the realm of Logris, and Sir Kehydius said that he would go into Brittany.

Now turn we unto Sir Dagonet again, that when he and his squires were upon horseback he deemed that the shepherds had sent that fool to array them so, because that they laughed at them, and so they rode unto the keepers of beasts and all to-beat them. Sir Tristram saw them beat that were wont to give him meat and drink, then he ran thither and gat Sir Dagonet by the head, and gave him such a fall to the earth that he bruised him sore so that he lay still. And then he wrast his sword out of his hand, and therewith he ran to one of his squires and smote off his head, and the other fled. And so Sir Tristram took his way with that sword in his hand, running as he had been wild wood. Then Sir Dagonet rode to King Mark and told him how he had sped in that forest. And therefore, said Sir Dagonet, beware, King Mark, that thou come not about that well in the forest, for there is a fool naked, and that fool and I fool met together, and he had almost slain me. Ah, said King Mark, that is Sir Matto le Breune, that fell out of his wit because he lost his lady; for when Sir Gaheris smote down Sir Matto and won his lady of him, never since was he in his mind, and that was pity, for he was a good knight.

CHAPTER XX

*How it was noised how Sir Tristram was dead, and how La
Beale Isoud would have slain herself.*

Then Sir Andred, that was cousin unto Sir Tristram, made a lady that
was his paramour to say and to noise it that she was with Sir Tristram
or ever he died. And this tale she brought unto King Mark's court,
that she buried him by a well, and that or he died he besought King
Mark to make his cousin, Sir Andred, king of the country of Liones,
of the which Sir Tristram was lord of. All this did Sir Andred because
he would have had Sir Tristram's lands. And when King Mark heard
tell that Sir Tristram was dead he wept and made great dole. But
when Queen Isoud heard of these tidings she made such sorrow that
she was nigh out of her mind; and so upon a day she thought to slay
herself and never to live after Sir Tristram's death. And so upon a day
La Beale Isoud gat a sword privily and bare it to her garden, and there
she pight the sword through a plum tree up to the hilt, so that it stuck
fast, and it stood breast high. And as she would have run upon the
sword and to have slain herself all this espied King Mark, how she
kneeled down and said: Sweet Lord Jesu, have mercy upon me, for I
may not live after the death of Sir Tristram de Liones, for he was my
first love and he shall be the last. And with these words came King
Mark and took her in his arms, and then he took up the sword, and
bare her away with him into a tower; and there he made her to be
kept, and watched her surely, and after that she lay long sick, nigh at
the point of death.

This meanwhile ran Sir Tristram naked in the forest with the sword
in his hand, and so he came to an hermitage, and there he laid him
down and slept; and in the meanwhile the hermit stole away his
sword, and laid meat down by him. Thus was he kept there ten days;
and at the last he departed and came to the herdmen again. And there
was a giant in that country that hight Tauleas, and for fear of Sir
Tristram more than seven year he durst never much go at large, but
for the most part he kept him in a sure castle of his own; and so this
Tauleas heard tell that Sir Tristram was dead, by the noise of the court

of King Mark. Then this Tauleas went daily at large. And so he happed upon a day he came to the herdmen wandering and langering, and there he set him down to rest among them. The meanwhile there came a knight of Cornwall that led a lady with him, and his name was Sir Dinant; and when the giant saw him he went from the herdmen and hid him under a tree, and so the knight came to that well, and there he alighted to repose him. And as soon as he was from his horse this giant Tauleas came betwixt this knight and his horse, and took the horse and leapt upon him. So forthwith he rode unto Sir Dinant and took him by the collar, and pulled him afore him upon his horse, and there would have stricken off his head. Then the herdmen said unto Sir Tristram: Help yonder knight. Help ye him, said Sir Tristram. We dare not, said the herdmen. Then Sir Tristram was ware of the sword of the knight thereas it lay; and so thither he ran and took up the sword and struck off Sir Tauleas' head, and so he yede his way to the herdmen.

CHAPTER XXI

How King Mark found Sir Tristram naked, and made him to be borne home to Tintagil, and how he was there known by a brachet.

Then the knight took up the giant's head and bare it with him unto King Mark, and told him what adventure betid him in the forest, and how a naked man rescued him from the grimly giant, Tauleas. Where had ye this adventure? said King Mark. Forsooth, said Sir Dinant, at the fair fountain in your forest where many adventurous knights meet, and there is the mad man. Well, said King Mark, I will see that wild man. So within a day or two King Mark commanded his knights and his hunters that they should be ready on the morn for to hunt, and so upon the morn he went unto that forest. And when the king came to that well he found there lying by that well a fair naked man, and a sword by him. Then King Mark blew and straked, and therewith his knights came to him; and then the king commanded his knights to: Take that naked man with fairness, and bring him to my castle. So they did softly and fair, and cast mantles upon Sir

Tristram, and so led him unto Tintagil; and there they bathed him, and washed him, and gave him hot suppings till they had brought him well to his remembrance; but all this while there was no creature that knew Sir Tristram, nor what man he was.

So it fell upon a day that the queen, La Beale Isoud, heard of such a man, that ran naked in the forest, and how the king had brought him home to the court. Then La Beale Isoud called unto her Dame Bragwaine and said: Come on with me, for we will go see this man that my lord brought from the forest the last day. So they passed forth, and spered where was the sick man. And then a squire told the queen that he was in the garden taking his rest, and reposing him against the sun. So when the queen looked upon Sir Tristram she was not remembered of him. But ever she said unto Dame Bragwaine: Meseemeth I should have seen him heretofore in many places. But as soon as Sir Tristram saw her he knew her well enough. And then he turned away his visage and wept.

Then the queen had always a little brachet with her that Sir Tristram gave her the first time that ever she came into Cornwall, and never would that brachet depart from her but if Sir Tristram was nigh thereas was La Beale Isoud; and this brachet was sent from the king's daughter of France unto Sir Tristram for great love. And anon as this little brachet felt a savour of Sir Tristram, she leapt upon him and licked his lears and his ears, and then she whined and quested, and she smelled at his feet and at his hands, and on all parts of his body that she might come to. Ah, my lady, said Dame Bragwaine unto La Beale Isoud, alas, alas, said she, I see it is mine own lord, Sir Tristram. And thereupon Isoud fell down in a swoon, and so lay a great while. And when she might speak she said: My lord Sir Tristram, blessed be God ye have your life, and now I am sure ye shall be discovered by this little brachet, for she will never leave you. And also I am sure as soon as my lord, King Mark, do know you he will banish you out of the country of Cornwall, or else he will destroy you; for God's sake, mine own lord, grant King Mark his will, and then draw you unto the court of King Arthur, for there are ye beloved, and ever when I may I shall send unto you; and when ye list ye may come to me, and at all times early and late I will be at your commandment, to live as poor a life as ever did queen or lady. O Madam, said Sir Tristram, go from me, for mickle anger and danger have I escaped for your love.

CHAPTER XXII

*How King Mark, by the advice of his council, banished Sir
Tristram out of Cornwall the term of ten years.*

Then the queen departed, but the brachet would not from him; and
therewithal came King Mark, and the brachet set upon him, and
bayed at them all. Therewithal Sir Andred spake and said: Sir, this is
Sir Tristram, I see by the brachet. Nay, said the king, I cannot
suppose that. Then the king asked him upon his faith what he was,
and what was his name. So God me help, said he, my name is Sir
Tristram de Liones; now do by me what ye list. Ah, said King Mark,
me repenteth of your recovery. And then he let call his barons to
judge Sir Tristram to the death. Then many of his barons would not
assent thereto, and in especial Sir Dinas, the Seneschal, and Sir Fergus.
And so by the advice of them all Sir Tristram was banished out of the
country for ten year, and thereupon he took his oath upon a book
before the king and his barons. And so he was made to depart out of
the country of Cornwall; and there were many barons brought him
unto his ship, of the which some were his friends and some his foes.
And in the meanwhile there came a knight of King Arthur's, his
name was Dinadan, and his coming was for to seek after Sir Tristram;
then they showed him where he was armed at all points going to the
ship. Now fair knight, said Sir Dinadan, or ye pass this court that ye
will joust with me I require thee. With a good will, said Sir Tristram,
an these lords will give me leave. Then the barons granted thereto,
and so they ran together, and there Sir Tristram gave Sir Dinadan a
fall. And then he prayed Sir Tristram to give him leave to go in his
fellowship. Ye shall be right welcome, said then Sir Tristram.

And so they took their horses and rode to their ships together, and
when Sir Tristram was in the sea he said: Greet well King Mark and
all mine enemies, and say them I will come again when I may; and
well am I rewarded for the fighting with Sir Marhaus, and delivered
all this country from servage; and well am I rewarded for the fetching
and costs of Queen Isoud out of Ireland, and the danger that I was in
first and last, and by the way coming home what danger I had to

bring again Queen Isoud from the Castle Pluere; and well am I rewarded when I fought with Sir Bleoberis for Sir Segwarides' wife; and well am I rewarded when I fought with Sir Blamore de Ganis for King Anguish, father unto La Beale Isoud; and well am I rewarded when I smote down the good knight, Sir Lamorak de Galis, at King Mark's request; and well am I rewarded when I fought with the King with the Hundred Knights, and the King of Northgalis, and both these would have put his land in servage, and by me they were put to a rebuke; and well am I rewarded for the slaying of Tauleas, the mighty giant, and many other deeds have I done for him, and now have I my warison. And tell King Mark that many noble knights of the Table Round have spared the barons of this country for my sake. Also am I not well rewarded when I fought with the good knight Sir Palomides and rescued Queen Isoud from him; and at that time King Mark said afore all his barons I should have been better rewarded. And forthwithal he took the sea.

CHAPTER XXIII

How a damosel sought help to help Sir Launcelot against thirty knights, and how Sir Tristram fought with them.

And at the next landing, fast by the sea, there met with Sir Tristram and with Sir Dinadan, Sir Ector de Maris and Sir Bors de Ganis; and there Sir Ector jousted with Sir Dinadan, and he smote him and his horse down. And then Sir Tristram would have jousted with Sir Bors, and Sir Bors said that he would not joust with no Cornish knights, for they are not called men of worship; and all this was done upon a bridge. And with this came Sir Bleoberis and Sir Driant, and Sir Bleoberis proffered to joust with Sir Tristram, and there Sir Tristram smote down Sir Bleoberis. Then said Sir Bors de Ganis: I wist never Cornish knight of so great valour nor so valiant as that knight that beareth the trappings embroidered with crowns. And then Sir Tristram and Sir Dinadan departed from them into a forest, and there met them a damosel that came for the love of Sir Launcelot to seek after some noble knights of King Arthur's court for to rescue Sir Launcelot. And so Sir Launcelot was ordained, for-by the treason of Queen Morgan le Fay to have slain Sir Launcelot, and for that cause she ordained thirty knights to lie in await for Sir Launcelot, and this damosel knew this treason. And for this cause the damosel came for to seek noble knights to help Sir Launcelot. For that night, or the day after, Sir Launcelot should come where these thirty knights were. And so this damosel met with Sir Bors and Sir Ector and with Sir Driant, and there she told them all four of the treason of Morgan le Fay; and then they promised her that they would be nigh where Sir Launcelot should meet with the thirty knights. And if so be they set upon him we will do rescues as we can.

So the damosel departed, and by adventure the damosel met with Sir Tristram and with Sir Dinadan, and there the damosel told them all the treason that was ordained for Sir Launcelot. Fair damosel, said Sir Tristram, bring me to that same place where they should meet with Sir Launcelot. Then said Sir Dinadan: What will ye do? it is not for us to fight with thirty knights, and wit you well I will not thereof; as to match one knight two or three is enough an they be men, but for to match fifteen knights that will I never undertake. Fie for shame, said Sir Tristram, do but your part. Nay, said Sir Dinadan, I will not thereof but if ye will lend me your shield, for ye bear a shield of Cornwall; and for the cowardice that is named to the knights of Cornwall, by your shields ye be ever forborne. Nay, said Sir Tristram, I will not depart from my shield for her sake that gave it me. But one thing, said Sir Tristram, I promise thee, Sir Dinadan, but if thou wilt promise me to abide with me, here I shall slay thee, for I desire no more of thee but answer one knight. And if thy heart will not serve thee, stand by and look upon me and them. Sir, said Sir Dinadan, I promise you to look upon and to do what I may to save myself, but I would I had not met with you.

So then anon these thirty knights came fast by these four knights, and they were ware of them, and either of other. And so these thirty knights let them pass, for this cause, that they would not wrath them, if case be that they had ado with Sir Launcelot; and the four knights let them pass to this intent, that they would see and behold what they would do with Sir Launcelot. And so the thirty knights passed on and came by Sir Tristram and by Sir Dinadan, and then Sir Tristram cried on high: Lo, here is a knight against you for the love of Sir Launcelot. And there he slew two with one spear and ten with his sword. And then came in Sir Dinadan and he did passing well, and so of the thirty knights there went but ten away, and they fled. All this battle saw Sir

Bors de Ganis and his three fellows, and then they saw well it was the same knight that jousted with them at the bridge; then they took their horses and rode unto Sir Tristram, and praised him and thanked him of his good deeds, and they all desired Sir Tristram to go with them to their lodging; and he said: Nay, he would not go to no lodging. Then they all four knights prayed him to tell them his name. Fair lords, said Sir Tristram, as at this time I will not tell you my name.

CHAPTER XXIV

How Sir Tristram and Sir Dinadan came to a lodging where they must joust with two knights.

Then Sir Tristram and Sir Dinadan rode forth their way till they came to the shepherds and to the herdmen, and there they asked them if they knew any lodging or harbour there nigh hand. Forsooth, sirs, said the herdmen, hereby is good lodging in a castle; but there is such a custom that there shall no knight be harboured but if he joust with two knights, and if he be but one knight he must joust with two. And as ye be therein soon shall ye be matched. There is shrewd harbour, said Sir Dinadan; lodge where ye will, for I will not lodge there. Fie for shame, said Sir Tristram, are ye not a knight of the Table Round? wherefore ye may not with your worship refuse your lodging. Not so, said the herdmen, for an ye be beaten and have the worse ye shall not be lodged there, and if ye beat them ye shall be well harboured. Ah, said Sir Dinadan, they are two sure knights. Then Sir Dinadan would not lodge there in no manner but as Sir Tristram required him of his knighthood; and so they rode thither. And to make short tale, Sir Tristram and Sir Dinadan smote them down both, and so they entered into the castle and had good cheer as they could think or devise.

And when they were unarmed, and thought to be merry and in good rest, there came in at the gates Sir Palomides and Sir Gaheris, requiring to have the custom of the castle. What array is this? said Sir Dinadan, I would have my rest. That may not be, said Sir Tristram; now must we needs defend the custom of this castle, insomuch as we have the better of the lords of this castle, and therefore, said Sir

Tristram, needs must ye make you ready. In the devil's name, said Sir Dinadan, came I into your company. And so they made them ready; and Sir Gaheris encountered with Sir Tristram, and Sir Gaheris had a fall; and Sir Palomides encountered with Sir Dinadan, and Sir Dinadan had a fall: then was it fall for fall. So then must they fight on foot. That would not Sir Dinadan, for he was so sore bruised of the fall that Sir Palomides gave him. Then Sir Tristram unlaced Sir Dinadan's helm, and prayed him to help him. I will not, said Sir Dinadan, for I am sore wounded of the thirty knights that we had but late ago to do withal. But ye fare, said Sir Dinadan unto Sir Tristram, as a madman and as a man that is out of his mind that would cast himself away, and I may curse the time that ever I saw you, for in all the world are not two such knights that be so wood as is Sir Launcelot and ye Sir Tristram; for once I fell in the fellowship of Sir Launcelot as I have done now with you, and he set me a work that a quarter of a year I kept my bed. Jesu defend me, said Sir Dinadan, from such two knights, and specially from your fellowship. Then, said Sir Tristram, I will fight with them both. Then Sir Tristram bade them come forth both, for I will fight with you. Then Sir Palomides and Sir Gaheris dressed them, and smote at them both. Then Dinadan smote at Sir Gaheris a stroke or two, and turned from him. Nay, said Sir Palomides, it is too much shame for us two knights to fight with one. And then he did bid Sir Gaheris stand aside with that knight that hath no list to fight. Then they rode together and fought long, and at the last Sir Tristram doubled his strokes, and drove Sir Palomides aback more than three strides. And then by one assent Sir Gaheris and Sir Dinadan went betwixt them, and departed them insunder. And then by assent of Sir Tristram they would have lodged together. But Sir Dinadan would not lodge in that castle. And then he cursed the time that ever he came in their fellowship, and so he took his horse, and his harness, and departed.

Then Sir Tristram prayed the lords of that castle to lend him a man to bring him to a lodging, and so they did, and overtook Sir Dinadan, and rode to their lodging two mile thence with a good man in a priory, and there they were well at ease. And that same night Sir Bors and Sir Bleoberis, and Sir Ector and Sir Driant, abode still in the same place thereas Sir Tristram fought with the thirty knights; and there they met with Sir Launcelot the same night, and had made promise to lodge with Sir Colgrevance the same night.

CHAPTER XXV

*How Sir Tristram jousted with Sir Kay and Sir Sagramore
le Desirous, and how Sir Gawaine turned Sir Tristram
from Morgan le Fay.*

But anon as the noble knight, Sir Launcelot, heard of the shield of
Cornwall, then wist he well that it was Sir Tristram that fought with
his enemies. And then Sir Launcelot praised Sir Tristram, and called
him the man of most worship in the world. So there was a knight in
that priory that hight Pellinore, and he desired to wit the name of Sir
Tristram, but in no wise he could not; and so Sir Tristram departed
and left Sir Dinadan in the priory, for he was so weary and so sore
bruised that he might not ride. Then this knight, Sir Pellinore, said to
Sir Dinadan: Sithen that ye will not tell me that knight's name I will
ride after him and make him to tell me his name, or he shall die
therefore. Beware, sir knight, said Sir Dinadan, for an ye follow him
ye shall repent it. So that knight, Sir Pellinore, rode after Sir Tristram
and required him of jousts. Then Sir Tristram smote him down and
wounded him through the shoulder, and so he passed on his way.
And on the next day following Sir Tristram met with pursuivants, and
they told him that there was made a great cry of tournament between
King Carados of Scotland and the King of North Wales, and either
should joust against other at the Castle of Maidens; and these
pursuivants sought all the country after the good knights, and in
especial King Carados let make seeking for Sir Launcelot du Lake, and
the King of Northgalis let seek after Sir Tristram de Liones. And at
that time Sir Tristram thought to be at that jousts; and so by adventure
they met with Sir Kay, the Seneschal, and Sir Sagramore le Desirous;
and Sir Kay required Sir Tristram to joust, and Sir Tristram in a
manner refused him, because he would not be hurt nor bruised against
the great jousts that should be before the Castle of Maidens, and
therefore thought to repose him and to rest him. And alway Sir Kay
cried: Sir knight of Cornwall, joust with me, or else yield thee to me
as recreant. When Sir Tristram heard him say so he turned to him, and
then Sir Kay refused him and turned his back. Then Sir Tristram said:

As I find thee I shall take thee. Then Sir Kay turned with evil will, and Sir Tristram smote Sir Kay down, and so he rode forth.

Then Sir Sagramore le Desirous rode after Sir Tristram, and made him to joust with him, and there Sir Tristram smote down Sir Sagramore le Desirous from his horse, and rode his way; and the same day he met with a damosel that told him that he should win great worship of a knight adventurous that did much harm in all that country. When Sir Tristram heard her say so, he was glad to go with her to win worship. So Sir Tristram rode with that damosel a six mile, and then met him Sir Gawaine, and therewithal Sir Gawaine knew the damosel, that she was a damosel of Queen Morgan le Fay. Then Sir Gawaine understood that she led that knight to some mischief. Fair knight, said Sir Gawaine, whither ride you now with that damosel? Sir, said Sir Tristram, I wot not whither I shall ride but as the damosel will lead me. Sir, said Sir Gawaine, ye shall not ride with her, for she and her lady did never good, but ill. And then Sir Gawaine pulled out his sword and said: Damosel, but if thou tell me anon for what cause thou leadest this knight with thee thou shalt die for it right anon: I know all your lady's treason, and yours. Mercy, Sir Gawaine, she said, and if ye will save my life I will tell you. Say on, said Sir Gawaine, and thou shalt have thy life. Sir, she said, Queen Morgan le Fay, my lady, hath ordained a thirty ladies to seek and espy after Sir Launcelot or Sir Tristram, and by the trains of these ladies, who that may first meet any of these two knights they should turn them unto Morgan le Fay's castle, saying that they should do deeds of worship; and if any of the two knights came there, there be thirty knights lying and watching in a tower to wait upon Sir Launcelot or upon Sir Tristram. Fie for shame, said Sir Gawaine, that ever such false treason should be wrought or used in a queen, and a king's sister, and a king and queen's daughter.

CHAPTER XXVI

*How Sir Tristram and Sir Gawaine rode to have foughten
with the thirty knights, but they durst not come out.*

Sir, said Sir Gawaine, will ye stand with me, and we will see the
malice of these thirty knights. Sir, said Sir Tristram, go ye to them, an
it please you, and ye shall see I will not fail you, for it is not long ago
since I and a fellow met with thirty knights of that queen's fellowship;
and God speed us so that we may win worship. So then Sir Gawaine
and Sir Tristram rode toward the castle where Morgan le Fay was,
and ever Sir Gawaine deemed well that he was Sir Tristram de
Liones, because he heard that two knights had slain and beaten thirty
knights. And when they came afore the castle Sir Gawaine spake on
high and said: Queen Morgan le Fay, send out your knights that ye
have laid in a watch for Sir Launcelot and for Sir Tristram. Now, said
Sir Gawaine, I know your false treason, and through all places where
that I ride men shall know of your false treason; and now let see, said
Sir Gawaine, whether ye dare come out of your castle, ye thirty
knights. Then the queen spake and all the thirty knights at once, and
said: Sir Gawaine, full well wottest thou what thou dost and sayest;
for by God we know thee passing well, but all that thou speakest and
dost, thou sayest it upon pride of that good knight that is there with
thee. For there be some of us that know full well the hands of that
knight over all well. And wit thou well, Sir Gawaine, it is more for
his sake than for thine that we will not come out of this castle. For
wit ye well, Sir Gawaine, the knight that beareth the arms of
Cornwall, we know him and what he is.

Then Sir Gawaine and Sir Tristram departed and rode on their
ways a day or two together; and there by adventure, they met with
Sir Kay and Sir Sagramore le Desirous. And then they were glad of
Sir Gawaine, and he of them, but they wist not what he was with the
shield of Cornwall, but by deeming. And thus they rode together a
day or two. And then they were ware of Sir Breuse Saunce Pité
chasing a lady for to have slain her, for he had slain her paramour
afore. Hold you all still, said Sir Gawaine, and show none of you

forth, and ye shall see me reward yonder false knight; for an he espy you he is so well horsed that he will escape away. And then Sir Gawaine rode betwixt Sir Breuse and the lady, and said: False knight, leave her, and have ado with me. When Sir Breuse saw no more but Sir Gawaine he feutred his spear, and Sir Gawaine against him; and there Sir Breuse overthrew Sir Gawaine, and then he rode over him, and overthwart him twenty times to have destroyed him; and when Sir Tristram saw him do so villainous a deed, he hurled out against him. And when Sir Breuse saw him with the shield of Cornwall he knew him well that it was Sir Tristram, and then he fled, and Sir Tristram followed after him; and Sir Breuse Saunce Pité was so horsed that he went his way quite, and Sir Tristram followed him long, for he would fain have been avenged upon him. And so when he had long chased him, he saw a fair well, and thither he rode to repose him, and tied his horse till a tree.

CHAPTER XXVII

How damosel Bragwaine found Tristram sleeping by a well, and how she delivered letters to him from La Beale Isoud.

And then he pulled off his helm and washed his visage and his hands, and so he fell asleep. In the meanwhile came a damosel that had sought Sir Tristram many ways and days within this land. And when she came to the well she looked upon him, and had forgotten him as in remembrance of Sir Tristram, but by his horse she knew him, that hight Passe-Brewel that had been Sir Tristram's horse many years. For when he was mad in the forest Sir Fergus kept him. So this lady, Dame Bragwaine, abode still till he was awake. So when she saw him wake she saluted him, and he her again, for either knew other of old acquaintance; then she told him how she had sought him long and broad, and there she told him how she had letters from Queen La Beale Isoud. Then anon Sir Tristram read them, and wit ye well he was glad, for therein was many a piteous complaint. Then Sir Tristram said: Lady Bragwaine, ye shall ride with me till that tournament be done at the Castle of Maidens, and then shall bear letters and tidings with you. And then Sir Tristram took his horse and sought lodging, and there he met with a good ancient knight and prayed him to lodge with him. Right so came Gouvernail unto Sir Tristram, that was glad of that lady. So this old knight's name was Sir Pellounes, and he told of the great tournament that should be at the Castle of Maidens. And there Sir Launcelot and thirty-two knights of his blood had ordained shields of Cornwall. And right so there came one unto Sir Pellounes, and told him that Sir Persides de Bloise was come home; then that knight held up his hands and thanked God of his coming home. And there Sir Pellounes told Sir Tristram that in two years he had not seen his son, Sir Persides. Sir, said Sir Tristram, I know your son well enough for a good knight.

So on a time Sir Tristram and Sir Persides came to their lodging both at once, and so they unarmed them, and put upon them their clothing. And then these two knights each welcomed other. And when Sir Persides understood that Sir Tristram was of Cornwall, he said he was once in Cornwall: And there I jousted afore King Mark; and so it happed me at that time to overthrow ten knights, and then came to me Sir Tristram de Liones and overthrew me, and took my lady away from me, and that shall I never forget, but I shall remember me an ever I see my time. Ah, said Sir Tristram, now I understand that ye hate Sir Tristram. What deem ye, ween ye that Sir Tristram is not able to withstand your malice? Yes, said Sir Persides, I know well that Sir Tristram is a noble knight and a much better knight than I, yet shall I not owe him my good will. Right as they stood thus talking at a bay-window of that castle, they saw many knights riding to and fro toward the tournament. And then was Sir Tristram ware of a likely knight riding upon a great black horse, and a black-covered shield. What knight is that, said Sir Tristram, with the black horse and the black shield? he seemeth a good knight. I know him well, said Sir Persides, he is one of the best knights of the world. Then is it Sir Launcelot, said Tristram. Nay, said Sir Persides, it is Sir Palomides, that is yet unchristened.

CHAPTER XXVIII

How Sir Tristram had a fall with Sir Palomides, and how
Launcelot overthrew two knights.

Then they saw much people of the country salute Sir Palomides. And within a while after there came a squire of the castle, that told Sir Pellounes that was lord of that castle, that a knight with a black shield had smitten down thirteen knights. Fair brother, said Sir Tristram unto Sir Persides, let us cast upon us cloaks, and let us go see the play. Not so, said Sir Persides, we will not go like knaves thither, but we will ride like men and good knights to withstand our enemies. So they armed them, and took their horses and great spears, and thither they went thereas many knights assayed themself before the tourna-ment. And anon Sir Palomides saw Sir Persides, and then he sent a squire unto him and said: Go thou to the yonder knight with the green shield and therein a lion of gold, and say him I require him to joust with me, and tell him that my name is Sir Palomides. When Sir Persides understood that request of Sir Palomides, he made him ready, and there anon they met together, but Sir Persides had a fall. Then Sir Tristram dressed him to be revenged upon Sir Palomides, and that saw Sir Palomides that was ready and so was not Sir Tristram, and took him at an advantage and smote him over his horse's tail when he had no spear in his rest. Then stert up Sir Tristram and took his horse lightly, and was wroth out of measure, and sore ashamed of that fall. Then Sir Tristram sent unto Sir Palomides by Gouvernail, and prayed him to joust with him at his request. Nay, said Sir Palomides, as at this time I will not joust with that knight, for I know him better than he weeneth. And if he be wroth he may right it to-morn at the Castle of Maidens, where he may see me and many other knights.

With that came Sir Dinadan, and when he saw Sir Tristram wroth he list not to jape. Lo, said Sir Dinadan, here may a man prove, be a man never so good yet may he have a fall, and he was never so wise but he might be overseen, and he rideth well that never fell. So Sir Tristram was passing wroth, and said to Sir Persides and to Sir

Dinadan: I will revenge me. Right so as they stood talking there, there came by Sir Tristram a likely knight riding passing soberly and heavily with a black shield. What knight is that? said Sir Tristram unto Sir Persides. I know him well, said Sir Persides, for his name is Sir Briant of North Wales; so he passed on among other knights of North Wales. And there came in Sir Launcelot du Lake with a shield of the arms of Cornwall, and he sent a squire unto Sir Briant, and required him to joust with him. Well, said Sir Briant, sithen I am required to joust I will do what I may; and there Sir Launcelot smote down Sir Briant from his horse a great fall. And then Sir Tristram marvelled what knight he was that bare the shield of Cornwall. Whatsoever he be, said Sir Dinadan, I warrant you he is of King Ban's blood, the which be knights of the most noble prowess in the world, for to account so many for so many. Then there came two knights of Northgalis, that one hight Hew de la Montaine, and the other Sir Madok de la Montaine, and they challenged Sir Launcelot foot-hot. Sir Launcelot not refusing them but made him ready, with one spear he smote them down both over their horses' croups; and so Sir Launcelot rode his way. By the good lord, said Sir Tristram, he is a good knight that beareth the shield of Cornwall, and meseemeth he rideth in the best manner that ever I saw knight ride.

Then the King of Northgalis rode unto Sir Palomides and prayed him heartily for his sake to joust with that knight that hath done us of Northgalis despite. Sir, said Sir Palomides, I am full loath to have ado with that knight, and cause why is, for as to-morn the great tournament shall be; and therefore I will keep myself fresh by my will. Nay, said the King of Northgalis, I pray you require him of jousts. Sir, said Sir Palomides, I will joust at your request, and require that knight to joust with me, and often I have seen a man have a fall at his own request.

CHAPTER XXIX

*How Sir Launcelot jousted with Palomides and overthrew
him, and after he was assailed with twelve knights.*

Then Sir Palomides sent unto Sir Launcelot a squire, and required
him of jousts. Fair fellow, said Sir Launcelot, tell me thy lord's name.
Sir, said the squire, my lord's name is Sir Palomides, the good knight.
In good hour, said Sir Launcelot, for there is no knight that I saw this
seven years that I had liefer ado withal than with him. And so either
knights made them ready with two great spears. Nay, said Sir
Dinadan, ye shall see that Sir Palomides will quit him right well. It
may be so, said Sir Tristram, but I undertake that knight with the
shield of Cornwall shall give him a fall. I believe it not, said Sir
Dinadan. Right so they spurred their horses and feutred their spears,
and either hit other, and Sir Palomides brake a spear upon Sir
Launcelot, and he sat and moved not; but Sir Launcelot smote him so
lightly that he made his horse to avoid the saddle, and the stroke
brake his shield and the hauberk, and had he not fallen he had been
slain. How now, said Sir Tristram, I wist well by the manner of their
riding both that Sir Palomides should have a fall.

Right so Sir Launcelot rode his way, and rode to a well to drink
and to repose him, and they of Northgalis espied him whither he
rode; and then there followed him twelve knights for to have
mischieved him, for this cause that upon the morn at the tournament
of the Castle of Maidens that he should not win the victory. So they
came upon Sir Launcelot suddenly, and unnethe he might put upon
him his helm and take his horse, but they were in hands with him;
and then Sir Launcelot gat his spear, and rode through them, and
there he slew a knight and brake a spear in his body. Then he drew
his sword and smote upon the right hand and upon the left hand, so
that within a few strokes he had slain other three knights, and the
remnant that abode he wounded them sore all that did abide. Thus
Sir Launcelot escaped from his enemies of North Wales, and then Sir
Launcelot rode his way till a friend, and lodged him till on the morn;
for he would not the first day have ado in the tournament because of

his great labour. And on the first day he was with King Arthur thereas
he was set on high upon a scaffold to discern who was best worthy of
his deeds. So Sir Launcelot was with King Arthur, and jousted not
the first day.

CHAPTER XXX

How Sir Tristram behaved him the first day of the tournament, and there he had the prize.

Now turn we unto Sir Tristram de Liones, that commanded
Gouvernail, his servant, to ordain him a black shield with none other
remembrance therein. And so Sir Persides and Sir Tristram departed
from their host Sir Pellounes, and they rode early toward the
tournament, and then they drew them to King Carados' side, of
Scotland; and anon knights began the field what of King Northgalis'
part, and what of King Carados' part, and there began great party.
Then there was hurling and rashing. Right so came in Sir Persides
and Sir Tristram, and so they did fare that they put the King of
Northgalis aback. Then came in Sir Bleoberis de Ganis and Sir
Gaheris with them of Northgalis, and then was Sir Persides smitten
down and almost slain, for more than forty horsemen went over him.
For Sir Bleoberis did great deeds of arms, and Sir Gaheris failed him
not. When Sir Tristram beheld them, and saw them do such deeds of
arms, he marvelled what they were. Also Sir Tristram thought shame
that Sir Persides was so done to; and then he gat a great spear in his
hand, and then he rode to Sir Gaheris and smote him down from his
horse. And then was Sir Bleoberis wroth, and gat a spear and rode
against Sir Tristram in great ire; and there Sir Tristram met with him,
and smote Sir Bleoberis from his horse. So then the King with the
Hundred Knights was wroth, and he horsed Sir Bleoberis and Sir
Gaheris again, and there began a great medley; and ever Sir Tristram
held them passing short, and ever Sir Bleoberis was passing busy upon
Sir Tristram; and there came Sir Dinadan against Sir Tristram, and Sir
Tristram gave him such a buffet that he swooned in his saddle. Then
anon Sir Dinadan came to Sir Tristram and said: Sir, I know thee
better than thou weenest; but here I promise thee my troth I will

never come against thee more, for I promise thee that sword of thine shall never come on mine helm.

With that came Sir Bleoberis, and Sir Tristram gave him such a buffet that down he laid his head; and then he caught him so sore by the helm that he pulled him under his horse's feet. And then King Arthur blew to lodging. Then Sir Tristram departed to his pavilion, and Sir Dinadan rode with him; and Sir Persides and King Arthur then, and the kings upon both parties, marvelled what knight that was with the black shield. Many said their advice, and some knew him for Sir Tristram, and held their peace and would nought say. So that first day King Arthur, and all the kings and lords that were judges, gave Sir Tristram the prize; howbeit they knew him not, but named him the Knight with the Black Shield.

CHAPTER XXXI

How Sir Tristram returned against King Arthur's party because he saw Sir Palomides on that party.

Then upon the morn Sir Palomides returned from the King of Northgalis, and rode to King Arthur's side, where was King Carados, and the King of Ireland, and Sir Launcelot's kin, and Sir Gawaine's kin. So Sir Palomides sent the damosel unto Sir Tristram that he sent to seek him when he was out of his mind in the forest, and this damosel asked Sir Tristram what he was and what was his name? As for that, said Sir Tristram, tell Sir Palomides ye shall not wit as at this time unto the time I have broken two spears upon him. But let him wit thus much, said Sir Tristram, that I am the same knight that he smote down in over-evening* at the tournament; and tell him plainly on what party that Sir Palomides be I will be of the contrary party. Sir, said the damosel, ye shall understand that Sir Palomides will be on King Arthur's side, where the most noble knights of the world be. In the name of God, said Sir Tristram, then will I be with the King of Northgalis, because Sir Palomides will be on King Arthur's side, and else I would not but for his sake. So when King Arthur was come

* 'the evening afore'. Wynkyn de Worde.

they blew unto the field; and then there began a great party, and so King Carados jousted with the King of the Hundred Knights, and there King Carados had a fall: then was there hurling and rushing, and right so came in knights of King Arthur's, and they bare aback the King of Northgalis' knights.

Then Sir Tristram came in, and began so roughly and so bigly that there was none might withstand him, and thus Sir Tristram dured long. And at the last Sir Tristram fell among the fellowship of King Ban, and there fell upon him Sir Bors de Ganis, and Sir Ector de Maris, and Sir Blamore de Ganis, and many other knights. And then Sir Tristram smote on the right hand and on the left hand, that all lords and ladies spake of his noble deeds. But at the last Sir Tristram should have had the worse had not the King with the Hundred Knights been. And then he came with his fellowship and rescued Sir Tristram, and brought him away from those knights that bare the shields of Cornwall. And then Sir Tristram saw another fellowship by themself, and there were a forty knights together, and Sir Kay, the Seneschal, was their governor. Then Sir Tristram rode in amongst them, and there he smote down Sir Kay from his horse; and there he fared among those knights like a greyhound among conies.

Then Sir Launcelot found a knight that was sore wounded upon the head. Sir, said Sir Launcelot, who wounded you so sore? Sir, he said, a knight that beareth a black shield, and I may curse the time that ever I met with him, for he is a devil and no man. So Sir Launcelot departed from him and thought to meet with Sir Tristram, and so he rode with his sword drawn in his hand to seek Sir Tristram; and then he espied him how he hurled here and there, and at every stroke Sir Tristram wellnigh smote down a knight. O mercy Jesu! said the king, sith the times I bare arms saw I never no knight do so marvellous deeds of arms. And if I should set upon this knight, said Sir Launcelot to himself, I did shame to myself, and therewithal Sir Launcelot put up his sword. And then the King with the Hundred Knights and an hundred more of North Wales set upon the twenty of Sir Launcelot's kin: and they twenty knights held them ever together as wild swine, and none would fail other. And so when Sir Tristram beheld the noblesse of these twenty knights he marvelled of their good deeds, for he saw by their fare and by their rule that they had liefer die than avoid the field. Now Jesu, said Sir Tristram, well may he be valiant and full of prowess that hath such a sort of noble knights unto his kin, and full like is he to be a noble man that is their leader and governor. He meant by it Sir Launcelot du Lake. So when Sir Tristram had beholden them long he thought shame to see two hundred knights battering upon twenty knights. Then Sir Tristram rode unto the King with the Hundred Knights and said: Sir, leave your fighting with those twenty knights, for ye win no worship of them, ye be so many and they so few; and wit ye well they will not out of the field I see by their cheer and countenance; and worship get ye none an ye slay them. Therefore leave your fighting with them, for I to increase my worship I will ride to the twenty knights and help them with all my might and power. Nay, said the King with the Hundred Knights, ye shall not do so; now I see your courage and courtesy I will withdraw my knights for your pleasure, for evermore a good knight will favour another, and like will draw to like.

CHAPTER XXXII

How Sir Tristram found Palomides by a well, and brought him with him to his lodging.

Then the King with the Hundred Knights withdrew his knights. And all this while, and long to-fore, Sir Launcelot had watched upon Sir Tristram with a very purpose to have fellowshipped with him. And then suddenly Sir Tristram, Sir Dinadan, and Gouvernail, his man, rode their way into the forest, that no man perceived where they went. So then King Arthur blew unto lodging, and gave the King of Northgalis the prize because Sir Tristram was upon his side. Then Sir Launcelot rode here and there, so wood as lion that fauted his fill, because he had lost Sir Tristram, and so he returned unto King Arthur. And then in all the field was a noise that with the wind it might be heard two mile thence, how the lords and ladies cried: The Knight with the Black Shield hath won the field. Alas, said King Arthur, where is that knight become? It is shame to all those in the field so to let him escape away from you; but with gentleness and courtesy ye might have brought him unto me to the Castle of Maidens. Then the noble King Arthur went unto his knights and comforted them in the best wise that he could, and said: My fair fellows, be not dismayed, howbeit ye have lost the field this day. And many were hurt and sore wounded, and many were whole. My fellows, said King Arthur, look that ye be of good cheer, for to-morn I will be in the field with you and revenge you of your enemies. So that night King Arthur and his knights reposed themself.

The damosel that came from La Beale Isoud unto Sir Tristram, all the while the tournament was a-doing she was with Queen Guenever, and ever the queen asked her for what cause she came into that country. Madam, she answered, I come for none other cause but from my lady La Beale Isoud to wit of your welfare. For in no wise she would not tell the queen that she came for Sir Tristram's sake. So this lady, Dame Bragwaine, took her leave of Queen Guenever, and she rode after Sir Tristram. And as she rode through the forest she heard a great cry; then she commanded her squire to go into the forest to wit what was that noise. And so he came to a well, and there he found a knight bounden till a tree crying as he had been wood, and his horse and his harness standing by him. And when he espied that squire, therewith he abraid and brake himself loose, and took his sword in his hand, and ran to have slain the squire. Then he took his horse and fled all that ever he might unto Dame Bragwaine, and told her of his adventure. Then she rode unto Sir Tristram's pavilion, and told Sir Tristram what adventure she had found in the forest. Alas, said Sir Tristram, upon my head there is some good knight at mischief.

Then Sir Tristram took his horse and his sword and rode thither, and there he heard how the knight complained unto himself and said: I, woful knight Sir Palomides, what misadventure befalleth me, that thus am defoiled with falsehood and treason, through Sir Bors and Sir Ector. Alas, he said, why live I so long! And then he gat his sword in his hands, and made many strange signs and tokens; and so through his raging he threw his sword into that fountain. Then Sir Palomides wailed and wrang his hands. And at the last for pure sorrow he ran into that fountain, over his belly, and sought after his sword. Then Sir Tristram saw that, and ran upon Sir Palomides, and held him in his arms fast. What art thou, said Palomides, that holdeth me so? I am a man of this forest that would thee none harm. Alas, said Sir Palomides, I may never win worship where Sir Tristram is; for ever where he is an I be there, then get I no worship; and if he be away for the most part I have the gree, unless that Sir Launcelot be there or Sir

Lamorak. Then Sir Palomides said: Once in Ireland Sir Tristram put me to the worse, and another time in Cornwall, and in other places in this land. What would ye do, said Sir Tristram, an ye had Sir Tristram? I would fight with him, said Sir Palomides, and ease my heart upon him; and yet, to say thee sooth, Sir Tristram is the gentlest knight in this world living. What will ye do, said Sir Tristram, will ye go with me to your lodging? Nay, said he, I will go to the King with the Hundred Knights, for he rescued me from Sir Bors de Ganis and Sir Ector, and else had I been slain traitorly. Sir Tristram said him such kind words that Sir Palomides went with him to his lodging. Then Gouvernail went to-fore, and charged Dame Bragwaine to go out of the way to her lodging. And bid ye Sir Persides that he make him no quarrels. And so they rode together till they came to Sir Tristram's pavilion, and there Sir Palomides had all the cheer that might be had all that night. But in no wise Sir Palomides might not know what was Sir Tristram; and so after supper they yede to rest, and Sir Tristram for great travail slept till it was day. And Sir Palomides might not sleep for anguish; and in the dawning of the day he took his horse privily, and rode his way unto Sir Gaheris and unto Sir Sagramore le Desirous, where they were in their pavilions; for they three were fellows at the beginning of the tournament. And then upon the morn the king blew unto the tournament upon the third day.

CHAPTER XXXIII

How Sir Tristram smote down Sir Palomides, and how he jousted with King Arthur, and other feats.

So the King of Northgalis and the King with the Hundred Knights, they two encountered with King Carados and with the King of Ireland; and there the King with the Hundred Knights smote down King Carados, and the King of Northgalis smote down the King of Ireland. With that came in Sir Palomides, and when he came he made great work, for by his indented shield he was well known. So came in King Arthur, and did great deeds of arms together, and put the King of Northgalis and the King with the Hundred Knights to the worse.

With this came in Sir Tristram with his black shield, and anon he jousted with Sir Palomides, and there by fine force Sir Tristram smote Sir Palomides over his horse's croup. Then King Arthur cried: Knight with the Black Shield, make thee ready to me, and in the same wise Sir Tristram smote King Arthur. And then by force of King Arthur's knights the King and Sir Palomides were horsed again. Then King Arthur with a great eager heart he gat a spear in his hand, and there upon the one side he smote Sir Tristram over his horse. Then foot-hot Sir Palomides came upon Sir Tristram, as he was upon foot, to have overridden him. Then Sir Tristram was ware of him, and there he stooped aside, and with great ire he gat him by the arm, and pulled him down from his horse. Then Sir Palomides lightly arose, and then they dashed together mightily with their swords; and many kings, queens, and lords, stood and beheld them. And at the last Sir Tristram smote Sir Palomides upon the helm three mighty strokes, and at every stroke that he gave him he said: This for Sir Tristram's sake. With that Sir Palomides fell to the earth grovelling.

Then came the King with the Hundred Knights, and brought Sir Tristram an horse, and so was he horsed again. By then was Sir Palomides horsed, and with great ire he jousted upon Sir Tristram with his spear as it was in the rest, and gave him a great dash with his sword. Then Sir Tristram avoided his spear, and gat him by the neck with his both hands, and pulled him clean out of his saddle, and so he bare him afore him the length of ten spears, and then in the presence of them all he let him fall at his adventure. Then Sir Tristram was ware of King Arthur with a naked sword in his hand, and with his spear Sir Tristram ran upon King Arthur; and then King Arthur boldly abode him and with his sword he smote a-two his spear, and therewithal Sir Tristram stonied; and so King Arthur gave him three or four strokes or he might get out his sword, and at the last Sir Tristram drew his sword and [either] assailed other passing hard. With that the great press departed [them]. Then Sir Tristram rode here and there and did his great pain, that eleven of the good knights of the blood of King Ban, that was of Sir Launcelot's kin, that day Sir Tristram smote down; that all the estates marvelled of his great deeds and all cried upon the Knight with the Black Shield.

CHAPTER XXXIV

*How Sir Launcelot hurt Sir Tristram, and how after Sir
Tristram smote down Sir Palomides.*

Then this cry was so large that Sir Launcelot heard it. And then he gat
a great spear in his hand and came towards the cry. Then Sir
Launcelot cried: The Knight with the Black Shield, make thee ready
to joust with me. When Sir Tristram heard him say so he gat his spear
in his hand, and either abashed down their heads, and came together
as thunder; and Sir Tristram's spear brake in pieces, and Sir Launcelot
by malfortune struck Sir Tristram on the side a deep wound nigh to
the death; but yet Sir Tristram avoided not his saddle, and so the spear
brake. Therewithal Sir Tristram that was wounded gat out his sword,
and he rushed to Sir Launcelot, and gave him three great strokes
upon the helm that the fire sprang thereout, and Sir Launcelot
abashed his head lowly toward his saddle-bow. And therewithal Sir
Tristram departed from the field, for he felt him so wounded that he
weened he should have died; and Sir Dinadan espied him and
followed him into the forest. Then Sir Launcelot abode and did many
marvellous deeds.

So when Sir Tristram was departed by the forest's side he alighted,
and unlaced his harness and freshed his wound; then weened Sir
Dinadan that he should have died. Nay, nay, said Sir Tristram,
Dinadan never dread thee, for I am heart-whole, and of this wound I
shall soon be whole, by the mercy of God. By that Sir Dinadan was
ware where came Palomides riding straight upon them. And then Sir
Tristram was ware that Sir Palomides came to have destroyed him.
And so Sir Dinadan gave him warning, and said: Sir Tristram, my
lord, ye are so sore wounded that ye may not have ado with him,
therefore I will ride against him and do to him what I may, and if I be
slain ye may pray for my soul; and in the meanwhile ye may
withdraw you and go into the castle, or in the forest, that he shall not
meet with you. Sir Tristram smiled and said: I thank you, Sir
Dinadan, of your good will, but ye shall wit that I am able to handle
him. And then anon hastily he armed him, and took his horse, and a

great spear in his hand, and said to Sir Dinadan: Adieu; and rode toward Sir Palomides a soft pace. Then when Sir Palomides saw that, he made countenance to amend his horse, but he did it for this cause, for he abode Sir Gaheris that came after him. And when he was come he rode toward Sir Tristram. Then Sir Tristram sent unto Sir Palomides, and required him to joust with him; and if he smote down Sir Palomides he would do no more to him; and if it so happened that Sir Palomides smote down Sir Tristram, he bade him do his utterance. So they were accorded. Then they met together, and Sir Tristram smote down Sir Palomides that he had a grievous fall, so that he lay still as he had been dead. And then Sir Tristram ran upon Sir Gaheris, and he would not have jousted; but whether he would or not Sir Tristram smote him over his horse's croup, that he lay still as though he had been dead. And then Sir Tristram rode his way and left Sir Persides' squire within the pavilions, and Sir Tristram and Sir Dinadan rode to an old knight's place to lodge them. And that old knight had five sons at the tournament, for whom he prayed God heartily for their coming home. And so, as the French book saith, they came home all five well beaten.

And when Sir Tristram departed into the forest Sir Launcelot held alway the stour like hard, as a man araged that took no heed to himself, and wit ye well there was many a noble knight against him. And when King Arthur saw Sir Launcelot do so marvellous deeds of arms he then armed him, and took his horse and his armour, and rode into the field to help Sir Launcelot; and so many knights came in with King Arthur. And to make short tale in conclusion, the King of Northgalis and the King of the Hundred Knights were put to the worse; and because Sir Launcelot abode and was the last in the field the prize was given him. But Sir Launcelot would neither for king, queen, nor knight, have the prize, but where the cry was cried through the field: Sir Launcelot, Sir Launcelot hath won the field this day, Sir Launcelot let make another cry contrary: Sir Tristram hath won the field, for he began first, and last he hath endured, and so hath he done the first day, the second, and the third day.

CHAPTER XXXV

*How the prize of the third day was given to Sir Launcelot,
and Sir Launcelot gave it to Sir Tristram.*

Then all the estates and degrees high and low said of Sir Launcelot
great worship, for the honour that he did unto Sir Tristram; and for
that honour doing to Sir Tristram he was at that time more praised
and renowned than an he had overthrown five hundred knights; and
all the people wholly for this gentleness, first the estates both high and
low, and after the commonalty cried at once: Sir Launcelot hath won
the field whosoever say nay. Then was Sir Launcelot wroth and
ashamed, and so therewithal he rode to King Arthur. Alas, said the
king, we are all dismayed that Sir Tristram is thus departed from us.
By God, said King Arthur, he is one of the noblest knights that ever I
saw hold spear or sword in hand, and the most courteoust knight in
his fighting; for full hard I saw him, said King Arthur, when he smote
Sir Palomides upon the helm thrice, that he abashed his helm with his
strokes, and also he said: Here is a stroke for Sir Tristram, and thus
thrice he said. Then King Arthur, Sir Launcelot, and Sir Dodinas le
Savage took their horses to seek Sir Tristram, and by the means of Sir
Persides he had told King Arthur where Sir Tristram was in his
pavilion. But when they came there, Sir Tristram and Sir Dinadan
were gone.

Then King Arthur and Sir Launcelot were heavy, and returned
again to the Castle of Maidens making great dole for the hurt of Sir
Tristram, and his sudden departing. So God me help, said King
Arthur, I am more heavy that I cannot meet with him than for all the
hurts that all my knights have had at the tournament. Right so came
Sir Gaheris and told King Arthur how Sir Tristram had smitten down
Sir Palomides, and it was at Sir Palomides' own request. Alas, said
King Arthur, that was great dishonour to Sir Palomides, inasmuch as
Sir Tristram was sore wounded, and now may we all, kings, and
knights, and men of worship, say that Sir Tristram may be called a
noble knight, and one of the best knights that ever I saw the days of
my life. For I will that ye all, kings and knights, know, said King

Arthur, that I never saw knight do so marvellously as he hath done these three days; for he was the first that began and that longest held on, save this last day. And though he was hurt, it was a manly adventure of two noble knights, and when two noble men encounter needs must the one have the worse, like as God will suffer at that time. As for me, said Sir Launcelot, for all the lands that ever my father left me I would not have hurt Sir Tristram an I had known him at that time; that I hurt him was for I saw not his shield. For an I had seen his black shield, I would not have meddled with him for many causes; for late he did as much for me as ever did knight, and that is well known that he had ado with thirty knights, and no help save Sir Dinadan. And one thing shall I promise, said Sir Launcelot, Sir Palomides shall repent it as in his unkindly dealing for to follow that noble knight that I by mishap hurted thus. Sir Launcelot said all the worship that might be said by Sir Tristram. Then King Arthur made a great feast to all that would come. And thus we let pass King Arthur, and a little we will turn unto Sir Palomides, that after he had a fall of Sir Tristram, he was nigh-hand araged out of his wit for despite of Sir Tristram. And so he followed him by adventure. And as he came by a river, in his woodness he would have made his horse to have leapt over; and the horse failed footing and fell in the river, wherefore Sir Palomides was adread lest he should have been drowned; and then he avoided his horse, and swam to the land, and let his horse go down by adventure.

CHAPTER XXXVI

How Palomides came to the castle where Sir Tristram was, and of the quest that Sir Launcelot and ten knights made for Sir Tristram.

And when he came to the land he took off his harness, and sat roaring and crying as a man out of his mind. Right so came a damosel even by Sir Palomides, that was sent from Sir Gawaine and his brother unto Sir Mordred, that lay sick in the same place with that old knight where Sir Tristram was. For, as the French book saith, Sir Persides hurt so Sir Mordred a ten days afore; and had it not been for the love of Sir Gawaine and his brother, Sir Persides had slain Sir Mordred.

And so this damosel came by Sir Palomides, and she and he had language together, the which pleased neither of them; and so the damosel rode her ways till she came to the old knight's place, and there she told that old knight how she met with the woodest knight by adventure that ever she met withal. What bare he in his shield? said Sir Tristram. It was indented with white and black, said the damosel. Ah, said Sir Tristram, that was Sir Palomides, the good knight. For well I know him, said Sir Tristram, for one of the best knights living in this realm. Then that old knight took a little hackney, and rode for Sir Palomides, and brought him unto his own manor; and full well knew Sir Tristram Sir Palomides, but he said but little, for at that time Sir Tristram was walking upon his feet, and well amended of his hurts; and always when Sir Palomides saw Sir Tristram he would behold him full marvellously, and ever him seemed that he had seen him. Then would he say unto Sir Dinadan: An ever I may meet with Sir Tristram he shall not escape mine hands. I marvel, said Sir Dinadan, that ye boast behind Sir Tristram, for it is but late that he was in your hands, and ye in his hands; why would ye not hold him when ye had him? for I saw myself twice or thrice that ye gat but little worship of Sir Tristram. Then was Sir Palomides ashamed. So leave we them a little while in the old castle with the old knight Sir Darras.

Now shall we speak of King Arthur, that said to Sir Launcelot: Had not ye been we had not lost Sir Tristram, for he was here daily unto the time ye met with him, and in an evil time, said Arthur, ye encountered with him. My lord Arthur, said Launcelot, ye put upon me that I should be cause of his departition; God knoweth it was against my will. But when men be hot in deeds of arms oft they hurt their friends as well as their foes. And my lord, said Sir Launcelot, ye shall understand that Sir Tristram is a man that I am loath to offend, for he hath done for me more than ever I did for him as yet. But then Sir Launcelot made bring forth a book: and then Sir Launcelot said: Here we are ten knights that will swear upon a book never to rest one night where we rest another this twelvemonth until that we find Sir Tristram. And as for me, said Sir Launcelot, I promise you upon this book that an I may meet with him, either with fairness or foulness I shall bring him to this court, or else I shall die therefore. And the names of these ten knights that had undertaken this quest were these following: First was Sir Launcelot, Sir Ector de Maris, Sir

Bors de Ganis, and Bleoberis, and Sir Blamore de Ganis, and Lucan the Butler, Sir Uwaine, Sir Galihud, Lionel, and Galiodin. So these ten noble knights departed from the court of King Arthur, and so they rode upon their quest together until they came to a cross where departed four ways, and there departed the fellowship in four to seek Sir Tristram.

And as Sir Launcelot rode by adventure he met with Dame Bragwaine that was sent into that country to seek Sir Tristram, and she fled as fast as her palfrey might go. So Sir Launcelot met with her and asked her why she fled. Ah, fair knight, said Dame Bragwaine, I flee for dread of my life, for here followeth me Sir Breuse Saunce Pité to slay me. Hold you nigh me, said Sir Launcelot. Then when Sir Launcelot saw Sir Breuse Saunce Pité, Sir Launcelot cried unto him, and said: False knight, destroyer of ladies and damosels, now thy last days be come. When Sir Breuse Saunce Pité saw Sir Launcelot's shield he knew it well, for at that time he bare not the arms of Cornwall, but he bare his own shield. And then Sir Breuse fled, and Sir Launcelot followed after him. But Sir Breuse was so well horsed that when him list to flee he might well flee, and also abide when him list. And then Sir Launcelot returned unto Dame Bragwaine, and she thanked him of his great labour.

CHAPTER XXXVII

How Sir Tristram, Sir Palomides, and Sir Dinadan were taken and put in prison.

Now will we speak of Sir Lucan the butler, that by fortune he came riding to the same place thereas was Sir Tristram, and in he came in none other intent but to ask harbour. Then the porter asked what was his name. Tell your lord that my name is Sir Lucan, the butler, a Knight of the Round Table. So the porter went unto Sir Darras, lord of the place, and told him who was there to ask harbour. Nay, nay, said Sir Daname, that was nephew to Sir Darras, say him that he shall not be lodged here, but let him wit that I, Sir Daname, will meet with him anon, and bid him make him ready. So Sir Daname came forth on horseback, and there they met together with spears, and Sir

Lucan smote down Sir Daname over his horse's croup, and then he fled into that place, and Sir Lucan rode after him, and asked after him many times.

Then Sir Dinadan said to Sir Tristram: It is shame to see the lord's cousin of this place defoiled. Abide, said Sir Tristram, and I shall redress it. And in the meanwhile Sir Dinadan was on horseback, and he jousted with Lucan the butler, and there Sir Lucan smote Dinadan through the thick of the thigh, and so he rode his way; and Sir Tristram was wroth that Sir Dinadan was hurt, and followed after, and thought to avenge him; and within a while he overtook Sir Lucan, and bade him turn; and so they met together so that Sir Tristram hurt Sir Lucan passing sore and gave him a fall. With that came Sir Uwaine, a gentle knight, and when he saw Sir Lucan so hurt he called Sir Tristram to joust with him. Fair knight, said Sir Tristram, tell me your name I require you. Sir knight, wit ye well my name is Sir Uwaine le Fise de Roy Ureine. Ah, said Sir Tristram, by my will I would not have ado with you at no time. Ye shall not so, said Sir Uwaine, but ye shall have ado with me. And then Sir Tristram saw none other bote, but rode against him, and overthrew Sir Uwaine and hurt him in the side, and so he departed unto his lodging again. And when Sir Dinadan understood that Sir Tristram had hurt Sir Lucan he would have ridden after Sir Lucan for to have slain him, but Sir Tristram would not suffer him. Then Sir Uwaine let ordain an horse litter, and brought Sir Lucan to the abbey of Ganis, and the castle thereby hight the Castle of Ganis, of the which Sir Bleoberis was lord. And at that castle Sir Launcelot promised all his fellows to meet in the quest of Sir Tristram.

So when Sir Tristram was come to his lodging there came a damosel that told Sir Darras that three of his sons were slain at that tournament, and two grievously wounded that they were never like to help themself. And all this was done by a noble knight that bare the black shield, and that was he that bare the prize. Then came there one and told Sir Darras that the same knight was within, him that bare the black shield. Then Sir Darras yede unto Sir Tristram's chamber, and there he found his shield and showed it to the damosel. Ah sir, said the damosel, that same is he that slew your three sons. Then without any tarrying Sir Darras put Sir Tristram, and Sir Palomides, and Sir Dinadan, within a strong prison, and there Sir Tristram was like to have died of great sickness; and every day Sir Palomides would reprove Sir Tristram of old hate betwixt them. And ever Sir Tristram spake fair and said little. But when Sir Palomides saw the falling of sickness of Sir Tristram, then was he heavy for him, and comforted him in all the best wise he could. And as the French book saith, there came forty knights to Sir Darras that were of his own kin, and they would have slain Sir Tristram and his two fellows, but Sir Darras would not suffer that, but kept them in prison, and meat and drink they had. So Sir Tristram endured there great pain, for sickness had undertaken him, and that is the greatest pain a prisoner may have. For all the while a prisoner may have his health of body he may endure under the mercy of God and in hope of good deliverance; but when sickness toucheth a prisoner's body, then may a prisoner say all wealth is him bereft, and then he hath cause to wail and to weep. Right so did Sir Tristram when sickness had undertaken him, for then he took such sorrow that he had almost slain himself.

CHAPTER XXXVIII

*How King Mark was sorry for the good renown of
Sir Tristram. Some of King Arthur's knights
jousted with knights of Cornwall.*

Now will we speak, and leave Sir Tristram, Sir Palomides, and Sir Dinadan in prison, and speak we of other knights that sought after Sir Tristram many divers parts of this land. And some yede into Cornwall; and by adventure Sir Gaheris, nephew unto King Arthur, came unto King Mark, and there he was well received and sat at King Mark's own table and ate of his own mess. Then King Mark asked Sir Gaheris what tidings there were in the realm of Logris. Sir, said Sir Gaheris, the king reigneth as a noble knight; and now but late there was a great jousts and tournament as ever I saw any in the realm of Logris, and the most noble knights were at that jousts. But there was one knight that did marvellously three days, and he bare a black shield, and of all knights that ever I saw he proved the best knight. Then, said King Mark, that was Sir Launcelot, or Sir Palomides the paynim. Not so, said Sir Gaheris, for both Sir Launcelot and Sir Palomides were on the contrary party against the Knight with the

Black Shield. Then was it Sir Tristram, said the king. Yea, said Sir Gaheris. And therewithal the king smote down his head, and in his heart he feared sore that Sir Tristram should get him such worship in the realm of Logris wherethrough that he himself should not be able to withstand him. Thus Sir Gaheris had great cheer with King Mark, and with Queen La Beale Isoud, the which was glad of Sir Gaheris' words; for well she wist by his deeds and manners that it was Sir Tristram. And then the king made a feast royal, and to that feast came Sir Uwaine le Fise de Roy Ureine, and some called him Uwaine le Blanchemains. And this Sir Uwaine challenged all the knights of Cornwall. Then was the king wood wroth that he had no knights to answer him. Then Sir Andred, nephew unto King Mark, leapt up and said: I will encounter with Sir Uwaine. Then he yede and armed him and horsed him in the best manner. And there Sir Uwaine met with Sir Andred, and smote him down that he swooned on the earth. Then was King Mark sorry and wroth out of measure that he had no knight to revenge his nephew, Sir Andred.

So the king called unto him Sir Dinas, the Seneschal, and prayed him for his sake to take upon him to joust with Sir Uwaine. Sir, said Sir Dinas, I am full loath to have ado with any knight of the Round Table. Yet, said the king, for my love take upon thee to joust. So Sir Dinas made him ready, and anon they encountered together with great spears, but Sir Dinas was overthrown, horse and man, a great fall. Who was wroth but King Mark! Alas, he said, have I no knight that will encounter with yonder knight? Sir, said Sir Gaheris, for your sake I will joust. So Sir Gaheris made him ready, and when he was armed he rode into the field. And when Sir Uwaine saw Sir Gaheris' shield he rode to him and said: Sir, ye do not your part. For, sir, the first time ye were made Knight of the Round Table ye sware that ye should not have ado with your fellowship wittingly. And pardie, Sir Gaheris, ye knew me well enough by my shield, and so do I know you by your shield, and though ye would break your oath I would not break mine; for there is not one here, nor ye, that shall think I am afeard of you, but I durst right well have ado with you, and yet we be sisters' sons. Then was Sir Gaheris ashamed, and so therewithal every knight went their way, and Sir Uwaine rode into the country.

Then King Mark armed him, and took his horse and his spear, with a squire with him. And then he rode afore Sir Uwaine, and suddenly at a gap he ran upon him as he that was not ware of him, and there he

smote him almost through the body, and there left him. So within a
while there came Sir Kay and found Sir Uwaine, and asked him how
he was hurt. I wot not, said Sir Uwaine, why nor wherefore, but by
treason I am sure I gat this hurt; for here came a knight suddenly upon
me or that I was ware, and suddenly hurt me. Then there was come
Sir Andred to seek King Mark. Thou traitor knight, said Sir Kay, an I
wist it were thou that thus traitorly hast hurt this noble knight thou
shouldst never pass my hands. Sir, said Sir Andred, I did never hurt
him, and that I will report me to himself. Fie on you false knight, said
Sir Kay, for ye of Cornwall are nought worth. So Sir Kay made carry
Sir Uwaine to the Abbey of the Black Cross, and there he was healed.
And then Sir Gaheris took his leave of King Mark, but or he departed
he said: Sir king, ye did a foul shame unto you and your court, when
ye banished Sir Tristram out of this country, for ye needed not to have
doubted no knight an he had been here. And so he departed.

CHAPTER XXXIX

*Of the treason of King Mark, and how Sir Gaheris smote
him down and Andred his cousin.*

Then there came Sir Kay, the Seneschal, unto King Mark, and there
he had good cheer showing outward. Now, fair lords, said he, will ye
prove any adventure in the forest of Morris, in the which I know
well is as hard an adventure as I know any. Sir, said Sir Kay, I will
prove it. And Sir Gaheris said he would be avised, for King Mark was
ever full of treason: and therewithal Sir Gaheris departed and rode his
way. And by the same way that Sir Kay should ride he laid him down
to rest, charging his squire to wait upon Sir Kay; And warn me when
he cometh. So within a while Sir Kay came riding that way, and then
Sir Gaheris took his horse and met him, and said: Sir Kay, ye are not
wise to ride at the request of King Mark, for he dealeth all with
treason. Then said Sir Kay: I require you let us prove this adventure. I
shall not fail you, said Sir Gaheris. And so they rode that time till a
lake that was that time called the Perilous Lake, and there they abode
under the shaw of the wood.

The meanwhile King Mark within the castle of Tintagil avoided all his barons, and all other save such as were privy with him were avoided out of his chamber. And then he let call his nephew Sir Andred, and bade arm him and horse him lightly; and by that time it was midnight. And so King Mark was armed in black, horse and all; and so at a privy postern they two issued out with their varlets with them, and rode till they came to that lake. Then Sir Kay espied them first, and gat his spear, and proffered to joust. And King Mark rode against him, and smote each other full hard, for the moon shone as the bright day. And there at that jousts Sir Kay's horse fell down, for his horse was not so big as the king's horse, and Sir Kay's horse bruised him full sore. Then Sir Gaheris was wroth that Sir Kay had a fall. Then he cried: Knight, sit thou fast in thy saddle, for I will revenge my fellow. Then King Mark was afeard of Sir Gaheris, and so with evil will King Mark rode against him, and Sir Gaheris gave him such a stroke that he fell down. So then forthwithal Sir Gaheris ran unto Sir Andred and smote him from his horse quite, that his helm smote in the earth, and nigh had broken his neck. And therewithal Sir Gaheris alighted, and gat up Sir Kay. And then they yode both on foot to them, and bade them yield them, and tell their names outher they should die. Then with great pain Sir Andred spake first, and said: It is King Mark of Cornwall, therefore be ye ware what ye do, and I am Sir Andred, his cousin. Fie on you both, said Sir Gaheris, for a false traitor, and false treason hast thou wrought and he both, under the feigned cheer that ye made us! it were pity, said Sir Gaheris, that thou shouldst live any longer. Save my life, said King Mark, and I will make amends; and consider that I am a king anointed. It were the more shame, said Sir Gaheris, to save thy life; thou art a king anointed with cream, and therefore thou shouldst hold with all men of worship; and therefore thou art worthy to die. With that he lashed at King Mark without saying any more, and covered him with his shield and defended him as he might. And then Sir Kay lashed at Sir Andred, and therewithal King Mark yielded him unto Sir Gaheris. And then he kneeled adown, and made his oath upon the cross of the sword, that never while he lived he would be against errant-knights. And also he sware to be good friend unto Sir Tristram if ever he came into Cornwall.

By then Sir Andred was on the earth, and Sir Kay would have slain him. Let be, said Sir Gaheris, slay him not I pray you. It were pity, said Sir Kay, that he should live any longer, for this is nigh cousin unto Sir Tristram, and ever he hath been a traitor unto him, and by him he was exiled out of Cornwall, and therefore I will slay him, said Sir Kay. Ye shall not, said Sir Gaheris; sithen I have given the king his life, I pray you give him his life. And therewithal Sir Kay let him go. And so Sir Kay and Sir Gaheris rode their way unto Dinas, the Seneschal, for because they heard say that he loved well Sir Tristram. So they reposed them there, and soon after they rode unto the realm of Logris. And so within a little while they met with Sir Launcelot that always had Dame Bragwaine with him, to that intent he weened to have met the sooner with Sir Tristram; and Sir Launcelot asked what tidings in Cornwall, and whether they heard of Sir Tristram or not. Sir Kay and Sir Gaheris answered and said, that they heard not of him. Then they told Sir Launcelot word by word of their adventure. Then Sir Launcelot smiled and said: Hard it is to take out of the flesh that is bred in the bone; and so made them merry together.

CHAPTER XL

How after that Sir Tristram, Sir Palomides, and Sir Dinadan had been long in prison they were delivered.

Now leave we off this tale, and speak we of Sir Dinas that had within the castle a paramour, and she loved another knight better than him. And so when Sir Dinas went out a-hunting she slipped down by a towel, and took with her two brachets, and so she yede to the knight that she loved, and he her again. And when Sir Dinas came home and missed his paramour and his brachets, then was he the more wrother for his brachets than for the lady. So then he rode after the knight that had his paramour, and bade him turn and joust. So Sir Dinas smote him down, that with the fall he brake his leg and his arm. And then his lady and paramour cried Sir Dinas mercy, and said she would love him better than ever she did. Nay, said Sir Dinas, I shall never trust them that once betrayed me, and therefore, as ye have begun, so end, for I will never meddle with you. And so Sir Dinas departed, and took his brachets with him, and so rode to his castle.

Now will we turn unto Sir Launcelot, that was right heavy that he could never hear no tidings of Sir Tristram, for all this while he was in prison with Sir Darras, Palomides, and Dinadan. Then Dame Bragwaine took her leave to go into Cornwall, and Sir Launcelot, Sir Kay, and Sir Gaheris rode to seek Sir Tristram in the country of Surluse.

Now speaketh this tale of Sir Tristram and of his two fellows, for every day Sir Palomides brawled and said language against Sir Tristram. I marvel, said Sir Dinadan, of thee, Sir Palomides, an thou haddest Sir Tristram here thou wouldst do him no harm; for an a wolf and a sheep were together in a prison the wolf would suffer the sheep to be in peace. And wit thou well, said Sir Dinadan, this same is Sir Tristram at a word, and now must thou do thy best with him, and let see now if ye can skift it with your hands. Then was Sir Palomides abashed and said little. Sir Palomides, then said Sir Tristram, I have heard much of your maugre against me, but I will not meddle with you as at this time by my will, because I dread the lord of this place that hath us in governance; for an I dread him not more than I do thee, soon it should be skift: so they peaced themself. Right so came in a damosel and said: Knights, be of good cheer, for ye are sure of your lives, and that I heard say my lord, Sir Darras. Then were they glad all three, for daily they weened they should have died.

Then soon after this Sir Tristram fell sick that he weened to have died; then Sir Dinadan wept, and so did Sir Palomides under them both making great sorrow. So a damosel came in to them and found them mourning. Then she went unto Sir Darras, and told him how that mighty knight that bare the black shield was likely to die. That shall not be, said Sir Darras, for God defend when knights come to me for succour that I should suffer them to die within my prison. Therefore, said Sir Darras to the damosel, fetch that knight and his fellows afore me. And then anon Sir Darras saw Sir Tristram brought afore him. He said: Sir knight, me repenteth of thy sickness, for thou art called a full noble knight, and so it seemeth by thee; and wit ye well it shall never be said that Sir Darras shall destroy such a noble knight as thou art in prison, howbeit that thou hast slain three of my sons, whereby I was greatly aggrieved. But now shalt thou go and thy fellows, and your harness and horses have been fair and clean kept, and ye shall go where it liketh you, upon this covenant, that thou, knight, wilt promise me to be good friend to my sons two that be now alive, and also that thou tell me thy name. Sir, said he, as for me my name is Sir Tristram de Liones, and in Cornwall was I born, and nephew I am unto King Mark. And as for the death of your sons I might not do withal, for an they had been the next kin that I have I might have done none otherwise. And if I had slain them by treason or treachery I had been worthy to have died. All this I consider, said Sir Darras, that all that ye did was by force of knighthood, and that was the cause I would not put you to death. But sith ye be Sir Tristram, the good knight, I pray you heartily to be my good friend and to my sons. Sir, said Sir Tristram, I promise you by the faith of my body, ever while I live I will do you service, for ye have done to us but as a natural knight ought to do. Then Sir Tristram reposed him there till that he was amended of his sickness; and when he was big and strong they took their leave, and every knight took their horses, and so departed and rode together till they came to a cross way. Now fellows, said Sir Tristram, here will we depart in sundry ways. And because Sir Dinadan had the first adventure of him I will begin.

CHAPTER XLI

How Sir Dinadan rescued a lady from Sir Breuse Saunce Pité, and how Sir Tristram received a shield of Morgan le Fay.

So as Sir Dinadan rode by a well he found a lady making great dole. What aileth you? said Sir Dinadan. Sir knight, said the lady, I am the wofullest lady of the world, for within these five days here came a knight called Sir Breuse Saunce Pité, and he slew mine own brother, and ever since he hath kept me at his own will, and of all men in the world I hate him most; and therefore I require you of knighthood to avenge me, for he will not tarry, but be here anon. Let him come, said Sir Dinadan, and because of honour of all women I will do my part. With this came Sir Breuse, and when he saw a knight with his lady he was wood wroth. And then he said: Sir knight, keep thee from me. So they hurtled together as thunder, and either smote other passing sore, but Sir Dinadan put him through the shoulder a grievous wound, and or ever Sir Dinadan might turn him Sir Breuse was gone and fled. Then the lady prayed him to bring her to a castle there beside but four mile thence; and so Sir Dinadan brought her there, and she was welcome, for the lord of that castle was her uncle; and so Sir Dinadan rode his way upon his adventure.

Now turn we this tale unto Sir Tristram, that by adventure he came to a castle to ask lodging, wherein was Queen Morgan le Fay; and so when Sir Tristram was let into that castle he had good cheer all that night. And upon the morn when he would have departed the queen said: Wit ye well ye shall not depart lightly, for ye are here as a prisoner. Jesu defend! said Sir Tristram, for I was but late a prisoner. Fair knight, said the queen, ye shall abide with me till that I wit what ye are and from whence ye come. And ever the queen would set Sir Tristram on her own side, and her paramour on the other side. And ever Queen Morgan would behold Sir Tristram, and thereat the knight was jealous, and was in will suddenly to have run upon Sir Tristram with a sword, but he left it for shame. Then the queen said to Sir Tristram: Tell me thy name, and I shall suffer you to depart when ye will. Upon that covenant I tell you my name is Sir Tristram de Liones. Ah, said Morgan le Fay, an I wist that, thou shouldst not have departed so soon as thou shalt. But sithen I have made a promise I will hold it, with that thou wilt promise me to bear upon thee a shield that I shall deliver thee, unto the castle of the Hard Rock, where King Arthur had cried a great tournament, and there I pray you that ye will be, and to do for me as much deeds of arms as ye may do. For at the Castle of Maidens, Sir Tristram, ye did marvellous deeds of arms as ever I heard knight do. Madam, said Sir Tristram, let me see the shield that I shall bear. Then the shield was brought forth, and the field was goldish, with a king and a queen therein painted, and a knight standing above them, [one foot] upon the king's head and the other upon the queen's. Madam, said Sir Tristram, this is a fair shield and a mighty; but what signifieth this king and queen, and the knight standing upon both their heads? I shall tell you, said Morgan le Fay, it signifieth King Arthur and Queen Guenever, and a knight who holdeth them both in bondage and in servage. Who is that knight? said Sir Tristram. That shall ye not wit as at this time, said the queen. But as the French book saith, Queen Morgan loved Sir Launcelot best, and ever she desired him, and he would never love her nor do nothing at her request, and therefore she held many knights together for to have taken him by strength. And because she deemed that Sir Launcelot loved Queen Guenever paramour, and she him again, therefore Queen Morgan le Fay ordained that shield to put Sir Launcelot to a rebuke, to that intent that King Arthur might understand the love between them. Then Sir Tristram took that shield and promised her to bear it at the tournament at the Castle of the Hard Rock. But Sir Tristram knew not that that shield was ordained against Sir Launcelot, but afterward he knew it.

CHAPTER XLII

How Sir Tristram took with him the shield, and also how he slew the paramour of Morgan le Fay.

So then Sir Tristram took his leave of the queen, and took the shield with him. Then came the knight that held Queen Morgan le Fay, his name was Sir Hemison, and he made him ready to follow Sir Tristram. Fair friend, said Morgan, ride not after that knight, for ye shall not win no worship of him. Fie on him, coward, said Sir Hemison, for I wist never good knight come out of Cornwall but if it were Sir Tristram de Liones. What an that be he? said she. Nay, nay, said he, he is with La Beale Isoud, and this is but a daffish knight. Alas, my fair friend, ye shall find him the best knight that ever ye met withal, for I know him better than ye do. For your sake, said Sir Hemison, I shall slay him. Ah, fair friend, said the queen, me repenteth that ye will follow that knight, for I fear me sore of your again coming. With this, this knight rode his way wood wroth, and he rode after Sir Tristram as fast as he had been chased with knights. When Sir Tristram heard a knight come after him so fast he returned about, and saw a knight coming against him. And when he came nigh to Sir Tristram he cried on high: Sir knight, keep thee from me. Then they rushed together as it had been thunder, and Sir Hemison brised his spear upon Sir Tristram, but his harness was so good that he might not hurt him. And Sir Tristram smote him harder, and bare him through the body, and he fell over his horse's croup. Then Sir Tristram turned to have done more with his sword, but he saw so much blood go from him that him seemed he was likely to die, and so he departed from him and came to a fair manor to an old knight, and there Sir Tristram lodged.

CHAPTER XLIII

How Morgan le Fay buried her paramour, and how Sir
Tristram praised Sir Launcelot and his kin.

Now leave to speak of Sir Tristram, and speak we of the knight that
was wounded to the death. Then his varlet alighted, and took off his
helm, and then he asked his lord whether there were any life in him.
There is in me life, said the knight, but it is but little; and therefore
leap thou up behind me when thou hast holpen me up, and hold me
fast that I fall not, and bring me to Queen Morgan le Fay; for deep
draughts of death draw to my heart that I may not live, for I would
fain speak with her or I died: for else my soul will be in great peril an
I die. For[thwith] with great pain his varlet brought him to the castle,
and there Sir Hemison fell down dead. When Morgan le Fay saw
him dead she made great sorrow out of reason; and then she let
despoil him unto his shirt, and so she let him put into a tomb. And
about the tomb she let write: Here lieth Sir Hemison, slain by the
hands of Sir Tristram de Liones.

Now turn we unto Sir Tristram, that asked the knight his host if he
saw late any knights adventurous. Sir, he said, the last night here
lodged with me Ector de Maris and a damosel with him, and that
damosel told me that he was one of the best knights of the world.
That is not so, said Sir Tristram, for I know four better knights of his
own blood, and the first is Sir Launcelot du Lake, call him the best
knight, and Sir Bors de Ganis, Sir Bleoberis, Sir Blamore de Ganis,
and Sir Gaheris. Nay, said his host, Sir Gawaine is a better knight than
he. That is not so, said Sir Tristram, for I have met with them both,
and I felt Sir Gaheris for the better knight, and Sir Lamorak I call him
as good as any of them except Sir Launcelot. Why name ye not Sir
Tristram? said his host, for I account him as good as any of them. I
know not Sir Tristram, said Tristram. Thus they talked and bourded
as long as them list, and then went to rest. And on the morn Sir
Tristram departed, and took his leave of his host, and rode toward the
Roche Dure, and none adventure had Sir Tristram but that; and so he
rested not till he came to the castle, where he saw five hundred tents.

CHAPTER XLIV

*How Sir Tristram at a tournament bare the shield that
Morgan le Fay delivered to him.*

Then the King of Scots and the King of Ireland held against King
Arthur's knights, and there began a great medley. So came in Sir
Tristram and did marvellous deeds of arms, for there he smote down
many knights. And ever he was afore King Arthur with that shield.
And when King Arthur saw that shield he marvelled greatly in what
intent it was made; but Queen Guenever deemed as it was,
wherefore she was heavy. Then was there a damosel of Queen
Morgan in a chamber by King Arthur, and when she heard King
Arthur speak of that shield, then she spake openly unto King Arthur.
Sir King, wit ye well this shield was ordained for you, to warn you of
your shame and dishonour, and that longeth to you and your queen.
And then anon that damosel picked her away privily, that no man
wist where she was become. Then was King Arthur sad and wroth,
and asked from whence came that damosel. There was not one that
knew her nor wist where she was become. Then Queen Guenever
called to her Sir Ector de Maris, and there she made her complaint to
him, and said: I wot well this shield was made by Morgan le Fay in
despite of me and of Sir Launcelot, wherefore I dread me sore lest I
should be destroyed. And ever the king beheld Sir Tristram, that did
so marvellous deeds of arms that he wondered sore what knight he
might be, and well he wist it was not Sir Launcelot. And it was told
him that Sir Tristram was in Petit Britain with Isoud la Blanche
Mains, for he deemed, an he had been in the realm of Logris, Sir
Launcelot or some of his fellows that were in the quest of Sir Tristram
that they should have found him or that time. So King Arthur had
marvel what knight he might be. And ever Sir Arthur's eye was on
that shield. All that espied the queen, and that made her sore afeard.

Then ever Sir Tristram smote down knights wonderly to behold,
what upon the right hand and upon the left hand, that unnethe no
knight might withstand him. And the King of Scots and the King of
Ireland began to withdraw them. When Arthur espied that, he

thought that that knight with the strange shield should not escape him. Then he called unto him Sir Uwaine le Blanche Mains, and bade him arm him and make him ready. So anon King Arthur and Sir Uwaine dressed them before Sir Tristram, and required him to tell them where he had that shield. Sir, he said, I had it of Queen Morgan le Fay, sister unto King Arthur.

So here endeth this history of this book, for it is the first book of Sir Tristram de Liones and the second book of Sir Tristram followeth.

BOOK TEN

CHAPTER I

How Sir Tristram jousted, and smote down King Arthur,
because he told him not the cause why he bare that shield.

And if so be ye can descrive what ye bear, ye are worthy to bear the arms. As for that, said Sir Tristram, I will answer you; this shield was given me, not desired, of Queen Morgan le Fay; and as for me, I can not descrive these arms, for it is no point of my charge, and yet I trust to God to bear them with worship. Truly, said King Arthur, ye ought not to bear none arms but if ye wist what ye bear: but I pray you tell me your name. To what intent? said Sir Tristram. For I would wit, said Arthur. Sir, ye shall not wit as at this time. Then shall ye and I do battle together, said King Arthur. Why, said Sir Tristram, will ye do battle with me but if I tell you my name? and that little needeth you an ye were a man of worship, for ye have seen me this day have had great travail, and therefore ye are a villainous knight to ask battle of me, considering my great travail; howbeit I will not fail you, and have ye no doubt that I fear not you; though you think you have me at a great advantage yet shall I right well endure you. And therewithal King Arthur dressed his shield and his spear, and Sir Tristram against him, and they came so eagerly together. And there King Arthur brake his spear all to pieces upon Sir Tristram's shield. But Sir Tristram hit Arthur again, that horse and man fell to the earth. And there was King Arthur wounded on the left side, a great wound and a perilous.

Then when Sir Uwaine saw his lord Arthur lie on the ground sore wounded, he was passing heavy. And then he dressed his shield and his spear, and cried aloud unto Sir Tristram and said: Knight, defend thee. So they came together as thunder, and Sir Uwaine brised his spear all to pieces upon Sir Tristram's shield, and Sir Tristram smote him harder and sorer, with such a might that he bare him clean out of his saddle to the earth. With that Sir Tristram turned about and said: Fair knights, I had no need to joust with you, for I have had enough to do this day. Then arose Arthur and went to Sir Uwaine, and said to Sir Tristram: We have as we have deserved, for through our orgulyté we demanded battle of you, and yet we knew not your name. Nevertheless, by Saint Cross, said Sir Uwaine, he is a strong knight at mine advice as any is now living.

Then Sir Tristram departed, and in every place he asked and demanded after Sir Launcelot, but in no place he could not hear of him whether he were dead or alive; wherefore Sir Tristram made great dole and sorrow. So Sir Tristram rode by a forest, and then was he ware of a fair tower by a marsh on that one side, and on that other side a fair meadow. And there he saw ten knights fighting together. And ever the nearer he came he saw how there was but one knight did battle against nine knights, and that one did so marvellously that Sir Tristram had great wonder that ever one knight might do so great deeds of arms. And then within a little while he had slain half their horses and unhorsed them, and their horses ran in the fields and forest. Then Sir Tristram had so great pity of that one knight that endured so great pain, and ever he thought it should be Sir Palomides, by his shield. And so he rode unto the knights and cried unto them, and bade them cease of their battle, for they did themselves great shame so many knights to fight with one. Then answered the master of those knights, his name was called Breuse Saunce Pité, that was at that time the most mischievoust knight living, and said thus: Sir knight, what have ye ado with us to meddle? and therefore, an ye be wise, depart on your way as ye came, for this knight shall not escape us. That were pity, said Sir Tristram, that so good a knight as he is should be slain so cowardly; and therefore I warn you I will succour him with all my puissance.

CHAPTER II

How Sir Tristram saved Sir Palomides' life, and how they
promised to fight together within a fortnight.

So Sir Tristram alighted off his horse because they were on foot, that
they should not slay his horse, and then dressed his shield, with his
sword in his hand, and he smote on the right hand and on the left
hand passing sore, that well-nigh at every stroke he struck down a
knight. And when they espied his strokes they fled all with Breuse
Saunce Pité unto the tower, and Sir Tristram followed fast after with
his sword in his hand, but they escaped into the tower, and shut Sir
Tristram without the gate. And when Sir Tristram saw this he
returned aback unto Sir Palomides, and found him sitting under a
tree sore wounded. Ah, fair knight, said Sir Tristram, well be ye
found. Gramercy, said Sir Palomides, of your great goodness, for ye
have rescued me of my life, and saved me from my death. What is
your name? said Sir Tristram. He said: My name is Sir Palomides. O
Jesu, said Sir Tristram, thou hast a fair grace of me this day that I
should rescue thee, and thou art the man in the world that I most
hate; but now make thee ready, for I will do battle with thee. What is
your name? said Sir Palomides. My name is Sir Tristram, your mortal
enemy. It may be so, said Sir Palomides; but ye have done over much
for me this day that I should fight with you; for inasmuch as ye have
saved my life it will be no worship for you to have ado with me, for
ye are fresh and I am wounded sore, and therefore, an ye will needs
have ado with me, assign me a day and then I shall meet with you
without fail. Ye say well, said Sir Tristram, now I assign you to meet
me in the meadow by the river of Camelot, where Merlin set the
peron. So they were agreed.

Then Sir Tristram asked Sir Palomides why the ten knights did
battle with him. For this cause, said Sir Palomides; as I rode upon
mine adventures in a forest here beside I espied where lay a dead
knight, and a lady weeping beside him. And when I saw her making
such dole, I asked her who slew her lord. Sir, she said, the falsest
knight of the world now living, and he is the most villain that ever

man heard speak of, and his name is Sir Breuse Saunce Pité. Then for pity I made the damosel to leap on her palfrey, and I promised her to be her warrant, and to help her to inter her lord. And so, suddenly, as I came riding by this tower, there came out Sir Breuse Saunce Pité, and suddenly he struck me from my horse. And then or I might recover my horse this Sir Breuse slew the damosel. And so I took my horse again, and I was sore ashamed, and so began the medley betwixt us: and this is the cause wherefore we did this battle. Well, said Sir Tristram, now I understand the manner of your battle, but in any wise have remembrance of your promise that ye have made with me to do battle with me this day fortnight. I shall not fail you, said Sir Palomides. Well, said Sir Tristram, as at this time I will not fail you till that ye be out of the danger of your enemies.

So they mounted upon their horses, and rode together unto that forest, and there they found a fair well, with clear water bubbling. Fair sir, said Sir Tristram, to drink of that water have I courage; and then they alighted off their horses. And then were they ware by them where stood a great horse tied to a tree, and ever he neighed. And then were they ware of a fair knight armed, under a tree, lacking no piece of harness, save his helm lay under his head. By the good lord, said Sir Tristram, yonder lieth a well-faring knight; what is best to do? Awake him, said Sir Palomides. So Sir Tristram awaked him with the butt of his spear. And so the knight rose up hastily and put his helm upon his head, and gat a great spear in his hand; and without any more words he hurled unto Sir Tristram, and smote him clean from his saddle to the earth, and hurt him on the left side, that Sir Tristram lay in great peril. Then he walloped farther, and fetched his course, and came hurling upon Sir Palomides, and there he struck him a part through the body, that he fell from his horse to the earth. And then this strange knight left them there, and took his way through the forest. With this Sir Palomides and Sir Tristram were on foot, and gat their horses again, and either asked counsel of other, what was best to do. By my head, said Sir Tristram, I will follow this strong knight that thus hath shamed us. Well, said Sir Palomides, and I will repose me hereby with a friend of mine. Beware, said Sir Tristram unto Palomides, that ye fail not that day that ye have set with me to do battle, for, as I deem, ye will not hold your day, for I am much bigger than ye. As for that, said Sir Palomides, be it as it be may, for I fear you not, for an I be not sick nor prisoner, I will not fail you; but I have cause to have more doubt of you that ye will not meet with me, for ye ride after yonder strong knight. And if ye meet with him it is an hard adventure an ever ye escape his hands. Right so Sir Tristram and Sir Palomides departed, and either took their ways diverse.

CHAPTER III

How Sir Tristram sought a strong knight that had smitten him down, and many other knights of the Round Table.

And so Sir Tristram rode long after this strong knight. And at the last he saw where lay a lady overthwart a dead knight. Fair lady, said Sir Tristram, who hath slain your lord? Sir, she said, here came a knight riding, as my lord and I rested us here, and asked him of whence he was, and my lord said of Arthur's court. Therefore, said the strong knight, I will joust with thee, for I hate all these that be of Arthur's court. And my lord that lieth here dead amounted upon his horse, and the strong knight and my lord encountered together, and there he smote my lord throughout with his spear, and thus he hath brought me in great woe and damage. That me repenteth, said Sir Tristram, of your great anger; an it please you tell me your husband's name. Sir, said she, his name was Galardoun, that would have proved a good knight. So departed Sir Tristram from that dolorous lady, and had much evil lodging. Then on the third day Sir Tristram met with Sir Gawaine and with Sir Bleoberis in a forest at a lodge, and either were sore wounded. Then Sir Tristram asked Sir Gawaine and Sir Bleoberis if they met with such a knight, with such a cognisance, with a covered shield. Fair sir, said these knights, such a knight met with us to our great damage. And first he smote down my fellow, Sir Bleoberis, and sore wounded him because he bade me I should not have ado with him, for why he was overstrong for me. That strong knight took his words at scorn, and said he said it for mockery. And then they rode together, and so he hurt my fellow. And when he had done so I might not for shame but I must joust with him. And at the first course he smote me down and my horse to the earth. And there he had almost slain me, and from us he took his horse and departed, and in an evil time we met with him. Fair knights, said Sir Tristram, so he met with me, and with another knight that hight Palomides, and he smote us both down with one spear, and hurt us right sore. By my faith, said Sir Gawaine, by my counsel ye shall let him pass and seek him no further; for at the next feast of the Round Table, upon pain of my head ye shall find him there. By my faith, said Sir Tristram, I shall never rest till that I find him. And then Sir Gawaine asked him his name. Then he said: My name is Sir Tristram. And so either told other their names, and then departed Sir Tristram and rode his way.

And by fortune in a meadow Sir Tristram met with Sir Kay, the Seneschal, and Sir Dinadan. What tidings with you, said Sir Tristram, with you knights? Not good, said these knights. Why so? said Sir Tristram; I pray you tell me, for I ride to seek a knight. What cognisance beareth he? said Sir Kay. He beareth, said Sir Tristram, a covered shield close with cloth. By my head, said Sir Kay, that is the same knight that met with us, for this night we were lodged within a widow's house, and there was that knight lodged; and when he wist we were of Arthur's court he spoke great villainy by the king, and specially by the Queen Guenever, and then on the morn was waged battle with him for that cause. And at the first recounter, said Sir Kay, he smote me down from my horse and hurt me passing sore; and when my fellow, Sir Dinadan, saw me smitten down and hurt he would not revenge me, but fled from me; and thus he departed. And then Sir Tristram asked them their names, and so either told other their names. And so Sir Tristram departed from Sir Kay, and from Sir Dinadan, and so he passed through a great forest into a plain, till he was ware of a priory, and there he reposed him with a good man six days.

CHAPTER IV

How Sir Tristram smote down Sir Sagramore le Desirous and Sir Dodinas le Savage.

And then he sent his man that hight Gouvernail, and commanded him to go to a city thereby to fetch him new harness; for it was long time afore that that Sir Tristram had been refreshed, his harness was brised and broken. And when Gouvernail, his servant, was come with his apparel, he took his leave at the widow, and mounted upon his horse, and rode his way early on the morn. And by sudden adventure Sir Tristram met with Sir Sagramore le Desirous, and with Sir Dodinas le Savage. And these two knights met with Sir Tristram and questioned with him, and asked him if he would joust with them. Fair knights, said Sir Tristram, with a good will I would joust with you, but I have promised at a day set, near hand, to do battle with a strong knight; and therefore I am loath to have ado with you, for an it misfortuned me here to be hurt I should not be able to do my battle which I promised. As for that, said Sagramore, maugre your head, ye shall joust with us or ye pass from us. Well, said Sir Tristram, if ye enforce me thereto I must do what I may. And then they dressed their shields, and came running together with great ire. But through Sir Tristram's great force he struck Sir Sagramore from his horse. Then he hurled his horse farther, and said to Sir Dodinas: Knight, make thee ready; and so through fine force Sir Tristram struck Dodinas from his horse. And when he saw them lie on the earth he took his bridle, and rode forth on his way, and his man Gouvernail with him.

Anon as Sir Tristram was passed, Sir Sagramore and Sir Dodinas gat again their horses, and mounted up lightly and followed after Sir Tristram. And when Sir Tristram saw them come so fast after him he returned with his horse to them, and asked them what they would. It is not long ago sithen I smote you to the earth at your own request and desire: I would have ridden by you, but ye would not suffer me, and now meseemeth ye would do more battle with me. That is truth, said Sir Sagramore and Sir Dodinas, for we will be revenged of the despite ye have done to us. Fair knights, said Sir Tristram, that shall little need you, for all that I did to you ye caused it; wherefore I require you of your knighthood leave me as at this time, for I am sure an I do battle with you I shall not escape without great hurts, and as I suppose ye shall not escape all lotless. And this is the cause why I am so loath to have with you: for I must fight within these three days with a good knight, and as valiant as any is now living, and if I be hurt I shall not be able to do battle with him. What knight is that, said Sir Sagramore, that ye shall fight withal? Sirs, said he, it is a good knight called Sir Palomides. By my head, said Sir Sagramore and Sir Dodinas, ye have cause to dread him, for ye shall find him a passing good knight, and a valiant. And because ye shall have ado with him we will forbear you as at this time, and else ye should not escape us lightly. But, fair knight, said Sir Sagramore, tell us your name. Sir, said he, my name is Sir Tristram de Liones. Ah, said Sagramore and Sir Dodinas, well be ye found, for much worship have we heard of you. And then either took leave of other, and departed on their way.

CHAPTER V

How Sir Tristram met at the peron with Sir Launcelot, and how they fought together unknown.

Then departed Sir Tristram and rode straight unto Camelot, to the peron that Merlin had made to-fore, where Sir Lanceor, that was the king's son of Ireland, was slain by the hands of Balin. And in that same place was the fair lady Colombe slain, that was love unto Sir Lanceor; for after he was dead she took his sword and thrust it through her body. And by the craft of Merlin he made to inter this knight, Lanceor, and his lady, Colombe, under one stone. And at that time Merlin prophesied that in that same place should fight two the best knights that ever were in Arthur's days, and the best lovers. So when Sir Tristram came to the tomb where Lanceor and his lady were buried he looked about him after Sir Palomides. Then was he ware of a seemly knight came riding against him all in white, with a covered shield. When he came nigh Sir Tristram he said on high: Ye be welcome, sir knight, and well and truly have ye holden your promise. And then they dressed their shields and spears, and came together with all their might of their horses; and they met so fiercely that both their horses and knights fell to the earth, and as fast as they might avoided their horses, and put their shields afore them; and they struck together with bright swords, as men that were of might, and either wounded other wonderly sore, that the blood ran out upon the grass. And thus they fought the space of four hours, that never one would speak to other one word, and of their harness they had hewn off many pieces. O Lord Jesu, said Gouvernail, I marvel greatly of the strokes my master hath given to your master. By my head, said Sir Launcelot's servant, your master hath not given so many but your master has received as many or more. O Jesu, said Gouvernail, it is too much for Sir Palomides to suffer or Sir Launcelot, and yet pity it were that either of these good knights should destroy other's blood. So they stood and wept both, and made great dole when they saw the bright swords over-covered with blood of their bodies.

Then at the last spake Sir Launcelot and said: Knight, thou fightest wonderly well as ever I saw knight, therefore, an it please you, tell me your name. Sir, said Sir Tristram, that is me loath to tell any man my name. Truly, said Sir Launcelot, an I were required I was never loath to tell my name. It is well said, said Sir Tristram, then I require you to tell me your name? Fair knight, he said, my name is Sir Launcelot du Lake. Alas, said Sir Tristram, what have I done! for ye are the man in the world that I love best. Fair knight, said Sir Launcelot, tell me your name? Truly, said he, my name is Sir Tristram de Liones. O Jesu, said Sir Launcelot, what adventure is befallen me! And therewith Sir Launcelot kneeled down and yielded him up his sword. And therewithal Sir Tristram kneeled adown, and yielded him up his sword. And so either gave other the degree. And then they both forthwithal went to the stone, and set them down upon it, and took off their helms to cool them, and either kissed other an hundred times. And then anon after they took off their helms and rode to Camelot. And there they met with Sir Gawaine and with Sir Gaheris that had made promise to Arthur never to come again to the court till they had brought Sir Tristram with them.

CHAPTER VI

*How Sir Launcelot brought Sir Tristram to the court,
and of the great joy that the king and other made
for the coming of Sir Tristram.*

Return again, said Sir Launcelot, for your quest is done, for I have met with Sir Tristram: lo, here is his own person! Then was Sir Gawaine glad, and said to Sir Tristram: Ye are welcome, for now have ye eased me greatly of my labour. For what cause, said Sir Gawaine, came ye into this court? Fair sir, said Sir Tristram, I came into this country because of Sir Palomides; for he and I had assigned at this day to have done battle together at the peron, and I marvel I hear not of him. And thus by adventure my lord, Sir Launcelot, and I met together. With this came King Arthur, and when he wist that there was Sir Tristram, then he ran unto him and took him by the hand and said: Sir Tristram, ye are as welcome as any knight that ever came to this court. And when the king had heard how Sir Launcelot and he had foughten, and either had wounded other wonderly sore, then the king made great dole. Then Sir Tristram told the king how he came thither for to have had ado with Sir Palomides. And then he told the king how he had rescued him from the nine knights and Breuse Saunce Pité; and how he found a knight lying by a well, and that knight smote down Sir Palomides and me, but his shield was covered with a cloth. So Sir Palomides left me, and I followed after that knight; and in many places I found where he had slain knights, and for-jousted many. By my head, said Sir Gawaine, that same knight smote me down and Sir Bleoberis, and hurt us sore both, he with the covered shield. Ah, said Sir Kay, that knight smote me adown and hurt me passing sore, and fain would I have known him, but I might not. Jesu, mercy, said Arthur, what knight was that with the covered shield? I know not, said Sir Tristram; and so said they all. Now, said King Arthur, then wot I, for it is Sir Launcelot. Then they all looked upon Sir Launcelot and said: Ye have beguiled us with your covered shield. It is not the first time, said Arthur, he hath done so. My lord, said Sir Launcelot, truly wit ye well I was the same knight that bare the covered shield; and because I would not be known that I was of your court I said no worship of your house. That is truth, said Sir Gawaine, Sir Kay, and Sir Bleoberis.

Then King Arthur took Sir Tristram by the hand and went to the Table Round. Then came Queen Guenever and many ladies with her, and all the ladies said at one voice: Welcome, Sir Tristram! Welcome, said the damosels. Welcome, said knights. Welcome, said Arthur, for one of the best knights, and the gentlest of the world, and the man of most worship; for of all manner of hunting thou bearest the prize, and of all measures of blowing thou art the beginning, and of all the terms of hunting and hawking ye are the beginner, of all instruments of music ye are the best; therefore, gentle knight, said Arthur, ye are welcome to this court. And also, I pray you, said Arthur, grant me a boon. It shall be at your commandment, said Tristram. Well, said Arthur, I will desire of you that ye will abide in my court. Sir, said Sir Tristram, thereto is me loath, for I have ado in many countries. Not so, said Arthur, ye have promised it me, ye may not say nay. Sir, said Sir Tristram, I will as ye will. Then went Arthur unto the sieges about the Round Table, and looked in every siege the which were void that lacked knights. And then the king saw in the siege of Marhaus letters that said: This is the siege of the noble knight, Sir Tristram. And then Arthur made Sir Tristram Knight of the Table Round, with great nobley and great feast as might be thought. For Sir Marhaus was slain afore by the hands of Sir Tristram in an island; and that was well known at that time in the court of Arthur, for this Marhaus was a worthy knight. And for evil deeds that he did unto the country of Cornwall Sir Tristram and he fought. And they fought so long, tracing and traversing, till they fell bleeding to the earth; for they were so sore wounded that they might not stand for bleeding. And Sir Tristram by fortune recovered, and Sir Marhaus died through the stroke on the head. So leave we of Sir Tristram and speak we of King Mark.

CHAPTER VII

*How for the despite of Sir Tristram King Mark came with two
knights into England, and how he slew one of the knights.*

Then King Mark had great despite of the renown of Sir Tristram, and
then he chased him out of Cornwall: yet was he nephew unto King
Mark, but he had great suspicion unto Sir Tristram because of his
queen, La Beale Isoud; for him seemed that there was too much love
between them both. So when Sir Tristram departed out of Cornwall
into England King Mark heard of the great prowess that Sir Tristram
did there, the which grieved him sore. So he sent on his part men to
espy what deeds he did. And the queen sent privily on her part spies
to know what deeds he had done, for great love was between them
twain. So when the messengers were come home they told the truth
as they had heard, that he passed all other knights but if it were Sir
Launcelot. Then King Mark was right heavy of these tidings, and as
glad was La Beale Isoud. Then in great despite he took with him two
good knights and two squires, and disguised himself, and took his
way into England, to the intent for to slay Sir Tristram. And one of
these two knights hight Bersules, and the other knight was called
Amant. So as they rode King Mark asked a knight that he met, where
he should find King Arthur. He said: At Camelot. Also he asked that
knight after Sir Tristram, whether he heard of him in the court of
King Arthur. Wit you well, said that knight, ye shall find Sir Tristram
there for a man of as great worship as is now living; for through his
prowess he won the tournament of the Castle of Maidens that
standeth by the Hard Rock. And sithen he hath won with his own
hands thirty knights that were men of great honour. And the last
battle that ever he did he fought with Sir Launcelot; and that was a
marvellous battle. And not by force Sir Launcelot brought Sir
Tristram to the court, and of him King Arthur made passing great
joy, and so made him Knight of the Table Round; and his seat was
where the good knight's, Sir Marhaus, seat was. Then was King Mark
passing sorry when he heard of the honour of Sir Tristram; and so
they departed.

Then said King Mark unto his two knights: Now will I tell you my counsel: ye are the men that I trust most to alive, and I will that ye wit my coming hither is to this intent,—for to destroy Sir Tristram by wiles or by treason; and it shall be hard if ever he escape our hands. Alas, said Sir Bersules, what mean you? for ye be set in such a way ye are disposed shamefully; for Sir Tristram is the knight of most worship that we know living, and therefore I warn you plainly I will never consent to do him to the death; and therefore I will yield my service, and forsake you. When King Mark heard him say so, suddenly he drew his sword and said: Ah, traitor; and smote Sir Bersules on the head, that the sword went to his teeth. When Amant, the knight, saw him do that villainous deed, and his squires, they said it was foul done, and mischievously: Wherefore we will do thee no more service, and wit ye well, we will appeach thee of treason afore Arthur. Then was King Mark wonderly wroth and would have slain Amant; but he and the two squires held them together, and set nought by his malice. When King Mark saw he might not be revenged on them, he said thus unto the knight, Amant: Wit thou well, an thou appeach me of treason I shall thereof defend me afore King Arthur; but I require thee that thou tell not my name, that I am King Mark, whatsomever come of me. As for that, said Sir Amant, I will not discover your name; and so they departed, and Amant and his fellows took the body of Bersules and buried it.

CHAPTER VIII

*How King Mark came to a fountain where he found Sir
Lamorak complaining for the love of King Lot's wife.*

Then King Mark rode till he came to a fountain, and there he rested him, and stood in a doubt whether he would ride to Arthur's court or none, or return again to his country. And as he thus rested him by that fountain there came by him a knight well armed on horseback; and he alighted, and tied his horse until a tree, and set him down by the brink of the fountain; and there he made great languor and dole, and made the dolefullest complaint of love that ever man heard; and all this while was he not ware of King Mark. And this was a great part of his complaint: he cried and wept, saying: O fair Queen of Orkney, King Lot's wife, and mother of Sir Gawaine, and to Sir Gaheris, and mother to many other, for thy love I am in great pains. Then King Mark arose and went near him and said: Fair knight, ye have made a piteous complaint. Truly, said the knight, it is an hundred part more ruefuller than my heart can utter. I require you, said King Mark, tell me your name. Sir, said he, as for my name I will not hide it from no knight that beareth a shield, and my name is Sir Lamorak de Galis. But when Sir Lamorak heard King Mark speak, then wist he well by his speech that he was a Cornish knight. Sir, said Sir Lamorak, I understand by your tongue ye be of Cornwall, wherein there dwelleth the shamefullest king that is now living, for he is a great enemy to all good knights; and that proveth well, for he hath chased out of that country Sir Tristram, that is the worshipfullest knight that now is living, and all knights speak of him worship; and for jealousness of his queen he hath chased him out of his country. It is pity, said Sir Lamorak, that ever any such false knight-coward as King Mark is, should be matched with such a fair lady and good as La Beale Isoud is, for all the world of him speaketh shame, and of her worship that any queen may have. I have not ado in this matter, said King Mark, neither nought will I speak thereof. Well said, said Sir Lamorak. Sir, can ye tell me any tidings? I can tell you, said Sir Lamorak, that there shall be a great tournament in haste beside Camelot, at the Castle of Jagent; and the King with the Hundred Knights and the King of Ireland, as I suppose, make that tournament.

Then there came a knight that was called Sir Dinadan, and saluted them both. And when he wist that King Mark was a knight of Cornwall he reproved him for the love of King Mark a thousand fold more than did Sir Lamorak. Then he proffered to joust with King Mark. And he was full loath thereto, but Sir Dinadan edged him so, that he jousted with Sir Lamorak. And Sir Lamorak smote King Mark so sore that he bare him on his spear end over his horse's tail. And then King Mark arose again, and followed after Sir Lamorak. But Sir Dinadan would not joust with Sir Lamorak, but he told King Mark that Sir Lamorak was Sir Kay, the Seneschal. That is not so, said King Mark, for he is much bigger than Sir Kay; and so he followed and overtook him, and bade him abide. What will you do? said Sir Lamorak. Sir, he said, I will fight with a sword, for ye have shamed me with a spear; and therewith they dashed together with swords, and Sir Lamorak suffered him and forbare him. And King Mark was passing hasty, and smote thick strokes. Sir Lamorak saw he would not stint, and waxed somewhat wroth, and doubled his strokes, for he was one of the noblest knights of the world; and he beat him so on the helm that his head hung nigh on the saddle bow. When Sir Lamorak saw him fare so, he said: Sir knight, what cheer? meseemeth you have nigh your fill of fighting, it were pity to do you any more harm, for ye are but a mean knight, therefore I give you leave to go where ye list. Gramercy, said King Mark, for ye and I be not matches.

Then Sir Dinadan mocked King Mark and said: Ye are not able to match a good knight. As for that, said King Mark, at the first time I jousted with this knight ye refused him. Think ye that it is a shame to me? said Sir Dinadan: nay, sir, it is ever worship to a knight to refuse that thing that he may not attain, therefore your worship had been much more to have refused him as I did; for I warn you plainly he is able to beat such five as ye and I be; for ye knights of Cornwall are no men of worship as other knights are. And because ye are no men of worship ye hate all men of worship, for never was bred in your country such a knight as is Sir Tristram.

CHAPTER IX

How King Mark, Sir Lamorak, and Sir Dinadan came to a castle, and how King Mark was known there.

Then they rode forth all together, King Mark, Sir Lamorak, and Sir Dinadan, till that they came to a bridge, and at the end thereof stood a fair tower. Then saw they a knight on horseback well armed, brandishing a spear, crying and proffering himself to joust. Now, said Sir Dinadan unto King Mark, yonder are two brethren, that one hight Alein, and the other hight Trian, that will joust with any that passeth this passage. Now proffer yourself, said Dinadan to King Mark, for ever ye be laid to the earth. Then King Mark was ashamed, and therewith he feutred his spear, and hurtled to Sir Trian, and either brake their spears all to pieces, and passed through anon. Then Sir Trian sent King Mark another spear to joust more; but in no wise he would not joust no more. Then they came to the castle all three knights, and prayed the lord of the castle of harbour. Ye are right welcome, said the knights of the castle, for the love of the lord of this castle, the which hight Sir Tor le Fise Aries. And then they came into a fair court well repaired, and they had passing good cheer, till the lieutenant of this castle, that hight Berluse, espied King Mark of Cornwall. Then said Berluse: Sir knight, I know you better than you ween, for ye are King Mark that slew my father afore mine own eyen; and me had ye slain had I not escaped into a wood; but wit ye well, for the love of my lord of this castle I will neither hurt you nor harm you, nor none of your fellowship. But wit ye well, when ye are past this lodging I shall hurt you an I may, for ye slew my father traitorly. But first for the love of my lord, Sir Tor, and for the love of Sir Lamorak, the honourable knight that here is lodged, ye shall have none ill lodging; for it is pity that ever ye should be in the company of good knights; for ye are the most villainous knight or king that is now known alive, for ye are a destroyer of good knights, and all that ye do is but treason.

CHAPTER X

How Sir Berluse met with King Mark, and how Sir Dinadan took his part.

Then was King Mark sore ashamed, and said but little again. But when Sir Lamorak and Sir Dinadan wist that he was King Mark they were sorry of his fellowship. So after supper they went to lodging. So on the morn they arose early, and King Mark and Sir Dinadan rode together; and three mile from their lodging there met with them three knights, and Sir Berluse was one, and that other his two cousins. Sir Berluse saw King Mark, and then he cried on high: Traitor, keep thee from me, for wit thou well that I am Berluse. Sir knight, said Sir Dinadan, I counsel you to leave off at this time, for he is riding to King Arthur; and because I have promised to conduct him to my lord King Arthur needs must I take a part with him; howbeit I love not his condition, and fain I would be from him. Well, Dinadan, said Sir Berluse, me repenteth that ye will take part with him, but now do your best. And then he hurtled to King Mark, and smote him sore upon the shield, that he bare him clean out of his saddle to the earth. That saw Sir Dinadan, and he feutred his spear, and ran to one of Berluse's fellows, and smote him down off his saddle. Then Dinadan turned his horse, and smote the third knight in the same wise to the earth, for Sir Dinadan was a good knight on horseback; and there began a great battle, for Berluse and his fellows held them together strongly on foot. And so through the great force of Sir Dinadan King Mark had Berluse to the earth, and his two fellows fled; and had not been Sir Dinadan King Mark would have slain him. And so Sir Dinadan rescued him of his life, for King Mark was but a murderer. And then they took their horses and departed, and left Sir Berluse there sore wounded.

Then King Mark and Sir Dinadan rode forth a four leagues English, till that they came to a bridge where hoved a knight on horseback, armed and ready to joust. Lo, said Sir Dinadan unto King Mark, yonder hoveth a knight that will joust, for there shall none pass this bridge but he must joust with that knight. It is well, said King Mark, for this jousts falleth with thee. Sir Dinadan knew the knight well that he was a noble knight, and fain he would have jousted, but he had had liefer King Mark had jousted with him, but by no mean King Mark would not joust. Then Sir Dinadan might not refuse him in no manner. And then either dressed their spears and their shields, and smote together, so that through fine force Sir Dinadan was smitten to the earth; and lightly he rose up and gat his horse, and required that knight to do battle with swords. And he answered and said: Fair knight, as at this time I may not have ado with you no more, for the custom of this passage is such. Then was Sir Dinadan passing wroth that he might not be revenged of that knight; and so he departed, and in no wise would that knight tell his name. But ever Sir Dinadan thought he should know him by his shield that it should be Sir Tor.

CHAPTER XI

*How King Mark mocked Sir Dinadan, and how they met
with six knights of the Round Table.*

So as they rode by the way King Mark then began to mock Sir
Dinadan, and said: I weened you knights of the Table Round might
not in no wise find their matches. Ye say well, said Sir Dinadan; as for
you, on my life I call you none of the best knights; but sith ye have
such a despite at me I require you to joust with me to prove my
strength. Not so, said King Mark, for I will not have ado with you in
no manner; but I require you of one thing, that when ye come to
Arthur's court discover not my name, for I am there so hated. It is
shame to you, said Sir Dinadan, that ye govern you so shamefully; for
I see by you ye are full of cowardice, and ye are a murderer, and that
is the greatest shame that a knight may have; for never a knight being
a murderer hath worship, nor never shall have; for I saw but late
through my force ye would have slain Sir Berluse, a better knight
than ye, or ever ye shall be, and more of prowess. Thus they rode
forth talking till they came to a fair place, where stood a knight, and
prayed them to take their lodging with him. So at the request of that
knight they reposed them there, and made them well at ease, and had
great cheer. For all errant-knights were welcome to him, and
specially all those of Arthur's court. Then Sir Dinadan demanded his
host what was the knight's name that kept the bridge. For what cause
ask you it? said the host. For it is not long ago, said Sir Dinadan,
sithen he gave me a fall. Ah, fair knight, said his host, thereof have ye
no marvel, for he is a passing good knight, and his name is Sir Tor,
the son of Aries le Vaysher. Ah, said Sir Dinadan, was that Sir Tor?
for truly so ever me thought.

Right as they stood thus talking together they saw come riding to
them over a plain six knights of the court of King Arthur, well armed
at all points. And there by their shields Sir Dinadan knew them well.
The first was the good knight Sir Uwaine, the son of King Uriens,
the second was the noble knight Sir Brandiles, the third was Ozana le
Cure Hardy, the fourth was Uwaine les Aventurous, the fifth was Sir

Agravaine, the sixth Sir Mordred, brother to Sir Gawaine. When Sir Dinadan had seen these six knights he thought in himself he would bring King Mark by some wile to joust with one of them. And anon they took their horses and ran after these knights well a three mile English. Then was King Mark ware where they sat all six about a well, and ate and drank such meats as they had, and their horses walking and some tied, and their shields hung in divers places about them. Lo, said Sir Dinadan, yonder are knights-errant that will joust with us. God forbid, said King Mark, for they be six and we but two. As for that, said Sir Dinadan, let us not spare, for I will assay the foremost; and therewith he made him ready. When King Mark saw him do so, as fast as Sir Dinadan rode toward them, King Mark rode froward them with all his menial meiny. So when Sir Dinadan saw King Mark was gone, he set the spear out of the rest, and threw his shield upon his back, and came riding to the fellowship of the Table Round. And anon Sir Uwaine knew Sir Dinadan, and welcomed him, and so did all his fellowship.

CHAPTER XII

How the six knights sent Sir Dagonet to joust with King Mark, and how King Mark refused him.

And then they asked him of his adventures, and whether he had seen Sir Tristram or Sir Launcelot. So God me help, said Sir Dinadan, I saw none of them sithen I departed from Camelot. What knight is that, said Sir Brandiles, that so suddenly departed from you, and rode over yonder field? Sir, said he, it was a knight of Cornwall, and the most horrible coward that ever bestrode horse. What is his name? said all these knights. I wot not, said Sir Dinadan. So when they had reposed them, and spoken together, they took their horses and rode to a castle where dwelt an old knight that made all knights-errant good cheer. Then in the meanwhile that they were talking came into the castle Sir Griflet le Fise de Dieu, and there was he welcome; and they all asked him whether he had seen Sir Launcelot or Sir Tristram. Sirs, he answered, I saw him not sithen he departed from Camelot. So as Sir Dinadan walked and beheld the castle, thereby in a chamber he espied King Mark, and then he rebuked him, and asked him why he departed so. Sir, said he, for I durst not abide because they were so many. But how escaped ye? said King Mark. Sir, said Sir Dinadan, they were better friends than I weened they had been. Who is captain of that fellowship? said the king. Then for to fear him Sir Dinadan said that it was Sir Launcelot. O Jesu, said the king, might I know Sir Launcelot by his shield? Yea, said Dinadan, for he beareth a shield of silver and black bends. All this he said to fear the king, for Sir Launcelot was not in his fellowship. Now I pray you, said King Mark, that ye will ride in my fellowship. That is me loath to do, said Sir Dinadan, because ye forsook my fellowship.

Right so Sir Dinadan went from King Mark, and went to his own fellowship; and so they mounted upon their horses, and rode on their ways, and talked of the Cornish knight, for Dinadan told them that he was in the castle where they were lodged. It is well said, said Sir Griflet, for here have I brought Sir Dagonet, King Arthur's fool, that is the best fellow and the merriest in the world. Will ye do well? said Sir Dinadan: I have told the Cornish knight that here is Sir Launcelot, and the Cornish knight asked me what shield he bare. Truly, I told him that he bare the same shield that Sir Mordred beareth. Will ye do well? said Sir Mordred; I am hurt and may not well bear my shield nor harness, and therefore put my shield and my harness upon Sir Dagonet, and let him set upon the Cornish knight. That shall be done, said Sir Dagonet, by my faith. Then anon was Dagonet armed him in Mordred's harness and his shield, and he was set on a great horse, and a spear in his hand. Now, said Dagonet, show me the knight, and I trow I shall bear him down. So all these knights rode to a woodside, and abode till King Mark came by the way. Then they put forth Sir Dagonet, and he came on all the while his horse might run, straight upon King Mark. And when he came nigh King Mark, he cried as he were wood, and said: Keep thee, knight of Cornwall, for I will slay thee. Anon, as King Mark beheld his shield, he said to himself: Yonder is Sir Launcelot; alas, now am I destroyed; and therewithal he made his horse to run as fast as it might through thick and thin. And ever Sir Dagonet followed after King Mark, crying and rating him as a wood man, through a great forest. When Sir Uwaine and Sir Brandiles saw Dagonet so chase King Mark, they laughed all as they were wood. And then they took their horses, and rode after to see how Sir Dagonet sped, for they would not for no good that Sir

Dagonet were shent, for King Arthur loved him passing well, and made him knight with his own hands. And at every tournament he began to make King Arthur to laugh. Then the knights rode here and there, crying and chasing after King Mark, that all the forest rang of the noise.

CHAPTER XIII

How Sir Palomides by adventure met King Mark flying, and how he overthrew Dagonet and other knights.

So King Mark rode by fortune by a well, in the way where stood a knight-errant on horseback, armed at all points, with a great spear in his hand. And when he saw King Mark coming flying he said: Knight, return again for shame and stand with me, and I shall be thy warrant. Ah, fair knight, said King Mark, let me pass, for yonder cometh after me the best knight of the world, with the black bended shield. Fie, for shame, said the knight, he is none of the worthy knights, and if he were Sir Launcelot or Sir Tristram I should not doubt to meet the better of them both. When King Mark heard him say that word, he turned his horse and abode by him. And then that strong knight bare a spear to Dagonet, and smote him so sore that he bare him over his horse's tail, and nigh he had broken his neck. And anon after him came Sir Brandiles, and when he saw Dagonet have that fall he was passing wroth, and cried: Keep thee, knight, and so they hurtled together wonder sore. But the knight smote Sir Brandiles so sore that he went to the earth, horse and man. Sir Uwaine came after and saw all this. Jesu, said he, yonder is a strong knight. And then they feutred their spears, and this knight came so eagerly that he smote down Sir Uwaine. Then came Ozana with the hardy heart, and he was smitten down. Now, said Sir Griflet, by my counsel let us send to yonder errant-knight, and wit whether he be of Arthur's court, for as I deem it is Sir Lamorak de Galis. So they sent unto him, and prayed the strange knight to tell his name, and whether he were of Arthur's court or not. As for my name they shall not wit, but tell them I am a knight-errant as they are, and let them wit that I am no knight of King Arthur's court: and so the squire rode again unto them and told them his answer of him. By my head, said Sir Agravaine, he is one of the strongest knights that ever I saw, for he hath overthrown three noble knights, and needs we must encounter with him for shame. So Sir Agravaine feutred his spear, and that other was ready, and smote him down over his horse to the earth. And in the same wise he smote Sir Uwaine les Avoutres and also Sir Griflet. Then had he served them all but Sir Dinadan, for he was behind, and Sir Mordred was unarmed, and Dagonet had his harness.

So when this was done, this strong knight rode on his way a soft pace, and King Mark rode after him, praising him mickle; but he would answer no words, but sighed wonderly sore, hanging down his head, taking no heed to his words. Thus they rode well a three mile English, and then this knight called to him a varlet, and bade him ride until yonder fair manor, and recommend me to the lady of that castle and place, and pray her to send me refreshing of good meats and drinks. And if she ask thee what I am, tell her that I am the knight that followeth the glatisant beast: that is in English to say the questing beast; for that beast wheresomever he yede he quested in the belly with such a noise as it had been a thirty couple of hounds. Then the varlet went his way and came to the manor, and saluted the lady, and told her from whence he came. And when she understood that he came from the knight that followed the questing beast: O sweet Lord Jesu, she said, when shall I see that noble knight, my dear son Palomides? Alas, will he not abide with me? and therewith she swooned and wept, and made passing great dole. And then also soon as she might she gave the varlet all that he asked. And the varlet returned unto Sir Palomides, for he was a varlet of King Mark. And as soon as he came, he told the knight's name was Sir Palomides. I am well pleased, said King Mark, but hold thee still and say nothing. Then they alighted and set them down and reposed them a while. Anon withal King Mark fell asleep. When Sir Palomides saw him sound asleep he took his horse and rode his way, and said to them: I will not be in the company of a sleeping knight. And so he rode forth a great pace.

CHAPTER XIV

*How King Mark and Sir Dinadan heard Sir Palomides
making great sorrow and mourning for La Beale Isoud.*

Now turn we unto Sir Dinadan, that found these seven knights
passing heavy. And when he wist how that they sped, as heavy was
he. My lord Uwaine, said Dinadan, I dare lay my head it is Sir
Lamorak de Galis. I promise you all I shall find him an he may be
found in this country. And so Sir Dinadan rode after this knight; and
so did King Mark, that sought him through the forest. So as King
Mark rode after Sir Palomides he heard the noise of a man that made
great dole. Then King Mark rode as nigh that noise as he might and
as he durst. Then was he ware of a knight that was descended off his
horse, and had put off his helm, and there he made a piteous
complaint and a dolorous, of love.

Now leave we that, and talk we of Sir Dinadan, that rode to seek Sir
Palomides. And as he came within a forest he met with a knight, a
chaser of a deer. Sir, said Sir Dinadan, met ye with a knight with a
shield of silver and lions' heads? Yea, fair knight, said the other, with
such a knight met I with but a while agone, and straight yonder way
he yede. Gramercy, said Sir Dinadan, for might I find the track of his
horse I should not fail to find that knight. Right so as Sir Dinadan rode
in the even late he heard a doleful noise as it were of a man. Then Sir
Dinadan rode toward that noise; and when he came nigh that noise he
alighted off his horse, and went near him on foot. Then was he ware
of a knight that stood under a tree, and his horse tied by him, and the
helm off his head; and ever that knight made a doleful complaint as
ever made knight. And always he made his complaint of La Beale
Isoud, the Queen of Cornwall, and said: Ah, fair lady, why love I thee!
for thou art fairest of all other, and yet showest thou never love to me,
nor bounty. Alas, yet must I love thee. And I may not blame thee, fair
lady, for mine eyes be cause of this sorrow. And yet to love thee I am
but a fool, for the best knight of the world loveth thee, and ye him
again, that is Sir Tristram de Liones. And the falsest king and knight is
your husband, and the most coward and full of treason, is your lord,

King Mark. Alas, that ever so fair a lady and peerless of all other should be matched with the most villainous knight of the world. All this language heard King Mark, what Sir Palomides said by him; wherefore he was adread when he saw Sir Dinadan, lest he espied him, that he would tell Sir Palomides that he was King Mark; and therefore he withdrew him, and took his horse and rode to his men, where he commanded them to abide. And so he rode as fast as he might unto Camelot; and the same day he found there Amant, the knight, ready that afore Arthur had appealed him of treason; and so, lightly the king commanded them to do battle. And by misadventure King Mark smote Amant through the body. And yet was Amant in the righteous quarrel. And right so he took his horse and departed from the court for dread of Sir Dinadan, that he would tell Sir Tristram and Sir Palomides what he was. Then were there maidens that La Beale Isoud had sent to Sir Tristram, that knew Sir Amant well.

CHAPTER XV

How King Mark had slain Sir Amant wrongfully to-fore King Arthur, and Sir Launcelot fetched King Mark to King Arthur.

Then by the license of King Arthur they went to him and spake with him; for while the truncheon of the spear stuck in his body he spake: Ah, fair damosels, said Amant, recommend me unto La Beale Isoud, and tell her that I am slain for the love of her and of Sir Tristram. And there he told the damosels how cowardly King Mark had slain him, and Sir Bersules, his fellow. And for that deed I appealed him of treason, and here am I slain in a righteous quarrel; and all was because Sir Bersules and I would not consent by treason to slay the noble knight, Sir Tristram. Then the two maidens cried aloud that all the court might hear it, and said: O sweet Lord Jesu, that knowest all hid things, why sufferest Thou so false a traitor to vanquish and slay a true knight that fought in a righteous quarrel? Then anon it was sprung to the king, and the queen, and to all the lords, that it was King Mark that had slain Sir Amant, and Sir Bersules aforehand; wherefore they did their battle. Then was King Arthur wroth out of measure, and so were all the other knights. But when Sir Tristram knew all the matter he made great dole and sorrow out of measure, and wept for sorrow for the loss of the noble knights, Sir Bersules and of Sir Amant.

When Sir Launcelot espied Sir Tristram weep he went hastily to King Arthur, and said: Sir, I pray you give me leave to return again to yonder false king and knight. I pray you, said King Arthur, fetch him again, but I would not that ye slew him, for my worship. Then Sir Launcelot armed him in all haste, and mounted upon a great horse, and took a spear in his hand and rode after King Mark. And from thence a three mile English Sir Launcelot overtook him, and bade him: Turn recreant king and knight, for whether thou wilt or not thou shalt go with me to King Arthur's court. King Mark returned and looked upon Sir Launcelot, and said: Fair sir, what is your name? Wit thou well, said he, my name is Sir Launcelot, and therefore defend thee. And when King Mark wist that it was Sir Launcelot, and came so fast upon him with a spear, he cried then aloud: I yield me to thee, Sir Launcelot, honourable knight. But Sir Launcelot would not hear him, but came fast upon him. King Mark saw that, and made no defence, but tumbled adown out of his saddle to the earth as a sack, and there he lay still, and cried Sir Launcelot mercy. Arise, recreant knight and king. I will not fight, said King Mark, but whither that ye will I will go with you. Alas, alas, said Sir Launcelot, that I may not give thee one buffet for the love of Sir Tristram and of La Beale Isoud, and for the two knights that thou hast slain traitorly. And so he mounted upon his horse and brought him to King Arthur; and there King Mark alighted in that same place, and threw his helm from him upon the earth, and his sword, and fell flat to the earth of King Arthur's feet, and put him in his grace and mercy. So God me help, said Arthur, ye are welcome in a manner, and in a manner ye are not welcome. In this manner ye are welcome, that ye come hither maugre thy head, as I suppose. That is truth, said King Mark, and else I had not been here, for my lord, Sir Launcelot, brought me hither through his fine force, and to him am I yolden to as recreant. Well, said Arthur, ye understand ye ought to do me service, homage, and fealty. And never would ye do me none, but ever ye have been against me, and a destroyer of my knights; now, how will ye acquit you? Sir, said King Mark, right as your lordship will require me unto my power, I will make a large amends. For he was a speaker, and false thereunder. Then for great pleasure of Sir Tristram, to make them twain accorded, the king withheld King Mark as at that time, and made a broken love-day between them.

CHAPTER XVI

*How Sir Dinadan told Sir Palomides of the battle between
Sir Launcelot and Sir Tristram.*

Now turn we again unto Sir Palomides, how Sir Dinadan comforted
him in all that he might, from his great sorrow. What knight are ye?
said Sir Palomides. Sir, I am a knight-errant as ye be, that hath sought
you long by your shield. Here is my shield, said Sir Palomides, wit ye
well, an ye will ought, therewith I will defend it. Nay, said Sir
Dinadan, I will not have ado with you but in good manner. And if ye
will, ye shall find me soon ready. Sir, said Sir Dinadan, whitherward
ride you this way? By my head, said Sir Palomides, I wot not, but as
fortune leadeth me. Heard ye or saw ye ought of Sir Tristram? So
God me help, of Sir Tristram I both heard and saw, and not for then
we loved not inwardly well together, yet at my mischief Sir Tristram
rescued me from my death; and yet, or he and I departed, by both
our assents we assigned a day that we should have met at the stony
grave that Merlin set beside Camelot, and there to have done battle
together; howbeit I was letted, said Sir Palomides, that I might not
hold my day, the which grieveth me sore; but I have a large excuse.
For I was prisoner with a lord, and many other more, and that shall
Sir Tristram right well understand, that I brake it not of fear of
cowardice. And then Sir Palomides told Sir Dinadan the same day
that they should have met. So God me help, said Sir Dinadan, that
same day met Sir Launcelot and Sir Tristram at the same grave of
stone. And there was the most mightiest battle that ever was seen in
this land betwixt two knights, for they fought more than two hours.
And there they both bled so much blood that all men marvelled that
ever they might endure it. And so at the last, by both their assents,
they were made friends and sworn-brethren for ever, and no man can
judge the better knight. And now is Sir Tristram made a knight of the
Round Table, and he sitteth in the siege of the noble knight, Sir
Marhaus. By my head, said Sir Palomides, Sir Tristram is far bigger
than Sir Launcelot, and the hardier knight. Have ye assayed them
both? said Sir Dinadan. I have seen Sir Tristram fight, said Sir

Palomides, but never Sir Launcelot to my witting. But at the fountain where Sir Launcelot lay asleep, there with one spear he smote down Sir Tristram and me, said Palomides, but at that time they knew not either other. Fair knight, said Sir Dinadan, as for Sir Launcelot and Sir Tristram let them be, for the worst of them will not be lightly matched of no knights that I know living. No, said Sir Palomides, God defend, but an I had a quarrel to the better of them both I would with as good a will fight with him as with you. Sir, I require you tell me your name, and in good faith I shall hold you company till that we come to Camelot; and there shall ye have great worship now at this great tournament; for there shall be the Queen Guenever, and La Beale Isoud of Cornwall. Wit you well, sir knight, for the love of La Beale Isoud I will be there, and else not, but I will not have ado in King Arthur's court. Sir, said Dinadan, I shall ride with you and do you service, so you will tell me your name. Sir, ye shall understand my name is Sir Palomides, brother to Safere, the good and noble knight. And Sir Segwarides and I, we be Saracens born, of father and mother. Sir, said Sir Dinadan, I thank you much for the telling of your name. For I am glad of that I know your name, and I promise you by the faith of my body, ye shall not be hurt by me by my will, but rather be advanced. And thereto will I help you with all my power, I promise you, doubt ye not. And certainly on my life ye shall win great worship in the court of King Arthur, and be right welcome. So then they dressed on their helms and put on their shields, and mounted upon their horses, and took the broad way towards Camelot. And then were they ware of a castle that was fair and rich, and also passing strong as any was within this realm.

CHAPTER XVII

How Sir Lamorak jousted with divers knights of the castle wherein was Morgan le Fay.

Sir Palomides, said Dinadan, here is a castle that I know well, and therein dwelleth Queen Morgan le Fay, King Arthur's sister; and King Arthur gave her this castle, the which he hath repented him sithen a thousand times, for sithen King Arthur and she have been at debate and strife; but this castle could he never get nor win of her by no manner of engine; and ever as she might she made war on King Arthur. And all dangerous knights she withholdeth with her, for to destroy all these knights that King Arthur loveth. And there shall no knight pass this way but he must joust with one knight, or with two, or with three. And if it hap that King Arthur's knight be beaten, he shall lose his horse and his harness and all that he hath, and hard, if that he escape, but that he shall be prisoner. So God me help, said Palomides, this is a shameful custom, and a villainous usance for a queen to use, and namely to make such war upon her own lord, that is called the Flower of Chivalry that is christian or heathen; and with all my heart I would destroy that shameful custom. And I will that all the world wit she shall have no service of me. And if she send out any knights, as I suppose she will, for to joust, they shall have both their hands full. And I shall not fail you, said Sir Dinadan, unto my puissance, upon my life.

So as they stood on horseback afore the castle, there came a knight with a red shield, and two squires after him: and he came straight unto Sir Palomides, the good knight, and said to him: Fair and gentle knight-errant, I require thee for the love thou owest unto knighthood, that ye will not have ado here with these men of this castle; for this was Sir Lamorak that thus said. For I came hither to seek this deed, and it is my request; and therefore I beseech you, knight, let me deal, and if I be beaten revenge me. In the name of God, said Palomides, let see how ye will speed, and we shall behold you. Then anon came forth a knight of the castle, and proffered to joust with the Knight with the Red Shield. Anon they encountered together, and he with the red shield smote him so hard that he bare him over to the earth. Therewith anon came another knight of the castle, and he was smitten so sore that he avoided his saddle. And forthwithal came the third knight, and the Knight with the Red Shield smote him to the earth. Then came Sir Palomides, and besought him that he might help him to joust. Fair knight, said he unto him, suffer me as at this time to have my will, for an they were twenty knights I shall not doubt them. And ever there were upon the walls of the castle many lords and ladies that cried and said: Well have ye jousted, Knight with the Red Shield. But as soon as the knight had smitten them down, his squire took their horses, and avoided their saddles and bridles of the horses, and turned them into the forest, and made the knights to be kept to the end of the jousts. Right so came out of the castle the fourth knight, and freshly proffered to joust with the Knight with the Red Shield: and he was ready, and he smote him so hard that horse and man fell to the earth, and the knight's back brake with the fall, and his neck also. O Jesu, said Sir Palomides, that yonder is a passing good knight, and the best jouster that ever I saw. By my head, said Sir Dinadan, he is as good as ever was Sir Launcelot or Sir Tristram, what knight somever he be.

CHAPTER XVIII

How Sir Palomides would have jousted for Sir Lamorak with the knights of the castle.

Then forthwithal came a knight out of the castle, with a shield bended with black and with white. And anon the Knight with the Red Shield and he encountered so hard that he smote the knight of the castle through the bended shield and through the body, and brake the horse's back. Fair knight, said Sir Palomides, ye have overmuch on hand, therefore I pray you let me joust, for ye had need to be reposed. Why sir, said the knight, seem ye that I am weak and feeble? and sir, methinketh ye proffer me wrong, and to me shame, when I do well enough. I tell you now as I told you erst; for an they were twenty knights I shall beat them, and if I be beaten or slain then may ye revenge me. And if ye think that I be weary, and ye have an appetite to joust with me, I shall find you jousting enough. Sir, said Palomides, I said it not because I would joust with you, but meseemeth that ye have overmuch on hand. And therefore, an ye were gentle, said the Knight with the Red Shield, ye should not proffer me shame; therefore I require you to joust with me, and ye shall find that I am not weary. Sith ye require me, said Sir Palomides, take keep to yourself. Then they two knights came together as fast as their horses might run, and the knight smote Sir Palomides so sore on the shield that the spear went into his side a great wound, and a perilous. And therewithal Sir Palomides avoided his saddle. And that knight turned unto Sir Dinadan; and when he saw him coming he cried aloud, and said: Sir, I will not have ado with you; but for that he let it not, but came straight upon him. So Sir Dinadan for shame put forth his spear and all to-shivered it upon the knight. But he smote Sir Dinadan again so hard that he smote him clean from his saddle; but their horses he would not suffer his squires to meddle with, and because they were knights-errant.

Then he dressed him again to the castle, and jousted with seven knights more, and there was none of them might withstand him, but he bare him to the earth. And of these twelve knights he slew in plain jousts four. And the eight knights he made them to swear on the cross of a sword that they should never use the evil customs of the castle. And when he had made them to swear that oath he let them pass. And ever stood the lords and the ladies on the castle walls crying and saying: Knight with the Red Shield, ye have marvellously well done as ever we saw knight do. And therewith came a knight out of the castle unarmed, and said: Knight with the Red Shield, overmuch damage hast thou done to us this day, therefore return whither thou wilt, for here are no more will have ado with thee; for we repent sore that ever thou camest here, for by thee is fordone the old custom of this castle. And with that word he turned again into the castle, and shut the gates. Then the Knight with the Red Shield turned and called his squires, and so passed forth on his way, and rode a great pace.

And when he was past Sir Palomides went to Sir Dinadan, and said: I had never such a shame of one knight that ever I met; and therefore I cast me to ride after him, and to be revenged with my sword, for a-horseback I deem I shall get no worship of him. Sir Palomides, said Dinadan, ye shall not meddle with him by my counsel, for ye shall get no worship of him; and for this cause, ye have seen him this day have had overmuch to do, and overmuch travailed. By almighty Jesu, said Palomides, I shall never be at ease till that I have had ado with him. Sir, said Dinadan, I shall give you my beholding. Well, said Palomides, then shall ye see how we shall redress our mights. So they took their horses of their varlets, and rode after the Knight with the Red Shield; and down in a valley beside a fountain they were ware where he was alighted to repose him, and had done off his helm for to drink at the well.

CHAPTER XIX

*How Sir Lamorak jousted with Sir Palomides,
and hurt him grievously.*

Then Palomides rode fast till he came nigh him. And then he said:
Knight, remember ye of the shame ye did to me right now at the
castle, therefore dress thee, for I will have ado with thee. Fair knight,
said he to Palomides, of me ye win no worship, for ye have seen this
day that I have been travailed sore. As for that, said Palomides, I will
not let, for wit ye well I will be revenged. Well, said the knight, I
may happen to endure you. And therewithal he mounted upon his
horse, and took a great spear in his hand ready for to joust. Nay, said
Palomides, I will not joust, for I am sure at jousting I get no prize.
Fair knight, said that knight, it would beseem a knight to joust and to
fight on horseback. Ye shall see what I will do, said Palomides. And
therewith he alighted down upon foot, and dressed his shield afore
him and pulled out his sword. Then the Knight with the Red Shield
descended down from his horse, and dressed his shield afore him, and
so he drew out his sword. And then they came together a soft pace,
and wonderly they lashed together passing thick the mountenance of
an hour or ever they breathed. Then they traced and traversed, and
waxed wonderly wroth, and either behight other death; they hewed
so fast with their swords that they cut in down half their swords and
mails, that the bare flesh in some place stood above their harness. And
when Sir Palomides beheld his fellow's sword over-hylled with his
blood it grieved him sore: some while they foined, some while they
struck as wild men. But at the last Sir Palomides waxed faint, because
of his first wound that he had at the castle with a spear, for that
wound grieved him wonderly sore. Fair knight, said Palomides,
meseemeth we have assayed either other passing sore, and if it may
please thee, I require thee of thy knighthood tell me thy name. Sir,
said the knight to Palomides, that is me loath to do, for thou hast
done me wrong and no knighthood to proffer me battle, considering
my great travail, but an thou wilt tell me thy name I will tell thee
mine. Sir, said he, wit thou well my name is Palomides. Ah, sir, ye

shall understand my name is Sir Lamorak de Galis, son and heir unto
the good knight and king, King Pellinore, and Sir Tor, the good
knight, is my half brother. When Sir Palomides heard him say so he
kneeled down and asked mercy, For outrageously have I done to you
this day; considering the great deeds of arms I have seen you do,
shamefully and unknightly I have required you to do battle. Ah, Sir
Palomides, said Sir Lamorak, overmuch have ye done and said to me.
And therewith he embraced him with his both hands, and said:
Palomides, the worthy knight, in all this land is no better than ye, nor
more of prowess, and me repenteth sore that we should fight
together. So it doth not me, said Sir Palomides, and yet am I sorer
wounded than ye be; but as for that I shall soon thereof be whole.
But certainly I would not for the fairest castle in this land, but if thou
and I had met, for I shall love you the days of my life afore all other
knights except my brother, Sir Safere. I say the same, said Sir
Lamorak, except my brother, Sir Tor. Then came Sir Dinadan, and
he made great joy of Sir Lamorak. Then their squires dressed both
their shields and their harness, and stopped their wounds. And
thereby at a priory they rested them all night.

CHAPTER XX

*How it was told Sir Launcelot that Dagonet chased King
Mark, and how a knight overthrew him and six knights.*

Now turn we again. When Sir Ganis and Sir Brandiles with his
fellows came to the court of King Arthur they told the king, Sir
Launcelot, and Sir Tristram, how Sir Dagonet, the fool, chased King
Mark through the forest, and how the strong knight smote them
down all seven with one spear. There was great laughing and japing
at King Mark and at Sir Dagonet. But all these knights could not tell
what knight it was that rescued King Mark. Then they asked King
Mark if that he knew him, and he answered and said: He named
himself the Knight that followed the Questing Beast, and on that
name he sent one of my varlets to a place where was his mother; and
when she heard from whence he came she made passing great dole,
and discovered to my varlet his name, and said: Oh, my dear son, Sir

Palomides, why wilt thou not see me? And therefore, sir, said King Mark, it is to understand his name is Sir Palomides, a noble knight. Then were all these seven knights glad that they knew his name.

Now turn we again, for on the morn they took their horses, both Sir Lamorak, Palomides, and Dinadan, with their squires and varlets, till they saw a fair castle that stood on a mountain well closed, and thither they rode; and there they found a knight that hight Galahalt, that was lord of that castle, and there they had great cheer and were well eased. Sir Dinadan, said Sir Lamorak, what will ye do? Oh sir, said Dinadan, I will to-morrow to the court of King Arthur. By my head, said Sir Palomides, I will not ride these three days, for I am sore hurt, and much have I bled, and therefore I will repose me here. Truly, said Sir Lamorak, and I will abide here with you; and when ye ride, then will I ride, unless that ye tarry over long; then will I take my horse. Therefore I pray you, Sir Dinadan, abide and ride with us. Faithfully, said Dinadan, I will not abide, for I have such a talent to see Sir Tristram that I may not abide long from him. Ah, Dinadan, said Sir Palomides, now do I understand that ye love my mortal enemy, and therefore how should I trust you. Well, said Dinadan, I love my lord Sir Tristram, above all other, and him will I serve and do honour. So shall I, said Sir Lamorak, in all that may lie in my power.

So on the morn Sir Dinadan rode unto the court of King Arthur; and by the way as he rode he saw where stood an errant knight, and made him ready for to joust. Not so, said Dinadan, for I have no will to joust. With me shall ye joust, said the knight, or that ye pass this way. Whether ask ye jousts, by love or by hate? The knight answered: Wit ye well I ask it for love, and not for hate. It may well be so, said Sir Dinadan, but ye proffer me hard love when ye will joust with me with a sharp spear. But, fair knight, said Sir Dinadan, sith ye will joust with me, meet with me in the court of King Arthur, and there shall I joust with you. Well, said the knight, sith ye will not joust with me, I pray you tell me your name. Sir knight, said he, my name is Sir Dinadan. Ah, said the knight, full well know I you for a good knight and a gentle, and wit you well I love you heartily. Then shall there be no jousts, said Dinadan, betwixt us. So they departed. And the same day he came to Camelot, where lay King Arthur. And there he saluted the king and the queen, Sir Launcelot, and Sir Tristram; and all the court was glad of Sir Dinadan, for he was gentle, wise, and courteous, and a good knight. And in especial, the valiant

knight Sir Tristram loved Sir Dinadan passing well above all other
knights save Sir Launcelot.

Then the king asked Sir Dinadan what adventures he had seen. Sir,
said Dinadan, I have seen many adventures, and of some King Mark
knoweth, but not all. Then the king hearkened Sir Dinadan, how he
told that Sir Palomides and he were afore the castle of Morgan le Fay,
and how Sir Lamorak took the jousts afore them, and how he for-
jousted twelve knights, and of them four he slew, and how after he
smote down Sir Palomides and me both. I may not believe that, said
the king, for Sir Palomides is a passing good knight. That is very
truth, said Sir Dinadan, but yet I saw him better proved, hand for
hand. And then he told the king all that battle, and how Sir
Palomides was more weaker, and more hurt, and more lost of his
blood. And without doubt, said Sir Dinadan, had the battle longer
lasted, Palomides had been slain. O Jesu, said King Arthur, this is to
me a great marvel. Sir, said Tristram, marvel ye nothing thereof, for at
mine advice there is not a valianter knight in the world living, for I
know his might. And now I will say you, I was never so weary of
knight but if it were Sir Launcelot. And there is no knight in the
world except Sir Launcelot that did so well as Sir Lamorak. So God
me help, said the king, I would that knight, Sir Lamorak, came to this
Court. Sir, said Dinadan, he will be here in short space, and Sir
Palomides both, but I fear that Palomides may not yet travel.

CHAPTER XXI

*How King Arthur let do cry a jousts, and how Sir Lamorak
came in, and overthrew Sir Gawaine and many other.*

Then within three days after the king let make a jousting at a priory.
And there made them ready many knights of the Round Table, for
Sir Gawaine and his brethren made them ready to joust; but Tristram,
Launcelot, nor Dinadan, would not joust, but suffered Sir Gawaine,
for the love of King Arthur, with his brethren, to win the gree if they
might. Then on the morn they apparelled them to joust, Sir Gawaine
and his four brethren, and did there great deeds of arms. And Sir
Ector de Maris did marvellously well, but Sir Gawaine passed all that

fellowship; wherefore King Arthur and all the knights gave Sir Gawaine the honour at the beginning.

Right so King Arthur was ware of a knight and two squires, the which came out of a forest side, with a shield covered with leather, and then he came slyly and hurtled here and there, and anon with one spear he had smitten down two knights of the Round Table. Then with his hurtling he lost the covering of his shield, then was the king and all other ware that he bare a red shield. O Jesu, said King Arthur, see where rideth a stout knight, he with the red shield. And there was noise and crying: Beware the Knight with the Red Shield. So within a little while he had overthrown three brethren of Sir Gawaine's. So God me help, said King Arthur, meseemeth yonder is the best jouster that ever I saw. With that he saw him encounter with Sir Gawaine, and he smote him down with so great force that he made his horse to avoid his saddle. How now, said the king, Sir Gawaine hath a fall; well were me an I knew what knight he were with the red shield. I know him well, said Dinadan, but as at this time ye shall not know his name. By my head, said Sir Tristram, he jousted better than Sir Palomides, and if ye list to know his name, wit ye well his name is Sir Lamorak de Galis.

As they stood thus talking, Sir Gawaine and he encountered together again, and there he smote Sir Gawaine from his horse, and bruised him sore. And in the sight of King Arthur he smote down twenty knights, beside Sir Gawaine and his brethren. And so clearly was the prize given him as a knight peerless. Then slyly and marvellously Sir Lamorak withdrew him from all the fellowship into the forest side. All this espied King Arthur, for his eye went never from him. Then the king, Sir Launcelot, Sir Tristram, and Sir Dinadan, took their hackneys, and rode straight after the good knight, Sir Lamorak de Galis, and there found him. And thus said the king: Ah, fair knight, well be ye found. When he saw the king he put off his helm and saluted him, and when he saw Sir Tristram he alighted down off his horse and ran to him to take him by the thighs, but Sir Tristram would not suffer him, but he alighted or that he came, and either took other in arms, and made great joy of other. The king was glad, and also was all the fellowship of the Round Table, except Sir Gawaine and his brethren. And when they wist that he was Sir Lamorak, they had great despite at him, and were wonderly wroth with him that he had put them to dishonour that day.

Then Gawaine called privily in council all his brethren, and to them said thus: Fair brethren, here may ye see, whom that we hate King Arthur loveth, and whom that we love he hateth. And wit ye well, my fair brethren, that this Sir Lamorak will never love us, because we slew his father, King Pellinore, for we deemed that he slew our father, King of Orkney. And for the despite of Pellinore, Sir Lamorak did us a shame to our mother, therefore I will be revenged. Sir, said Sir Gawaine's brethren, let see how ye will or may be revenged, and ye shall find us ready. Well, said Gawaine, hold you still and we shall espy our time.

CHAPTER XXII

How King Arthur made King Mark to be accorded with
Sir Tristram, and how they departed toward Cornwall.

Now pass we our matter, and leave we Sir Gawaine, and speak of King Arthur, that on a day said unto King Mark: Sir, I pray you give me a gift that I shall ask you. Sir, said King Mark, I will give you whatsomever ye desire an it be in my power. Sir, gramercy, said Arthur. This I will ask you, that ye will be good lord unto Sir Tristram, for he is a man of great honour; and that ye will take him with you into Cornwall, and let him see his friends, and there cherish him for my sake. Sir, said King Mark, I promise you by the faith of my body, and by the faith that I owe to God and to you, I shall worship him for your sake in all that I can or may. Sir, said Arthur, and I will forgive you all the evil will that ever I ought you, an so be that you swear that upon a book before me. With a good will, said King Mark; and so he there sware upon a book afore him and all his knights, and therewith King Mark and Sir Tristram took either other by the hands hard knit together. But for all this King Mark thought falsely, as it proved after, for he put Sir Tristram in prison, and cowardly would have slain him.

Then soon after King Mark took his leave to ride into Cornwall, and Sir Tristram made him ready to ride with him, whereof the most part of the Round Table were wroth and heavy, and in especial Sir Launcelot, and Sir Lamorak, and Sir Dinadan, were wroth out of measure. For well they wist King Mark would slay or destroy Sir Tristram. Alas, said Dinadan, that my lord, Sir Tristram, shall depart. And Sir Tristram took such sorrow that he was amazed like a fool. Alas, said Sir Launcelot unto King Arthur, what have ye done, for ye shall lose the most man of worship that ever came into your court. It was his own desire, said Arthur, and therefore I might not do withal, for I have done all that I can and made them at accord. Accord, said Sir Launcelot, fie upon that accord, for ye shall hear that he shall slay Sir Tristram, or put him in a prison, for he is the most coward and the villainest king and knight that is now living.

And therewith Sir Launcelot departed, and came to King Mark, and said to him thus: Sir king, wit thou well the good knight Sir Tristram shall go with thee. Beware, I rede thee, of treason, for an thou mischief that knight by any manner of falsehood or treason, by the faith I owe to God and to the order of knighthood, I shall slay thee with mine own hands. Sir Launcelot, said the king, overmuch have ye said to me, and I have sworn and said over largely afore King Arthur in hearing of all his knights, that I shall not slay nor betray him. It were to me overmuch shame to break my promise. Ye say well, said Sir Launcelot, but ye are called so false and full of treason that no man may believe you. Forsooth it is known well wherefore ye came into this country, and for none other cause but for to slay Sir Tristram. So with great dole King Mark and Sir Tristram rode together, for it was by Sir Tristram's will and his means to go with King Mark, and all was for the intent to see La Beale Isoud, for without the sight of her Sir Tristram might not endure.

CHAPTER XXIII

How Sir Percivale was made knight of King Arthur, and how a dumb maid spake, and brought him to the Round Table.

Now turn we again unto Sir Lamorak, and speak we of his brethren, Sir Tor, which was King Pellinore's first son and begotten on the wife of Aries the cowherd, for he was a bastard; and Sir Aglovale was his first son begotten in wedlock; Sir Lamorak, Dornar, Percivale, these were his sons too in wedlock. So when King Mark and Sir

Tristram were departed from the court there was made great dole and sorrow for the departing of Sir Tristram. Then the king and his knights made no manner of joys eight days after. And at the eight days' end there came to the court a knight with a young squire with him. And when this knight was unarmed, he went to the king and required him to make the young squire a knight. Of what lineage is he come? said King Arthur. Sir, said the knight, he is the son of King Pellinore, that did you some time good service, and he is a brother unto Sir Lamorak de Galis, the good knight. Well, said the king, for what cause desire ye that of me that I should make him knight? Wit you well, my lord the king, that this young squire is brother to me as well as to Sir Lamorak, and my name is Aglavale. Sir Aglavale, said Arthur, for the love of Sir Lamorak, and for his father's love, he shall be made knight to-morrow. Now tell me, said Arthur, what is his name? Sir, said the knight, his name is Percivale de Galis. So on the morn the king made him knight in Camelot. But the king and all the knights thought it would be long or that he proved a good knight.

Then at the dinner, when the king was set at the table, and every knight after he was of prowess, the king commanded him to be set among mean knights; and so was Sir Percivale set as the king commanded. Then was there a maiden in the queen's court that was come of high blood, and she was dumb and never spake word. Right so she came straight into the hall, and went unto Sir Percivale, and took him by the hand and said aloud, that the king and all the knights might hear it: Arise, Sir Percivale, the noble knight and God's knight, and go with me; and so he did. And there she brought him to the right side of the Siege Perilous, and said, Fair knight, take here thy siege, for that siege appertaineth to thee and to none other. Right so she departed and asked a priest. And as she was confessed and houselled then she died. Then the king and all the court made great joy of Sir Percivale.

CHAPTER XXIV

How Sir Lamorak visited King Lot's wife, and how
Sir Gaheris slew her which was his own mother.

Now turn we unto Sir Lamorak, that much was there praised. Then,
by the mean of Sir Gawaine and his brethren, they sent for their
mother there besides, fast by a castle beside Camelot; and all was to
that intent to slay Sir Lamorak. The Queen of Orkney was there but
a while, but Sir Lamorak wist of their being, and was full fain; and for
to make an end of this matter, he sent unto her, and there betwixt
them was a night assigned that Sir Lamorak should come to her.
Thereof was ware Sir Gaheris, and there he rode afore the same
night, and waited upon Sir Lamorak, and then he saw where he came
all armed. And where Sir Lamorak alighted he tied his horse to a
privy postern, and so he went into a parlour and unarmed him; and
then he went unto the queen's bed, and she made of him passing
great joy, and he of her again, for either loved other passing sore. So
when the knight, Sir Gaheris, saw his time, he came to their bedside
all armed, with his sword naked, and suddenly gat his mother by the
hair and struck off her head.

When Sir Lamorak saw the blood dash upon him all hot, the
which he loved passing well, wit you well he was sore abashed and
dismayed of that dolorous knight. And therewithal, Sir Lamorak leapt
out of the bed in his shirt ; as a knight dismayed, saying thus: Ah, Sir
Gaheris, knight of the Table Round, foul and evil have ye done, and
to you great shame. Alas, why have ye slain your mother that bare
you? with more right ye should have slain me. The offence hast thou
done, said Gaheris, notwithstanding a man is born to offer his service;
but yet shouldst thou beware with whom thou meddlest, for thou
hast put me and my brethren to a shame, and thy father slew our
father; and thou to lie by our mother is too much shame for us to
suffer. And as for thy father, King Pellinore, my brother Sir Gawaine
and I slew him. Ye did him the more wrong, said Sir Lamorak, for
my father slew not your father, it was Balin le Savage: and as yet my
father's death is not revenged. Leave those words, said Sir Gaheris, for

an thou speak feloniously I will slay thee. But because thou art naked I am ashamed to slay thee. But wit thou well, in what place I may get thee I shall slay thee; and now my mother is quit of thee; and withdraw thee and take thine armour, that thou were gone. Sir Lamorak saw there was none other bote, but fast armed him, and took his horse and rode his way making great sorrow. But for the shame and dolour he would not ride to King Arthur's court, but rode another way.

But when it was known that Gaheris had slain his mother the king was passing wroth, and commanded him to go out of his court. Wit ye well Sir Gawaine was wroth that Gaheris had slain his mother and let Sir Lamorak escape. And for this matter was the king passing wroth, and so was Sir Launcelot, and many other knights. Sir, said Sir Launcelot, here is a great mischief befallen by felony, and by forecast treason, that your sister is thus shamefully slain. And I dare say that it was wrought by treason; and I dare say ye shall lose that good knight, Sir Lamorak, the which is great pity. I wot well and am sure, an Sir Tristram wist it, he would never more come within your court, the which should grieve you much more and all your knights. God defend, said the noble King Arthur, that I should lose Sir Lamorak or Sir Tristram, for then twain of my chief knights of the Table Round were gone. Sir, said Sir Launcelot, I am sure ye shall lose Sir Lamorak, for Sir Gawaine and his brethren will slay him by one mean or other; for they among them have concluded and sworn to slay him an ever they may see their time. That shall I let, said Arthur.

CHAPTER XXV

How Sir Agravaine and Sir Mordred met with a knight fleeing, and how they both were overthrown, and of Sir Dinadan.

Now leave we of Sir Lamorak, and speak of Sir Gawaine's brethren, and specially of Sir Agravaine and Sir Mordred. As they rode on their adventures they met with a knight fleeing, sore wounded; and they asked him what tidings. Fair knights, said he, here cometh a knight after me that will slay me. With that came Sir Dinadan riding to them by adventure, but he would promise them no help. But Sir Agravaine and Sir Mordred promised him to rescue him. Therewithal came that knight straight unto them, and anon he proffered to joust. That saw Sir Mordred and rode to him, but he struck Mordred over his horse's tail. That saw Sir Agravaine, and straight he rode toward that knight, and right so as he served Mordred so he served Agravaine, and said to them: Sirs, wit ye well both that I am Breuse Saunce Pité, that hath done this to you. And yet he rode over Agravaine five or six times. When Dinadan saw this, he must needs joust with him for shame. And so Dinadan and he encountered together, that with pure strength Sir Dinadan smote him over his horse's tail. Then he took his horse and fled, for he was on foot one of the valiantest knights in Arthur's days, and a great destroyer of all good knights.

Then rode Sir Dinadan unto Sir Mordred and unto Sir Agravaine. Sir knight, said they all, well have ye done, and well have ye revenged us, wherefore we pray you tell us your name. Fair sirs, ye ought to know my name, the which is called Sir Dinadan. When they understood that it was Dinadan they were more wroth than they were before, for they hated him out of measure because of Sir Lamorak. For Dinadan had such a custom that he loved all good knights that were valiant, and he hated all those that were destroyers of good knights. And there were none that hated Dinadan but those that ever were called murderers. Then spake the hurt knight that Breuse Saunce Pité had chased, his name was Dalan, and said: If thou be Dinadan thou slewest my father. It may well be so, said Dinadan, but then it was in my defence and at his request. By my head, said Dalan, thou shalt die therefore, and therewith he dressed his spear and his shield. And to make the shorter tale, Sir Dinadan smote him down off his horse, that his neck was nigh broken. And in the same wise he smote Sir Mordred and Sir Agravaine. And after, in the quest of the Sangreal, cowardly and feloniously they slew Dinadan, the which was great damage, for he was a great bourder and a passing good knight.

And so Sir Dinadan rode to a castle that hight Beale-Valet. And there he found Sir Palomides that was not yet whole of the wound that Sir Lamorak gave him. And there Dinadan told Palomides all the tidings that he heard and saw of Sir Tristram, and how he was gone with King Mark, and with him he hath all his will and desire. Therewith Sir Palomides waxed wroth, for he loved La Beale Isoud. And then he wist well that Sir Tristram enjoyed her.

CHAPTER XXVI

How King Arthur, the Queen, and Launcelot received letters
out of Cornwall, and of the answer again.

Now leave we Sir Palomides and Sir Dinadan in the Castle of Beale-Valet, and turn we again unto King Arthur. There came a knight out of Cornwall, his name was Fergus, a fellow of the Round Table. And there he told the king and Sir Launcelot good tidings of Sir Tristram, and there were brought goodly letters, and how he left him in the castle of Tintagil. Then came the damosel that brought goodly letters unto King Arthur and unto Sir Launcelot, and there she had passing good cheer of the king, and of the Queen Guenever, and of Sir Launcelot. Then they wrote goodly letters again. But Sir Launcelot bade ever Sir Tristram beware of King Mark, for ever he called him in his letters King Fox, as who saith, he fareth all with wiles and treason. Whereof Sir Tristram in his heart thanked Sir Launcelot. Then the damosel went unto La Beale Isoud, and bare her letters from the king and from Sir Launcelot, whereof she was in passing great joy. Fair damosel, said La Beale Isoud, how fareth my Lord Arthur and the Queen Guenever, and the noble knight, Sir Launcelot? She answered, and to make short tale: Much the better that ye and Sir Tristram be in joy. God reward them, said La Beale Isoud, for Sir Tristram suffereth great pain for me, and I for him.

So the damosel departed, and brought letters to King Mark. And when he had read them, and understood them, he was wroth with Sir Tristram, for he deemed that he had sent the damosel unto King Arthur. For Arthur and Launcelot in a manner threated King Mark. And as King Mark read these letters he deemed treason by Sir Tristram. Damosel, said King Mark, will ye ride again and bear letters from me unto King Arthur? Sir, she said, I will be at your commandment to ride when ye will. Ye say well, said the king; come again, said the king, to-morn, and fetch your letters. Then she departed and told them how she should ride again with letters unto Arthur. Then we pray you, said La Beale Isoud and Sir Tristram, that when ye have received your letters, that ye would come by us that we may see the privity of your letters. All that I may do, madam, ye wot well I must do for Sir Tristram, for I have been long his own maiden.

So on the morn the damosel went to King Mark to have had his letters and to depart. I am not avised, said King Mark, as at this time to send my letters Then privily and secretly he sent letters unto King Arthur, and unto Queen Guenever, and unto Sir Launcelot. So the varlet departed, and found the king and the queen in Wales, at Carlion. And as the king and the queen were at mass the varlet came with the letters. And when mass was done the king and the queen opened the letters privily by themself. And the beginning of the king's letters spake wonderly short unto King Arthur, and bade him entermete with himself and with his wife, and of his knights; for he was able enough to rule and keep his wife.

CHAPTER XXVII

How Sir Launcelot was wroth with the letter that he
received from King Mark, and of Dinadan
which made a lay of King Mark.

When King Arthur understood the letter, he mused of many things, and thought on his sister's words, Queen Morgan le Fay, that she had said betwixt Queen Guenever and Sir Launcelot. And in this thought he studied a great while. Then he bethought him again how his sister was his own enemy, and that she hated the queen and Sir Launcelot, and so he put all that out of his thought. Then King Arthur read the letter again, and the latter clause said that King Mark took Sir Tristram for his mortal enemy; wherefore he put Arthur out of doubt he would be revenged of Sir Tristram. Then was King Arthur wroth with King Mark. And when Queen Guenever read her letter and understood it, she was wroth out of measure, for the letter spake shame by her and by Sir Launcelot. And so privily she sent the letter unto Sir Launcelot. And when he wist the intent of the letter he was so wroth that he laid him down on his bed to sleep, whereof Sir Dinadan was ware, for it was his manner to be privy with all good knights. And as Sir Launcelot slept he stole the letter out of his hand, and read it word by word. And then he made great sorrow for anger.

And so Sir Launcelot awaked, and went to a window, and read the letter again, the which made him angry.

Sir, said Dinadan, wherefore be ye angry? discover your heart to me: forsooth ye wot well I owe you good will, howbeit I am a poor knight and a servitor unto you and to all good knights. For though I be not of worship myself I love all those that be of worship. It is truth, said Sir Launcelot, ye are a trusty knight, and for great trust I will show you my counsel. And when Dinadan understood all, he said: This is my counsel: set you right nought by these threats, for King Mark is so villainous, that by fair speech shall never man get of him. But ye shall see what I shall do; I will make a lay for him, and when it is made I shall make an harper to sing it afore him. So anon he went and made it, and taught it an harper that hight Eliot. And when he could sing it, he taught it to many harpers. And so by the will of Sir Launcelot, and of Arthur, the harpers went straight into Wales, and into Cornwall, to sing the lay that Sir Dinadan made by King Mark, the which was the worst lay that ever harper sang with harp or with any other instruments.

CHAPTER XXVIII

How Sir Tristram was hurt, and of a war made to King Mark; and of Sir Tristram how he promised to rescue him.

Now turn we again unto Sir Tristram and to King Mark. As Sir Tristram was at jousts and at tournament it fortuned he was sore hurt both with a spear and with a sword, but yet he won always the degree. And for to repose him he went to a good knight that dwelled in Cornwall, in a castle, whose name was Sir Dinas le Seneschal. Then by misfortune there came out of Sessoin a great number of men of arms, and an hideous host, and they entered nigh the Castle of Tintagil; and their captain's name was Elias, a good man of arms. When King Mark understood his enemies were entered into his land he made great dole and sorrow, for in no wise by his will King Mark would not send for Sir Tristram, for he hated him deadly.

So when his council was come they devised and cast many perils of the strength of their enemies. And then they concluded all at once, and said thus unto King Mark: Sir, wit ye well ye must send for Sir Tristram, the good knight, or else they will never be overcome. For by Sir Tristram they must be foughten withal, or else we row against the stream. Well, said King Mark, I will do by your counsel; but yet he was full loath thereto, but need constrained him to send for him. Then was he sent for in all haste that might be, that he should come to King Mark. And when he understood that King Mark had sent for him, he mounted upon a soft ambler and rode to King Mark. And when he was come the king said thus: Fair nephew, Sir Tristram, this is all. Here be come our enemies of Sessoin, that are here nigh hand, and without tarrying they must be met with shortly, or else they will destroy this country. Sir, said Sir Tristram, wit ye well all my power is at your commandment. And wit ye well, sir, these eight days I may bear none arms, for my wounds be not yet whole. And by that day I shall do what I may. Ye say well, said King Mark; then go ye again and repose you and make you fresh, and I shall go and meet the Sessoins with all my power.

So the king departed unto Tintagil, and Sir Tristram went to repose him. And the king made a great host, and departed them in three; the first part led Sir Dinas the Seneschal, and Sir Andred led the second part, and Sir Argius led the third part; and he was of the blood of King Mark. And the Sessoins had three great battles, and many good men of arms. And so King Mark by the advice of his knights issued out of the Castle of Tintagil upon his enemies. And Dinas, the good knight, rode out afore, and slew two knights with his own hands, and then began the battles. And there was marvellous breaking of spears and smiting of swords, and slew down many good knights. And ever was Sir Dinas the Seneschal the best of King Mark's party. And thus the battle endured long with great mortality. But at the last King Mark and Sir Dinas, were they never so loath, they withdrew them to the Castle of Tintagil with great slaughter of people; and the Sessoins followed on fast, that ten of them were put within the gates and four slain with the portcullis.

Then King Mark sent for Sir Tristram by a varlet, that told him all the mortality. Then he sent the varlet again, and bade him: Tell King Mark that I will come as soon as I am whole, for erst I may do him no good. Then King Mark had his answer. Therewith came Elias and bade the king yield up the castle: For ye may not hold it no while. Sir Elias, said the king, so will I yield up the castle if I be not soon rescued. Anon King Mark sent again for rescue to Sir Tristram. By then Sir Tristram was whole, and he had gotten him ten good knights of Arthur's; and with them he rode unto Tintagil. And when he saw the great host of Sessoins he marvelled wonder greatly. And then Sir Tristram rode by the woods and by the ditches as secretly as he might, till he came nigh the gates. And there dressed a knight to him when he saw that Sir Tristram would enter; and Sir Tristram smote him down dead, and so he served three more. And everych of these ten knights slew a man of arms. So Sir Tristram entered into the Castle of Tintagil. And when King Mark wist that Sir Tristram was come he was glad of his coming, and so was all the fellowship, and or him they made great joy.

CHAPTER XXIX

How Sir Tristram overcame the battle, and how Elias desired a man to fight body for body.

So on the morn Elias the captain came, and bade King Mark: Come out and do battle; for now the good knight Sir Tristram is entered it will be shame to thee, said Elias, for to keep thy walls. When King Mark understood this he was wroth and said no word, but went unto Sir Tristram and asked him his counsel. Sir, said Sir Tristram, will ye that I give him his answer? I will well, said King Mark. Then Sir Tristram said thus to the messenger: Bear thy lord word from the king and me, that we will do battle with him to-morn in the plain field. What is your name? said the messenger. Wit thou well my name is Sir Tristram de Liones. Therewithal the messenger departed and told his lord Elias all that he had heard. Sir, said Sir Tristram unto King Mark, I pray you give me leave to have the rule of the battle. I pray you take the rule, said King Mark. Then Sir Tristram let devise the battle in what manner that it should be. He let depart his host in six parties, and ordained Sir Dinas the Seneschal to have the foreward, and other knights to rule the remnant. And the same night Sir Tristram burnt all the Sessoins' ships unto the cold water. Anon, as Elias wist that, he said it was of Sir Tristram's doing: For he casteth that we shall never escape, mother son of us. Therefore, fair fellows, fight freely to-morrow, and miscomfort you nought; for any knight, though he be the best knight in the world, he may not have ado with us all.

Then they ordained their battle in four parties, wonderly well apparelled and garnished with men of arms. Thus they within issued, and they without set freely upon them; and there Sir Dinas did great deeds of arms. Not for then Sir Dinas and his fellowship were put to the worse. With that came Sir Tristram and slew two knights with one spear; then he slew on the right hand and on the left hand, that men marvelled that ever he might do such deeds of arms. And then he might see sometime the battle was driven a bow-draught from the castle, and sometime it was at the gates of the castle. Then came Elias the captain rushing here and there, and hit King Mark so sore upon the helm that he made him to avoid the saddle. And then Sir Dinas gat King Mark again to horseback. Therewithal came in Sir Tristram like a lion, and there he met with Elias, and he smote him so sore upon the helm that he avoided his saddle. And thus they fought till it was night, and for great slaughter and for wounded people everych party drew to their rest.

And when King Mark was come within the Castle of Tintagil he lacked of his knights an hundred, and they without lacked two hundred; and they searched the wounded men on both parties. And then they went to council; and wit you well either party were loath to fight more, so that either might escape with their worship. When Elias the captain understood the death of his men he made great dole; and when he wist that they were loath to go to battle again he was wroth out of measure. Then Elias sent word unto King Mark, in great despite, whether he would find a knight that would fight for him body for body. And if that he might slay King Mark's knight, he to have the truage of Cornwall yearly. And if that his knight slay mine, I fully release my claim forever. Then the messenger departed unto King Mark, and told him how that his lord Elias had sent him word to find a knight to do battle with him body for body. When King Mark understood the messenger, he bade him abide and he should have his answer. Then called he all the baronage together to wit what was the best counsel. They said all at once: To fight in a field we have no lust, for had not been Sir Tristram's prowess it had been likely that we never should have escaped; and therefore, sir, as we deem, it were well done to find a knight that would do battle with him, for he knightly proffereth.

CHAPTER XXX

How Sir Elias and Sir Tristram fought together for the
truage, and how Sir Tristram slew Elias in the field.

Not for then when all this was said, they could find no knight that
would do battle with him. Sir king, said they all, here is no knight
that dare fight with Elias. Alas, said King Mark, then am I utterly
ashamed and utterly destroyed, unless that my nephew Sir Tristram
will take the battle upon him. Wit you well, they said all, he had
yesterday overmuch on hand, and he is weary for travail, and sore
wounded. Where is he? said King Mark. Sir, said they, he is in his
bed to repose him. Alas, said King Mark, but I have the succour of
my nephew Sir Tristram, I am utterly destroyed for ever.

Therewith one went to Sir Tristram where he lay, and told him
what King Mark had said. And therewith Sir Tristram arose lightly,
and put on him a long gown, and came afore the king and all the
lords. And when he saw them all so dismayed he asked the king and
the lords what tidings were with them. Never worse, said the king.
And therewith he told him all, how he had word of Elias to find a
knight to fight for the truage of Cornwall, and none can I find. And
as for you, said the king and all the lords, we may ask no more of you
for shame; for through your hardiness yesterday ye saved all our lives.
Sir, said Sir Tristram, now I understand ye would have my succour,
reason would that I should do all that lieth in my power to do, saving
my worship and my life, howbeit I am sore bruised and hurt. And
sithen Sir Elias proffereth so largely, I shall fight with him, or else I
will be slain in the field, or else I will deliver Cornwall from the old
truage. And therefore lightly call his messenger and he shall be
answered, for as yet my wounds be green, and they will be sorer a
seven night after than they be now; and therefore he shall have his
answer that I will do battle to-morn with him.

Then was the messenger departed brought before King Mark.
Hark, my fellow, said Sir Tristram, go fast unto thy lord, and bid him
make true assurance on his part for the truage, as the king here shall
make on his part; and then tell thy lord, Sir Elias, that I, Sir Tristram,

King Arthur's knight, and knight of the Table Round, will as to-morn meet with thy lord on horseback, to do battle as long as my horse may endure, and after that to do battle with him on foot to the utterance. The messenger beheld Sir Tristram from the top to the toe; and therewithal he departed and came to his lord, and told him how he was answered of Sir Tristram. And therewithal was made hostage on both parties, and made it as sure as it might be, that whether party had the victory, so to end. And then were both hosts assembled on both parts of the field, without the Castle of Tintagil, and there was none but Sir Tristram and Sir Elias armed.

So when the appointment was made, they departed in-sunder, and they came together with all the might that their horses might run. And either knight smote other so hard that both horses and knights went to the earth. Not for then they both lightly arose and dressed their shields on their shoulders, with naked swords in their hands, and they dashed together that it seemed a flaming fire about them. Thus they traced, and traversed, and hewed on helms and hauberks, and cut away many cantels of their shields, and either wounded other passing sore, so that the hot blood fell freshly upon the earth. And by then they had foughten the mountenance of an hour Sir Tristram waxed faint and for-bled, and gave sore aback. That saw Sir Elias, and followed fiercely upon him, and wounded him in many places. And ever Sir Tristram traced and traversed, and went froward him here and there, and covered him with his shield as he might all weakly, that all men said he was overcome; for Sir Elias had given him twenty strokes against one.

Then was there laughing of the Sessoins' party, and great dole on King Mark's party. Alas, said the king, we are ashamed and destroyed all for ever: for as the book saith, Sir Tristram was never so matched, but if it were Sir Launcelot. Thus as they stood and beheld both parties, that one party laughing and the other party weeping, Sir Tristram remembered him of his lady, La Beale Isoud, that looked upon him, and how he was likely never to come in her presence. Then he pulled up his shield that erst hung full low. And then he dressed up his shield unto Elias, and gave him many sad strokes, twenty against one, and all to-brake his shield and his hauberk, that the hot blood ran down to the earth. Then began King Mark to laugh, and all Cornish men, and that other party to weep. And ever Sir Tristram said to Sir Elias: Yield thee.

Then when Sir Tristram saw him so staggering on the ground, he said: Sir Elias, I am right sorry for thee, for thou art a passing good knight as ever I met withal, except Sir Launcelot. Therewithal Sir Elias fell to the earth, and there died. What shall I do, said Sir Tristram unto King Mark, for this battle is at an end? Then they of Elias' party departed, and King Mark took of them many prisoners, to redress the harms and the scathes that he had of them; and the remnant he sent into their country to borrow out their fellows. Then was Sir Tristram searched and well healed. Yet for all this King Mark would fain have slain Sir Tristram. But for all that ever Sir Tristram saw or heard by King Mark, yet would he never beware of his treason, but ever he would be thereas La Beale Isoud was.

CHAPTER XXXI

How at a great feast that King Mark made an harper came and sang the lay that Dinadan had made.

Now will we pass of this matter, and speak we of the harpers that Sir Launcelot and Sir Dinadan had sent into Cornwall. And at the great feast that King Mark made for joy that the Sessoins were put out of his country, then came Eliot the harper with the lay that Dinadan had made, and secretly brought it unto Sir Tristram, and told him the lay that Dinadan had made by King Mark. And when Sir Tristram heard it, he said: O Lord Jesu, that Dinadan can make wonderly well and ill, thereas it shall be. Sir, said Eliot, dare I sing this song afore King Mark? Yea, on my peril, said Sir Tristram, for I shall be thy warrant. Then at the meat came in Eliot the harper, and because he was a curious harper men heard him sing the same lay that Dinadan had made, the which spake the most villainy by King Mark of his treason that ever man heard.

When the harper had sung his song to the end King Mark was wonderly wroth, and said: Thou harper, how durst thou be so bold on thy head to sing this song afore me. Sir, said Eliot, wit you well I am a minstrel, and I must do as I am commanded of these lords that I bear the arms of. And sir, wit ye well that Sir Dinadan, a knight of the Table Round, made this song, and made me to sing it afore you. Thou sayest well, said King Mark, and because thou art a minstrel thou shalt go quit, but I charge thee hie thee fast out of my sight. So the harper departed and went to Sir Tristram, and told him how he had sped. Then Sir Tristram let make letters as goodly as he could to Launcelot and to Sir Dinadan. And so he let conduct the harper out of the country. But to say that King Mark was wonderly wroth, he was, for he deemed that the lay that was sung afore him was made by Sir Tristram's counsel, wherefore he thought to slay him and all his well-willers in that country.

CHAPTER XXXII

How King Mark slew by treason his brother Boudwin, for good service that he had done to him.

Now turn we to another matter that fell between King Mark and his brother, that was called the good Prince Boudwin, that all the people of the country loved passing well. So it befell on a time that the miscreant Saracens landed in the country of Cornwall soon after these Sessoins were gone. And then the good Prince Boudwin, at the landing, he raised the country privily and hastily. And or it were day he let put wildfire in three of his own ships, and suddenly he pulled up the sail, and with the wind he made those ships to be driven among the navy of the Saracens. And to make short tale, those three ships set on fire all the ships, that none were saved. And at point of the day the good Prince Boudwin with all his fellowship set on the miscreants with shouts and cries, and slew to the number of forty thousand, and left none alive.

When King Mark wist this he was wonderly wroth that his brother should win such worship. And because this prince was better beloved than he in all that country, and that also Boudwin loved well Sir Tristram, therefore he thought to slay him. And thus, hastily, as a man out of his wit, he sent for Prince Boudwin and Anglides his wife, and bade them bring their young son with them, that he might see him. All this he did to the intent to slay the child as well as his father, for he was the falsest traitor that ever was born. Alas, for his goodness and for his good deeds this gentle Prince Boudwin was slain. So when he came with his wife Anglides, the king made them fair semblant till they had dined. And when they had dined King Mark sent for his brother and said thus: Brother, how sped you when the miscreants arrived by you? meseemeth it had been your part to have sent me word, that I might have been at that journey, for it had been reason that I had had the honour and not you. Sir, said the Prince Boudwin, it was so that an I had tarried till that I had sent for you those miscreants had destroyed my country. Thou liest, false traitor, said King Mark, for thou art ever about for to win worship from me, and put me to dishonour, and thou cherishest that I hate. And therewith he struck him to the heart with a dagger, that he never after spake word. Then the Lady Anglides made great dole, and swooned, for she saw her lord slain afore her face. Then was there no more to do but Prince Boudwin was despoiled and brought to burial. But Anglides privily gat her husband's doublet and his shirt, and that she kept secretly.

Then was there much sorrow and crying, and great dole made Sir Tristram, Sir Dinas, Sir Fergus, and so did all knights that were there; for that prince was passingly well beloved. So La Beale Isoud sent unto Anglides, the Prince Boudwin's wife, and bade her avoid lightly or else her young son, Alisander le Orphelin, should be slain. When she heard this, she took her horse and her child, and rode with such poor men as durst ride with her.

CHAPTER XXXIII

How Anglides, Boudwin's wife, escaped with her young son, Alisander le Orphelin, and came to the Castle of Arundel.

Notwithstanding, when King Mark had done this deed, yet he thought to do more vengeance; and with his sword in his hand, he sought from chamber to chamber, to seek Anglides and her young son. And when she was missed he called a good knight that hight Sadok, and charged him by pain of death to fetch Anglides again and her young son. So Sir Sadok departed and rode after Anglides. And within ten mile he overtook her, and bade her turn again and ride with him to King Mark. Alas, fair knight, she said, what shall ye win by my son's death or by mine? I have had overmuch harm and too great a loss. Madam, said Sadok, of your loss is dole and pity; but madam, said Sadok, would ye depart out of this country with your son, and keep him till he be of age, that he may revenge his father's death, then would I suffer you to depart from me, so you promise me to revenge the death of Prince Boudwin. Ah, gentle knight, Jesu thank thee, and if ever my son, Alisander le Orphelin, live to be a knight, he shall have his father's doublet and his shirt with the bloody marks, and I shall give him such a charge that he shall remember it while he liveth. And therewithal Sadok departed from her, and either betook other to God. And when Sadok came to King Mark he told him faithfully that he had drowned young Alisander her son; and thereof King Mark was full glad.

Now turn we unto Anglides, that rode both night and day by adventure out of Cornwall, and little and in few places she rested; but ever she drew southward to the seaside, till by fortune she came to a castle that is called Magouns, and now it is called Arundel, in Sussex. And the Constable of the castle welcomed her, and said she was welcome to her own castle; and there was Anglides worshipfully received, for the Constable's wife was nigh her cousin, and the Constable's name was Bellangere; and that same Constable told Anglides that the same castle was hers by right inheritance. Thus Anglides endured years and winters, till Alisander was big and strong; there was none so wight in all that country, neither there was none that might do no manner of mastery afore him.

CHAPTER XXXIV

How Anglides gave the bloody doublet to Alisander, her son, the same day that he was made knight, and the charge withal.

Then upon a day Bellangere the Constable came to Anglides and said: Madam, it were time my lord Alisander were made knight, for he is a passing strong young man. Sir, said she, I would he were made knight; but then must I give him the most charge that ever sinful mother gave to her child. Do as ye list, said Bellangere, and I shall give him warning that he shall be made knight. Now it will be well done that he may be made knight at our Lady Day in Lent. Be it so, said Anglides, and I pray you make ready therefore. So came the Constable to Alisander, and told him that he should at our Lady Day in Lent be made knight. I thank God, said Alisander; these are the best tidings that ever came to me. Then the Constable ordained twenty of the greatest gentlemen's sons, and the best born men of the country, that should be made knights that same day that Alisander was made knight. So on the same day that Alisander and his twenty fellows were made knights, at the offering of the mass there came Anglides unto her son and said thus: O fair sweet son, I charge thee upon my blessing, and of the high order of chivalry that thou takest here this day, that thou understand what I shall say and charge thee withal. Therewithal she pulled out a bloody doublet and a bloody shirt, that were be-bled with old blood. When Alisander saw this he stert aback and waxed pale, and said: Fair mother, what may this mean? I shall tell thee, fair son: this was thine own father's doublet and shirt, that he wore upon him that same day that he was slain. And there she told him why and wherefore, and how for his goodness King Mark slew him with his dagger afore mine own eyen. And therefore this shall be your charge that I shall give thee.

CHAPTER XXXV

How it was told to King Mark of Sir Alisander, and how he would have slain Sir Sadok for saving his life.

Now I require thee, and charge thee upon my blessing, and upon the high order of knighthood, that thou be revenged upon King Mark for the death of thy father. And therewithal she swooned. Then Alisander leapt to his mother, and took her up in his arms, and said: Fair mother, ye have given me a great charge, and here I promise you I shall be avenged upon King Mark when that I may; and that I promise to God and to you. So this feast was ended, and the Constable, by the advice of Anglides, let purvey that Alisander was well horsed and harnessed. Then he jousted with his twenty fellows that were made knights with him, but for to make a short tale, he overthrew all those twenty, that none might withstand him a buffet.

Then one of those knights departed unto King Mark, and told him all, how Alisander was made knight, and all the charge that his mother gave him, as ye have heard afore time. Alas, false treason, said King Mark, I weened that young traitor had been dead. Alas, whom may I trust? And therewithal King Mark took a sword in his hand, and sought Sir Sadok from chamber to chamber to slay him. When Sir Sadok saw King Mark come with his sword in his hand he said thus: Beware, King Mark, and come not nigh me; for wit thou well that I saved Alisander his life, of which I never repent me, for thou falsely and cowardly slew his father Boudwin, traitorly for his good deeds; wherefore I pray Almighty Jesu send Alisander might and strength to be revenged upon thee. And now beware King Mark of young Alisander, for he is made a knight. Alas, said King Mark, that ever I should hear a traitor say so afore me. And therewith four knights of King Mark's drew their swords to slay Sir Sadok, but anon Sir Sadok slew them all in King Mark's presence. And then Sir Sadok passed forth into his chamber, and took his horse and his harness, and rode on his way a good pace. For there was neither Sir Tristram, neither Sir Dinas, nor Sir Fergus, that would Sir Sadok any evil will. Then was King Mark wroth, and thought to destroy Sir Alisander and Sir Sadok that had saved him; for King Mark dreaded and hated Alisander most of any man living.

When Sir Tristram understood that Alisander was made knight, anon forthwithal he sent him a letter, praying him and charging him that he would draw him to the court of King Arthur, and that he put him in the rule and in the hands of Sir Launcelot. So this letter was sent to Alisander from his cousin, Sir Tristram. And at that time he thought to do after his commandment. Then King Mark called a knight that brought him the tidings from Alisander, and bade him abide still in that country. Sir, said that knight, so must I do, for in my own country I dare not come. No force, said King Mark, I shall give thee here double as much lands as ever thou hadst of thine own. But within short space Sir Sadok met with that false knight, and slew him. Then was King Mark wood wroth out of measure. Then he sent unto Queen Morgan le Fay, and to the Queen of Northgalis, praying them in his letters that they two sorceresses would set all the country in fire with ladies that were enchantresses, and by such that were dangerous knights, as Malgrin, Breuse Saunce Pité, that by no mean Alisander le Orphelin should escape, but either he should be taken or slain. This ordinance made King Mark for to destroy Alisander.

CHAPTER XXXVI

*How Sir Alisander won the prize at a tournament,
and of Morgan le Fay: and how he fought with
Sir Malgrin, and slew him.*

Now turn we again unto Sir Alisander, that at his departing his
mother took with him his father's bloody shirt. So that he bare with
him always till his death day, in tokening to think of his father's death.
So was Alisander purposed to ride to London, by the counsel of Sir
Tristram, to Sir Launcelot. And by fortune he went by the seaside,
and rode wrong. And there he won at a tournament the gree that
King Carados made. And there he smote down King Carados and
twenty of his knights, and also Sir Safere, a good knight that was Sir
Palomides' brother, the good knight. All this saw a damosel, and saw
the best knight joust that ever she saw. And ever as he smote down
knights he made them to swear to wear none harness in a
twelvemonth and a day. This is well said, said Morgan le Fay, this is
the knight that I would fain see. And so she took her palfrey, and
rode a great while, and then she rested her in her pavilion. So there
came four knights, two were armed, and two were unarmed, and
they told Morgan le Fay their names: the first was Elias de Gomeret,
the second was Cari de Gomeret, those were armed; that other twain
were of Camiliard, cousins unto Queen Guenever, and that one
hight Guy, and that other hight Garaunt, those were unarmed. There
these four knights told Morgan le Fay how a young knight had
smitten them down before a castle. For the maiden of that castle said
that he was but late made knight, and young. But as we suppose, but
if it were Sir Tristram, or Sir Launcelot, or Sir Lamorak, the good
knight, there is none that might sit him a buffet with a spear. Well,
said Morgan le Fay, I shall meet that knight or it be long time, an he
dwell in that country.

So turn we to the damosel of the castle, that when Alisander le
Orphelin had for-jousted the four knights, she called him to her, and
said thus: Sir knight, wilt thou for my sake joust and fight with a
knight, for my sake, of this country, that is and hath been long time

an evil neighbour to me? His name is Malgrin, and he will not suffer me to be married in no manner wise for all that I can do, or any knight for my sake. Damosel, said Alisander, an he come whiles I am here I will fight with him, and my poor body for your sake I will jeopard. And therewithal she sent for him, for he was at her commandment. And when either had a sight of other, they made them ready for to joust, and they came together eagerly, and Malgrin brised his spear upon Alisander, and Alisander smote him again so hard that he bare him quite from his saddle to the earth. But this Malgrin arose lightly, and dressed his shield and drew his sword, and bade him alight, saying: Though thou have the better of me on horseback, thou shalt find that I shall endure like a knight on foot. It is well said, said Alisander; and so lightly he avoided his horse and betook him to his varlet. And then they rushed together like two boars, and laid on their helms and shields long time, by the space of three hours, that never man could say which was the better knight.

And in the meanwhile came Morgan le Fay to the damosel of the castle, and they beheld the battle. But this Malgrin was an old roted knight, and he was called one of the dangerous knights of the world to do battle on foot, but on horseback there were many better. And ever this Malgrin awaited to slay Alisander, and so wounded him wonderly sore, that it was marvel that ever he might stand, for he had bled so much blood; for Alisander fought wildly, and not wittily. And that other was a felonious knight, and awaited him, and smote him sore. And sometime they rushed together with their shields like two boars or rams, and fell grovelling both to the earth. Now knight, said Malgrin, hold thy hand a while, and tell me what thou art. I will not, said Alisander, but if me list: but tell me thy name, and why thou keepest this country, or else thou shalt die of my hands. Wit thou well, said Malgrin, that for this maiden's love, of this castle, I have slain ten good knights by mishap; and by outrage and orgulité of myself I have slain ten other knights. So God me help, said Alisander, this is the foulest confession that ever I heard knight make, nor never heard I speak of other men of such a shameful confession; wherefore it were great pity and great shame unto me that I should let thee live any longer; therefore keep thee as well as ever thou mayest, for as I am true knight, either thou shalt slay me or else I shall slay thee, I promise thee faithfully.

Then they lashed together fiercely, and at the last Alisander smote

Malgrin to the earth. And then he raced off his helm, and smote off his head lightly. And when he had done and ended this battle, anon he called to him his varlet, the which brought him his horse. And then he, weening to be strong enough, would have mounted. And so she laid Sir Alisander in an horse litter, and led him into the castle, for he had no foot nor might to stand upon the earth; for he had sixteen great wounds, and in especial one of them was like to be his death.

CHAPTER XXXVII

How Queen Morgan le Fay had Alisander in her castle, and how she healed his wounds.

Then Queen Morgan le Fay searched his wounds, and gave such an ointment unto him that he should have died. And on the morn when she came to him he complained him sore; and then she put other ointments upon him, and then he was out of his pain. Then came the damosel of the castle, and said unto Morgan le Fay: I pray you help me that this knight might wed me, for he hath won me with his hands. Ye shall see, said Morgan le Fay, what I shall say. Then Morgan le Fay went unto Alisander, and bade in anywise that he should refuse this lady, an she desire to wed you, for she is not for you. So the damosel came and desired of him marriage. Damosel, said Orphelin, I thank you, but as yet I cast me not to marry in this country. Sir, she said, sithen ye will not marry me, I pray you insomuch as ye have won me, that ye will give me to a knight of this country that hath been my friend, and loved me many years. With all my heart, said Alisander, I will assent thereto. Then was the knight sent for, his name was Gerine le Grose. And anon he made them handfast, and wedded them.

Then came Queen Morgan le Fay to Alisander, and bade him arise, and put him in an horse litter, and gave him such a drink that in three days and three nights he waked never, but slept; and so she brought him to her own castle that at that time was called La Beale Regard. Then Morgan le Fay came to Alisander, and asked him if he would fain be whole. Who would be sick, said Alisander, an he might be whole? Well, said Morgan le Fay, then shall ye promise me by your knighthood that this day twelvemonth and a day ye shall not pass the compass of this castle, and without doubt ye shall lightly be whole. I assent, said Sir Alisander. And there he made her a promise: then was he soon whole. And when Alisander was whole, then he repented him of his oath, for he might not be revenged upon King Mark. Right so there came a damosel that was cousin to the Earl of Pase, and she was cousin to Morgan le Fay. And by right that castle of La Beale Regard should have been hers by true inheritance. So this damosel entered into this castle where lay Alisander, and there she found him upon his bed, passing heavy and all sad.

CHAPTER XXXVIII

How Alisander was delivered from Queen Morgan le Fay by the means of a damosel.

Sir knight, said the damosel, an ye would be merry I could tell you good tidings. Well were me, said Alisander, an I might hear of good tidings, for now I stand as a prisoner by my promise. Sir, she said, wit you well that ye be a prisoner, and worse than ye ween; for my lady, my cousin Queen Morgan le Fay, keepeth you here for none other intent but for to do her pleasure with you when it liketh her. O Jesu defend me, said Alisander, from such pleasure; for I had liefer cut away my hangers than I would do her such pleasure. As Jesu help me, said the damosel, an ye would love me and be ruled by me, I shall make your deliverance with your worship. Tell me, said Alisander, by what means, and ye shall have my love. Fair knight, said she, this castle of right ought to be mine, and I have an uncle the which is a mighty earl, he is Earl of Pase, and of all folks he hateth most Morgan le Fay; and I shall send unto him and pray him for my sake to destroy this castle for the evil customs that be used therein; and then will he come and set wild-fire on every part of the castle, and I shall get you out at a privy postern, and there shall ye have your horse and your harness. Ye say well, damosel, said Alisander. And then she said: Ye may keep the room of this castle this twelvemonth and a day, then break ye not your oath. Truly, fair damosel, said Alisander, ye say sooth. And then he kissed her, and did to her pleasaunce as it pleased them both at times and leisures.

So anon she sent unto her uncle and bade him come and destroy that castle, for as the book saith, he would have destroyed that castle afore time had not that damosel been. When the earl understood her letters he sent her word again that on such a day he would come and destroy that castle. So when that day came she showed Alisander a postern wherethrough he should flee into a garden, and there he should find his armour and his horse. When the day came that was set, thither came the Earl of Pase with four hundred knights, and set on fire all the parts of the castle, that or they ceased they left not a stone standing. And all this while that the fire was in the castle he abode in the garden. And when the fire was done he let make a cry that he would keep that piece of earth thereas the castle of La Beale Regard was a twelvemonth and a day, from all manner knights that would come.

So it happed there was a duke that hight Ansirus, and he was of the kin of Sir Launcelot. And this knight was a great pilgrim, for every third year he would be at Jerusalem. And because he used all his life to go in pilgrimage men called him Duke Ansirus the Pilgrim. And this duke had a daughter that hight Alice, that was a passing fair woman, and because of her father she was called Alice la Beale Pilgrim. And anon as she heard of this cry she went unto Arthur's court, and said openly in hearing of many knights, that what knight may overcome that knight that keepeth that piece of earth shall have me and all my lands.

When the knights of the Round Table heard her say thus many were glad, for she was passing fair and of great rents. Right so she let cry in castles and towns as fast on her side as Alisander did on his side. Then she dressed her pavilion straight by the piece of the earth that Alisander kept. So she was not so soon there but there came a knight of Arthur's court that hight Sagramore le Desirous, and he proffered to joust with Alisander; and they encountered, and Sagramore le Desirous brised his spear upon Sir Alisander, but Sir Alisander smote him so hard that he avoided his saddle. And when La Beale Alice saw him joust so well, she thought him a passing goodly knight on horseback. And then she leapt out of her pavilion, and took Sir Alisander by the bridle, and thus she said: Fair knight, I require thee of thy knighthood show me thy visage. I dare well, said Alisander, show my visage. And then he put off his helm; and she saw his visage, she said: O sweet Jesu, thee I must love, and never other. Then show me your visage, said he.

CHAPTER XXXIX

How Alisander met with Alice la Beale Pilgrim,
and how he jousted with two knights;
and after of him and of Sir Mordred.

Then she unwimpled her visage. And when he saw her he said: Here have I found my love and my lady. Truly, fair lady, said he, I promise you to be your knight, and none other that beareth the life. Now, gentle knight, said she, tell me your name. My name is, said he, Alisander le Orphelin. Now, damosel, tell me your name, said he. My name is, said she, Alice la Beale Pilgrim. And when we be more at our heart's ease, both ye and I shall tell other of what blood we be come. So there was great love betwixt them. And as they thus talked there came a knight that hight Harsouse le Berbuse, and asked part of Sir Alisander's spears. Then Sir Alisander encountered with him, and at the first Sir Alisander smote him over his horse's croup. And then there came another knight that hight Sir Hewgon, and Sir Alisander smote him down as he did that other. Then Sir Hewgon proffered to do battle on foot. Sir Alisander overcame him with three strokes, and there would have slain him had he not yielded him. So then Alisander made both those knights to swear to wear none armour in a twelvemonth and a day.

Then Sir Alisander alighted down, and went to rest him and repose him. Then the damosel that helped Sir Alisander out of the castle, in her play told Alice all together how he was prisoner in the castle of La Beale Regard, and there she told her how she got him out of prison. Sir, said Alice la Beale Pilgrim, meseemeth ye are much beholding to this maiden. That is truth, said Sir Alisander. And there Alice told him of what blood she was come. Sir, wit ye well, she said, that I am of the blood of King Ban, that was father unto Sir Launcelot. Y-wis, fair lady, said Alisander, my mother told me that my father was brother unto a king, and I nigh cousin unto Sir Tristram.

Then this while came there three knights, that one hight Vains, and the other hight Harvis de les Marches, and the third hight Perin de la Montaine. And with one spear Sir Alisander smote them down all three, and gave them such falls that they had no list to fight upon foot. So he made them to swear to wear none arms in a twelvemonth. So when they were departed Sir Alisander beheld his lady Alice on horseback as he stood in her pavilion. And then was he so enamoured upon her that he wist not whether he were on horseback or on foot.

Right so came the false knight Sir Mordred, and saw Sir Alisander was assotted upon his lady; and therewithal he took his horse by the bridle, and led him here and there, and had cast to have led him out of that place to have shamed him. When the damosel that helped him out of that castle saw how shamefully he was led, anon she let arm her, and set a shield upon her shoulder; and therewith she mounted upon his horse, and gat a naked sword in her hand, and she thrust unto Alisander with all her might, and she gave him such a buffet that he thought the fire flew out of his eyen. And when Alisander felt that stroke he looked about him, and drew his sword. And when she saw that, she fled, and so did Mordred into the forest, and the damosel fled into the pavilion. So when Alisander understood himself how the false knight would have shamed him had not the damosel been, then was he wroth with himself that Sir Mordred was so escaped his hands. But then Sir Alisander and Alice had good game at the damosel, how sadly she hit him upon the helm.

Then Sir Alisander jousted thus day by day, and on foot he did many battles with many knights of King Arthur's court, and with many knights strangers. Therefore to tell all the battles that he did it were overmuch to rehearse, for every day within that twelvemonth he had ado with one knight or with other, and some day he had ado with three or with four; and there was never knight that put him to the worse. And at the twelvemonth's end he departed with his lady, Alice la Beale Pilgrim. And the damosel would never go from him, and so they went into their country of Benoye, and lived there in great joy.

CHAPTER XL

How Sir Galahalt did do cry a jousts in Surluse, and Queen Guenever's knights should joust against all that would come.

But as the book saith, King Mark would never stint till he had slain him by treason. And by Alice he gat a child that hight Bellengerus le Beuse. And by good fortune he came to the court of King Arthur, and proved a passing good knight; and he revenged his father's death, for the false King Mark slew both Sir Tristram and Alisander falsely and feloniously. And it happed so that Alisander had never grace nor fortune to come to King Arthur's court. For an he had come to Sir Launcelot, all knights said that knew him, he was one of the strongest knights that was in Arthur's days, and great dole was made for him. So let we of him pass, and turn we to another tale.

So it befell that Sir Galahalt, the haut prince, was lord of the country of Surluse, whereof came many good knights. And this noble prince was a passing good man of arms, and ever he held a noble fellowship together. And then he came to Arthur's court and told him his intent, how this was his will, how he would let cry a jousts in the country of Surluse, the which country was within the lands of King Arthur, and there he asked leave to let cry a jousts. I will give you leave, said King Arthur; but wit thou well, said King Arthur, I may not be there. Sir, said Queen Guenever, please it you to give me leave to be at that jousts. With right good will, said Arthur; for Sir Galahalt, the haut prince, shall have you in governance. Sir, said Galahalt, I will as ye will. Sir, then [said] the queen, I will take with me [Sir Launcelot] and such knights as please me best. Do as ye list, said King Arthur. So anon she commanded Sir Launcelot to make him ready with such knights as he thought best.

So in every good town and castle of this land was made a cry, that in the country of Surluse Sir Galahalt should make a joust that should last eight days, and how the haut prince, with the help of Queen Guenever's knights, should joust against all manner of men that would come. When this cry was known, kings and princes, dukes and earls, barons and noble knights, made them ready to be at that jousts. And at the day of jousting there came in Sir Dinadan disguised, and did many great deeds of arms.

CHAPTER XLI

How Sir Launcelot fought in the tournament, and how Sir Palomides did arms there for a damosel.

Then at the request of Queen Guenever and of King Bagdemagus Sir Launcelot came into the range, but he was disguised, and that was the cause that few folk knew him; and there met with him Sir Ector de Maris, his own brother, and either brake their spears upon other to their hands. And then either gat another spear. And then Sir Launcelot smote down Sir Ector de Maris, his own brother. That saw Sir Bleoberis, and he smote Sir Launcelot such a buffet upon the helm that he wist not well where he was. Then Sir Launcelot was wroth, and smote Sir Bleoberis so sore upon the helm that his head bowed down backward. And he smote eft another buffet, that he avoided his saddle; and so he rode by, and thrust forth to the thickest. When the King of Northgalis saw Sir Ector and Bleoberis lie on the ground then was he wroth, for they came on his party against them of Surluse. So the King of Northgalis ran to Sir Launcelot, and brake a spear upon him all to pieces. Therewith Sir Launcelot overtook the King of Northgalis, and smote him such a buffet on the helm with his sword that he made him to avoid his horse; and anon the king was horsed again. So both the King Bagdemagus' and the King of Northgalis' party hurled to other; and then began a strong medley, but they of Northgalis were far bigger.

When Sir Launcelot saw his party go to the worst he thrang into the thickest press with a sword in his hand; and there he smote down on the right hand and on the left hand, and pulled down knights and raced off their helms, that all men had wonder that ever one knight might do such deeds of arms. When Sir Meliagaunce, that was son unto King Bagdemagus, saw how Sir Launcelot fared he marvelled greatly. And when he understood that it was he, he wist well that he was disguised for his sake. Then Sir Meliagaunce prayed a knight to slay Sir Launcelot's horse, either with sword or with spear. At that time King Bagdemagus met with a knight that hight Sauseise, a good knight, to whom he said: Now fair Sauseise, encounter with my son Meliagaunce and give him large payment, for I would he were well beaten of thy hands, that he might depart out of this field. And then Sir Sauseise encountered with Sir Meliagaunce, and either smote other down. And then they fought on foot, and there Sauseise had won Sir Meliagaunce, had there not come rescues. So then the haut prince blew to lodging, and every knight unarmed him and went to the great feast.

Then in the meanwhile there came a damosel to the haut prince, and complained that there was a knight that hight Goneries that withheld her all her lands. Then the knight was there present, and cast his glove to her or to any that would fight in her name. So the damosel took up the glove all heavily for default of a champion. Then there came a varlet to her and said: Damosel, will ye do after me? Full fain, said the damosel. Then go you unto such a knight that lieth here beside in an hermitage, and that followeth the Questing Beast, and pray him to take the battle upon him, and anon I wot well he will grant you.

So anon she took her palfrey, and within a while she found that knight, that was Sir Palomides. And when she required him he armed him and rode with her, and made her to go to the haut prince, and to ask leave for her knight to do battle. I will well, said the haut prince. Then the knights were ready in the field to joust on horseback; and either gat a spear in their hands, and met so fiercely together that their spears all to-shivered. Then they flang out swords, and Sir Palomides smote Sir Goneries down to the earth. And then he raced off his helm and smote off his head. Then they went to supper, and the damosel loved Palomides as paramour, but the book saith she was of his kin. So then Palomides disguised himself in this manner, in his shield he bare the Questing Beast, and in all his trappings. And when he was thus ready, he sent to the haut prince to give him leave to joust with other knights, but he was adoubted of Sir Launcelot. The haut prince sent him word again that he should be welcome and that Sir Launcelot should not joust with him. Then Sir Galahalt, the haut prince, let cry what knight somever he were that smote down Sir Palomides should have his damosel to himself.

CHAPTER XLII

How Sir Galahalt and Palomides fought together, and of Sir Dinadan and Sir Galahalt.

Here beginneth the second day. Anon as Sir Palomides came into the field, Sir Galahalt, the haut prince, was at the range end, and met with Sir Palomides, and he with him, with great spears. And then they came so hard together that their spears all to-shivered, but Sir Galahalt smote him so hard that he bare him backward over his horse, but yet he lost not his stirrups. Then they drew their swords and lashed together many sad strokes, that many worshipful knights left their business to behold them. But at the last Sir Galahalt, the haut prince, smote a stroke of might unto Palomides, sore upon the helm; but the helm was so hard that the sword might not bite, but slipped and smote off the head of the horse of Sir Palomides. When the haut prince wist and saw the good knight fall unto the earth he was ashamed of that stroke. And therewith he alighted down off his own horse, and prayed the good knight, Palomides, to take that horse of his gift, and to forgive him that deed. Sir, said Palomides, I thank you of your great goodness, for ever of a man of worship a knight shall never have disworship; and so he mounted upon that horse, and the haut prince had another anon. Now, said the haut prince, I release to you that maiden, for ye have won her. Ah, said Palomides, the damosel and I be at your commandment.

So they departed, and Sir Galahalt did great deeds of arms. And right so came Dinadan and encountered with Sir Galahalt, and either came to other so fast with their spears that their spears brake to their hands. But Dinadan had weened the haut prince had been more weary than he was. And then he smote many sad strokes at the haut prince; but when Dinadan saw he might not get him to the earth he said: My lord, I pray you leave me, and take another. The haut prince knew not Dinadan, and left goodly for his fair words. And so they departed; but soon there came another and told the haut prince that it was Dinadan. Forsooth, said the prince, therefore am I heavy that he is so escaped from me, for with his mocks and japes now shall I never have done with him. And then Galahalt rode fast after him, and bade him: Abide, Dinadan, for King Arthur's sake. Nay, said Dinadan, so God me help, we meet no more together this day. Then in that wrath the haut prince met with Meliagaunce, and he smote him in the throat that an he had fallen his neck had broken; and with the same spear he smote down another knight. Then came in they of Northgalis and many strangers, and were like to have put them of Surluse to the worse, for Sir Galahalt, the haut prince, had ever much in hand. So there came the good knight, Semound the Valiant, with forty knights, and he beat them all aback. Then the Queen Guenever and Sir Launcelot let blow to lodging, and every knight unarmed him, and dressed him to the feast.

CHAPTER XLIII

How Sir Archade appealed Sir Palomides of treason, and how Sir Palomides slew him.

When Palomides was unarmed he asked lodging for himself and the damosel. Anon the haut prince commanded them to lodging. And he was not so soon in his lodging but there came a knight that hight Archade, he was brother unto Goneries that Palomides slew afore in the damosel's quarrel. And this knight, Archade, called Sir Palomides traitor, and appealed him for the death of his brother. By the leave of the haut prince, said Palomides, I shall answer thee. When Sir Galahalt understood their quarrel he bade them go to dinner: And as soon as ye have dined look that either knight be ready in the field. So when they had dined they were armed both, and took their horses, and the queen, and the prince, and Sir Launcelot, were set to behold them; and so they let run their horses, and there Sir Palomides bare Archade on his spear over his horse's tail. And then Palomides alighted and drew his sword, but Sir Archade might not arise; and there Sir Palomides raced off his helm, and smote off his head. Then the haut prince and Queen Guenever went unto supper. Then King Bagdemagus sent away his son Meliagaunce because Sir Launcelot should not meet with him, for he hated Sir Launcelot, and that knew he not.

CHAPTER XLIV

*Of the third day, and how Sir Palomides jousted with
Sir Lamorak, and other things.*

Now beginneth the third day of jousting; and at that day King
Bagdemagus made him ready; and there came against him King
Marsil, that had in gift an island of Sir Galahalt the haut prince; and
this island had the name Pomitain. Then it befell that King
Bagdemagus and King Marsil of Pomitain met together with spears,
and King Marsil had such a buffet that he fell over his horse's croup.
Then came there in a knight of King Marsil to revenge his lord, and
King Bagdemagus smote him down, horse and man, to the earth. So
there came an earl that hight Arrouse, and Sir Breuse, and an hundred
knights with them of Pomitain, and the King of Northgalis was with
them; and all these were against them of Surluse. And then there
began great battle, and many knights were cast under horses' feet.
And ever King Bagdemagus did best, for he first began, and ever he
held on. Gaheris, Gawaine's brother, smote ever at the face of King
Bagdemagus; and at the last King Bagdemagus hurtled down Gaheris,
horse and man.

Then by adventure Sir Palomides, the good knight, met with Sir
Blamore de Ganis, Sir Bleoberis' brother. And either smote other
with great spears, that both their horses and knights fell to the earth.
But Sir Blamore had such a fall that he had almost broken his neck,
for the blood brast out at nose, mouth, and his ears, but at the last he
recovered well by good surgeons. Then there came in the Duke
Chaleins of Clarance; and in his governance there came a knight that
hight Elis la Noire; and there encountered with him King Bagdemagus,
and he smote Elis that he made him to avoid his saddle. So the Duke
Chaleins of Clarance did there great deeds of arms, and of so late as he
came in the third day there was no man did so well except King
Bagdemagus and Sir Palomides, that the prize was given that day to
King Bagdemagus. And then they blew unto lodging, and unarmed
them, and went to the feast. Right so came Dinadan, and mocked
and japed with King Bagdemagus that all knights laughed at him, for

he was a fine japer, and well loving all good knights.

So anon as they had dined there came a varlet bearing four spears on his back; and he came to Palomides, and said thus: Here is a knight by hath sent you the choice of four spears, and requireth you for your lady's sake to take that one half of these spears, and joust with him in the field. Tell him, said Palomides, I will not fail him. When Sir Galahalt wist of this, he bade Palomides make him ready. So the Queen Guenever, the haut prince, and Sir Launcelot, they were set upon scaffolds to give the judgment of these two knights. Then Sir Palomides and the strange knight ran so eagerly together that their spears brake to their hands. Anon withal either of them took a great spear in his hand and all to-shivered them in pieces. And then either took a greater spear, and then the knight smote down Sir Palomides, horse and man, to the earth. And as he would have passed over him the strange knight's horse stumbled and fell down upon Palomides. Then they drew their swords and lashed together wonderly sore a great while.

Then the haut prince and Sir Launcelot said they saw never two knights fight better than they did; but ever the strange knight doubled his strokes, and put Palomides aback; therewithal the haut prince cried: Ho: and then they went to lodging. And when they were unarmed they knew it was the noble knight Sir Lamorak. When Sir Launcelot knew that it was Sir Lamorak he made much of him, for above all earthly men he loved him best except Sir Tristram. Then Queen Guenever commended him, and so did all other good knights make much of him, except Sir Gawaine's brethren. Then Queen Guenever said unto Sir Launcelot: Sir, I require you that an ye joust any more, that ye joust with none of the blood of my lord Arthur. So he promised he would not as at that time.

CHAPTER XLV

Of the fourth day, and of many great feats of arms.

Here beginneth the fourth day. Then came into the field the King with the Hundred Knights, and all they of Northgalis, and the Duke Chaleins of Clarance, and King Marsil of Pomitain, and there came

Safere, Palomides' brother, and there he told him tidings of his mother. And his name was called the Earl, and so he appealed him afore King Arthur: For he made war upon our father and mother, and there I slew him in plain battle. So they went into the field, and the damosel with them; and there came to encounter again them Sir Bleoberis de Ganis, and Sir Ector de Maris. Sir Palomides encountered with Sir Bleoberis, and either smote other down. And in the same wise did Sir Safere and Sir Ector, and the two couples did battle on foot. Then came in Sir Lamorak, and he encountered with the King with the Hundred Knights, and smote him quite over his horse's tail. And in the same wise he served the King of Northgalis, and also he smote down King Marsil. And so or ever he stint he smote down with his spear and with his sword thirty knights. When Duke Chaleins saw Lamorak do so great prowess he would not meddle with him for shame; and then he charged all his knights in pain of death that none of you touch him; for it were shame to all good knights an that knight were shamed.

Then the two kings gathered them together, and all they set upon Sir Lamorak; and he failed them not, but rushed here and there, smiting on the right hand and on the left, and raced off many helms, so that the haut prince and Queen Guenever said they saw never knight do such deeds of arms on horseback. Alas, said Launcelot to King Bagdemagus, I will arm me and help Sir Lamorak. And I will ride with you, said King Bagdemagus. And when they two were horsed they came to Sir Lamorak that stood among thirty knights; and well was him that might reach him a buffet, and ever he smote again mightily. Then came there into the press Sir Launcelot, and he threw down Sir Mador de la Porte. And with the truncheon of that spear he threw down many knights. And King Bagdemagus smote on the left hand and on the right hand marvellously well. And then the three kings fled aback. Therewithal then Sir Galahalt let blow to lodging, and all the heralds gave Sir Lamorak the prize. And all this while fought Palomides, Sir Bleoberis, Sir Safere, Sir Ector on foot; never were there four knights evener matched. And then they were departed, and had unto their lodging, and unarmed them, and so they went to the great feast.

But when Sir Lamorak was come into the court Queen Guenever took him in her arms and said: Sir, well have ye done this day. Then came the haut prince, and he made of him great joy, and so did

Dinadan, for he wept for joy; but the joy that Sir Launcelot made of Sir Lamorak there might no man tell. Then they went unto rest, and on the morn the haut prince let blow unto the field.

CHAPTER XLVI

Of the fifth day, and how Sir Lamorak behaved him.

Here beginneth the fifth day. So it befell that Sir Palomides came in the morntide, and proffered to joust thereas King Arthur was in a castle there besides Surluse; and there encountered with him a worshipful duke, and there Sir Palomides smote him over his horse's croup. And this duke was uncle unto King Arthur. Then Sir Elise's son rode unto Palomides, and Palomides served Elise in the same wise. When Sir Uwaine saw this he was wroth. Then he took his horse and encountered with Sir Palomides, and Palomides smote him so hard that he went to the earth, horse and man. And for to make a short tale, he smote down three brethren of Sir Gawaine, that is for to say Mordred, Gaheris, and Agravaine. O Jesu, said Arthur, this is a great despite of a Saracen that he shall smite down my blood. And therewithal King Arthur was wood wroth, and thought to have made him ready to joust.

That espied Sir Lamorak, that Arthur and his blood were discomfit; and anon he was ready, and asked Palomides if he would any more joust. Why should I not? said Palomides. Then they hurtled together, and brake their spears, and all to-shivered them, that all the castle rang of their dints. Then either gat a greater spear in his hand, and they came so fiercely together; but Sir Palomides' spear all to-brast and Sir Lamorak's did hold. Therewithal Sir Palomides lost his stirrups and lay upright on his horse's back. And then Sir Palomides returned again and took his damosel, and Sir Safere returned his way.

So, when he was departed, King Arthur came to Sir Lamorak and thanked him of his goodness, and prayed him to tell him his name. Sir, said Lamorak, wit thou well, I owe you my service, but as at this time I will not abide here, for I see of mine enemies many about me. Alas, said Arthur, now wot I well it is Sir Lamorak de Galis. O Lamorak, abide with me, and by my crown I shall never fail thee: and not so hardy in Gawaine's head, nor none of his brethren, to do thee any wrong. Sir, said Sir Lamorak, wrong have they done me, and to you both. That is truth, said the king, for they slew their own mother and my sister, the which me sore grieveth: it had been much fairer and better that ye had wedded her, for ye are a king's son as well as they. O Jesu, said the noble knight Sir Lamorak unto Arthur, her death shall I never forget. I promise you, and make mine avow unto God, I shall revenge her death as soon as I see time convenable. And if it were not at the reverence of your highness I should now have been revenged upon Sir Gawaine and his brethren. Truly, said Arthur, I will make you at accord. Sir, said Lamorak, as at this time I may not abide with you, for I must to the jousts, where is Sir Launcelot, and the haut prince Sir Galahalt.

Then there was a damosel that was daughter to King Bandes. And there was a Saracen knight that hight Corsabrin, and he loved the damosel, and in no wise he would suffer her to be married; for ever this Corsabrin noised her, and named her that she was out of her mind; and thus he let her that she might not be married.

CHAPTER XLVII

How Sir Palomides fought with Corsabrin for a lady, and how Palomides slew Corsabrin.

So by fortune this damosel heard tell that Palomides did much for damosels' sake; so she sent to him a pensel, and prayed him to fight with Sir Corsabrin for her love, and he should have her and her lands of her father's that should fall to her. Then the damosel sent unto Corsabrin, and bade him go unto Sir Palomides that was a paynim as well as he, and she gave him warning that she had sent him her pensel, and if he might overcome Palomides she would wed him. When Corsabrin wist of her deeds then was he wood wroth and angry, and rode unto Surluse where the haut prince was, and there he found Sir Palomides ready, the which had the pensel. So there they waged battle either with other afore Galahalt. Well, said the haut prince, this day must noble knights joust, and at-after dinner we shall see how ye can speed.

Then they blew to jousts; and in came Dinadan, and met with Sir
Gerin, a good knight, and he threw him down over his horse's croup;
and Sir Dinadan overthrew four knights more; and there he did great
deeds of arms, for he was a good knight, but he was a scoffer and a
japer, and the merriest knight among fellowship that was that time
living. And he had such a custom that he loved every good knight,
and every good knight loved him again. So then when the haut
prince saw Dinadan do so well, he sent unto Sir Launcelot and bade
him strike down Sir Dinadan: And when that ye have done so bring
him afore me and the noble Queen Guenever. Then Sir Launcelot
did as he was required. Then Sir Lamorak and he smote down many
knights, and raced off helms, and drove all the knights afore them.
And so Sir Launcelot smote down Sir Dinadan, and made his men to
unarm him, and so brought him to the queen and the haut prince,
and they laughed at Dinadan so sore that they might not stand. Well,
said Sir Dinadan, yet have I no shame, for the old shrew, Sir
Launcelot, smote me down. So they went to dinner, [and] all the
court had good sport at Dinadan.

Then when the dinner was done they blew to the field to behold
Sir Palomides and Corsabrin. Sir Palomides pight his pensel in midst
of the field; and then they hurtled together with their spears as it were
thunder, and either smote other to the earth. And then they pulled
out their swords, and dressed their shields, and lashed together
mightily as mighty knights, that well-nigh there was no piece of
harness would hold them, for this Corsabrin was a passing felonious
knight. Corsabrin, said Palomides, wilt thou release me yonder
damosel and the pensel? Then was Corsabrin wroth out of measure,
and gave Palomides such a buffet that he kneeled on his knee. Then
Palomides arose lightly, and smote him upon the helm that he fell
down right to the earth. And therewith he raced off his helm and
said: Corsabrin, yield thee or else thou shalt die of my hands. Fie on
thee, said Corsabrin, do thy worst. Then he smote off his head. And
therewithal came a stink of his body when the soul departed, that
there might nobody abide the savour. So was the corpse had away
and buried in a wood, because he was a paynim. Then they blew
unto lodging, and Palomides was unarmed.

Then he went unto Queen Guenever, to the haut prince, and to
Sir Launcelot. Sir, said the haut prince, here have ye seen this day a
great miracle by Corsabrin, what savour there was when the soul

departed from the body. Therefore, sir, we will require you to take the baptism upon you, and I promise you all knights will set the more by you, and say more worship by you. Sir, said Palomides, I will that ye all know that into this land I came to be christened, and in my heart I am christened, and christened will I be. But I have made such an avow that I may not be christened till I have done seven true battles for Jesu's sake, and then will I be christened; and I trust God will take mine intent, for I mean truly. Then Sir Palomides prayed Queen Guenever and the haut prince to sup with him. And so they did, both Sir Launcelot and Sir Lamorak, and many other good knights. So on the morn they heard their mass, and blew the field, and then knights made them ready.

CHAPTER XLVIII

Of the sixth day, and what then was done.

Here beginneth the sixth day. Then came therein Sir Gaheris, and there encountered with him Sir Ossaise of Surluse, and Sir Gaheris smote him over his horse's croup. And then either party encountered with other, and there were many spears broken, and many knights cast under feet. So there came in Sir Dornard and Sir Aglovale, that were brethren unto Sir Lamorak, and they met with other two knights, and either smote other so hard that all four knights and horses fell to the earth. When Sir Lamorak saw his two brethren down he was wrath out of measure, and then he gat a great spear in his hand, and therewithal he smote down four good knights, and then his spear brake. Then he pulled out his sword, and smote about him on the right hand and on the left hand, and raced off helms and pulled down knights, that all men marvelled of such deeds of arms as he did, for he fared so that many knights fled. Then he horsed his brethren again, and said: Brethren, ye ought to be ashamed to fall so off your horses! what is a knight but when he is on horseback? I set not by a knight when he is on foot, for all battles on foot are but pillers' battles. For there should no knight fight on foot but if it were for treason, or else he were driven thereto by force; therefore, brethren, sit fast on your horses, or else fight never more afore me.

With that came in the Duke Chaleins of Clarance, and there encountered with him the Earl Ulbawes of Surluse, and either of them smote other down. Then the knights of both parties horsed their lords again, for Sir Ector and Bleoberis were on foot, waiting on the Duke Chaleins. And the King with the Hundred Knights was with the Earl of Ulbawes. With that came Gaheris and lashed to the King with the Hundred Knights, and he to him again. Then came the Duke Chaleins and departed them.

Then they blew to lodging, and the knights unarmed them and drew them to their dinner; and at the midst of their dinner in came Dinadan and began to rail. Then he beheld the haut prince, that seemed wroth with some fault that he saw; for he had a custom he loved no fish, and because he was served with fish, the which he hated, therefore he was not merry. When Sir Dinadan had espied the haut prince, he espied where was a fish with a great head, and that he gat betwixt two dishes, and served the haut prince with that fish. And then he said thus: Sir Galahalt, well may I liken you to a wolf, for he will never eat fish, but flesh; then the haut prince laughed at his words. Well, well, said Dinadan to Launcelot, what devil do ye in this country, for here may no mean knights win no worship for thee. Sir Dinadan, said Launcelot, I ensure thee I shall no more meet with thee nor with thy great spear, for I may not sit in my saddle when that spear hitteth me. And if I be happy I shall beware of that boistous body that thou bearest. Well, said Launcelot, make good watch ever: God forbid that ever we meet but if it be at a dish of meat. Then laughed the queen and the haut prince, that they might not sit at their table; thus they made great joy till on the morn, and then they heard mass, and blew to field. And Queen Guenever and all the estates were set, and judges armed clean with their shields to keep the right.

CHAPTER XLIX

Of the seventh battle, and how Sir Launcelot, being disguised
like a maid, smote down Sir Dinadan.

Now beginneth the seventh battle. There came in the Duke
Cambines, and there encountered with him Sir Aristance, that was
counted a good knight, and they met so hard that either bare other
down, horse and man. Then came there the Earl of Lambaile and
helped the duke again to horse. Then came there Sir Ossaise of
Surluse, and he smote the Earl Lambaile down from his horse. Then
began they to do great deeds of arms, and many spears were broken,
and many knights were cast to the earth. Then the King of Northgalis
and the Earl Ulbawes smote together that all the judges thought it
was like mortal death. This meanwhile Queen Guenever, and the
haut prince, and Sir Launcelot, made there Sir Dinadan make him
ready to joust. I would, said Dinadan, ride into the field, but then one
of you twain will meet with me. Per dieu, said the haut prince, ye
may see how we sit here as judges with our shields, and always mayest
thou behold whether we sit here or not.

So Sir Dinadan departed and took his horse, and met with many
knights, and did passing well. And as he was departed, Sir Launcelot
disguised himself, and put upon his armour a maiden's garment
freshly attired. Then Sir Launcelot made Sir Galihodin to lead him
through the range, and all men had wonder what damosel it was.
And so as Sir Dinadan came into the range, Sir Launcelot, that was in
the damosel's array, gat Galihodin's spear, and ran unto Sir Dinadan.
And always Sir Dinadan looked up thereas Sir Launcelot was, and
then he saw one sit in the stead of Sir Launcelot, armed. But when
Dinadan saw a manner of a damosel he dread perils that it was Sir
Launcelot disguised, but Sir Launcelot came on him so fast that he
smote him over his horse's croup; and then with great scorns they
gat Sir Dinadan into the forest there beside, and there they dispoiled
him unto his shirt, and put upon him a woman's garment, and so
brought him into the field: and so they blew unto lodging. And
every knight went and unarmed them. Then was Sir Dinadan

brought in among them all. And when Queen Guenever saw Sir Dinadan brought so among them all, then she laughed that she fell down, and so did all that there were. Well, said Dinadan to Launcelot, thou art so false that I can never beware of thee. Then by all the assent they gave Sir Launcelot the prize, the next was Sir Lamorak de Galis, the third was Sir Palomides, the fourth was King Bagdemagus; so these four knights had the prize, and there was great joy, and great nobley in all the court.

And on the morn Queen Guenever and Sir Launcelot departed unto King Arthur, but in no wise Sir Lamorak would not go with them. I shall undertake, said Sir Launcelot, that an ye will go with us King Arthur shall charge Sir Gawaine and his brethren never to do you hurt. As for that, said Sir Lamorak, I will not trust Sir Gawaine nor none of his brethren; and wit ye well, Sir Launcelot, an it were not for my lord King Arthur's sake, I should match Sir Gawaine and his brethren well enough. But to say that I should trust them, that shall I never, and therefore I pray you recommend me unto my lord Arthur, and unto all my lords of the Round Table. And in what place that ever I come I shall do you service to my power: and sir, it is but late that I revenged that, when my lord Arthur's kin were put to the worse by Sir Palomides. Then Sir Lamorak departed from Sir Launcelot, and either wept at their departing.

CHAPTER L

How by treason Sir Tristram was brought to a tournament for to have been slain, and how he was put in prison.

Now turn we from this matter, and speak we of Sir Tristram, of whom this book is principally of, and leave we the king and the queen, Sir Launcelot, and Sir Lamorak, and here beginneth the treason of King Mark, that he ordained against Sir Tristram. There was cried by the coasts of Cornwall a great tournament and jousts, and all was done by Sir Galahalt the haut prince and King Bagdemagus, to the intent to slay Launcelot, or else utterly destroy him and shame him, because Sir Launcelot had always the higher degree; therefore this prince and this king made this jousts against Sir

Launcelot. And thus their counsel was discovered unto King Mark, whereof he was full glad.

Then King Mark bethought him that he would have Sir Tristram unto that tournament disguised that no man should know him, to that intent that the haut prince should ween that Sir Tristram were Sir Launcelot. So at these jousts came in Sir Tristram. And at that time Sir Launcelot was not there, but when they saw a knight disguised do such deeds of arms, they weened it had been Sir Launcelot. And in especial King Mark said it was Sir Launcelot plainly. Then they set upon him, both King Bagdemagus, and the haut prince, and their knights, that it was wonder that ever Sir Tristram might endure that pain. Notwithstanding for all the pain that he had, Sir Tristram won the degree at that tournament, and there he hurt many knights and bruised them, and they hurt him and bruised him wonderly sore. So when the jousts were all done they knew well that it was Sir Tristram de Liones; and all that were on King Mark's party were glad that Sir Tristram was hurt, and the remnant were sorry of his hurt; for Sir Tristram was not so behated as was Sir Launcelot within the realm of England.

Then came King Mark unto Sir Tristram and said: Fair nephew, I am sorry of your hurts. Gramercy my lord, said Sir Tristram. Then King Mark made Sir Tristram to be put in an horse bier in great sign of love, and said: Fair cousin, I shall be your leech myself. And so he rode forth with Sir Tristram, and brought him to a castle by daylight. And then King Mark made Sir Tristram to eat. And then after he gave him a drink, the which as soon as he had drunk he fell asleep. And when it was night he made him to be carried to another castle, and there he put him in a strong prison, and there he ordained a man and a woman to give him his meat and drink. So there he was a great while.

Then was Sir Tristram missed, and no creature wist where he was become. When La Beale Isoud heard how he was missed, privily she went unto Sir Sadok, and prayed him to espy where was Sir Tristram. Then when Sadok wist how Sir Tristram was missed, and anon espied that he was put in prison by King Mark and the traitors of Magouns, then Sadok and two of his cousins laid them in an ambushment, fast by the Castle of Tintagil, in arms. And as by fortune, there came riding King Mark and four of his nephews, and a certain of the traitors of Magouns. When Sir Sadok espied them he brake out of the bushment, and set there upon them. And when

King Mark espied Sir Sadok he fled as fast as he might, and there Sir Sadok slew all the four nephews unto King Mark. But these traitors of Magouns slew one of Sadok's cousins with a great wound in the neck, but Sadok smote the other to the death. Then Sir Sadok rode upon his way unto a castle that was called Liones, and there he espied of the treason and felony of King Mark. So they of that castle rode with Sir Sadok till that they came to a castle that hight Arbray, and there in the town they found Sir Dinas the Seneschal, that was a good knight. But when Sir Sadok had told Sir Dinas of all the treason of King Mark he defied such a king, and said he would give up his lands that he held of him. And when he said these words all manner knights said as Sir Dinas said. Then by his advice, and of Sir Sadok's, he let stuff all the towns and castles within the country of Liones, and assembled all the people that they might make.

CHAPTER LI

How King Mark let do counterfeit letters from the Pope, and how Sir Percivale delivered Sir Tristram out of prison.

Now turn we unto King Mark, that when he was escaped from Sir Sadok he rode unto the Castle of Tintagil, and there he made great cry and noise, and cried unto harness all that might bear arms. Then they sought and found where were dead four cousins of King Mark's, and the traitor of Magouns. Then the king let inter them in a chapel. Then the king let cry in all the country that held of him, to go unto arms, for he understood to the war he must needs. When King Mark heard and understood how Sir Sadok and Sir Dinas were arisen in the country of Liones he remembered of wiles and treason. Lo thus he did: he let make and counterfeit letters from the Pope, and did make a strange clerk to bear them unto King Mark; the which letters specified that King Mark should make him ready, upon pain of cursing, with his host to come to the Pope, to help to go to Jerusalem, for to make war upon the Saracens.

When this clerk was come by the mean of the king, anon withal King Mark sent these letters unto Sir Tristram and bade him say thus: that an he would go war upon the miscreants, he should be had out of prison, and to have all his power. When Sir Tristram understood this letter, then he said thus to the clerk: Ah, King Mark, ever hast thou been a traitor, and ever will be; but, Clerk, said Sir Tristram, say thou thus unto King Mark: Since the Apostle Pope hath sent for him, bid him go thither himself; for tell him, traitor king as he is, I will not go at his commandment, get I out of prison as I may, for I see I am well rewarded for my true service. Then the clerk returned unto King Mark, and told him of the answer of Sir Tristram. Well, said King Mark, yet shall he be beguiled. So he went into his chamber, and counterfeit letters; and the letters specified that the Pope desired Sir Tristram to come himself, to make war upon the miscreants. When the clerk was come again to Sir Tristram and took him these letters, then Sir Tristram beheld these letters, and anon espied they were of King Mark's counterfeiting. Ah, said Sir Tristram, false hast thou been ever, King Mark, and so wilt thou end. Then the clerk departed from Sir Tristram and came to King Mark again.

By then there were come four wounded knights within the Castle of Tintagil, and one of them his neck was nigh broken in twain. Another had his arm stricken away, the third was borne through with a spear, the fourth had his teeth stricken in twain. And when they came afore King Mark they cried and said: King, why fleest thou not, for all this country is arisen clearly against thee? Then was King Mark wroth out of measure.

And in the meanwhile there came into the country Sir Percivale de Galis to seek Sir Tristram. And when he heard that Sir Tristram was in prison, Sir Percivale made clearly the deliverance of Sir Tristram by his knightly means. And when he was so delivered he made great joy of Sir Percivale, and so each one of other. Sir Tristram said unto Sir Percivale: An ye will abide in these marches I will ride with you. Nay, said Percivale, in this country I may not tarry, for I must needs into Wales. So Sir Percivale departed from Sir Tristram, and rode straight unto King Mark, and told him how he had delivered Sir Tristram; and also he told the king that he had done himself great shame for to put Sir Tristram in prison, for he is now the knight of most renown in this world living. And wit thou well the noblest knights of the world love Sir Tristram, and if he will make war upon you ye may not abide it. That is truth, said King Mark, but I may not love Sir Tristram because he loveth my queen and my wife, La Beale Isoud. Ah, fie for shame, said Sir Percivale, say ye never so more. Are ye not uncle unto Sir Tristram, and he your nephew? Ye should never think that so noble a knight as Sir Tristram is, that he would do himself so great a villainy to hold his uncle's wife; howbeit, said Sir Percivale, he may love your queen sinless, because she is called one of the fairest ladies of the world.

Then Sir Percivale departed from King Mark. So when he was departed King Mark bethought him of more treason: notwithstanding King Mark granted Sir Percivale never by no manner of means to hurt Sir Tristram. So anon King Mark sent unto Sir Dinas the Seneschal that he should put down all the people that he had raised, for he sent him an oath that he would go himself unto the Pope of Rome to war upon the miscreants; and this is a fairer war than thus to arise the people against your king. When Sir Dinas understood that King Mark would go upon the miscreants, then Sir Dinas in all the haste put down all the people; and when the people were departed every man to his home, then King Mark espied where was Sir Tristram with La Beale Isoud; and there by treason King Mark let take him and put him in prison, contrary to his promise that he made unto Sir Percivale.

When Queen Isoud understood that Sir Tristram was in prison she made as great sorrow as ever made lady or gentlewoman. Then Sir Tristram sent a letter unto La Beale Isoud, and prayed her to be his good lady; and if it pleased her to make a vessel ready for her and him, he would go with her unto the realm of Logris, that is this land. When La Beale Isoud understood Sir Tristram's letters and his intent, she sent him another, and bade him be of good comfort, for she would do make the vessel ready, and all thing to purpose.

Then La Beale Isoud sent unto Sir Dinas, and to Sadok, and prayed them in anywise to take King Mark, and put him in prison, unto the time that she and Sir Tristram were departed unto the realm of Logris. When Sir Dinas the Seneschal understood the treason of King Mark he promised her again, and sent her word that King Mark should be put in prison. And as they devised it so it was done. And then Sir Tristram was delivered out of prison; and anon in all the haste Queen Isoud and Sir Tristram went and took their counsel with that they would have with them when they departed.

CHAPTER LII

*How Sir Tristram and La Beale Isoud came unto England,
and how Sir Launcelot brought them to Joyous Gard.*

Then La Beale Isoud and Sir Tristram took their vessel, and came by water into this land. And so they were not in this land four days but there came a cry of a jousts and tournament that King Arthur let make. When Sir Tristram heard tell of that tournament he disguised himself, and La Beale Isoud, and rode unto that tournament. And when he came there he saw many knights joust and tourney; and so Sir Tristram dressed him to the range, and to make short conclusion, he overthrew fourteen knights of the Round Table. When Sir Launcelot saw these knights thus overthrown, Sir Launcelot dressed him to Sir Tristram. That saw La Beale Isoud how Sir Launcelot was come into the field. Then La Beale Isoud sent unto Sir Launcelot a ring, and bade him wit that it was Sir Tristram de Liones. When Sir Launcelot understood that there was Sir Tristram he was full glad, and would not joust. Then Sir Launcelot espied whither Sir Tristram yede, and after him he rode; and then either made of other great joy. And so Sir Launcelot brought Sir Tristram and La Beale Isoud unto Joyous Gard, that was his own castle, that he had won with his own hands. And there Sir Launcelot put them in to wield for their own. And wit ye well that castle was garnished and furnished for a king and a queen royal there to have sojourned. And Sir Launcelot charged all his people to honour them and love them as they would do himself.

So Sir Launcelot departed unto King Arthur; and then he told Queen Guenever how he that jousted so well at the last tournament was Sir Tristram. And there he told her how he had with him La Beale Isoud maugre King Mark, and so Queen Guenever told all this unto King Arthur. When King Arthur wist that Sir Tristram was escaped and come from King Mark, and had brought La Beale Isoud with him, then was he passing glad. So because of Sir Tristram King Arthur let make a cry, that on May Day should be a jousts before the castle of Lonazep; and that castle was fast by Joyous Gard. And thus Arthur devised, that all the knights of this land, and of Cornwall, and of North Wales, should joust against all these countries, Ireland, Scotland, and the remnant of Wales, and the country of Gore, and Surluse, and of Listinoise, and they of Northumberland, and all they that held lands of Arthur on this half the sea. When this cry was made many knights were glad and many were unglad. Sir, said Launcelot unto Arthur, by this cry that ye have made ye will put us that be about you in great jeopardy, for there be many knights that have great envy to us; therefore when we shall meet at the day of jousts there will be hard shift among us. As for that, said Arthur, I care not; there shall we prove who shall be best of his hands. So when Sir Launcelot understood wherefore King Arthur made this jousting, then he made such purveyance that La Beale Isoud should behold the jousts in a secret place that was honest for her estate.

Now turn we unto Sir Tristram and to La Beale Isoud, how they made great joy daily together with all manner of mirths that they could devise; and every day Sir Tristram would go ride a-hunting, for Sir Tristram was that time called the best chaser of the world, and the noblest blower of an horn of all manner of measures; for as books report, of Sir Tristram came all the good terms of venery and hunting, and all the sizes and measures of blowing of an horn; and of him we had first all the terms of hawking, and which were beasts of chase and beasts of venery, and which were vermins, and all the blasts that long to all manner of games. First to the uncoupling, to the seeking, to the rechate, to the flight, to the death, and to strake, and many other blasts and terms, that all manner of gentlemen have cause to the world's end to praise Sir Tristram, and to pray for his soul.

CHAPTER LIII

*How by the counsel of La Beale Isoud Sir Tristram rode
armed, and how he met with Sir Palomides.*

So on a day La Beale Isoud said unto Sir Tristram: I marvel me much, said she, that ye remember not yourself, how ye be here in a strange country, and here be many perilous knights; and well ye wot that King Mark is full of treason; and that ye will ride thus to chase and to hunt unarmed ye might be destroyed. My fair lady and my love, I cry you mercy, I will no more do so. So then Sir Tristram rode daily a-hunting armed, and his men bearing his shield and his spear. So on a day a little afore the month of May, Sir Tristram chased an hart passing eagerly, and so the hart passed by a fair well. And then Sir Tristram alighted and put off his helm to drink of that bubbly water. Right so he heard and saw the Questing Beast come to the well. When Sir Tristram saw that beast he put on his helm, for he deemed he should hear of Sir Palomides, for that beast was his quest. Right so Sir Tristram saw where came a knight armed, upon a noble courser, and he saluted him, and they spake of many things; and this knight's name was Breuse Saunce Pité. And right so withal there came unto them the noble knight Sir Palomides, and either saluted other, and spake fair to other.

Fair knights, said Sir Palomides, I can tell you tidings. What is that? said those knights. Sirs, wit ye well that King Mark is put in prison by his own knights, and all was for love of Sir Tristram; for King Mark had put Sir Tristram twice in prison, and once Sir Percivale delivered the noble knight Sir Tristram out of prison. And at the last time Queen La Beale Isoud delivered him, and went clearly away with him into this realm; and all this while King Mark, the false traitor, is in prison. Is this truth? said Palomides; then shall we hastily hear of Sir Tristram. And as for to say that I love La Beale Isoud paramours, I dare make good that I do, and that she hath my service above all other ladies, and shall have the term of my life.

And right so as they stood talking they saw afore them where came a knight all armed, on a great horse, and one of his men bare his shield, and the other his spear. And anon as that knight espied them he gat his shield and his spear and dressed him to joust. Fair fellows, said Sir Tristram, yonder is a knight will joust with us, let see which of us shall encounter with him, for I see well he is of the court of King Arthur. It shall not be long or he be met withal, said Sir Palomides, for I found never no knight in my quest of this glasting beast, but an he would joust I never refused him. As well may I, said Breuse Saunce Pité, follow that beast as ye. Then shall ye do battle with me, said Palomides.

So Sir Palomides dressed him unto that other knight, Sir Bleoberis, that was a full noble knight, nigh kin unto Sir Launcelot. And so they met so hard that Sir Palomides fell to the earth, horse and all. Then Sir Bleoberis cried aloud and said thus: Make thee ready thou false traitor knight, Breuse Saunce Pité, for wit thou certainly I will have ado with thee to the utterance for the noble knights and ladies that thou hast falsely betrayed. When this false knight and traitor, Breuse Saunce Pité, heard him say so, he took his horse by the bridle and fled his way as fast as ever his horse might run, for sore he was of him afeard. When Sir Bleoberis saw him flee he followed fast after, through thick and through thin. And by fortune as Sir Breuse fled, he saw even afore him three knights of the Table Round, of the which the one hight Sir Ector de Maris, the other hight Sir Percivale de Galis, the third hight Sir Harry le Fise Lake, a good knight and an hardy. And as for Sir Percivale, he was called that time of his time one of the best knights of the world, and the best assured. When Breuse saw these knights he rode straight unto them, and cried unto them and prayed them of rescues. What need have ye? said Sir Ector. Ah, fair knights, said Sir Breuse, here followeth me the most traitor knight, and most coward, and most of villainy; his name is Breuse Saunce Pité, and if he may get me he will slay me without mercy and pity. Abide with us, said Sir Percivale, and we shall warrant you.

Then were they ware of Sir Bleoberis that came riding all that he might. Then Sir Ector put himself forth to joust afore them all. When Sir Bleoberis saw that they were four knights and he but himself, he stood in a doubt whether he would turn or hold his way. Then he said to himself: I am a knight of the Table Round, and rather than I should shame mine oath and my blood I will hold my way whatsoever fall thereof. And then Sir Ector dressed his spear, and smote either other passing sore, but Sir Ector fell to the earth. That saw Sir Percivale, and he dressed his horse toward him all that he might drive but Sir Percivale had such a stroke that horse and man fell to the earth. When Sir Harry saw that they were both to the earth then he said to himself: Never was Breuse of such prowess. So Sir Harry dressed his horse, and they met together so strongly that both the horses and knights fell to the earth, but Sir Bleoberis' horse began to recover again. That saw Breuse and he came hurtling, and smote him over and over, and would have slain him as he lay on the ground. Then Sir Harry le Fise Lake arose lightly, and took the bridle of Sir Breuse's horse, and said: Fie for shame! strike never a knight when he is at the earth, for this knight may be called no shameful knight of his deeds, for yet as men may see thereas he lieth on the ground he hath done worshipfully, and put to the worse passing good knights.

Therefore will I not let, said Sir Breuse. Thou shalt not choose, said Sir Harry, as at this time. Then when Sir Breuse saw that he might not choose nor have his will he spake fair. Then Sir Harry let him go. And then anon he made his horse to run over Sir Bleoberis, and rashed him to the earth like if he would have slain him. When Sir Harry saw him do so villainously he cried: Traitor knight, leave off for shame. And as Sir Harry would have taken his horse to fight with Sir Breuse, then Sir Breuse ran upon him as he was half upon his horse, and smote him down, horse and man, to the earth, and had near slain Sir Harry, the good knight. That saw Sir Percivale, and then he cried: Traitor knight, what dost thou? And when Sir Percivale was upon his horse Sir Breuse took his horse and fled all that ever he might, and Sir Percivale and Sir Harry followed after him fast, but ever the longer they chased the farther were they behind.

Then they turned again and came to Sir Ector de Maris and to Sir Bleoberis. Ah, fair knights, said Bleoberis, why have ye succoured that false knight and traitor? Why, said Sir Harry, what knight is he? for well I wot it is a false knight, said Sir Harry, and a coward and a felonious knight. Sir, said Bleoberis, he is the most coward knight, and a devourer of ladies and a destroyer of good knights, and especially of Arthur's. What is your name? said Sir Ector. My name is Sir Bleoberis de Ganis. Alas, fair cousin, said Ector, forgive it me, for I am Sir Ector de Maris. Then Sir Percivale and Sir Harry made great joy that they met with Bleoberis, but all they were heavy that Sir Breuse was escaped them, whereof they made great dole.

CHAPTER LIV

Of Sir Palomides, and how he met with Sir Bleoberis and with Sir Ector, and of Sir Percivale.

Right so as they stood thus there came Sir Palomides, and when he saw the shield of Bleoberis lie on the earth, then said Palomides: He that oweth that shield let him dress him to me, for he smote me down here fast by at a fountain, and therefore I will fight for him on foot. I am ready, said Bleoberis, here to answer thee, for wit thou well, sir knight, it was I, and my name is Bleoberis de Ganis. Well art thou met, said Palomides, and wit thou well my name is Palomides the Saracen; and either of them hated other to the death. Sir Palomides, said Ector, wit thou well there is neither thou nor none knight that beareth the life that slayeth any of our blood but he shall die for it; therefore an thou list to fight go seek Sir Launcelot or Sir Tristram, and there shall ye find your match. With them have I met, said Palomides, but I had never no worship of them. Was there never no manner of knight, said Sir Ector, but they that ever matched with you? Yes, said Palomides, there was the third, a good knight as any of them, and of his age he was the best that ever I found; for an he might have lived till he had been an hardier man there liveth no knight now such, and his name was Sir Lamorak de Galis. And as he had jousted at a tournament there he overthrew me and thirty knights more, and there he won the degree. And at his departing there met him Sir Gawaine and his brethren, and with great pain they slew him feloniously, unto all good knights' great damage. Anon as Sir Percivale heard that his brother was dead, Sir Lamorak, he fell over his horse's mane swooning, and there he made the greatest dole that ever made knight. And when Sir Percivale arose he said: Alas, my good and noble brother Sir Lamorak, now shall we never meet, and I trow in all the wide world a man may not find such a knight as he was of his age; and it is too much to suffer the death of our father King Pellinore, and now the death of our good brother Sir Lamorak.

Then in the meanwhile there came a varlet from the court of King Arthur, and told them of the great tournament that should be at Lonazep, and how these lands, Cornwall and Northgalis, should be against all them that would come.

CHAPTER LV

How Sir Tristram met with Sir Dinadan, and of their devices, and what he said to Sir Gawaine's brethren.

Now turn we unto Sir Tristram, that as he rode a-hunting he met with Sir Dinadan, that was come into that country to seek Sir Tristram. Then Sir Dinadan told Sir Tristram his name, but Sir Tristram would not tell him his name, wherefore Sir Dinadan was wroth. For such a foolish knight as ye are, said Sir Dinadan, I saw but late this day lying by a well, and he fared as he slept; and there he lay like a fool grinning, and would not speak, and his shield lay by him, and his horse stood by him; and well I wot he was a lover. Ah, fair sir, said Sir Tristram, are ye not a lover? Marry, fie on that craft! said Sir Dinadan. That is evil said, said Sir Tristram, for a knight may never be of prowess but if he be a lover. It is well said, said Sir Dinadan; now tell me your name, sith ye be a lover, or else I shall do battle with you. As for that, said Sir Tristram, it is no reason to fight with me but I tell you my name; and as for that my name shall ye not wit as at this time. Fie for shame, said Dinadan, art thou a knight and durst not tell thy name to me? therefore I will fight with thee. As for that, said Sir Tristram, I will be advised, for I will not do battle but if me list. And if I do battle, said Sir Tristram, ye are not able to withstand me. Fie on thee, coward, said Sir Dinadan.

And thus as they hoved still, they saw a knight come riding against them. Lo, said Sir Tristram, see where cometh a knight riding, will joust with you. Anon, as Sir Dinadan beheld him he said: That is the same doted knight that I saw lie by the well, neither sleeping nor waking. Well, said Sir Tristram, I know that knight well with the covered shield of azure, he is the king's son of Northumberland, his name is Epinegris; and he is as great a lover as I know, and he loveth the king's daughter of Wales, a full fair lady. And now I suppose, said Sir Tristram, an ye require him he will joust with you, and then shall ye prove whether a lover be a better knight, or ye that will not love no lady. Well, said Dinadan, now shalt thou see what I shall do. Therewithal Sir Dinadan spake on high and said: Sir knight, make thee ready to joust with me, for it is the custom of errant knights one to joust with other. Sir, said Epinegris, is that the rule of you errant knights for to make a knight to joust, will he or nill? As for that, said Dinadan, make thee ready, for here is for me. And therewithal they spurred their horses and met together so hard that Epinegris smote down Sir Dinadan. Then Sir Tristram rode to Sir Dinadan and said: How now, meseemeth the lover hath well sped. Fie on thee, coward, said Sir Dinadan, and if thou be a good knight revenge me. Nay, said Sir Tristram, I will not joust as at this time, but take your horse and let us go hence. God defend me, said Sir Dinadan, from thy fellowship, for I never sped well since I met with thee: and so they departed. Well, said Sir Tristram, peradventure I could tell you tidings of Sir Tristram. God defend me, said Dinadan, from thy fellowship, for Sir Tristram were mickle the worse an he were in thy company: and then they departed. Sir, said Sir Tristram, yet it may happen I shall meet with you in other places.

So rode Sir Tristram unto Joyous Gard, and there he heard in that town great noise and cry. What is this noise? said Sir Tristram. Sir, said they, here is a knight of this castle that hath been long among us, and right now he is slain with two knights, and for none other cause but that our knight said that Sir Launcelot were a better knight than Sir Gawaine. That was a simple cause, said Sir Tristram, for to slay a good knight for to say well by his master. That is little remedy to us, said the men of the town. For an Sir Launcelot had been here soon we should have been revenged upon the false knights.

When Sir Tristram heard them say so he sent for his shield and for his spear, and lightly within a while he had overtaken them, and bade them turn and amend that they had misdone. What amends wouldst thou have? said the one knight. And therewith they took their course, and either met other so hard that Sir Tristram smote down that knight over his horse's tail. Then the other knight dressed him to Sir Tristram, and in the same wise he served the other knight. And then they gat off their horses as well as they might, and dressed their shields and swords to do their battle to the utterance. Knights, said Sir Tristram, ye shall tell me of whence ye are, and what be your names, for such men ye might be ye should hard escape my hands; and ye might be such men of such a country that for all your evil deeds ye should pass quit. Wit thou well, sir knight, said they, we fear not to tell thee our names, for my name is Sir Agravaine, and my name is Gaheris, brethren unto the good knight Sir Gawaine, and we be nephews unto King Arthur. Well, said Sir Tristram, for King Arthur's sake I shall let you pass as at this time. But it is shame, said Sir Tristram, that Sir Gawaine and ye be come of so great a blood that ye four brethren are so named as ye be, for ye be called the greatest destroyers and murderers of good knights that be now in this realm; for it is but as I heard say that Sir Gawaine and ye slew among you a better knight than ever ye were, that was the noble knight Sir Lamorak de Galis. An it had pleased God, said Sir Tristram, I would I had been by Sir Lamorak at his death. Then shouldst thou have gone the same way, said Sir Gaheris. Fair knight, said Sir Tristram, there must have been many more knights than ye are. And therewithal Sir Tristram departed from them toward Joyous

Gard. And when he was departed they took their horses, and the one said to the other: We will overtake him and be revenged upon him in the despite of Sir Lamorak.

CHAPTER LVI

How Sir Tristram smote down Sir Agravaine and Sir Gaheris, and how Sir Dinadan was sent for by La Beale Isoud.

So when they had overtaken Sir Tristram, Sir Agravaine bade him: Turn, traitor knight. That is evil said, said Sir Tristram; and therewith he pulled out his sword, and smote Sir Agravaine such a buffet upon the helm that he tumbled down off his horse in a swoon, and he had a grievous wound. And then he turned to Gaheris, and Sir Tristram smote his sword and his helm together with such a might that Gaheris fell out of his saddle: and so Sir Tristram rode unto Joyous Gard, and there he alighted and unarmed him. So Sir Tristram told La Beale Isoud of all his adventure, as ye have heard to-fore. And when she heard him tell of Sir Dinadan: Sir, said she, is not that he that made the song by King Mark? That same is he, said Sir Tristram, for he is the best bourder and japer, and a noble knight of his hands, and the best fellow that I know, and all good knights love his fellowship. Alas, sir, said she, why brought ye not him with you? Have ye no care, said Sir Tristram, for he rideth to seek me in this country; and therefore he will not away till he have met with me. And there Sir Tristram told La Beale Isoud how Sir Dinadan held against all lovers. Right so there came in a varlet and told Sir Tristram how there was come an errant knight into the town, with such colours upon his shield. That is Sir Dinadan, said Sir Tristram; wit ye what ye shall do, said Sir Tristram: send ye for him, my Lady Isoud, and I will not be seen, and ye shall hear the merriest knight that ever ye spake withal, and the maddest talker; and I pray you heartily that ye make him good cheer.

Then anon La Beale Isoud sent into the town, and prayed Sir Dinadan that he would come into the castle and repose him there with a lady. With a good will, said Sir Dinadan; and so he mounted upon his horse and rode into the castle; and there he alighted, and was unarmed, and brought into the castle. Anon La Beale Isoud came unto him, and either saluted other; then she asked him of whence that he was. Madam, said Dinadan, I am of the court of King Arthur, and knight of the Table Round, and my name is Sir Dinadan. What do ye in this country? said La Beale Isoud. Madam, said he, I seek Sir Tristram the good knight, for it was told me that he was in this country. It may well be, said La Beale Isoud, but I am not ware of him. Madam, said Dinadan, I marvel of Sir Tristram and mo other lovers, what aileth them to be so mad and so sotted upon women. Why, said La Beale Isoud, are ye a knight and be no lover? it is shame to you: wherefore ye may not be called a good knight [but] if ye make a quarrel for a lady. God defend me, said Dinadan, for the joy of love is too short, and the sorrow thereof, and what cometh thereof, dureth over long. Ah, said La Beale Isoud, say ye not so, for here fast by was the good knight Sir Bleoberis, that fought with three knights at once for a damosel's sake, and he won her afore the King of Northumberland. It was so, said Sir Dinadan, for I know him well for a good knight and a noble, and come of noble blood; for all be noble knights of whom he is come of, that is Sir Launcelot du Lake.

Now I pray you, said La Beale Isoud, tell me will you fight for my love with three knights that do me great wrong? and insomuch as ye be a knight of King Arthur's I require you to do battle for me. Then Sir Dinadan said: I shall say you ye be as fair a lady as ever I saw any, and much fairer than is my lady Queen Guenever, but wit ye well at one word, I will not fight for you with three knights, Jesu defend me. Then Isoud laughed, and had good game at him. So he had all the cheer that she might make him, and there he lay all that night. And on the morn early Sir Tristram armed him, and La Beale Isoud gave him a good helm; and then he promised her that he would meet with Sir Dinadan, and they two would ride together into Lonazep, where the tournament should be: And there shall I make ready for you where ye shall see the tournament. Then departed Sir Tristram with two squires that bare his shield and his spears that were great and long.

CHAPTER LVII

How Sir Dinadan met with Sir Tristram, and with jousting with Sir Palomides, Sir Dinadan knew him.

Then after that Sir Dinadan departed, and rode his way a great pace until he had overtaken Sir Tristram. And when Sir Dinadan had overtaken him he knew him anon, and he hated the fellowship of him above all other knights. Ah, said Sir Dinadan, art thou that coward knight that I met with yesterday? keep thee, for thou shalt joust with me maugre thy head. Well, said Sir Tristram, and I am loath to joust. And so they let their horses run, and Sir Tristram missed of him a-purpose, and Sir Dinadan brake a spear upon Sir Tristram, and therewith Sir Dinadan dressed him to draw out his sword. Not so, said Sir Tristram, why are ye so wroth? I will not fight. Fie on thee, coward, said Dinadan, thou shamest all knights. As for that, said Sir Tristram, I care not, for I will wait upon you and be under your protection; for because ye are so good a knight ye may save me. The devil deliver me of thee, said Sir Dinadan, for thou art as goodly a man of arms and of thy person as ever I saw, and the most coward that ever I saw. What wilt thou do with those great spears that thou carriest with thee? I shall give them, said Sir Tristram, to some good knight when I come to the tournament; and if I see you do best, I shall give them to you.

So thus as they rode talking they saw where came an errant knight afore them, that dressed him to joust. Lo, said Sir Tristram, yonder is one will joust; now dress thee to him. Ah, shame betide thee, said Sir Dinadan. Nay, not so, said Tristram, for that knight beseemeth a shrew. Then shall I, said Sir Dinadan. And so they dressed their shields and their spears, and they met together so hard that the other knight smote down Sir Dinadan from his horse. Lo, said Sir Tristram, it had been better ye had left. Fie on thee, coward, said Sir Dinadan. Then Sir Dinadan started up and gat his sword in his hand, and proffered to do battle on foot. Whether in love or in wrath? said the other knight. Let us do battle in love, said Sir Dinadan. What is your name, said that knight, I pray you tell me. Wit ye well my name is Sir

Dinadan. Ah, Dinadan, said that knight, and my name is Gareth, the youngest brother unto Sir Gawaine. Then either made of other great cheer, for this Gareth was the best knight of all the brethren, and he proved a good knight. Then they took their horses, and there they spake of Sir Tristram, how such a coward he was; and every word Sir Tristram heard and laughed them to scorn.

Then were they ware where came a knight afore them well horsed and well armed, and he made him ready to joust. Fair knights, said Sir Tristram, look betwixt you who shall joust with yonder knight, for I warn you I will not have ado with him. Then shall I, said Sir Gareth. And so they encountered together, and there that knight smote down Sir Gareth over his horse's croup. How now, said Sir Tristram unto Sir Dinadan, dress thee now and revenge the good knight Gareth. That shall I not, said Sir Dinadan, for he hath stricken down a much bigger knight than I am. Ah, said Sir Tristram, now Sir Dinadan, I see and feel well your heart faileth you, therefore now shall ye see what I shall do. And then Sir Tristram hurtled unto that knight, and smote him quite from his horse. And when Sir Dinadan saw that, he marvelled greatly; and then he deemed that it was Sir Tristram.

Then this knight that was on foot pulled out his sword to do battle. What is your name? said Sir Tristram. Wit ye well, said that knight, my name is Sir Palomides. What knight hate ye most? said Sir Tristram. Sir knight, said he, I hate Sir Tristram to the death, for an I may meet with him the one of us shall die. Ye say well, said Sir Tristram, and wit ye well that I am Sir Tristram de Liones, and now do your worst. When Sir Palomides heard him say so he was astonied. And then he said thus: I pray you, Sir Tristram, forgive me all mine evil will, and if I live I shall do you service above all other knights that be living; and whereas I have owed you evil will me sore repenteth. I wot not what aileth me, for meseemeth that ye are a good knight, and none other knight that named himself a good knight should not hate you; therefore I require you, Sir Tristram, take no displeasure at mine unkind words. Sir Palomides, said Sir Tristram, ye say well, and well I wot ye are a good knight, for I have seen ye proved; and many great enterprises have ye taken upon you, and well achieved them; therefore, said Sir Tristram, an ye have any evil will to me, now may ye right it, for I am ready at your hand. Not so, my lord Sir Tristram, I will do you knightly service in all thing as ye will command. And right so I will take you, said Sir Tristram. And so they rode forth on their ways talking of many things. O my lord Sir Tristram, said Dinadan, foul have ye mocked me, for God knoweth I came into this country for your sake, and by the advice of my lord Sir Launcelot; and yet would not Sir Launcelot tell me the certainty of you, where I should find you. Truly, said Sir Tristram, Sir Launcelot wist well where I was, for I abode within his own castle.

CHAPTER LVIII

How they approached the Castle Lonazep, and of other devices of the death of Sir Lamorak.

Thus they rode until they were ware of the Castle Lonazep. And then were they ware of four hundred tents and pavilions, and marvellous great ordinance. So God me help, said Sir Tristram, yonder I see the greatest ordinance that ever I saw. Sir, said Palomides, meseemeth that there was as great an ordinance at the Castle of Maidens upon the rock, where ye won the prize, for I saw myself where ye for-jousted thirty knights. Sir, said Dinadan, and in Surluse, at that tournament that Galahalt of the Long Isles made, the which there dured seven days, was as great a gathering as is here, for there were many nations. Who was the best? said Sir Tristram. Sir, it was Sir Launcelot du Lake and the noble knight, Sir Lamorak de Galis, and Sir Launcelot won the degree. I doubt not, said Sir Tristram, but he won the degree, so he had not been overmatched with many knights; and of the death of Sir Lamorak, said Sir Tristram, it was over great pity, for I dare say he was the cleanest mighted man and the best winded of his age that was alive; for I knew him that he was the biggest knight that ever I met withal, but if it were Sir Launcelot. Alas, said Sir Tristram, full woe is me for his death. And if they were not the cousins of my lord Arthur that slew him, they should die for it, and all those that were consenting to his death. And for such things, said Sir Tristram, I fear to draw unto the court of my lord Arthur; I will that ye wit it, said Sir Tristram unto Gareth.

Sir, I blame you not, said Gareth, for well I understand the vengeance of my brethren Sir Gawaine, Agravaine, Gaheris, and Mordred. But as for me, said Sir Gareth, I meddle not of their matters, therefore there is none of them that loveth me. And for I understand they be murderers of good knights I left their company; and God would I had been by, said Gareth, when the noble knight, Sir Lamorak, was slain. Now as Jesu be my help, said Sir Tristram, it is well said of you, for I had liefer than all the gold betwixt this and Rome I had been there. Y-wis,* said Palomides, and so would I had been there, and yet had I never the degree at no jousts nor tournament thereas he was, but he put me to the worse, or on foot or on horseback; and that day that he was slain he did the most deeds of arms that ever I saw knight do in all my life days. And when him was given the degree by my lord Arthur, Sir Gawaine and his three brethren, Agravaine, Gaheris, and Sir Mordred, set upon Sir Lamorak in a privy place, and there they slew his horse. And so they fought with him on foot more than three hours, both before him and behind him; and Sir Mordred gave him his death wound behind him at his back, and all to-hew him: for one of his squires told me that saw it. Fie upon treason, said Sir Tristram, for it killeth my heart to hear this tale. So it doth mine, said Gareth; brethren as they be mine I shall never love them, nor draw in their fellowship for that deed.

Now speak we of other deeds, said Palomides, and let him be, for his life ye may not get again. That is the more pity, said Dinadan, for Sir Gawaine and his brethren, except you Sir Gareth, hate all the good knights of the Round Table for the most part; for well I wot an they might privily, they hate my lord Sir Launcelot and all his kin, and great privy despite they have at him; and that is my lord Sir Launcelot well ware of, and that causeth him to have the good knights of his kin about him.

* 'Y-wis' (certainly); Caxton, 'ye wis'; Wynkyn de Worde, 'truly'.

CHAPTER LIX

How they came to Humber bank, and how they found a ship
there, wherein lay the body of King Hermance.

Sir, said Palomides, let us leave of this matter, and let us see how we shall do at this tournament. By mine advice, said Palomides, let us four hold together against all that will come. Not by my counsel, said Sir Tristram, for I see by their pavilions there will be four hundred knights, and doubt ye not, said Sir Tristram, but there will be many good knights; and be a man never so valiant nor so big, yet he may be overmatched. And so have I seen knights done many times; and when they weened best to have won worship they lost it, for manhood is not worth but if it be medled with wisdom. And as for me, said Sir Tristram, it may happen I shall keep mine own head as well as another.

So thus they rode until that they came to Humber bank, where they heard a cry and a doleful noise. Then were they ware in the wind where came a rich vessel hilled over with red silk, and the vessel landed fast by them. Therewith Sir Tristram alighted and his knights. And so Sir Tristram went afore and entered into that vessel. And when he came within he saw a fair bed richly covered, and thereupon lay a dead seemly knight, all armed save the head, was all be-bled with deadly wounds upon him, the which seemed to be a passing good knight. How may this be, said Sir Tristram, that this knight is thus slain? Then Sir Tristram was ware of a letter in the dead knight's hand. Master mariners, said Sir Tristram, what meaneth that letter? Sir, said they, in that letter ye shall hear and know how he was slain, and for what cause, and what was his name. But sir, said the mariners, wit ye well that no man shall take that letter and read it but if he be a good knight, and that he will faithfully promise to revenge his death, else shall there be no knight see that letter open. Wit ye well, said Sir Tristram, that some of us may revenge his death as well as other, and if it be so as ye mariners say his death shall be revenged. And therewith Sir Tristram took the letter out of the knight's hand, and it said thus: Hermance, king and lord of the Red City, I send unto all knights errant, recommending unto you noble knights of Arthur's court. I beseech them all among them to find one knight that will fight for my sake with two brethren that I brought up of nought, and feloniously and traitorly they have slain me; wherefore I beseech one good knight to revenge my death. And he that revengeth my death I will that he have my Red City and all my castles.

Sir, said the mariners, wit ye well this king and knight that here lieth was a full worshipful man and of full great prowess, and full well he loved all manner knights errants. So God me help, said Sir Tristram, here is a piteous case, and full fain would I take this enterprise upon me; but I have made such a promise that needs I must be at this great tournament, or else I am shamed. For well I wot for my sake in especial my lord Arthur let make this jousts and tournament in this country; and well I wot that many worshipful people will be there at that tournament for to see me; therefore I fear me to take this enterprise upon me that I shall not come again by time to this jousts. Sir, said Palomides, I pray you give me this enterprise, and ye shall see me achieve it worshipfully, other else I shall die in this quarrel. Well, said Sir Tristram, and this enterprise I give you, with this, that ye be with me at this tournament that shall be as this day seven night. Sir, said Palomides, I promise you that I shall be with you by that day if I be unslain or unmaimed.

CHAPTER LX

How Sir Tristram with his fellowship came and were with an host which after fought with Sir Tristram; and other matters.

Then departed Sir Tristram, Gareth, and Sir Dinadan, and left Sir Palomides in the vessel; and so Sir Tristram beheld the mariners how they sailed overlong Humber. And when Sir Palomides was out of their sight they took their horses and beheld about them. And then were they ware of a knight that came riding against them unarmed, and nothing about him but a sword. And when this knight came nigh them he saluted them, and they him again. Fair knights, said that knight, I pray you insomuch as ye be knights errant, that ye will come and see my castle, and take such as ye find there; I pray you heartily. And so they rode with him until his castle, and there they were brought into the hall, that was well apparelled; and so they were there unarmed, and set at a board; and when this knight saw Sir Tristram, anon he knew him. And then this knight waxed pale and wroth at Sir Tristram. When Sir Tristram saw his host make such cheer he marvelled and said: Sir, mine host, what cheer make you? Wit thou well, said he, I fare the worse for thee, for I know thee, Sir Tristram de Liones, thou slewest my brother; and therefore I give thee summons I will slay thee an ever I may get thee at large. Sir knight, said Sir Tristram, I am never advised that ever I slew any brother of yours; and if ye say that I did I will make amends unto my power. I will none amends, said the knight, but keep thee from me.

So when he had dined Sir Tristram asked his arms, and departed. And so they rode on their ways, and within a while Sir Dinadan saw where came a knight well armed and well horsed, without shield. Sir Tristram, said Sir Dinadan, take keep to yourself, for I dare undertake yonder cometh your host that will have ado with you. Let him come, said Sir Tristram, I shall abide him as well as I may. Anon the knight, when he came nigh Sir Tristram, he cried and bade him abide and keep him. So they hurtled together, but Sir Tristram smote the other knight so sore that he bare him over his horse's croup. That knight arose lightly and took his horse again, and so rode fiercely to Sir Tristram, and smote him twice hard upon the helm. Sir knight, said Sir Tristram, I pray you leave off and smite me no more, for I would be loath to deal with you an I might choose, for I have your meat and your drink within my body. For all that he would not leave; and then Sir Tristram gave him such a buffet upon the helm that he fell up-so-down from his horse, that the blood brast out at the ventails of his helm, and so he lay still likely to be dead. Then Sir Tristram said: Me repenteth of this buffet that I smote so sore, for as I suppose he is dead. And so they left him and rode on their ways.

So they had not ridden but a while, but they saw riding against them two full likely knights, well armed and well horsed, and goodly servants about them. The one was Berrant le Apres, and he was called the King with the Hundred Knights; and the other was Sir Segwarides, which were renowned two noble knights. So as they came either by other the king looked upon Sir Dinadan, that at that time he had Sir Tristram's helm upon his shoulder, the which helm the king had seen to-fore with the Queen of Northgalis, and that queen the king loved as paramour; and that helm the Queen of Northgalis had given to La Beale Isoud, and the queen La Beale Isoud gave it to Sir Tristram. Sir knight, said Berrant, where had ye that helm? What would ye? said Sir Dinadan. For I will have ado with thee, said the king, for the love of her that owed that helm, and therefore keep you. So they departed and came together with all their mights of their horses, and there the King with the Hundred Knights smote Sir Dinadan, horse and all, to the earth; and then he commanded his servant: Go and take thou his helm off, and keep it. So the varlet went to unbuckle his helm. What helm, what wilt thou do? said Sir Tristram, leave that helm. To what intent, said the king, will ye, sir knight, meddle with that helm? Wit you well, said Sir Tristram, that helm shall not depart from me or it be dearer bought. Then make you ready, said Sir Berrant unto Sir Tristram. So they hurtled together, and there Sir Tristram smote him down over his horse's tail; and then the king arose lightly, and gat his horse lightly again. And then he struck fiercely at Sir Tristram many great strokes. And then Sir Tristram gave Sir Berrant such a buffet upon the helm that he fell down over his horse sore stonied. Lo, said Dinadan, that helm is unhappy to us twain, for I had a fall for it, and now, sir king, have ye another fall.

Then Segwarides asked: Who shall joust with me? I pray thee, said Sir Gareth unto Dinadan, let me have this jousts. Sir, said Dinadan, I pray you take it as for me. That is no reason, said Tristram, for this jousts should be yours. At a word, said Dinadan, I will not thereof. Then Gareth dressed him to Sir Segwarides, and there Sir Segwarides smote Gareth and his horse to the earth. Now, said Sir Tristram to Dinadan, joust with yonder knight. I will not thereof, said Dinadan. Then will I, said Sir Tristram. And then Sir Tristram ran to him, and gave him a fall; and so they left them on foot, and Sir Tristram rode unto Joyous Gard, and there Sir Gareth would not of his courtesy have gone into this castle, but Sir Tristram would not suffer him to depart. And so they alighted and unarmed them, and had great cheer. But when Dinadan came afore La Beale Isoud he cursed the time that ever he bare Sir Tristram's helm, and there he told her how Sir Tristram had mocked him. Then was there laughing and japing at Sir Dinadan, that they wist not what to do with him.

CHAPTER LXI

How Palomides went for to fight with two brethren for the death of King Hermance.

Now will we leave them merry within Joyous Gard, and speak we of Sir Palomides. Then Sir Palomides sailed evenlong Humber to the coasts of the sea, where was a fair castle. And at that time it was early in the morning, afore day. Then the mariners went unto Sir Palomides that slept fast. Sir knight, said the mariners, ye must arise, for here is a castle there ye must go into. I assent me, said Sir Palomides; and therewithal he arrived. And then he blew his horn that the mariners had given him. And when they within the castle heard that horn they put forth many knights; and there they stood upon the walls, and said with one voice: Welcome be ye to this castle. And then it waxed clear day, and Sir Palomides entered into the castle. And within a while he was served with many divers meats. Then Sir Palomides heard about him much weeping and great dole. What may this mean? said Sir Palomides; I love not to hear such a sorrow, and fain I would know what it meaneth. Then there came afore him one whose name was Sir Ebel, that said thus: Wit ye well, sir knight, this dole and sorrow is here made every day, and for this cause: we had a king that hight Hermance, and he was King of the Red City, and this king that was lord was a noble knight, large and liberal of his expense; and in the world he loved nothing so much as he did errant knights of King Arthur's court, and all jousting, hunting, and all manner of knightly games; for so kind a king and knight had never the rule of poor people as he was; and because of his goodness and gentleness we bemoan him, and ever shall. And all kings and estates may beware by our lord, for he was destroyed in his own default; for had he cherished them of his blood he had yet lived with great riches and rest: but all estates may beware by our king. But alas, said Ebel, that we shall give all other warning by his death.

Tell me, said Palomides, and in what manner was your lord slain, and by whom. Sir, said Sir Ebel, our king brought up of children two men that now are perilous knights; and these two knights our king had so in charity, that he loved no man nor trusted no man of his blood, nor none other that was about him. And by these two knights our king was governed, and so they ruled him peaceably and his lands, and never would they suffer none of his blood to have no rule with our king. And also he was so free and so gentle, and they so false and deceivable, that they ruled him peaceably; and that espied the lords of our king's blood, and departed from him unto their own livelihood. Then when these two traitors understood that they had driven all the lords of his blood from him, they were not pleased with that rule, but then they thought to have more, as ever it is an old saw: Give a churl rule and thereby he will not be sufficed; for whatsomever he be that is ruled by a villein born, and the lord of the soil to be a gentleman born, the same villein shall destroy all the gentlemen about him: therefore all estates and lords, beware whom ye take about you. And if ye be a knight of King Arthur's court remember this tale, for this is the end and conclusion. My lord and king rode unto the forest hereby by the advice of these traitors, and there he chased at the red deer, armed at all pieces full like a good knight; and so for labour he waxed dry, and then he alighted, and drank at a well. And when he was alighted, by the assent of these two traitors, that one that hight Helius he suddenly smote our king through the body with a spear, and so they left him there. And when they were departed, then by fortune I came to the well, and found my lord and king wounded to the death. And when I heard his complaint, I let bring him to the water side, and in that same ship I put him alive; and when my lord King Hermance was in that vessel, he required me for the true faith I owed unto him for to write a letter in this manner.

CHAPTER LXII

The copy of the letter written for to revenge the king's death, and how Sir Palomides fought for to have the battle.

Recommending unto King Arthur and to all his knights errant, beseeching them all that insomuch as I, King Hermance, King of the Red City, thus am slain by felony and treason, through two knights of mine own, and of mine own bringing up and of mine own making, that some worshipful knight will revenge my death, insomuch I have been ever to my power well willing unto Arthur's court. And who that will adventure his life with these two traitors for my sake in one battle, I, King Hermance, King of the Red City, freely give him all my lands and rents that ever I wielded in my life. This letter, said Ebel, I wrote by my lord's commandment, and then he received his Creator; and when he was dead, he commanded me or ever he were cold to put that letter fast in his hand. And then he commanded me to put forth that same vessel down Humber, and I should give these mariners in commandment never to stint until that they came unto Logris, where all the noble knights shall assemble at this time. And there shall some good knight have pity on me to revenge my death, for there was never king nor lord falslier nor traitorlier slain than I am here to my death. Thus was the complaint of our King Hermance. Now, said Sir Ebel, ye know all how our lord was betrayed, we require you for God's sake have pity upon his death, and worshipfully revenge his death, and then may ye wield all these lands. For we all wit well that an ye may slay these two traitors, the Red City and all those that be therein will take you for their lord.

Truly, said Sir Palomides, it grieveth my heart for to hear you tell this doleful tale; and to say the truth I saw the same letter that ye speak of, and one of the best knights on the earth read that letter to me, and by his commandment I came hither to revenge your king's death; and therefore have done, and let me wit where I shall find those traitors, for I shall never be at ease in my heart till I be in hands with them. Sir, said Sir Ebel, then take your ship again, and that ship must bring you unto the Delectable Isle, fast by the Red City, and we in this castle shall pray for you, and abide your again-coming. For this same castle, an ye speed well, must needs be yours; for our King Hermance let make this castle for the love of the two traitors, and so we kept it with strong hand, and therefore full sore are we threated. Wot ye what ye shall do, said Sir Palomides; whatsomever come of me, look ye keep well this castle. For an it misfortune me so to be slain in this quest I am sure there will come one of the best knights of the world for to revenge my death, and that is Sir Tristram de Liones, or else Sir Launcelot du Lake.

Then Sir Palomides departed from that castle. And as he came nigh the city, there came out of a ship a goodly knight armed against him, with his shield on his shoulder, and his hand upon his sword. And anon as he came nigh Sir Palomides he said: Sir knight, what seek ye here? leave this quest for it is mine, and mine it was or ever it was yours, and therefore I will have it. Sir knight, said Palomides, it may well be that this quest was yours or it was mine, but when the letter was taken out of the dead king's hand, at that time by likelihood there was no knight had undertaken to revenge the death of the king. And so at that time I promised to revenge his death, and so I shall or else I am ashamed. Ye say well, said the knight, but wit ye well then will I fight with you, and who be the better knight of us both, let him take the battle upon hand. I assent me, said Sir Palomides. And then they dressed their shields, and pulled out their swords, and lashed together many sad strokes as men of might; and this fighting was more than an hour, but at the last Sir Palomides waxed big and better winded, so that then he smote that knight such a stroke that he made him to kneel upon his knees. Then that knight spake on high and said: Gentle knight, hold thy hand. Sir Palomides was goodly and withdrew his hand. Then this knight said: Wit ye well, knight, that thou art better worthy to have this battle than I, and require thee of knighthood tell me thy name. Sir, my name is Palomides, a knight of King Arthur's, and of the Table Round, that hither I came to revenge the death of this dead king.

CHAPTER LXIII

Of the preparation of Sir Palomides and the two brethren that should fight with him.

Well be ye found, said the knight to Palomides, for of all knights that be alive, except three, I had liefest have you. The first is Sir Launcelot du Lake, and Sir Tristram de Liones, the third is my nigh cousin, Sir Lamorak de Galis. And I am brother unto King Hermance that is dead, and my name is Sir Hermind. Ye say well, said Sir Palomides, and ye shall see how I shall speed; and if I be there slain go ye to my lord Sir Launcelot, or else to my lord Sir Tristram, and pray them to revenge my death, for as for Sir Lamorak him shall ye never see in this world. Alas, said Sir Hermind, how may that be? He is slain, said Sir Palomides, by Sir Gawaine and his brethren. So God me help, said Hermind, there was not one for one that slew him. That is truth, said Sir Palomides, for they were four dangerous knights that slew him, as Sir Gawaine, Sir Agravaine, Sir Gaheris, and Sir Mordred, but Sir Gareth, the fifth brother was away, the best knight of them all. And so Sir Palomides told Hermind all the manner, and how they slew Sir Lamorak all only by treason.

So Sir Palomides took his ship, and arrived up at the Delectable Isle. And in the meanwhile Sir Hermind that was the king's brother, he arrived up at the Red City, and there he told them how there was come a knight of King Arthur's to avenge King Hermance's death: And his name is Sir Palomides, the good knight, that for the most part he followeth the beast Glatisant. Then all the city made great joy, for mickle had they heard of Sir Palomides, and of his noble prowess. So let they ordain a messenger, and sent unto the two brethren, and bade them to make them ready, for there was a knight come that would fight with them both. So the messenger went unto them where they were at a castle there beside; and there he told them how there was a knight come of King Arthur's court to fight with them both at once. He is welcome, said they; but tell us, we pray you, if it be Sir Launcelot or any of his blood? He is none of that blood, said the messenger. Then we care the less, said the two brethren, for with none of the blood of Sir Launcelot we keep not to have ado withal. Wit ye well, said the messenger, that his name is Sir Palomides, that yet is unchristened, a noble knight. Well, said they, an he be now unchristened he shall never be christened. So they appointed to be at the city within two days.

And when Sir Palomides was come to the city they made passing great joy of him, and then they beheld him, and saw that he was well made, cleanly and bigly, and unmaimed of his limbs, and neither too young nor too old. And so all the people praised him; and though he was not christened yet he believed in the best manner, and was full faithful and true of his promise, and well conditioned; and because he made his avow that he would never be christened unto the time that he had achieved the beast Glatisant, the which was a full wonderful beast, and a great signification; for Merlin prophesied much of that beast. And also Sir Palomides avowed never to take full christendom unto the time that he had done seven battles within the lists.

So within the third day there came to the city these two brethren, the one hight Helius, the other hight Helake, the which were men of great prowess; howbeit that they were false and full of treason, and but poor men born, yet were they noble knights of their hands. And with them they brought forty knights, to that intent that they should be big enough for the Red City. Thus came the two brethren with great bobaunce and pride, for they had put the Red City in fear and damage. Then they were brought to the lists, and Sir Palomides came into the place and said thus: Be ye the two brethren, Helius and Helake, that slew your king and lord, Sir Hermance, by felony and treason, for whom that I am come hither to revenge his death? Wit thou well, said Sir Helius and Sir Helake, that we are the same knights that slew King Hermance; and wit thou well, Sir Palomides Saracen, that we shall handle thee so or thou depart that thou shalt wish that thou wert christened. It may well be, said Sir Palomides, for yet I would not die or I were christened; and yet so am I not afeard of you both, but I trust to God that I shall die a better christian man than any of you both; and doubt ye not, said Sir Palomides, either ye or I shall be left dead in this place.

CHAPTER LXIV

Of the battle between Sir Palomides and the two brethren, and how the two brethren were slain.

Then they departed, and the two brethren came against Sir Palomides, and he against them, as fast as their horses might run. And by fortune Sir Palomides smote Helake through his shield and through the breast more than a fathom. All this while Sir Helius held up his spear, and for pride and orgulité he would not smite Sir Palomides with his spear; but when he saw his brother lie on the earth, and saw he might not help himself, then he said unto Sir Palomides: Help thyself. And therewith he came hurtling unto Sir Palomides with his spear, and smote him quite from his saddle. Then Sir Helius rode over Sir Palomides twice or thrice. And therewith Sir Palomides was ashamed, and gat the horse of Sir Helius by the bridle, and therewithal the horse areared, and Sir Palomides halp after, and so they fell both to the earth; but anon Sir Helius stert up lightly, and there he smote Sir Palomides a great stroke upon the helm, that he kneeled upon his own knee. Then they lashed together many sad strokes, and traced and traversed now backward, now sideling, hurtling together like two boars, and that same time they fell both grovelling to the earth.

Thus they fought still without any reposing two hours, and never breathed; and then Sir Palomides waxed faint and weary, and Sir Helius waxed passing strong, and doubled his strokes, and drove Sir Palomides overthwart and endlong all the field, that they of the city when they saw Sir Palomides in this case they wept and cried, and made great dole, and the other party made as great joy. Alas, said the men of the city, that this noble knight should thus be slain for our king's sake. And as they were thus weeping and crying, Sir Palomides that had suffered an hundred strokes, that it was wonder that he stood on his feet, at the last Sir Palomides beheld as he might the common people, how they wept for him; and then he said to himself: Ah, fie for shame, Sir Palomides, why hangest thou thy head so low; and therewith he bare up his shield, and looked Sir Helius in the visage, and he smote him a great stroke upon the helm, and after that another and another. And then he smote Sir Helius with such a might that he fell to the earth grovelling; and then he raced off his helm from his head, and there he smote him such a buffet that he departed his head from the body. And then were the people of the city the joyfullest people that might be. So they brought him to his lodging with great solemnity, and there all the people became his men. And then Sir Palomides prayed them all to take keep unto all the lordship of King Hermance: For, fair sirs, wit ye well I may not as at this time abide with you, for I must in all haste be with my lord King Arthur at the Castle of Lonazep, the which I have promised. Then was the people full heavy at his departing, for all that city proffered Sir Palomides the third part of their goods so that he would abide with them; but in no wise as at that time he would not abide.

And so Sir Palomides departed, and so he came unto the castle thereas Sir Ebel was lieutenant. And when they in the castle wist how Sir Palomides had sped, there was a joyful meiny; and so Sir Palomides departed, and came to the castle of Lonazep. And when he wist that Sir Tristram was not there he took his way over Humber, and came unto Joyous Gard, whereas Sir Tristram was and La Beale Isoud. Sir Tristram had commanded that what knight errant came within the Joyous Gard, as in the town, that they should warn Sir Tristram. So there came a man of the town, and told Sir Tristram how there was a knight in the town, a passing goodly man. What manner of man is he, said Sir Tristram, and what sign beareth he? So the man told Sir Tristram all the tokens of him. That is Palomides, said Dinadan. It may well be, said Sir Tristram. Go ye to him, said Sir Tristram unto Dinadan. So Dinadan went unto Sir Palomides, and there either made other great joy, and so they lay together that night. And on the morn early came Sir Tristram and Sir Gareth, and took them in their beds, and so they arose and brake their fast.

CHAPTER LXV

How Sir Tristram and Sir Palomides met Breuse Saunce Pité, and how Sir Tristram and La Beale Isoud went unto Lonazep.

And then Sir Tristram desired Sir Palomides to ride into the fields and woods. So they were accorded to repose them in the forest. And when they had played them a great while they rode unto a fair well; and anon they were ware of an armed knight that came riding against them, and there either saluted other. Then this armed knight spake to Sir Tristram, and asked what were these knights that were lodged in Joyous Gard. I wot not what they are, said Sir Tristram. What knights be ye? said that knight, for meseemeth ye be no knights errant, because ye ride unarmed. Whether we be knights or not we list not to tell thee our name. Wilt thou not tell me thy name? said that knight; then keep thee, for thou shalt die of my hands. And therewith he got his spear in his hands, and would have run Sir Tristram through. That saw Sir Palomides, and smote his horse traverse in midst of the side, that man and horse fell to the earth. And therewith Sir Palomides alighted and pulled out his sword to have slain him. Let be, said Sir Tristram, slay him not, the knight is but a fool, it were shame to slay him. But take away his spear, said Sir Tristram, and let him take his horse and go where that he will.

So when this knight arose he groaned sore of the fall, and so he took his horse, and when he was up he turned then his horse, and required Sir Tristram and Sir Palomides to tell him what knights they were. Now wit ye well, said Sir Tristram, that my name is Sir Tristram de Liones, and this knight's name is Sir Palomides. When he wist what they were he took his horse with the spurs, because they should not ask him his name, and so rode fast away through thick and thin. Then came there by them a knight with a bended shield of azure, whose name was Epinogris, and he came toward them a great wallop. Whither are ye riding? said Sir Tristram. My fair lords, said Epinogris, I follow the falsest knight that beareth the life; wherefore I require you tell me whether ye saw him, for he beareth a shield with a case of red over it. So God me help, said Tristram, such a knight departed from us not a quarter of an hour agone; we pray you tell us his name. Alas, said Epinogris, why let ye him escape from you? and he is so great a foe unto all errant knights: his name is Breuse Saunce Pité. Ah, fie for shame, said Sir Palomides, alas that ever he escaped mine hands, for he is the man in the world that I hate most. Then every knight made great sorrow to other; and so Epinogris departed and followed the chase after him.

Then Sir Tristram and his three fellows rode unto Joyous Gard; and there Sir Tristram talked unto Sir Palomides of his battle, how he sped at the Red City, and as ye have heard afore so was it ended. Truly, said Sir Tristram, I am glad ye have well sped, for ye have done worshipfully. Well, said Sir Tristram, we must forward to-morn. And then he devised how it should be; and Sir Tristram devised to send his two pavilions to set them fast by the well of Lonazep, and therein shall be the queen La Beale Isoud. It is well said, said Sir Dinadan, but when Sir Palomides heard of that his heart was ravished out of measure: notwithstanding he said but little. So when they came to Joyous Gard Sir Palomides would not have gone into the castle, but as Sir Tristram took him by the finger, and led him into the castle. And when Sir Palomides saw La Beale Isoud he was ravished so that he might unnethe speak. So they went unto meat, but Palomides might not eat, and there was all the cheer that might be had. And on the morn they were apparelled to ride toward Lonazep.

So Sir Tristram had three squires, and La Beale Isoud had three gentlewomen, and both the queen and they were richly apparelled; and other people had they none with them, but varlets to bear their shields and their spears. And thus they rode forth. So as they rode they saw afore them a rout of knights; it was the knight Galihodin with twenty knights with him. Fair fellows, said Galihodin, yonder come four knights, and a rich and a well fair lady: I am in will to take

that lady from them. That is not of the best counsel, said one of
Galihodin's men, but send ye to them and wit what they will say; and
so it was done. There came a squire unto Sir Tristram, and asked
them whether they would joust or else to lose their lady. Not so, said
Sir Tristram, tell your lord I bid him come as many as we be, and win
her and take her. Sir, said Palomides, an it please you let me have this
deed, and I shall undertake them all four. I will that ye have it, said Sir
Tristram, at your pleasure. Now go and tell your lord Galihodin, that
this same knight will encounter with him and his fellows.

CHAPTER LXVI

How Sir Palomides jousted with Sir Galihodin, and after with Sir Gawaine, and smote them down.

Then this squire departed and told Galihodin; and then he dressed his
shield, and put forth a spear, and Sir Palomides another; and there Sir
Palomides smote Galihodin so hard that he smote both horse and
man to the earth. And there he had an horrible fall. And then came
there another knight, and in the same wise he served him; and so he
served the third and the fourth, that he smote them over their horses'
croups, and always Sir Palomides' spear was whole. Then came six
knights more of Galihodin's men, and would have been avenged
upon Sir Palomides. Let be, said Sir Galihodin, not so hardy, none of
you all meddle with this knight, for he is a man of great bounté and
honour, and if he would ye were not able to meddle with him. And
right so they held them still. And ever Sir Palomides was ready to
joust; and when he saw they would no more he rode unto Sir
Tristram. Right well have ye done, said Sir Tristram, and worshipfully have ye done as a good knight should. This Galihodin was nigh
cousin unto Galahalt, the haut prince; and this Galihodin was a king
within the country of Surluse.

So as Sir Tristram, Sir Palomides, and La Beale Isoud rode together
they saw afore them four knights, and every man had his spear in his
hand: the first was Sir Gawaine, the second Sir Uwaine, the third Sir
Sagramore le Desirous, and the fourth was Dodinas le Savage. When
Sir Palomides beheld them, that the four knights were ready to joust,

he prayed Sir Tristram to give him leave to have ado with them all so long as he might hold him on horseback. And if that I be smitten down I pray you revenge me. Well, said Sir Tristram, I will as ye will, and ye are not so fain to have worship but I would as fain increase your worship. And therewithal Sir Gawaine put forth his spear, and Sir Palomides another; and so they came so eagerly together that Sir Palomides smote Sir Gawaine to the earth, horse and all; and in the same wise he served Uwaine, Sir Dodinas, and Sagramore. All these four knights Sir Palomides smote down with divers spears. And then Sir Tristram departed toward Lonazep.

And when they were departed then came thither Galihodin with his ten knights unto Sir Gawaine, and there he told him all how he had sped. I marvel, said Sir Gawaine, what knights they be, that are so arrayed in green. And that knight upon the white horse smote me down, said Galihodin, and my three fellows. And so he did to me, said Gawaine; and well I wot, said Sir Gawaine, that either he upon the white horse is Sir Tristram or else Sir Palomides, and that gay beseen lady is Queen Isoud. Thus they talked of one thing and of other.

And in the meanwhile Sir Tristram passed on till that he came to the well where his two pavilions were set; and there they alighted, and there they saw many pavilions and great array. Then Sir Tristram left there Sir Palomides and Sir Gareth with La Beale Isoud, and Sir Tristram and Sir Dinadan rode to Lonazep to hearken tidings; and Sir Tristram rode upon Sir Palomides' white horse. And when he came into the castle Sir Dinadan heard a great horn blow, and to the horn drew many knights. Then Sir Tristram asked a knight: What meaneth the blast of that horn? Sir, said that knight, it is all those that shall hold against King Arthur at this tournament. The first is the King of Ireland, and the King of Surluse, the King of Listinoise, the King of Northumberland, and the King of the best part of Wales, with many other countries. And these draw them to a council, to understand what governance they shall be of; but the King of Ireland, whose name was Marhalt, and father to the good knight Sir Marhaus that Sir Tristram slew, had all the speech that Sir Tristram might hear it. He said: Lords and fellows, let us look to ourself, for wit ye well King Arthur is sure of many good knights, or else he would not with so few knights have ado with us; therefore by my counsel let every king have a standard and a cognisance by himself, that every knight draw to their natural lord, and then may every king and captain help his knights if they have need. When Sir Tristram had heard all their counsel he rode unto King Arthur for to hear of his counsel.

CHAPTER LXVII

How Sir Tristram and his fellowship came into the tournament of Lonazep; and of divers jousts and matters.

But Sir Tristram was not so soon come into the place, but Sir Gawaine and Sir Galihodin went to King Arthur, and told him: That same green knight in the green harness with the white horse smote us two down, and six of our fellows this same day. Well, said Arthur. And then he called Sir Tristram and asked him what was his name. Sir, said Sir Tristram, ye shall hold me excused as at this time, for ye shall not wit my name. And there Sir Tristram returned and rode his way. I have marvel, said Arthur, that yonder knight will not tell me his name, but go thou, Griflet le Fise de Dieu, and pray him to speak with me betwixt us. Then Sir Griflet rode after him and overtook him, and said him that King Arthur prayed him for to speak with him secretly apart. Upon this covenant, said Sir Tristram, I will speak with him; that I will turn again so that ye will ensure me not to desire to hear my name. I shall undertake, said Sir Griflet, that he will not greatly desire it of you. So they rode together until they came to King Arthur. Fair sir, said King Arthur, what is the cause ye will not tell me your name? Sir, said Sir Tristram, without a cause I will not hide my name. Upon what party will ye hold? said King Arthur. Truly, my lord, said Sir Tristram, I wot not yet on what party I will be on, until I come to the field, and there as my heart giveth me, there will I hold; but to-morrow ye shall see and prove on what party I shall come. And therewithal he returned and went to his pavilions.

And upon the morn they armed them all in green, and came into the field; and there young knights began to joust, and did many worshipful deeds. Then spake Gareth unto Sir Tristram, and prayed him to give him leave to break his spear, for him thought shame to bear his spear whole again When Sir Tristram heard him say so he laughed, and said: I pray you do your best. Then Sir Gareth gat a spear and proffered to joust. That saw a knight that was nephew unto the King of the Hundred Knights; his name was Selises, and a good man of arms. So this knight Selises then dressed him unto Sir Gareth, and they two met together so hard that either smote other down, his horse and all, to the earth, so they were both bruised and hurt; and there they lay till the King with the Hundred Knights halp Selises up, and Sir Tristram and Sir Palomides halp up Gareth again. And so they rode with Sir Gareth unto their pavilions, and then they pulled off his helm.

And when La Beale Isoud saw Sir Gareth bruised in the face she asked him what ailed him. Madam, said Sir Gareth, I had a great buffet, and as I suppose I gave another, but none of my fellows, God thank them, would not rescue me. Forsooth, said Palomides, it longed not to none of us as this day to joust, for there have not this day jousted no proved knights, and needly ye would joust. And when the other party saw ye proffered yourself to joust they sent one to you, a passing good knight of his age, for I know him well, his name is Selises; and worshipfully ye met with him, and neither of you are dishonoured, and therefore refresh yourself that ye may be ready and whole to joust to-morrow. As for that, said Gareth, I shall not fail you an I may bestride mine horse.

CHAPTER LXVIII

How Sir Tristram and his fellowship jousted, and of the noble feats that they did in that tourneying.

Now upon what party, said Tristram, is it best we be withal as to-morn? Sir, said Palomides, ye shall have mine advice to be against King Arthur as to-morn, for on his party will be Sir Launcelot and many good knights of his blood with him. And the more men of worship that they be, the more worship we shall win. That is full knightly spoken, said Sir Tristram; and right so as ye counsel me, so will we do. In the name of God, said they all. So that night they were lodged with the best. And on the morn when it was day they were arrayed all in green trappings, shields and spears, and La Beale Isoud in the same colour, and her three damosels. And right so these four knights came into the field endlong and through. And so they led La Beale Isoud thither as she should stand and behold all the jousts in a bay window; but always she was wimpled that no man might see her visage. And then these three knights rode straight unto the party of the King of Scots.

When King Arthur had seen them do all this he asked Sir Launcelot what were these knights and that queen. Sir, said Launcelot, I cannot say you in certain, but if Sir Tristram be in this country, or Sir Palomides, wit ye well it be they in certain, and La Beale Isoud. Then Arthur called to him Sir Kay and said: Go lightly and wit how many knights there be here lacking of the Table Round, for by the sieges thou mayst know. So went Sir Kay and saw by the writings in the sieges that there lacked ten knights. And these be their names that be not here. Sir Tristram, Sir Palomides, Sir Percivale, Sir Gaheris, Sir Epinogris, Sir Mordred, Sir Dinadan, Sir La Cote Male Taile, and Sir Pelleas the noble knight. Well, said Arthur, some of these I dare undertake are here this day against us.

Then came therein two brethren, cousins unto Sir Gawaine, the one hight Sir Edward, that other hight Sir Sadok, the which were two good knights; and they asked of King Arthur that they might have the first jousts, for they were of Orkney. I am pleased, said King Arthur. Then Sir Edward encountered with the King of Scots, in whose party was Sir Tristram and Sir Palomides; and Sir Edward smote the King of Scots quite from his horse, and Sir Sadok smote down the King of North Wales, and gave him a wonder great fall, that there was a great cry on King Arthur's party, and that made Sir Palomides passing wroth. And so Sir Palomides dressed his shield and his spear, and with all his might he met with Sir Edward of Orkney, that he smote him so hard that his horse might not stand on his feet, and so they hurtled to the earth; and then with the same spear Sir Palomides smote down Sir Sadok over his horse's croup. O Jesu, said Arthur, what knight is that arrayed all in green? he jousteth mightily. Wit you well, said Sir Gawaine, he is a good knight, and yet shall ye see him joust better or he depart. And yet shall ye see, said Sir Gawaine, another bigger knight, in the same colour, than he is; for that same knight, said Sir Gawaine, that smote down right now my four cousins, he smote me down within these two days, and seven fellows more.

This meanwhile as they stood thus talking there came into the place Sir Tristram upon a black horse, and or ever he stint he smote down with one spear four good knights of Orkney that were of the kin of Sir Gawaine; and Sir Gareth and Sir Dinadan everych of them smote down a good knight. Jesu, said Arthur, yonder knight upon the black horse doth mightily and marvellously well. Abide you, said Sir Gawaine; that knight with the black horse began not yet. Then Sir Tristram made to horse again the two kings that Edward and Sadok had unhorsed at the beginning. And then Sir Tristram drew his sword and rode into the thickest of the press against them of Orkney; and there he smote down knights, and rashed off helms, and pulled away their shields, and hurtled down many knights: he fared so that Sir Arthur and all knights had great marvel when they saw one knight do so great deeds of arms. And Sir Palomides failed not upon the other side, but did so marvellously well that all men had wonder. For there King Arthur likened Sir Tristram that was on the black horse like to a wood lion, and likened Sir Palomides upon the white horse unto a wood leopard, and Sir Gareth and Sir Dinadan unto eager wolves. But the custom was such among them that none of the kings would help other, but all the fellowship of every standard to help other as they might; but ever Sir Tristram did so much deeds of arms that they of Orkney waxed weary of him, and so withdrew them unto Lonazep.

CHAPTER LXIX

*How Sir Tristram was unhorsed and smitten down by
Sir Launcelot, and after that Sir Tristram
smote down King Arthur.*

Then was the cry of heralds and all manner of common people: The Green Knight hath done marvellously, and beaten all them of Orkney. And there the heralds numbered that Sir Tristram that sat upon the black horse had smitten down with spears and swords thirty knights; and Sir Palomides had smitten down twenty knights, and the most part of these fifty knights were of the house of King Arthur, and proved knights. So God me help, said Arthur unto Sir Launcelot, this is a great shame to us to see four knights beat so many knights of mine; and therefore make you ready, for we will have ado with them. Sir, said Launcelot, wit ye well that there are two passing good

knights, and great worship were it not to us now to have ado with
them, for they have this day sore travailed. As for that, said Arthur, I
will be avenged; and therefore take with you Sir Bleoberis and Sir
Ector, and I will be the fourth, said Arthur. Sir, said Launcelot, ye
shall find me ready, and my brother Sir Ector, and my cousin Sir
Bleoberis. And so when they were ready and on horseback: Now
choose, said Sir Arthur unto Sir Launcelot, with whom that ye will
encounter withal. Sir, said Launcelot, I will meet with the green
knight upon the black horse, that was Sir Tristram; and my cousin Sir
Bleoberis shall match the green knight upon the white horse, that was
Sir Palomides; and my brother Sir Ector shall match with the green
knight upon the white horse, that was Sir Gareth. Then must I, said
Sir Arthur, have ado with the green knight upon the grisled horse,
and that was Sir Dinadan. Now every man take heed to his fellow,
said Sir Launcelot. And so they trotted on together, and there
encountered Sir Launcelot against Sir Tristram. So Sir Launcelot
smote Sir Tristram so sore upon the shield that he bare horse and man
to the earth; but Sir Launcelot weened that it had been Sir Palomides,
and so he passed forth. And then Sir Bleoberis encountered with Sir
Palomides, and he smote him so hard upon the shield that Sir
Palomides and his white horse rustled to the earth. Then Sir Ector de
Maris smote Sir Gareth so hard that down he fell off his horse. And
the noble King Arthur encountered with Sir Dinadan, and he smote
him quite from his saddle. And then the noise turned awhile how the
green knights were slain down.

When the King of Northgalis saw that Sir Tristram had a fall, then
he remembered him how great deeds of arms Sir Tristram had done.
Then he made ready many knights, for the custom and cry was such,
that what knight were smitten down, and might not be horsed again
by his fellows, outher by his own strength, that as that day he should
be prisoner unto the party that had smitten him down. So came in
the King of Northgalis, and he rode straight unto Sir Tristram; and
when he came nigh him he alighted down suddenly and betook Sir
Tristram his horse, and said thus: Noble knight, I know thee not of
what country that thou art, but for the noble deeds that thou hast
done this day take there my horse, and let me do as well I may; for, as
Jesu me help, thou art better worthy to have mine horse than I
myself. Gramercy, said Sir Tristram, and if I may I shall quite you:
look that ye go not far from us, and as I suppose, I shall win you

another horse. And therewith Sir Tristram mounted upon his horse, and there he met with King Arthur, and he gave him such a buffet upon the helm with his sword that King Arthur had no power to keep his saddle. And then Sir Tristram gave the King of Northgalis King Arthur's horse: then was there great press about King Arthur for to horse him again; but Sir Palomides would not suffer King Arthur to be horsed again, but ever Sir Palomides smote on the right hand and on the left hand mightily as a noble knight. And this meanwhile Sir Tristram rode through the thickest of the press, and smote down knights on the right hand and on the left hand, and raced off helms, and so passed forth unto his pavilions, and left Sir Palomides on foot; and Sir Tristram changed his horse and disguised himself all in red, horse and harness.

CHAPTER LXX

*How Sir Tristram changed his harness and it was
all red, and how he demeaned him, and how
Sir Palomides slew Launcelot's horse.*

And when the queen La Beale Isoud saw that Sir Tristram was unhorsed, and she wist not where he was, then she wept greatly. But Sir Tristram, when he was ready, came dashing lightly into the field, and then La Beale Isoud espied him. And so he did great deeds of arms; with one spear, that was great, Sir Tristram smote down five knights or ever he stint. Then Sir Launcelot espied him readily, that it was Sir Tristram, and then he repented him that he had smitten him down; and so Sir Launcelot went out of the press to repose him and lightly he came again. And now when Sir Tristram came into the press, through his great force he put Sir Palomides upon his horse, and Sir Gareth, and Sir Dinadan, and then they began to do marvellously; but Sir Palomides nor none of his two fellows knew not who had holpen them on horseback again. But ever Sir Tristram was nigh them and succoured them, and they [knew] not him, because he was changed into red armour: and all this while Sir Launcelot was away.

So when La Beale Isoud knew Sir Tristram again upon his horse-back she was passing glad, and then she laughed and made good cheer. And as it happened, Sir Palomides looked up toward her where she lay in the window, and he espied how she laughed; and therewith he took such a rejoicing that he smote down, what with his spear and with his sword, all that ever he met; for through the sight of her he was so enamoured in her love that he seemed at that time, that an both Sir Tristram and Sir Launcelot had been both against him they should have won no worship of him; and in his heart, as the book saith, Sir Palomides wished that with his worship he might have ado with Sir Tristram before all men, because of La Beale Isoud. Then Sir Palomides began to double his strength, and he did so marvellously that all men had wonder of him, and ever he cast up his eye unto La Beale Isoud. And when he saw her make such cheer he fared like a lion, that there might no man withstand him; and then Sir Tristram beheld him, how that Sir Palomides bestirred him; and then he said unto Sir Dinadan: So God me help, Sir Palomides is a passing good knight and a well enduring, but such deeds saw I him never do, nor never heard I tell that ever he did so much in one day. It is his day, said Dinadan; and he would say no more unto Sir Tristram; but to himself he said: An if ye knew for whose love he doth all those deeds of arms, soon would Sir Tristram abate his courage. Alas, said Sir Tristram, that Sir Palomides is not christened. So said King Arthur, and so said all those that beheld him. Then all people gave him the prize, as for the best knight that day, that he passed Sir Launcelot outher Sir Tristram. Well, said Dinadan to himself, all this worship that Sir Palomides hath here this day he may thank the Queen Isoud, for had she been away this day Sir Palomides had not gotten the prize this day.

Right so came into the field Sir Launcelot du Lake, and saw and heard the noise and cry and the great worship that Sir Palomides had. He dressed him against Sir Palomides, with a great mighty spear and a long, and thought to smite him down. And when Sir Palomides saw Sir Launcelot come upon him so fast, he ran upon Sir Launcelot as fast with his sword as he might; and as Sir Launcelot should have stricken him he smote his spear aside, and smote it a-two with his sword. And Sir Palomides rushed unto Sir Launcelot, and thought to have put him to a shame; and with his sword he smote his horse's neck that Sir Launcelot rode upon, and then Sir Launcelot fell to the earth. Then was the cry huge and great: See how Sir Palomides the Saracen hath smitten down Sir Launcelot's horse. Right then were there many knights wroth with Sir Palomides because he had done that deed; therefore many knights held there against that it was unknightly done in a tournament to kill an horse wilfully, but that it had been done in plain battle, life for life.

CHAPTER LXXI

How Sir Launcelot said to Sir Palomides, and how the prize of that day was given unto Sir Palomides.

When Sir Ector de Maris saw Sir Launcelot his brother have such a despite, and so set on foot, then he gat a spear eagerly, and ran against Sir Palomides, and he smote him so hard that he bare him quite from his horse. That saw Sir Tristram, that was in red harness, and he smote down Sir Ector de Maris quite from his horse. Then Sir Launcelot dressed his shield upon his shoulder, and with his sword naked in his hand, and so came straight upon Sir Palomides fiercely and said: Wit thou well thou hast done me this day the greatest despite that ever any worshipful knight did to me in tournament or in jousts, and therefore I will be avenged upon thee, therefore take keep to yourself. Ah, mercy, noble knight, said Palomides, and forgive me mine unkindly deeds, for I have no power nor might to withstand you, and I have done so much this day that well I wot I did never so much, nor never shall in my life-days; and therefore, most noble knight, I require thee spare me as at this day, and I promise you I shall ever be your knight while I live: an ye put me from my worship now, ye put me from the greatest worship that ever I had or ever shall have in my life-days. Well, said Sir Launcelot, I see, for to say thee sooth, ye have done marvellously well this day; and I understand a part for whose love ye do it, and well I wot that love is a great mistress. And if my lady were here as she nis not, wit you well, said Sir Launcelot, ye should not bear away the worship. But beware your love be not discovered, for an Sir Tristram may know it ye will repent it; and sithen my quarrel is not here, ye shall have this day the worship as for me; considering the great travail and pain that ye have had this day, it were no worship for me to put you from it. And therewithal Sir Launcelot suffered Sir Palomides to depart.

Then Sir Launcelot by great force and might gat his own horse maugre twenty knights. So when Sir Launcelot was horsed he did many marvels, and so did Sir Tristram, and Sir Palomides in like wise. Then Sir Launcelot smote down with a spear Sir Dinadan, and the King of Scotland, and the King of Wales, and the King of Northumberland, and the King of Listinoise. So then Sir Launcelot and his fellows smote down well a forty knights. Then came the King of Ireland and the King of the Straight Marches to rescue Sir Tristram and Sir Palomides. There began a great medley, and many knights were smitten down on both parties; and always Sir Launcelot spared Sir Tristram, and he spared him. And Sir Palomides would not meddle with Sir Launcelot, and so there was hurtling here and there. And then King Arthur sent out many knights of the Table Round; and Sir Palomides was ever in the foremost front, and Sir Tristram did so strongly well that the king and all other had marvel. And then the king let blow to lodging; and because Sir Palomides began first, and never he went nor rode out of the field to repose, but ever he was doing marvellously well either on foot or on horseback, and longest during, King Arthur and all the kings gave Sir Palomides the honour and the gree as for that day.

Then Sir Tristram commanded Sir Dinadan to fetch the queen La Beale Isoud, and bring her to his two pavilions that stood by the well. And so Dinadan did as he was commanded. But when Sir Palomides understood and wist that Sir Tristram was in the red armour, and on a red horse, wit ye well that he was glad, and so was Sir Gareth and Sir Dinadan, for they all weened that Sir Tristram had been taken prisoner. And then every knight drew to his inn. And then King Arthur and every knight spake of those knights; but above all men they gave Sir Palomides the prize, and all knights that knew Sir Palomides had wonder of his deeds. Sir, said Sir Launcelot unto Arthur, as for Sir Palomides an he be the green knight I dare say as for this day he is best worthy to have the degree, for he reposed him never, nor never changed his weeds, and he began first and longest held on. And yet, well I wot, said Sir Launcelot, that there was a better knight than he, and that shall be proved or we depart, upon pain of my life. Thus they talked on either party; and so Sir Dinadan railed with Sir Tristram and said: What the devil is upon thee this day? for Sir Palomides' strength feebled never this day, but ever he doubled his strength.

CHAPTER LXXII

How Sir Dinadan provoked Sir Tristram to do well.

And thou, Sir Tristram, farest all this day as though thou hadst been asleep, and therefore I call thee coward. Well, Dinadan, said Sir Tristram, I was never called coward or now of no earthly knight in my life; and wit thou well, sir, I call myself never the more coward though Sir Launcelot gave me a fall, for I outcept him of all knights. And doubt ye not Sir Dinadan, an Sir Launcelot have a quarrel good, he is too over good for any knight that now is living; and yet of his sufferance, largess, bounty, and courtesy, I call him knight peerless: and so Sir Tristram was in manner wroth with Sir Dinadan. But all this language Sir Dinadan said because he would anger Sir Tristram, for to cause him to awake his spirits and to be wroth; for well knew Sir Dinadan that an Sir Tristram were thoroughly wroth Sir Palomides should not get the prize upon the morn. And for this intent Sir Dinadan said all this railing and language against Sir Tristram. Truly, said Sir Palomides, as for Sir Launcelot, of his noble knighthood, courtesy, and prowess, and gentleness, I know not his peer; for this day, said Sir Palomides, I did full uncourteously unto Sir Launcelot, and full unknightly, and full knightly and courteously he did to me again; for an he had been as ungentle to me as I was to him, this day I had won no worship. And therefore, said Palomides, I shall be Sir Launcelot's knight while my life lasteth. This talking was in the houses of kings. But all kings, lords, and knights, said, of clear knighthood, and of pure strength, of bounty, of courtesy, Sir Launcelot and Sir Tristram bare the prize above all knights that ever were in Arthur's days. And there were never knights in Arthur's days did half so many deeds as they did; as the book saith, no ten knights did not half the deeds that they did, and there was never knight in their days that required Sir Launcelot or Sir Tristram of any quest, so it were not to their shame, but they performed their desire.

CHAPTER LXXIII

How King Arthur and Sir Launcelot came to see La Beale Isoud, and how Palomides smote down King Arthur.

So on the morn Sir Launcelot departed, and Sir Tristram was ready, and La Beale Isoud with Sir Palomides and Sir Gareth. And so they rode all in green full freshly beseen unto the forest. And Sir Tristram left Sir Dinadan sleeping in his bed. And so as they rode it happed the king and Launcelot stood in a window, and saw Sir Tristram ride and Isoud. Sir, said Launcelot, yonder rideth the fairest lady of the world except your queen, Dame Guenever. Who is that? said Sir Arthur. Sir, said he, it is Queen Isoud that, out-taken my lady your queen, she is makeless. Take your horse, said Arthur, and array you at all rights as I will do, and I promise you, said the king, I will see her. Then anon they were armed and horsed, and either took a spear and rode unto the forest. Sir, said Launcelot, it is not good that ye go too nigh them, for wit ye well there are two as good knights as now are living, and therefore, sir, I pray you be not too hasty. For peradventure there will be some knights be displeased an we come suddenly upon them. As for that, said Arthur, I will see her, for I take no force whom I grieve. Sir, said Launcelot, ye put yourself in great jeopardy. As for that, said the king, we will take the adventure. Right so anon the king rode even to her, and saluted her, and said: God you save. Sir, said she, ye are welcome. Then the king beheld her, and liked her wonderly well.

With that came Sir Palomides unto Arthur, and said: Uncourteous knight, what seekest thou here? thou art uncourteous to come upon a lady thus suddenly, therefore withdraw thee. Sir Arthur took none heed of Sir Palomides' words, but ever he looked still upon Queen Isoud. Then was Sir Palomides wroth, and therewith he took a spear, and came hurtling upon King Arthur, and smote him down with a spear. When Sir Launcelot saw that despite of Sir Palomides, he said to himself: I am loath to have ado with yonder knight, and not for his own sake but for Sir Tristram. And one thing I am sure of, if I smite down Sir Palomides I must have ado with Sir Tristram, and that were overmuch for me to match them both, for they are two noble knights;

notwithstanding, whether I live or I die, needs must I revenge my lord, and so will I, whatsomever befall of me. And therewith Sir Launcelot cried to Sir Palomides: Keep thee from me. And then Sir Launcelot and Sir Palomides rushed together with two spears strongly, but Sir Launcelot smote Sir Palomides so hard that he went quite out of his saddle, and had a great fall. When Sir Tristram saw Sir Palomides have that fall, he said to Sir Launcelot: Sir knight, keep thee, for I must joust with thee. As for to joust with me, said Sir Launcelot, I will not fail you, for no dread I have of you; but I am loath to have ado with you an I might choose, for I will that ye wit that I must revenge my special lord that was unhorsed unwarly and unknightly. And therefore, though I revenged that fall, take ye no displeasure therein, for he is to me such a friend that I may not see him shamed.

Anon Sir Tristram understood by his person and by his knightly words that it was Sir Launcelot du Lake, and verily Sir Tristram deemed that it was King Arthur, he that Sir Palomides had smitten down. And then Sir Tristram put his spear from him, and put Sir Palomides again on horseback, and Sir Launcelot put King Arthur on horseback and so departed. So God me help, said Sir Tristram unto Palomides, ye did not worshipfully when ye smote down that knight so suddenly as ye did. And wit ye well ye did yourself great shame, for the knights came hither of their gentleness to see a fair lady; and that is every good knight's part, to behold a fair lady; and ye had not ado to play such masteries afore my lady. Wit thou well it will turn to anger, for he that ye smote down was King Arthur, and that other was the good knight Sir Launcelot. But I shall not forget the words of Sir Launcelot when that he called him a man of great worship, thereby I wist that it was King Arthur. And as for Sir Launcelot, an there had been five hundred knights in the meadow, he would not have refused them, and yet he said he would refuse me. By that again I wist that it was Sir Launcelot, for ever he forbeareth me in every place, and showeth me great kindness; and of all knights, I out-take none, say what men will say, he beareth the flower of all chivalry, say it him whosomever will. An he be well angered, and that him list to do his utterance without any favour, I know him not alive but Sir Launcelot is over hard for him, be it on horseback or on foot. I may never believe, said Palomides, that King Arthur will ride so privily as a poor errant knight. Ah, said Sir Tristram, ye know not my lord Arthur, for all knights may learn to be a knight of him. And therefore ye may be sorry, said Sir Tristram, of your unkindly deeds to so noble a king. And a thing that is done may not be undone, said Palomides. Then Sir Tristram sent Queen Isoud unto her lodging in the priory, there to behold all the tournament.

CHAPTER LXXIV

How the second day Palomides forsook Sir Tristram, and went to the contrary party against him.

Then there was a cry unto all knights, that when they heard an horn blow they should make jousts as they did the first day. And like as the brethren Sir Edward and Sir Sadok began the jousts the first day, Sir Uwaine the king's son Urien and Sir Lucanere de Buttelere began the jousts the second day. And at the first encounter Sir Uwaine smote down the King's son of Scots; and Sir Lucanere ran against the King of Wales, and they brake their spears all to pieces; and they were so fierce both, that they hurtled together that both fell to the earth. Then they of Orkney horsed again Sir Lucanere. And then came in Sir Tristram de Liones; and then Sir Tristram smote down Sir Uwaine and Sir Lucanere; and Sir Palomides smote down other two knights; and Sir Gareth smote down other two knights. Then said Sir Arthur unto Sir Launcelot: See yonder three knights do passingly well, and namely the first that jousted. Sir, said Launcelot, that knight began not yet, but ye shall see him this day do marvellously. And then came into the place the duke's son of Orkney, and then they began to do many deeds of arms.

When Sir Tristram saw them so begin, he said to Palomides: How feel ye yourself? may ye do this day as ye did yesterday? Nay, said Palomides, I feel myself so weary, and so sore bruised of the deeds of yesterday, that I may not endure as I did yesterday. That me repenteth, said Sir Tristram, for I shall lack you this day. Sir Palomides said: Trust not to me, for I may not do as I did. All these words said Palomides for to beguile Sir Tristram. Sir, said Sir Tristram unto Sir Gareth, then must I trust upon you; wherefore I pray you be not far from me to rescue me. An need be, said Sir Gareth, I shall not fail you in all that I may do. Then Sir Palomides rode by himself; and then in despite of Sir Tristram he put himself in the thickest press among them of Orkney, and there he did so marvellously deeds of arms that all men had wonder of him, for there might none stand him a stroke.

When Sir Tristram saw Sir Palomides do such deeds, he marvelled and said to himself: He is weary of my company. So Sir Tristram beheld him a great while and did but little else, for the noise and cry was so huge and great that Sir Tristram marvelled from whence came the strength that Sir Palomides had there in the field. Sir, said Sir Gareth unto Sir Tristram, remember ye not of the words that Sir Dinadan said to you yesterday, when he called you a coward; forsooth, sir, he said it for none ill, for ye are the man in the world that he most loveth, and all that he said was for your worship. And therefore, said Sir Gareth to Sir Tristram, let me know this day what ye be; and wonder ye not so upon Sir Palomides, for he enforceth himself to win all the worship and honour from you. I may well believe it, said Sir Tristram. And sithen I understand his evil will and his envy, ye shall see, if that I enforce myself, that the noise shall be left that now is upon him.

Then Sir Tristram rode into the thickest of the press, and then he did so marvellously well, and did so great deeds of arms, that all men said that Sir Tristram did double so much deeds of arms as Sir Palomides had done aforehand. And then the noise went plain from Sir Palomides, and all the people cried upon Sir Tristram. O Jesu, said the people, see how Sir Tristram smiteth down with his spear so many knights. And see, said they all, how many knights he smiteth down with his sword, and of how many knights he rashed off their helms and their shields; and so he beat them all of Orkney afore him. How now, said Sir Launcelot unto King Arthur, I told you that this day there would a knight play his pageant. Yonder rideth a knight ye may see he doth knightly, for he hath strength and wind. So God me help, said Arthur to Launcelot, ye say sooth, for I saw never a better knight, for he passeth far Sir Palomides. Sir, wit ye well, said Launcelot, it must be so of right, for it is himself, that noble knight Sir Tristram. I may right well believe it, said Arthur.

But when Sir Palomides heard the noise and the cry was turned from him, he rode out on a part and beheld Sir Tristram. And when Sir Palomides saw Sir Tristram do so marvellously well he wept passingly sore for despite, for he wist well he should no worship win that day; for well knew Sir Palomides, when Sir Tristram would put forth his strength and his manhood, be should get but little worship that day.

CHAPTER LXXV

How Sir Tristram departed off the field, and awaked Sir Dinadan, and changed his array into black.

Then came King Arthur, and the King of Northgalis, and Sir Launcelot du Lake; and Sir Bleoberis, Sir Bors de Ganis, Sir Ector de Maris, these three knights came into the field with Sir Launcelot. And then Sir Launcelot with the three knights of his kin did so great deeds of arms that all the noise began upon Sir Launcelot. And so they beat the King of Wales and the King of Scots far aback, and made them to avoid the field; but Sir Tristram and Sir Gareth abode still in the field and endured all that ever there came, that all men had wonder that any knight might endure so many strokes. But ever Sir Launcelot, and his three kinsmen by the commandment of Sir Launcelot, forbare Sir Tristram. Then said Sir Arthur: Is that Sir Palomides that endureth so well? Nay, said Sir Launcelot, wit ye well it is the good knight Sir Tristram, for yonder ye may see Sir Palomides beholdeth and hoveth, and doth little or nought. And sir, ye shall understand that Sir Tristram weeneth this day to beat us all out of the field. And as for me, said Sir Launcelot, I shall not beat him, beat him whoso will. Sir, said Launcelot unto Arthur, ye may see how Sir Palomides hoveth yonder, as though he were in a dream; wit ye well he is full heavy that Tristram doth such deeds of arms. Then is he but a fool, said Arthur, for never was Sir Palomides, nor never shall be, of such prowess as Sir Tristram. And if he have any envy at Sir Tristram, and cometh in with him upon his side he is a false knight.

As the king and Sir Launcelot thus spake, Sir Tristram rode privily out of the press, that none espied him but La Beale Isoud and Sir Palomides, for they two would not let off their eyes upon Sir Tristram. And when Sir Tristram came to his pavilions he found Sir Dinadan in his bed asleep. Awake, said Tristram, ye ought to be ashamed so to sleep when knights have ado in the field. Then Sir Dinadan arose lightly and said: What will ye that I shall do? Make you ready, said Sir Tristram, to ride with me into the field. So when Sir Dinadan was armed he looked upon Sir Tristram's helm and on his shield, and when he saw so many strokes upon his helm and upon his shield he said: In good time was I thus asleep, for had I been with you I must needs for shame there have followed you; more for shame than any prowess that is in me; that I see well now by those strokes that I should have been truly beaten as I was yesterday. Leave your japes, said Sir Tristram, and come off, that [we] were in the field again. What, said Sir Dinadan, is your heart up? yesterday ye fared as though ye had dreamed. So then Sir Tristram was arrayed in black harness. O Jesu, said Dinadan, what aileth you this day? meseemeth ye be wilder than ye were yesterday. Then smiled Sir Tristram and said to Dinadan: Await well upon me; if ye see me overmatched look that ye be ever behind me, and I shall make you ready way by God's grace. So Sir Tristram and Sir Dinadan took their horses. All this espied Sir Palomides, both their going and their coming, and so did La Beale Isoud, for she knew Sir Tristram above all other.

CHAPTER LXXVI

How Sir Palomides changed his shield and his armour for to hurt Sir Tristram, and how Sir Launcelot did to Sir Tristram.

Then when Sir Palomides saw that Sir Tristram was disguised, then he thought to do him a shame. So Sir Palomides rode to a knight that was sore wounded, that sat under a fair well from the field. Sir knight, said Sir Palomides, I pray you to lend me your armour and your shield, for mine is over-well known in this field, and that hath done me great damage; and ye shall have mine armour and my shield that is as sure as yours. I will well, said the knight, that ye have mine armour and my shield, if they may do you any avail. So Sir Palomides armed him hastily in that knight's armour and his shield that shone as any crystal or silver, and so he came riding into the field. And then there was neither Sir Tristram nor none of King Arthur's party that knew Sir Palomides. And right so as Sir Palomides was come into the field Sir Tristram smote down three knights, even in the sight of Sir Palomides. And then Sir Palomides rode against Sir Tristram, and either met other with great spears, that they brast to their hands. And then they dashed together with swords eagerly. Then Sir Tristram had marvel what knight he was that did battle so knightly with him. Then was Sir Tristram wroth, for he felt him passing strong, so that he deemed he might not have ado with the remnant of the knights, because of the strength of Sir Palomides. So they lashed together and gave many sad strokes together, and many knights marvelled what knight he might be that so encountered with the black knight, Sir Tristram. Full well knew La Beale Isoud that there was Sir Palomides that fought with Sir Tristram, for she espied all in her window where that she stood, as Sir Palomides changed his harness with the wounded knight. And then she began to weep so heartily for the despite of Sir Palomides that there she swooned.

Then came in Sir Launcelot with the knights of Orkney. And when the other party had espied Sir Launcelot, they cried: Return, return, here cometh Sir Launcelot du Lake. So there came knights and said: Sir Launcelot, ye must needs fight with yonder knight in the black harness, that was Sir Tristram, for he hath almost overcome that good knight that fighteth with him with the silver shield, that was Sir Palomides. Then Sir Launcelot rode betwixt Sir Tristram and Sir Palomides, and Sir Launcelot said to Palomides: Sir knight, let me have the battle, for ye have need to be reposed. Sir Palomides knew Sir Launcelot well, and so did Sir Tristram, but because Sir Launcelot was far hardier knight than himself therefore he was glad, and suffered Sir Launcelot to fight with Sir Tristram. For well wist he that Sir Launcelot knew not Sir Tristram, and there he hoped that Sir Launcelot should beat or shame Sir Tristram, whereof Sir Palomides was full fain. And so Sir Launcelot gave Sir Tristram many sad strokes, but Sir Launcelot knew not Sir Tristram, but Sir Tristram knew well Sir Launcelot. And thus they fought long together, that La Beale Isoud was well-nigh out of her mind for sorrow.

Then Sir Dinadan told Sir Gareth how that knight in the black harness was Sir Tristram: And this is Launcelot that fighteth with him, that must needs have the better of him, for Sir Tristram hath had too much travail this day. Then let us smite him down, said Sir Gareth. So it is better that we do, said Sir Dinadan, than Sir Tristram be shamed, for yonder hoveth the strong knight with the silver shield to fall upon Sir Tristram if need be. Then forthwithal Gareth rushed upon Sir Launcelot, and gave him a great stroke upon his helm so hard that he was astonied. And then came Sir Dinadan with a spear, and he smote Sir Launcelot such a buffet that horse and all fell to the earth. O Jesu, said Sir Tristram to Sir Gareth and Sir Dinadan, fie for shame, why did ye smite down so good a knight as he is, and namely when I had ado with him? now ye do yourself great shame, and him no disworship; for I held him reasonable hot, though ye had not holpen me.

Then came Sir Palomides that was disguised, and smote down Sir Dinadan from his horse. Then Sir Launcelot, because Sir Dinadan had smitten him aforehand, then Sir Launcelot assailed Sir Dinadan passing sore, and Sir Dinadan defended him mightily. But well understood Sir Tristram that Sir Dinadan might not endure Sir Launcelot, wherefore Sir Tristram was sorry. Then came Sir Palomides fresh upon Sir Tristram. And when Sir Tristram saw him come, he thought to deliver him at once, because that he would help Sir Dinadan, because he stood in great peril with Sir Launcelot. Then Sir Tristram hurtled unto Sir Palomides and gave him a great buffet, and then Sir Tristram gat Sir Palomides and pulled him down underneath him. And so fell Sir Tristram with him; and Sir Tristram leapt up lightly and left Sir Palomides, and went betwixt Sir Launcelot and Dinadan, and then they began to do battle together.

Right so Sir Dinadan gat Sir Tristram's horse, and said on high that Sir Launcelot might hear it: My lord Sir Tristram, take your horse. And when Sir Launcelot heard him name Sir Tristram: O Jesu, said Launcelot, what have I done? I am dishonoured. Ah, my lord Sir Tristram, said Launcelot, why were ye disguised? ye have put yourself in great peril this day; but I pray you noble knight to pardon me, for an I had known you we had not done this battle. Sir, said Sir Tristram, this is not the first kindness ye showed me. So they were both horsed again.

Then all the people on the one side gave Sir Launcelot the honour and the degree, and on the other side all the people gave to the noble knight Sir Tristram the honour and the degree; but Launcelot said nay thereto: For I am not worthy to have this honour, for I will report me unto all knights that Sir Tristram hath been longer in the field than I, and he hath smitten down many more knights this day than I have done. And therefore I will give Sir Tristram my voice and my name, and so I pray all my lords and fellows so to do. Then there was the whole voice of dukes and earls, barons and knights, that Sir Tristram this day is proved the best knight.

CHAPTER LXXVII

*How Sir Tristram departed with La Beale Isoud, and how
Palomides followed and excused him.*

Then they blew unto lodging, and Queen Isoud was led unto her
pavilions. But wit you well she was wroth out of measure with Sir
Palomides, for she saw all his treason from the beginning to the
ending. And all this while neither Sir Tristram, neither Sir Gareth nor
Dinadan, knew not of the treason of Sir Palomides; but afterward ye
shall hear that there befell the greatest debate betwixt Sir Tristram and
Sir Palomides that might be.

So when the tournament was done, Sir Tristram, Gareth, and
Dinadan, rode with La Beale Isoud to these pavilions. And ever Sir
Palomides rode with them in their company disguised as he was. But
when Sir Tristram had espied him that he was the same knight with
the shield of silver that held him so hot that day: Sir knight, said Sir
Tristram, wit ye well here is none that hath need of your fellowship,
and therefore I pray you depart from us. Sir Palomides answered
again as though he had not known Sir Tristram: Wit you well, sir
knight, from this fellowship will I never depart, for one of the best
knights of the world commanded me to be in this company, and till
he discharge me of my service I will not be discharged. By that Sir
Tristram knew that it was Sir Palomides. Ah, Sir Palomides, said the
noble knight Sir Tristram, are ye such a knight? Ye have been named
wrong, for ye have long been called a gentle knight, and as this day ye
have showed me great ungentleness, for ye had almost brought me
unto my death. But, as for you, I suppose I should have done well
enough, but Sir Launcelot with you was overmuch; for I know no
knight living but Sir Launcelot is over good for him, an he will do his
uttermost. Alas, said Sir Palomides, are ye my lord Sir Tristram? Yea
sir, and that ye know well enough. By my knighthood, said
Palomides, until now I knew you not; I weened that ye had been the
King of Ireland, for well I wot ye bare his arms. His arms I bare, said
Sir Tristram, and that will I stand by, for I won them once in a field
of a full noble knight, his name was Sir Marhaus; and with great pain

I won that knight, for there was none other recover, but Sir Marhaus died through false leeches; and yet was he never yolden to me. Sir, said Palomides, I weened ye had been turned upon Sir Launcelot's party, and that caused me to turn. Ye say well, said Sir Tristram, and so I take you, and I forgive you.

So then they rode into their pavilions; and when they were alighted they unarmed them and washed their faces and hands, and so yode unto meat, and were set at their table. But when Isoud saw Sir Palomides she changed then her colours, and for wrath she might not speak. Anon Sir Tristram espied her countenance and said: Madam, for what cause make ye us such cheer? we have been sore travailed this day. Mine own lord, said La Beale Isoud, for God's sake be ye not displeased with me, for I may none otherwise do; for I saw this day how ye were betrayed and nigh brought to your death. Truly, sir, I saw every deal, how and in what wise, and therefore, sir, how should I suffer in your presence such a felon and traitor as Sir Palomides; for I saw him with mine eyes, how he beheld you when ye went out of the field. For ever he hoved still upon his horse till he saw you come in againward. And then forthwithal I saw him ride to the hurt knight, and changed harness with him, and then straight I saw him how he rode into the field. And anon as he had found you he encountered with you, and thus wilfully Sir Palomides did battle with you; and as for him, sir, I was not greatly afraid, but I dread sore Launcelot, that knew you not. Madam, said Palomides, ye may say whatso ye will, I may not contrary you, but by my knighthood I knew not Sir Tristram. Sir Palomides, said Sir Tristram, I will take your excuse, but well I wot ye spared me but little, but all is pardoned on my part. Then La Beale Isoud held down her head and said no more at that time.

CHAPTER LXXVIII

*How King Arthur and Sir Launcelot came unto their
pavilions as they sat at supper, and of Sir Palomides.*

And therewithal two knights armed came unto the pavilion, and
there they alighted both, and came in armed at all pieces. Fair knights,
said Sir Tristram, ye are to blame to come thus armed at all pieces
upon me while we are at our meat; if ye would anything when we
were in the field there might ye have eased your hearts. Not so, said
the one of those knights, we come not for that intent, but wit ye well
Sir Tristram, we be come hither as your friends. And I am come here,
said the one, for to see you, and this knight is come for to see La
Beale Isoud. Then said Sir Tristram: I require you do off your helms
that I may see you. That will we do at your desire, said the knights.
And when their helms were off, Sir Tristram thought that he should
know them.

Then said Sir Dinadan privily unto Sir Tristram: Sir, that is Sir
Launcelot du Lake that spake unto you first, and the other is my lord
King Arthur. Then, said Sir Tristram unto La Beale Isoud, Madam
arise, for here is my lord, King Arthur. Then the king and the queen
kissed, and Sir Launcelot and Sir Tristram braced either other in arms,
and then there was joy without measure; and at the request of La
Beale Isoud, King Arthur and Launcelot were unarmed, and then
there was merry talking. Madam, said Sir Arthur, it is many a day
sithen that I have desired to see you, for ye have been praised so far;
and now I dare say ye are the fairest that ever I saw, and Sir Tristram
is as fair and as good a knight as any that I know; therefore me
beseemeth ye are well beset together. Sir, God thank you, said the
noble knight, Sir Tristram, and Isoud; of your great goodness and
largess ye are peerless. Thus they talked of many things and of all the
whole jousts. But for what cause, said King Arthur, were ye, Sir
Tristram, against us? Ye are a knight of the Table Round; of right ye
should have been with us. Sir, said Sir Tristram, here is Dinadan, and
Sir Gareth your own nephew, caused me to be against you. My lord
Arthur, said Gareth, I may well bear the blame, but it were Sir

Tristram's own deeds. That may I repent, said Dinadan, for this unhappy Sir Tristram brought us to this tournament, and many great buffets he caused us to have. Then the king and Launcelot laughed that they might not sit.

What knight was that, said Arthur, that held you so short, this with the shield of silver? Sir, said Sir Tristram, here he sitteth at this board. What, said Arthur, was it Sir Palomides? Wit ye well it was he, said La Beale Isoud. So God me help, said Arthur, that was unknightly done of you of so good a knight, for I have heard many people call you a courteous knight. Sir, said Palomides, I knew not Sir Tristram, for he was so disguised. So God me help, said Launcelot, it may well be, for I knew not Sir Tristram; but I marvel why ye turned on our party. That was done for the same cause, said Launcelot. As for that, said Sir Tristram, I have pardoned him, and I would be right loath to leave his fellowship, for I love right well his company: so they left off and talked of other things,

And in the evening King Arthur and Sir Launcelot departed unto their lodging; but wit ye well Sir Palomides had envy heartily, for all that night he had never rest in his bed, but wailed and wept out of measure. So on the morn Sir Tristram, Gareth, and Dinadan arose early, and they went unto Sir Palomides' chamber, and there they found him fast asleep, for he had all night watched, and it was seen upon his cheeks that he had wept full sore. Say nothing, said Sir Tristram, for I am sure he hath taken anger and sorrow for the rebuke that I gave to him, and La Beale Isoud.

CHAPTER LXXIX

How Sir Tristram and Sir Palomides did the next day,
and how King Arthur was unhorsed.

Then Sir Tristram let call Sir Palomides, and bade him make him ready, for it was time to go to the field. When they were ready they were armed, and clothed all in red, both Isoud and all they; and so they led her passing freshly through the field, into the priory where was her lodging. And then they heard three blasts blow, and every king and knight dressed him unto the field. And the first that was

ready to joust was Sir Palomides and Sir Kainus le Strange, a knight of
the Table Round. And so they two encountered together, but Sir
Palomides smote Sir Kainus so hard that he smote him quite over his
horse's croup. And forthwithal Sir Palomides smote down another
knight, and brake then his spear, and pulled out his sword and did
wonderly well. And then the noise began greatly upon Sir Palomides.
Lo, said King Arthur, yonder Palomides beginneth to play his
pageant. So God me help, said Arthur, he is a passing good knight.
And right as they stood talking thus, in came Sir Tristram as thunder,
and he encountered with Sir Kay the Seneschal, and there he smote
him down quite from his horse; and with that same spear Sir Tristram
smote down three knights more, and then he pulled out his sword
and did marvellously. Then the noise and cry changed from Sir
Palomides and turned to Sir Tristram, and all the people cried: O
Tristram, O Tristram. And then was Sir Palomides clean forgotten.

How now, said Launcelot unto Arthur, yonder rideth a knight that
playeth his pageants. So God me help, said Arthur to Launcelot, ye
shall see this day that yonder two knights shall here do this day
wonders. Sir, said Launcelot, the one knight waiteth upon the other,
and enforceth himself through envy to pass the noble knight Sir
Tristram, and he knoweth not of the privy envy the which Sir
Palomides hath to him; for all that the noble Sir Tristram doth is
through clean knighthood. And then Sir Gareth and Dinadan did
wonderly great deeds of arms, as two noble knights, so that King
Arthur spake of them great honour and worship; and the kings and
knights of Sir Tristram's side did passingly well, and held them truly
together. Then Sir Arthur and Sir Launcelot took their horses and
dressed them, and gat into the thickest of the press. And there Sir
Tristram unknowing smote down King Arthur, and then Sir
Launcelot would have rescued him, but there were so many upon Sir
Launcelot that they pulled him down from his horse. And then the
King of Ireland and the King of Scots with their knights did their pain
to take King Arthur and Sir Launcelot prisoner. When Sir Launcelot
heard them say so, he fared as it had been an hungry lion, for he fared
so that no knight durst nigh him.

Then came Sir Ector de Maris, and he bare a spear against Sir
Palomides, and brast it upon him all to shivers. And then Sir Ector
came again and gave Sir Palomides such a dash with a sword that he
stooped down upon his saddle bow. And forthwithal Sir Ector pulled

down Sir Palomides under his feet; and then Sir Ector de Maris gat Sir Launcelot du Lake an horse, and brought it to him, and bade him mount upon him; but Sir Palomides leapt afore and gat the horse by the bridle, and leapt into the saddle. So God me help, said Launcelot, ye are better worthy to have that horse than I. Then Sir Ector brought Sir Launcelot another horse. Gramercy, said Launcelot unto his brother. And so when he was horsed again, with one spear he smote down four knights. And then Sir Launcelot brought to King Arthur one of the best of the four horses. Then Sir Launcelot with King Arthur and a few of his knights of Sir Launcelot's kin did marvellous deeds; for that time, as the book recordeth, Sir Launcelot smote down and pulled down thirty knights. Notwithstanding the other party held them so fast together that King Arthur and his knights were overmatched. And when Sir Tristram saw that, what labour King Arthur and his knights, and in especial the noble deeds that Sir Launcelot did with his own hands, he marvelled greatly.

CHAPTER LXXX

How Sir Tristram turned to King Arthur's side, and how Palomides would not.

Then Sir Tristram called unto him Sir Palomides, Sir Gareth, and Sir Dinadan, and said thus to them: My fair fellows, wit ye well that I will turn unto King Arthur's party, for I saw never so few men do so well, and it will be shame unto us knights that be of the Round Table to see our lord King Arthur, and that noble knight Sir Launcelot, to be dishonoured. It will be well done, said Sir Gareth and Sir Dinadan. Do your best, said Palomides, for I will not change my party that I came in withal. That is for my sake, said Sir Tristram; God speed you in your journey. And so departed Sir Palomides from them. Then Sir Tristram, Gareth, and Dinadan, turned with Sir Launcelot. And then Sir Launcelot smote down the King of Ireland quite from his horse; and so Sir Launcelot smote down the King of Scots, and the King of Wales; and then Sir Arthur ran unto Sir Palomides and smote him quite from his horse; and then Sir Tristram bare down all that he met. Sir Gareth and Sir Dinadan did there as noble knights; then all the parties began to flee. Alas, said Palomides, that ever I should see this day, for now have I lost all the worship that I won; and then Sir Palomides went his way wailing, and so withdrew him till he came to a well, and there he put his horse from him, and did off his armour, and wailed and wept like as he had been a wood man. Then many knights gave the prize to Sir Tristram, and there were many that gave the prize unto Sir Launcelot. Fair lords, said Sir Tristram, I thank you of the honour ye would give me, but I pray you heartily that ye would give your voice to Sir Launcelot, for by my faith, said Sir Tristram, I will give Sir Launcelot my voice. But Sir Launcelot would not have it, and so the prize was given betwixt them both.

Then every man rode to his lodging, and Sir Bleoberis and Sir Ector rode with Sir Tristram and La Beale Isoud unto their pavilions. Then as Sir Palomides was at the well wailing and weeping, there came by him flying the kings of Wales and of Scotland, and they saw Sir Palomides in that arage. Alas, said they, that so noble a man as ye be should be in this array. And then those kings gat Sir Palomides' horse again, and made him to arm him and mount upon his horse, and so he rode with them, making great dole. So when Sir Palomides came nigh the pavilions thereas Sir Tristram and La Beale Isoud was in, then Sir Palomides prayed the two kings to abide him there the while that he spake with Sir Tristram. And when he came to the port of the pavilions, Sir Palomides said on high: Where art thou, Sir Tristram de Liones? Sir, said Dinadan, that is Palomides. What, Sir Palomides, will ye not come in here among us? Fie on thee, traitor, said Palomides, for wit you well an it were daylight as it is night I should slay thee, mine own hands. And if ever I may get thee, said Palomides, thou shalt die for this day's deed. Sir Palomides, said Sir Tristram, ye wite me with wrong, for had ye done as I did ye had won worship. But sithen ye give me so large warning I shall be well ware of you. Fie on thee, traitor, said Palomides, and therewith departed.

Then on the morn Sir Tristram, Bleoberis, and Sir Ector de Maris, Sir Gareth, Sir Dinadan, what by water and what by land, they brought La Beale Isoud unto Joyous Gard, and there reposed them a seven night, and made all the mirths and disports that they could devise. And King Arthur and his knights drew unto Camelot, and Sir Palomides rode with the two kings; and ever he made the greatest dole that any man could think, for he was not all only so dolorous for the departing from La Beale Isoud, but he was a part as sorrowful to depart from the fellowship of Sir Tristram; for Sir Tristram was so kind and so gentle that when Sir Palomides remembered him thereof he might never be merry.

CHAPTER LXXXI

How Sir Bleoberis and Sir Ector reported to
Queen Guenever of the beauty of La Beale Isoud.

So at the seven nights' end Sir Bleoberis and Sir Ector departed from Sir Tristram and from the queen; and these two good knights had great gifts; and Sir Gareth and Sir Dinadan abode with Sir Tristram. And when Sir Bleoberis and Sir Ector were come there as the Queen Guenever was lodged, in a castle by the seaside, and through the grace of God the queen was recovered of her malady, then she asked the two knights from whence they came. They said that they came from Sir Tristram and from La Beale Isoud. How doth Sir Tristram, said the queen, and La Beale Isoud? Truly, said those two knights, he doth as a noble knight should do; and as for the Queen Isoud, she is peerless of all ladies; for to speak of her beauty, bounté, and mirth, and of her goodness, we saw never her match as far as we have ridden and gone. O mercy Jesu, said Queen Guenever, so saith all the people that have seen her and spoken with her. God would that I had part of her conditions; and it is misfortuned me of my sickness while that tournament endured. And as I suppose I shall never see in all my life such an assembly of knights and ladies as ye have done.

Then the knights told her how Palomides won the degree at the first day with great noblesse; and the second day Sir Tristram won the degree; and the third day Sir Launcelot won the degree. Well, said Queen Guenever, who did best all these three days? So God me help, said these knights, Sir Launcelot and Sir Tristram had least dishonour. And wit ye well Sir Palomides did passing well and mightily; but he turned against the party that he came in withal, and that caused him to lose a great part of his worship, for it seemed that Sir Palomides is passing envious. Then shall he never win worship, said Queen Guenever, for an it happeth an envious man once to win worship he shall be dishonoured twice therefore; and for this cause all men of worship hate an envious man, and will show him no favour, and he that is courteous, and kind, and gentle, hath favour in every place.

CHAPTER LXXXII

How Epinogris complained by a well, and how Sir Palomides came and found him, and of their both sorrowing.

Now leave we of this matter and speak we of Sir Palomides, that rode and lodged him with the two kings, whereof the kings were heavy. Then the King of Ireland sent a man of his to Sir Palomides, and gave him a great courser, and the King of Scotland gave him great gifts; and fain they would have had Sir Palomides to have abiden with them, but in no wise he would abide; and so he departed, and rode as adventures would guide him, till it was nigh noon. And then in a forest by a well Sir Palomides saw where lay a fair wounded knight and his horse bounden by him; and that knight made the greatest dole that ever he heard man make, for ever he wept, and therewith he sighed as though he would die. Then Sir Palomides rode near him and saluted him mildly and said: Fair knight, why wail ye so? let me lie down and wail with you, for doubt not I am much more heavier than ye are; for I dare say, said Palomides, that my sorrow is an hundred fold more than yours is, and therefore let us complain either to other. First, said the wounded knight, I require you tell me your name, for an thou be none of the noble knights of the Round Table thou shalt never know my name, whatsomever come of me. Fair knight, said Palomides, such as I am, be it better or be it worse, wit thou well that my name is Sir Palomides, son and heir unto King Astlabor, and Sir Safere and Sir Segwarides are my two brethren; and wit thou well as for myself I was never christened, but my two brethren are truly christened. O noble knight, said that knight, well is me that I have met with you; and wit ye well my name is Epinogris, the king's son of Northumberland. Now sit down, said Epinogris, and let us either complain to other.

Then Sir Palomides began his complaint. Now shall I tell you, said Palomides, what woe I endure. I love the fairest queen and lady that ever bare life, and wit ye well her name is La Beale Isoud, King Mark's wife of Cornwall. That is great folly, said Epinogris, for to love Queen Isoud, for one of the best knights of the world loveth her, that is Sir Tristram de Liones. That is truth, said Palomides, for no man knoweth that matter better than I do, for I have been in Sir Tristram's fellowship this month, and with La Beale Isoud together; and alas, said Palomides, unhappy man that I am, now have I lost the fellowship of Sir Tristram for ever, and the love of La Beale Isoud for ever, and I am never like to see her more, and Sir Tristram and I be either to other mortal enemies. Well, said Epinogris, sith that ye loved La Beale Isoud, loved she you ever again by anything that ye could think or wit, or else did ye rejoice her ever in any pleasure? Nay, by my knighthood, said Palomides, I never espied that ever she loved me more than all the world, nor never had I pleasure with her, but the last day she gave me the greatest rebuke that ever I had, the which shall never go from my heart. And yet I well deserved that rebuke, for I did not knightly, and therefore I have lost the love of her and of Sir Tristram for ever; and I have many times enforced myself to do many deeds for La Beale Isoud's sake, and she was the causer of my worship-winning. Alas, said Sir Palomides, now have I lost all the worship that ever I won, for never shall me befall such prowess as I had in the fellowship of Sir Tristram.

CHAPTER LXXXIII

How Sir Palomides brought Sir Epinogris his lady; and how Sir Palomides and Sir Safere were assailed.

Nay, nay, said Epinogris, your sorrow is but japes to my sorrow; for I rejoiced my lady and won her with my hands, and lost her again: alas that day! Thus first I won her, said Epinogris; my lady was an earl's daughter, and as the earl and two knights came from the tournament of Lonazep, for her sake I set upon this earl and on his two knights, my lady there being present; and so by fortune there I slew the earl and one of the knights, and the other knight fled, and so that night I had my lady. And on the morn as she and I reposed us at this well-side there came there to me an errant knight, his name was Sir Helior le Preuse, an hardy knight, and this Sir Helior challenged me to fight for my lady. And then we went to battle first upon horse and after on foot, but at the last Sir Helior wounded me so that he left me for dead, and so he took my lady with him; and thus my sorrow is more than yours, for I have rejoiced and ye rejoiced never. That is truth, said Palomides, but sith I can never recover myself I shall promise you if I can meet with Sir Helior I shall get you your lady again, or else he shall beat me.

Then Sir Palomides made Sir Epinogris to take his horse, and so they rode to an hermitage, and there Sir Epinogris rested him. And in the meanwhile Sir Palomides walked privily out to rest him under the leaves, and there beside he saw a knight come riding with a shield that he had seen Sir Ector de Maris bear beforehand; and there came after him a ten knights, and so these ten knights hoved under the leaves for heat. And anon after there came a knight with a green shield and therein a white lion, leading a lady upon a palfrey. Then this knight with the green shield that seemed to be master of the ten knights, he rode fiercely after Sir Helior, for it was he that hurt Sir Epinogris. And when he came nigh Sir Helior he bade him defend his lady. I will defend her, said Helior, unto my power. And so they ran together so mightily that either of these knights smote other down, horse and all, to the earth; and then they won up lightly and drew their swords and their shields, and lashed together mightily more than an hour. All this Sir Palomides saw and beheld, but ever at the last the knight with Sir Ector's shield was bigger, and at the last this knight smote Sir Helior down, and then that knight unlaced his helm to have stricken off his head. And then he cried mercy, and prayed him to save his life, and bade him take his lady. Then Sir Palomides dressed him up, because he wist well that that same lady was Epinogris' lady, and he promised him to help him.

Then Sir Palomides went straight to that lady, and took her by the hand, and asked her whether she knew a knight that hight Epinogris. Alas, she said, that ever he knew me or I him, for I have for his sake lost my worship, and also his life grieveth me most of all. Not so, lady, said Palomides, come on with me, for here is Epinogris in this hermitage. Ah! well is me, said the lady, an he be alive. Whither wilt thou with that lady? said the knight with Sir Ector's shield. I will do with her what me list, said Palomides. Wit you well, said that knight, thou speakest over large, though thou seemest me to have at advantage, because thou sawest me do battle but late. Thou weenest, sir knight, to have that lady away from me so lightly? nay, think it never not; an thou were as good a knight as is Sir Launcelot, or as is Sir Tristram, or Sir Palomides, but thou shalt win her dearer than ever did I. And so they went unto battle upon foot, and there they gave many sad strokes, and either wounded other passing sore, and thus they fought still more than an hour.

Then Sir Palomides had marvel what knight he might be that was so strong and so well breathed during, and thus said Palomides: Knight, I require thee tell me thy name. Wit thou well, said that knight, I dare tell thee my name, so that thou wilt tell me thy name. I will, said Palomides. Truly, said that knight, my name is Safere, son of King Astlabor, and Sir Palomides and Sir Segwarides are my brethren. Now, and wit thou well, my name is Sir Palomides. Then Sir Safere kneeled down upon his knees, and prayed him of mercy; and then they unlaced their helms and either kissed other weeping. And in the meanwhile Sir Epinogris arose out of his bed, and heard them by the strokes, and so he armed him to help Sir Palomides if need were.

CHAPTER LXXXIV

How Sir Palomides and Sir Safere conducted Sir Epinogris to his castle, and of other adventures.

Then Sir Palomides took the lady by the hand and brought her to Sir Epinogris, and there was great joy betwixt them, for either swooned for joy. When they were met: Fair knight and lady, said Sir Safere, it were pity to depart you; Jesu send you joy either of other. Gramercy, gentle knight, said Epinogris; and much more thanks be to my lord Sir Palomides, that thus hath through his prowess made me to get my lady. Then Sir Epinogris required Sir Palomides and Sir Safere, his brother, to ride with them unto his castle, for the safeguard of his person. Sir, said Palomides, we will be ready to conduct you because that ye are sore wounded; and so was Epinogris and his lady horsed, and his lady behind him upon a soft ambler. And then they rode unto his castle, where they had great cheer and joy, as great as ever Sir Palomides and Sir Safere had in their life-days.

So on the morn Sir Safere and Sir Palomides departed, and rode as fortune led them, and so they rode all that day until after noon. And at the last they heard a great weeping and a great noise down in a manor. Sir, said then Sir Safere, let us wit what noise this is. I will well, said Sir Palomides. And so they rode forth till that they came to a fair gate of a manor, and there sat an old man saying his prayers and beads. Then Sir Palomides and Sir Safere alighted and left their horses, and went within the gates, and there they saw full many goodly men weeping. Fair sirs, said Palomides, wherefore weep ye and make this sorrow? Anon one of the knights of the castle beheld Sir Palomides and knew him, and then went to his fellows and said: Fair fellows, wit ye well all, we have in this castle the same knight that slew our lord at Lonazep, for I know him well; it is Sir Palomides. Then they went unto harness, all that might bear harness, some on horseback and some on foot, to the number of three score. And when they were ready they came freshly upon Sir Palomides and upon Sir Safere with a great noise, and said thus: Keep thee, Sir Palomides, for thou art known, and by right thou must be dead, for thou hast slain our lord; and therefore wit ye well we will slay thee, therefore defend thee.

Then Sir Palomides and Sir Safere, the one set his back to the other, and gave many great strokes, and took many great strokes; and thus they fought with a twenty knights and forty gentlemen and yeomen nigh two hours. But at the last though they were loath, Sir Palomides and Sir Safere were taken and yolden, and put in a strong prison; and within three days twelve knights passed upon them, and they found Sir Palomides guilty, and Sir Safere not guilty, of their lord's death. And when Sir Safere should be delivered there was great dole betwixt Sir Palomides and him, and many piteous complaints that Sir Safere made at his departing, there is no maker can rehearse the tenth part. Fair brother, said Palomides, let be thy dolour and thy sorrow. And if I be ordained to die a shameful death, welcome be it; but an I had wist of this death that I am deemed unto, I should never have been yolden. So Sir Safere departed from his brother with the greatest dolour and sorrow that ever made knight.

And on the morn they of the castle ordained twelve knights to ride with Sir Palomides unto the father of the same knight that Sir Palomides slew; and so they bound his legs under an old steed's belly. And then they rode with Sir Palomides unto a castle by the seaside, that hight Pelownes, and there Sir Palomides should have justice. Thus was their ordinance; and so they rode with Sir Palomides fast by the castle of Joyous Gard. And as they passed by that castle there came riding out of that castle by them one that knew Sir Palomides. And when that knight saw Sir Palomides bounden upon a crooked courser, the knight asked Sir Palomides for what cause he was led so. Ah, my fair fellow and knight, said Palomides, I ride toward my death for the slaying of a knight at a tournament of Lonazep; and if I had not departed from my lord Sir Tristram, as I ought not to have done, now might I have been sure to have had my life saved; but I pray you, sir knight, recommend me unto my lord, Sir Tristram, and unto my lady, Queen Isoud, and say to them if ever I trespassed to them I ask them forgiveness. And also I beseech you recommend me unto my lord, King Arthur, and to all the fellowship of the Round Table, unto my power. Then that knight wept for pity of Sir Palomides; and therewithal he rode unto Joyous Gard as fast as his horse might run, and lightly that knight descended down off his horse and went unto Sir Tristram, and there he told him all as ye have heard, and ever the knight wept as he had been mad.

CHAPTER LXXXV

How Sir Tristram made him ready to rescue Sir Palomides, but Sir Launcelot rescued him or he came.

When Sir Tristram heard how Sir Palomides went to his death, he was heavy to hear that, and said: Howbeit that I am wroth with Sir Palomides, yet will not I suffer him to die so shameful a death, for he is a full noble knight. And then anon Sir Tristram was armed and took his horse and two squires with him, and rode a great pace toward the castle of Pelownes where Sir Palomides was judged to death. And these twelve knights that led Sir Palomides passed by a well whereas Sir Launcelot was, which was alighted there, and had tied his horse to a tree, and taken off his helm to drink of that well; and when he saw these knights, Sir Launcelot put on his helm and suffered them to pass by him. And then was he ware of Sir Palomides bounden, and led shamefully to his death. O Jesu, said Launcelot, what misadventure is befallen him that he is thus led toward his death? Forsooth, said Launcelot, it were shame to me to suffer this noble knight so to die an I might help him, therefore I will help him whatsomever come of it, or else I shall die for Sir Palomides' sake. And then Sir Launcelot mounted upon his horse, and gat his spear in his hand, and rode after the twelve knights that led Sir Palomides. Fair knights, said Sir Launcelot, whither lead ye that knight? it beseemeth him full ill to ride bounden. Then these twelve knights suddenly turned their horses and said to Sir Launcelot: Sir knight, we counsel thee not to meddle with this knight, for he hath deserved death, and unto death he is judged. That me repenteth, said Launcelot, that I may not borrow him with fairness, for he is over good a knight to die such a shameful death. And therefore, fair knights, said Sir Launcelot, keep you as well as ye can, for I will rescue that knight or die for it.

Then they began to dress their spears, and Sir Launcelot smote the foremost down, horse and man, and so he served three more with one spear; and then that spear brast, and therewithal Sir Launcelot drew his sword, and then he smote on the right hand and on the left hand. Then within a while he left none of those twelve knights, but he had laid them to the earth, and the most part of them were sore wounded. And then Sir Launcelot took the best horse that he found, and loosed Sir Palomides and set him upon that horse; and so they returned again unto Joyous Gard, and then was Sir Palomides ware of Sir Tristram how he came riding. And when Sir Launcelot saw him he knew him well, but Sir Tristram knew him not because Sir Launcelot had on his shoulder a golden shield. So Sir Launcelot made him ready to joust with Sir Tristram, that Sir Tristram should not ween that he were Sir Launcelot. Then Sir Palomides cried aloud to Sir Tristram: O my lord, I require you joust not with this knight, for this good knight hath saved me from my death. When Sir Tristram heard him say so he came a soft trotting pace toward them. And then Sir Palomides said: My lord, Sir Tristram, much am I beholding unto you of your great goodness, that would proffer your noble body to rescue me undeserved, for I have greatly offended you. Notwith-standing, said Sir Palomides, here met we with this noble knight that worshipfully and manly rescued me from twelve knights, and smote them down all and wounded them sore.

CHAPTER LXXXVI

*How Sir Tristram and Launcelot, with Palomides, came to
Joyous Gard; and of Palomides and Sir Tristram.*

Fair knight, said Sir Tristram unto Sir Launcelot, of whence be ye? I
am a knight errant, said Sir Launcelot, that rideth to seek many
adventures. What is your name? said Sir Tristram. Sir, at this time I
will not tell you. Then Sir Launcelot said unto Sir Tristram and to
Palomides: Now either of you are met together I will depart from
you. Not so, said Sir Tristram; I pray you of knighthood to ride with
me unto my castle. Wit you well, said Sir Launcelot, I may not ride
with you, for I have many deeds to do in other places, that at this
time I may not abide with you. Ah, mercy Jesu, said Sir Tristram, I
require you as ye be a true knight to the order of knighthood, play
you with me this night. Then Sir Tristram had a grant of Sir
Launcelot: howbeit though he had not desired him he would have
ridden with them, outher soon have come after them; for Sir
Launcelot came for none other cause into that country but for to see
Sir Tristram. And when they were come within Joyous Gard they
alighted, and their horses were led into a stable; and then they
unarmed them. And when Sir Launcelot was unhelmed, Sir Tristram
and Sir Palomides knew him. Then Sir Tristram took Sir Launcelot
in arms, and so did La Beale Isoud; and Palomides kneeled down
upon his knees and thanked Sir Launcelot. When Sir Launcelot saw
Sir Palomides kneel he lightly took him up and said thus: Wit thou
well, Sir Palomides, I and any knight in this land, of worship ought of
very right succour and rescue so noble a knight as ye are proved and
renowned, throughout all this realm endlong and overthwart. And
then was there joy among them, and the oftener that Sir Palomides
saw La Beale Isoud the heavier he waxed day by day.

Then Sir Launcelot within three or four days departed, and with
him rode Sir Ector de Maris; and Dinadan and Sir Palomides were
there left with Sir Tristram a two months and more. But ever Sir
Palomides faded and mourned, that all men had marvel wherefore he
faded so away. So upon a day, in the dawning, Sir Palomides went

into the forest by himself alone; and there he found a well, and then he looked into the well, and in the water he saw his own visage, how he was disturbed and defaded, nothing like that he was. What may this mean? said Sir Palomides, and thus he said to himself: Ah, Palomides, Palomides, why art thou defaded, thou that was wont to be called one of the fairest knights of the world? I will no more lead this life, for I love that I may never get nor recover. And therewithal he laid him down by the well. And then he began to make a rhyme of La Beale Isoud and him.

And in the meanwhile Sir Tristram was that same day ridden into the forest to chase the hart of greese; but Sir Tristram would not ride a-hunting never more unarmed, because of Sir Breuse Saunce Pité. And so as Sir Tristram rode into that forest up and down, he heard one sing marvellously loud, and that was Sir Palomides that lay by the well. And then Sir Tristram rode softly thither, for he deemed there was some knight errant that was at the well. And when Sir Tristram came nigh him he descended down from his horse and tied his horse fast till a tree, and then he came near him on foot; and anon he was ware where lay Sir Palomides by the well and sang loud and merrily; and ever the complaints were of that noble queen, La Beale Isoud, the which was marvellously and wonderfully well said, and full dolefully and piteously made. And all the whole song the noble knight, Sir Tristram, heard from the beginning to the ending, the which grieved and troubled him sore.

But then at the last, when Sir Tristram had heard all Sir Palomides' complaints, he was wroth out of measure, and thought for to slay him thereas he lay. Then Sir Tristram remembered himself that Sir Palomides was unarmed, and of the noble name that Sir Palomides had, and the noble name that himself had, and then he made a restraint of his anger; and so he went unto Sir Palomides a soft pace and said: Sir Palomides, I have heard your complaint, and of thy treason that thou hast owed me so long, and wit thou well therefore thou shalt die; and if it were not for shame of knighthood thou shouldest not escape my hands, for now I know well thou hast awaited me with treason. Tell me, said Sir Tristram, how thou wilt acquit thee? Sir, said Palomides, thus I will acquit me: as for Queen La Beale Isoud, ye shall wit well that I love her above all other ladies in this world; and well I wot it shall befall me as for her love as befell to the noble knight Sir Kehydius, that died for the love of La Beale

Isoud. And now, Sir Tristram, I will that ye wit that I have loved La Beale Isoud many a day, and she hath been the causer of my worship, and else I had been the most simplest knight in the world. For by her, and because of her, I have won the worship that I have; for when I remembered me of La Beale Isoud I won the worship wheresomever I came for the most part; and yet had I never reward nor bounté of her the days of my life, and yet have I been her knight guerdonless. And therefore, Sir Tristram, as for any death I dread not, for I had as lief die as to live. And if I were armed as thou art, I should lightly do battle with thee. Well have ye uttered your treason, said Tristram. I have done to you no treason, said Palomides, for love is free for all men, and though I have loved your lady, she is my lady as well as yours; howbeit I have wrong if any wrong be, for ye rejoice her, and have your desire of her, and so had I never nor never am like to have, and yet shall I love her to the uttermost days of my life as well as ye.

CHAPTER LXXXVII

How there was a day set between Sir Tristram and Sir Palomides for to fight, and how Sir Tristram was hurt.

Then said Sir Tristram: I will fight with you to the uttermost. I grant, said Palomides, for in a better quarrel keep I never to fight, for an I die of your hands, of a better knight's hands may I not be slain. And sithen I understand that I shall never rejoice La Beale Isoud, I have as good will to die as to live. Then set ye a day, said Sir Tristram, that we shall do battle. This day fifteen days, said Palomides, will I meet with you hereby, in the meadow under Joyous Gard. Fie for shame, said Sir Tristram, will ye set so long day? let us fight to-morn. Not so, said Palomides, for I am meagre, and have been long sick for the love of La Beale Isoud, and therefore I will repose me till I have my strength again. So then Sir Tristram and Sir Palomides promised faithfully to meet at the well that day fifteen days. I am remembered, said Sir Tristram to Palomides, that ye brake me once a promise when that I rescued you from Breuse Saunce Pité and nine knights; and then ye promised me to meet me at the peron and the grave beside Camelot, whereas at that time ye failed of your promise. Wit you well, said Palomides unto Sir Tristram, I was at that day in prison, so that I might not hold my promise. So God me help, said Sir Tristram, an ye had holden your promise this work had not been here now at this time.

Right so departed Sir Tristram and Sir Palomides. And so Sir Palomides took his horse and his harness, and he rode unto King Arthur's court; and there Sir Palomides gat him four knights and four sergeants-of-arms, and so he returned againward unto Joyous Gard. And in the meanwhile Sir Tristram chased and hunted at all manner of venery; and about three days afore the battle should be, as Sir Tristram chased an hart, there was an archer shot at the hart, and by misfortune he smote Sir Tristram in the thick of the thigh, and the arrow slew Sir Tristram's horse and hurt him. When Sir Tristram was so hurt he was passing heavy, and wit ye well he bled sore; and then he took another horse, and rode unto Joyous Gard with great heaviness, more for the promise that he had made with Sir Palomides, as to do battle with him within three days after, than for any hurt of his thigh. Wherefore there was neither man nor woman that could cheer him with anything that they could make to him, neither Queen La Beale Isoud; for ever he deemed that Sir Palomides had smitten him so that he should not be able to do battle with him at the day set.

CHAPTER LXXXVIII

How Sir Palomides kept his day to have foughten, but Sir Tristram might not come; and other things.

But in no wise there was no knight about Sir Tristram that would believe that ever Sir Palomides would hurt Sir Tristram, neither by his own hands nor by none other consenting. Then when the fifteenth day was come, Sir Palomides came to the well with four knights with him of Arthur's court, and three sergeants-of-arms. And for this intent Sir Palomides brought the knights with him and the sergeants-of-arms, for they should bear record of the battle betwixt Sir Tristram and Sir Palomides. And the one sergeant brought in his helm, the other his spear, the third his sword. So thus Palomides came into the field, and there he abode nigh two hours; and then he sent a squire unto Sir Tristram, and desired him to come into the field to hold his promise.

When the squire was come to Joyous Gard, anon as Sir Tristram heard of his coming he let command that the squire should come to his presence thereas he lay in his bed. My lord Sir Tristram, said Palomides' squire, wit you well my lord, Palomides, abideth you in the field, and he would wit whether ye would do battle or not. Ah, my fair brother, said Sir Tristram, wit thou well that I am right heavy for these tidings; therefore tell Sir Palomides an I were well at ease I would not lie here, nor he should have no need to send for me an I might either ride or go; and for thou shalt say that I am no liar – Sir Tristram showed him his thigh that the wound was six inches deep. And now thou hast seen my hurt, tell thy lord that this is no feigned matter, and tell him that I had liefer than all the gold of King Arthur that I were whole; and tell Palomides as soon as I am whole I shall seek him endlong and overthwart, and that I promise you as I am true knight; and if ever I may meet with him, he shall have battle of me his fill. And with this the squire departed; and when Palomides wist that Tristram was hurt he was glad and said: Now I am sure I shall have no shame, for I wot well I should have had hard handling of him, and by likely I must needs have had the worse, for he is the hardest knight in battle that now is living except Sir Launcelot.

And then departed Sir Palomides whereas fortune led him, and within a month Sir Tristram was whole of his hurt. And then he took his horse, and rode from country to country, and all strange adventures he achieved wheresomever he rode; and always he enquired for Sir Palomides, but of all that quarter of summer Sir Tristram could never meet with Sir Palomides. But thus as Sir Tristram sought and enquired after Sir Palomides Sir Tristram achieved many great battles, wherethrough all the noise fell to Sir Tristram, and it ceased of Sir Launcelot; and therefore Sir Launcelot's brethren and his kinsmen would have slain Sir Tristram because of his fame. But when Sir Launcelot wist how his kinsmen were set, he said to them openly: Wit you well, that an the envy of you all be so hardy to wait upon my lord, Sir Tristram, with any hurt, shame, or villainy, as I am true knight I shall slay the best of you with mine own hands. Alas, fie for shame, should ye for his noble deeds await upon him to slay him. Jesu defend, said Launcelot, that ever any noble knight as Sir Tristram is should be destroyed with treason. Of this noise and fame sprang into Cornwall, and among them of Liones, whereof they were passing glad, and made great joy. And then they of Liones sent letters unto Sir Tristram of recommendation, and many great gifts to maintain Sir Tristram's estate; and ever, between, Sir Tristram resorted unto Joyous Gard whereas La Beale Isoud was, that loved him as her life.

Here endeth the tenth book which is of
Sir Tristram. And here followeth the eleventh
book which is of Sir Launcelot.

BOOK ELEVEN

CHAPTER I

How Sir Launcelot rode on his adventure, and how he holp
a dolorous lady from her pain, and how that
he fought with a dragon.

Now leave we Sir Tristram de Liones, and speak we of Sir Launcelot du Lake, and of Sir Galahad, Sir Launcelot's son, how he was gotten, and in what manner, as the book of French rehearseth. Afore the time that Sir Galahad was gotten or born, there came in an hermit unto King Arthur upon Whitsunday, as the knights sat at the Table Round. And when the hermit saw the Siege Perilous, he asked the king and all the knights why that siege was void. Sir Arthur and all the knights answered: There shall never none sit in that siege but one, but if he be destroyed. Then said the hermit: Wot ye what is he? Nay, said Arthur and all the knights, we wot not who is he that shall sit therein. Then wot I, said the hermit, for he that shall sit there is unborn and ungotten, and this same year he shall be gotten that shall sit there in that Siege Perilous, and he shall win the Sangreal. When this hermit had made this mention he departed from the court of King Arthur.

And then after this feast Sir Launcelot rode on his adventure, till on a time by adventure he passed over the pont of Corbin; and there he saw the fairest tower that ever he saw, and there-under was a fair town full of people; and all the people, men and women, cried at once: Welcome, Sir Launcelot du Lake, the flower of all knighthood, for by thee all we shall be holpen out of danger. What mean ye, said Sir Launcelot, that ye cry so upon me? Ah, fair knight, said they all, here is within this tower a dolorous lady that hath been there in pains many winters and days, for ever she boileth in scalding water; and but late, said all the people, Sir Gawaine was here and he might not help her, and so he left her in pain. So may I, said Sir Launcelot, leave her in pain as well as Sir Gawaine did. Nay, said the people, we know well that it is Sir Launcelot that shall deliver her. Well, said Launcelot, then shew me what I shall do.

Then they brought Sir Launcelot into the tower; and when he came to the chamber thereas this lady was, the doors of iron unlocked and unbolted. And so Sir Launcelot went into the chamber that was as hot as any stew. And there Sir Launcelot took the fairest lady by the hand that ever he saw, and she was naked as a needle; and by enchantment Queen Morgan le Fay and the Queen of Northgalis had put her there in that pains, because she was called the fairest lady of that country; and there she had been five years, and never might she be delivered out of her great pains unto the time the best knight of the world had taken her by the hand. Then the people brought her clothes. And when she was arrayed, Sir Launcelot thought she was the fairest lady of the world, but if it were Queen Guenever.

Then this lady said to Sir Launcelot: Sir, if it please you will ye go with me hereby into a chapel that we may give loving and thanking unto God? Madam, said Sir Launcelot, come on with me, I will go with you. So when they came there and gave thankings to God all the people, both learned and lewd, gave thankings unto God and him, and said: Sir knight, since ye have delivered this lady, ye shall deliver us from a serpent there is here in a tomb. Then Sir Launcelot took his shield and said: Bring me thither, and what I may do unto the pleasure of God and you I will do. So when Sir Launcelot came thither he saw written upon the tomb letters of gold that said thus: Here shall come a leopard of king's blood, and he shall slay this serpent, and this leopard shall engender a lion in this foreign country, the which lion shall pass all other knights. So then Sir Launcelot lift up the tomb, and there came out an horrible and a fiendly dragon, spitting fire out of his mouth. Then Sir Launcelot drew his sword and fought with the dragon long, and at the last with great pain Sir Launcelot slew that dragon. Therewithal came King Pelles, the good and noble knight, and saluted Sir Launcelot, and he him again. Fair knight, said the king, what is your name? I require you of your knighthood tell me!

CHAPTER II

How Sir Launcelot came to Pelles, and of the Sangreal,
and of Elaine, King Pelles' daughter.

Sir, said Launcelot, wit you well my name is Sir Launcelot du Lake. And my name is, said the king, Pelles, king of the foreign country, and cousin nigh unto Joseph of Armathie. And then either of them made much of other, and so they went into the castle to take their repast. And anon there came in a dove at a window, and in her mouth there seemed a little censer of gold. And therewithal there was such a savour as all the spicery of the world had been there. And forthwithal there was upon the table all manner of meats and drinks that they could think upon. So came in a damosel passing fair and young, and she bare a vessel of gold betwixt her hands; and thereto the king kneeled devoutly, and said his prayers, and so did all that were there. O Jesu, said Sir Launcelot, what may this mean? This is, said the king, the richest thing that any man hath living. And when this thing goeth about, the Round Table shall be broken; and wit thou well, said the king, this is the holy Sangreal that ye have here seen. So the king and Sir Launcelot led their life the most part of that day. And fain would King Pelles have found the mean to have had Sir Launcelot to have lain by his daughter, fair Elaine. And for this intent: the king knew well that Sir Launcelot should get a child upon his daughter, the which should be named Sir Galahad the good knight, by whom all the foreign country should be brought out of danger, and by him the Holy Greal should be achieved.

Then came forth a lady that hight Dame Brisen, and she said unto the king: Sir, wit ye well Sir Launcelot loveth no lady in the world but all only Queen Guenever; and therefore work ye by counsel, and I shall make him to lie with your daughter, and he shall not wit but that he lieth with Queen Guenever. O fair lady, Dame Brisen, said the king, hope ye to bring this about? Sir, said she, upon pain of my life let me deal; for this Brisen was one of the greatest enchantresses that was at that time in the world living. Then anon by Dame Brisen's wit she made one to come to Sir Launcelot that he knew well. And this man brought him a ring from Queen Guenever like as it had come from her, and such one as she was wont for the most part to wear; and when Sir Launcelot saw that token wit ye well he was never so fain. Where is my lady? said Sir Launcelot. In the Castle of Case, said the messenger, but five mile hence. Then Sir Launcelot thought to be there the same night. And then this Brisen by the commandment of King Pelles let send Elaine to this castle with twenty-five knights unto the Castle of Case. Then Sir Launcelot against night rode unto that castle, and there anon he was received worshipfully with such people, to his seeming, as were about Queen Guenever secret.

So when Sir Launcelot was alighted, he asked where the queen was. So Dame Brisen said she was in her bed; and then the people were avoided, and Sir Launcelot was led unto his chamber. And then Dame Brisen brought Sir Launcelot a cup full of wine; and anon as he had drunken that wine he was so assotted and mad that he might make no delay, but withouten any let he went to bed; and he weened that maiden Elaine had been Queen Guenever. Wit you well that Sir Launcelot was glad, and so was that lady Elaine that she had gotten Sir Launcelot in her arms. For well she knew that same night should be gotten upon her Galahad that should prove the best knight of the world; and so they lay together until underne of the morn; and all the windows and holes of that chamber were stopped that no manner of day might be seen. And then Sir Launcelot remembered him, and he arose up and went to the window.

CHAPTER III

How Sir Launcelot was displeased when he knew that he had lain by Dame Elaine, and how she was delivered of Galahad.

And anon as he had unshut the window the enchantment was gone; then he knew himself that he had done amiss. Alas, he said, that I have lived so long; now I am shamed. So then he gat his sword in his hand and said: Thou traitress, what art thou that I have lain by all this night? thou shalt die right here of my hands. Then this fair lady Elaine skipped out of her bed all naked, and kneeled down afore Sir

Launcelot, and said: Fair courteous knight, come of king's blood, I require you have mercy upon me, and as thou art renowned the most noble knight of the world, slay me not, for I have in my womb him by thee that shall be the most noblest knight of the world. Ah, false traitress, said Sir Launcelot, why hast thou betrayed me? anon tell me what thou art. Sir, she said, I am Elaine, the daughter of King Pelles. Well, said Sir Launcelot, I will forgive you this deed; and therewith he took her up in his arms, and kissed her, for she was as fair a lady, and thereto lusty and young, and as wise, as any was that time living. So God me help, said Sir Launcelot, I may not wite this to you; but her that made this enchantment upon me as between you and me, an I may find her, that same Lady Brisen, she shall lose her head for witchcrafts, for there was never knight deceived so as I am this night. And so Sir Launcelot arrayed him, and armed him, and took his leave mildly at that lady young Elaine, and so he departed. Then she said: My lord Sir Launcelot, I beseech you see me as soon as ye may, for I have obeyed me unto the prophecy that my father told me. And by his commandment to fulfil this prophecy I have given the greatest riches and the fairest flower that ever I had, and that is my maidenhood that I shall never have again; and therefore, gentle knight, owe me your goodwill.

And so Sir Launcelot arrayed him and was armed, and took his leave mildly at that young lady Elaine; and so he departed, and rode till he came to the Castle of Corbin, where her father was. And as fast as her time came she was delivered of a fair child, and they christened him Galahad; and wit ye well that child was well kept and well nourished, and he was named Galahad because Sir Launcelot was so named at the fountain stone; and after that the Lady of the Lake confirmed him Sir Launcelot du Lake.

Then after this lady was delivered and churched, there came a knight unto her, his name was Sir Bromel la Pleche, the which was a great lord; and he had loved that lady long, and he evermore desired her to wed her; and so by no mean she could put him off, till on a day she said to Sir Bromel: Wit thou well, sir knight, I will not love you, for my love is set upon the best knight of the world. Who is he? said Sir Bromel. Sir, she said, it is Sir Launcelot du Lake that I love and none other, and therefore woo me no longer. Ye say well, said Sir Bromel, and sithen ye have told me so much, ye shall have but little joy of Sir Launcelot, for I shall slay him wheresomever I meet him. Sir, said the Lady Elaine, do to him no treason. Wit ye well, my lady, said Bromel, and I promise you this twelvemonth I shall keep the pont of Corbin for Sir Launcelot's sake, that he shall neither come nor go unto you, but I shall meet with him.

CHAPTER IV

*How Sir Bors came to Dame Elaine and saw Galahad,
and how he was fed with the Sangreal.*

Then as it fell by fortune and adventure, Sir Bors de Ganis, that was nephew unto Sir Launcelot, came over that bridge; and there Sir Bromel and Sir Bors jousted, and Sir Bors smote Sir Bromel such a buffet that he bare him over his horse's croup. And then Sir Bromel, as an hardy knight, pulled out his sword, and dressed his shield to do battle with Sir Bors. And then Sir Bors alighted and avoided his horse, and there they dashed together many sad strokes; and long thus they fought, till at the last Sir Bromel was laid to the earth, and there Sir Bors began to unlace his helm to slay him. Then Sir Bromel cried Sir Bors mercy, and yielded him. Upon this covenant thou shalt have thy life, said Sir Bors, so thou go unto Sir Launcelot upon Whitsunday that next cometh, and yield thee unto him as knight recreant. I will do it, said Sir Bromel, and that he sware upon the cross of the sword. And so he let him depart, and Sir Bors rode unto King Pelles, that was within Corbin.

And when the king and Elaine his daughter wist that Sir Bors was nephew unto Sir Launcelot, they made him great cheer. Then said Dame Elaine: We marvel where Sir Launcelot is, for he came never here but once. Marvel not, said Sir Bors, for this half year he hath been in prison with Queen Morgan le Fay, King Arthur's sister. Alas, said Dame Elaine, that me repenteth. And ever Sir Bors beheld that child in her arms, and ever him seemed it was passing like Sir Launcelot. Truly, said Elaine, wit ye well this child he gat upon me. Then Sir Bors wept for joy, and he prayed to God it might prove as good a knight as his father was. And so came in a white dove, and she bare a little censer of gold in her mouth, and there was all manner of meats and drinks: and a maiden bare that Sangreal, and she said openly: Wit you well, Sir Bors, that this child is Galahad, that shall sit in the Siege Perilous, and achieve the Sangreal, and he shall be much better than ever was Sir Launcelot du Lake, that is his own father. And then they kneeled down and made their devotions, and there was such a savour as all the spicery in the world had been there. And when the dove took her flight, the maiden vanished with the Sangreal as she came.

Sir, said Sir Bors unto King Pelles, this castle may be named the Castle Adventurous, for here be many strange adventures. That is sooth, said the king, for well may this place be called the adventures place, for there come but few knights here that go away with any worship; be he never so strong, here he may be proved; and but late Sir Gawaine, the good knight, gat but little worship here. For I let you wit, said King Pelles, here shall no knight win no worship but if he be of worship himself and of good living, and that loveth God and dreadeth God, and else he getteth no worship here, be he never so hardy. That is wonderful thing, said Sir Bors. What ye mean in this country I wot not, for ye have many strange adventures, and therefore I will lie in this castle this night. Ye shall not do so, said King Pelles, by my counsel, for it is hard an ye escape without a shame. I shall take the adventure that will befall me, said Sir Bors. Then I counsel you, said the king, to be confessed clean. As for that, said Sir Bors, I will be shriven with a good will. So Sir Bors was confessed, and for all women Sir Bors was a virgin, save for one, that was the daughter of King Brangoris, and on her he gat a child that hight Elaine, and save for her Sir Bors was a clean maiden.

And so Sir Bors was led unto bed in a fair large chamber, and many doors were shut about the chamber. When Sir Bors espied all those doors, he avoided all the people, for he might have nobody with him; but in no wise Sir Bors would unarm him, but so he laid him down upon the bed. And right so he saw come in a light, that he might well see a spear great and long that came straight upon him pointling, and to Sir Bors seemed that the head of the spear brent like a taper. And anon, or Sir Bors wist, the spear head smote him into the shoulder an handbreadth in deepness, and that wound grieved Sir Bors passing sore. And then he laid him down again for pain; and anon therewithal there came a knight armed with his shield on his shoulder and his sword in his hand, and he bade Sir Bors: Arise, sir knight, and fight with me. I am sore hurt, he said, but yet I shall not fail thee. And then Sir Bors started up and dressed his shield; and then they lashed together mightily a great while; and at the last Sir Bors bare him backward until that he came unto a chamber door, and there that knight yede into that chamber and rested him a great while. And when he had reposed him he came out freshly again, and began new battle with Sir Bors mightily and strongly.

CHAPTER V

*How Sir Bors made Sir Pedivere to yield him,
and of marvellous adventures that he had,
and how he achieved them.*

Then Sir Bors thought he should no more go into that chamber to rest him, and so Sir Bors dressed him betwixt the knight and that chamber door, and there Sir Bors smote him down, and then that knight yielded him. What is your name? said Sir Bors. Sir, said he, my name is Pedivere of the Straight Marches. So Sir Bors made him to swear at Whitsunday next coming to be at the court of King Arthur, and yield him there as a prisoner as an overcome knight by the hands of Sir Bors. So thus departed Sir Pedivere of the Straight Marches. And then Sir Bors laid him down to rest, and then he heard and felt much noise in that chamber; and then Sir Bors espied that there came in, he wist not whether at the doors nor windows, shot of arrows and of quarrels so thick that he marvelled, and many fell upon him and hurt him in the bare places.

And then Sir Bors was ware where came in an hideous lion; so Sir Bors dressed him unto the lion, and anon the lion bereft him his shield, and with his sword Sir Bors smote off the lion's head. Right so Sir Bors forthwithal saw a dragon in the court passing horrible, and there seemed letters of gold written in his forehead; and Sir Bors thought that the letters made a signification of King Arthur. Right so there came an horrible leopard and an old, and there they fought long, and did great battle together. And at the last the dragon spit out of his mouth as it had been an hundred dragons; and lightly all the small dragons slew the old dragon and tare him all to pieces.

Anon withal there came an old man into the hall, and he sat him down in a fair chair, and there seemed to be two adders about his neck; and then the old man had an harp, and there he sang an old song how Joseph of Armathie came into this land. Then when he had sung, the old man bade Sir Bors go from thence. For here shall ye have no more adventures; and full worshipfully have ye done, and better shall ye do hereafter. And then Sir Bors seemed that there came the whitest dove with a little golden censer in her mouth. And anon therewithal the tempest ceased and passed, that afore was marvellous to hear. So was all that court full of good savours. Then Sir Bors saw four children bearing four fair tapers, and an old man in the midst of the children with a censer in his own hand, and a spear in his other hand, and that spear was called the Spear of Vengeance.

CHAPTER VI

How Sir Bors departed; and how Sir Launcelot was rebuked of Queen Guenever, and of his excuse.

Now, said that old man to Sir Bors, go ye to your cousin, Sir Launcelot, and tell him of this adventure the which had been most convenient for him of all earthly knights; but sin is so foul in him he may not achieve such holy deeds, for had not been his sin he had passed all the knights that ever were in his days; and tell thou Sir Launcelot, of all worldly adventures he passeth in manhood and prowess all other, but in this spiritual matters he shall have many his better. And then Sir Bors saw four gentlewomen come by him, purely beseen: and he saw where that they entered into a chamber where was great light as it were a summer light; and the women kneeled down afore an altar of silver with four pillars, and as it had been a bishop kneeled down afore that table of silver. And as Sir Bors looked over his head he saw a sword like silver, naked, hoving over his head, and the clearness thereof smote so in his eyes that as at that time Sir Bors was blind; and there he heard a voice that said: Go hence, thou Sir Bors, for as yet thou art not worthy for to be in this place. And then he yede backward to his bed till on the morn. And on the morn King Pelles made great joy of Sir Bors; and then he departed and rode to Camelot, and there he found Sir Launcelot du

Lake, and told him of the adventures that he had seen with King Pelles at Corbin.

So the noise sprang in Arthur's court that Launcelot had gotten a child upon Elaine, the daughter of King Pelles, wherefore Queen Guenever was wroth, and gave many rebukes to Sir Launcelot, and called him false knight. And then Sir Launcelot told the queen all, and how he was made to lie by her by enchantment in likeness of the queen. So the queen held Sir Launcelot excused. And as the book saith, King Arthur had been in France, and had made war upon the mighty King Claudas, and had won much of his lands. And when the king was come again he let cry a great feast, that all lords and ladies of all England should be there, but if it were such as were rebellious against him.

CHAPTER VII

How Dame Elaine, Galahad's mother, came in great estate
unto Camelot, and how Sir Launcelot behaved him there.

And when Dame Elaine, the daughter of King Pelles, heard of this feast she went to her father and required him that he would give her leave to ride to that feast. The king answered: I will well ye go thither, but in any wise as ye love me and will have my blessing, that ye be well beseen in the richest wise; and look that ye spare not for no cost; ask and ye shall have all that you needeth. Then by the advice of Dame Brisen, her maiden, all thing was apparelled unto the purpose, that there was never no lady more richlier beseen. So she rode with twenty knights, and ten ladies, and gentlewomen, to the number of an hundred horses. And when she came to Camelot, King Arthur and Queen Guenever said, and all the knights, that Dame Elaine was the fairest and the best beseen lady that ever was seen in that court. And anon as King Arthur wist that she was come he met her and saluted her, and so did the most part of all the knights of the Round Table, both Sir Tristram, Sir Bleoberis, and Sir Gawaine, and many more that I will not rehearse. But when Sir Launcelot saw her he was so ashamed, and that because he drew his sword on the morn when he had lain by her, that he would not salute her nor speak to her; and yet Sir Launcelot thought she was the fairest woman that ever he saw in his life-days.

But when Dame Elaine saw Sir Launcelot that would not speak unto her she was so heavy that she weened her heart would have to-brast; for wit you well, out of measure she loved him. And then Elaine said unto her woman, Dame Brisen: The unkindness of Sir Launcelot slayeth me near. Ah, peace, madam, said Dame Brisen, I will undertake that this night he shall lie with you, an ye would hold you still. That were me liefer, said Dame Elaine, than all the gold that is above the earth. Let me deal, said Dame Brisen. So when Elaine was brought unto Queen Guenever either made other good cheer by countenance, but nothing with hearts. But all men and women spake of the beauty of Dame Elaine, and of her great riches.

Then, at night, the queen commanded that Dame Elaine should sleep in a chamber nigh her chamber, and all under one roof; and so it was done as the queen commanded. Then the queen sent for Sir Launcelot and bade him come to her chamber that night: Or else I am sure, said the queen, that ye will go to your lady's bed, Dame Elaine, by whom ye gat Galahad. Ah, madam, said Sir Launcelot, never say ye so, for that I did was against my will. Then, said the queen, look that ye come to me when I send for you. Madam, said Launcelot, I shall not fail you, but I shall be ready at your commandment. This bargain was soon done and made between them, but Dame Brisen knew it by her crafts, and told it to her lady, Dame Elaine. Alas, said she, how shall I do? Let me deal, said Dame Brisen, for I shall bring him by the hand even to your bed, and he shall ween that I am Queen Guenever's messenger. Now well is me, said Dame Elaine, for all the world I love not so much as I do Sir Launcelot.

CHAPTER VIII

*How Dame Brisen by enchantment brought Sir Launcelot to
Dame Elaine's bed, and how Queen Guenever rebuked him.*

So when time came that all folks were abed, Dame Brisen came to Sir
Launcelot's bed's side and said: Sir Launcelot du Lake, sleep you? My
lady, Queen Guenever, lieth and awaiteth upon you. O my fair lady,
said Sir Launcelot, I am ready to go with you where ye will have me.
So Sir Launcelot threw upon him a long gown, and his sword in his
hand; and then Dame Brisen took him by the finger and led him to
her lady's bed, Dame Elaine; and then she departed and left them in
bed together. Wit you well the lady was glad, and so was Sir
Launcelot, for he weened that he had had another in his arms.

Now leave we them kissing and clipping, as was kindly thing; and
now speak we of Queen Guenever that sent one of her women unto
Sir Launcelot's bed; and when she came there she found the bed
cold, and he was away; so she came to the queen and told her all.
Alas, said the queen, where is that false knight become? Then the
queen was nigh out of her wit, and then she writhed and weltered as
a mad woman, and might not sleep a four or five hours. Then Sir
Launcelot had a condition that he used of custom, he would clatter in
his sleep, and speak oft of his lady, Queen Guenever. So as Sir
Launcelot had waked as long as it had pleased him, then by course of
kind he slept, and Dame Elaine both. And in his sleep he talked and
clattered as a jay, of the love that had been betwixt Queen Guenever
and him. And so as he talked so loud the queen heard him thereas she
lay in her chamber; and when she heard him so clatter she was nigh
wood and out of her mind, and for anger and pain wist not what to
do. And then she coughed so loud that Sir Launcelot awaked, and he
knew her hemming. And then he knew well that he lay not by the
queen; and therewith he leapt out of his bed as he had been a wood
man, in his shirt, and the queen met him in the floor; and thus she
said: False traitor knight that thou art, look thou never abide in my
court, and avoid my chamber, and not so hardy, thou false traitor
knight that thou art, that ever thou come in my sight. Alas, said Sir

Launcelot; and therewith he took such an heartly sorrow at her words that he fell down to the floor in a swoon. And therewithal Queen Guenever departed. And when Sir Launcelot awoke of his swoon, he leapt out at a bay window into a garden, and there with thorns he was all to-scratched in his visage and his body; and so he ran forth he wist not whither, and was wild wood as ever was man; and so he ran two year, and never man might have grace to know him.

CHAPTER IX

How Dame Elaine was commanded by Queen Guenever to avoid the court, and how Sir Launcelot became mad.

Now turn we unto Queen Guenever and to the fair Lady Elaine, that when Dame Elaine heard the queen so to rebuke Sir Launcelot, and also she saw how he swooned, and how he leaped out at a bay window, then she said unto Queen Guenever: Madam, ye are greatly to blame for Sir Launcelot, for now have ye lost him, for I saw and heard by his countenance that he is mad for ever. Alas, madam, ye do great sin, and to yourself great dishonour, for ye have a lord of your own, and therefore it is your part to love him; for there is no queen in this world hath such another king as ye have. And, if ye were not, I might have the love of my lord Sir Launcelot; and cause I have to love him for he had my maidenhood, and by him I have borne a fair son, and his name is Galahad, and he shall be in his time the best knight of the world. Dame Elaine, said the queen, when it is daylight I charge you and command you to avoid my court; and for the love ye owe unto Sir Launcelot discover not his counsel, for an ye do, it will be his death. As for that, said Dame Elaine, I dare undertake he is marred for ever, and that have ye made; for ye, nor I, are like to rejoice him; for he made the most piteous groans when he leapt out at yonder bay window that ever I heard man make. Alas, said fair Elaine, and alas, said the Queen Guenever, for now I wot well we have lost him for ever.

So on the morn Dame Elaine took her leave to depart, and she would no longer abide. Then King Arthur brought her on her way with mo than an hundred knights through a forest. And by the way she told Sir Bors de Ganis all how it betid that same night, and how Sir Launcelot leapt out at a window, araged out of his wit. Alas, said Sir Bors, where is my lord, Sir Launcelot, become? Sir, said Elaine, I wot ne'er. Alas, said Sir Bors, betwixt you both ye have destroyed that good knight. As for me, said Dame Elaine, I said never nor did never thing that should in any wise displease him, but with the rebuke that Queen Guenever gave him I saw him swoon to the earth; and when he awoke he took his sword in his hand, naked save his shirt, and leapt out at a window with the grisliest groan that ever I heard man make. Now farewell, Dame Elaine, said Sir Bors, and hold my lord Arthur with a tale as long as ye can, for I will turn again to Queen Guenever and give her a hete; and I require you, as ever ye will have my service, make good watch and espy if ever ye may see my lord Sir Launcelot. Truly, said fair Elaine, I shall do all that I may do, for as fain would I know and wit where he is become, as you, or any of his kin, or Queen Guenever; and cause great enough have I thereto as well as any other. And wit ye well, said fair Elaine to Sir Bors, I would lose my life for him rather than he should be hurt; but alas, I cast me never for to see him, and the chief causer of this is Dame Guenever. Madam, said Dame Brisen, the which had made the enchantment before betwixt Sir Launcelot and her, I pray you heartily, let Sir Bors depart, and hie him with all his might as fast as he may to seek Sir Launcelot, for I warn you he is clean out of his mind; and yet he shall be well holpen an but by miracle.

Then wept Dame Elaine, and so did Sir Bors de Ganis; and so they departed, and Sir Bors rode straight unto Queen Guenever. And when she saw Sir Bors she wept as she were wood. Fie on your weeping, said Sir Bors de Ganis, for ye weep never but when there is no bote. Alas, said Sir Bors, that ever Sir Launcelot's kin saw you, for now have ye lost the best knight of our blood, and he that was all our leader and our succour; and I dare say and make it good that all kings, christian nor heathen, may not find such a knight, for to speak of his nobleness and courtesy, with his beauty and his gentleness. Alas, said Sir Bors, what shall we do that be of his blood? Alas, said Sir Ector de Maris. Alas, said Lionel.

CHAPTER X

What sorrow Queen Guenever made for Sir Launcelot,
and how he was sought by knights of his kin.

And when the queen heard them say so she fell to the earth in a dead
swoon. And then Sir Bors took her up, and dawed her; and when she
was awaked she kneeled afore the three knights, and held up both her
hands, and besought them to seek him. And spare not for no goods
but that he be found, for I wot he is out of his mind. And Sir Bors,
Sir Ector, and Sir Lionel departed from the queen, for they might not
abide no longer for sorrow. And then the queen sent them treasure
enough for their expenses, and so they took their horses and their
armour, and departed. And then they rode from country to country,
in forests, and in wilderness, and in wastes; and ever they laid watch
both at forests and at all manner of men as they rode, to hearken and
spere after him, as he that was a naked man, in his shirt, with a sword
in his hand. And thus they rode nigh a quarter of a year, endlong and
overthwart, in many places, forests and wilderness, and oft-times
were evil lodged for his sake; and yet for all their labour and seeking
could they never hear word of him. And wit you well these three
knights were passing sorry.

Then at the last Sir Bors and his fellows met with a knight that
hight Sir Melion de Tartare. Now fair knight, said Sir Bors, whither
be ye away? for they knew either other afore time. Sir, said Melion, I
am in the way toward the court of King Arthur. Then we pray you,
said Sir Bors, that ye will tell my lord Arthur, and my lady, Queen
Guenever, and all the fellowship of the Round Table, that we cannot
in no wise hear tell where Sir Launcelot is become. Then Sir Melion
departed from them, and said that he would tell the king, and the
queen, and all the fellowship of the Round Table, as they had desired
him. So when Sir Melion came to the court of King Arthur he told
the king, and the queen, and all the fellowship of the Round Table,
what Sir Bors had said of Sir Launcelot. Then Sir Gawaine, Sir
Uwaine, Sir Sagramore le Desirous, Sir Aglovale, and Sir Percivale de
Galis took upon them by the great desire of King Arthur, and in

especial by the queen, to seek throughout all England, Wales, and Scotland, to find Sir Launcelot, and with them rode eighteen knights mo to bear them fellowship; and wit ye well, they lacked no manner of spending; and so were they three and twenty knights.

Now turn we to Sir Launcelot, and speak we of his care and woe, and what pain he there endured; for cold, hunger, and thirst, he had plenty. And thus as these noble knights rode together, they by one assent departed, and then they rode by two, by three, and by four, and by five, and ever they assigned where they should meet. And so Sir Aglovale and Sir Percivale rode together unto their mother that was a queen in those days. And when she saw her two sons, for joy she wept tenderly. And then she said: Ah, my dear sons, when your father was slain he left me four sons, of the which now be twain slain. And for the death of my noble son, Sir Lamorak, shall my heart never be glad. And then she kneeled down upon her knees to-fore Aglovale and Sir Percivale, and besought them to abide at home with her. Ah, sweet mother, said Sir Percivale, we may not, for we be come of king's blood of both parties, and therefore, mother, it is our kind to haunt arms and noble deeds. Alas, my sweet sons, then she said, for your sakes I shall lose my liking and lust, and then wind and weather I may not endure, what for the death of your father, King Pellinore, that was shamefully slain by the hands of Sir Gawaine, and his brother, Sir Gaheris: and they slew him not manly but by treason. Ah, my dear sons, this is a piteous complaint for me of your father's death, considering also the death of Sir Lamorak, that of knighthood had but few fellows. Now, my dear sons, have this in your mind. Then there was but weeping and sobbing in the court when they should depart, and she fell a-swooning in midst of the court.

CHAPTER XI

How a servant of Sir Aglovale's was slain, and what vengeance Sir Aglovale and Sir Percivale did therefore.

And when she was awaked she sent a squire after them with spending enough. And so when the squire had overtaken them, they would not suffer him to ride with them, but sent him home again to comfort their mother, praying her meekly of her blessing. And so this squire was benighted, and by misfortune he happened to come to a castle where dwelled a baron. And so when the squire was come into the castle, the lord asked him from whence he came, and whom he served. My lord, said the squire, I serve a good knight that is called Sir Aglovale: the squire said it to good intent, weening unto him to have been more forborne for Sir Aglovale's sake, than he had said he had served the queen, Aglovale's mother. Well, my fellow, said the lord of that castle, for Sir Aglovale's sake thou shalt have evil lodging, for Sir Aglovale slew my brother, and therefore thou shalt die on part of payment. And then that lord commanded his men to have him away and slay him; and so they did, and so pulled him out of the castle, and there they slew him without mercy.

Right so on the morn came Sir Aglovale and Sir Percivale riding by a churchyard, where men and women were busy, and beheld the dead squire, and they thought to bury him. What is there, said Sir Aglovale, that ye behold so fast? A good man stert forth and said: Fair knight, here lieth a squire slain shamefully this night. How was he slain, fair fellow? said Sir Aglovale. My fair sir, said the man, the lord of this castle lodged this squire this night; and because he said he was servant unto a good knight that is with King Arthur, his name is Sir Aglovale, therefore the lord commanded to slay him, and for this cause is he slain. Gramercy, said Sir Aglovale, and ye shall see his death revenged lightly; for I am that same knight for whom this squire was slain.

Then Sir Aglovale called unto him Sir Percivale, and bade him alight lightly; and so they alighted both, and betook their horses to their men, and so they yede on foot into the castle. And all so soon as they were within the castle gate Sir Aglovale bade the porter: Go thou unto thy lord and tell him that I am Sir Aglovale for whom this squire was slain this night. Anon the porter told this to his lord, whose name was Goodewin. Anon he armed him, and then he came into the court and said: Which of you is Sir Aglovale? Here I am, said Aglovale: for what cause slewest thou this night my mother's squire? I slew him, said Sir Goodewin, because of thee, for thou slewest my brother, Sir Gawdelin. As for thy brother, said Sir Aglovale, I avow it I slew him, for he was a false knight and a betrayer of ladies and of good knights; and for the death of my squire thou shalt die. I defy thee, said Sir Goodewin. Then they lashed together as eagerly as it had been two lions, and Sir Percivale he fought with all the remnant that would fight. And within a while Sir Percivale had slain all that would withstand him; for Sir Percivale dealt so his strokes that were so rude that there durst no man abide him. And within a while Sir Aglovale had Sir Goodewin at the earth, and there he unlaced his helm, and struck off his head. And then they departed and took their horses; and then they let carry the dead squire unto a priory, and there they interred him.

CHAPTER XII

How Sir Percivale departed secretly from his brother,
and how he loosed a knight bound with a chain,
and of other doings.

And when this was done they rode into many countries, ever inquiring after Sir Launcelot, but never they could hear of him; and at the last they came to a castle that hight Cardican, and there Sir Percivale and Sir Aglovale were lodged together. And privily about midnight Sir Percivale came to Aglovale's squire and said: Arise and make thee ready, for ye and I will ride away secretly. Sir, said the squire, I would full fain ride with you where ye would have me, but an my lord, your brother, take me he will slay me. As for that care thou not, for I shall be thy warrant.

And so Sir Percivale rode till it was after noon, and then he came upon a bridge of stone, and there he found a knight that was bound with a chain fast about the waist unto a pillar of stone. O fair knight, said that bound knight, I require thee loose me of my bonds. What knight are ye, said Sir Percivale, and for what cause are ye so bound? Sir, I shall tell you, said that knight: I am a knight of the Table Round, and my name is Sir Persides; and thus by adventure I came this way, and here I lodged in this castle at the bridge foot, and therein dwelleth an uncourteous lady; and because she proffered me to be her paramour, and I refused her, she set her men upon me suddenly or ever I might come to my weapon; and thus they bound me, and here I wot well I shall die but if some man of worship break my bands. Be ye of good cheer, said Sir Percivale, and because ye are a knight of the Round Table as well as I, I trust to God to break your bands. And therewith Sir Percivale pulled out his sword and struck at the chain with such a might that he cut a-two the chain, and through Sir Persides' hauberk and hurt him a little. O Jesu, said Sir Persides, that was a mighty stroke as ever I felt one, for had not the chain been ye had slain me.

And therewithal Sir Persides saw a knight coming out of a castle all that ever he might fling. Beware, sir, said Sir Persides, yonder cometh a man that will have ado with you. Let him come, said Sir Percivale. And so he met with that knight in midst of the bridge; and Sir Percivale gave him such a buffet that he smote him quite from his horse and over a part of the bridge, that, had not been a little vessel under the bridge, that knight had been drowned. And then Sir Percivale took the knight's horse and made Sir Persides to mount up him; and so they rode unto the castle, and bade the lady deliver Sir Persides' servants, or else he would slay all that ever he found; and so for fear she delivered them all. Then was Sir Percivale ware of a lady that stood in that tower. Ah, madam, said Sir Percivale, what use and custom is that in a lady to destroy good knights but if they will be your paramour? Forsooth this is a shameful custom of a lady, and if I had not a great matter in my hand I should fordo your evil customs.

And so Sir Persides brought Sir Percivale unto his own castle, and there he made him great cheer all that night. And on the morn, when Sir Percivale had heard mass and broken his fast, he bade Sir Persides ride unto King Arthur: And tell the king how that ye met with me; and tell my brother, Sir Aglovale, how I rescued you; and bid him seek not after me, for I am in the quest to seek Sir Launcelot du Lake, and though he seek me he shall not find me; and tell him I will never see him, nor the court, till I have found Sir Launcelot. Also tell Sir Kay the Seneschal, and to Sir Mordred, that I trust to Jesu to be of as great worthiness as either of them, for tell them I shall never forget their mocks and scorns that they did to me that day that I was made knight; and tell them I will never see that court till men speak more worship of me than ever men did of any of them both. And so Sir Persides departed from Sir Percivale, and then he rode unto King Arthur, and told there of Sir Percivale. And when Sir Aglovale heard him speak of his brother Sir Percivale, he said: He departed from me unkindly.

CHAPTER XIII

How Sir Percivale met with Sir Ector, and how they fought long, and each had almost slain other.

Sir, said Sir Persides, on my life he shall prove a noble knight as any now is living. And when he saw Sir Kay and Sir Mordred, Sir Persides said thus: My fair lords both, Sir Percivale greeteth you well both, and he sent you word by me that he trusteth to God or ever he come to the court again to be of as great noblesse as ever were ye both, and mo men to speak of his noblesse than ever they did of you. It may well be, said Sir Kay and Sir Mordred, but at that time when he was made knight he was full unlike to prove a good knight. As for that, said King Arthur, he must needs prove a good knight, for his father and his brethren were noble knights.

And now will we turn unto Sir Percivale that rode long; and in a forest he met a knight with a broken shield and a broken helm; and as soon as either saw other readily they made them ready to joust, and so hurtled together with all the might of their horses, and met together so hard, that Sir Percivale was smitten to the earth. And then Sir Percivale arose lightly, and cast his shield on his shoulder and drew his sword, and bade the other knight: Alight, and do we battle unto the uttermost. Will ye more? said that knight. And therewith he alighted, and put his horse from him; and then they came together an easy pace, and there they lashed together with noble swords, and sometime they struck and sometime they foined, and either gave other many great wounds. Thus they fought near half a day, and never rested but right little, and there was none of them both that had less wounds than fifteen, and they bled so much that it was marvel they stood on their feet. But this knight that fought with Sir Percivale was a proved knight and a wise-fighting knight, and Sir Percivale was young and strong, not knowing in fighting as the other was

Then Sir Percivale spoke first, and said: Sir knight, hold thy hand a while still, for we have fought for a simple matter and quarrel overlong, and therefore I require thee tell me thy name, for I was never or this time matched. So God me help, said that knight, and never or this time was there never knight that wounded me so sore as thou hast done, and yet have I fought in many battles; and now shalt thou wit that I am a knight of the Table Round, and my name is Sir Ector de Maris, brother unto the good knight, Sir Launcelot du Lake. Alas, said Sir Percivale, and my name is Sir Percivale de Galis that hath made my quest to seek Sir Launcelot, and now I am siker that I shall never finish my quest, for ye have slain me with your hands. It is not so, said Sir Ector, for I am slain by your hands, and may not live. Therefore I require you, said Sir Ector unto Sir Percivale, ride ye hereby to a priory, and bring me a priest that I may receive my Saviour, for I may not live. And when ye come to the court of King Arthur tell not my brother, Sir Launcelot, how that ye slew me, for then he would be your mortal enemy, but ye may say that I was slain in my quest as I sought him. Alas, said Sir Percivale, ye say that never will be, for I am so faint for bleeding that I may unnethe stand, how should I then take my horse?

CHAPTER XIV

How by miracle they were both made whole by the coming of the holy vessel of Sangreal.

Then they made both great dole out of measure. This will not avail, said Sir Percivale. And then he kneeled down and made his prayer devoutly unto Almighty Jesu, for he was one of the best knights of the world that at that time was, in whom the very faith stood most in. Right so there came by the holy vessel of the Sangreal with all manner of sweetness and savour; but they could not readily see who that bare that vessel, but Sir Percivale had a glimmering of the vessel and of the maiden that bare it, for he was a perfect clean maiden; and forthwithal they both were as whole of hide and limb as ever they were in their life-days: then they gave thankings to God with great mildness. O Jesu, said Sir Percivale, what may this mean, that we be thus healed, and right now we were at the point of dying? I wot full well, said Sir Ector, what it is; it is an holy vessel that is borne by a maiden, and therein is part of the holy blood of our Lord Jesu Christ, blessed mote he be. But it may not be seen, said Sir Ector, but if it be by a perfect man. So God me help, said Sir Percivale, I saw a damosel, as me thought, all in white, with a vessel in both her hands, and forthwithal I was whole.

So then they took their horses and their harness, and amended their harness as well as they might that was broken; and so they mounted upon their horses, and rode talking together. And there Sir Ector de Maris told Sir Percivale how he had sought his brother, Sir Launcelot, long, and never could hear witting of him: In many strange adventures have I been in this quest. And so either told other of their adventures.

**Here endeth the eleventh book.
And here followeth the twelfth book.**

BOOK TWELVE

CHAPTER I

*How Sir Launcelot in his madness took a sword and
fought with a knight, and leapt in a bed.*

And now leave we of a while of Sir Ector and of Sir Percivale, and
speak we of Sir Launcelot that suffered and endured many sharp
showers, that ever ran wild wood from place to place, and lived by
fruit and such as he might get, and drank water two year; and other
clothing had he but little but his shirt and his breech. Thus as Sir
Launcelot wandered here and there he came in a fair meadow where
he found a pavilion; and there by, upon a tree, there hung a white
shield, and two swords hung thereby, and two spears leaned there by
a tree. And when Sir Launcelot saw the swords, anon he leapt to the
one sword, and took it in his hand, and drew it out. And then he
lashed at the shield, that all the meadow rang of the dints, that he gave
such a noise as ten knights had foughten together.

Then came forth a dwarf, and leapt unto Sir Launcelot, and would
have had the sword out of his hand. And then Sir Launcelot took him
by the both shoulders and threw him to the ground upon his neck,
that he had almost broken his neck; and therewithal the dwarf cried
help. Then came forth a likely knight, and well apparelled in scarlet
furred with minever. And anon as he saw Sir Launcelot he deemed
that he should be out of his wit. And then he said with fair speech:
Good man, lay down that sword, for as meseemeth thou hadst more
need of sleep and of warm clothes than to wield that sword. As for
that, said Sir Launcelot, come not too nigh, for an thou do, wit thou
well I will slay thee.

And when the knight of the pavilion saw that, he stert backward
within the pavilion. And then the dwarf armed him lightly; and so
the knight thought by force and might to take the sword from Sir

Launcelot, and so he came stepping out; and when Sir Launcelot saw
him come so all armed with his sword in his hand, then Sir Launcelot
flew to him with such a might, and hit him upon the helm such a
buffet, that the stroke troubled his brains, and therewith the sword
brake in three. And the knight fell to the earth as he had been dead,
the blood brasting out of his mouth, the nose, and the ears. And then
Sir Launcelot ran into the pavilion, and rushed even into the warm
bed; and there was a lady in that bed, and she gat her smock, and ran
out of the pavilion. And when she saw her lord lie at the ground like
to be dead, then she cried and wept as she had been mad. Then with
her noise the knight awaked out of his swoon, and looked up weakly
with his eyes; and then he asked her, where was that mad man that
had given him such a buffet: For such a buffet had I never of man's
hand. Sir, said the dwarf, it is not worship to hurt him, for he is a man
out of his wit; and doubt ye not he hath been a man of great worship,
and for some heartly sorrow that he hath taken, he is fallen mad; and
me beseemeth, said the dwarf, he resembleth much unto Sir
Launcelot, for him I saw at the great tournament beside Lonazep.
Jesu defend, said that knight, that ever that noble knight, Sir
Launcelot, should be in such a plight; but whatsomever he be, said
that knight, harm will I none do him: and this knight's name was
Bliant. Then he said unto the dwarf: Go thou fast on horseback, unto
my brother Sir Selivant, that is at the Castle Blank, and tell him of
mine adventure, and bid him bring with him an horse litter, and then
will we bear this knight unto my castle.

CHAPTER II

*How Sir Launcelot was carried in an horse litter, and how
Sir Launcelot rescued Sir Bliant, his host.*

So the dwarf rode fast, and he came again and brought Sir Selivant
with him, and six men with an horse litter; and so they took up the
feather bed with Sir Launcelot, and so carried all away with them
unto the Castle Blank, and he never awaked till he was within the
castle. And then they bound his hands and his feet, and gave him
good meats and good drinks, and brought him again to his strength

and his fairness; but in his wit they could not bring him again, nor to know himself. Thus was Sir Launcelot there more than a year and a half, honestly arrayed and fair faren withal.

Then upon a day this lord of that castle, Sir Bliant, took his arms, on horseback, with a spear, to seek adventures. And as he rode in a forest there met with him two knights adventurous, the one was Breuse Saunce Pité, and his brother, Sir Bertelot; and these two ran both at once upon Sir Bliant, and brake their spears upon his body. And then they drew out swords and made great battle, and fought long together. But at the last Sir Bliant was sore wounded, and felt himself faint; and then he fled on horseback toward his castle. And as they came hurling under the castle whereas Sir Launcelot lay in a window, [he] saw how two knights laid upon Sir Bliant with their swords. And when Sir Launcelot saw that, yet as wood as he was he was sorry for his lord, Sir Bliant. And then Sir Launcelot brake the chains from his legs and off his arms, and in the breaking he hurt his hands sore; and so Sir Launcelot ran out at a postern, and there he met with the two knights that chased Sir Bliant; and there he pulled down Sir Bertelot with his bare hands from his horse, and therewithal he wrothe his sword out of his hand; and so he leapt unto Sir Breuse, and gave him such a buffet upon the head that he tumbled backward over his horse's croup. And when Sir Bertelot saw there his brother have such a fall, he gat a spear in his hand, and would have run Sir Launcelot through: that saw Sir Bliant, and struck off the hand of Sir Bertelot. And then Sir Breuse and Sir Bertelot gat their horses and fled away.

When Sir Selivant came and saw what Sir Launcelot had done for his brother, then he thanked God, and so did his brother, that ever they did him any good. But when Sir Bliant saw that Sir Launcelot was hurt with the breaking of his irons, then was he heavy that ever he bound him. Bind him no more, said Sir Selivant, for he is happy and gracious. Then they made great joy of Sir Launcelot, and they bound him no more; and so he abode there an half year and more. And on the morn early Sir Launcelot was ware where came a great boar with many hounds nigh him. But the boar was so big there might no hounds tear him; and the hunters came after, blowing their horns, both upon horseback and some upon foot; and then Sir Launcelot was ware where one alighted and tied his horse to a tree, and leaned his spear against the tree.

CHAPTER III

*How Sir Launcelot fought against a boar and slew him, and
how he was hurt, and brought unto an hermitage.*

So came Sir Launcelot and found the horse bounden till a tree, and a
spear leaning against a tree, and a sword tied to the saddle bow; and
then Sir Launcelot leapt into the saddle and gat that spear in his hand,
and then he rode after the boar; and then Sir Launcelot was ware
where the boar set his arse to a tree fast by an hermitage. Then Sir
Launcelot ran at the boar with his spear, and therewith the boar
turned him nimbly, and rove out the lungs and the heart of the horse,
so that Launcelot fell to the earth; and, or ever Sir Launcelot might
get from the horse, the boar rove him on the brawn of the thigh up
to the hough bone. And then Sir Launcelot was wroth, and up he gat
upon his feet, and drew his sword, and he smote off the boar's head at
one stroke. And therewithal came out the hermit, and saw him have
such a wound. Then the hermit came to Sir Launcelot and
bemoaned him, and would have had him home unto his hermitage;
but when Sir Launcelot heard him speak, he was so wroth with his
wound that he ran upon the hermit to have slain him, and the hermit
ran away. And when Sir Launcelot might not overget him, he threw
his sword after him, for Sir Launcelot might go no further for
bleeding; then the hermit turned again, and asked Sir Launcelot how
he was hurt. Fellow, said Sir Launcelot, this boar hath bitten me sore.
Then come with me, said the hermit, and I shall heal you. Go thy
way, said Sir Launcelot, and deal not with me.

Then the hermit ran his way, and there he met with a good knight
with many men. Sir, said the hermit, here is fast by my place the
goodliest man that ever I saw, and he is sore wounded with a boar,
and yet he hath slain the boar. But well I wot, said the hermit, and he
be not holpen, that goodly man shall die of that wound, and that
were great pity. Then that knight at the desire of the hermit gat a cart,
and in that cart that knight put the boar and Sir Launcelot, for Sir
Launcelot was so feeble that they might right easily deal with him;
and so Sir Launcelot was brought unto the hermitage, and there the

hermit healed him of his wound. But the hermit might not find Sir Launcelot's sustenance, and so he impaired and waxed feeble, both of his body and of his wit: for the default of his sustenance he waxed more wooder than he was aforehand.

And then upon a day Sir Launcelot ran his way into the forest; and by adventure he came to the city of Corbin, where Dame Elaine was, that bare Galahad, Sir Launcelot's son. And so when he was entered into the town he ran through the town to the castle; and then all the young men of that city ran after Sir Launcelot, and there they threw turves at him, and gave him many sad strokes. And ever as Sir Launcelot might overreach any of them, he threw them so that they would never come in his hands no more; for of some he brake the legs and the arms, and so fled into the castle; and then came out knights and squires and rescued Sir Launcelot. And when they beheld him and looked upon his person, they thought they saw never so goodly a man. And when they saw so many wounds upon him, all they deemed that he had been a man of worship. And then they ordained him clothes to his body, and straw underneath him, and a little house. And then every day they would throw him meat, and set him drink, but there was but few would bring him meat to his hands.

<h2 style="text-align:center">CHAPTER IV</h2>

How Sir Launcelot was known by Dame Elaine, and was borne into a chamber and after healed by the Sangreal.

So it befell that King Pelles had a nephew, his name was Castor; and so he desired of the king to be made knight, and so at the request of this Castor the king made him knight at the feast of Candlemas. And when Sir Castor was made knight, that same day he gave many gowns. And then Sir Castor sent for the fool – that was Sir Launcelot. And when he was come afore Sir Castor, he gave Sir Launcelot a robe of scarlet and all that longed unto him. And when Sir Launcelot was so arrayed like a knight, he was the seemliest man in all the court, and none so well made. So when he saw his time he went into the garden, and there Sir Launcelot laid him down by a well and slept. And so at-after noon Dame Elaine and her maidens came into the garden to play them; and as they roamed up and down one of Dame Elaine's maidens espied where lay a goodly man by the well sleeping, and anon showed him to Dame Elaine. Peace, said Dame Elaine, and say no word: and then she brought Dame Elaine where he lay. And when that she beheld him, anon she fell in remembrance of him, and knew him verily for Sir Launcelot; and therewithal she fell a-weeping so heartily that she sank even to the earth; and when she had thus wept a great while, then she arose and called her maidens and said she was sick.

And so she yede out of the garden, and she went straight to her father, and there she took him apart by herself; and then she said: O father, now have I need of your help, and but if that ye help me farewell my good days for ever. What is that, daughter? said King Pelles. Sir, she said, thus is it: in your garden I went for to sport, and there, by the well, I found Sir Launcelot du Lake sleeping. I may not believe that, said King Pelles. Sir, she said, truly he is there, and meseemeth he should be distract out of his wit. Then hold you still, said the king, and let me deal. Then the king called to him such as he most trusted, a four persons, and Dame Elaine, his daughter. And when they came to the well and beheld Sir Launcelot, anon Dame Brisen knew him. Sir, said Dame Brisen, we must be wise how we deal with him, for this knight is out of his mind, and if we awake him rudely what he will do we all know not; but ye shall abide, and I shall throw such an enchantment upon him that he shall not awake within the space of an hour; and so she did.

Then within a little while after, the king commanded that all people should avoid, that none should be in that way thereas the king would come. And so when this was done, these four men and these ladies laid hand on Sir Launcelot, and so they bare him into a tower, and so into a chamber where was the holy vessel of the Sangreal, and by force Sir Launcelot was laid by that holy vessel; and there came an holy man and unhilled that vessel, and so by miracle and by virtue of that holy vessel Sir Launcelot was healed and recovered. And when that he was awaked he groaned and sighed, and complained greatly that he was passing sore.

CHAPTER V

*How Sir Launcelot, after that he was whole and had his
mind, he was ashamed, and how that Elaine
desired a castle for him.*

And when Sir Launcelot saw King Pelles and Elaine, he waxed
ashamed and said thus: O Lord Jesu, how came I here? for God's
sake, my lord, let me wit how I came here. Sir, said Dame Elaine,
into this country ye came like a madman, clean out of your wit, and
here have ye been kept as a fool; and no creature here knew what ye
were, until by fortune a maiden of mine brought me unto you
whereas ye lay sleeping by a well, and anon as I verily beheld you I
knew you. And then I told my father, and so were ye brought afore
this holy vessel, and by the virtue of it thus were ye healed. O Jesu,
mercy, said Sir Launcelot; if this be sooth, how many there be that
know of my woodness! So God me help, said Elaine, no more but
my father, and I, and Dame Brisen. Now for Christ's love, said Sir
Launcelot, keep it in counsel, and let no man know it in the world,
for I am sore ashamed that I have been thus miscarried; for I am
banished out of the country of Logris for ever, that is for to say the
country of England.

And so Sir Launcelot lay more than a fortnight or ever that he
might stir for soreness. And then upon a day he said unto Dame
Elaine these words: Lady Elaine, for your sake I have had much
travail, care, and anguish, it needeth not to rehearse it, ye know how.
Notwithstanding I know well I have done foul to you when that I
drew my sword to you, to have slain you, upon the morn when I had
lain with you. And all was the cause, that ye and Dame Brisen made
me for to lie by you maugre mine head; and as ye say, that night
Galahad your son was begotten. That is truth, said Dame Elaine.
Now will ye for my love, said Sir Launcelot, go unto your father and
get me a place of him wherein I may dwell? for in the court of King
Arthur may I never come. Sir, said Dame Elaine, I will live and die
with you, and only for your sake; and if my life might not avail you
and my death might avail you, wit you well I would die for your

sake. And I will go to my father, and I am sure there is nothing that I can desire of him but I shall have it. And where ye be, my lord Sir Launcelot, doubt ye not but I will be with you with all the service that I may do. So forthwithal she went to her father and said, Sir, my lord, Sir Launcelot, desireth to be here by you in some castle of yours. Well daughter, said the king, sith it is his desire to abide in these marches he shall be in the Castle of Bliant, and there shall ye be with him, and twenty of the fairest ladies that be in the country, and they shall all be of the great blood, and ye shall have ten knights with you; for, daughter, I will that ye wit we all be honoured by the blood of Sir Launcelot.

CHAPTER VI

How Sir Launcelot came into the Joyous Isle, and there he named himself Le Chevaler Mal Fet.

Then went Dame Elaine unto Sir Launcelot, and told him all how her father had devised for him and her. Then came the knight Sir Castor, that was nephew unto King Pelles, unto Sir Launcelot, and asked him what was his name. Sir, said Sir Launcelot, my name is Le Chevaler Mal Fet, that is to say the knight that hath trespassed. Sir, said Sir Castor, it may well be so, but ever meseemeth your name should be Sir Launcelot du Lake, for or now I have seen you. Sir, said Launcelot, ye are not as a gentle knight: I put case my name were Sir Launcelot, and that it list me not to discover my name, what should it grieve you here to keep my counsel, and ye be not hurt thereby? but wit thou well an ever it lie in my power I shall grieve you, and that I promise you truly. Then Sir Castor kneeled down and besought Sir Launcelot of mercy: For I shall never utter what ye be, while that ye be in these parts. Then Sir Launcelot pardoned him.

And then, after this, King Pelles with ten knights, and Dame Elaine, and twenty ladies, rode unto the Castle of Bliant that stood in an island beclosed in iron, with a fair water deep and large. And when they were there Sir Launcelot let call it the Joyous Isle; and there was he called none otherwise but Le Chevaler Mal Fet, the knight that hath trespassed. Then Sir Launcelot let make him a shield all of sable, and a queen crowned in the midst, all of silver, and a knight clean armed kneeling afore her. And every day once, for any mirths that all the ladies might make him, he would once every day look toward the realm of Logris, where King Arthur and Queen Guenever was. And then would he fall upon a weeping as his heart should to-brast.

So it fell that time Sir Launcelot heard of a jousting fast by his castle, within three leagues. Then he called unto him a dwarf, and he bade him go unto that jousting: And or ever the knights depart, look thou make there a cry, in hearing of all the knights, that there is one knight in the Joyous Isle, that is the Castle of Bliant, and say his name is Le Chevaler Mal Fet, that will joust against knights that will come. And who that putteth that knight to the worse shall have a fair maid and a gerfalcon.

CHAPTER VII

Of a great tourneying in the Joyous Isle, and how Sir Percivale and Sir Ector came thither, and Sir Percivale fought with him.

So when this cry was made, unto Joyous Isle drew knights to the number of five hundred; and wit ye well there was never seen in Arthur's days one knight that did so much deeds of arms as Sir Launcelot did three days together; for as the book maketh truly mention, he had the better of all the five hundred knights, and there was not one slain of them. And after that Sir Launcelot made them all a great feast.

And in the meanwhile came Sir Percivale de Galis and Sir Ector de Maris under that castle that was called the Joyous Isle. And as they beheld that gay castle they would have gone to that castle, but they might not for the broad water, and bridge could they find none. Then they saw on the other side a lady with a sperhawk on her hand, and Sir Percivale called unto her, and asked that lady who was in that castle. Fair knights, she said, here within this castle is the fairest lady in this land, and her name is Elaine. Also we have in this castle the fairest knight and the mightiest man that is I dare say living, and he called himself Le Chevaler Mal Fet. How came he into these marches? said

Sir Percivale. Truly, said the damosel, he came into this country like a mad man, with dogs and boys chasing him through the city of Corbin, and by the holy vessel of the Sangreal he was brought into his wit again; but he will not do battle with no knight, but by underne or by noon. And if ye list to come into the castle, said the lady, ye must ride unto the further side of the castle and there shall ye find a vessel that will bear you and your horse. Then they departed, and came unto the vessel. And then Sir Percivale alighted, and said to Sir Ector de Maris: Ye shall abide me here until that I wit what manner a knight he is; for it were shame unto us, inasmuch as he is but one knight, an we should both do battle with him. Do ye as ye list, said Sir Ector, and here I shall abide you until that I hear of you.

Then passed Sir Percivale the water, and when he came to the castle gate he bade the porter: Go thou to the good knight within the castle, and tell him here is come an errant knight to joust with him. Sir, said the porter, ride ye within the castle, and there is a common place for jousting, that lords and ladies may behold you. So anon as Sir Launcelot had warning he was soon ready; and there Sir Percivale and Sir Launcelot encountered with such a might, and their spears were so rude, that both the horses and the knights fell to the earth. Then they avoided their horses, and flang out noble swords, and hewed away cantels of their shields, and hurtled together with their shields like two boars, and either wounded other passing sore. At the last Sir Percivale spake first when they had foughten there more than two hours. Fair knight, said Sir Percivale, I require thee tell me thy name, for I met never with such a knight. Sir, said Sir Launcelot, my name is Le Chevaler Mal Fet. Now tell me your name, said Sir Launcelot, I require you, gentle knight. Truly, said Sir Percivale, my name is Sir Percivale de Galis, that was brother unto the good knight, Sir Lamorak de Galis, and King Pellinore was our father, and Sir Aglovale is my brother. Alas, said Sir Launcelot, what have I done to fight with you that art a knight of the Round Table, that sometime was your fellow?

CHAPTER VIII

*How each of them knew other, and of their great courtesy,
and how his brother Sir Ector came unto him,
and of their joy.*

And therewithal Sir Launcelot kneeled down upon his knees, and
threw away his shield and his sword from him. When Sir Percivale
saw him do so he marvelled what he meant. And then thus he said:
Sir knight, whatsomever thou be, I require thee upon the high order
of knighthood, tell me thy true name. Then he said: So God me
help, my name is Sir Launcelot du Lake, King Ban's son of Benoy.
Alas, said Sir Percivale, what have I done? I was sent by the queen for
to seek you, and so I have sought you nigh this two year, and yonder
is Sir Ector de Maris, your brother, abideth me on the other side of
the yonder water. Now, for God's sake, said Sir Percivale, forgive me
mine offences that I have here done. It is soon forgiven, said
Sir Launcelot.

Then Sir Percivale sent for Sir Ector de Maris; and when Sir
Launcelot had a sight of him, he ran unto him and took him in his
arms; and then Sir Ector kneeled down, and either wept upon other,
that all had pity to behold them. Then came Dame Elaine, and she
there made them great cheer as might lie in her power; and there she
told Sir Ector and Sir Percivale how and in what manner Sir
Launcelot came into that country, and how he was healed; and there
it was known how long Sir Launcelot was with Sir Bliant and with
Sir Selivant, and how he first met with them, and how he departed
from them because of a boar; and how the hermit healed Sir
Launcelot of his great wound, and how that he came to Corbin.

CHAPTER IX

How Sir Bors and Sir Lionel came to King Brandegore,
and how Sir Bors took his son Helin le Blank,
and of Sir Launcelot.

Now leave we Sir Launcelot in the Joyous Isle with the Lady Dame Elaine, and Sir Percivale and Sir Ector playing with them, and turn we to Sir Bors de Ganis and Sir Lionel, that had sought Sir Launcelot nigh by the space of two year, and never could they hear of him. And as they thus rode, by adventure they came to the house of Brandegore, and there Sir Bors was well known, for he had gotten a child upon the king's daughter fifteen year to-fore, and his name was Helin le Blank. And when Sir Bors saw that child it liked him passing well. And so those knights had good cheer of the King Brandegore. And on the morn Sir Bors came afore King Brandegore and said: Here is my son Helin le Blank, that as it is said he is my son; and sith it is so, I will that ye wit that I will have him with me unto the court of King Arthur. Sir, said the king, ye may well take him with you, but he is over tender of age. As for that, said Sir Bors, I will have him with me, and bring him to the house of most worship of the world. So when Sir Bors should depart there was made great sorrow for the departing of Helin le Blank, and great weeping was there made. But Sir Bors and Sir Lionel departed, and within a while they came to Camelot, where was King Arthur. And when King Arthur understood that Helin le Blank was Sir Bors' son, and nephew unto King Brandegore, then King Arthur let him make knight of the Round Table; and so he proved a good knight and an adventurous.

Now will we turn to our matter of Sir Launcelot. It befell upon a day Sir Ector and Sir Percivale came to Sir Launcelot and asked him what he would do, and whether he would go with them unto King Arthur or not. Nay, said Sir Launcelot, that may not be by no mean, for I was so entreated at the court that I cast me never to come there more. Sir, said Sir Ector, I am your brother, and ye are the man in the world that I love most; and if I understood that it were your disworship, ye may understand I would never counsel you thereto;

but King Arthur and all his knights, and in especial Queen Guenever, made such dole and sorrow that it was marvel to hear and see. And ye must remember the great worship and renown that ye be of, how that ye have been more spoken of than any other knight that is now living; for there is none that beareth the name now but ye and Sir Tristram. Therefore brother, said Sir Ector, make you ready to ride to the court with us, and I dare say there was never knight better welcome to the court than ye; and I wot well and can make it good, said Sir Ector, it hath cost my lady, the queen, twenty thousand pound the seeking of you. Well brother, said Sir Launcelot, I will do after your counsel, and ride with you.

So then they took their horses and made them ready, and took their leave at King Pelles and at Dame Elaine. And when Sir Launcelot should depart Dame Elaine made great sorrow. My lord, Sir Launcelot, said Dame Elaine, at this same feast of Pentecost shall your son and mine, Galahad, be made knight, for he is fully now fifteen winter old. Do as ye list, said Sir Launcelot; God give him grace to prove a good knight. As for that, said Dame Elaine, I doubt not he shall prove the best man of his kin except one. Then shall he be a man good enough, said Sir Launcelot.

CHAPTER X

How Sir Launcelot with Sir Percivale and Sir Ector came to the court, and of the great joy of him.

Then they departed, and within five days' journey they came to Camelot, that is called in English, Winchester. And when Sir Launcelot was come among them, the king and all the knights made great joy of him. And there Sir Percivale de Galis and Sir Ector de Maris began and told the whole adventures: that Sir Launcelot had been out of his mind the time of his absence, and how he called himself Le Chevaler Mal Fet, the knight that had trespassed; and in three days Sir Launcelot smote down five hundred knights. And ever as Sir Ector and Sir Percivale told these tales of Sir Launcelot, Queen Guenever wept as she should have died. Then the queen made great cheer. O Jesu, said King Arthur, I marvel for what cause ye, Sir

Launcelot, went out of your mind. I and many others deem it was for the love of fair Elaine, the daughter of King Pelles, by whom ye are noised that ye have gotten a child, and his name is Galahad, and men say he shall do marvels. My lord, said Sir Launcelot, if I did any folly I have that I sought. And therewithal the king spake no more. But all Sir Launcelot's kin knew for whom he went out of his mind. And then there were great feasts made and great joy; and many great lords and ladies, when they heard that Sir Launcelot was come to the court again, they made great joy.

CHAPTER XI

How La Beale Isoud counselled Sir Tristram to go unto the court, to the great feast of Pentecost.

Now will we leave off this matter, and speak we of Sir Tristram, and of Sir Palomides that was the Saracen unchristened. When Sir Tristram was come home unto Joyous Gard from his adventures, all this while that Sir Launcelot was thus missed, two year and more, Sir Tristram bare the renown through all the realm of Logris, and many strange adventures befell him, and full well and manly and worshipfully he brought them to an end. So when he was come home La Beale Isoud told him of the great feast that should be at Pentecost next following, and there she told him how Sir Launcelot had been missed two year, and all that while he had been out of his mind, and how he was holpen by the holy vessel, the Sangreal. Alas, said Sir Tristram, that caused some debate betwixt him and Queen Guenever. Sir, said Dame Isoud, I know it all, for Queen Guenever sent me a letter in the which she wrote me all how it was, for to require you to seek him. And now, blessed be God, said La Beale Isoud, he is whole and sound and come again to the court.

Thereof am I glad, said Sir Tristram, and now shall ye and I make us ready, for both ye and I will be at the feast. Sir, said Isoud, an it please you I will not be there, for through me ye be marked of many good knights, and that caused you to have much more labour for my sake than needeth you. Then will I not be there, said Sir Tristram, but if ye be there. God defend, said La Beale Isoud, for then shall I be spoken of shame among all queens and ladies of estate; for ye that are called one of the noblest knights of the world, and ye a knight of the Round Table, how may ye be missed at that feast? What shall be said among all knights? See how Sir Tristram hunteth, and hawketh, and cowereth within a castle with his lady, and forsaketh your worship. Alas, shall some say, it is pity that ever he was made knight, or that ever he should have the love of a lady. Also what shall queens and ladies say of me? It is pity that I have my life, that I will hold so noble a knight as ye are from his worship. So God me help, said Sir Tristram unto La Beale Isoud, it is passing well said of you and nobly counselled; and now I well understand that ye love me; and like as ye have counselled me I will do a part thereafter. But there shall no man nor child ride with me, but myself. And so will I ride on Tuesday next coming, and no more harness of war but my spear and my sword.

CHAPTER XII

How Sir Tristram departed unarmed and met with
Sir Palomides, and how they smote each other, and how
Sir Palomides forbare him.

And so when the day came Sir Tristram took his leave at La Beale Isoud, and she sent with him four knights, and within half a mile he sent them again: and within a mile after Sir Tristram saw afore him where Sir Palomides had stricken down a knight, and almost wounded him to the death. Then Sir Tristram repented him that he was not armed, and then he hoved still. With that Sir Palomides knew Sir Tristram, and cried on high: Sir Tristram, now be we met, for or we depart we will redress our old sores. As for that, said Sir Tristram, there was yet never Christian man might make his boast that ever I fled from him; and wit ye well, Sir Palomides, thou that art a Saracen shall never make thy boast that Sir Tristram de Liones shall flee from thee. And therewith Sir Tristram made his horse to run, and with all his might he came straight upon Sir Palomides, and brast his spear upon him an hundred pieces. And forthwithal Sir Tristram drew his sword. And then he turned his horse and struck at Palomides six great strokes upon his helm; and then Sir Palomides stood still, and beheld Sir Tristram, and marvelled of his woodness, and of his folly. And then Sir Palomides said to himself: An Sir Tristram were armed, it were hard to cease him of this battle, and if I turn again and slay him I am ashamed wheresomever that I go.

Then Sir Tristram spake and said: Thou coward knight, what castest thou to do; why wilt thou not do battle with me? for have thou no doubt I shall endure all thy malice. Ah, Sir Tristram, said Palomides, full well thou wottest I may not fight with thee for shame, for thou art here naked and I am armed, and if I slay thee, dishonour shall be mine. And well thou wottest, said Sir Palomides to Sir Tristram, I know thy strength and thy hardiness to endure against a good knight. That is truth, said Sir Tristram, I understand thy valiantness well. Ye say well, said Sir Palomides; now, I require you, tell me a question that I shall say to you. Tell me what it is, said Sir Tristram, and I shall answer you the truth, as God me help. I put case, said Sir Palomides, that ye were armed at all rights as well as I am, and I naked as ye be, what would you do to me now, by your true knighthood? Ah, said Sir Tristram, now I understand thee well, Sir Palomides, for now must I say mine own judgment, and as God me bless, that I shall say shall not be said for no fear that I have of thee. But this is all: wit Sir Palomides, as at this time thou shouldest depart from me, for I would not have ado with thee. No more will I, said Palomides, and therefore ride forth on thy way. As for that I may choose, said Sir Tristram, either to ride or to abide. But Sir Palomides, said Sir Tristram, I marvel of one thing, that thou that art so good a knight, that thou wilt not be christened, and thy brother, Sir Safere, hath been christened many a day.

CHAPTER XIII

How that Sir Tristram gat him harness of a knight which was hurt, and how he overthrew Sir Palomides.

As for that, said Sir Palomides, I may not yet be christened, for one avow that I have made many years agone; howbeit in my heart I believe in Jesu Christ and his mild mother Mary; but I have but one battle to do, and when that is done I will be baptised with a good will. By my head, said Tristram, as for one battle thou shalt not seek it no longer. For God defend, said Sir Tristram, that through my default thou shouldst longer live thus a Saracen, for yonder is a knight that ye, Sir Palomides, have hurt and smitten down. Now help me that I were armed in his armour, and I shall soon fulfil thine avows. As ye will, said Palomides, so it shall be.

So they rode both unto that knight that sat upon a bank, and then Sir Tristram saluted him, and he weakly saluted him again. Sir knight, said Sir Tristram, I require you tell me your right name. Sir, he said, my name is Sir Galleron of Galway, and knight of the Table Round. So God me help, said Sir Tristram, I am right heavy of your hurts; but this is all, I must pray you to lend me all your whole armour, for ye see I am unarmed, and I must do battle with this knight. Sir, said the hurt knight, ye shall have it with a good will; but ye must beware, for I warn you that knight is wight. Sir, said Galleron, I pray you tell me your name, and what is that knight's name that hath beaten me. Sir, as for my name it is Sir Tristram de Liones, and as for the knight's name that hath hurt you is Sir Palomides, brother to the good knight Sir Safere, and yet is Sir Palomides unchristened. Alas, said Sir Galleron, that is pity that so good a knight and so noble a man of arms should be unchristened. So God me help, said Sir Tristram, either he shall slay me or I him but that he shall be christened or ever we depart insunder. My lord Sir Tristram, said Sir Galleron, your renown and worship is well known through many realms, and God save you this day from shenship and shame.

Then Sir Tristram unarmed Galleron, the which was a noble knight, and had done many deeds of arms, and he was a large knight of flesh and bone. And when he was unarmed he stood upon his feet, for he was bruised in the back with a spear; yet so as Sir Galleron might, he armed Sir Tristram. And then Sir Tristram mounted upon his own horse, and in his hand he gat Sir Galleron's spear; and therewithal Sir Palomides was ready. And so they came hurtling together, and either smote other in midst of their shields; and therewithal Sir Palomides' spear brake, and Sir Tristram smote down the horse; and Sir Palomides, as soon as he might, avoided his horse, and dressed his shield, and pulled out his sword. That saw Sir Tristram, and therewithal he alighted and tied his horse till a tree.

CHAPTER XIV

*How Sir Tristram and Sir Palomides fought long together,
and after accorded, and how Sir Tristram made
him to be christened.*

And then they came together as two wild boars, lashing together, tracing and traversing as noble men that oft had been well proved in battle; but ever Sir Palomides dread the might of Sir Tristram, and therefore he suffered him to breathe him. Thus they fought more than two hours, but often Sir Tristram smote such strokes at Sir Palomides that he made him to kneel; and Sir Palomides brake and cut away many pieces of Sir Tristram's shield; and then Sir Palomides wounded Sir Tristram, for he was a well fighting man. Then Sir Tristram was wood wroth out of measure, and rushed upon Sir Palomides with such a might that Sir Palomides fell grovelling to the earth; and therewithal he leapt up lightly upon his feet, and then Sir Tristram wounded Palomides sore through the shoulder. And ever Sir Tristram fought still in like hard, and Sir Palomides failed not, but gave him many sad strokes. And at the last Sir Tristram doubled his strokes, and by fortune Sir Tristram smote Sir Palomides' sword out of his hand, and if Sir Palomides had stooped for his sword he had been slain.

Then Palomides stood still and beheld his sword with a sorrowful heart. How now, said Sir Tristram unto Palomides, now have I thee at advantage as thou haddest me this day; but it shall never be said in no court, nor among good knights, that Sir Tristram shall slay any knight that is weaponless; and therefore take thou thy sword, and let us make an end of this battle. As for to do this battle, said Palomides, I dare right well end it, but I have no great lust to fight no more. And for this cause, said Palomides: mine offence to you is not so great but that we may be friends. All that I have offended is and was for the love of La Beale Isoud. And as for her, I dare say she is peerless above all other ladies, and also I proffered her never no dishonour; and by her I have gotten the most part of my worship. And sithen I offended never as to her own person, and as for the offence that I have done, it was against your own person, and for that offence ye have given me this day many sad strokes, and some I have given you again; and now I dare say I felt never man of your might, nor so well breathed, but if it were Sir Launcelot du Lake; wherefore I require you, my lord, forgive me all that I have offended unto you; and this same day have me to the next church, and first let me be clean confessed, and after see you now that I be truly baptised. And then will we all ride together unto the court of Arthur, that we be there at the high feast. Now take your horse, said Sir Tristram, and as ye say so it shall be, and all thine evil will God forgive it you, and I do. And here within this mile is the Suffragan of Carlisle that shall give you the sacrament of baptism.

Then they took their horses and Sir Galleron rode with them. And when they came to the Suffragan Sir Tristram told him their desire. Then the Suffragan let fill a great vessel with water, and when he had hallowed it he then confessed clean Sir Palomides, and Sir Tristram and Sir Galleron were his godfathers. And then soon after they departed, riding toward Camelot, where King Arthur and Queen Guenever was, and for the most part all the knights of the Round Table. And so the king and all the court were glad that Sir Palomides was christened. And at the same feast in came Galahad and sat in the Siege Perilous. And so therewithal departed and dissevered all the knights of the Round Table. And Sir Tristram returned again unto Joyous Gard, and Sir Palomides followed the Questing Beast.

Here endeth the second book of Sir Tristram that was drawn out of French into English. But here is no rehearsal of the third book. And here followeth the noble tale of the Sangreal, that called is the Holy Vessel; and the signification of the blessed blood of our Lord Jesus Christ, blessed mote it be, the which was brought into this land by Joseph of Aramathie. Therefore on all sinful souls blessed Lord have thou mercy.

Explicit liber xii. Et incipit Decimustercius.

BOOK THIRTEEN

CHAPTER I

How at the vigil of the Feast of Pentecost entered into the hall before King Arthur a damosel, and desired Sir Launcelot for to come and dub a knight, and how he went with her.

At the vigil of Pentecost, when all the fellowship of the Round Table were come unto Camelot and there heard their service, and the tables were set ready to the meat, right so entered into the hall a full fair gentlewoman on horseback, that had ridden full fast, for her horse was all besweated. Then she there alighted, and came before the king and saluted him; and he said: Damosel, God thee bless. Sir, said she, for God's sake say me where Sir Launcelot is. Yonder ye may see him, said the king. Then she went unto Launcelot and said: Sir Launcelot, I salute you on King Pelles' behalf, and I require you come on with me hereby into a forest. Then Sir Launcelot asked her with whom she dwelled. I dwell, said she, with King Pelles. What will ye with me? said Launcelot. Ye shall know, said she, when ye come thither. Well, said he, I will gladly go with you. So Sir Launcelot bade his squire saddle his horse and bring his arms; and in all haste he did his commandment.

Then came the queen unto Launcelot, and said: Will ye leave us at this high feast? Madam, said the gentlewoman, wit ye well he shall be with you to-morn by dinner time. If I wist, said the queen, that he should not be with us here to-morn he should not go with you by my good will. Right so departed Sir Launcelot with the gentle-woman, and rode until that he came into a forest and into a great valley, where they saw an abbey of nuns; and there was a squire ready and opened the gates, and so they entered and descended off their horses; and there came a fair fellowship about Sir Launcelot, and welcomed him, and were passing glad of his coming. And then they led him unto the Abbess's chamber and unarmed him; and right so he was ware upon a bed lying two of his cousins, Sir Bors and Sir Lionel, and then he waked them; and when they saw him they made great joy. Sir, said Sir Bors unto Sir Launcelot, what adventure hath brought you hither, for we weened to-morn to have found you at Camelot? As God me help, said Sir Launcelot, a gentlewoman brought me hither, but I know not the cause.

In the meanwhile that they thus stood talking together, therein came twelve nuns that brought with them Galahad, the which was passing fair and well made, that unnethe in the world men might not find his match: and all those ladies wept. Sir, said they all, we bring you here this child the which we have nourished, and we pray you to make him a knight, for of a more worthier man's hand may he not receive the order of knighthood. Sir Launcelot beheld the young squire and saw him seemly and demure as a dove, with all manner of good features, that he weened of his age never to have seen so fair a man of form. Then said Sir Launcelot: Cometh this desire of himself? He and all they said yea. Then shall he, said Sir Launcelot, receive the high order of knighthood as to-morn at the reverence of the high feast. That night Sir Launcelot had passing good cheer; and on the morn at the hour of prime, at Galahad's desire, he made him knight and said: God make him a good man, for of beauty faileth you not as any that liveth.

CHAPTER II

How the letters were found written in the Siege Perilous, and of the marvellous adventure of the sword in a stone.

Now fair sir, said Sir Launcelot, will ye come with me unto the court of King Arthur? Nay, said he, I will not go with you as at this time. Then he departed from them and took his two cousins with him, and so they came unto Camelot by the hour of underne on Whitsunday. By that time the king and the queen were gone to the minster to hear their service. Then the king and the queen were passing glad of Sir Bors and Sir Lionel, and so was all the fellowship. So when the king and all the knights were come from service, the barons espied in the sieges of the Round Table all about, written with golden letters: Here ought to sit he, and he ought to sit here. And thus they went so long till that they came to the Siege Perilous, where they found letters newly written of gold which said: Four hundred winters and four and fifty accomplished after the passion of our Lord Jesu Christ ought this siege to be fulfilled. Then all they said: This is a marvellous thing and an adventurous. In the name of God, said Sir Launcelot; and then accompted the term of the writing from the birth of our Lord unto that day. It seemeth me, said Sir Launcelot, this siege ought to be fulfilled this same day, for this is the feast of Pentecost after the four hundred and four and fifty year; and if it would please all parties, I would none of these letters were seen this day, till he be come that ought to enchieve this adventure. Then made they to ordain a cloth of silk, for to cover these letters in the Siege Perilous.

Then the king bade haste unto dinner. Sir, said Sir Kay the Steward, if ye go now unto your meat ye shall break your old custom of your court, for ye have not used on this day to sit at your meat or that ye have seen some adventure. Ye say sooth, said the king, but I had so great joy of Sir Launcelot and of his cousins, which be come to the court whole and sound, so that I bethought me not of mine old custom. So, as they stood speaking, in came a squire and said unto the king: Sir, I bring unto you marvellous tidings. What be they? said the king. Sir, there is here beneath at the river a great stone which I saw fleet above the water, and therein I saw sticking a sword. The king said: I will see that marvel. So all the knights went with him, and when they came to the river they found there a stone fleeting, as it were of red marble, and therein stuck a fair rich sword, and in the pommel thereof were precious stones wrought with subtle letters of gold. Then the barons read the letters which said in this wise: Never shall man take me hence, but only he by whose side I ought to hang, and he shall be the best knight of the world.

When the king had seen the letters, he said unto Sir Launcelot: Fair Sir, this sword ought to be yours, for I am sure ye be the best knight of the world. Then Sir Launcelot answered full soberly: Certes, sir, it is not my sword; also, Sir, wit ye well I have no hardiness to set my hand to it, for it longed not to hang by my side. Also, who that assayeth to take the sword and faileth of it, he shall receive a wound by that sword that he shall not be whole long after. And I will that ye wit that this same day shall the adventures of the Sangreal, that is called the Holy Vessel, begin.

CHAPTER III

How Sir Gawaine assayed to draw out the sword, and how an old man brought in Galahad.

Now, fair nephew, said the king unto Sir Gawaine, assay ye, for my love. Sir, he said, save your good grace I shall not do that. Sir, said the king, assay to take the sword and at my commandment. Sir, said Gawaine, your commandment I will obey. And therewith he took up the sword by the handles, but he might not stir it. I thank you, said the king to Sir Gawaine. My lord Sir Gawaine, said Sir Launcelot, now wit ye well this sword shall touch you so sore that ye shall will ye had never set your hand thereto for the best castle of this realm. Sir, he said, I might not withsay mine uncle's will and commandment. But when the king heard this he repented it much, and said unto Sir Percivale that he should assay, for his love. And he said: Gladly, for to bear Sir Gawaine fellowship. And therewith he set his hand on the sword and drew it strongly, but he might not move it. Then were there no* mo that durst be so hardy to set their hands thereto. Now may ye go to your dinner, said Sir Kay unto the king, for a marvellous adventure have ye seen. So the king and all went unto the court, and every knight knew his own place, and set him therein, and young men that were knights served them.

So when they were served, and all sieges fulfilled save only the Siege Perilous, anon there befell a marvellous adventure, that all the doors and windows of the palace shut by themself. Not for then the hall was not greatly darked; and therewith they were* all* abashed both one and other. Then King Arthur spake first and said: By God, fair fellows and lords, we have seen this day marvels, but or night I suppose we shall see greater marvels.

In the meanwhile came in a good old man, and an ancient, clothed all in white, and there was no knight knew from whence he came. And with him he brought a young knight, both on foot, in red arms, without sword or shield, save a scabbard hanging by his side. And

* Omitted by Caxton, supplied from Wynkyn de Worde.

these words he said: Peace be with you, fair lords. Then the old man said unto Arthur: Sir, I bring here a young knight, the which is of king's lineage, and of the kindred of Joseph of Aramathie, whereby the marvels of this court, and of strange realms, shall be fully accomplished.

CHAPTER IV

How the old man brought Galahad to the Siege Perilous and set him therein, and how all the knights marvelled.

The king was right glad of his words, and said unto the good man: Sir, ye be right welcome, and the young knight with you. Then the old man made the young man to unarm him, and he was in a coat of red sendal, and bare a mantle upon his shoulder that was furred with ermine, and put that upon him. And the old knight said unto the young knight: Sir, follow me. And anon he led him unto the Siege Perilous, where beside sat Sir Launcelot; and the good man lift up the cloth, and found there letters that said thus: This is the siege of Galahad, the haut prince. Sir, said the old knight, wit ye well that place is yours. And then he set him down surely in that siege. And then he said to the old man: Sir, ye may now go your way, for well have ye done that ye were commanded to do; and recommend me unto my grandsire, King Pelles, and unto my lord Petchere, and say them on my behalf, I shall come and see them as soon as ever I may. So the good man departed; and there met him twenty noble squires, and so took their horses and went their way.

Then all the knights of the Table Round marvelled greatly of Sir Galahad, that he durst sit there in that Siege Perilous, and was so tender of age; and wist not from whence he came but all only by God; and said: This is he by whom the Sangreal shall be enchieved, for there sat never none but he, but he were mischieved. Then Sir Launcelot beheld his son and had great joy of him. Then Bors told his fellows: upon pain of my life this young knight shall come unto great worship. This noise was great in all the court, so that it came to the queen. Then she had marvel what knight it might be that durst adventure him to sit in the Siege Perilous. Many said unto the queen he resembled much unto Sir Launcelot. I may well suppose, said the queen, that Sir Launcelot begat him on King Pelles' daughter, by the which he was made to lie by, by enchantment, and his name is Galahad. I would fain see him, said the queen, for he must needs be a noble man, for so is his father that him begat, I report me unto all the Table Round.

So when the meat was done that the king and all were risen, the king yede unto the Siege Perilous and lift up the cloth, and found there the name of Galahad; and then he showed it unto Sir Gawaine, and said: Fair nephew, now have we among us Sir Galahad, the good knight that shall worship us all; and upon pain of my life he shall enchieve the Sangreal, right as Sir Launcelot had done us to understand. Then came King Arthur unto Galahad and said: Sir, ye be welcome, for ye shall move many good knights to the quest of the Sangreal, and ye shall enchieve that never knights might bring to an end. Then the king took him by the hand, and went down from the palace to show Galahad the adventures of the stone.

CHAPTER V

How King Arthur showed the stone hoving on the water to Galahad, and how he drew out the sword.

The queen heard thereof, and came after with many ladies, and showed them the stone where it hoved on the water. Sir, said the king unto Sir Galahad, here is a great marvel as ever I saw, and right good knights have assayed and failed. Sir, said Galahad, that is no marvel, for this adventure is not theirs but mine; and for the surety of this sword I brought none with me, for here by my side hangeth the scabbard. And anon he laid his hand on the sword, and lightly drew it out of the stone, and put it in the sheath, and said unto the king: Now it goeth better than it did aforehand. Sir, said the king, a shield God shall send you. Now have I that sword that sometime was the good knight's, Balin le Savage, and he was a passing good man of his hands; and with this sword he slew his brother Balan, and that was great pity, for he was a good knight, and either slew other through a dolorous stroke that Balin gave unto my grandfather King Pelles, the which is not yet whole, nor not shall be till I heal him.

Therewith the king and all espied where came riding down the river a lady on a white palfrey toward them. Then she saluted the king and the queen, and asked if that Sir Launcelot was there. And then he answered himself: I am here, fair lady. Then she said all with weeping: How your great doing is changed sith this day in the morn. Damosel, why say you so? said Launcelot. I say you sooth, said the damosel, for ye were this day the best knight of the world, but who should say so now, he should be a liar, for there is now one better than ye, and well it is proved by the adventures of the sword whereto ye durst not set to your hand; and that is the change and leaving of your name. Wherefore I make unto you a remembrance, that ye shall not ween from henceforth that ye be the best knight of the world. As touching unto that, said Launcelot, I know well I was never the best. Yes, said the damosel, that were ye, and are yet, of any sinful man of the world. And, Sir king, Nacien, the hermit, sendeth thee word, that thee shall befall the greatest worship that ever befell king in Britain; and I say you wherefore, for this day the Sangreal appeared in thy house and fed thee and all thy fellowship of the Round Table. So she departed and went that same way that she came.

CHAPTER VI

How King Arthur had all the knights together for to joust in the meadow beside Camelot or they departed.

Now, said the king, I am sure at this quest of the Sangreal shall all ye of the Table Round depart, and never shall I see you again whole together; therefore I will see you all whole together in the meadow of Camelot to joust and to tourney, that after your death men may speak of it that such good knights were wholly together such a day. As unto that counsel and at the king's request they accorded all, and took on their harness that longed unto jousting. But all this moving of the king was for this intent, for to see Galahad proved; for the king deemed he should not lightly come again unto the court after his departing. So were they assembled in the meadow, both more and less. Then Sir Galahad, by the prayer of the king and the queen, did upon him a noble jesseraunce, and also he did on his helm, but shield would he take none for no prayer of the king. And then Sir Gawaine and other knights prayed him to take a spear. Right so he did; and the queen was in a tower with all her ladies, for to behold that tournament. Then Sir Galahad dressed him in midst of the meadow, and began to break spears marvellously, that all men had wonder of him; for he there surmounted all other knights, for within a while he had defouled many good knights of the Table Round save twain, that was Sir Launcelot and Sir Percivale.

CHAPTER VII

How the queen desired to see Galahad; and how after, all the knights were replenished with the Holy Sangreal, and how they avowed the enquest of the same.

Then the king, at the queen's request, made him to alight and to unlace his helm, that the queen might see him in the visage. When she beheld him she said: Soothly I dare well say that Sir Launcelot begat him, for never two men resembled more in likeness, therefore it nis no marvel though he be of great prowess. So a lady that stood by the queen said: Madam, for God's sake ought he of right to be so good a knight? Yea, forsooth, said the queen, for he is of all parties come of the best knights of the world and of the highest lineage; for Sir Launcelot is come but of the eighth degree from our Lord Jesu Christ, and Sir Galahad is of the ninth degree from our Lord Jesu Christ, therefore I dare say they be the greatest gentlemen of the world.

And then the king and all estates went home unto Camelot, and so went to evensong to the great minster, and so after upon that to supper, and every knight sat in his own place as they were toforehand. Then anon they heard cracking and crying of thunder, that them thought the place should all to-drive. In the midst of this blast entered a sunbeam more clearer by seven times than ever they saw day, and all they were alighted of the grace of the Holy Ghost. Then began every knight to behold other, and either saw other, by their seeming, fairer than ever they saw afore. Not for then there was no knight might speak one word a great while, and so they looked every man on other as they had been dumb. Then there entered into the hall the Holy Grail covered with white samite, but there was none might see it, nor who bare it. And there was all the hall fulfilled with good odours, and every knight had such meats and drinks as he best loved in this world. And when the Holy Grail had been borne through the hall, then the holy vessel departed suddenly, that they wist not where it became: then had they all breath to speak. And then the king yielded thankings to God, of His good grace that he had sent them. Certes, said the king, we ought to thank our Lord Jesu greatly for that he hath showed us this day, at the reverence of this high feast of Pentecost.

Now, said Sir Gawaine, we have been served this day of what meats and drinks we thought on; but one thing beguiled us, we might not see the Holy Grail, it was so preciously covered. Wherefore I will make here avow, that to-morn, without longer abiding, I shall labour in the quest of the Sangreal, that I shall hold me out a twelvemonth and a day, or more if need be, and never shall I return again unto the court till I have seen it more openly than it hath been seen here; and if I may not speed I shall return again as he that may not be against the will of our Lord Jesu Christ.

When they of the Table Round heard Sir Gawaine say so, they arose up the most part and made such avows as Sir Gawaine had made. Anon as King Arthur heard this he was greatly displeased, for he wist well they might not again-say their avows. Alas, said King Arthur unto Sir Gawaine, ye have nigh slain me with the avow and promise that ye have made; for through you ye have bereft me the fairest fellowship and the truest of knighthood that ever were seen together in any realm of the world; for when they depart from hence I am sure they all shall never meet more in this world, for they shall die many in the quest. And so it forthinketh me a little, for I have loved them as well as my life, wherefore it shall grieve me right sore, the departition of this fellowship: for I have had an old custom to have them in my fellowship.

CHAPTER VIII

*How great sorrow was made of the king and the queen
and ladies for the departing of the knights,
and how they departed.*

And therewith the tears fell in his eyes. And then he said: Gawaine, Gawaine, ye have set me in great sorrow, for I have great doubt that my true fellowship shall never meet here more again. Ah, said Sir Launcelot, comfort yourself; for it shall be unto us a great honour and much more than if we died in any other places, for of death we be siker. Ah, Launcelot, said the king, the great love that I have had unto you all the days of my life maketh me to say such doleful words; for never Christian king had never so many worthy men at his table as I have had this day at the Round Table, and that is my great sorrow.

When the queen, ladies, and gentlewomen, wist these tidings, they had such sorrow and heaviness that there might no tongue tell it, for those knights had held them in honour and chierté. But among all other Queen Guenever made great sorrow. I marvel, said she, my lord would suffer them to depart from him. Thus was all the court troubled for the love of the departition of those knights. And many of those ladies that loved knights would have gone with their lovers; and so had they done, had not an old knight come among them in religious clothing; and then he spake all on high and said: Fair lords, which have sworn in the quest of the Sangreal, thus sendeth you Nacien, the hermit, word, that none in this quest lead lady nor gentlewoman with him, for it is not to do in so high a service as they labour in; for I warn you plain, he that is not clean of his sins he shall not see the mysteries of our Lord Jesu Christ. And for this cause they left these ladies and gentlewomen.

After this the queen came unto Galahad and asked him of whence he was, and of what country. He told her of whence he was. And son unto Launcelot, she said he was. As to that, he said neither yea nor nay. So God me help, said the queen, of your father ye need not to shame you, for he is the goodliest knight, and of the best men of the world come, and of the strain, of all parties, of kings. Wherefore ye ought of right to be, of your deeds, a passing good man; and certainly, she said, ye resemble him much. Then Sir Galahad was a little ashamed and said: Madam, sith ye know in certain, wherefore do ye ask it me? for he that is my father shall be known openly and all betimes. And then they went to rest them. And in the honour of the highness of Galahad he was led into King Arthur's chamber, and there rested in his own bed.

And as soon as it was day the king arose, for he had no rest of all that night for sorrow. Then he went unto Gawaine and to Sir Launcelot that were arisen for to hear mass. And then the king again said: Ah Gawaine, Gawaine, ye have betrayed me; for never shall my court be amended by you, but ye will never be sorry for me as I am for you. And therewith the tears began to run down by his visage. And therewith the king said: Ah, knight Sir Launcelot, I require thee thou counsel me, for I would that this quest were undone, an it might be. Sir, said Sir Launcelot, ye saw yesterday so many worthy knights that then were sworn that they may not leave it in no manner of wise. That wot I well, said the king, but it shall so heavy me at their departing that I wot well there shall no manner of joy remedy me. And then the king and the queen went unto the minster. So anon Launcelot and Gawaine commanded their men to bring their arms. And when they all were armed save their shields and their helms, then they came to their fellowship, which were all ready in the same wise, for to go to the minster to hear their service.

Then after the service was done the king would wit how many had undertaken the quest of the Holy Grail; and to accompt them he prayed them all. Then found they by the tale an hundred and fifty, and all were knights of the Round Table. And then they put on their helms and departed, and recommended them all wholly unto the queen; and there was weeping and great sorrow. Then the queen departed into her chamber and held her, so that no man should perceive her great sorrows. When Sir Launcelot missed the queen he went till her chamber, and when she saw him she cried aloud: O Launcelot, Launcelot, ye have betrayed me and put me to the death, for to leave thus my lord. Ah, madam, I pray you be not displeased, for I shall come again as soon as I may with my worship. Alas, said she, that ever I saw you; but he that suffered upon the cross for all mankind, he be unto you good conduct and safety, and all the whole fellowship.

Right so departed Sir Launcelot, and found his fellowship that abode his coming. And so they mounted upon their horses and rode through the streets of Camelot; and there was weeping of rich and poor, and the king turned away and might not speak for weeping. So within a while they came to a city, and a castle that hight Vagon. There they entered into the castle, and the lord of that castle was an old man that hight Vagon, and he was a good man of his living, and set open the gates, and made them all the cheer that he might. And so on the morn they were all accorded that they should depart everych from other; and on the morn they departed with weeping cheer, and every knight took the way that him liked best.

CHAPTER IX

How Galahad gat him a shield, and how they sped that presumed to take down the said shield.

Now rideth Sir Galahad yet without shield, and so he rode four days without any adventure. And at the fourth day after evensong he came to a White Abbey, and there he was received with great reverence, and led unto a chamber, and there was he unarmed; and then was he ware of two* knights of the Table Round, one was Sir Bagdemagus, and* that* other* was Sir Uwaine. And when they saw him they went unto Galahad and made of him great solace, and so they went unto supper. Sirs, said Sir Galahad, what adventure brought you hither? Sir, said they, it is told us that within this place is a shield that no man may bear about his neck but he be mischieved outher dead within three days, or maimed for ever. Ah sir, said King Bagdemagus, I shall it bear to-morrow for to assay this adventure. In the name of God, said Sir Galahad. Sir, said Bagdemagus, an I may not enchieve the adventure of this shield ye shall take it upon you, for I am sure ye shall not fail. Sir, said Galahad, I right well agree me thereto, for I have no shield. So on the morn they arose and heard mass. Then Bagdemagus asked where the adventurous shield was. Anon a monk led him behind an altar where the shield hung as white as any snow, but in the midst was a red

* Omitted by Caxton, supplied from Wynkyn de Worde.

cross. Sir, said the monk, this shield ought not to be hanged about no knight's neck but he be the worthiest knight of the world; therefore I counsel you knights to be well advised. Well, said Bagdemagus, I wot well that I am not the best knight of the world, but yet I shall assay to bear it, and so bare it out of the minster. And then he said unto Galahad: An it please you abide here still, till ye wit how that I speed. I shall abide you, said Galahad. Then King Bagdemagus took with him a good squire, to bring tidings unto Sir Galahad how he sped.

Then when they had ridden a two mile and came to a fair valley afore an hermitage, then they saw a knight come from that part in white armour, horse and all; and he came as fast as his horse might run, and his spear in his rest, and Bagdemagus dressed his spear against him and brake it upon the white knight. But the other struck him so hard that he brast the mails, and sheef him through the right shoulder, for the shield covered him not as at that time; and so he bare him from his horse. And therewith he alighted and took the white shield from him, saying: Knight, thou hast done thyself great folly, for this shield ought not to be borne but by him that shall have no peer that liveth. And then he came to Bagdemagus' squire and said: Bear this shield unto the good knight Sir Galahad, that thou left in the abbey, and greet him well by me. Sir, said the squire, what is your name? Take thou no heed of my name, said the knight, for it is not for thee to know nor for none earthly man. Now, fair sir, said the squire, at the reverence of Jesu Christ, tell me for what cause this shield may not be borne but if the bearer thereof be mischieved. Now sith thou hast conjured me so, said the knight, this shield behoveth unto no man but unto Galahad. And the squire went unto Bagdemagus and asked whether he were sore wounded or not. Yea forsooth, said he, I shall escape hard from the death. Then he fetched his horse, and brought him with great pain unto an abbey. Then was he taken down softly and unarmed, and laid in a bed, and there was looked to his wounds. And as the book telleth, he lay there long, and escaped hard with the life.

CHAPTER X

How Galahad departed with the shield, and how King
Evelake had received the shield of Joseph of Aramathie.

Sir Galahad, said the squire, that knight that wounded Bagdemagus sendeth you greeting, and bade that ye should bear this shield, wherethrough great adventures should befall. Now blessed be God and fortune, said Galahad. And then he asked his arms, and mounted upon his horse, and hung the white shield about his neck, and commended them unto God. And Sir Uwaine said he would bear him fellowship if it pleased him. Sir, said Galahad, that may ye not, for I must go alone, save this squire shall bear me fellowship: and so departed Uwaine.

Then within a while came Galahad thereas the White Knight abode him by the hermitage, and everych saluted other courteously. Sir, said Galahad, by this shield be many marvels fallen. Sir, said the knight, it befell after the passion of our Lord Jesu Christ thirty-two year, that Joseph of Aramathie, the gentle knight, the which took down our Lord off the holy Cross, at that time he departed from Jerusalem with a great party of his kindred with him. And so he laboured till that they came to a city that hight Sarras. And at that same hour that Joseph came to Sarras there was a king that hight Evelake, that had great war against the Saracens, and in especial against one Saracen, the which was King Evelake's cousin, a rich king and a mighty, which marched nigh this land, and his name was called Tolleme la Feintes. So on a day these two met to do battle. Then Joseph, the son of Joseph of Aramathie, went to King Evelake and told him he should be discomfit and slain, but if he left his belief of the old law and believed upon the new law. And then there he showed him the right belief of the Holy Trinity, to the which he agreed unto with all his heart; and there this shield was made for King Evelake, in the name of Him that died upon the Cross. And then through his good belief he had the better of King Tolleme. For when Evelake was in the battle there was a cloth set afore the shield, and when he was in the greatest peril he let put away the cloth, and then his enemies saw a figure of a man on the Cross, wherethrough they all were discomfit. And so it befell that a man of King Evelake's was smitten his hand off, and bare that hand in his other hand; and Joseph called that man unto him and bade him go with good devotion touch the Cross. And as soon as that man had touched the Cross with his hand it was as whole as ever it was to-fore. Then soon after there fell a great marvel, that the cross of the shield at one time vanished away that no man wist where it became. And then King Evelake was baptised, and for the most part all the people of that city. So, soon after Joseph would depart, and King Evelake would go with him, whether he wold or nold. And so by fortune they came into this land, that at that time was called Great Britain; and there they found a great felon paynim, that put Joseph into prison. And so by fortune tidings came unto a worthy man that hight Mondrames, and he assembled all his people for the great renown he had heard of Joseph; and so he came into the land of Great Britain and disherited this felon paynim and consumed him, and therewith delivered Joseph out of prison. And after that all the people were turned to the Christian faith.

CHAPTER XI

How Joseph made a cross on the white shield with his blood, and how Galahad was by a monk brought to a tomb.

Not long after that Joseph was laid in his deadly bed. And when King Evelake saw that he made much sorrow, and said: For thy love I have left my country, and sith ye shall depart out of this world, leave me some token of yours that I may think on you. Joseph said: That will I do full gladly; now bring me your shield that I took you when ye went into battle against King Tolleme. Then Joseph bled sore at the nose, so that he might not by no mean be staunched. And there upon that shield he made a cross of his own blood. Now may ye see a remembrance that I love you, for ye shall never see this shield but ye shall think on me, and it shall be always as fresh as it is now. And never shall man bear this shield about his neck but he shall repent it, unto the time that Galahad, the good knight, bear it; and the last of my lineage shall have it about his neck, that shall do many marvellous deeds. Now, said King Evelake, where shall I put this shield, that this worthy knight may have it? Ye shall leave it thereas Nacien, the hermit, shall be put after his death; for thither shall that good knight come the fifteenth day after that he shall receive the order of knighthood: and so that day that they set is this time that he have his shield, and in the same abbey lieth Nacien, the hermit. And then the White Knight vanished away.

Anon as the squire had heard these words, he alighted off his hackney and kneeled down at Galahad's feet, and prayed him that he might go with him till he had made him knight. Yea,* I would not refuse you. Then will ye make me a knight? said the squire, and that order, by the grace of God, shall be well set in me. So Sir Galahad granted him, and turned again unto the abbey where they came from; and there men made great joy of Sir Galahad. And anon as he was alighted there was a monk brought him unto a tomb in a churchyard, where there was such a noise that who that heard it should verily nigh be mad or lose his strength: and sir, they said, we deem it is a fiend.

CHAPTER XII

Of the marvel that Sir Galahad saw and heard in the tomb, and how he made Melias knight.

Now lead me thither, said Galahad. And so they did, all armed save his helm. Now, said the good man, go to the tomb and lift it up. So he did, and heard a great noise; and piteously he said, that all men might hear it: Sir Galahad, the servant of Jesu Christ, come thou not nigh me, for thou shalt make me go again there where I have been so long. But Galahad was nothing afraid, but lifted up the stone; and there came out so foul a smoke, and after he saw the foulest figure leap thereout that ever he saw in the likeness of a man; and then he blessed him and wist well it was a fiend. Then heard he a voice say: Galahad, I see there environ about thee so many angels that my

---

* Caxton 'Yf', for which 'Yea' seems the easiest emendation that will save the sense.

power may not dere thee. Right so Sir Galahad saw a body all armed lie in that tomb, and beside him a sword. Now, fair brother, said Galahad, let us remove this body, for it is not worthy to lie in this churchyard, for he was a false Christian man. And therewith they all departed and went to the abbey. And anon as he was unarmed a good man came and set him down by him and said: Sir, I shall tell you what betokeneth all that ye saw in the tomb; for that covered body betokeneth the duresse of the world, and the great sin that Our Lord found in the world. For there was such wretchedness that the father loved not the son, nor the son loved not the father; and that was one of the causes that Our Lord took flesh and blood of a clean maiden, for our sins were so great at that time that well-nigh all was wickedness. Truly, said Galahad, I believe you right well.

So Sir Galahad rested him there that night; and upon the morn he made the squire knight, and asked him his name, and of what kindred he was come. Sir, said he, men calleth me Melias de Lile, and I am the son of the King of Denmark. Now, fair sir, said Galahad, sith that ye be come of kings and queens, now look that knighthood be well set in you, for ye ought to be a mirror unto all chivalry. Sir, said Sir Melias, ye say sooth. But, sir, sithen ye have made me a knight ye must of right grant me my first desire that is reasonable. Ye say sooth, said Galahad. Melias said: Then that ye will suffer me to ride with you in this quest of the Sangreal, till that some adventure depart us. I grant you, sir.

Then men brought Sir Melias his armour and his spear and his horse, and so Sir Galahad and he rode forth all that week or they found any adventure. And then upon a Monday in the morning, as they were departed from an abbey, they came to a cross which departed two ways, and in that cross were letters written that said thus: Now, ye knights errant, the which goeth to seek knights adventurous, see here two ways; that one way defendeth thee that thou ne go that way, for he shall not go out of the way again but if he be a good man and a worthy knight; and if thou go on the left hand, thou shalt not lightly there win prowess, for thou shalt in this way be soon assayed. Sir, said Melias to Galahad, if it like you to suffer me to take the way on the left hand, tell me, for there I shall well prove my strength. It were better, said Galahad, ye rode not that way, for I deem I should better escape in that way than ye. Nay, my lord, I pray you let me have that adventure. Take it in God's name, said Galahad.

CHAPTER XIII

Of the adventure that Melias had, and how Galahad
revenged him, and how Melias was carried into an abbey.

And then rode Melias into an old forest, and therein he rode two days
and more. And then he came into a fair meadow, and there was a fair
lodge of boughs. And then he espied in that lodge a chair, wherein
was a crown of gold, subtly wrought. Also there were cloths covered
upon the earth, and many delicious meats set thereon. Sir Melias
beheld this adventure, and thought it marvellous, but he had no
hunger, but of the crown of gold he took much keep; and therewith
he stooped down and took it up, and rode his way with it. And anon
he saw a knight came riding after him that said: Knight, set down that
crown which is not yours, and therefore defend you. Then Sir Melias
blessed him and said: Fair lord of heaven, help and save thy new-
made knight. And then they let their horses run as fast as they might,
so that the other knight smote Sir Melias through hauberk and
through the left side, that he fell to the earth nigh dead. And then he
took the crown and went his way; and Sir Melias lay still and had no
power to stir.

In the meanwhile by fortune there came Sir Galahad and found him
there in peril of death. And then he said: Ah Melias, who hath
wounded you? therefore it had been better to have ridden the other
way. And when Sir Melias heard him speak: Sir, he said, for God's
love let me not die in this forest, but bear me unto the abbey here
beside, that I may be confessed and have my rights. It shall be done,
said Galahad, but where is he that hath wounded you? With that Sir
Galahad heard in the leaves cry on high: Knight, keep thee from me.
Ah sir, said Melias, beware, for that is he that hath slain me. Sir
Galahad answered: Sir knight, come on your peril. Then either dressed
to other, and came together as fast as their horses might run, and
Galahad smote him so that his spear went through his shoulder, and
smote him down off his horse, and in the falling Galahad's spear brake.

With that came out another knight out of the leaves, and brake a
spear upon Galahad or ever he might turn him. Then Galahad drew

out his sword and smote off the left arm of him, so that it fell to the earth. And then he fled, and Sir Galahad pursued fast after him. And then he turned again unto Sir Melias, and there he alighted and dressed him softly on his horse to-fore him, for the truncheon of his spear was in his body; and Sir Galahad stert up behind him, and held him in his arms, and so brought him to the abbey, and there unarmed him and brought him to his chamber. And then he asked his Saviour. And when he had received Him he said unto Sir Galahad: Sir, let death come when it pleaseth him. And therewith he drew out the truncheon of the spear out of his body: and then he swooned.

Then came there an old monk which sometime had been a knight, and beheld Sir Melias. And anon he ransacked him; and then he said unto Sir Galahad: I shall heal him of his wound, by the grace of God, within the term of seven weeks. Then was Sir Galahad glad, and unarmed him, and said he would abide there three days. And then he asked Sir Melias how it stood with him. Then he said he was turned unto helping, God be thanked.

CHAPTER XIV

How Sir Galahad departed, and how he was commanded to go to the Castle of Maidens to destroy the wicked custom.

Now will I depart, said Galahad, for I have much on hand, for many good knights be full busy about it, and this knight and I were in the same quest of the Sangreal. Sir, said a good man, for his sin he was thus wounded; and I marvel, said the good man, how ye durst take upon you so rich a thing as the high order of knighthood without clean confession, and that was the cause ye were bitterly wounded. For the way on the right hand betokeneth the highway of our Lord Jesu Christ, and the way of a good true good liver. And the other way betokeneth the way of sinners and of misbelievers. And when the devil saw your pride and presumption, for to take you in the quest of the Sangreal, that made you to be overthrown, for it may not be enchieved but by virtuous living. Also, the writing on the cross was a signification of heavenly deeds, and of knightly deeds in God's works, and no knightly deeds in worldly works. And pride is head of all deadly sins, that caused this knight to depart from Galahad. And where thou tookest the crown of gold thou sinnest in covetise and in theft: all this were no knightly deeds. And this Galahad, the holy knight, the which fought with the two knights, the two knights signify the two deadly sins which were wholly in this knight Melias; and they might not withstand you, for ye are without deadly sin.

Now departed Galahad from thence, and betaught them all unto God. Sir Melias said: My lord Galahad, as soon as I may ride I shall seek you. God send you health, said Galahad, and so took his horse and departed, and rode many journeys forward and backward, as adventure would lead him. And at the last it happened him to depart from a place or a castle the which was named Abblasoure; and he had heard no mass, the which he was wont ever to hear or ever he departed out of any castle or place, and kept that for a custom. Then Sir Galahad came unto a mountain where he found an old chapel, and found there nobody, for all, all was desolate; and there he kneeled to-fore the altar, and besought God of wholesome counsel. So as he prayed he heard a voice that said: Go thou now, thou adventurous knight, to the Castle of Maidens, and there do thou away the wicked customs.

CHAPTER XV

How Sir Galahad fought with the knights of the castle, and destroyed the wicked custom.

When Sir Galahad heard this he thanked God, and took his horse; and he had not ridden but half a mile, he saw in the valley afore him a strong castle with deep ditches, and there ran beside it a fair river that hight Severn; and there he met with a man of great age, and either saluted other, and Galahad asked him the castle's name. Fair sir, said he, it is the Castle of Maidens. That is a cursed castle, said Galahad, and all they that be conversant therein, for all pity is out thereof, and all hardiness and mischief is therein. Therefore, I counsel you, sir knight, to turn again. Sir, said Galahad, wit you well I shall not turn again. Then looked Sir Galahad on his arms that nothing failed him, and then he put his shield afore him; and anon there met him seven fair maidens, the which said unto him: Sir knight, ye ride here in a great folly, for ye have the water to pass over. Why should I not pass the water? said Galahad. So rode he away from them and met with a squire that said: Knight, those knights in the castle defy you, and defenden you ye go no further till that they wit what ye would. Fair sir, said Galahad, I come for to destroy the wicked custom of this castle. Sir, an ye will abide by that ye shall have enough to do. Go you now, said Galahad, and haste my needs.

Then the squire entered into the castle. And anon after there came out of the castle seven knights, and all were brethren. And when they saw Galahad they cried: Knight, keep thee, for we assure thee nothing but death. Why, said Galahad, will ye all have ado with me at once? Yea, said they, thereto mayst thou trust. Then Galahad put forth his spear and smote the foremost to the earth, that near he brake his neck. And therewithal the other smote him on his shield great strokes, so that their spears brake. Then Sir Galahad drew out his sword, and set upon them so hard that it was marvel to see it, and so through great force he made them to forsake the field; and Galahad chased them till they entered into the castle, and so passed through the castle at another gate.

And there met Sir Galahad an old man clothed in religious clothing, and said: Sir, have here the keys of this castle. Then Sir Galahad opened the gates, and saw so much people in the streets that he might not number them, and all said: Sir, ye be welcome, for long have we abiden here our deliverance. Then came to him a gentlewoman and said: These knights be fled, but they will come again this night, and here to begin again their evil custom. What will ye that I shall do? said Galahad. Sir, said the gentlewoman, that ye send after all the knights hither that hold their lands of this castle, and make them to swear for to use the customs that were used heretofore of old time. I will well, said Galahad. And there she brought him an horn of ivory, bounden with gold richly, and said: Sir, blow this horn which will be heard two mile about this castle. When Sir Galahad had blown the horn he set him down upon a bed.

Then came a priest to Galahad, and said: Sir, it is past a seven year agone that these seven brethren came into this castle, and harboured with the lord of this castle, that hight the Duke Lianour, and he was lord of all this country. And when they espied the duke's daughter, that was a full fair woman, then by their false covin they made debate betwixt themself, and the duke of his goodness would have departed them, and there they slew him and his eldest son. And then they took the maiden and the treasure of the castle. And then by great force they held all the knights of this castle against their will under their obeissance, and in great service and truage, robbing and pilling the poor common people of all that they had. So it happened on a day the duke's daughter said: Ye have done unto me great wrong to slay mine own father, and my brother, and thus to hold our lands: not for then, she said, ye shall not hold this castle for many years, for by one knight ye shall be overcome. Thus she prophesied seven years agone. Well, said the seven knights, sithen ye say so, there shall never lady nor knight pass this castle but they shall abide maugre their heads, or die therefore, till that knight be come by whom we shall lose this castle. And therefore is it called the Maidens' Castle, for they have devoured many maidens. Now, said Galahad, is she here for whom this castle was lost? Nay sir, said the priest, she was dead within these three nights after that she was thus enforced; and sithen have they kept her younger sister, which endureth great pains with mo other ladies.

By this were the knights of the country come, and then he made them do homage and fealty to the king's daughter, and set them in great ease of heart. And in the morn there came one to Galahad and told him how that Gawaine, Gareth, and Uwaine, had slain the seven brethren. I suppose well, said Sir Galahad, and took his armour and his horse, and commended them unto God.

CHAPTER XVI

How Sir Gawaine came to the abbey for to follow Galahad, and how he was shriven to a hermit.

Now, saith the tale, after Sir Gawaine departed, he rode many journeys, both toward and froward. And at the last he came to the abbey where Sir Galahad had the white shield, and there Sir Gawaine learned the way to sewe after Sir Galahad; and so he rode to the abbey where Melias lay sick, and there Sir Melias told Sir Gawaine of the marvellous adventures that Sir Galahad did. Certes, said Sir Gawaine, I am not happy that I took not the way that he went, for an

I may meet with him I will not depart from him lightly, for all marvellous adventures Sir Galahad enchieveth. Sir, said one of the monks, he will not of your fellowship. Why? said Sir Gawaine. Sir, said he, for ye be wicked and sinful, and he is full blessed. Right as they thus stood talking there came in riding Sir Gareth. And then they made joy either of other. And on the morn they heard mass, and so departed. And by the way they met with Sir Uwaine les Avoutres, and there Sir Uwaine told Sir Gawaine how he had met with none adventure sith he departed from the court. Nor we, said Sir Gawaine. And either promised other of the three knights not to depart while they were in that quest, but if fortune caused it.

So they departed and rode by fortune till that they came by the Castle of Maidens; and there the seven brethren espied the three knights, and said: Sithen, we be flemed by one knight from this castle, we shall destroy all the knights of King Arthur's that we may overcome, for the love of Sir Galahad. And therewith the seven knights set upon the three knights, and by fortune Sir Gawaine slew one of the brethren, and each one of his fellows slew another, and so slew the remnant. And then they took the way under the castle, and there they lost the way that Sir Galahad rode, and there everych of them departed from other; and Sir Gawaine rode till he came to an hermitage, and there he found the good man saying his evensong of Our Lady; and there Sir Gawaine asked harbour for charity, and the good man granted it him gladly.

Then the good man asked him what he was. Sir, he said, I am a knight of King Arthur's that am in the quest of the Sangreal, and my name is Sir Gawaine. Sir, said the good man, I would wit how it standeth betwixt God and you. Sir, said Sir Gawaine, I will with a good will show you my life if it please you; and there he told the hermit how a monk of an abbey called me wicked knight. He might well say it, said the hermit, for when ye were first made knight ye should have taken you to knightly deeds and virtuous living, and ye have done the contrary, for ye have lived mischievously many winters; and Sir Galahad is a maid and sinned never, and that is the cause he shall enchieve where he goeth that ye nor none such shall not attain, nor none in your fellowship, for ye have used the most untruest life that ever I heard knight live. For certes had ye not been so wicked as ye are, never had the seven brethren been slain by you and your two fellows. For Sir Galahad himself alone beat them all seven the day to-fore, but his living is such he shall slay no man lightly. Also I may say you the Castle of Maidens betokeneth the good souls that were in prison afore the Incarnation of Jesu Christ. And the seven nights betoken the seven deadly sins that reigned that time in the world; and I may liken the good Galahad unto the son of the High Father, that lighted within a maid, and bought all the souls out of thrall, so did Sir Galahad deliver all the maidens out of the woful castle.

Now, Sir Gawaine, said the good man, thou must do penance for thy sin. Sir, what penance shall I do? Such as I will give, said the good man. Nay, said Sir Gawaine, I may do no penance; for we knights adventurous oft suffer great woe and pain. Well, said the good man, and then he held his peace. And on the morn Sir Gawaine departed from the hermit, and betaught him unto God. And by adventure he met with Sir Aglovale and Sir Griflet, two knights of the Table Round. And they two rode four days without finding of any adventure, and at the fifth day they departed. And everych held as fell them by adventure. Here leaveth the tale of Sir Gawaine and his fellows, and speak we of Sir Galahad.

CHAPTER XVII

How Sir Galahad met with Sir Launcelot and Sir Percivale, and smote them down, and departed from them.

So when Sir Galahad was departed from the Castle of Maidens he rode till he came to a waste forest, and there he met with Sir Launcelot and Sir Percivale, but they knew him not, for he was new disguised. Right so Sir Launcelot, his father, dressed his spear and brake it upon Sir Galahad, and Galahad smote him so again that he smote down horse and man. And then he drew his sword, and dressed him unto Sir Percivale, and smote him so on the helm, that it rove to the coif of steel; and had not the sword swerved Sir Percivale had been slain, and with the stroke he fell out of his saddle. This jousts was done to-fore the hermitage where a recluse dwelled. And when she saw Sir Galahad ride, she said: God be with thee, best knight of the world. Ah certes, said she, all aloud that Launcelot and Percivale might hear it:

An yonder two knights had known thee as well as I do they would not have encountered with thee. Then Sir Galahad heard her say so he was adread to be known: therewith he smote his horse with his spurs and rode a great pace froward them. Then perceived they both that he was Galahad; and up they gat on their horses, and rode fast after him, but in a while he was out of their sight. And then they turned again with heavy cheer. Let us spere some tidings, said Percivale, at yonder recluse. Do as ye list, said Sir Launcelot.

When Sir Percivale came to the recluse she knew him well enough, and Sir Launcelot both. But Sir Launcelot rode overthwart and endlong in a wild forest, and held no path but as wild adventure led him. And at the last he came to a stony cross which departed two ways in waste land; and by the cross was a stone that was of marble, but it was so dark that Sir Launcelot might not wit what it was. Then Sir Launcelot looked by him, and saw an old chapel, and there he weened to have found people; and Sir Launcelot tied his horse till a tree, and there he did off his shield and hung it upon a tree, and then went to the chapel door, and found it waste and broken. And within he found a fair altar, full richly arrayed with cloth of clean silk, and there stood a fair clean candlestick, which bare six great candles, and the candlestick was of silver. And when Sir Launcelot saw this light he had great will for to enter into the chapel, but he could find no place where he might enter; then was he passing heavy and dismayed. Then he returned and came to his horse and did off his saddle and bridle, and let him pasture, and unlaced his helm, and ungirt his sword, and laid him down to sleep upon his shield to-fore the cross.

CHAPTER XVIII

How Sir Launcelot, half sleeping and half waking,
saw a sick man borne in a litter, and how he
was healed with the Sangreal.

And so he fell asleep; and half waking and sleeping he saw come by him two palfreys all fair and white, the which bare a litter, therein lying a sick knight. And when he was nigh the cross he there abode still. All this Sir Launcelot saw and beheld, for he slept not verily; and he heard him say: O sweet Lord, when shall this sorrow leave me? and when shall the holy vessel come by me, wherethrough I shall be blessed? For I have endured thus long, for little trespass. A full great while complained the knight thus, and always Sir Launcelot heard it. With that Sir Launcelot saw the candlestick with the six tapers come before the cross, and he saw nobody that brought it. Also there came a table of silver, and the holy vessel of the Sangreal, which Launcelot had seen aforetime in King Pescheour's house. And therewith the sick knight set him up, and held up both his hands, and said: Fair sweet Lord, which is here within this holy vessel; take heed unto me that I may be whole of this malady. And therewith on his hands and on his knees he went so nigh that he touched the holy vessel and kissed it, and anon he was whole; and then he said: Lord God, I thank thee, for I am healed of this sickness.

So when the holy vessel had been there a great while it went unto the chapel with the chandelier and the light, so that Launcelot wist not where it was become; for he was overtaken with sin that he had no power to rise again the holy vessel; wherefore after that many men said of him shame, but he took repentance after that. Then the sick knight dressed him up and kissed the cross: anon his squire brought him his arms, and asked his lord how he did. Certes, said he, I thank God right well, through the holy vessel I am healed. But I have marvel of this sleeping knight that had no power to awake when this holy vessel was brought hither. I dare right well say, said the squire, that he dwelleth in some deadly sin whereof he was never confessed. By my faith, said the knight, whatsomever he be he is unhappy, for as

I deem he is of the fellowship of the Round Table, the which is entered into the quest of the Sangreal. Sir, said the squire, here I have brought you all your arms save your helm and your sword, and therefore by mine assent now may ye take this knight's helm and his sword: and so he did. And when he was clean armed he took Sir Launcelot's horse, for he was better than his; and so departed they from the cross.

CHAPTER XIX

How a voice spake to Sir Launcelot, and how he found his horse and his helm borne away, and after went afoot.

Then anon Sir Launcelot waked, and set him up, and bethought him what he had seen there, and whether it were dreams or not. Right so heard he a voice that said: Sir Launcelot, more harder than is the stone, and more bitter than is the wood, and more naked and barer than is the leaf of the fig tree; therefore go thou from hence, and withdraw thee from this holy place. And when Sir Launcelot heard this he was passing heavy and wist not what to do, and so departed sore weeping, and cursed the time that he was born. For then he deemed never to have had worship more. For those words went to his heart, till that he knew wherefore he was called so. Then Sir Launcelot went to the cross and found his helm, his sword, and his horse taken away. And then he called himself a very wretch, and most unhappy of all knights; and there he said: My sin and my wickedness have brought me unto great dishonour. For when I sought worldly adventures for worldly desires, I ever enchieved them and had the better in every place, and never was I discomfit in no quarrel, were it right or wrong. And now I take upon me the adventures of holy things, and now I see and understand that mine old sin hindereth me and shameth me, so that I had no power to stir nor speak when the holy blood appeared afore me. So thus he sorrowed till it was day, and heard the fowls sing: then somewhat he was comforted. But when Sir Launcelot missed his horse and his harness then he wist well God was displeased with him.

Then he departed from the cross on foot into a forest; and so by prime he came to an high hill, and found an hermitage and a hermit therein which was going unto mass. And then Launcelot kneeled down and cried on Our Lord mercy for his wicked works. So when mass was done Launcelot called him, and prayed him for charity for to hear his life. With a good will, said the good man. Sir, said he, be ye of King Arthur's court and of the fellowship of the Round Table? Yea forsooth, and my name is Sir Launcelot du Lake that hath been right well said of, and now my good fortune is changed, for I am the most wretch of the world. The hermit beheld him and had marvel how he was so abashed. Sir, said the hermit, ye ought to thank God more than any knight living, for He hath caused you to have more worldly worship than any knight that now liveth. And for your presumption to take upon you in deadly sin for to be in His presence, where His flesh and His blood was, that caused you ye might not see it with worldly eyes; for He will not appear where such sinners be, but if it be unto their great hurt and unto their great shame; and there is no knight living now that ought to give God so great thank as ye, for He hath given you beauty, seemliness, and great strength above all other knights; and therefore ye are the more beholding unto God than any other man, to love Him and dread Him, for your strength and manhood will little avail you an God be against you.

CHAPTER XX

How Sir Launcelot was shriven, and what sorrow he made, and of the good ensamples which were showed him.

Then Sir Launcelot wept with heavy cheer, and said: Now I know well ye say me sooth. Sir, said the good man, hide none old sin from me. Truly, said Sir Launcelot, that were me full loath to discover. For this fourteen year I never discovered one thing that I have used, and that may I now wite my shame and my disadventure. And then he told there that good man all his life. And how he had loved a queen unmeasurably and out of measure long. And all my great deeds of arms that I have done, I did for the most part for the queen's sake, and for her sake would I do battle were it right or wrong; and never did I battle all only for God's sake, but for to win worship and to cause me to be the better beloved, and little or nought I thanked God of it. Then Sir Launcelot said: I pray you counsel me. I will counsel you, said the hermit, if ye will ensure me that ye will never come in that queen's fellowship as much as ye may forbear. And then Sir Launcelot promised him he nold, by the faith of his body. Look that your heart and your mouth accord, said the good man, and I shall ensure you ye shall have more worship than ever ye had.

Holy father, said Sir Launcelot, I marvel of the voice that said to me marvellous words, as ye have heard to-forehand. Have ye no marvel, said the good man, thereof, for it seemeth well God loveth you; for men may understand a stone is hard of kind, and namely one more than another; and that is to understand by thee, Sir Launcelot, for thou wilt not leave thy sin for no goodness that God hath sent thee; therefore thou art more than any stone, and never wouldst thou be made nesh nor by water nor by fire, and that is the heat of the Holy Ghost may not enter in thee. Now take heed, in all the world men shall not find one knight to whom Our Lord hath given so much of grace as He hath given you, for He hath given you fairness with seemliness, He hath given thee wit, discretion to know good from evil, He hath given thee prowess and hardiness, and given thee to work so largely that thou hast had at all days the better wheresomever thou came; and now Our Lord will suffer thee no longer, but that thou shalt know Him whether thou wilt or nylt. And why the voice called thee bitterer than wood, for where overmuch sin dwelleth, there may be but little sweetness, wherefore thou art likened to an old rotten tree.

Now have I showed thee why thou art harder than the stone and bitterer than the tree. Now shall I show thee why thou art more naked and barer than the fig tree. It befell that Our Lord on Palm Sunday preached in Jerusalem, and there He found in the people that all hardness was harboured in them, and there He found in all the town not one that would harbour him. And then He went without the town, and found in midst of the way a fig tree, the which was right fair and well garnished of leaves, but fruit had it none. Then Our Lord cursed the tree that bare no fruit; that betokeneth the fig tree unto Jerusalem, that had leaves and no fruit. So thou, Sir Launcelot, when the Holy Grail was brought afore thee, He found in thee no fruit, nor good thought nor good will, and defouled with lechery. Certes, said Sir Launcelot, all that you have said is true, and from henceforward I cast me, by the grace of God, never to be so wicked as I have been, but as to follow knighthood and to do feats of arms.

Then the good man enjoined Sir Launcelot such penance as he might do and to sewe knighthood, and so assoiled him, and prayed Sir Launcelot to abide with him all that day. I will well, said Sir Launcelot, for I have neither helm, nor horse, nor sword. As for that, said the good man, I shall help you or to-morn at even of an horse, and all that longed unto you. And then Sir Launcelot repented him greatly.

Here leaveth off the history of Sir Launcelot. And here followeth of Sir Percivale de Galis, which is the fourteenth book.

BOOK FOURTEEN

CHAPTER I

How Sir Percivale came to a recluse and asked counsel, and how she told him that she was his aunt.

Now saith the tale, that when Sir Launcelot was ridden after Sir Galahad, the which had all these adventures above said, Sir Percivale turned again unto the recluse, where he deemed to have tidings of that knight that Launcelot followed. And so he kneeled at her window, and the recluse opened it and asked Sir Percivale what he would. Madam, he said, I am a knight of King Arthur's court, and my name is Sir Percivale de Galis. When the recluse heard his name she had great joy of him, for mickle she had loved him to-fore any other knight, for she ought to do so, for she was his aunt. And then she commanded the gates to be opened, and there he had all the cheer that she might make him, and all that was in her power was at his commandment.

So on the morn Sir Percivale went to the recluse and asked her if she knew that knight with the white shield. Sir, said she, why would ye wit? Truly, madam, said Sir Percivale, I shall never be well at ease till that I know of that knight's fellowship, and that I may fight with him, for I may not leave him so lightly, for I have the shame yet. Ah, Percivale, said she, would ye fight with him? I see well ye have great will to be slain as your father was, through outrageousness. Madam, said Sir Percivale, it seemeth by your words that ye know me. Yea, said she, I well ought to know you, for I am your aunt, although I be in a priory place. For some called me sometime the Queen of the Waste Lands, and I was called the queen of most riches in the world; and it pleased me never my riches so much as doth my poverty. Then Sir Percivale wept for very pity when that he knew it was his aunt. Ah, fair nephew, said she, when heard ye tidings of your mother?

Truly, said he, I heard none of her, but I dream of her much in my sleep; and therefore I wot not whether she be dead or alive. Certes, fair nephew, said she, your mother is dead, for after your departing from her she took such a sorrow that anon, after she was confessed, she died. Now, God have mercy on her soul, said Sir Percivale, it sore forthinketh me; but all we must change the life. Now, fair aunt, tell me what is the knight? I deem it be he that bare the red arms on Whitsunday. Wit you well, said she, that this is he, for otherwise ought he not to do, but to go in red arms; and that same knight hath no peer, for he worketh all by miracle, and he shall never be overcome of none earthly man's hand.

CHAPTER II

How Merlin likened the Round Table to the world, and how the knights that should achieve the Sangreal should be known.

Also Merlin made the Round Table in tokening of roundness of the world, for by the Round Table is the world signified by right, for all the world, Christian and heathen, repair unto the Round Table; and when they are chosen to be of the fellowship of the Round Table they think them more blessed and more in worship than if they had gotten half the world; and ye have seen that they have lost their fathers and their mothers, and all their kin, and their wives and their children, for to be of your fellowship. It is well seen by you; for since ye have departed from your mother ye would never see her, ye found such fellowship at the Round Table. When Merlin had ordained the Round Table he said, by them which should be fellows of the Round Table the truth of the Sangreal should be well known. And men asked him how men might know them that should best do and to enchieve the Sangreal? Then he said there should be three white bulls that should enchieve it, and the two should be maidens, and the third should be chaste. And that one of the three should pass his father as much as the lion passeth the leopard, both of strength and hardiness.

They that heard Merlin say so said thus unto Merlin: Sithen there shall be such a knight, thou shouldest ordain by thy crafts a siege, that no man should sit in it but he all only that shall pass all other knights.

Then Merlin answered that he would do so. And then he made the Siege Perilous, in the which Galahad sat in at his meat on Whitsunday last past. Now, madam, said Sir Percivale, so much have I heard of you that by my good will I will never have ado with Sir Galahad but by way of kindness; and for God's love, fair aunt, can ye teach me some way where I may find him? for much would I love the fellowship of him. Fair nephew, said she, ye must ride unto a castle the which is called Goothe, where he hath a cousin-germain, and there may ye be lodged this night. And as he teacheth you, seweth after as fast as ye can; and if he can tell you no tidings of him, ride straight unto the Castle of Carbonek, where the maimed king is there lying, for there shall ye hear true tidings of him.

CHAPTER III

How Sir Percivale came into a monastery, where he found
King Evelake, which was an old man.

Then departed Sir Percivale from his aunt, either making great sorrow. And so he rode till evensong time. And then he heard a clock smite; and then he was ware of an house closed well with walls and deep ditches, and there he knocked at the gate and was let in, and he alighted and was led unto a chamber, and soon he was unarmed. And there he had right good cheer all that night; and on the morn he heard his mass, and in the monastery he found a priest ready at the altar. And on the right side he saw a pew closed with iron, and behind the altar he saw a rich bed and a fair, as of cloth of silk and gold.

Then Sir Percivale espied that therein was a man or a woman, for the visage was covered; then he left off his looking and heard his service. And when it came to the sacring, he that lay within that parclos dressed him up, and uncovered his head; and then him beseemed a passing old man, and he had a crown of gold upon his head, and his shoulders were naked and unhilled unto his navel. And then Sir Percivale espied his body was full of great wounds, both on the shoulders, arms, and visage. And ever he held up his hands against Our Lord's body, and cried: Fair, sweet Father, Jesu Christ, forget not me. And so he lay down, but always he was in his prayers and orisons;

and him seemed to be of the age of three hundred winter. And when the mass was done the priest took Our Lord's body and bare it to the sick king. And when he had used it he did off his crown, and commanded the crown to be set on the altar.

Then Sir Percivale asked one of the brethren what he was. Sir, said the good man, ye have heard much of Joseph of Aramathie, how he was sent by Jesu Christ into this land for to teach and preach the holy Christian faith; and therefore he suffered many persecutions the which the enemies of Christ did unto him, and in the city of Sarras he converted a king whose name was Evelake. And so this king came with Joseph into this land, and ever he was busy to be thereas the Sangreal was; and on a time he nighed it so nigh that Our Lord was displeased with him, but ever he followed it more and more, till God struck him almost blind. Then this king cried mercy, and said: Fair Lord, let me never die till the good knight of my blood of the ninth degree be come, that I may see him openly that he shall enchieve the Sangreal, that I may kiss him.

CHAPTER IV

How Sir Percivale saw many men of arms bearing a dead knight, and how he fought against them.

When the king thus had made his prayers he heard a voice that said: Heard be thy prayers, for thou shalt not die till he have kissed thee. And when that knight shall come the clearness of your eyes shall come again, and thou shalt see openly, and thy wounds shall be healed, and erst shall they never close. And this befell of King Evelake, and this same king hath lived this three hundred winters this holy life, and men say the knight is in the court that shall heal him. Sir, said the good man, I pray you tell me what knight that ye be, and if ye be of King Arthur's court and of the Table Round. Yea forsooth, said he, and my name is Sir Percivale de Galis. And when the good man understood his name he made great joy of him.

And then Sir Percivale departed and rode till the hour of noon. And he met in a valley about a twenty men of arms, which bare in a bier a knight deadly slain. And when they saw Sir Percivale they asked him of whence he was. And he answered: Of the court of King Arthur. Then they cried all at once: Slay him. Then Sir Percivale smote the first to the earth and his horse upon him. And then seven of the knights smote upon his shield all at once, and the remnant slew his horse so that he fell to the earth. So had they slain him or taken him had not the good knight, Sir Galahad, with the red arms come there by adventure into those parts. And when he saw all those knights upon one knight he cried: Save me that knight's life. And then he dressed him toward the twenty men of arms as fast as his horse might drive, with his spear in the rest, and smote the foremost horse and man to the earth. And when his spear was broken he set his hand to his sword, and smote on the right hand and on the left hand that it was marvel to see, and at every stroke he smote one down or put him to a rebuke, so that they would fight no more but fled to a thick forest, and Sir Galahad followed them.

And when Sir Percivale saw him chase them so, he made great sorrow that his horse was away. And then he wist well it was Sir Galahad. And then he cried aloud: Ah fair knight, abide and suffer me to do thankings unto thee, for much have ye done for me. But ever Sir Galahad rode so fast that at the last he passed out of his sight. And as fast as Sir Percivale might he went after him on foot, crying. And then he met with a yeoman riding upon an hackney, the which led in his hand a great steed blacker than any bear. Ah, fair friend, said Sir Percivale, as ever I may do for you, and to be your true knight in the first place ye will require me, that ye will lend me that black steed, that I might overtake a knight the which rideth afore me. Sir knight, said the yeoman, I pray you hold me excused of that, for that I may not do. For wit ye well, the horse is such a man's horse, that an I lent it you or any man, that he would slay me. Alas, said Sir Percivale, I had never so great sorrow as I have had for losing of yonder knight. Sir, said the yeoman, I am right heavy for you, for a good horse would beseem you well; but I dare not deliver you this horse but if ye would take him from me. That will I not do, said Sir Percivale. And so they departed; and Sir Percivale set him down under a tree, and made sorrow out of measure. And as he was there, there came a knight riding on the horse that the yeoman led, and he was clean armed.

CHAPTER V

*How a yeoman desired him to get again an horse, and how
Sir Percivale's hackney was slain, and how he gat an horse.*

And anon the yeoman came pricking after as fast as ever he might,
and asked Sir Percivale if he saw any knight riding on his black steed.
Yea, sir, forsooth, said he; why, sir, ask ye me that? Ah, sir, that steed
he hath benome me with strength; wherefore my lord will slay me in
what place he findeth me. Well, said Sir Percivale, what wouldst thou
that I did? Thou seest well that I am on foot, but an I had a good
horse I should bring him soon again. Sir, said the yeoman, take mine
hackney and do the best ye can, and I shall sewe you on foot to wit
how that ye shall speed. Then Sir Percivale alighted upon that
hackney, and rode as fast as he might, and at the last he saw that
knight. And then he cried: Knight, turn again; and he turned and set
his spear against Sir Percivale, and he smote the hackney in the midst
of the breast that he fell down dead to the earth, and there he had a
great fall, and the other rode his way. And then Sir Percivale was
wood wroth, and cried: Abide, wicked knight; coward and false-
hearted knight, turn again and fight with me on foot. But he
answered not, but passed on his way.

When Sir Percivale saw he would not turn he cast away his helm
and sword, and said: Now am I a very wretch, cursed and most
unhappy above all other knights. So in this sorrow he abode all that
day till it was night; and then he was faint, and laid him down and
slept till it was midnight; and then he awaked and saw afore him a
woman which said unto him right fiercely: Sir Percivale, what dost
thou here? He answered, I do neither good nor great ill. If thou wilt
ensure me, said she, that thou wilt fulfil my will when I summon
thee, I shall lend thee mine own horse which shall bear thee whither
thou wilt. Sir Percivale was glad of her proffer, and ensured her to
fulfil all her desire. Then abide me here, and I shall go and fetch you
an horse. And so she came soon again and brought an horse with her
that was inly black. When Percivale beheld that horse he marvelled
that it was so great and so well apparelled; and not for then he was so

hardy, and he leapt upon him, and took none heed of himself. And so anon as he was upon him he thrust to him with his spurs, and so he rode by a forest, and the moon shone clear. And within an hour and less he bare him four days' journey thence, until he came to a rough water the which roared, and his horse would have borne him into it.

CHAPTER VI

Of the great danger that Sir Percivale was in by his horse,
and how he saw a serpent and a lion fight.

And when Sir Percivale came nigh the brim, and saw the water so boistous, he doubted to overpass it. And then he made a sign of the cross in his forehead. When the fiend felt him so charged he shook off Sir Percivale, and he went into the water crying and roaring, making great sorrow, and it seemed unto him that the water brent. Then Sir Percivale perceived it was a fiend, the which would have brought him unto his perdition. Then he commended himself unto God, and prayed Our Lord to keep him from all such temptations; and so he prayed all that night till on the morn that it was day; then he saw that he was in a wild mountain the which was closed with the sea nigh all about, that he might see no land about him which might relieve him, but wild beasts.

And then he went into a valley, and there he saw a young serpent bring a young lion by the neck, and so he came by Sir Percivale. With that came a great lion crying and roaring after the serpent. And as fast as Sir Percivale saw this he marvelled, and hied him thither, but anon the lion had overtaken the serpent and began battle with him. And then Sir Percivale thought to help the lion, for he was the more natural beast of the two; and therewith he drew his sword, and set his shield afore him, and there he gave the serpent such a buffet that he had a deadly wound. When the lion saw that, he made no resemblaunt to fight with him, but made him all the cheer that a beast might make a man. Then Percivale perceived that, and cast down his shield which was broken; and then he did off his helm for to gather wind, for he was greatly enchafed with the serpent: and the lion went alway about him fawning as a spaniel. And then he stroked him on the neck and on the shoulders. And then he thanked God of the fellowship of that beast. And about noon the lion took his little whelp and trussed him and bare him there he came from.

Then was Sir Percivale alone. And as the tale telleth, he was one of the men of the world at that time which most believed in Our Lord Jesu Christ, for in those days there were but few folks that believed in God perfectly. For in those days the son spared not the father no more than a stranger. And so Sir Percivale comforted himself in our Lord Jesu, and besought God no temptation should bring him out of God's service, but to endure as his true champion. Thus when Sir Percivale had prayed he saw the lion come toward him, and then he couched down at his feet. And so all that night the lion and he slept together; and when Sir Percivale slept he dreamed a marvellous dream, that there two ladies met with him, and that one sat upon a lion, and that other sat upon a serpent, and that one of them was young, and the other was old; and the youngest him thought said: Sir Percivale, my lord saluteth thee, and sendeth thee word that thou array thee and make thee ready, for to-morn thou must fight with the strongest champion of the world. And if thou be overcome thou shall not be quit for losing of any of thy members, but thou shalt be shamed for ever to the world's end. And then he asked her what was her lord. And she said the greatest lord of all the world: and so she departed suddenly that he wist not where.

CHAPTER VII

Of the vision that Sir Percivale saw, and how his vision was expounded, and of his lion.

Then came forth the other lady that rode upon the serpent, and she said: Sir Percivale, I complain me of you that ye have done unto me, and have not offended unto you. Certes, madam, he said, unto you nor no lady I never offended. Yes, said she, I shall tell you why. I have nourished in this place a great while a serpent, which served me a great while, and yesterday ye slew him as he gat his prey. Say me for what cause ye slew him, for the lion was not yours. Madam, said Sir Percivale, I know well the lion was not mine, but I did it for the lion is of more gentler nature than the serpent, and therefore I slew him; meseemeth I did not amiss against you. Madam, said he, what would ye that I did? I would, said she, for the amends of my beast that ye become my man. And then he answered: That will I not grant you. No, said she, truly ye were never but my servant sin ye received the homage of Our Lord Jesu Christ. Therefore, I ensure you in what place I may find you without keeping I shall take you, as he that sometime was my man. And so she departed from Sir Percivale and left him sleeping, the which was sore travailed of his advision. And on the morn he arose and blessed him, and he was passing feeble.

Then was Sir Percivale ware in the sea, and saw a ship come sailing toward him; and Sir Percivale went unto the ship and found it covered within and without with white samite. And at the board stood an old man clothed in a surplice, in likeness of a priest. Sir, said Sir Percivale, ye be welcome. God keep you, said the good man. Sir, said the old man, of whence be ye? Sir, said Sir Percivale, I am of King Arthur's court, and a knight of the Table Round, the which am in the quest of the Sangreal; and here am I in great duresse, and never like to escape out of this wilderness. Doubt not, said the good man, an ye be so true a knight as the order of chivalry requireth, and of heart as ye ought to be, ye should not doubt that none enemy should slay you. What are ye? said Sir Percivale. Sir, said the old man, I am of a strange country, and hither I come to comfort you.

Sir, said Sir Percivale, what signifieth my dream that I dreamed this night? And there he told him altogether: She which rode upon the lion betokeneth the new law of holy church, that is to understand, faith, good hope, belief, and baptism. For she seemed younger than the other it is great reason, for she was born in the resurrection and the passion of Our Lord Jesu Christ. And for great love she came to thee to warn thee of thy great battle that shall befall thee. With whom, said Sir Percivale, shall I fight? With the most champion of the world, said the old man; for as the lady said, but if thou quit thee well thou shalt not be quit by losing of one member, but thou shalt be shamed to the world's end. And she that rode on the serpent signifieth the old law, and that serpent betokeneth a fiend. And why she blamed thee that thou slewest her servant, it betokeneth nothing; the serpent that thou slewest betokeneth the devil that thou rodest upon to the rock. And when thou madest a sign of the cross, there thou slewest him, and put away his power.

And when she asked thee amends and to become her man, and thou saidst thou wouldst not, that was to make thee to believe on her and leave thy baptism. So he commanded Sir Percivale to depart, and so he leapt over the board and the ship, and all went away he wist not whither. Then he went up unto the rock and found the lion which always kept him fellowship, and he stroked him upon the back and had great joy of him.

CHAPTER VIII

How Sir Percivale saw a ship coming to him-ward, and how the lady of the ship told him of her disheritance.

By that Sir Percivale had abiden there till mid-day he saw a ship came rowing in the sea, as all the wind of the world had driven it. And so it drove under that rock. And when Sir Percivale saw this he hied him thither, and found the ship covered with silk more blacker than any bear, and therein was a gentlewoman of great beauty, and she was clothed richly that none might be better. And when she saw Sir Percivale she said: Who brought you in this wilderness where ye be never like to pass hence, for ye shall die here for hunger and mischief? Damosel, said Sir Percivale, I serve the best man of the world, and in his service he will not suffer me to die, for who that knocketh shall enter, and who that asketh shall have, and who that seeketh him he hideth him not. But then she said: Sir Percivale, wot ye what I am? Yea, said he. Now who taught you my name? said she. Now, said Sir Percivale, I know you better than ye ween. And I came out of the waste forest where I found the Red Knight with the white shield, said the damosel. Ah, damosel, said he, with that knight would I meet passing fain. Sir knight, said she, an ye will ensure me by the faith that ye owe unto knighthood that ye shall do my will what time I summon you, and I shall bring you unto that knight. Yea, said he, I shall promise you to fulfil your desire. Well, said she, now shall I tell you. I saw him in the forest chasing two knights unto a water, the which is called Mortaise; and they drove him into the water for dread of death, and the two knights passed over, and the Red Knight passed after, and there his horse was drenched, and he, through great strength, escaped unto the land: thus she told him, and Sir Percivale was passing glad thereof.

Then she asked him if he had ate any meat late. Nay, madam, truly I ate no meat nigh this three days, but late here I spake with a good man that fed me with his good words and holy, and refreshed me greatly. Ah, sir knight, said she, that same man is an enchanter and a multiplier of words. For an ye believe him ye shall plainly be shamed, and die in this rock for pure hunger, and be eaten with wild beasts; and ye be a young man and a goodly knight, and I shall help you an ye will. What are ye, said Sir Percivale, that proffered me thus great kindness? I am, said she, a gentlewoman that am disherited, which was sometime the richest woman of the world. Damosel, said Sir Percivale, who hath disherited you? for I have great pity of you. Sir, said she, I dwelled with the greatest man of the world, and he made me so fair and clear that there was none like me; and of that great beauty I had a little pride more than I ought to have had. Also I said a word that pleased him not. And then he would not suffer me to be any longer in his company, and so drove me from mine heritage, and so disherited me, and he had never pity of me nor of none of my council, nor of my court. And sithen, sir knight, it hath befallen me so, and through me and mine I have benome him many of his men, and made them to become my men. For they ask never nothing of me but I give it them, that and much more. Thus I and all my servants were against him night and day. Therefore I know now no good knight, nor no good man, but I get them on my side an I may. And for that I know that thou art a good knight, I beseech you to help me; and for ye be a fellow of the Round Table, wherefore ye ought not to fail no gentlewoman which is disherited, an she besought you of help.

CHAPTER IX

*How Sir Percivale promised her help, and how he required
her of love, and how he was saved from the fiend.*

Then Sir Percivale promised her all the help that he might; and then she thanked him. And at that time the weather was hot. Then she called unto her a gentlewoman and bade her bring forth a pavilion;

and so she did, and pight it upon the gravel. Sir, said she, now may ye rest you in this heat of the day. Then he thanked her, and she put off his helm and his shield, and there he slept a great while. And then he awoke and asked her if she had any meat, and she said: Yea, also ye shall have enough. And so there was set enough upon the table, and thereon so much that he had marvel, for there was all manner of meats that he could think on. Also he drank there the strongest wine that ever he drank, him thought, and therewith he was a little chafed more than he ought to be; with that he beheld the gentlewoman, and him thought she was the fairest creature that ever he saw. And then Sir Percivale proffered her love, and prayed her that she would be his. Then she refused him, in a manner, when he required her, for the cause he should be the more ardent on her, and ever he ceased not to pray her of love. And when she saw him well enchafed, then she said: Sir Percivale, wit you well I shall not fulfil your will but if ye swear from henceforth ye shall be my true servant, and to do nothing but that I shall command you. Will ye ensure me this as ye be a true knight? Yea, said he, fair lady, by the faith of my body. Well, said she, now shall ye do with me whatso it please you; and now wit ye well ye are the knight in the world that I have most desire to.

And then two squires were commanded to make a bed in midst of the pavilion. And anon she was unclothed and laid therein. And then Sir Percivale laid him down by her naked; and by adventure and grace he saw his sword lie on the ground naked, in whose pommel was a red cross and the sign of the crucifix therein, and bethought him on his knighthood and his promise made to-forehand unto the good man; then he made a sign of the cross in his forehead, and therewith the pavilion turned up-so-down, and then it changed unto a smoke, and a black cloud, and then he was adread and cried aloud:

CHAPTER X

How Sir Percivale for penance rove himself through the thigh; and how she was known for the devil.

Fair sweet Father, Jesu Christ, ne let me not be shamed, the which was nigh lost had not thy good grace been. And then he looked into a ship, and saw her enter therein, which said: Sir Percivale, ye have betrayed me. And so she went with the wind roaring and yelling, that it seemed all the water brent after her. Then Sir Percivale made great sorrow, and drew his sword unto him, saying: Sithen my flesh will be my master I shall punish it; and therewith he rove himself through the thigh that the blood stert about him, and said: O good Lord, take this in recompensation of that I have done against thee, my Lord. So then he clothed him and armed him, and called himself a wretch, saying: How nigh was I lost, and to have lost that I should never have gotten again, that was my virginity, for that may never be recovered after it is once lost. And then he stopped his bleeding wound with a piece of his shirt.

Thus as he made his moan he saw the same ship come from Orient that the good man was in the day afore, and the noble knight was ashamed with himself, and therewith he fell in a swoon. And when he awoke he went unto him weakly, and there he saluted this good man. And then he asked Sir Percivale: How hast thou done sith I departed? Sir, said he, here was a gentlewoman and led me into deadly sin. And there he told him altogether. Knew ye not the maid? said the good man. Sir, said he, nay, but well I wot the fiend sent her hither to shame me. O good knight, said he, thou art a fool, for that gentlewoman was the master fiend of hell, the which hath power above all devils, and that was the old lady that thou sawest in thine advision riding on the serpent. Then he told Sir Percivale how our Lord Jesu Christ beat him out of heaven for his sin, the which was the most brightest angel of heaven, and therefore he lost his heritage. And that was the champion that thou foughtest withal, the which had overcome thee had not the grace of God been. Now beware Sir Percivale, and take this for an ensample. And then the good man vanished away. Then Sir Percivale took his arms, and entered into the ship, and so departed from thence.

Here endeth the fourteenth book, which is of Sir
Percivale. And here followeth of Sir Launcelot,
which is the fifteenth book.

BOOK FIFTEEN

CHAPTER I

How Sir Launcelot came to a chapel, where he found dead, in a white shirt, a man of religion, of an hundred winter old.

When the hermit had kept Sir Launcelot three days, the hermit gat him an horse, an helm, and a sword. And then he departed about the hour of noon. And then he saw a little house. And when he came near he saw a chapel, and there beside he saw an old man that was clothed all in white full richly; and then Sir Launcelot said: God save you. God keep you, said the good man, and make you a good knight. Then Sir Launcelot alighted and entered into the chapel, and there he saw an old man dead, in a white shirt of passing fine cloth.

Sir, said the good man, this man that is dead ought not to be in such clothing as ye see him in, for in that he brake the oath of his order, for he hath been more than a hundred winter a man of a religion. And then the good man and Sir Launcelot went into the chapel; and the good man took a stole about his neck, and a book, and then he conjured on that book; and with that they saw in an hideous figure and horrible, that there was no man hard-hearted nor so hard but he should have been afeard. Then said the fiend: Thou hast travailed me greatly; now tell me what thou wilt with me. I will, said the good man, that thou tell me how my fellow became dead, and whether he be saved or damned. Then he said with an horrible voice: He is not lost but saved. How may that be? said the good man; it seemed to me that he lived not well, for he brake his order for to wear a shirt where he ought to wear none, and who that trespasseth against our order doth not well. Not so, said the fiend, this man that lieth here dead was come of a great lineage. And there was a lord that hight the Earl de Vale, that held great war against this man's nephew, the which hight Aguarus. And so this Aguarus saw the earl was bigger

than he. Then he went for to take counsel of his uncle, the which
lieth here dead as ye may see. And then he asked leave, and went out
of his hermitage for to maintain his nephew against the mighty earl;
and so it happed that this man that lieth here dead did so much by his
wisdom and hardiness that the earl was taken, and three of his lords,
by force of this dead man.

CHAPTER II

*Of a dead man, how men would have hewn him, and it would
not be, and how Sir Launcelot took the hair of the dead man.*

Then was there peace betwixt the earl and this Aguarus, and great
surety that the earl should never war against him. Then this dead man
that here lieth came to this hermitage again; and then the earl made
two of his nephews for to be avenged upon this man. So they came
on a day, and found this dead man at the sacring of his mass, and they
abode him till he had said mass. And then they set upon him and drew
out swords to have slain him; but there would no sword bite on him
more than upon a gad of steel, for the high Lord which he served He
him preserved. Then made they a great fire, and did off all his clothes,
and the hair off his back. And then this dead man hermit said unto
them: Ween you to burn me? It shall not lie in your power nor to
perish me as much as a thread, an there were any on my body. No?
said one of them, it shall be assayed. And then they despoiled him, and
put upon him this shirt, and cast him in a fire, and there he lay all that
night till it was day in that fire, and was not dead, and so in the morn I
came and found him dead; but I found neither thread nor skin tamed,
and so took him out of the fire with great fear, and laid him here as ye
may see. And now may ye suffer me to go my way, for I have said
you the sooth. And then he departed with a great tempest.

Then was the good man and Sir Launcelot more gladder than they
were to-fore. And then Sir Launcelot dwelled with that good man
that night. Sir, said the good man, be ye not Sir Launcelot du Lake?
Yea, sir, said he. What seek ye in this country? Sir, said Sir Launcelot,
I go to seek the adventures of the Sangreal. Well, said he, seek it ye
may well, but though it were here ye shall have no power to see it no

more than a blind man should see a bright sword, and that is long on your sin, and else ye were more abler than any man living. And then Sir Launcelot began to weep. Then said the good man: Were ye confessed sith ye entered into the quest of the Sangreal? Yea, sir, said Sir Launcelot. Then upon the morn when the good man had sung his mass, then they buried the dead man. Then Sir Launcelot said: Father, what shall I do? Now, said the good man, I require you take this hair that was this holy man's and put it next thy skin, and it shall prevail thee greatly. Sir, and I will do it, said Sir Launcelot. Also I charge you that ye eat no flesh as long as ye be in the quest of the Sangreal, nor ye shall drink no wine, and that ye hear mass daily an ye may do it. So he took the hair and put it upon him, and so departed at evensong-time.

And so rode he into a forest, and there he met with a gentlewoman riding upon a white palfrey, and then she asked him: Sir knight, whither ride ye? Certes, damosel, said Launcelot, I wot not whither I ride but as fortune leadeth me. Ah, Sir Launcelot, said she, I wot what adventure ye seek, for ye were afore time nearer than ye be now, and yet shall ye see it more openly than ever ye did, and that shall ye understand in short time. Then Sir Launcelot asked her where he might be harboured that night. Ye shall not find this day nor night, but to-morn ye shall find harbour good, and ease of that ye be in doubt of. And then he commended her unto God. Then he rode till that he came to a Cross, and took that for his host as for that night.

CHAPTER III

Of an advision that Sir Launcelot had, and how he told it to an hermit, and desired counsel of him.

And so he put his horse to pasture, and did off his helm and his shield, and made his prayers unto the Cross that he never fall in deadly sin again. And so he laid him down to sleep. And anon as he was asleep it befell him there an advision, that there came a man afore him all by compass of stars, and that man had a crown of gold on his head, and that man led in his fellowship seven kings and two knights. And all these worshipped the Cross, kneeling upon their knees, holding up their hands toward the heaven. And all they said: Fair sweet Father of heaven, come and visit us, and yield unto us everych as we have deserved.

Then looked Launcelot up to the heaven, and him seemed the clouds did open, and an old man came down, with a company of angels, and alighted among them, and gave unto everych his blessing, and called them his servants, and good and true knights. And when this old man had said thus he came to one of those knights, and said: I have lost all that I have set in thee, for thou hast ruled thee against me as a warrior, and used wrong wars with vain-glory, more for the pleasure of the world than to please me, therefore thou shalt be confounded without thou yield me my treasure. All this advision saw Sir Launcelot at the Cross.

And on the morn he took his horse and rode till midday; and there by adventure he met with the same knight that took his horse, helm, and his sword, when he slept when the Sangreal appeared afore the Cross. When Sir Launcelot saw him he saluted him not fair, but cried on high: Knight, keep thee, for thou hast done to me great unkindness. And then they put afore them their spears, and Sir Launcelot came so fiercely upon him that he smote him and his horse down to the earth, that he had nigh broken his neck. Then Sir Launcelot took the knight's horse that was his own aforehand, and descended from the horse he sat upon, and mounted upon his own horse, and tied the knight's own horse to a tree, that he might find that horse when that he was arisen. Then Sir Launcelot rode till night, and by adventure he met an hermit, and each of them saluted other; and there he rested with that good man all night, and gave his horse such as he might get. Then said the good man unto Launcelot: Of whence be ye? Sir, said he, I am of Arthur's court, and my name is Sir Launcelot du Lake that am in the quest of the Sangreal, and therefore I pray you to counsel me of a vision the which I had at the Cross. And so he told him all.

CHAPTER IV

*How the hermit expounded to Sir Launcelot his advision,
and told him that Sir Galahad was his son.*

Lo, Sir Launcelot, said the good man, there thou mightest understand the high lineage that thou art come of, and thine advision betokeneth. After the passion of Jesu Christ forty year, Joseph of Aramathie preached the victory of King Evelake, that he had in the battles the better of his enemies. And of the seven kings and the two knights: the first of them is called Nappus, an holy man; and the second hight Nacien, in remembrance of his grandsire, and in him dwelled our Lord Jesu Christ; and the third was called Helias le Grose; and the fourth hight Lisais; and the fifth hight Jonas, he departed out of his country and went into Wales, and took there the daughter of Manuel, whereby he had the land of Gaul, and he came to dwell in this country. And of him came King Launcelot thy grandsire, the which there wedded the king's daughter of Ireland, and he was as worthy a man as thou art, and of him came King Ban, thy father, the which was the last of the seven kings. And by thee, Sir Launcelot, it signifieth that the angels said thou were none of the seven fellowships. And the last was the ninth knight, he was signified to a lion, for he should pass all manner of earthly knights, that is Sir Galahad, the which thou gat on King Pelles' daughter; and thou ought to thank God more than any other man living, for of a sinner earthly thou hast no peer as in knighthood, nor never shall be. But little thank hast thou given to God for all the great virtues that God hath lent thee. Sir, said Launcelot, ye say that that good knight is my son. That oughtest thou to know and no man better, said the good man, for thou knewest the daughter of King Pelles fleshly, and on her thou begattest Galahad, and that was he that at the feast of Pentecost sat in the Siege Perilous; and therefore make thou it known openly that he is one of thy begetting on King Pelles' daughter, for that will be your worship and honour, and to all thy kindred. And I counsel you in no place press not upon him to have ado with him. Well, said Launcelot, meseemeth that good knight should pray for me unto the High

Father, that I fall not to sin again. Trust thou well, said the good man, thou farest mickle the better for his prayer; but the son shall not bear the wickedness of the father, nor the father shall not bear the wickedness of the son, but everych shall bear his own burden. And therefore beseek thou only God, and He will help thee in all thy needs. And then Sir Launcelot and he went to supper, and so laid him to rest, and the hair pricked so Sir Launcelot's skin which grieved him full sore, but he took it meekly, and suffered the pain. And so on the morn he heard his mass and took his arms, and so took his leave.

CHAPTER V

How Sir Launcelot jousted with many knights, and how he was taken.

And then mounted upon his horse, and rode into a forest, and held no highway. And as he looked afore him he saw a fair plain, and beside that a fair castle, and afore the castle were many pavilions of silk and of diverse hue. And him seemed that he saw there five hundred knights riding on horseback; and there were two parties: they that were of the castle were all on black horses and their trappings black, and they that were without were all on white horses and trappings, and everych hurtled to other that it marvelled Sir Launcelot. And at the last him thought they of the castle were put to the worse.

Then thought Sir Launcelot for to help there the weaker party in increasing of his chivalry. And so Sir Launcelot thrust in among the party of the castle, and smote down a knight, horse and man, to the earth. And then he rashed here and there, and did marvellous deeds of arms. And then he drew out his sword, and struck many knights to the earth, so that all those that saw him marvelled that ever one knight might do so great deeds of arms. But always the white knights held them nigh about Sir Launcelot, for to tire him and wind him. But at the last, as a man may not ever endure, Sir Launcelot waxed so faint of fighting and travailing, and was so weary of his great deeds, that* he might not lift up his arms for to give one stroke, so that he

* So Wynkyn de Worde: Caxton 'but'.

weened never to have borne arms; and then they all took and led him away into a forest, and there made him to alight and to rest him. And then all the fellowship of the castle were overcome for the default of him. Then they said all unto Sir Launcelot: Blessed be God that ye be now of our fellowship, for we shall hold you in our prison; and so they left him with few words. And then Sir Launcelot made great sorrow, For never or now was I never at tournament nor jousts but I had the best, and now I am shamed; and then he said: Now I am sure that I am more sinfuller than ever I was.

Thus he rode sorrowing, and half a day he was out of despair, till that he came into a deep valley. And when Sir Launcelot saw he might not ride up into the mountain, he there alighted under an apple tree, and there he left his helm and his shield, and put his horse unto pasture. And then he laid him down to sleep. And then him thought there came an old man afore him, the which said: Ah, Launcelot of evil faith and poor belief, wherefore is thy will turned so lightly toward thy deadly sin? And when he had said thus he vanished away, and Launcelot wist not where he was become. Then he took his horse, and armed him; and as he rode by the way he saw a chapel where was a recluse, which had a window that she might see up to the altar. And all aloud she called Launcelot, for that he seemed a knight errant. And then he came, and she asked him what he was, and of what place, and where about he went to seek.

CHAPTER VI

How Sir Launcelot told his advision to a woman,
and how she expounded it to him.

And then he told her altogether word by word, and the truth how it befell him at the tournament. And after told her his advision that he had had that night in his sleep, and prayed her to tell him what it might mean, for he was not well content with it. Ah, Launcelot, said she, as long as ye were knight of earthly knighthood ye were the most marvellous man of the world, and most adventurous. Now, said the lady, sithen ye be set among the knights of heavenly adventures, if adventure fell thee contrary at that tournament have thou no marvel, for that tournament yesterday was but a tokening of Our Lord. And not for then there was none enchantment, for they at the tournament were earthly knights. The tournament was a token to see who should have most knights, either Eliazar, the son of King Pelles, or Argustus, the son of King Harlon. But Eliazar was all clothed in white, and Argustus was covered in black, the which were [over]come.

All what this betokeneth I shall tell you. The day of Pentecost, when King Arthur held his court, it befell that earthly kings and knights took a tournament together, that is to say the quest of the Sangreal. The earthly knights were they the which were clothed all in black, and the covering betokeneth the sins whereof they be not confessed. And they with the covering of white betokeneth virginity, and they that chose chastity. And thus was the quest begun in them. Then thou beheld the sinners and the good men, and when thou sawest the sinners overcome, thou inclinest to that party for bobaunce and pride of the world, and all that must be left in that quest, for in this quest thou shalt have many fellows and thy betters. For thou art so feeble of evil trust and good belief, this made it when thou were there where they took thee and led thee into the forest. And anon there appeared the Sangreal unto the white knights, but thou was so feeble of good belief and faith that thou mightest not abide it for all the teaching of the good man, but anon thou turnest to the sinners, and that caused thy misadventure that thou should'st know good from evil and vain glory of the world, the which is not worth a pear. And for great pride thou madest great sorrow that thou hadst not overcome all the white knights with the covering of white, by whom was betokened virginity and chastity; and therefore God was wroth with you, for God loveth no such deeds in this quest. And this advision signifieth that thou were of evil faith and of poor belief, the which will make thee to fall into the deep pit of hell if thou keep thee not. Now have I warned thee of thy vain glory and of thy pride, that thou hast many times erred against thy Maker. Beware of everlasting pain, for of all earthly knights I have most pity of thee, for I know well thou hast not thy peer of any earthly sinful man.

And so she commended Sir Launcelot to dinner. And after dinner he took his horse and commended her to God, and so rode into a deep valley, and there he saw a river and an high mountain. And through the water he must needs pass, the which was hideous; and then in the name of God he took it with good heart. And when he came over he saw an armed knight, horse and man black as any bear; without any word he smote Sir Launcelot's horse to the earth; and so he passed on, he wist not where he was become. And then he took his helm and his shield, and thanked God of his adventure.

Here leaveth off the story of Sir Launcelot, and speak we of Sir Gawaine, the which is the sixteenth book.

BOOK SIXTEEN

CHAPTER I

How Sir Gawaine was nigh weary of the quest of the Sangreal, and of his marvellous dream.

When Sir Gawaine was departed from his fellowship he rode long without any adventure. For he found not the tenth part of adventure as he was wont to do. For Sir Gawaine rode from Whitsuntide until Michaelmas and found none adventure that pleased him. So on a day it befell Gawaine met with Sir Ector de Maris, and either made great joy of other that it were marvel to tell. And so they told everych other, and complained them greatly that they could find none adventure. Truly, said Sir Gawaine unto Sir Ector, I am nigh weary of this quest, and loath I am to follow further in strange countries. One thing marvelled me, said Sir Ector, I have met with twenty knights, fellows of mine, and all they complain as I do. I have marvel, said Sir Gawaine, where that Sir Launcelot, your brother, is. Truly, said Sir Ector, I cannot hear of him, nor of Sir Galahad, Percivale, nor Sir Bors. Let them be, said Sir Gawaine, for they four have no peers. And if one thing were not in Sir Launcelot he had no fellow of none earthly man; but he is as we be, but if he took more pain upon him. But an these four be met together they will be loath that any man meet with them; for an they fail of the Sangreal it is in waste of all the remnant to recover it.

Thus Ector and Gawaine rode more than eight days, and on a Saturday they found an old chapel, the which was wasted that there seemed no man thither repaired; and there they alighted, and set their spears at the door, and in they entered into the chapel, and there made their orisons a great while, and set them down in the sieges of the chapel. And as they spake of one thing and other, for heaviness they fell asleep, and there befell them both marvellous adventures. Sir

Gawaine him seemed he came into a meadow full of herbs and flowers, and there he saw a rack of bulls, an hundred and fifty, that were proud and black, save three of them were all white, and one had a black spot, and the other two were so fair and so white that they might be no whiter. And these three bulls which were so fair were tied with two strong cords. And the remnant of the bulls said among them: Go we hence to seek better pasture. And so some went, and some came again, but they were so lean that they might not stand upright; and of the bulls that were so white, that one came again and no mo. But when this white bull was come again among these other there rose up a great cry for lack of wind that failed them; and so they departed one here and another there: this advision befell Gawaine that night.

CHAPTER II

Of the advision of Sir Ector, and how he jousted with Sir Uwaine les Avoutres, his sworn brother.

But to Ector de Maris befell another vision the contrary. For it seemed him that his brother, Sir Launcelot, and he alighted out of a chair and leapt upon two horses, and the one said to the other: Go we seek that we shall not find. And him thought that a man beat Sir Launcelot, and despoiled him, and clothed him in another array, the which was all full of knots, and set him upon an ass, and so he rode till he came to the fairest well that ever he saw; and Sir Launcelot alighted and would have drunk of that well. And when he stooped to drink of the water the water sank from him. And when Sir Launcelot saw that, he turned and went thither as the head came from. And in the meanwhile he trowed that himself and Sir Ector rode till that they came to a rich man's house where there was a wedding. And there he saw a king the which said: Sir knight, here is no place for you. And then he turned again unto the chair that he came from.

Thus within a while both Gawaine and Ector awaked, and either told other of their advision, the which marvelled them greatly. Truly, said Ector, I shall never be merry till I hear tidings of my brother Launcelot. Now as they sat thus talking they saw an hand showing

unto the elbow, and was covered with red samite, and upon that
hung a bridle not right rich, and held within the fist a great candle
which burned right clear, and so passed afore them, and entered into
the chapel, and then vanished away and they wist not where. And
anon came down a voice which said: Knights of full evil faith and of
poor belief, these two things have failed you, and therefore ye may
not come to the adventures of the Sangreal.

Then first spake Gawaine and said: Ector, have ye heard these
words? Yea truly, said Sir Ector, I heard all. Now go we, said Sir
Ector, unto some hermit that will tell us of our advision, for it
seemeth me we labour all in vain. And so they departed and rode into
a valley, and there met with a squire which rode on an hackney, and
they saluted him fair. Sir, said Gawaine, can thou teach us to any
hermit? Here is one in a little mountain, but it is so rough there may
no horse go thither, and therefore ye must go upon foot; there shall
ye find a poor house, and there is Nacien the hermit, which is the
holiest man in this country. And so they departed either from other.

And then in a valley they met with a knight all armed, which
proffered them to joust as far as he saw them. In the name of God,
said Sir Gawaine, sith I departed from Camelot there was none
proffered me to joust but once. And now, sir, said Ector, let me joust
with him. Nay, said Gawaine, ye shall not but if I be beat; it shall not
for-think me then if ye go after me. And then either embraced other
to joust and came together as fast as their horses might run, and brast
their shields and the mails, and the one more than the other; and
Gawaine was wounded in the left side, but the other knight was
smitten through the breast, and the spear came out on the other side,
and so they fell both out of their saddles, and in the falling they brake
both their spears.

Anon Gawaine arose and set his hand to his sword, and cast his
shield afore him. But all for naught was it, for the knight had no power
to arise against him. Then said Gawaine: Ye must yield you as an
overcome man, or else I may slay you. Ah, sir knight, said he, I am but
dead, for God's sake and of your gentleness lead me here unto an
abbey that I may receive my Creator. Sir, said Gawaine, I know no
house of religion hereby. Sir, said the knight, set me on an horse to-
fore you, and I shall teach you. Gawaine set him up in the saddle, and
he leapt up behind him for to sustain him, and so came to an abbey
where they were well received; and anon he was unarmed, and

received his Creator. Then he prayed Gawaine to draw out the truncheon of the spear out of his body. Then Gawaine asked him what he was, that knew him not. I am, said he, of King Arthur's court, and was a fellow of the Round Table, and we were brethren sworn together; and now Sir Gawaine, thou hast slain me, and my name is Uwaine les Avoutres, that sometime was son unto King Uriens, and was in the quest of the Sangreal; and now forgive it thee God, for it shall ever be said that the one sworn brother hath slain the other.

CHAPTER III

How Sir Gawaine and Sir Ector came to an hermitage to be confessed, and how they told to the hermit their advisions.

Alas, said Gawaine, that ever this misadventure is befallen me. No force, said Uwaine, sith I shall die this death, of a much more worshipfuller man's hand might I not die; but when ye come to the court recommend me unto my lord, King Arthur, and all those that be left alive, and for old brotherhood think on me. Then began Gawaine to weep, and Ector also. And then Uwaine himself and Sir Gawaine drew out the truncheon of the spear, and anon departed the soul from the body. Then Sir Gawaine and Sir Ector buried him as men ought to bury a king's son, and made write upon his name, and by whom he was slain.

Then departed Gawaine and Ector, as heavy as they might for their misadventure, and so rode till that they came to the rough mountain, and there they tied their horses and went on foot to the hermitage. And when they were come up they saw a poor house, and beside the chapel a little courtelage, where Nacien the hermit gathered worts, as he which had tasted none other meat of a great while. And when he saw the errant knights he came toward them and saluted them, and they him again. Fair lords, said he, what adventure brought you hither? Sir, said Gawaine, to speak with you for to be confessed. Sir, said the hermit, I am ready. Then they told him so much that he wist well what they were. And then he thought to counsel them if he might.

Then began Gawaine first and told him of his advision that he had

had in the chapel, and Ector told him all as it is afore rehearsed. Sir, said the hermit unto Sir Gawaine, the fair meadow and the rack therein ought to be understood the Round Table, and by the meadow ought to be understood humility and patience, those be the things which be always green and quick; for men may no time overcome humility and patience, therefore was the Round Table founded; and the chivalry hath been at all times so by the fraternity which was there that she might not be overcome; for men said she was founded in patience and in humility. At the rack ate an hundred and fifty bulls; but they ate not in the meadow, for their hearts should be set in humility and patience, and the bulls were proud and black save only three. By the bulls is to understand the fellowship of the Round Table, which for their sin and their wickedness be black. Blackness is to say without good or virtuous works. And the three bulls which were white save only one that was spotted: the two white betoken Sir Galahad and Sir Percivale, for they be maidens clean and without spot; and the third that had a spot signifieth Sir Bors de Ganis, which trespassed but once in his virginity, but sithen he kept himself so well in chastity that all is forgiven him and his misdeeds. And why those three were tied by the necks, they be three knights in virginity and chastity, and there is no pride smitten in them. And the black bulls which said: Go we hence, they were those which at Pentecost at the high feast took upon them to go in the quest of the Sangreal without confession: they might not enter in the meadow of humility and patience. And therefore they returned into waste countries, that signifieth death, for there shall die many of them: everych of them shall slay other for sin, and they that shall escape shall be so lean that it shall be marvel to see them. And of the three bulls without spot, the one shall come again, and the other two never.

CHAPTER IV

How the hermit expounded their advision.

Then spake Nacien unto Ector: Sooth it is that Launcelot and ye came down off one chair: the chair betokeneth mastership and lordship which ye came down from. But ye two knights, said the hermit, ye go to seek that ye shall never find, that is the Sangreal; for it is the secret thing of our Lord Jesu Christ. What is to mean that Sir Launcelot fell down off his horse: he hath left pride and taken him to humility, for he hath cried mercy loud for his sin, and sore repented him, and our Lord hath clothed him in his clothing which is full of knots, that is the hair that he weareth daily. And the ass that he rode upon is a beast of humility, for God would not ride upon no steed, nor upon no palfrey; so in ensample that an ass betokeneth meekness, that thou sawest Sir Launcelot ride on in thy sleep. And the well whereas the water sank from him when he should have taken thereof, and when he saw he might not have it, he returned thither from whence he came, for the well betokeneth the high grace of God, the more men desire it to take it, the more shall be their desire. So when he came nigh the Sangreal, he meeked him that he held him not a man worthy to be so nigh the Holy Vessel, for he had been so defouled in deadly sin by the space of many years; yet when he kneeled to drink of the well, there he saw great providence of the Sangreal. And for he had served so long the devil, he shall have vengeance four-and-twenty days long, for that he hath been the devil's servant four-and-twenty years. And then soon after he shall return unto Camelot out of this country, and he shall say a part of such things as he hath found.

Now will I tell you what betokeneth the hand with the candle and the bridle: that is to understand the Holy Ghost where charity is ever, and the bridle signifieth abstinence. For when she is bridled in Christian man's heart she holdeth him so short that he falleth not in deadly sin. And the candle which showeth clearness and sight signifieth the right way of Jesu Christ. And when he went and said: Knights of poor faith and of wicked belief, these three things failed, charity, abstinence, and truth; therefore ye may not attain that high adventure of the Sangreal.

CHAPTER V

Of the good counsel that the hermit gave to them.

Certes, said Gawaine, soothly have ye said, that I see it openly. Now, I pray you, good man and holy father, tell me why we met not with so many adventures as we were wont to do, and commonly have the better. I shall tell you gladly, said the good man; the adventure of the Sangreal which ye and many other have undertaken the quest of it and find it not, the cause is for it appeareth not to sinners. Wherefore marvel not though ye fail thereof, and many other. For ye be an untrue knight, and a great murderer, and to good men signifieth other things than murder. For I dare say, as sinful as Sir Launcelot hath been, sith that he went into the quest of the Sangreal he slew never man, nor nought shall, till that he come unto Camelot again, for he hath taken upon him for to forsake sin. And nere that he nis not stable, but by his thought he is likely to turn again, he should be next to enchieve it save Galahad, his son. But God knoweth his thought and his unstableness, and yet shall he die right an holy man, and no doubt he hath no fellow of no earthly sinful man. Sir, said Gawaine, it seemeth me by your words that for our sins it will not avail us to travel in this quest. Truly, said the good man, there be an hundred such as ye be that never shall prevail, but to have shame. And when they had heard these voices they commended him unto God.

Then the good man called Gawaine, and said: It is long time passed sith that ye were made knight, and never sithen thou servedst thy Maker, and now thou art so old a tree that in thee is neither life nor fruit; wherefore bethink thee that thou yield to Our Lord the bare rind, sith the fiend hath the leaves and the fruit. Sir, said Gawaine, an I had leisure I would speak with you, but my fellow here, Sir Ector, is gone, and abideth me yonder beneath the hill. Well, said the good man, thou were better to be counselled. Then departed Gawaine and came to Ector, and so took their horses and rode till they came to a forester's house, which harboured them right well. And on the morn they departed from their host, and rode long or they could find any adventure.

CHAPTER VI

*How Sir Bors met with an hermit, and how he was confessed
to him, and of his penance enjoined to him.*

When Bors was departed from Camelot he met with a religious man riding on an ass, and Sir Bors saluted him. Anon the good man knew him that he was one of the knights-errant that was in the quest of the Sangreal. What are ye? said the good man. Sir, said he, I am a knight that fain would be counselled in the quest of the Sangreal, for he shall have much earthly worship that may bring it to an end. Certes, said the good man, that is sooth, for he shall be the best knight of the world, and the fairest of all the fellowship. But wit you well there shall none attain it but by cleanness, that is pure confession.

So rode they together till that they came to an hermitage. And there he prayed Bors to dwell all that night with him. And so he alighted and put away his armour, and prayed him that he might be confessed; and so they went into the chapel, and there he was clean confessed, and they ate bread and drank water together. Now, said the good man, I pray thee that thou eat none other till that thou sit at the table where the Sangreal shall be. Sir, said he, I agree me thereto, but how wit ye that I shall sit there. Yes, said the good man, that know I, but there shall be but few of your fellows with you. All is welcome, said Sir Bors, that God sendeth me. Also, said the good man, instead of a shirt, and in sign of chastisement, ye shall wear a garment; therefore I pray you do off all your clothes and your shirt: and so he did. And then he took him a scarlet coat, so that should be instead of his shirt till he had fulfilled the quest of the Sangreal; and the good man found in him so marvellous a life and so stable, that he marvelled and felt that he was never corrupt in fleshly lusts, but in one time that he begat Elian le Blank.

Then he armed him, and took his leave, and so departed. And so a little from thence he looked up into a tree, and there he saw a passing great bird upon an old tree, and it was passing dry, without leaves; and the bird sat above, and had birds, the which were dead for hunger. So smote he himself with his beak, the which was great and sharp. And so the great bird bled till that he died among his birds. And the young birds took the life by the blood of the great bird. When Bors saw this he wist well it was a great tokening; for when he saw the great bird arose not, then he took his horse and yede his way. So by evensong, by adventure he came to a strong tower and an high, and there was he lodged gladly.

CHAPTER VII

How Sir Bors was lodged with a lady, and how he took upon him for to fight against a champion for her land.

And when he was unarmed they led him into an high tower where was a lady, young, lusty, and fair. And she received him with great joy, and made him to sit down by her, and so was he set to sup with flesh and many dainties. And when Sir Bors saw that, he bethought him on his penance, and bade a squire to bring him water. And so he brought him, and he made sops therein and ate them. Ah, said the lady, I trow ye like not my meat. Yes, truly, said Sir Bors, God thank you, madam, but I may eat none other meat this day. Then she spake no more as at that time, for she was loath to displease him. Then after supper they spake of one thing and other.

With that came a squire and said: Madam, ye must purvey you to-morn for a champion, for else your sister will have this castle and also your lands, except ye can find a knight that will fight to-morn in your quarrel against Pridam le Noire. Then she made sorrow and said: Ah, Lord God, wherefore granted ye to hold my land, whereof I should now be disherited without reason and right? And when Sir Bors had heard her say thus, he said: I shall comfort you. Sir, said she, I shall tell you there was here a king that hight Aniause, which held all this land in his keeping. So it mishapped he loved a gentlewoman a great deal elder than I. So took he her all this land to her keeping, and all his men to govern; and she brought up many evil customs whereby she put to death a great part of his kinsmen. And when he saw that, he let chase her out of this land, and betook it me, and all this land in my demesnes. But anon as that worthy king was dead, this other lady began to war upon me, and hath destroyed many of my men, and turned them against me, that I have well-nigh no man left me; and I have nought else but this high tower that she left me. And yet she hath promised me to have this tower, without I can find a knight to fight with her champion.

Now tell me, said Sir Bors, what is that Pridam le Noire? Sir, said she, he is the most doubted man of this land. Now may ye send her word that ye have found a knight that shall fight with that Pridam le Noire in God's quarrel and yours. Then that lady was not a little glad, and sent word that she was purveyed, and that night Bors had good cheer; but in no bed he would come, but laid him on the floor, nor never would do otherwise till that he had met with the quest of the Sangreal.

CHAPTER VIII

Of an advision which Sir Bors had that night, and how he fought and overcame his adversary.

And anon as he was asleep him befell a vision, that there came to him two birds, the one as white as a swan, and the other was marvellous black; but it was not so great as the other, but in the likeness of a Raven. Then the white bird came to him, and said: An thou wouldst give me meat and serve me I should give thee all the riches of the world, and I shall make thee as fair and as white as I am. So the white bird departed, and there came the black bird to him, and said: An thou wolt, serve me to-morrow and have me in no despite though I be black, for wit thou well that more availeth my blackness than the other's whiteness. And then he departed.

And he had another vision: him thought that he came to a great place which seemed a chapel, and there he found a chair set on the left side, which was worm-eaten and feeble. And on the right hand were two flowers like a lily, and the one would have benome the other's whiteness, but a good man departed them that the one touched not the other; and then out of every flower came out many flowers, and fruit great plenty. Then him thought the good man said: Should not he do great folly that would let these two flowers perish for to succour the rotten tree, that it fell not to the earth? Sir, said he, it seemeth me that this wood might not avail. Now keep thee, said the good man, that thou never see such adventure befall thee.

Then he awaked and made a sign of the cross in midst of the forehead, and so rose and clothed him. And there came the lady of the place, and she saluted him, and he her again, and so went to a chapel and heard their service. And there came a company of knights, that the lady had sent for, to lead Sir Bors unto battle. Then asked he his arms. And when he was armed she prayed him to take a little morsel to dine. Nay, madam, said he, that shall I not do till I have done my battle, by the grace of God. And so he leapt upon his horse, and departed, all the knights and men with him. And as soon as these two ladies met together, she which Bors should fight for complained her, and said: Madam, ye have done me wrong to bereave me of my lands that King Aniause gave me, and full loath I am there should be any battle. Ye shall not choose, said the other lady, or else your knight withdraw him.

Then there was the cry made, which party had the better of the two knights, that his lady should rejoice all the land. Now departed the one knight here, and the other there. Then they came together with such a raundon that they pierced their shields and their hauberks, and the spears flew in pieces, and they wounded either other sore. Then hurtled they together, so that they fell both to the earth, and their horses betwixt their legs; and anon they arose, and set hands to their swords, and smote each one other upon the heads, that they made great wounds and deep, that the blood went out of their bodies. For there found Sir Bors greater defence in that knight more than he weened. For that Pridam was a passing good knight, and he wounded Sir Bors full evil, and he him again; but ever this Pridam held the stour in like hard. That perceived Sir Bors, and suffered him till he was nigh attaint. And then he ran upon him more and more, and the other went back for dread of death. So in his withdrawing he fell upright, and Sir Bors drew his helm so strongly that he rent it from his head, and gave him great strokes with the flat of his sword upon the visage, and bade him yield him or he should slay him. Then he cried him mercy and said: Fair knight, for God's love slay me not, and I shall ensure thee never to war against thy lady, but be alway toward her. Then Bors let him be; then the old lady fled with all her knights.

CHAPTER IX

How the lady was returned to her lands by the battle of
Sir Bors, and of his departing, and how he met Sir Lionel
taken and beaten with thorns, and also of a maid which
should have been devoured.

So then came Bors to all those that held lands of his lady, and said he
should destroy them but if they did such service unto her as longed to
their lands. So they did their homage, and they that would not were
chased out of their lands. Then befell that young lady to come to her
estate again, by the mighty prowess of Sir Bors de Ganis. So when all
the country was well set in peace, then Sir Bors took his leave and
departed; and she thanked him greatly, and would have given him
great riches, but he refused it.

Then he rode all that day till night, and came to an harbour to a
lady which knew him well enough, and made of him great joy.
Upon the morn, as soon as the day appeared, Bors departed from
thence, and so rode into a forest unto the hour of midday, and there
befell him a marvellous adventure. So he met at the departing of the
two ways two knights that led Lionel, his brother, all naked, bounden
upon a strong hackney, and his hands bounden to-fore his breast.
And everych of them held in his hands thorns wherewith they went
beating him so sore that the blood trailed down more than in an
hundred places of his body, so that he was all blood to-fore and
behind, but he said never a word; as he which was great of heart he
suffered all that ever they did to him, as though he had felt none
anguish.

Anon Sir Bors dressed him to rescue him that was his brother; and
so he looked upon the other side of him, and saw a knight which
brought a fair gentlewoman, and would have set her in the thickest
place of the forest for to have been the more surer out of the way
from them that sought him. And she which was nothing assured cried
with an high voice: Saint Mary succour your maid. And anon she
espied where Sir Bors came riding. And when she came nigh him she
deemed him a knight of the Round Table, whereof she hoped to

have some comfort; and then she conjured him: By the faith that he ought unto Him in whose service thou art entered in, and for the faith ye owe unto the high order of knighthood, and for the noble King Arthur's sake, that I suppose made thee knight, that thou help me, and suffer me not to be shamed of this knight. When Bors heard her say thus he had so much sorrow there he nist not what to do. For if I let my brother be in adventure he must be slain, and that would I not for all the earth. And if I help not the maid she is shamed for ever, and also she shall lose her virginity the which she shall never get again. Then lift he up his eyes and said weeping: Fair sweet Lord Jesu Christ, whose liege man I am, keep Lionel, my brother, that these knights slay him not, and for pity of you, and for Mary's sake, I shall succour this maid.

CHAPTER X

How Sir Bors left to rescue his brother, and rescued the damosel; and how it was told him that Lionel was dead.

Then dressed he him unto the knight the which had the gentlewoman, and then he cried: Sir knight, let your hand off that maiden, or ye be but dead. And then he set down the maiden, and was armed at all pieces save he lacked his spear. Then he dressed his shield, and drew out his sword, and Bors smote him so hard that it went through his shield and habergeon on the left shoulder. And through great strength he beat him down to the earth, and at the pulling out of Bors' spear there he swooned. Then came Bors to the maid and said: How seemeth it you? of this knight ye be delivered at this time. Now sir, said she, I pray you lead me thereas this knight had me. So shall I do gladly: and took the horse of the wounded knight, and set the gentlewoman upon him, and so brought her as she desired. Sir knight, said she, ye have better sped than ye weened, for an I had lost my maidenhead, five hundred men should have died for it. What knight was he that had you in the forest? By my faith, said she, he is my cousin. So wot I never with what engine the fiend enchafed him, for yesterday he took me from my father privily; for I, nor none of my father's men, mistrusted him not, and if he had had my maidenhead he should have died for the sin, and his body shamed and dishonoured for ever. Thus as she stood talking with him there came twelve knights seeking after her, and anon she told them all how Bors had delivered her; then they made great joy, and besought him to come to her father, a great lord, and he should be right welcome. Truly, said Bors, that may not be at this time, for I have a great adventure to do in this country. So he commended them unto God and departed.

Then Sir Bors rode after Lionel, his brother, by the trace of their horses, thus he rode seeking a great while. Then he overtook a man clothed in a religious clothing, and rode on a strong black horse blacker than a berry, and said: Sir knight, what seek you? Sir, said he, I seek my brother that I saw within a while beaten with two knights. Ah, Bors, discomfort you not, nor fall into no wanhope, for I shall tell you tidings such as they be, for truly he is dead. Then showed he him a new slain body lying in a bush, and it seemed him well that it was the body of Lionel; and then he made such a sorrow that he fell to the earth all in a swoon, and lay a great while there. And when he came to himself he said: Fair brother, sith the company of you and me is departed shall I never have joy in my heart, and now He which I have taken unto my master, He be my help. And when he had said thus he took his body lightly in his arms, and put it upon the arson of his saddle. And then he said to the man: Canst thou tell me unto some chapel where that I may bury this body? Come on, said he, here is one fast by; and so long they rode till they saw a fair tower, and afore it there seemed an old feeble chapel. And then they alighted both, and put him into a tomb of marble.

CHAPTER XI

How Sir Bors told his dream to a priest, which he had
dreamed, and of the counsel that the priest gave to him.

Now leave we him here, said the good man, and go we to our harbour till to-morrow; we will come here again to do him service. Sir, said Bors, be ye a priest? Yea forsooth, said he. Then I pray you tell me a dream that befell to me the last night. Say on, said he. Then he began so much to tell him of the great bird in the forest, and after told him of his birds, one white, another black, and of the rotten tree, and of the white flowers. Sir, I shall tell you a part now, and the other deal to-morrow. The white fowl betokeneth a gentlewoman, fair and rich, which loved thee paramours, and hath loved thee long; and if thou warn her love she shall go die anon, if thou have no pity on her. That signifieth the great bird, the which shall make thee to warn her. Now for no fear that thou hast, ne for no dread that thou hast of God, thou shalt not warn her, but thou wouldst not do it for to be holden chaste, for to conquer the loos of the vain glory of the world; for that shall befall thee now an thou warn her, that Launcelot, the good knight, thy cousin, shall die. And therefore men shall now say that thou art a manslayer, both of thy brother, Sir Lionel, and of thy cousin, Sir Launcelot du Lake, the which thou mightest have saved and rescued easily, but thou weenedst to rescue a maid which pertaineth nothing to thee. Now look thou whether it had been greater harm of thy brother's death, or else to have suffered her to have lost her maidenhood. Then asked he him: Hast thou heard the tokens of thy dream the which I have told to you? Yea forsooth, said Sir Bors, all your exposition and declaring of my dream I have well understood and heard. Then said the man in this black clothing: Then is it in thy default if Sir Launcelot, thy cousin, die. Sir, said Bors, that were me loath, for wit ye well there is nothing in the world but I had liefer do it than to see my lord, Sir Launcelot du Lake, to die in my default. Choose ye now the one or the other, said the good man.

And then he led Sir Bors into an high tower, and there he found knights and ladies: those ladies said he was welcome, and so they unarmed him. And when he was in his doublet men brought him a mantle furred with ermine, and put it about him; and then they made him such cheer that he had forgotten all his sorrow and anguish, and only set his heart in these delights and dainties, and took no thought more for his brother, Sir Lionel, neither of Sir Launcelot du Lake, his cousin. And anon came out of a chamber to him the fairest lady than ever he saw, and more richer beseen than ever he saw Queen Guenever or any other estate. Lo, said they, Sir Bors, here is the lady unto whom we owe all our service, and I trow she be the richest lady and the fairest of all the world, and the which loveth you best above all other knights, for she will have no knight but you. And when he understood that language he was abashed. Not for then she saluted him, and he her; and then they sat down together and spake of many

things, in so much that she besought him to be her love, for she had
loved him above all earthly men, and she should make him richer
than ever was man of his age. When Bors understood her words he
was right evil at ease, which in no manner would not break chastity,
so wist not he how to answer her.

CHAPTER XII

*How the devil in a woman's likeness would have had Sir
Bors to have lain by her, and how by God's grace he escaped.*

Alas, said she, Bors, shall ye not do my will? Madam, said Bors, there
is no lady in the world whose will I will fulfil as of this thing, for my
brother lieth dead which was slain right late. Ah Bors, said she, I have
loved you long for the great beauty I have seen in you, and the great
hardiness that I have heard of you, that needs ye must lie by me this
night, and therefore I pray you grant it me. Truly, said he, I shall not
do it in no manner wise. Then she made him such sorrow as though
she would have died. Well Bors, said she, unto this have ye brought
me, nigh to mine end. And therewith she took him by the hand, and
bade him behold her. And ye shall see how I shall die for your love.
Ah, said then he, that shall I never see.

Then she departed and went up into an high battlement, and led
with her twelve gentlewomen; and when they were above, one of
the gentlewomen cried, and said: Ah, Sir Bors, gentle knight have
mercy on us all, and suffer my lady to have her will, and if ye do not
we must suffer death with our lady, for to fall down off this high
tower, and if ye suffer us thus to die for so little a thing all ladies and
gentlewomen will say of you dishonour. Then looked he upward,
they seemed all ladies of great estate, and richly and well beseen.
Then had he of them great pity; not for that he was uncounselled in
himself that liefer he had they all had lost their souls than he his, and
with that they fell adown all at once unto the earth. And when he
saw that, he was all abashed, and had thereof great marvel. With that
he blessed his body and his visage. And anon he heard a great noise
and a great cry, as though all the fiends of hell had been about him;
and therewith he saw neither tower, nor lady, nor gentlewoman, nor

no chapel where he brought his brother to. Then held he up both his hands to the heaven, and said: Fair Father God, I am grievously escaped; and then he took his arms and his horse and rode on his way.

Then he heard a clock smite on his right hand; and thither he came to an abbey on his right hand, closed with high walls, and there was let in. Then they supposed that he was one of the quest of the Sangreal, so they led him into a chamber and unarmed him. Sirs, said Sir Bors, if there be any holy man in this house I pray you let me speak with him. Then one of them led him unto the Abbot, which was in a chapel. And then Sir Bors saluted him, and he him again. Sir, said Bors, I am a knight-errant; and told him all the adventure which he had seen. Sir Knight, said the Abbot, I wot not what ye be, for I weened never that a knight of your age might have been so strong in the grace of our Lord Jesu Christ. Not for then ye shall go unto your rest, for I will not counsel you this day, it is too late, and to-morrow I shall counsel you as I can.

CHAPTER XIII

Of the holy communication of an Abbot to Sir Bors, and how the Abbot counselled him.

And that night was Sir Bors served richly; and on the morn early he heard mass, and the Abbot came to him, and bade him good morrow, and Bors to him again. And then he told him he was a fellow of the quest of the Sangreal, and how he had charge of the holy man to eat bread and water. Then [said the Abbot]: Our Lord Jesu Christ showed him unto you in the likeness of a soul that suffered great anguish for us, since He was put upon the cross, and bled His heart-blood for mankind: there was the token and the likeness of the Sangreal that appeared afore you, for the blood that the great fowl bled revived the chickens from death to life. And by the bare tree is betokened the world which is naked and without fruit but if it come of Our Lord. Also the lady for whom ye fought for, and King Aniause which was lord there-to-fore, betokeneth Jesu Christ which is the King of the world. And that ye fought with the champion for the lady, this it betokeneth: for when ye took the battle for the lady, by her shall ye understand the new law of Jesu Christ and Holy Church; and by the other lady ye shall understand the old law and the fiend, which all day warreth against Holy Church, therefore ye did your battle with right. For ye be Jesu Christ's knights, therefore ye ought to be defenders of Holy Church. And by the black bird might ye understand Holy Church, which sayeth I am black, but he is fair. And by the white bird might men understand the fiend, and I shall tell you how the swan is white without-forth, and black within: it is hypocrisy which is without yellow or pale, and seemeth without-forth the servants of Jesu Christ, but they be within so horrible of filth and sin, and beguile the world evil. Also when the fiend appeared to thee in likeness of a man of religion, and blamed thee that thou left thy brother for a lady, so led thee where thou seemed thy brother was slain, but he is yet alive; and all was for to put thee in error, and bring thee unto wanhope and lechery, for he knew thou were tender hearted, and all was for thou shouldst not find the blessed adventure of the Sangreal. And the third fowl betokeneth the strong battle against the fair ladies which were all devils. Also the dry tree and the white lily: the dry tree betokeneth thy brother Lionel, which is dry without virtue, and therefore many men ought to call him the rotten tree, and the worm-eaten tree, for he is a murderer and doth contrary to the order of knighthood. And the two white flowers signify two maidens, the one is a knight which was wounded the other day, and the other is the gentlewoman which ye rescued; and why the other flower drew nigh the other, that was the knight which would have defouled her and himself both. And Sir Bors, ye had been a great fool and in great peril for to have seen those two flowers perish for to succour the rotten tree, for an they had sinned together they had been damned; and for that ye rescued them both, men might call you a very knight and servant of Jesu Christ.

CHAPTER XIV

*How Sir Bors met with his brother Sir Lionel,
and how Sir Lionel would have slain Sir Bors.*

Then went Sir Bors from thence and commended the Abbot unto
God. And then he rode all that day, and harboured with an old lady.
And on the morn he rode to a castle in a valley, and there he met with
a yeoman going a great pace toward a forest. Say me, said Sir Bors,
canst thou tell me of any adventure? Sir, said he, here shall be under
this castle a great and a marvellous tournament. Of what folks shall it
be? said Sir Bors. The Earl of Plains shall be in the one party, and the
lady's nephew of Hervin on the other party. Then Bors thought to be
there if he might meet with his brother Sir Lionel, or any other of his
fellowship, which were in the quest of the Sangreal. And then he
turned to an hermitage that was in the entry of the forest.

And when he was come thither he found there Sir Lionel, his
brother, which sat all armed at the entry of the chapel door for to
abide there harbour till on the morn that the tournament shall be.
And when Sir Bors saw him he had great joy of him, that it were
marvel to tell of his joy. And then he alighted off his horse, and said:
Fair sweet brother, when came ye hither? Anon as Lionel saw him he
said: Ah Bors, ye may not make none avaunt, but as for you I might
have been slain; when ye saw two knights leading me away beating
me, ye left me for to succour a gentlewoman, and suffered me in peril
of death; for never erst ne did no brother to another so great an
untruth. And for that misdeed now I ensure you but death, for well
have ye deserved it; therefore keep thee from henceforward, and that
shall ye find as soon as I am armed. When Sir Bors understood his
brother's wrath he kneeled down to the earth and cried him mercy,
holding up both his hands, and prayed him to forgive him his evil
will. Nay, said Lionel, that shall never be an I may have the higher
hand, that I make mine avow to God, thou shalt have death for it, for
it were pity ye lived any longer.

Right so he went in and took his harness, and mounted upon his
horse, and came to-fore him and said: Bors, keep thee from me, for I

shall do to thee as I would to a felon or a traitor, for ye be the
untruest knight that ever came out of so worthy an house as was King
Bors de Ganis which was our father, therefore start upon thy horse,
and so shall ye be most at your advantage. And but if ye will I will run
upon you thereas ye stand upon foot, and so the shame shall be mine
and the harm yours, but of that shame ne reck I nought.

When Sir Bors saw that he must fight with his brother or else to
die, he nist what to do; then his heart counselled him not thereto,
inasmuch as Lionel was born or he, wherefore he ought to bear him
reverence; yet kneeled he down afore Lionel's horse's feet, and said:
Fair sweet brother, have mercy upon me and slay me not, and have
in remembrance the great love which ought to be between us twain.
What Sir Bors said to Lionel he rought not, for the fiend had brought
him in such a will that he should slay him. Then when Lionel saw he
would none other, and that he would not have risen to give him
battle, he rashed over him so that he smote Bors with his horse, feet
upward, to the earth, and hurt him so sore that he swooned of
distress, the which he felt in himself to have died without confession.
So when Lionel saw this, he alighted off his horse to have smitten off
his head. And so he took him by the helm, and would have rent it
from his head. Then came the hermit running unto him, which was a
good man and of great age, and well had heard all the words that
were between them, and so fell down upon Sir Bors.

CHAPTER XV

How Sir Colgrevance fought against Sir Lionel for to save Sir Bors, and how the hermit was slain.

Then he said to Lionel: Ah gentle knight, have mercy upon me and
on thy brother, for if thou slay him thou shalt be dead of sin, and that
were sorrowful, for he is one of the worthiest knights of the world,
and of the best conditions. So God help me, said Lionel, sir priest, but
if ye flee from him I shall slay you, and he shall never the sooner be
quit. Certes, said the good man, I have liefer ye slay me than him, for
my death shall not be great harm, not half so much as of his. Well, said
Lionel, I am greed; and set his hand to his sword and smote him so

hard that his head yede backward. Not for that he restrained him of his evil will, but took his brother by the helm, and unlaced it to have stricken off his head, and had slain him without fail. But so it happed, Colgrevance, a fellow of the Round Table, came at that time thither as Our Lord's will was. And when he saw the good man slain he marvelled much what it might be. And then he beheld Lionel would have slain his brother, and knew Sir Bors which he loved right well. Then stert he down and took Lionel by the shoulders, and drew him strongly aback from Bors, and said: Lionel, will ye slay your brother, the worthiest knight of the world and that should no good man suffer. Why, said Lionel, will ye let me? therefore if ye entermete you in this I shall slay you, and him after. Why, said Colgrevance, is this sooth that ye will slay him? Slay him will I, said he, whoso say the contrary, for he hath done so much against me that he hath well deserved it. And so ran upon him, and would have smitten him through the head, and Sir Colgrevance ran betwixt them, and said: An ye be so hardy to do so more, we two shall meddle together.

When Lionel understood his words he took his shield afore him, and asked him what that he was. And he told him, Colgrevance, one of his fellows. Then Lionel defied him, and gave him a great stroke through the helm. Then he drew his sword, for he was a passing good knight, and defended him right manfully. So long dured the battle that Bors rose up all anguishly, and beheld [how] Colgrevance, the good knight, fought with his brother for his quarrel; then was he full sorry and heavy, and thought if Colgrevance slew him that was his brother he should never have joy; and if his brother slew Colgrevance the shame should ever be mine. Then would he have risen to have departed them, but he had not so much might to stand on foot; so he abode him so long till Colgrevance had the worse, for Lionel was of great chivalry and right hardy, for he had pierced the hauberk and the helm, that he abode but death, for he had lost much of his blood that it was marvel that he might stand upright. Then beheld he Sir Bors which sat dressing him upward and said: Ah, Bors, why come ye not to cast me out of peril of death, wherein I have put me to succour you which were right now nigh the death? Certes, said Lionel, that shall not avail you, for none of you shall bear others warrant, but that ye shall die both of my hand. When Bors heard that, he did so much, he rose and put on his helm. Then perceived he first the hermit-priest which was slain, then made he a marvellous sorrow upon him.

CHAPTER XVI

How Sir Lionel slew Sir Colgrevance, and how after he would have slain Sir Bors.

Then oft Colgrevance cried upon Sir Bors: Why will ye let me die here for your sake? if it please you that I die for you the death, it will please me the better for to save a worthy man. With that word Sir Lionel smote off the helm from his head. Then Colgrevance saw that he might not escape; then he said: Fair sweet Jesu, that I have misdone have mercy upon my soul, for such sorrow that my heart suffereth for goodness, and for alms deed that I would have done here, be to me aligement of penance unto my soul's health. At these words Lionel smote him so sore that he bare him to the earth. So he had slain Colgrevance he ran upon his brother as a fiendly man, and gave him such a stroke that he made him stoop. And he that was full of humility prayed him for God's love to leave this battle: For an it befell, fair brother, that I slew you or ye me, we should be dead of that sin. Never God me help but if I have on you mercy, an I may have the better hand. Then drew Bors his sword, all weeping, and said: Fair brother, God knoweth mine intent. Ah, fair brother, ye have done full evil this day to slay such an holy priest the which never trespassed. Also ye have slain a gentle knight, and one of our fellows. And well wot ye that I am not afeard of you greatly, but I dread the wrath of God, and this is an unkindly war, therefore God show miracle upon us both. Now God have mercy upon me though I defend my life against my brother: with that Bors lift up his hand and would have smitten his brother.

CHAPTER XVII

How there came a voice which charged Sir Bors to touch him
not, and of a cloud that came between them.

And then he heard a voice that said: Flee Bors, and touch him not, or else thou shalt slay him. Right so alighted a cloud betwixt them in likeness of a fire and a marvellous flame, that both their two shields brent. Then were they sore afraid, that they fell both to the earth, and lay there a great while in a swoon. And when they came to themself, Bors saw that his brother had no harm; then he held up both his hands, for he dread God had taken vengeance upon him. With that he heard a voice say: Bors, go hence, and bear thy brother no longer fellowship, but take thy way anon right to the sea, for Sir Percivale abideth thee there. Then he said to his brother: Fair sweet brother, forgive me for God's love all that I have trespassed unto you. Then he answered: God forgive it thee and I do gladly.

So Sir Bors departed from him and rode the next way to the sea. And at the last by fortune he came to an abbey which was nigh the sea. That night Bors rested him there; and in his sleep there came a voice to him and bade him go to the sea. Then he stert up and made a sign of the cross in the midst of his forehead, and took his harness, and made ready his horse, and mounted upon him; and at a broken wall he rode out, and rode so long till that he came to the sea. And on the strand he found a ship covered all with white samite, and he alighted, and betook him to Jesu Christ. And as soon as he entered into the ship, the ship departed into the sea, and went so fast that him seemed the ship went flying, but it was soon dark so that he might know no man, and so he slept till it was day. Then he awaked, and saw in midst of the ship a knight lie all armed save his helm. Then knew he that it was Sir Percivale of Wales, and then he made of him right great joy; but Sir Percivale was abashed of him, and he asked him what he was. Ah, fair sir, said Bors, know ye me not? Certes, said he, I marvel how ye came hither, but if Our Lord brought ye hither Himself. Then Sir Bors smiled and did off his helm. Then Percivale knew him, and either made great joy of other, that it was marvel to hear. Then Bors told him how he came into the ship, and by whose admonishment; and either told other of their temptations, as ye have heard to-forehand. So went they downward in the sea, one while backward, another while forward, and everych comforted other, and oft were in their prayers. Then said Sir Percivale: We lack nothing but Galahad, the good knight.

And thus endeth the sixteenth book, which is of Sir Gawaine, Ector de Maris, and Sir Bors de Ganis, and Sir Percivale. And here followeth the seventeenth book, which is of the noble knight Sir Galahad.

BOOK SEVENTEEN

CHAPTER I

How Sir Galahad fought at a tournament, and how he was known of Sir Gawaine and Sir Ector de Maris.

Now saith this story, when Galahad had rescued Percivale from the twenty knights, he yede tho into a waste forest wherein he rode many journeys; and he found many adventures the which he brought to an end, whereof the story maketh here no mention. Then he took his way to the sea on a day, and it befell as he passed by a castle where was a wonder tournament, but they without had done so much that they within were put to the worse, yet were they within good knights enough. When Galahad saw that those within were at so great a mischief that men slew them at the entry of the castle, then he thought to help them, and put a spear forth and smote the first that he fell to the earth, and the spear brake to pieces. Then he drew his sword and smote thereas they were thickest, and so he did wonderful deeds of arms that all they marvelled. Then it happed that Gawaine and Sir Ector de Maris were with the knights without. But when they espied the white shield with the red cross the one said to the other: Yonder is the good knight, Sir Galahad, the haut prince: now he should be a great fool which should meet with him to fight. So by adventure he came by Sir Gawaine, and he smote him so hard that he clave his helm and the coif of iron unto his head, so that Gawaine fell to the earth; but the stroke was so great that it slanted down to the earth and carved the horse's shoulder in two.

When Ector saw Gawaine down he drew him aside, and thought it no wisdom for to abide him, and also for natural love, that he was his uncle. Thus through his great hardiness he beat aback all the knights without. And then they within came out and chased them all about. But when Galahad saw there would none turn again he stole away privily, so that none wist where he was become. Now by my head, said Gawaine to Ector, now are the wonders true that were said of Launcelot du Lake, that the sword which stuck in the stone should give me such a buffet that I would not have it for the best castle in this world; and soothly now it is proved true, for never ere had I such a stroke of man's hand. Sir, said Ector, meseemeth your quest is done. And yours is not done, said Gawaine, but mine is done, I shall seek no further. Then Gawaine was borne into a castle and unarmed him, and laid him in a rich bed, and a leech found that he might live, and to be whole within a month. Thus Gawaine and Ector abode together, for Sir Ector would not away till Gawaine were whole.

And the good knight, Galahad, rode so long till he came that night to the Castle of Carboneck; and it befell him thus that he was benighted in an hermitage. So the good man was fain when he saw he was a knight-errant. So when they were at rest there came a gentlewoman knocking at the door, and called Galahad, and so the good man came to the door to wit what she would. Then she called the hermit: Sir Ulfin, I am a gentlewoman that would speak with the knight which is with you. Then the good man awaked Galahad, and bade him: Arise, and speak with a gentlewoman that seemeth hath great need of you. Then Galahad went to her and asked her what she would. Galahad, said she, I will that ye arm you, and mount upon your horse and follow me, for I shall show you within these three days the highest adventure that ever any knight saw. Anon Galahad armed him, and took his horse, and commended him to God, and bade the gentlewoman go, and he would follow thereas she liked.

CHAPTER II

How Sir Galahad rode with a damosel, and came to the ship whereas Sir Bors and Sir Percivale were in.

So she rode as fast as her palfrey might bear her, till that she came to the sea, the which was called Collibe. And at the night they came unto a castle in a valley, closed with a running water, and with strong walls and high; and so she entered into the castle with Galahad, and there had he great cheer, for the lady of that castle was the damosel's lady. So when he was unarmed, then said the damosel: Madam, shall we abide here all this day? Nay, said she, but till he hath dined and till he hath slept a little. So he ate and slept a while till that the maid called him, and armed him by torchlight. And when the maid was horsed and he both, the lady took Galahad a fair child and rich; and so they departed from the castle till they came to the seaside; and there they found the ship where Bors and Percivale were in, the which cried on the ship's board: Sir Galahad, ye be welcome, we have abiden you long. And when he heard them he asked them what they were. Sir, said she, leave your horse here, and I shall leave mine; and took their saddles and their bridles with them, and made a cross on them, and so entered into the ship. And the two knights received them both with great joy, and everych knew other; and so the wind arose, and drove them through the sea in a marvellous pace. And within a while it dawned.

Then did Galahad off his helm and his sword, and asked of his fellows from whence came that fair ship. Truly, said they, ye wot as well as we, but of God's grace; and then they told everych to other of all their hard adventures, and of their great temptations. Truly, said Galahad, ye are much bounden to God, for ye have escaped great adventures; and had not the gentlewoman been I had not come here, for as for you I weened never to have found you in these strange countries. Ah Galahad, said Bors, if Launcelot, your father, were here then were we well at ease, for then meseemed we failed nothing. That may not be, said Galahad, but if it pleased Our Lord.

By then the ship went from the land of Logris, and by adventure it arrived up betwixt two rocks passing great and marvellous; but there they might not land, for there was a swallow of the sea, save there was another ship, and upon it they might go without danger. Go we thither, said the gentlewoman, and there shall we see adventures, for so is Our Lord's will. And when they came thither they found the ship rich enough, but they found neither man nor woman therein. But they found in the end of the ship two fair letters written, which said a dreadful word and a marvellous: Thou man, which shall enter into this ship, beware thou be in steadfast belief, for I am Faith, and therefore beware how thou enterest, for an thou fail I shall not help thee. Then said the gentlewoman: Percivale, wot ye what I am? Certes, said he, nay, to my witting. Wit ye well, said she, that I am thy sister, which am daughter of King Pellinore, and therefore wit ye well ye are the man in the world that I most love; and if ye be not in perfect belief of Jesu Christ enter not in no manner of wise, for then should ye perish the ship, for he is so perfect he will suffer no sinner in him. When Percivale understood that she was his very sister he was inwardly glad, and said: Fair sister, I shall enter therein, for if I be a miscreature or all untrue knight there shall I perish.

CHAPTER III

How Sir Galahad entered into the ship, and of a fair bed therein, with other marvellous things, and of a sword.

In the meanwhile Galahad blessed him, and entered therein; and then next the gentlewoman, and then Sir Bors and Sir Percivale. And when they were in, it was so marvellous fair and rich that they marvelled; and in midst of the ship was a fair bed, and Galahad went thereto, and found there a crown of silk. And at the feet was a sword, rich and fair, and it was drawn out of the sheath half a foot and more; and the sword was of divers fashions, and the pommel was of stone, and there was in him all manner of colours that any man might find, and everych of the colours had divers virtues; and the scales of the haft were of two ribs of divers beasts, the one beast was a serpent which was conversant in Calidone, and is called the Serpent of the fiend; and the bone of him is of such a virtue that there is no hand that handleth him shall never be weary nor hurt. And the other beast is a fish which is not right great, and haunteth the flood of Euphrates; and that fish is called Ertanax, and his bones be of such a manner of kind that who that handleth them shall have so much will that he shall never be weary, and he shall not think on joy nor sorrow that he hath had, but only that thing that he beholdeth before him. And as for this sword there shall never man begrip him at the handles but one; but he shall pass all other. In the name of God, said Percivale, I shall assay to handle it. So he set his hand to the sword, but he might not begrip it. By my faith, said he, now have I failed. Bors set his hand thereto and failed.

Then Galahad beheld the sword and saw letters like blood that said: Let see who shall assay to draw me out of my sheath, but if he be more hardier than any other; and who that draweth me, wit ye well that he shall never fail of shame of his body, or to be wounded to the death. By my faith, said Galahad, I would draw this sword out of the sheath, but the offending is so great that I shall not set my hand thereto. Now sirs, said the gentlewoman, wit ye well that the drawing of this sword is warned to all men save all only to you. Also this ship arrived in the realm of Logris; and that time was deadly war between King Labor, which was father unto the maimed king, and King Hurlame, which was a Saracen. But then was he newly christened, so that men held him afterward one of the wittiest men of the world. And so upon a day it befell that King Labor and King Hurlame had assembled their folk upon the sea where this ship was arrived; and there King Hurlame was discomfit, and his men slain; and he was afeard to be dead, and fled to his ship, and there found this sword and drew it, and came out and found King Labor, the man in the world of all Christendom in whom was then the greatest faith. And when King Hurlame saw King Labor he dressed this sword, and smote him upon the helm so hard that he clave him and his horse to the earth with the first stroke of his sword. And it was in the realm of Logris; and so befell great pestilence and great harm to both realms. For sithen increased neither corn, nor grass, nor well-nigh no fruit, nor in the water was no fish; wherefore men call it the lands of the two marches, the waste land, for that dolorous stroke. And when King Hurlame saw this sword so carving, he turned again to fetch the scabbard, and so came into this ship and entered, and put up the sword in the sheath. And as soon as he had done it he fell down dead afore the bed. Thus was the sword proved, that none ne drew it but he were dead or maimed. So lay he there till a maiden came into the ship and cast him out, for there was no man so hardy of the world to enter into that ship for the defence.

CHAPTER IV

Of the marvels of the sword and of the scabbard.

And then beheld they the scabbard, it seemed to be of a serpent's skin, and thereon were letters of gold and silver. And the girdle was but poorly to come to, and not able to sustain such a rich sword. And the letters said: He which shall wield me ought to be more harder than any other, if he bear me as truly as me ought to be borne. For the body of him which I ought to hang by, he shall not be shamed in no place while he is girt with this girdle, nor never none be so hardy to do away this girdle; for it ought not be done away but by the hands of a maid, and that she be a king's daughter and queen's, and she must be a maid all the days of her life, both in will and in deed. And if she break her virginity she shall die the most villainous death that ever died any woman. Sir, said Percivale, turn this sword that we may see what is on the other side. And it was red as blood, with black letters as any coal, which said: He that shall praise me most, most shall he find me to blame at a great need; and to whom I should be most debonair shall I be most felon, and that shall be at one time.

Fair brother, said she to Percivale, it befell after a forty year after the passion of Jesu Christ that Nacien, the brother-in-law of King Mordrains, was borne into a town more than fourteen days' journey from his country, by the commandment of Our Lord, into an isle, into the parts of the West, that men cleped the Isle of Turnance. So befell it that he found this ship at the entry of a rock, and he found the bed and this sword as we have heard now. Not for then he had not so much hardiness to draw it; and there he dwelled an eight days, and at the ninth day there fell a great wind which departed him out of the isle, and brought him to another isle by a rock, and there he found the greatest giant that ever man might see. Therewith came that horrible giant to slay him; and then he looked about him and might not flee, and he had nothing to defend him with. So he ran to his sword, and when he saw it naked he praised it much, and then he shook it, and therewith he brake it in the midst. Ah, said Nacien, the thing that I most praised ought I now most to blame, and therewith he threw the pieces of his sword over his bed. And after he leapt over the board to fight with the giant, and slew him.

And anon he entered into the ship again, and the wind arose, and drove him through the sea, that by adventure he came to another ship where King Mordrains was, which had been tempted full evil with a fiend in the Port of Perilous Rock. And when that one saw the other they made great joy of other, and either told other of their adventure, and how the sword failed him at his most need. When Mordrains saw the sword he praised it much: But the breaking was not to do but by wickedness of thy selfward, for thou art in some sin. And there he took the sword, and set the pieces together, and they soldered as fair as ever they were to-fore; and there put he the sword in the sheath, and laid it down on the bed. Then heard they a voice that said: Go out of this ship a little while, and enter into the other, for dread ye fall in deadly sin, for and ye be found in deadly sin ye may not escape but perish: and so they went into the other ship. And as Nacien went over the board he was smitten with a sword on the right foot, that he fell down noseling to the ship's board; and therewith he said: O God, how am I hurt. And then there came a voice and said: Take thou that for thy forfeit that thou didst in drawing of this sword, therefore thou receivest a wound, for thou were never worthy to handle it, as the writing maketh mention. In the name of God, said Galahad, ye are right wise of these works.

CHAPTER V

How King Pelles was smitten through both thighs because he drew the sword, and other marvellous histories.

Sir, said she, there was a king that hight Pelles, the maimed king. And while he might ride he supported much Christendom and Holy Church. So upon a day he hunted in a wood of his which lasted unto the sea; and at the last he lost his hounds and his knights save only one: and there he and his knight went till that they came toward Ireland, and there he found the ship. And when he saw the letters and understood them, yet he entered, for he was right perfect of his life, but his knight had none hardiness to enter; and there found he this sword, and drew it out as much as ye may see. So therewith entered a spear wherewith he was smitten him through both the thighs, and never sith might he be healed, nor nought shall to-fore we come to him. Thus, said she, was not King Pelles, your grandsire, maimed for his hardiness? In the name of God, damosel, said Galahad.

So they went toward the bed to behold all about it, and above the head there hung two swords. Also there were two spindles which were as white as any snow, and other that were as red as blood, and other above green as any emerald: of these three colours were the spindles, and of natural colour within, and without any painting. These spindles, said the damosel, were when sinful Eve came to gather fruit, for which Adam and she were put out of paradise, she took with her the bough on which the apple hung on. Then perceived she that the branch was fair and green, and she remembered her the loss which came from the tree. Then she thought to keep the branch as long as she might. And for she had no coffer to keep it in, she put it in the earth. So by the will of Our Lord the branch grew to a great tree within a little while, and was as white as any snow, branches, boughs, and leaves: that was a token a maiden planted it. But after God came to Adam, and bade him know his wife fleshly as nature required. So lay Adam with his wife under the same tree; and anon the tree which was white was full green as any grass, and all that came out of it; and in the same time that they medled together there was Abel begotten: thus was the tree long of green colour. And so it befell many days after, under the same tree Caym slew Abel, whereof befell great marvel. For anon as Abel had received the death under the green tree, it lost the green colour and became red; and that was in tokening of the blood. And anon all the plants died thereof, but the tree grew and waxed marvellously fair, and it was the fairest tree and the most delectable that any man might behold and see; and so died the plants that grew out of it to-fore that Abel was slain under it. So long dured the tree till that Solomon, King David's son, reigned, and held the land after his father. This Solomon was wise, and knew all the virtues of stones and trees, and so he knew the course of the stars, and many other divers things. This Solomon had an evil wife, wherethrough he weened that there had been no good woman, and so he despised them in his books. So answered a voice him once: Solomon, if heaviness come to a man by a woman, ne reck thou never; for yet shall there come a woman whereof there shall come greater joy to man an hundred times more than this heaviness giveth sorrow; and that woman shall be born of thy lineage. Tho when Solomon heard these words he held himself but a fool, and the truth he perceived by old books. Also the Holy Ghost showed him the coming of the glorious Virgin Mary. Then asked he of the voice, if it should be in the yerde of his lineage. Nay, said the voice, but there shall come a man which shall be a maid, and the last of your blood, and he shall be as good a knight as Duke Josua, thy brother-in-law.

CHAPTER VI

How Solomon took David's sword by the counsel of his wife, and of other matters marvellous.

Now have I certified thee of that thou stoodest in doubt. Then was Solomon glad that there should come any such of his lineage; but ever he marvelled and studied who that should be, and what his name might be. His wife perceived that he studied, and thought she would know it at some season; and so she waited her time, and asked of him the cause of his studying, and there he told her altogether how the voice told him. Well, said she, I shall let make a ship of the best wood and most durable that men may find. So Solomon sent for all the carpenters of the land, and the best. And when they had made the ship the lady said to Solomon: Sir, said she, since it is so that this knight ought to pass all knights of chivalry which have been to-fore him and shall come after him, moreover I shall tell you, said she, ye shall go into Our Lord's temple, where is King David's sword, your father, the which is the marvelloust and the sharpest that ever was taken in any knight's hand. Therefore take that, and take off the pommel, and thereto make ye a pommel of precious stones, that it be so subtly made that no man perceive it but that they be all one; and after make there an hilt so marvellously and wonderly that no man may know it; and after make a marvellous sheath. And when ye have made all this I shall let make a girdle thereto, such as shall please me.

All this King Solomon did let make as she devised, both the ship and all the remnant. And when the ship was ready in the sea to sail,

the lady let make a great bed and marvellous rich, and set her upon
the bed's head, covered with silk, and laid the sword at the feet, and
the girdles were of hemp, and therewith the king was angry. Sir, wit
ye well, said she, that I have none so high a thing which were worthy
to sustain so high a sword, and a maid shall bring other knights
thereto, but I wot not when it shall be, nor what time. And there she
let make a covering to the ship, of cloth of silk that should never rot
for no manner of weather. Yet went that lady and made a carpenter
to come to the tree which Abel was slain under. Now, said she, carve
me out of this tree as much wood as will make me a spindle. Ah
madam, said he, this is the tree the which our first mother planted.
Do it, said she or else I shall destroy thee. Anon as he began to work
there came out drops of blood; and then would he have left, but she
would not suffer him, and so he took away as much wood as might
make a spindle: and so she made him to take as much of the green
tree and of the white tree. And when these three spindles were
shapen she made them to be fastened upon the selar of the bed.
When Solomon saw this, he said to his wife: Ye have done
marvellously, for though all the world were here right now, he could
not devise wherefore all this was made, but Our Lord Himself; and
thou that hast done it wottest not what it shall betoken. Now let it
be, said she, for ye shall hear tidings sooner than ye ween. Now shall
ye hear a wonderful tale of King Solomon and his wife.

CHAPTER VII

A wonderful tale of King Solomon and his wife.

That night lay Solomon before the ship with little fellowship. And
when he was asleep him thought there came from heaven a great
company of angels, and alighted into the ship, and took water which
was brought by an angel, in a vessel of silver, and sprent all the ship.
And after he came to the sword, and drew letters on the hilt. And
after went to the ship's board, and wrote there other letters which
said: Thou man that wilt enter within me, beware that thou be full
within the faith, for I ne am but Faith and Belief. When Solomon
espied these letters he was abashed, so that he durst not enter, and so

drew him aback; and the ship was anon shoven in the sea, and he went so fast that he lost sight of him within a little while. And then a little voice said: Solomon, the last knight of thy lineage shall rest in this bed. Then went Solomon and awaked his wife, and told her of the adventures of the ship.

Now saith the history that a great while the three fellows beheld the bed and the three spindles. Then they were at certain that they were of natural colours without painting. Then they lift up a cloth which was above the ground, and there found a rich purse by seeming. And Percivale took it, and found therein a writ and so he read it, and devised the manner of the spindles and of the ship, whence it came, and by whom it was made. Now, said Galahad, where shall we find the gentlewoman that shall make new girdles to the sword? Fair sir, said Percivale's sister, dismay you not, for by the leave of God I shall let make a girdle to the sword, such one as shall long thereto. And then she opened a box, and took out girdles which were seemly wrought with golden threads, and upon that were set full precious stones, and a rich buckle of gold. Lo, lords, said she, here is a girdle that ought to be set about the sword. And wit ye well the greatest part of this girdle was made of my hair, which I loved well while that I was a woman of the world. But as soon as I wist that this adventure was ordained me I clipped off my hair, and made this girdle in the name of God. Ye be well found, said Sir Bors, for certes ye have put us out of great pain, wherein we should have entered ne had your tidings been.

Then went the gentlewoman and set it on the girdle of the sword. Now, said the fellowship, what is the name of the sword, and what shall we call it? Truly, said she, the name of the sword is the Sword with the Strange Girdles; and the sheath, Mover of Blood; for no man that hath blood in him ne shall never see the one part of the sheath which was made of the Tree of Life. Then they said to Galahad: In the name of Jesu Christ, and pray you that ye gird you with this sword which hath been desired so much in the realm of Logris. Now let me begin, said Galahad, to grip this sword for to give you courage; but wit ye well it longeth no more to me than it doth to you. And then he gripped about it with his fingers a great deal; and then she girt him about the middle with the sword. Now reck I not though I die, for now I hold me one of the blessed maidens of the world, which hath made the worthiest knight of the world. Damosel, said Galahad, ye have done so much that I shall be your knight all the days of my life.

Then they went from that ship, and went to the other. And anon the wind drove them into the sea a great pace, but they had no victuals: but it befell that they came on the morn to a castle that men call Carteloise, that was in the marches of Scotland. And when they had passed the port, the gentlewoman said: Lords, here be men arriven that, an they wist that ye were of King Arthur's court, ye should be assailed anon. Damosel, said Galahad, He that cast us out of the rock shall deliver us from them.

CHAPTER VIII

How Galahad and his fellows came to a castle, and how they were fought withal, and how they slew their adversaries, and other matters.

So it befell as they spoke thus there came a squire by them, and asked what they were; and they said they were of King Arthur's house. Is that sooth? said he. Now by my head, said he, ye be ill arrayed; and then turned he again unto the cliff fortress. And within a while they heard an horn blow. Then a gentlewoman came to them, and asked them of whence they were; and they told her. Fair lords, said she, for God's love turn again if ye may, for ye be come unto your death. Nay, they said, we will not turn again, for He shall help us in whose service we be entered in. Then as they stood talking there came knights well armed, and bade them yield them or else to die. That yielding, said they, shall be noyous to you. And therewith they let their horses run, and Sir Percivale smote the foremost to the earth, and took his horse, and mounted thereupon, and the same did Galahad. Also Bors served another so, for they had no horses in that country, for they left their horses when they took their ship in other countries. And so when they were horsed then began they to set upon them; and they of the castle fled into the strong fortress, and the three knights after them into the castle, and so alighted on foot, and with their swords slew them down, and gat into the hall.

Then when they beheld the great multitude of people that they had slain, they held themself great sinners. Certes, said Bors, I ween an God had loved them that we should not have had power to have slain them thus. But they have done so much against Our Lord that He would not suffer them to reign no longer. Say ye not so, said Galahad, for if they misdid against God, the vengeance is not ours, but to Him which hath power thereof.

So came there out of a chamber a good man which was a priest, and bare God's body in a cup. And when he saw them which lay dead in the hall he was all abashed; and Galahad did off his helm and kneeled down, and so did his two fellows. Sir, said they, have ye no dread of us, for we be of King Arthur's court. Then asked the good man how they were slain so suddenly, and they told it him. Truly, said the good man, an ye might live as long as the world might endure, ne might ye have done so great an alms-deed as this. Sir, said Galahad, I repent me much, inasmuch as they were christened. Nay, repent you not, said he, for they were not christened, and I shall tell you how that I wot of this castle. Here was Lord Earl Hernox not but one year, and he had three sons, good knights of arms, and a daughter, the fairest gentlewoman that men knew. So those three knights loved their sister so sore that they brent in love, and so they lay by her, maugre her head. And for she cried to her father they slew her, and took their father and put him in prison, and wounded him nigh to the death, but a cousin of hers rescued him. And then did they great untruth: they slew clerks and priests, and made beat down chapels, that Our Lord's service might not be served nor said. And this same day her father sent to me for to be confessed and houseled; but such shame had never man as I had this day with the three brethren, but the earl bade me suffer, for he said they should not long endure, for three servants of Our Lord should destroy them, and now it is brought to an end. And by this may ye wit that Our Lord is not displeased with your deeds. Certes, said Galahad, an it had not pleased Our Lord, never should we have slain so many men in so little a while.

And then they brought the Earl Hernox out of prison into the midst of the hall, that knew Galahad anon, and yet he saw him never afore but by revelation of Our Lord.

CHAPTER IX

How the three knights, with Percivale's sister, came unto the same forest, and of an hart and four lions, and other things.

Then began he to weep right tenderly, and said: Long have I abiden your coming, but for God's love hold me in your arms, that my soul may depart out of my body in so good a man's arms as ye be. Gladly, said Galahad. And then one said on high, that all heard: Galahad, well hast thou avenged me on God's enemies. Now behoveth thee to go to the Maimed King as soon as thou mayest, for he shall receive by thee health which he hath abiden so long. And therewith the soul departed from the body, and Galahad made him to be buried as him ought to be.

Right so departed the three knights, and Percivale's sister with them. And so they came into a waste forest, and there they saw afore them a white hart which four lions led. Then they took them to assent for to follow after for to know whither they repaired; and so they rode after a great pace till that they came to a valley, and thereby was an hermitage where a good man dwelled, and the hart and the lions entered also. So when they saw all this they turned to the chapel, and saw the good man in a religious weed and in the armour of Our Lord, for he would sing mass of the Holy Ghost; and so they entered in and heard mass. And at the secrets of the mass they three saw the hart become a man, the which marvelled them, and set him upon the altar in a rich siege; and saw the four lions were changed, the one to the form of a man, the other to the form of a lion, and the third to an eagle, and the fourth was changed unto an ox. Then took they their siege where the hart sat, and went out through a glass window, and there was nothing perished nor broken; and they heard a voice say: In such a manner entered the Son of God in the womb of a maid Mary, whose virginity ne was perished ne hurt. And when they heard these words they fell down to the earth and were astonied; and therewith was a great clearness.

And when they were come to theirself again they went to the good man and prayed him that he would say them truth. What thing have ye seen? said he. And they told him all that they had seen. Ah lords, said he, ye be welcome; now wot I well ye be the good knights the which shall bring the Sangreal to an end; for ye be they unto whom Our Lord shall show great secrets. And well ought Our Lord be signified to an hart, for the hart when he is old he waxeth young again in his white skin. Right so cometh again Our Lord from death to life, for He lost earthly flesh that was the deadly flesh, which He had taken in the womb of the blessed Virgin Mary; and for that cause appeared Our Lord as a white hart without spot. And the four that were with Him is to understand the four evangelists which set in writing a part of Jesu Christ's deeds that He did sometime when He was among you an earthly man; for wit ye well never erst ne might no knight know the truth, for ofttimes or this Our Lord showed Him unto good men and unto good knights, in likeness of an hart, but I suppose from henceforth ye shall see no more. And then they joyed much, and dwelled there all that day. And upon the morrow when they had heard mass they departed and commended the good man to God: and so they came to a castle and passed by. So there came a knight armed after them and said: Lords, hark what I shall say to you.

CHAPTER X

How they were desired of a strange custom, the which they would not obey; wherefore they fought and slew many knights.

This gentlewoman that ye lead with you is a maid? Sir, said she, a maid I am. Then he took her by the bridle and said: By the Holy Cross, ye shall not escape me to-fore ye have yolden the custom of this castle. Let her go, said Percivale, ye be not wise, for a maid in what place she cometh is free. So in the meanwhile there came out a ten or twelve knights armed, out of the castle, and with them came gentlewomen which held a dish of silver. And then they said: This gentlewoman must yield us the custom of this castle. Sir, said a knight, what maid passeth hereby shall give this dish full of blood of her right arm. Blame have ye, said Galahad, that brought up such customs, and so God me save, I ensure you of this gentlewoman ye shall fail while that I live. So God me help, said Percivale, I had liefer be slain. And I also, said Sir Bors. By my troth, said the knight, then shall ye die, for ye may not endure against us though ye were the best knights of the world.

Then let they run each to other, and the three fellows beat the ten knights, and then set their hands to their swords and beat them down and slew them. Then there came out of the castle a three score knights armed. Fair lords, said the three fellows, have mercy on yourself and have not ado with us. Nay, fair lords, said the knights of the castle, we counsel you to withdraw you, for ye be the best knights of the world, and therefore do no more, for ye have done enough. We will let you go with this harm, but we must needs have the custom. Certes, said Galahad, for nought speak ye. Well, said they, will ye die? We be not yet come thereto, said Galahad. Then began they to meddle together, and Galahad, with the strange girdles, drew his sword, and smote on the right hand and on the left hand, and slew what that ever abode him, and did such marvels that there was none that saw him but weened he had been none earthly man, but a monster. And his two fellows halp him passing well, and so they held the journey everych in like hard till it was night: then must they needs depart.

So came in a good knight, and said to the three fellows: If ye will come in to-night and take such harbour as here is ye shall be right welcome, and we shall ensure you by the faith of our bodies, and as we be true knights, to leave you in such estate to-morrow as we find you, without any falsehood. And as soon as ye know of the custom we dare say ye will accord therefore. For God's love, said the gentlewoman, go thither and spare not for me. Go we, said Galahad; and so they entered into the chapel. And when they were alighted they made great joy of them. So within a while the three knights asked the custom of the castle and wherefore it was. What it is, said they, we will say you sooth.

CHAPTER XI

*How Sir Percivale's sister bled a dish full of blood for to heal
a lady, wherefore she died; and how that the body
was put in a ship.*

There is in this castle a gentlewoman which we and this castle is hers,
and many other. So it befell many years agone there fell upon her a
malady; and when she had lain a great while she fell unto a measle,
and of no leech she could have no remedy. But at the last an old man
said an she might have a dish full of blood of a maid and a clean virgin
in will and in work, and a king's daughter, that blood should be her
health, and for to anoint her withal; and for this thing was this custom
made. Now, said Percivale's sister, fair knights, I see well that this
gentlewoman is but dead. Certes, said Galahad, an ye bleed so much
ye may die. Truly, said she, an I die for to heal her I shall get me great
worship and soul's health, and worship to my lineage, and better is
one harm than twain. And therefore there shall be no more battle,
but to-morn I shall yield you your custom of this castle. And then
there was great joy more than there was to-fore, for else had there
been mortal war upon the morn; notwithstanding she would none
other, whether they wold or nold.

That night were the three fellows eased with the best; and on the
morn they heard mass, and Sir Percivale's sister bade bring forth the
sick lady. So she was, the which was evil at ease. Then said she: Who
shall let me blood? So one came forth and let her blood, and she bled
so much that the dish was full. Then she lift up her hand and blessed
her; and then she said to the lady: Madam, I am come to the death for
to make you whole, for God's love pray for me. With that she fell in
a swoon. Then Galahad and his two fellows start up to her, and lift
her up and staunched her, but she had bled so much that she might
not live. Then she said when she was awaked: Fair brother Percivale,
I die for the healing of this lady, so I require you that ye bury me not
in this country, but as soon as I am dead put me in a boat at the next
haven, and let me go as adventure will lead me; and as soon as ye
three come to the City of Sarras, there to enchieve the Holy Grail, ye

shall find me under a tower arrived, and there bury me in the spiritual place; for I say you so much, there Galahad shall be buried, and ye also, in the same place.

Then Percivale understood these words, and granted it her, weeping. And then said a voice: Lords and fellows, to-morrow at the hour of prime ye three shall depart everych from other, till the adventure bring you to the Maimed King. Then asked she her Saviour; and as soon as she had received it the soul departed from the body. So the same day was the lady healed, when she was anointed withal. Then Sir Percivale made a letter of all that she had holpen them as in strange adventures, and put it in her right hand, and so laid her in a barge, and covered it with black silk; and so the wind arose, and drove the barge from the land, and all knights beheld it till it was out of their sight. Then they drew all to the castle, and so forthwith there fell a sudden tempest and a thunder, lightning, and rain, as all the earth would have broken. So half the castle turned up-so-down. So it passed evensong or the tempest was ceased.

Then they saw afore them a knight armed and wounded hard in the body and in the head, that said: O God, succour me for now it is need. After this knight came another knight and a dwarf, which cried to them afar: Stand, ye may not escape. Then the wounded knight held up his hands to God that he should not die in such tribulation. Truly, said Galahad, I shall succour him for His sake that he calleth upon. Sir, said Bors, I shall do it, for it is not for you, for he is but one knight. Sir, said he, I grant. So Sir Bors took his horse, and commended him to God, and rode after, to rescue the wounded knight. Now turn we to the two fellows.

CHAPTER XII

How Galahad and Percivale found in a castle many tombs of maidens that had bled to death.

Now saith the story that all night Galahad and Percivale were in a chapel in their prayers, for to save Sir Bors. So on the morrow they dressed them in their harness toward the castle, to wit what was fallen of them therein. And when they came there they found neither man

nor woman that he ne was dead by the vengeance of Our Lord. With
that they heard a voice that said: This vengeance is for blood-
shedding of maidens. Also they found at the end of the chapel a
churchyard, and therein might they see a three score fair tombs, and
that place was so fair and so delectable that it seemed them there had
been none tempest, for there lay the bodies of all the good maidens
which were martyred for the sick lady's sake. Also they found the
names of everych, and of what blood they were come, and all were
of kings' blood, and twelve of them were kings' daughters. Then they
departed and went into a forest. Now, said Percivale unto Galahad,
we must depart, so pray we Our Lord that we may meet together in
short time: then they did off their helms and kissed together, and
wept at their departing.

CHAPTER XIII

*How Sir Launcelot entered into the ship where Sir Percivale's
sister lay dead, and how he met with Sir Galahad, his son.*

Now saith the history, that when Launcelot was come to the water of
Mortoise, as it is rehearsed before, he was in great peril, and so he laid
him down and slept, and took the adventure that God would send
him. So when he was asleep there came a vision unto him and said:
Launcelot, arise up and take thine armour, and enter into the first ship
that thou shalt find. And when he heard these words he start up and
saw great clearness about him. And then he lift up his hand and
blessed him, and so took his arms and made him ready; and so by
adventure he came by a strand, and found a ship the which was
without sail or oar. And as soon as he was within the ship there he felt
the most sweetness that ever he felt, and he was fulfilled with all thing
that he thought on or desired. Then he said: Fair sweet Father, Jesu
Christ, I wot not in what joy I am, for this joy passeth all earthly joys
that ever I was in. And so in this joy he laid him down to the ship's
board, and slept till day. And when he awoke he found there a fair
bed, and therein lying a gentlewoman dead, the which was Sir
Percivale's sister. And as Launcelot devised her, he espied in her right
hand a writ, the which he read, the which told him all the adventures

that ye have heard to-fore, and of what lineage she was come. So with this gentlewoman Sir Launcelot was a month and more. If ye would ask how he lived, He that fed the people of Israel with manna in the desert, so was he fed; for every day when he had said his prayers he was sustained with the grace of the Holy Ghost.

So on a night he went to play him by the water side, for he was somewhat weary of the ship. And then he listened and heard an horse come, and one riding upon him. And when he came nigh he seemed a knight. And so he let him pass, and went thereas the ship was; and there he alighted, and took the saddle and the bridle and put the horse from him, and went into the ship. And then Launcelot dressed unto him, and said: Ye be welcome. And he answered and saluted him again, and asked him: What is your name? for much my heart giveth unto you. Truly, said he, my name is Launcelot du Lake. Sir, said he, then be ye welcome, for ye were the beginner of me in this world. Ah, said he, are ye Galahad? Yea, forsooth, said he; and so he kneeled down and asked him his blessing, and after took off his helm and kissed him. And there was great joy between them, for there is no tongue can tell the joy that they made either of other, and many a friendly word spoken between, as kin would, the which is no need here to be rehearsed. And there everych told other of their adventures and marvels that were befallen to them in many journeys sith that they departed from the court.

Anon, as Galahad saw the gentlewoman dead in the bed, he knew her well enough, and told great worship of her, that she was the best maid living, and it was great pity of her death. But when Launcelot heard how the marvellous sword was gotten, and who made it, and all the marvels rehearsed afore, then he prayed Galahad, his son, that he would show him the sword, and so he did; and anon he kissed the pommel, and the hilt, and the scabbard. Truly, said Launcelot, never erst knew I of so high adventures done, and so marvellous and strange. So dwelt Launcelot and Galahad within that ship half a year, and served God daily and nightly with all their power; and often they arrived in isles far from folk, where there repaired none but wild beasts, and there they found many strange adventures and perilous, which they brought to an end; but for those adventures were with wild beasts, and not in the quest of the Sangreal, therefore the tale maketh here no mention thereof, for it would be too long to tell of all those adventures that befell them.

CHAPTER XIV

*How a knight brought unto Sir Galahad a horse, and bade
him come from his father, Sir Launcelot.*

So after, on a Monday, it befell that they arrived in the edge of a
forest to-fore a cross; and then saw they a knight armed all in white,
and was richly horsed, and led in his right hand a white horse; and so
he came to the ship, and saluted the two knights on the High Lord's
behalf, and said: Galahad, sir, ye have been long enough with your
father, come out of the ship, and start upon this horse, and go where
the adventures shall lead thee in the quest of the Sangreal. Then he
went to his father and kissed him sweetly, and said: Fair sweet father,
I wot not when I shall see you more till I see the body of Jesu Christ.
I pray you, said Launcelot, pray ye to the High Father that He hold
me in His service. And so he took his horse, and there they heard a
voice that said: Think for to do well, for the one shall never see the
other before the dreadful day of doom. Now, son Galahad, said
Launcelot, since we shall depart, and never see other, I pray to the
High Father to conserve me and you both. Sir, said Galahad, no
prayer availeth so much as yours. And therewith Galahad entered
into the forest.

And the wind arose, and drove Launcelot more than a month
throughout the sea, where he slept but little, but prayed to God that
he might see some tidings of the Sangreal. So it befell on a night, at
midnight, he arrived afore a castle, on the back side, which was rich
and fair, and there was a postern opened toward the sea, and was
open without any keeping, save two lions kept the entry; and the
moon shone clear. Anon Sir Launcelot heard a voice that said:
Launcelot, go out of this ship and enter into the castle, where thou
shalt see a great part of thy desire. Then he ran to his arms, and so
armed him, and so went to the gate and saw the lions. Then set he
hand to his sword and drew it. Then there came a dwarf suddenly,
and smote him on the arm so sore that the sword fell out of his hand.
Then heard he a voice say: O man of evil faith and poor belief,
wherefore trowest thou more on thy harness than in thy Maker, for

He might more avail thee than thine armour, in whose service that thou art set. Then said Launcelot: Fair Father Jesu Christ, I thank thee of Thy great mercy that Thou reprovest me of my misdeed; now see I well that ye hold me for your servant. Then took he again his sword and put it up in his sheath, and made a cross in his forehead, and came to the lions, and they made semblaunt to do him harm. Notwithstanding he passed by them without hurt, and entered into the castle to the chief fortress, and there were they all at rest. Then Launcelot entered in so armed, for he found no gate nor door but it was open. And at the last he found a chamber whereof the door was shut, and he set his hand thereto to have opened it, but he might not.

CHAPTER XV

How Sir Launcelot was to-fore the door of the chamber wherein the Holy Sangreal was.

Then he enforced him mickle to undo the door. Then he listened and heard a voice which sang so sweetly that it seemed none earthly thing; and him thought the voice said: Joy and honour be to the Father of Heaven. Then Launcelot kneeled down to-fore the chamber, for well wist he that there was the Sangreal within that chamber. Then said he: Fair sweet Father, Jesu Christ, if ever I did thing that pleased Thee, Lord for Thy pity never have me not in despite for my sins done aforetime, and that Thou show me something of that I seek. And with that he saw the chamber door open, and there came out a great clearness, that the house was as bright as all the torches of the world had been there.

So came he to the chamber door, and would have entered. And anon a voice said to him: Flee, Launcelot, and enter not, for thou oughtest not to do it; and if thou enter thou shalt for-think it. Then he withdrew him aback right heavy. Then looked he up in the midst of the chamber, and saw a table of silver, and the Holy Vessel, covered with red samite, and many angels about it, whereof one held a candle of wax burning, and the other held a cross, and the ornaments of an altar. And before the Holy Vessel he saw a good man clothed as a priest. And it seemed that he was at the sacring of the mass. And it seemed to Launcelot that above the priest's hands were three men, whereof the two put the youngest by likeness between the priest's hands; and so he lift it up right high, and it seemed to show so to the people. And then Launcelot marvelled not a little, for him thought the priest was so greatly charged of the figure that him seemed that he should fall to the earth. And when he saw none about him that would help him, then came he to the door a great pace, and said: Fair Father Jesu Christ, ne take it for no sin though I help the good man which hath great need of help.

Right so entered he into the chamber, and came toward the table of silver; and when he came nigh he felt a breath, that him thought it was intermeddled with fire, which smote him so sore in the visage that him thought it brent his visage; and therewith he fell to the earth, and had no power to arise, as he that was so araged, that had lost the power of his body, and his hearing, and his seeing. Then felt he many hands about him, which took him up and bare him out of the chamber door, without any amending of his swoon, and left him there, seeming dead to all people.

So upon the morrow when it was fair day they within were arisen, and found Launcelot lying afore the chamber door. All they marvelled how that he came in, and so they looked upon him, and felt his pulse to wit whether there were any life in him; and so they found life in him, but he might not stand nor stir no member that he had. And so they took him by every part of the body, and bare him into a chamber, and laid him in a rich bed, far from all folk; and so he lay four days. Then the one said he was alive, and the other said, Nay. In the name of God, said an old man, for I do you verily to wit he is not dead, but he is so full of life as the mightiest of you all; and therefore I counsel you that he be well kept till God send him life again.

CHAPTER XVI

How Sir Launcelot had lain four-and-twenty days and as many nights as a dead man, and other divers matters.

In such manner they kept Launcelot four-and-twenty days and all so many nights, that ever he lay still as a dead man; and at the twenty-fifth day befell him after midday that he opened his eyes. And when he saw folk he made great sorrow, and said: Why have ye awaked me, for I was more at ease than I am now. O Jesu Christ, who might be so blessed that might see openly thy great marvels of secretness there where no sinner may be! What have ye seen? said they about him. I have seen, said he, so great marvels that no tongue may tell, and more than any heart can think, and had not my son been here afore me I had seen much more.

Then they told him how he had lain there four-and-twenty days and nights. Then him thought it was punishment for the four-and-twenty years that he had been a sinner, wherefore Our Lord put him in penance four-and-twenty days and nights. Then looked Sir Launcelot afore him, and saw the hair which he had borne nigh a year, for that he for-thought him right much that he had broken his promise unto the hermit, which he had avowed to do. Then they asked how it stood with him. Forsooth, said he, I am whole of body, thanked be Our Lord; therefore, sirs, for God's love tell me where I am. Then said they all that he was in the castle of Carbonek.

Therewith came a gentlewoman and brought him a shirt of small linen cloth, but he changed not there, but took the hair to him again. Sir, said they, the quest of the Sangreal is achieved now right in you, that never shall ye see of the Sangreal no more than ye have seen. Now I thank God, said Launcelot, of His great mercy of that I have seen, for it sufficeth me; for as I suppose no man in this world hath lived better than I have done to enchieve that I have done. And therewith he took the hair and clothed him in it, and above that he put a linen shirt, and after a robe of scarlet, fresh and new. And when he was so arrayed they marvelled all, for they knew him that he was Launcelot, the good knight. And then they said all: O my lord Sir

Launcelot, be that ye? And he said: Truly I am he.

Then came word to King Pelles that the knight that had lain so long dead was Sir Launcelot. Then was the king right glad, and went to see him. And when Launcelot saw him come he dressed him against him, and there made the king great joy of him. And there the king told him tidings that his fair daughter was dead. Then Launcelot was right heavy of it, and said: Sir, me forthinketh the death of your daughter, for she was a full fair lady, fresh and young. And well I wot she bare the best knight that is now on the earth, or that ever was sith God was born. So the king held him there four days, and on the morrow he took his leave at King Pelles and at all the fellowship, and thanked them of their great labour.

Right so as they sat at their dinner in the chief salle, then was so befallen that the Sangreal had fulfilled the table with all manner of meats that any heart might think. So as they sat they saw all the doors and the windows of the place were shut without man's hand, whereof they were all abashed, and none wist what to do.

And then it happed suddenly a knight came to the chief door and knocked, and cried: Undo the door. But they would not. And ever he cried: Undo; but they would not. And at last it noyed them so much that the king himself arose and came to a window there where the knight called. Then he said: Sir knight, ye shall not enter at this time while the Sangreal is here, and therefore go into another; for certes ye be none of the knights of the quest, but one of them which hath served the fiend, and hast left the service of Our Lord: and he was passing wroth at the king's words. Sir knight, said the king, sith ye would so fain enter, say me of what country ye be. Sir, said he, I am of the realm of Logris, and my name is Ector de Maris, and brother unto my lord, Sir Launcelot. In the name of God, said the king, me for-thinketh of what I have said, for your brother is here within. And when Ector de Maris understood that his brother was there, for he was the man in the world that he most dread and loved, and then he said: Ah God, now doubleth my sorrow and shame. Full truly said the good man of the hill unto Gawaine and to me of our dreams. Then went he out of the court as fast as his horse might, and so throughout the castle.

CHAPTER XVII

How Sir Launcelot returned towards Logris, and of other adventures which he saw in the way.

Then King Pelles came to Sir Launcelot and told him tidings of his brother, whereof he was sorry, that he wist not what to do. So Sir Launcelot departed, and took his arms, and said he would go see the realm of Logris, which I have not seen in twelve months. And therewith he commended the king to God, and so rode through many realms. And at the last he came to a white abbey, and there they made him that night great cheer; and on the morn he rose and heard mass. And afore an altar he found a rich tomb, which was newly made; and then he took heed, and saw the sides written with gold which said: Here lieth King Bagdemagus of Gore, which King Arthur's nephew slew; and named him, Sir Gawaine. Then was not he a little sorry, for Launcelot loved him much more than any other, and had it been any other than Gawaine he should not have escaped from death to life; and said to himself: Ah Lord God, this is a great hurt unto King Arthur's court, the loss of such a man. And then he departed and came to the abbey where Galahad did the adventure of the tombs, and won the white shield with the red cross; and there had he great cheer all that night.

And on the morn he turned unto Camelot, where he found King Arthur and the queen. But many of the knights of the Round Table were slain and destroyed, more than half. And so three were come home, Ector, Gawaine, and Lionel, and many other that need not to be rehearsed. And all the court was passing glad of Sir Launcelot, and the king asked him many tidings of his son Galahad. And there Launcelot told the king of his adventures that had befallen him since he departed. And also he told him of the adventures of Galahad, Percivale, and Bors, which that he knew by the letter of the dead damosel, and as Galahad had told him. Now God would, said the king, that they were all three here. That shall never be, said Launcelot, for two of them shall ye never see, but one of them shall come again.

Now leave we this story and speak of Galahad.

CHAPTER XVIII

How Galahad came to King Mordrains, and of other matters and adventures.

Now, saith the story, Galahad rode many journeys in vain. And at the last he came to the abbey where King Mordrains was, and when he heard that, he thought he would abide to see him. And upon the morn, when he had heard mass, Galahad came unto King Mordrains, and anon the king saw him, which had lain blind of long time. And then he dressed him against him, and said: Galahad, the servant of Jesu Christ, whose coming I have abiden so long, now embrace me and let me rest on thy breast, so that I may rest between thine arms, for thou art a clean virgin above all knights, as the flower of the lily in whom virginity is signified, and thou art the rose the which is the flower of all good virtues, and in colour of fire. For the fire of the Holy Ghost is taken so in thee that my flesh which was all dead of oldness is become young again. Then Galahad heard his words, then he embraced him and all his body. Then said he: Fair Lord Jesu Christ, now I have my will. Now I require thee, in this point that I am in, thou come and visit me. And anon Our Lord heard his prayer: therewith the soul departed from the body.

And then Galahad put him in the earth as a king ought to be, and so departed and so came into a perilous forest where he found the well the which boileth with great waves, as the tale telleth to-fore. And as soon as Galahad set his hand thereto it ceased, so that it brent no more, and the heat departed. For that it brent it was a sign of lechery, the which was that time much used. But that heat might not abide his pure virginity. And this was taken in the country for a miracle. And so ever after was it called Galahad's well.

Then by adventure he came into the country of Gore, and into the abbey where Launcelot had been to-forehand, and found the tomb of King Bagdemagus, but he was founder thereof, Joseph of Aramathie's son; and the tomb of Simeon where Launcelot had failed. Then he looked into a croft under the minster, and there he saw a tomb which brent full marvellously. Then asked he the brethren what it was. Sir, said they, a marvellous adventure that may not be brought unto none end but by him that passeth of bounty and of knighthood all them of the Round Table. I would, said Galahad, that ye would lead me thereto. Gladly, said they, and so led him till a cave. And he went down upon greses, and came nigh the tomb. And then the flaming failed, and the fire staunched, the which many a day had been great. Then came there a voice that said: Much are ye beholden to thank Our Lord, the which hath given you a good hour, that ye may draw out the souls of earthly pain, and to put them into the joys of paradise. I am of your kindred, the which hath dwelled in this heat this three hundred winter and four-and-fifty to be purged of the sin that I did against Joseph of Aramathie. Then Galahad took the body in his arms and bare it into the minster. And that night lay Galahad in the abbey; and on the morn he gave him service, and put him in the earth afore the high altar.

CHAPTER XIX

How Sir Percivale and Sir Bors met with Sir Galahad, and how they came to the castle of Carbonek, and other matters.

So departed he from thence, and commended the brethren to God; and so he rode five days till that he came to the Maimed King. And ever followed Percivale the five days, asking where he had been; and so one told him how the adventures of Logris were enchieved. So on a day it befell that they came out of a great forest, and there they met at traverse with Sir Bors, the which rode alone. It is none need to tell if they were glad; and them he saluted, and they yielded him honour and good adventure, and everych told other. Then said Bors: It is mo than a year and an half that I ne lay ten times where men dwelled, but in wild forests and in mountains, but God was ever my comfort.

Then rode they a great while till that they came to the castle of Carbonek. And when they were entered within the castle King Pelles knew them; then there was great joy, for they wist well by their coming that they had fulfilled the quest of the Sangreal. Then Eliazar, King Pelles' son, brought to-fore them the broken sword wherewith Joseph was stricken through the thigh. Then Bors set his hand thereto, if that he might have soldered it again; but it would not be. Then he took it to Percivale, but he had no more power thereto than he. Now have ye it again, said Percivale to Galahad, for an it be ever enchieved by any bodily man ye must do it. And then he took the pieces and set them together, and they seemed that they had never been broken, and as well as it had been first forged. And when they within espied that the adventure of the sword was enchieved, then they gave the sword to Bors, for it might not be better set; for he was a good knight and a worthy man.

And a little afore even the sword arose great and marvellous, and was full of great heat that many men fell for dread. And anon alighted a voice among them, and said: They that ought not to sit at the table of Jesu Christ arise, for now shall very knights be fed. So they went thence, all save King Pelles and Eliazar, his son, the which were holy men, and a maid which was his niece; and so these three fellows and they three were there, no mo. Anon they saw knights all armed came in at the hall door, and did off their helms and their arms, and said unto Galahad: Sir, we have hied right much for to be with you at this table where the holy meat shall be departed. Then said he: Ye be welcome, but of whence be ye? So three of them said they were of Gaul, and other three said they were of Ireland, and the other three said they were of Denmark. So as they sat thus there came out a bed of tree, of a chamber, the which four gentlewomen brought; and in the bed lay a good man sick, and a crown of gold upon his head; and there in the midst of the place they set him down, and went again their way. Then he lift up his head, and said: Galahad, Knight, ye be welcome, for much have I desired your coming, for in such pain and in such anguish I have been long. But now I trust to God the term is come that my pain shall be allayed, that I shall pass out of this world so as it was promised me long ago. Therewith a voice said: There be two among you that be not in the quest of the Sangreal, and therefore depart ye.

CHAPTER XX

*How Galahad and his fellows were fed of the Holy Sangreal,
and how Our Lord appeared to them, and other things.*

Then King Pelles and his son departed. And therewithal beseemed
them that there came a man, and four angels from heaven, clothed in
likeness of a bishop, and had a cross in his hand; and these four angels
bare him up in a chair, and set him down before the table of silver
whereupon the Sangreal was; and it seemed that he had in midst of
his forehead letters the which said: See ye here Joseph, the first bishop
of Christendom, the same which Our Lord succoured in the city of
Sarras in the spiritual place. Then the knights marvelled, for that
bishop was dead more than three hundred year to-fore. O knights,
said he, marvel not, for I was sometime an earthly man. With that
they heard the chamber door open, and there they saw angels; and
two bare candles of wax, and the third a towel, and the fourth a spear
which bled marvellously, that three drops fell within a box which he
held with his other hand. And they set the candles upon the table,
and the third the towel upon the vessel, and the fourth the holy spear
even upright upon the vessel. And then the bishop made semblaunt
as though he would have gone to the sacring of the mass. And then
he took an ubblie which was made in likeness of bread. And at the
lifting up there came a figure in likeness of a child, and the visage was
as red and as bright as any fire, and smote himself into the bread, so
that they all saw it that the bread was formed of a fleshly man; and
then he put it into the Holy Vessel again, and then he did that longed
to a priest to do to a mass. And then he went to Galahad and kissed
him, and bade him go and kiss his fellows: and so he did anon. Now,
said he, servants of Jesu Christ, ye shall be fed afore this table with
sweet meats that never knights tasted. And when he had said, he
vanished away. And they set them at the table in great dread, and
made their prayers.

Then looked they and saw a man come out of the Holy Vessel, that
had all the signs of the passion of Jesu Christ, bleeding all openly, and
said: My knights, and my servants, and my true children, which be

come out of deadly life into spiritual life, I will now no longer hide me from you, but ye shall see now a part of my secrets and of my hidden things: now hold and receive the high meat which ye have so much desired. Then took he himself the Holy Vessel and came to Galahad; and he kneeled down, and there he received his Saviour, and after him so received all his fellows; and they thought it so sweet that it was marvellous to tell. Then said he to Galahad: Son, wottest thou what I hold betwixt my hands? Nay, said he, but if ye will tell me. This is, said he, the holy dish wherein I ate the lamb on Sheer-Thursday. And now hast thou seen that thou most desired to see, but yet hast thou not seen it so openly as thou shalt see it in the city of Sarras in the spiritual place. Therefore thou must go hence and bear with thee this Holy Vessel; for this night it shall depart from the realm of Logris, that it shall never be seen more here. And wottest thou wherefore? For he is not served nor worshipped to his right by them of this land, for they be turned to evil living; therefore I shall disherit them of the honour which I have done them. And therefore go ye three to-morrow unto the sea, where ye shall find your ship ready, and with you take the sword with the strange girdles, and no more with you but Sir Percivale and Sir Bors. Also I will that ye take with you of the blood of this spear for to anoint the Maimed King, both his legs and all his body, and he shall have his health. Sir, said Galahad, why shall not these other fellows go with us? For this cause: for right as I departed my apostles one here and another there, so I will that ye depart; and two of you shall die in my service, but one of you shall come again and tell tidings. Then gave he them his blessing and vanished away.

CHAPTER XXI

How Galahad anointed with the blood of the spear the Maimed King, and of other adventures.

And Galahad went anon to the spear which lay upon the table, and touched the blood with his fingers, and came after to the Maimed King and anointed his legs. And therewith he clothed him anon, and start upon his feet out of his bed as an whole man, and thanked Our

Lord that He had healed him. And that was not to the world-ward, for anon he yielded him to a place of religion of white monks, and was a full holy man. That same night about midnight came a voice among them which said: My sons and not my chief sons, my friends and not my warriors, go ye hence where ye hope best to do and as I bade you. Ah, thanked be Thou, Lord, that Thou wilt vouchsafe to call us, Thy sinners. Now may we well prove that we have not lost our pains. And anon in all haste they took their harness and departed. But the three knights of Gaul, one of them hight Claudine, King Claudas' son, and the other two were great gentlemen. Then prayed Galahad to everych of them, that if they come to King Arthur's court that they should salute my lord, Sir Launcelot, my father, and all the fellowship* of the Round Table; and prayed them if that they came on that part that they should not forget it.

Right so departed Galahad, Percivale and Bors with him; and so they rode three days, and then they came to a rivage, and found the ship whereof the tale speaketh of to-fore. And when they came to the board they found in the midst the table of silver which they had left with the Maimed King, and the Sangreal which was covered with red samite. Then were they glad to have such things in their fellowship; and so they entered and made great reverence thereto; and Galahad fell in his prayer long time to Our Lord, that at what time he asked, that he should pass out of this world. So much he prayed till a voice said to him: Galahad, thou shalt have thy request; and when thou askest the death of thy body thou shalt have it, and then shalt thou find the life of the soul. Percivale heard this, and prayed him, of fellowship that was between them, to tell him wherefore he asked such things. That shall I tell you, said Galahad; the other day when we saw a part of the adventures of the Sangreal I was in such a joy of heart, that I trow never man was that was earthly. And therefore I wot well, when my body is dead my soul shall be in great joy to see the blessed Trinity every day, and the majesty of Our Lord, Jesu Christ.

So long were they in the ship that they said to Galahad: Sir, in this bed ought ye to lie, for so saith the scripture. And so he laid him down and slept a great while; and when he awaked he looked afore him and saw the city of Sarras. And as they would have landed they

---

* So Wynkyn de Worde; Caxton 'of them'.

saw the ship wherein Percivale had put his sister in. Truly, said Percivale, in the name of God, well hath my sister holden us covenant. Then took they out of the ship the table of silver, and he took it to Percivale and to Bors, to go to-fore, and Galahad came behind. And right so they went to the city, and at the gate of the city they saw an old man crooked. Then Galahad called him and bade him help to bear this heavy thing. Truly, said the old man, it is ten year ago that I might not go but with crutches. Care thou not, said Galahad, and arise up and show thy good will. And so he assayed, and found himself as whole as ever he was. Than ran he to the table, and took one part against Galahad. And anon arose there great noise in the city, that a cripple was made whole by knights marvellous that entered into the city.

Then anon after, the three knights went to the water, and brought up into the palace Percivale's sister, and buried her as richly as a king's daughter ought to be. And when the king of the city, which was cleped Estorause, saw the fellowship, he asked them of whence they were, and what thing it was that they had brought upon the table of silver. And they told him the truth of the Sangreal, and the power which that God had sent there. Then the king was a tyrant, and was come of the line of paynims, and took them and put them in prison in a deep hole.

CHAPTER XXII

How they were fed with the Sangreal while they were in prison, and how Galahad was made king.

But as soon as they were there Our Lord sent them the Sangreal, through whose grace they were always fulfilled while that they were in prison. So at the year's end it befell that this King Estorause lay sick, and felt that he should die. Then he sent for the three knights, and they came afore him; and he cried them mercy of that he had done to them, and they forgave it him goodly; and he died anon. When the king was dead all the city was dismayed, and wist not who might be their king. Right so as they were in counsel there came a voice among them, and bade them choose the youngest knight of them three to be their king: For he shall well maintain you and all yours. So they made Galahad king by all the assent of the holy city, and else they would have slain him. And when he was come to behold the land, he let make above the table of silver a chest of gold and of precious stones, that hilled the Holy Vessel. And every day early the three fellows would come afore it, and make their prayers.

Now at the year's end, and the self day after Galahad had borne the crown of gold, he arose up early and his fellows, and came to the palace, and saw to-fore them the Holy Vessel, and a man kneeling on his knees in likeness of a bishop, that had about him a great fellowship of angels, as it had been Jesu Christ himself; and then he arose and began a mass of Our Lady. And when he came to the sacrament of the mass, and had done, anon he called Galahad, and said to him: Come forth the servant of Jesu Christ, and thou shalt see that thou hast much desired to see. And then he began to tremble right hard when the deadly flesh began to behold the spiritual things. Then he held up his hands toward heaven and said: Lord, I thank thee, for now I see that that hath been my desire many a day. Now, blessed Lord, would I not longer live, if it might please thee, Lord. And therewith the good man took Our Lord's body betwixt his hands, and proffered it to Galahad, and he received it right gladly and meekly. Now wottest thou what I am? said the good man. Nay, said Galahad. I am Joseph of Aramathie, the which Our Lord hath sent here to thee to bear thee fellowship; and wottest thou wherefore that he hath sent me more than any other? For thou hast resembled me in two things; in that thou hast seen the marvels of the Sangreal, in that thou hast been a clean maiden, as I have been and am.

And when he had said these words Galahad went to Percivale and kissed him, and commended him to God; and so he went to Sir Bors and kissed him, and commended him to God, and said: Fair lord, salute me to my lord, Sir Launcelot, my father, and as soon as ye see him, bid him remember of this unstable world. And therewith he kneeled down to-fore the table and made his prayers, and then suddenly his soul departed to Jesu Christ, and a great multitude of angels bare his soul up to heaven, that the two fellows might well behold it. Also the two fellows saw come from heaven an hand, but they saw not the body. And then it came right to the Vessel, and took it and the spear, and so bare it up to heaven. Sithen was there never man so hardy to say that he had seen the Sangreal.

CHAPTER XXIII

Of the sorrow that Percivale and Bors made when Galahad
was dead: and of Percivale how he died, and other matters.

When Percivale and Bors saw Galahad dead they made as much
sorrow as ever did two men. And if they had not been good men
they might lightly have fallen in despair. And the people of the
country and of the city were right heavy. And then he was buried;
and as soon as he was buried Sir Percivale yielded him to an
hermitage out of the city, and took a religious clothing. And Bors was
alway with him, but never changed he his secular clothing, for that he
purposed him to go again into the realm of Logris. Thus a year and
two months lived Sir Percivale in the hermitage a full holy life, and
then passed out of this world; and Bors let bury him by his sister and
by Galahad in the spiritualities.

When Bors saw that he was in so far countries as in the parts of
Babylon he departed from Sarras, and armed him and came to the
sea, and entered into a ship; and so it befell him in good adventure he
came into the realm of Logris; and he rode so fast till he came to
Camelot where the king was. And then was there great joy made of
him in the court, for they weened all he had been dead, forasmuch as
he had been so long out of the country. And when they had eaten,
the king made great clerks to come afore him, that they should
chronicle of the high adventures of the good knights. When Bors had
told him of the adventures of the Sangreal, such as had befallen him
and his three fellows, that was Launcelot, Percivale, Galahad, and
himself, there Launcelot told the adventures of the Sangreal that he
had seen. All this was made in great books, and put up in almeries at
Salisbury. And anon Sir Bors said to Sir Launcelot: Galahad, your
own son, saluted you by me, and after you King Arthur and all the
court, and so did Sir Percivale, for I buried them with mine own
hands in the city of Sarras. Also, Sir Launcelot, Galahad prayed you to
remember of this unsiker world as ye behight him when ye were
together more than half a year. This is true, said Launcelot; now I
trust to God his prayer shall avail me.

Then Launcelot took Sir Bors in his arms, and said: Gentle cousin, ye are right welcome to me, and all that ever I may do for you and for yours ye shall find my poor body ready at all times, while the spirit is in it, and that I promise you faithfully, and never to fail. And wit ye well, gentle cousin, Sir Bors, that ye and I will never depart asunder whilst our lives may last. Sir, said he, I will as ye will.

Thus endeth the history of the Sangreal, that was briefly drawn out of French into English, the which is a story chronicled for one of the truest and the holiest that is in this world, the which is the xvii. book.

And here followeth the eighteenth book.

BOOK EIGHTEEN

CHAPTER I

Of the joy King Arthur and the queen had of the achievement of the Sangreal; and how Launcelot fell to his old love again.

So after the quest of the Sangreal was fulfilled, and all knights that were left alive were come again unto the Table Round, as the book of the Sangreal maketh mention, then was there great joy in the court; and in especial King Arthur and Queen Guenever made great joy of the remnant that were come home, and passing glad was the king and the queen of Sir Launcelot and of Sir Bors, for they had been passing long away in the quest of the Sangreal.

Then, as the book saith, Sir Launcelot began to resort unto Queen Guenever again, and forgat the promise and the perfection that he made in the quest. For, as the book saith, had not Sir Launcelot been in his privy thoughts and in his mind so set inwardly to the queen as he was in seeming outward to God, there had no knight passed him in the quest of the Sangreal; but ever his thoughts were privily on the queen, and so they loved together more hotter than they did toforehand, and had such privy draughts together, that many in the court spake of it, and in especial Sir Agravaine, Sir Gawaine's brother, for he was ever open-mouthed.

So befell that Sir Launcelot had many resorts of ladies and damosels that daily resorted unto him, that besought him to be their champion, and in all such matters of right Sir Launcelot applied him daily to do for the pleasure of Our Lord, Jesu Christ. And ever as much as he might he withdrew him from the company and fellowship of Queen Guenever, for to eschew the slander and noise; wherefore the queen waxed wroth with Sir Launcelot. And upon a day she called Sir Launcelot unto her chamber, and said thus: Sir Launcelot, I see and feel daily that thy love beginneth to slake, for thou hast no joy to be in my presence, but ever thou art out of this court, and quarrels and matters thou hast nowadays for ladies and gentlewomen more than ever thou wert wont to have aforehand.

Ah madam, said Launcelot, in this ye must hold me excused for divers causes; one is, I was but late in the quest of the Sangreal; and I thank God of his great mercy, and never of my desert, that I saw in that my quest as much as ever saw any sinful man, and so was it told me. And if I had not had my privy thoughts to return to your love again as I do, I had seen as great mysteries as ever saw my son Galahad, outher Percivale, or Sir Bors; and therefore, madam, I was but late in that quest. Wit ye well, madam, it may not be yet lightly forgotten the high service in whom I did my diligent labour. Also, madam, wit ye well that there be many men speak of our love in this court, and have you and me greatly in await, as Sir Agravaine and Sir Mordred; and madam, wit ye well I dread them more for your sake than for any fear I have of them myself, for I may happen to escape and rid myself in a great need, where ye must abide all that will be said unto you. And then if that ye fall in any distress through wilful folly, then is there none other remedy or help but by me and my blood. And wit ye well, madam, the boldness of you and me will bring us to great shame and slander; and that were me loath to see you dishonoured. And that is the cause I take upon me more for to do for damosels and maidens than ever I did to-fore, that men should understand my joy and my delight is my pleasure to have ado for damosels and maidens.

CHAPTER II

How the queen commanded Sir Launcelot to avoid the court, and of the sorrow that Launcelot made.

All this while the queen stood still and let Sir Launcelot say what he would. And when he had all said she brast out a-weeping, and so she sobbed and wept a great while. And when she might speak she said: Launcelot, now I well understand that thou art a false recreant knight and a common lecher, and lovest and holdest other ladies, and by me thou hast disdain and scorn. For wit thou well, she said, now I understand thy falsehood, and therefore shall I never love thee no more. And never be thou so hardy to come in my sight; and right here I discharge thee this court, that thou never come within it; and I forfend thee my fellowship, and upon pain of thy head that thou see me no more. Right so Sir Launcelot departed with great heaviness, that unnethe he might sustain himself for great dole-making.

Then he called Sir Bors, Sir Ector de Maris, and Sir Lionel, and told them how the queen had forfended him the court, and so he was in will to depart into his own country. Fair sir, said Sir Bors de Ganis, ye shall not depart out of this land by mine advice. Ye must remember in what honour ye are renowned, and called the noblest knight of the world; and many great matters ye have in hand. And women in their hastiness will do ofttimes that sore repenteth them; and therefore by mine advice ye shall take your horse, and ride to the good hermitage here beside Windsor, that sometime was a good knight, his name is Sir Brasias, and there shall ye abide till I send you word of better tidings. Brother, said Sir Launcelot, wit ye well I am full loath to depart out of this realm, but the queen hath defended me so highly, that meseemeth she will never be my good lady as she hath been. Say ye never so, said Sir Bors, for many times or this time she hath been wroth with you, and after it she was the first that repented it. Ye say well, said Launcelot, for now will I do by your counsel, and take mine horse and my harness, and ride to the hermit Sir Brasias, and there will I repose me until I hear some manner of tidings from you; but, fair brother, I pray you get me the love of my lady, Queen Guenever, an ye may. Sir, said Sir Bors, ye need not to move me of such matters, for well ye wot I will do what I may to please you.

And then the noble knight, Sir Launcelot, departed with right heavy cheer suddenly, that none earthly creature wist of him, nor where he was become, but Sir Bors. So when Sir Launcelot was departed, the queen outward made no manner of sorrow in showing to none of his blood nor to none other. But wit ye well, inwardly, as the book saith, she took great thought, but she bare it out with a proud countenance as though she felt nothing nor danger.

CHAPTER III

*How at a dinner that the queen made there was a knight
enpoisoned, which Sir Mador laid on the queen.*

And then the queen let make a privy dinner in London unto the
knights of the Round Table. And all was for to show outward that
she had as great joy in all other knights of the Table Round as she had
in Sir Launcelot. All only at that dinner she had Sir Gawaine and his
brethren, that is for to say Sir Agravaine, Sir Gaheris, Sir Gareth, and
Sir Mordred. Also there was Sir Bors de Ganis, Sir Blamore de Ganis,
Sir Bleoberis de Ganis, Sir Galihud, Sir Galihodin, Sir Ector de Maris,
Sir Lionel, Sir Palomides, Safere his brother, Sir La Cote Male Taile,
Sir Persant, Sir Ironside, Sir Brandiles, Sir Kay le Seneschal, Sir
Mador de la Porte, Sir Patrise, a knight of Ireland, Aliduk, Sir
Astamore, and Sir Pinel le Savage, the which was cousin to Sir
Lamorak de Galis, the good knight that Sir Gawaine and his brethren
slew by treason. And so these four-and-twenty knights should dine
with the queen in a privy place by themself, and there was made a
great feast of all manner of dainties.

But Sir Gawaine had a custom that he used daily at dinner and at
supper, that he loved well all manner of fruit, and in especial apples
and pears. And therefore whosomever dined or feasted Sir Gawaine
would commonly purvey for good fruit for him, and so did the
queen for to please Sir Gawaine; she let purvey for him all manner of
fruit, for Sir Gawaine was a passing hot knight of nature. And this
Pinel hated Sir Gawaine because of his kinsman Sir Lamorak de Galis;
and therefore for pure envy and hate Sir Pinel enpoisoned certain
apples for to enpoison Sir Gawaine. And so this was well unto the
end of the meat; and so it befell by misfortune a good knight named
Patrise, cousin unto Sir Mador de la Porte, to take a poisoned apple.
And when he had eaten it he swelled so till he brast, and there Sir
Patrise fell down suddenly dead among them.

Then every knight leapt from the board ashamed, and araged for
wrath, nigh out of their wits. For they wist not what to say;
considering Queen Guenever made the feast and dinner, they all had

suspicion unto her. My lady, the queen, said Gawaine, wit ye well, madam, that this dinner was made for me, for all folks that know my condition understand that I love well fruit, and now I see well I had near been slain; therefore, madam, I dread me lest ye will be shamed. Then the queen stood still and was sore abashed, that she nist not what to say. This shall not so be ended, said Sir Mador de la Porte, for here have I lost a full noble knight of my blood; and therefore upon this shame and despite I will be revenged to the utterance. And there openly Sir Mador appealed the queen of the death of his cousin, Sir Patrise. Then stood they all still, that none would speak a word against him, for they all had great suspicion unto the queen because she let make that dinner. And the queen was so abashed that she could none other ways do, but wept so heartily that she fell in a swoon. With this noise and cry came to them King Arthur, and when he wist of that trouble he was a passing heavy man.

CHAPTER IV

*How Sir Mador appeached the queen of treason, and there
was no knight would fight for her at the first time.*

And ever Sir Mador stood still afore the king, and ever he appealed the queen of treason; for the custom was such that time that all manner of shameful death was called treason. Fair lords, said King Arthur, me repenteth of this trouble, but the case is so I may not have ado in this matter, for I must be a rightful judge; and that repenteth me that I may not do battle for my wife, for as I deem this deed came never by her. And therefore I suppose she shall not be all distained, but that some good knight shall put his body in jeopardy for my queen rather than she shall be brent in a wrong quarrel. And therefore, Sir Mador, be not so hasty, for it may happen she shall not be all friendless; and therefore desire thou thy day of battle, and she shall purvey her of some good knight that shall answer you, or else it were to me great shame, and to all my court.

My gracious lord, said Sir Mador, ye must hold me excused, for though ye be our king in that degree, ye are but a knight as we are, and ye are sworn unto knighthood as well as we; and therefore I beseech you that ye be not displeased, for there is none of the four-and-twenty knights that were bidden to this dinner but all they have great suspicion unto the queen. What say ye all, my lords? said Sir Mador. Then they answered by and by that they could not excuse the queen; for why she made the dinner, and either it must come by her or by her servants. Alas, said the queen, I made this dinner for a good intent, and never for none evil, so Almighty God me help in my right, as I was never purposed to do such evil deeds, and that I report me unto God.

My lord, the king, said Sir Mador, I require you as ye be a righteous king give me a day that I may have justice. Well, said the king, I give the day this day fifteen days that thou be ready armed on horseback in the meadow beside Westminster. And if it so fall that there be any knight to encounter with you, there mayst thou do the best, and God speed the right. And if it so fall that there be no knight at that day, then must my queen be burnt, and there she shall be ready to have her judgment. I am answered, said Sir Mador. And every knight went where it liked them.

So when the king and the queen were together the king asked the queen how this case befell. The queen answered: So God me help, I wot not how or in what manner. Where is Sir Launcelot? said King Arthur; an he were here he would not grudge to do battle for you. Sir, said the queen, I wot not where he is, but his brother and his kinsmen deem that he be not within this realm. That me repenteth, said King Arthur, for an he were here he would soon stint this strife. Then I will counsel you, said the king, and unto Sir Bors: That ye will do battle for her for Sir Launcelot's sake, and upon my life he will not refuse you. For well I see, said the king, that none of these four-and-twenty knights that were with you at your dinner where Sir Patrise was slain, that will do battle for you, nor none of them will say well of you, and that shall be a great slander for you in this court. Alas, said the queen, and I may not do withal, but now I miss Sir Launcelot, for an he were here he would put me soon to my heart's ease. What aileth you, said the king, ye cannot keep Sir Launcelot upon your side? For wit ye well, said the king, who that hath Sir Launcelot upon his part hath the most man of worship in the world upon his side. Now go your way, said the king unto the queen, and require Sir Bors to do battle for you for Sir Launcelot's sake.

CHAPTER V

*How the queen required Sir Bors to fight for her, and how he
granted upon condition; and how he warned Sir Launcelot thereof.*

So the queen departed from the king, and sent for Sir Bors into her
chamber. And when he was come she besought him of succour.
Madam, said he, what would ye that I did? for I may not with my
worship have ado in this matter, because I was at the same dinner, for
dread that any of those knights would have me in suspicion. Also,
madam, said Sir Bors, now miss ye Sir Launcelot, for he would not
have failed you neither in right nor in wrong, as ye have well proved
when ye have been in danger; and now ye have driven him out of this
country, by whom ye and all we were daily worshipped by; therefore,
madam, I marvel how ye dare for shame require me to do any thing
for you, in so much ye have chased him out of your country by
whom we were borne up and honoured. Alas, fair knight, said the
queen, I put me wholly in your grace, and all that is done amiss I will
amend as ye will counsel me. And therewith she kneeled down upon
both her knees, and besought Sir Bors to have mercy upon her:
Outher I shall have a shameful death, and thereto I never offended.

Right so came King Arthur, and found the queen kneeling afore Sir
Bors; then Sir Bors pulled her up, and said: Madam, ye do me great
dishonour. Ah, gentle knight, said the king, have mercy upon my
queen, courteous knight, for I am now in certain she is untruly
defamed. And therefore, courteous knight, said the king, promise her
to do battle for her, I require you for the love of Sir Launcelot. My
lord, said Sir Bors, ye require me the greatest thing that any man may
require me; and wit ye well if I grant to do battle for the queen I shall
wrath many of my fellowship of the Table Round. But as for that, said
Bors, I will grant my lord that for my lord Sir Launcelot's sake, and for
your sake I will at that day be the queen's champion unless that there
come by adventure a better knight than I am to do battle for her. Will
ye promise me this, said the king, by your faith? Yea sir, said Sir Bors,
of that I will not fail you, nor her both, but if there come a better
knight than I am, and then shall he have the battle. Then was the king

and the queen passing glad, and so departed, and thanked him heartily.

So then Sir Bors departed secretly upon a day, and rode unto Sir Launcelot thereas he was with the hermit, Sir Brasias, and told him of all their adventure. Ah Jesu, said Sir Launcelot, this is come happily as I would have it, and therefore I pray you make you ready to do battle, but look that ye tarry till ye see me come, as long as ye may. For I am sure Mador is an hot knight when he is enchafed, for the more ye suffer him the hastier will he be to battle. Sir, said Bors, let me deal with him, doubt ye not ye shall have all your will. Then departed Sir Bors from him and came to the court again. Then was it noised in all the court that Sir Bors should do battle for the queen; wherefore many knights were displeased with him, that he would take upon him to do battle in the queen's quarrel; for there were but few knights in all the court but they deemed the queen was in the wrong, and that she had done that treason.

So Sir Bors answered thus to his fellows of the Table Round: Wit ye well, my fair lords, it were shame to us all an we suffered to see the most noble queen of the world to be shamed openly, considering her lord and our lord is the man of most worship in the world, and most christened, and he hath ever worshipped us all in all places. Many answered him again: As for our most noble King Arthur, we love him and honour him as well as ye do, but as for Queen Guenever we love her not, because she is a destroyer of good knights. Fair lords, said Sir Bors, meseemeth ye say not as ye should say, for never yet in my days knew I never nor heard say that ever she was a destroyer of any good knight. But at all times as far as ever I could know she was a maintainer of good knights; and ever she hath been large and free of her goods to all good knights, and the most bounteous lady of her gifts and her good grace, that ever I saw or heard speak of. And therefore it were shame, said Sir Bors, to us all to our most noble king's wife, an we suffered her to be shamefully slain. And wit ye well, said Sir Bors, I will not suffer it, for I dare say so much, the queen is not guilty of Sir Patrise's death, for she owed him never none ill will, nor none of the four-and-twenty knights that were at that dinner; for I dare say for good love she bade us to dinner, and not for no mal engine, and that I doubt not shall be proved hereafter, for howsomever the game goeth, there was treason among us. Then some said to Sir Bors: We may well believe your words. And so some of them were well pleased, and some were not so.

CHAPTER VI

How at the day Sir Bors made him ready for to fight for the queen; and when he would fight how another discharged him.

The day came on fast until the even that the battle should be. Then the queen sent for Sir Bors and asked him how he was disposed. Truly madam, said he, I am disposed in likewise as I promised you, that is for to say I shall not fail you, unless by adventure there come a better knight than I am to do battle for you, then, madam, am I discharged of my promise. Will ye, said the queen, that I tell my lord Arthur thus? Do as it shall please you, madam. Then the queen went unto the king and told him the answer of Sir Bors. Have ye no doubt, said the king, of Sir Bors, for I call him now one of the best knights of the world, and the most profitablest man. And thus it passed on until the morn, and the king and the queen and all manner of knights that were there at that time drew them unto the meadow beside Westminster where the battle should be. And so when the king was come with the queen and many knights of the Round Table, then the queen was put there in the Constable's ward, and a great fire made about an iron stake, that an Sir Mador de la Porte had the better, she should be burnt: such custom was used in those days, that neither for favour, neither for love nor affinity, there should be none other but righteous judgment, as well upon a king as upon a knight, and as well upon a queen as upon another poor lady.

So in this meanwhile came in Sir Mador de la Porte, and took his oath afore the king, that the queen did this treason until his cousin Sir Patrise, and unto his oath he would prove it with his body, hand for hand, who that would say the contrary. Right so came in Sir Bors de Ganis, and said: That as for Queen Guenever she is in the right, and that will I make good with my hands that she is not culpable of this treason that is put upon her. Then make thee ready, said Sir Mador, and we shall prove whether thou be in the right or I. Sir Mador, said Sir Bors, wit thou well I know you for a good knight. Not for then I shall not fear you so greatly, but I trust to God I shall be able to withstand your malice. But this much have I promised my lord

Arthur and my lady the queen, that I shall do battle for her in this case to the uttermost, unless that there come a better knight than I am and discharge me. Is that all? said Sir Mador, either come thou off and do battle with me, or else say nay. Take your horse, said Sir Bors, and as I suppose, ye shall not tarry long but ye shall be answered.

Then either departed to their tents and made them ready to horseback as they thought best. And anon Sir Mador came into the field with his shield on his shoulder and his spear in his hand; and so rode about the place crying unto Arthur: Bid your champion come forth an he dare. Then was Sir Bors ashamed and took his horse and came to the lists' end. And then was he ware where came from a wood there fast by a knight all armed, upon a white horse, with a strange shield of strange arms; and he came riding all that he might run, and so he came to Sir Bors, and said thus: Fair knight, I pray you be not displeased, for here must a better knight than ye are have this battle, therefore I pray you withdraw you. For wit ye well I have had this day a right great journey, and this battle ought to be mine, and so I promised you when I spake with you last, and with all my heart I thank you of your good will. Then Sir Bors rode unto King Arthur and told him how there was a knight come that would have the battle for to fight for the queen. What knight is he? said the king. I wot not, said Sir Bors, but such covenant he made with me to be here this day. Now my lord, said Sir Bors, here am I discharged.

CHAPTER VII

How Sir Launcelot fought against Sir Mador for the queen, and how he overcame Sir Mador, and discharged the queen.

Then the king called to that knight, and asked him if he would fight for the queen. Then he answered to the king: Therefore came I hither, and therefore, sir king, he said, tarry me no longer, for I may not tarry. For anon as I have finished this battle I must depart hence, for I have ado many matters elsewhere. For wit you well, said that knight, this is dishonour to you all knights of the Round Table, to see and know so noble a lady and so courteous a queen as Queen

Guenever is, thus to be rebuked and shamed amongst you. Then they all marvelled what knight that might be that so took the battle upon him. For there was not one that knew him, but if it were Sir Bors.

Then said Sir Mador de la Porte unto the king: Now let me wit with whom I shall have ado withal. And then they rode to the lists' end, and there they couched their spears, and ran together with all their might, and Sir Mador's spear brake all to pieces, but the other's spear held, and bare Sir Mador's horse and all backward to the earth a great fall. But mightily and suddenly he avoided his horse and put his shield afore him, and then drew his sword, and bade the other knight alight and do battle with him on foot. Then that knight descended from his horse lightly like a valiant man, and put his shield afore him and drew his sword; and so they came eagerly unto battle, and either gave other many great strokes, tracing and traversing, racing and foining, and hurtling together with their swords as it were wild boars. Thus were they fighting nigh an hour, for this Sir Mador was a strong knight, and mightily proved in many strong battles. But at the last this knight smote Sir Mador grovelling upon the earth, and the knight stepped near him to have pulled Sir Mador flatling upon the ground; and therewith suddenly Sir Mador arose, and in his rising he smote that knight through the thick of the thighs that the blood ran out fiercely. And when he felt himself so wounded, and saw his blood, he let him arise upon his feet. And then he gave him such a buffet upon the helm that he fell to the earth flatling, and therewith he strode to him to have pulled off his helm off his head. And then Sir Mador prayed that knight to save his life, and so he yielded him as overcome, and released the queen of his quarrel. I will not grant thee thy life, said that knight, only that thou freely release the queen for ever, and that no mention be made upon Sir Patrise's tomb that ever Queen Guenever consented to that treason. All this shall be done, said Sir Mador, I clearly discharge my quarrel for ever.

Then the knights parters of the lists took up Sir Mador, and led him to his tent, and the other knight went straight to the stair-foot where sat King Arthur; and by that time was the queen come to the king, and either kissed other heartily. And when the king saw that knight, he stooped down to him, and thanked him, and in likewise did the queen; and the king prayed him to put off his helmet, and to repose him, and to take a sop of wine. And then he put off his helm to drink, and then every knight knew him that it was Sir Launcelot du Lake.

Anon as the king wist that, he took the queen in his hand, and yode unto Sir Launcelot, and said: Sir, grant mercy of your great travail that ye have had this day for me and for my queen. My lord, said Sir Launcelot, wit ye well I ought of right ever to be in your quarrel, and in my lady the queen's quarrel, to do battle; for ye are the man that gave me the high order of knighthood, and that day my lady, your queen, did me great worship, and else I had been shamed; for that same day ye made me knight, through my hastiness I lost my sword, and my lady, your queen, found it, and lapped it in her train, and gave me my sword when I had need thereto, and else had I been shamed among all knights; and therefore, my lord Arthur, I promised her at that day ever to be her knight in right outher in wrong. Grant mercy, said the king, for this journey; and wit ye well, said the king, I shall acquit your goodness.

And ever the queen beheld Sir Launcelot, and wept so tenderly that she sank almost to the ground for sorrow that he had done to her so great goodness where she showed him great unkindness. Then the knights of his blood drew unto him, and there either of them made great joy of other. And so came all the knights of the Table Round that were there at that time, and welcomed him. And then Sir Mador was had to leech-craft, and Sir Launcelot was healed of his wound. And then there was made great joy and mirths in that court.

CHAPTER VIII

How the truth was known by the Maiden of the Lake, and of divers other matters.

And so it befell that the damosel of the lake, her name was Nimue, the which wedded the good knight Sir Pelleas, and so she came to the court; for ever she did great goodness unto King Arthur and to all his knights through her sorcery and enchantments. And so when she heard how the queen was an-angered for the death of Sir Patrise, then she told it openly that she was never guilty; and there she disclosed by whom it was done, and named him, Sir Pinel; and for what cause he did it, there it was openly disclosed; and so the queen was excused, and the knight Pinel fled into his country. Then was it openly known that Sir Pinel enpoisoned the apples at the feast to that intent to have destroyed Sir Gawaine, because Sir Gawaine and his brethren destroyed Sir Lamorak de Galis, to the which Sir Pinel was cousin unto. Then was Sir Patrise buried in the church of Westminster in a tomb, and thereupon was written: Here lieth Sir Patrise of Ireland, slain by Sir Pinel le Savage, that enpoisoned apples to have slain Sir Gawaine, and by misfortune Sir Patrise ate one of those apples, and then suddenly he brast. Also there was written upon the tomb that Queen Guenever was appealed of treason of the death of Sir Patrise, by Sir Mador de la Porte; and there was made mention how Sir Launcelot fought with him for Queen Guenever, and overcame him in plain battle. All this was written upon the tomb of Sir Patrise in excusing of the queen. And then Sir Mador sued daily and long, to have the queen's good grace; and so by the means of Sir Launcelot he caused him to stand in the queen's good grace, and all was forgiven.

Thus it passed on till our Lady Day, Assumption. Within a fifteen days of that feast the king let cry a great jousts and a tournament that should be at that day at Camelot, that is Winchester; and the king let cry that he and the King of Scots would joust against all that would come against them. And when this cry was made, thither came many knights. So there came thither the King of Northgalis, and King Anguish of Ireland, and the King with the Hundred Knights, and Galahad, the haut prince, and the King of Northumberland, and many other noble dukes and earls of divers countries. So King Arthur made him ready to depart to these jousts, and would have had the queen with him, but at that time she would not, she said, for she was sick and might not ride at that time. That me repenteth, said the king, for this seven year ye saw not such a noble fellowship together except at Whitsuntide when Galahad departed from the court. Truly, said the queen to the king, ye must hold me excused, I may not be there, and that me repenteth. And many deemed the queen would not be there because of Sir Launcelot du Lake, for Sir Launcelot would not ride with the king, for he said that he was not whole of the wound the which Sir Mador had given him; wherefore the king was heavy and passing wroth. And so he departed toward Winchester with his fellowship; and so by the way the king lodged in a town called Astolat, that is now in English called Guildford, and there the king lay in the castle.

So when the king was departed the queen called Sir Launcelot to her, and said thus: Sir Launcelot, ye are greatly to blame thus to hold you behind my lord; what, trow ye, what will your enemies and mine say and deem? nought else but, See how Sir Launcelot holdeth him ever behind the king, and so doth the queen, for that they would have their pleasure together. And thus will they say, said the queen to Sir Launcelot, have ye no doubt thereof.

CHAPTER IX

How Sir Launcelot rode to Astolat, and received a sleeve to wear upon his helm at the request of a maid.

Madam, said Sir Launcelot, I allow your wit, it is of late come since ye were wise. And therefore, madam, at this time I will be ruled by your counsel, and this night I will take my rest, and to-morrow by time I will take my way toward Winchester. But wit you well, said Sir Launcelot to the queen, that at that jousts I will be against the king, and against all his fellowship. Ye may there do as ye list, said the queen, but by my counsel ye shall not be against your king and your fellowship. For therein be full many hard knights of your blood, as ye wot well enough, it needeth not to rehearse them. Madam, said Sir Launcelot, I pray you that ye be not displeased with me, for I will take the adventure that God will send me.

And so upon the morn early Sir Launcelot heard mass and brake his fast, and so took his leave of the queen and departed. And then he rode so much until he came to Astolat, that is Guildford; and there it happed him in the eventide he came to an old baron's place that hight Sir Bernard of Astolat. And as Sir Launcelot entered into his lodging, King Arthur espied him as he did walk in a garden beside the castle, how he took his lodging, and knew him full well. It is well, said King Arthur unto the knights that were with him in that garden beside the castle, I have now espied one knight that will play his play at the jousts to the which we be gone toward; I undertake he will do marvels. Who is that, we pray you tell us? said many knights that were there at that time. Ye shall not wit for me, said the king, as at this time. And so the king smiled, and went to his lodging.

So when Sir Launcelot was in his lodging, and unarmed him in his chamber, the old baron and hermit came to him making his reverence, and welcomed him in the best manner; but the old knight knew not Sir Launcelot. Fair sir, said Sir Launcelot to his host, I would pray you to lend me a shield that were not openly known, for mine is well known. Sir, said his host, ye shall have your desire, for meseemeth ye be one of the likeliest knights of the world, and therefore I shall show you friendship. Sir, wit you well I have two sons that were but late made knights, and the eldest hight Sir Tirre, and he was hurt that same day he was made knight, that he may not ride, and his shield ye shall have; for that is not known I dare say but here, and in no place else. And my youngest son hight Lavaine, and if it please you, he shall ride with you unto that jousts; and he is of his age strong and wight, for much my heart giveth unto you that ye should be a noble knight, therefore I pray you, tell me your name, said Sir Bernard. As for that, said Sir Launcelot, ye must hold me excused as at this time, and if God give me grace to speed well at the jousts I shall come again and tell you. But I pray you, said Sir Launcelot, in any wise let me have your son, Sir Lavaine, with me, and that I may have his brother's shield. All this shall be done, said Sir Bernard.

This old baron had a daughter that was called that time the Fair Maiden of Astolat. And ever she beheld Sir Launcelot wonderfully; and as the book saith, she cast such a love unto Sir Launcelot that she could never withdraw her love, wherefore she died, and her name was Elaine le Blank. So thus as she came to and fro she was so hot in her love that she besought Sir Launcelot to wear upon him at the jousts a token of hers. Fair damosel, said Sir Launcelot, an if I grant you that, ye may say I do more for your love than ever I did for lady or damosel. Then he remembered him he would go to the jousts disguised. And because he had never fore that time borne no manner of token of no damosel, then he bethought him that he would bear one of her, that none of his blood thereby might know him, and then he said: Fair maiden, I will grant you to wear a token of yours upon mine helmet, and therefore what it is, show it me. Sir, she said, it is a red sleeve of mine, of scarlet, well embroidered with great pearls: and so she brought it him. So Sir Launcelot received it, and said: Never did I erst so much for no damosel. And then Sir Launcelot betook the fair maiden his shield in keeping, and prayed her to keep that until that he came again; and so that night he had merry rest and great cheer, for ever the damosel Elaine was about Sir Launcelot all the while she might be suffered.

CHAPTER X

How the tourney began at Winchester, and what knights were at the jousts; and other things.

So upon a day, on the morn, King Arthur and all his knights departed, for their king had tarried three days to abide his noble knights. And so when the king was ridden, Sir Launcelot and Sir Lavaine made them ready to ride, and either of them had white shields, and the red sleeve Sir Launcelot let carry with him. And so they took their leave at Sir Bernard, the old baron, and at his daughter, the Fair Maiden of Astolat. And then they rode so long till that they came to Camelot, that time called Winchester; and there was great press of kings, dukes, earls, and barons, and many noble knights. But there Sir Launcelot was lodged privily by the means of Sir Lavaine with a rich burgess, that no man in that town was ware what they were. And so they reposed them there till our Lady Day, Assumption, as the great feast should be. So then trumpets blew unto the field, and King Arthur was set on high upon a scaffold to behold who did best. But as the French book saith, the king would not suffer Sir Gawaine to go from him, for never had Sir Gawaine the better an Sir Launcelot were in the field; and many times was Sir Gawaine rebuked when Launcelot came into any jousts disguised.

Then some of the kings, as King Anguish of Ireland and the King of Scots, were that time turned upon the side of King Arthur. And then on the other party was the King of Northgalis, and the King with the Hundred Knights, and the King of Northumberland, and Sir Galahad, the haut prince. But these three kings and this duke were passing weak to hold against King Arthur's party, for with him were the noblest knights of the world. So then they withdrew them either party from other, and every man made him ready in his best manner to do what he might.

Then Sir Launcelot made him ready, and put the red sleeve upon his head, and fastened it fast; and so Sir Launcelot and Sir Lavaine departed out of Winchester privily, and rode until a little leaved wood behind the party that held against King Arthur's party, and there they held them still till the parties smote together. And then came in the King of Scots and the King of Ireland on Arthur's party, and against them came the King of Northumberland, and the King with the Hundred Knights smote down the King of Northumberland, and the King with the Hundred Knights smote down King Anguish of Ireland. Then Sir Palomides that was on Arthur's party encountered with Sir Galahad, and either of them smote down other, and either party halp their lords on horseback again. So there began a strong assail upon both parties And then came in Sir Brandiles, Sir Sagramore le Desirous, Sir Dodinas le Savage, Sir Kay le Seneschal, Sir Griflet le Fise de Dieu, Sir Mordred, Sir Meliot de Logris, Sir Ozanna le Cure Hardy, Sir Safere, Sir Epinogris, Sir Galleron of Galway. All these fifteen knights were knights of the Table Round. So these with more other came in together, and beat aback the King of Northumberland and the King of Northgalis. When Sir Launcelot saw this, as he hoved in a little leaved wood, then he said unto Sir Lavaine: See yonder is a company of good knights, and they hold them together as boars that were chafed with dogs. That is truth, said Sir Lavaine.

CHAPTER XI

How Sir Launcelot and Sir Lavaine entered in the field against them of King Arthur's court, and how Launcelot was hurt.

Now, said Sir Launcelot, an ye will help me a little, ye shall see yonder fellowship that chaseth now these men in our side, that they shall go as fast backward as they went forward. Sir, spare not, said Sir Lavaine, for I shall do what I may. Then Sir Launcelot and Sir Lavaine came in at the thickest of the press, and there Sir Launcelot smote down Sir Brandiles, Sir Sagramore, Sir Dodinas, Sir Kay, Sir Griflet, and all this he did with one spear; and Sir Lavaine smote down Sir Lucan le Butler and Sir Bedevere. And then Sir Launcelot gat another spear, and there he smote down Sir Agravaine, Sir Gaheris, and Sir

Mordred, and Sir Meliot de Logris; and Sir Lavaine smote Ozanna le Cure Hardy. And then Sir Launcelot drew his sword, and there he smote on the right hand and on the left hand, and by great force he unhorsed Sir Safere, Sir Epinogris, and Sir Galleron; and then the knights of the Table Round withdrew them aback, after they had gotten their horses as well as they might. O mercy Jesu, said Sir Gawaine, what knight is yonder that doth so marvellous deeds of arms in that field? I wot well what he is, said King Arthur, but as at this time I will not name him. Sir, said Sir Gawaine, I would say it were Sir Launcelot by his riding and his buffets that I see him deal, but ever meseemeth it should not be he, for that he beareth the red sleeve upon his head; for I wist him never bear token at no jousts, of lady nor gentlewoman. Let him be, said King Arthur, he will be better known, and do more, or ever he depart.

Then the party that was against King Arthur were well comforted, and then they held them together that beforehand were sore rebuked. Then Sir Bors, Sir Ector de Maris, and Sir Lionel called unto them the knights of their blood, as Sir Blamore de Ganis, Sir Bleoberis, Sir Aliduke, Sir Galihud, Sir Galihodin, Sir Bellangere le Beuse. So these nine knights of Sir Launcelot's kin thrust in mightily, for they were all noble knights; and they, of great hate and despite that they had unto him, thought to rebuke that noble knight Sir Launcelot, and Sir Lavaine, for they knew them not; and so they came hurling together, and smote down many knights of Northgalis and of Northumberland. And when Sir Launcelot saw them fare so, he gat a spear in his hand; and there encountered with him all at once Sir Bors, Sir Ector, and Sir Lionel, and all they three smote him at once with their spears. And with force of themself they smote Sir Launcelot's horse to the earth; and by misfortune Sir Bors smote Sir Launcelot through the shield into the side, and the spear brake, and the head left still in his side.

When Sir Lavaine saw his master lie on the ground, he ran to the King of Scots and smote him to the earth; and by great force he took his horse, and brought him to Sir Launcelot, and maugre of them all he made him to mount upon that horse. And then Launcelot gat a spear in his hand, and there he smote Sir Bors, horse and man, to the earth. In the same wise he served Sir Ector and Sir Lionel; and Sir Lavaine smote down Sir Blamore de Ganis. And then Sir Launcelot drew his sword, for he felt himself so sore y-hurt that he weened there to have had his death. And then he smote Sir Bleoberis such a buffet on the helm that he fell down to the earth in a swoon. And in the same wise he served Sir Aliduke and Sir Galihud. And Sir Lavaine smote down Sir Bellangere, that was the son of Alisander le Orphelin.

And by this was Sir Bors horsed, and then he came with Sir Ector and Sir Lionel, and all they three smote with swords upon Sir Launcelot's helmet. And when he felt their buffets and his wound, the which was so grievous, then he thought to do what he might while he might endure. And then he gave Sir Bors such a buffet that he made him bow his head passing low; and therewithal he raced off his helm, and might have slain him; and so pulled him down, and in the same wise he served Sir Ector and Sir Lionel. For as the book saith he might have slain them, but when he saw their visages his heart might not serve him thereto, but left them there. And then afterward he hurled into the thickest press of them all, and did there the marvelloust deeds of arms that ever man saw or heard speak of, and ever Sir Lavaine, the good knight, with him. And there Sir Launcelot with his sword smote down and pulled down, as French book maketh mention, mo than thirty knights, and the most part were of the Table Round; and Sir Lavaine did full well that day, for he smote down ten knights of the Table Round.

CHAPTER XII

How Sir Launcelot and Sir Lavaine departed out of the field,
and in what jeopardy Launcelot was.

Mercy Jesu, said Sir Gawaine to Arthur, I marvel what knight that he is with the red sleeve. Sir, said King Arthur, he will be known or he depart. And then the king blew unto lodging, and the prize was given by heralds unto the knight with the white shield that bare the red sleeve. Then came the King with the Hundred Knights, the King of Northgalis, and the King of Northumberland, and Sir Galahad, the haut prince, and said unto Sir Launcelot: Fair knight, God thee bless, for much have ye done this day for us, therefore we pray you that ye will come with us that ye may receive the honour and the prize as ye have worshipfully deserved it. My fair lords, said Sir Launcelot, wit you well if I have deserved thanks I have sore bought it, and that me repenteth, for I am like never to escape with my life; therefore, fair lords, I pray you that ye will suffer me to depart where me liketh, for I am sore hurt. I take none force of none honour, for I had liefer to repose me than to be lord of all the world. And therewithal he groaned piteously, and rode a great wallop away-ward from them until he came under a wood's side.

And when he saw that he was from the field nigh a mile, that he was sure he might not be seen, then he said with an high voice: O gentle knight, Sir Lavaine, help me that this truncheon were out of my side, for it sticketh so sore that it nigh slayeth me. O mine own lord, said Sir Lavaine, I would fain do that might please you, but I dread me sore an I pull out the truncheon that ye shall be in peril of death. I charge you, said Sir Launcelot, as ye love me, draw it out. And therewithal he descended from his horse, and right so did Sir Lavaine; and forthwithal Sir Lavaine drew the truncheon out of his side, and he gave a great shriek and a marvellous grisly groan, and the blood brast out nigh a pint at once, that at the last he sank down upon his buttocks, and so swooned pale and deadly. Alas, said Sir Lavaine, what shall I do? And then he turned Sir Launcelot into the wind, but so he lay there nigh half an hour as he had been dead.

And so at the last Sir Launcelot cast up his eyes, and said: O Lavaine, help me that I were on my horse, for here is fast by within this two mile a gentle hermit that sometime was a full noble knight and a great lord of possessions. And for great goodness he hath taken him to wilful poverty, and forsaken many lands, and his name is Sir Baudwin of Brittany, and he is a full noble surgeon and a good leech. Now let see, help me up that I were there, for ever my heart giveth me that I shall never die of my cousin-germain's hands. And then with great pain Sir Lavaine halp him upon his horse. And then they rode a great wallop together, and ever Sir Launcelot bled that it ran down to the earth; and so by fortune they came to that hermitage the which was under a wood, and a great cliff on the other side, and a fair water running under it. And then Sir Lavaine beat on the gate with the butt of his spear, and cried fast: Let in for Jesu's sake.

And there came a fair child to them, and asked them what they would. Fair son, said Sir Lavaine, go and pray thy lord, the hermit, for God's sake to let in here a knight that is full sore wounded; and this day tell thy lord I saw him do more deeds of arms than ever I heard say that any man did. So the child went in lightly, and then he brought the hermit, the which was a passing good man. When Sir Lavaine saw him he prayed him for God's sake of succour. What knight is he? said the hermit. Is he of the house of King Arthur, or not? I wot not, said Sir Lavaine, what is he, nor what is his name but well I wot I saw him do marvellously this day as of deeds of arms. On whose party was he? said the hermit. Sir, said Sir Lavaine, he was this day against King Arthur, and there he won the prize of all the knights of the Round Table. I have seen the day, said the hermit, I would have loved him the worse because he was against my lord, King Arthur, for sometime I was one of the fellowship of the Round Table, but I thank God now I am otherwise disposed. But where is he? let me see him. Then Sir Lavaine brought the hermit to him.

CHAPTER XIII

How Launcelot was brought to an hermit for to be healed of his wound, and of other matters.

And when the hermit beheld him, as he sat leaning upon his saddle-bow ever bleeding piteously, and ever the knight-hermit thought that he should know him, but he could not bring him to knowledge because he was so pale for bleeding. What knight are ye, said the hermit, and where were ye born? My fair lord, said Sir Launcelot, I am a stranger and a knight adventurous, that laboureth throughout many realms for to win worship. Then the hermit advised him better, and saw by a wound on his cheek that he was Sir Launcelot. Alas, said the hermit, mine own lord why lain you your name from me? Forsooth I ought to know you of right, for ye are the most noblest knight of the world, for well I know you for Sir Launcelot. Sir, said he, sith ye know me, help me an ye may, for God's sake, for I would be out of this pain at once, either to death or to life. Have ye no doubt, said the hermit, ye shall live and fare right well. And so the hermit called to him two of his servants, and so he and his servants bare him into the hermitage, and lightly unarmed him, and laid him in his bed. And then anon the hermit staunched his blood, and made him to drink good wine, so that Sir Launcelot was well refreshed and knew himself; for in those days it was not the guise of hermits as is nowadays, for there were none hermits in those days but that they had been men of worship and of prowess; and those hermits held great household, and refreshed people that were in distress.

Now turn we unto King Arthur, and leave we Sir Launcelot in the hermitage. So when the kings were come together on both parties, and the great feast should be holden, King Arthur asked the King of Northgalis and their fellowship, where was that knight that bare the red sleeve: Bring him afore me that he may have his laud, and honour, and the prize, as it is right. Then spake Sir Galahad, the haut prince, and the King with the Hundred Knights: We suppose that knight is mischieved, and that he is never like to see you nor none of us all, and that is the greatest pity that ever we wist of any knight. Alas, said Arthur, how may this be, is he so hurt? What is his name? said King Arthur. Truly, said they all, we know not his name, nor from whence he came, nor whither he would. Alas, said the king, this be to me the worst tidings that came to me this seven year, for I would not for all the lands I wield to know and wit it were so that that noble knight were slain. Know ye him? said they all. As for that, said Arthur, whether I know him or know him not, ye shall not know for me what man he is, but Almighty Jesu send me good tidings of him. And so said they all. By my head, said Sir Gawaine, if it so be that the good knight be so sore hurt, it is great damage and pity to all this land, for he is one of the noblest knights that ever I saw in a field handle a spear or a sword; and if he may be found I shall find him, for I am sure he nis not far from this town. Bear you well, said King Arthur, an ye may find him, unless that he be in such a plight that he may not wield himself. Jesu defend, said Sir Gawaine, but wit I shall what he is, an I may find him.

Right so Sir Gawaine took a squire with him upon hackneys, and rode all about Camelot within six or seven mile, but so he came again and could hear no word of him. Then within two days King Arthur and all the fellowship returned unto London again. And so as they rode by the way it happed Sir Gawaine at Astolat to lodge with Sir Bernard thereas was Sir Launcelot lodged. And so as Sir Gawaine was in his chamber to repose him Sir Bernard, the old baron, came unto him, and his daughter Elaine, to cheer him and to ask him what tidings, and who did best at that tournament of Winchester. So God me help, said Sir Gawaine, there were two knights that bare two white shields, but the one of them bare a red sleeve upon his head, and certainly he was one of the best knights that ever I saw joust in field. For I dare say, said Sir Gawaine, that one knight with the red sleeve smote down forty knights of the Table Round, and his fellow did right well and worshipfully. Now blessed be God, said the Fair Maiden of Astolat, that that knight sped so well, for he is the man in the world that I first loved, and truly he shall be last that ever I shall love. Now, fair maid, said Sir Gawaine, is that good knight your love? Certainly sir, said she, wit ye well he is my love. Then know ye his name? said Sir Gawaine. Nay truly, said the damosel, I know not his name nor from whence he cometh, but to say that I love him, I promise you and God that I love him. How had ye knowledge of him first? said Sir Gawaine.

CHAPTER XIV

How Sir Gawaine was lodged with the lord of Astolat, and there had knowledge that it was Sir Launcelot that bare the red sleeve.

Then she told him as ye have heard to-fore, and how her father betook him her brother to do him service, and how her father lent him her brother's, Sir Tirre's, shield: And here with me he left his own shield. For what cause did he so? said Sir Gawaine. For this cause, said the damosel, for his shield was too well known among many noble knights. Ah fair damosel, said Sir Gawaine, please it you let me have a sight of that shield. Sir, said she, it is in my chamber, covered with a case, and if ye will come with me ye shall see it. Not so, said Sir Bernard till his daughter, let send for it.

So when the shield was come, Sir Gawaine took off the case, and when he beheld that shield he knew anon that it was Sir Launcelot's shield, and his own arms. Ah Jesu mercy, said Sir Gawaine, now is my heart more heavier than ever it was to-fore. Why? said Elaine. For I have great cause, said Sir Gawaine. Is that knight that oweth this shield your love? Yea truly, said she, my love he is, God would I were his love. So God me speed, said Sir Gawaine, fair damosel ye have right, for an he be your love ye love the most honourable knight of the world, and the man of most worship. So me thought ever, said the damosel, for never or that time, for no knight that ever I saw, loved I never none erst. God grant, said Sir Gawaine, that either of you may rejoice other, but that is in a great adventure. But truly, said Sir Gawaine unto the damosel, ye may say ye have a fair grace, for why I have known that noble knight this four-and-twenty year, and never or that day, I nor none other knight, I dare make good, saw nor heard say that ever he bare token or sign of no lady, gentlewoman, ne maiden, at no jousts nor tournament. And therefore fair maiden, said Sir Gawaine, ye are much beholden to him to give him thanks. But I dread me, said Sir Gawaine, that ye shall never see him in this world, and that is great pity that ever was of earthly knight. Alas, said she, how may this be, is he slain? I say not so, said Sir Gawaine, but wit ye well he is grievously wounded, by all manner of signs, and by men's sight more likelier to be dead than to be alive; and wit ye well he is the noble knight, Sir Launcelot, for by this shield I know him. Alas, said the Fair Maiden of Astolat, how may this be, and what was his hurt? Truly, said Sir Gawaine, the man in the world that loved him best hurt him so; and I dare say, said Sir Gawaine, an that knight that hurt him knew the very certainty that he had hurt Sir Launcelot, it would be the most sorrow that ever came to his heart.

Now fair father, said then Elaine, I require you give me leave to ride and to seek him, or else I wot well I shall go out of my mind, for I shall never stint till that I find him and my brother, Sir Lavaine. Do as it liketh you, said her father, for me sore repenteth of the hurt of that noble knight. Right so the maid made her ready and before Sir Gawaine, making great dole.

Then on the morn Sir Gawaine came to King Arthur, and told him how he had found Sir Launcelot's shield in the keeping of the Fair Maiden of Astolat. All that knew I aforehand, said King Arthur, and that caused me I would not suffer you to have ado at the great jousts, for I espied, said King Arthur, when he came in till his lodging full late in the evening in Astolat. But marvel have I, said Arthur, that ever he would bear any sign of any damosel, for or now I never heard say nor knew that ever he bare any token of none earthly woman. By my head, said Sir Gawaine, the Fair Maiden of Astolat loveth him marvellously well; what it meaneth I cannot say, and she is ridden after to seek him. So the king and all came to London, and there Sir Gawaine openly disclosed to all the court that it was Sir Launcelot that jousted best.

CHAPTER XV

Of the sorrow that Sir Bors had for the hurt of Launcelot;
and of the anger that the queen had because
Launcelot bare the sleeve.

And when Sir Bors heard that, wit ye well he was an heavy man, and
so were all his kinsmen. But when Queen Guenever wist that Sir
Launcelot bare the red sleeve of the Fair Maiden of Astolat she was
nigh out of her mind for wrath. And then she sent for Sir Bors de
Ganis in all the haste that might be. So when Sir Bors was come to-
fore the queen, then she said: Ah Sir Bors, have ye heard say how
falsely Sir Launcelot hath betrayed me? Alas madam, said Sir Bors, I
am afeard he hath betrayed himself and us all. No force, said the
queen, though he be destroyed, for he is a false traitor-knight.
Madam, said Sir Bors, I pray you say ye not so, for wit you well I may
not hear such language of him. Why Sir Bors, said she, should I not
call him traitor when he bare the red sleeve upon his head at
Winchester, at the great jousts? Madam, said Sir Bors, that sleeve-
bearing repenteth me sore, but I dare say he did it to none evil intent,
but for this cause he bare the red sleeve that none of his blood should
know him. For or then we, nor none of us all, never knew that ever
he bare token or sign of maid, lady, ne gentlewoman. Fie on him,
said the queen, yet for all his pride and bobaunce there ye proved
yourself his better. Nay madam, say ye never more so, for he beat me
and my fellows, and might have slain us an he had would. Fie on
him, said the queen, for I heard Sir Gawaine say before my lord
Arthur that it were marvel to tell the great love that is between the
Fair Maiden of Astolat and him. Madam, said Sir Bors, I may not
warn Sir Gawaine to say what it pleased him; but I dare say, as for my
lord, Sir Launcelot, that he loveth no lady, gentlewoman, nor maid,
but all he loveth in like much. And therefore madam, said Sir Bors,
ye may say what ye will, but wit ye well I will haste me to seek him,
and find him wheresomever he be, and God send me good tidings of
him. And so leave we them there, and speak we of Sir Launcelot that
lay in great peril.

So as fair Elaine came to Winchester she sought there all about, and by fortune Sir Lavaine was ridden to play him, to enchafe his horse. And anon as Elaine saw him she knew him, and then she cried aloud until him. And when he heard her anon he came to her, and then she asked her brother how did my lord, Sir Launcelot. Who told you, sister, that my lord's name was Sir Launcelot? Then she told him how Sir Gawaine by his shield knew him. So they rode together till that they came to the hermitage, and anon she alighted.

So Sir Lavaine brought her in to Sir Launcelot; and when she saw him lie so sick and pale in his bed she might not speak, but suddenly she fell to the earth down suddenly in a swoon, and there she lay a great while. And when she was relieved, she shrieked and said: My lord, Sir Launcelot, alas why be ye in this plight? and then she swooned again. And then Sir Launcelot prayed Sir Lavaine to take her up: And bring her to me. And when she came to herself Sir Launcelot kissed her, and said: Fair maiden, why fare ye thus? ye put me to pain; wherefore make ye no more such cheer, for an ye be come to comfort me ye be right welcome; and of this little hurt that I have I shall be right hastily whole by the grace of God. But I marvel, said Sir Launcelot, who told you my name? Then the fair maiden told him all how Sir Gawaine was lodged with her father: And there by your shield he discovered your name. Alas, said Sir Launcelot, that me repenteth that my name is known, for I am sure it will turn unto anger. And then Sir Launcelot compassed in his mind that Sir Gawaine would tell Queen Guenever how he bare the red sleeve, and for whom; that he wist well would turn into great anger.

So this maiden Elaine never went from Sir Launcelot, but watched him day and night, and did such attendance to him, that the French book saith there was never woman did more kindlier for man than she. Then Sir Launcelot prayed Sir Lavaine to make aspies in Winchester for Sir Bors if he came there, and told him by what tokens he should know him, by a wound in his forehead. For well I am sure, said Sir Launcelot, that Sir Bors will seek me, for he is the same good knight that hurt me.

CHAPTER XVI

How Sir Bors sought Launcelot and found him in the
hermitage, and of the lamentation between them.

Now turn we unto Sir Bors de Ganis that came unto Winchester to
seek after his cousin Sir Launcelot. And so when he came to
Winchester, anon there were men that Sir Lavaine had made to lie in
a watch for such a man, and anon Sir Lavaine had warning; and then
Sir Lavaine came to Winchester and found Sir Bors, and there he told
him what he was, and with whom he was, and what was his name.
Now fair knight, said Sir Bors, I require you that ye will bring me to
my lord, Sir Launcelot. Sir, said Sir Lavaine, take your horse, and
within this hour ye shall see him. And so they departed, and came to
the hermitage.

And when Sir Bors saw Sir Launcelot lie in his bed pale and
discoloured, anon Sir Bors lost his countenance, and for kindness and
pity he might not speak, but wept tenderly a great while. And then
when he might speak he said thus: O my lord, Sir Launcelot, God
you bless, and send you hasty recover; and full heavy am I of my
misfortune and of mine unhappiness, for now I may call myself
unhappy. And I dread me that God is greatly displeased with me, that
he would suffer me to have such a shame for to hurt you that are all
our leader, and all our worship; and therefore I call myself unhappy.
Alas that ever such a caitiff-knight as I am should have power by
unhappiness to hurt the most noblest knight of the world. Where I so
shamefully set upon you and overcharged you, and where ye might
have slain me, ye saved me; and so did not I, for I and your blood did
to you our utterance. I marvel, said Sir Bors, that my heart or my
blood would serve me, wherefore my lord, Sir Launcelot, I ask your
mercy. Fair cousin, said Sir Launcelot, ye be right welcome; and wit
ye well, overmuch ye say for to please me, the which pleaseth me
not, for why I have the same I sought; for I would with pride have
overcome you all, and there in my pride I was near slain, and that was
in mine own default, for I might have given you warning of my
being there. And then had I had no hurt, for it is an old said saw,

there is hard battle thereas kin and friends do battle either against other, there may be no mercy but mortal war. Therefore, fair cousin, said Sir Launcelot, let this speech overpass, and all shall be welcome that God sendeth; and let us leave off this matter and let us speak of some rejoicing, for this that is done may not be undone; and let us find a remedy how soon that I may be whole.

Then Sir Bors leaned upon his bedside, and told Sir Launcelot how the queen was passing wroth with him, because he wore the red sleeve at the great jousts; and there Sir Bors told him all how Sir Gawaine discovered it: By your shield that ye left with the Fair Maiden of Astolat. Then is the queen wroth, said Sir Launcelot, and therefore am I right heavy, for I deserved no wrath, for all that I did was because I would not be known. Right so excused I you, said Sir Bors, but all was in vain, for she said more largelier to me than I to you now. But is this she, said Sir Bors, that is so busy about you, that men call the Fair Maiden of Astolat? She it is, said Sir Launcelot, that by no means I cannot put her from me. Why should ye put her from you? said Sir Bors, she is a passing fair damosel, and a well beseen, and well taught; and God would, fair cousin, said Sir Bors, that ye could love her, but as to that I may not, nor I dare not, counsel you. But I see well, said Sir Bors, by her diligence about you that she loveth you entirely. That me repenteth, said Sir Launcelot. Sir, said Sir Bors, she is not the first that hath lost her pain upon you, and that is the more pity: and so they talked of many more things. And so within three days or four Sir Launcelot was big and strong again.

CHAPTER XVII

How Sir Launcelot armed him to assay if he might bear arms, and how his wounds brast out again.

Then Sir Bors told Sir Launcelot how there was sworn a great tournament and jousts betwixt King Arthur and the King of Northgalis, that should be upon All Hallowmass Day, beside Winchester. Is that truth? said Sir Launcelot; then shall ye abide with me still a little while until that I be whole, for I feel myself right big and strong. Blessed be God, said Sir Bors. Then were they there nigh a month together, and ever this maiden Elaine did ever her diligent labour night and day unto Sir Launcelot, that there was never child nor wife more meeker to her father and husband than was that Fair Maiden of Astolat; wherefore Sir Bors was greatly pleased with her.

So upon a day, by the assent of Sir Launcelot, Sir Bors, and Sir Lavaine, they made the hermit to seek in woods for divers herbs, and so Sir Launcelot made fair Elaine to gather herbs for him to make him a bain. In the meanwhile Sir Launcelot made him to arm him at all pieces; and there he thought to assay his armour and his spear, for his hurt or not. And so when he was upon his horse he stirred him fiercely, and the horse was passing lusty and fresh because he was not laboured a month afore. And then Sir Launcelot couched that spear in the rest. That courser leapt mightily when he felt the spurs; and he that was upon him, the which was the noblest horse of the world, strained him mightily and stably, and kept still the spear in the rest; and therewith Sir Launcelot strained himself so straitly, with so great force, to get the horse forward, that the button of his wound brast both within and without; and therewithal the blood came out so fiercely that he felt himself so feeble that he might not sit upon his horse. And then Sir Launcelot cried unto Sir Bors: Ah, Sir Bors and Sir Lavaine, help, for I am come to mine end. And therewith he fell down on the one side to the earth like a dead corpse. And then Sir Bors and Sir Lavaine came to him with sorrow-making out of measure. And so by fortune the maiden Elaine heard their mourning, and then she came thither; and when she found Sir Launcelot there armed in that place she cried and wept as she had been wood; and then she kissed him, and did what she might to awake him. And then she rebuked her brother and Sir Bors, and called them false traitors, why they would take him out of his bed; there she cried, and said she would appeal them of his death.

With this came the holy hermit, Sir Baudwin of Brittany, and when he found Sir Launcelot in that plight he said but little, but wit ye well he was wroth; and then he bade them: Let us have him in. And so they all bare him unto the hermitage, and unarmed him, and laid him in his bed; and evermore his wound bled piteously, but he stirred no limb of him. Then the knight-hermit put a thing in his nose and a little deal of water in his mouth. And then Sir Launcelot waked of his swoon, and then the hermit staunched his bleeding. And when he might speak he asked Sir Launcelot why he put his life in jeopardy. Sir, said Sir Launcelot, because I weened I had been strong, and also Sir Bors told me that there should be at All Hallowmass a great jousts betwixt King Arthur and the King of Northgalis, and therefore I thought to assay it myself, whether I might be there or not. Ah, Sir Launcelot, said the hermit, your heart and your courage will never be done until your last day, but ye shall do now by my counsel. Let Sir Bors depart from you, and let him do at that tournament what he may: And by the grace of God, said the knight-hermit, by that the tournament be done and ye come hither again, Sir Launcelot shall be as whole as ye, so that he will be governed by me.

CHAPTER XVIII

How Sir Bors returned and told tidings of Sir Launcelot; and of the tourney, and to whom the prize was given.

Then Sir Bors made him ready to depart from Sir Launcelot; and then Sir Launcelot said: Fair cousin, Sir Bors, recommend me unto all them unto whom me ought to recommend me unto. And I pray you, enforce yourself at that jousts that ye may be best, for my love; and here shall I abide you at the mercy of God till ye come again. And so Sir Bors departed and came to the court of King Arthur, and told them in what place he had left Sir Launcelot. That me repenteth, said the king, but since he shall have his life we all may thank God. And there Sir Bors told the queen in what jeopardy Sir Launcelot was when he would assay his horse. And all that he did, madam, was for the love of you, because he would have been at this tournament. Fie on him, recreant knight, said the queen, for wit ye well I am right sorry an he shall have his life. His life shall he have, said Sir Bors, and who that would otherwise, except you, madam, we that be of his blood should help to short their lives. But madam, said Sir Bors, ye have been oft-times displeased with my lord, Sir Launcelot, but at all times at the end ye find him a true knight: and so he departed.

And then every knight of the Round Table that were there at that time present made them ready to be at that jousts at All Hallowmass, and thither drew many knights of divers countries. And as All

Hallowmass drew near, thither came the King of Northgalis, and the King with the Hundred Knights, and Sir Galahad, the haut prince, of Surluse, and thither came King Anguish of Ireland, and the King of Scots. So these three kings came on King Arthur's party. And so that day Sir Gawaine did great deeds of arms, and began first. And the heralds numbered that Sir Gawaine smote down twenty knights. Then Sir Bors de Ganis came in the same time, and he was numbered that he smote down twenty knights; and therefore the prize was given betwixt them both, for they began first and longest endured. Also Sir Gareth, as the book saith, did that day great deeds of arms, for he smote down and pulled down thirty knights. But when he had done these deeds he tarried not but so departed, and therefore he lost his prize. And Sir Palomides did great deeds of arms that day, for he smote down twenty knights, but he departed suddenly, and men deemed Sir Gareth and he rode together to some manner adventures.

So when this tournament was done Sir Bors departed, and rode till he came to Sir Launcelot, his cousin; and then he found him walking on his feet, and there either made great joy of other; and so Sir Bors told Sir Launcelot of all the jousts like as ye have heard. I marvel, said Sir Launcelot, that Sir Gareth, when he had done such deeds of arms, that he would not tarry. Thereof we marvelled all, said Sir Bors, for but if it were you, or Sir Tristram, or Sir Lamorak de Galis, I saw never knight bear down so many in so little a while as did Sir Gareth: and anon he was gone we wist not where. By my head, said Sir Launcelot, he is a noble knight, and a mighty man and well breathed; and if he were well assayed, said Sir Launcelot, I would deem he were good enough for any knight that beareth the life; and he is a gentle knight, courteous, true, and bounteous, meek, and mild, and in him is no manner of mal engin, but plain, faithful, and true.

So then they made them ready to depart from the hermit. And so upon a morn they took their horses and Elaine le Blank with them; and when they came to Astolat there were they well lodged, and had great cheer of Sir Bernard, the old baron, and of Sir Tirre, his son. And so upon the morn when Sir Launcelot should depart, fair Elaine brought her father with her, and Sir Lavaine, and Sir Tirre, and thus she said:

CHAPTER XIX

Of the great lamentation of the Fair Maid of Astolat when
Launcelot should depart, and how she died for his love.

My lord, Sir Launcelot, now I see ye will depart; now fair knight and
courteous knight, have mercy upon me, and suffer me not to die for
thy love. What would ye that I did? said Sir Launcelot. I would have
you to my husband, said Elaine. Fair damosel, I thank you, said Sir
Launcelot, but truly, said he, I cast me never to be wedded man.
Then, fair knight, said she, will ye be my paramour? Jesu defend me,
said Sir Launcelot, for then I rewarded your father and your brother
full evil for their great goodness. Alas, said she, then must I die for
your love. Ye shall not so, said Sir Launcelot, for wit ye well, fair
maiden, I might have been married an I had would, but I never
applied me to be married yet; but because, fair damosel, that ye love
me as ye say ye do, I will for your good will and kindness show you
some goodness, and that is this, that wheresomever ye will beset your
heart upon some good knight that will wed you, I shall give you
together a thousand pound yearly to you and to your heirs; thus
much will I give you, fair madam, for your kindness, and always
while I live to be your own knight. Of all this, said the maiden, I will
none, for but if ye will wed me, or else be my paramour at the least,
wit you well, Sir Launcelot, my good days are done. Fair damosel,
said Sir Launcelot, of these two things ye must pardon me.

Then she shrieked shrilly, and fell down in a swoon; and then
women bare her into her chamber, and there she made over much
sorrow; and then Sir Launcelot would depart, and there he asked Sir
Lavaine what he would do. What should I do, said Sir Lavaine, but
follow you, but if ye drive me from you, or command me to go from
you. Then came Sir Bernard to Sir Launcelot and said to him: I
cannot see but that my daughter Elaine will die for your sake. I may
not do withal, said Sir Launcelot, for that me sore repenteth, for I
report me to yourself, that my proffer is fair; and me repenteth, said
Sir Launcelot, that she loveth me as she doth; I was never the causer
of it, for I report me to your son I early ne late proffered her bounté

nor fair behests; and as for me, said Sir Launcelot, I dare do all that a knight should do that she is a clean maiden for me, both for deed and for will. And I am right heavy of her distress, for she is a full fair maiden, good and gentle, and well taught. Father, said Sir Lavaine, I dare make good she is a clean maiden as for my lord Sir Launcelot; but she doth as I do, for sithen I first saw my lord Sir Launcelot, I could never depart from him, nor nought I will an I may follow him.

Then Sir Launcelot took his leave, and so they departed, and came unto Winchester. And when Arthur wist that Sir Launcelot was come whole and sound the king made great joy of him, and so did Sir Gawaine and all the knights of the Round Table except Sir Agravaine and Sir Mordred. Also Queen Guenever was wood wroth with Sir Launcelot, and would by no means speak with him, but estranged herself from him; and Sir Launcelot made all the means that he might for to speak with the queen, but it would not be.

Now speak we of the Fair Maiden of Astolat that made such sorrow day and night that she never slept, ate, nor drank, and ever she made her complaint unto Sir Launcelot. So when she had thus endured a ten days, that she feebled so that she must needs pass out of this world, then she shrived her clean, and received her Creator. And ever she complained still upon Sir Launcelot. Then her ghostly father bade her leave such thoughts. Then she said, why should I leave such thoughts? Am I not an earthly woman? And all the while the breath is in my body I may complain me, for my belief is I do none offence though I love an earthly man; and I take God to my record I loved never none but Sir Launcelot du Lake, nor never shall, and a clean maiden I am for him and for all other; and sithen it is the sufferance of God that I shall die for the love of so noble a knight, I beseech the High Father of Heaven to have mercy upon my soul, and upon mine innumerable pains that I suffered may be allegeance of part of my sins. For sweet Lord Jesu, said the fair maiden, I take Thee to record, on Thee I was never great offencer against thy laws; but that I loved this noble knight, Sir Launcelot, out of measure, and of myself, good Lord, I might not withstand the fervent love wherefore I have my death.

And then she called her father, Sir Bernard, and her brother, Sir Tirre, and heartily she prayed her father that her brother might write a letter like as she did indite it: and so her father granted her. And when the letter was written word by word like as she devised, then she prayed her father that she might be watched until she were dead. And while my body is hot let this letter be put in my right hand, and my hand bound fast with the letter until that I be cold; and let me be put in a fair bed with all the richest clothes that I have about me, and so let my bed and all my richest clothes be laid with me in a chariot unto the next place where Thames is; and there let me be put within a barget, and but one man with me, such as ye trust to steer me thither, and that my barget be covered with black samite over and over: thus father I beseech you let it be done. So her father granted it her faithfully, all things should be done like as she had devised. Then her father and her brother made great dole, for when this was done anon she died. And so when she was dead the corpse and the bed all was led the next way unto Thames, and there a man, and the corpse, and all, were put into Thames; and so the man steered the barget unto Westminster, and there he rowed a great while to and fro or any espied it.

CHAPTER XX

*How the corpse of the Maid of Astolat arrived to-fore
King Arthur, and of the burying, and how
Sir Launcelot offered the mass-penny.*

So by fortune King Arthur and the Queen Guenever were speaking together at a window, and so as they looked into Thames they espied this black barget, and had marvel what it meant. Then the king called Sir Kay, and showed it him. Sir, said Sir Kay, wit you well there is some new tidings. Go thither, said the king to Sir Kay, and take with you Sir Brandiles and Agravaine, and bring me ready word what is there. Then these four knights departed and came to the barget and went in; and there they found the fairest corpse lying in a rich bed, and a poor man sitting in the barget's end, and no word would he speak. So these four knights returned unto the king again, and told him what they found. That fair corpse will I see, said the king. And so then the king took the queen by the hand, and went thither.

Then the king made the barget to be holden fast, and then the king and the queen entered with certain knights with them; and there he saw the fairest woman lie in a rich bed, covered unto her middle with many rich clothes, and all was of cloth of gold, and she lay as though she had smiled. Then the queen espied a letter in her right hand, and told it to the king. Then the king took it and said: Now am I sure this letter will tell what she was, and why she is come hither. So then the king and the queen went out of the barget, and so commanded a certain man to wait upon the barget.

And so when the king was come within his chamber, he called many knights about him, and said that he would wit openly what was written within that letter. Then the king brake it, and made a clerk to read it, and this was the intent of the letter. Most noble knight, Sir Launcelot, now hath death made us two at debate for your love. I was your lover, that men called the Fair Maiden of Astolat; therefore unto all ladies I make my moan, yet pray for my soul and bury me at least, and offer ye my mass-penny: this is my last request. And a clean maiden I died, I take God to witness: pray for my soul, Sir Launcelot, as thou art peerless. This was all the substance in the letter. And when it was read, the king, the queen, and all the knights wept for pity of the doleful complaints. Then was Sir Launcelot sent for; and when he was come King Arthur made the letter to be read to him.

And when Sir Launcelot heard it word by word, he said: My lord Arthur, wit ye well I am right heavy of the death of this fair damosel: God knoweth I was never causer of her death by my willing, and that will I report me to her own brother: here he is, Sir Lavaine. I will not say nay, said Sir Launcelot, but that she was both fair and good, and much I was beholden unto her, but she loved me out of measure. Ye might have showed her, said the queen, some bounty and gentleness that might have preserved her life. Madam, said Sir Launcelot, she would none other ways be answered but that she would be my wife, outher else my paramour; and of these two I would not grant her, but I proffered her, for her good love that she showed me, a thousand pound yearly to her, and to her heirs, and to wed any manner knight that she could find best to love in her heart. For madam, said Sir Launcelot, I love not to be constrained to love; for love must arise of the heart, and not by no constraint. That is truth, said the king, and many [a] knight's love is free in himself, and never will be bounden, for where he is bounden he looseth himself.

Then said the king unto Sir Launcelot: It will be your worship that ye oversee that she be interred worshipfully. Sir, said Sir Launcelot, that shall be done as I can best devise. And so many knights yede thither to behold that fair maiden. And so upon the morn she was interred richly, and Sir Launcelot offered her mass-penny; and all the knights of the Table Round that were there at that time offered with Sir Launcelot. And then the poor man went again with the barget. Then the queen sent for Sir Launcelot, and prayed him of mercy, for why that she had been wroth with him causeless. This is not the first time, said Sir Launcelot, that ye had been displeased with me causeless, but, madam, ever I must suffer you, but what sorrow I endure I take no force. So this passed on all that winter, with all manner of hunting and hawking, and jousts and tourneys were many betwixt many great lords, and ever in all places Sir Lavaine gat great worship, so that he was nobly renowned among many knights of the Table Round.

CHAPTER XXI

Of great jousts done all a Christmas, and of a great jousts and tourney ordained by King Arthur, and of Sir Launcelot.

Thus it passed on till Christmas, and then every day there was jousts made for a diamond, who that jousted best should have a diamond. But Sir Launcelot would not joust but if it were at a great jousts cried. But Sir Lavaine jousted there all that Christmas passingly well, and best was praised, for there were but few that did so well. Wherefore all manner of knights deemed that Sir Lavaine should be made knight of the Table Round at the next feast of Pentecost. So at-after Christmas King Arthur let call unto him many knights, and there they advised together to make a party and a great tournament and jousts. And the King of Northgalis said to Arthur, he would have on his party King Anguish of Ireland, and the King with the Hundred Knights, and the King of Northumberland, and Sir Galahad, the haut prince. And so these four kings and this mighty duke took part against King Arthur and the knights of the Table Round. And the cry was made that the day of the jousts should be beside Westminster upon Candlemas Day, whereof many knights were glad, and made them ready to be at that jousts in the freshest manner.

Then Queen Guenever sent for Sir Launcelot, and said thus: I warn you that ye ride no more in no jousts nor tournaments but that your kinsmen may know you. And at these jousts that shall be ye shall have of me a sleeve of gold; and I pray you for my sake enforce yourself there, that men may speak of you worship; but I charge you as ye will have my love, that ye warn your kinsmen that ye will bear that day the sleeve of gold upon your helmet. Madam, said Sir Launcelot, it shall be done. And so either made great joy of other. And when Sir Launcelot saw his time he told Sir Bors that he would depart, and have no more with him but Sir Lavaine, unto the good hermit that dwelt in that forest of Windsor; his name was Sir Brasias; and there he thought to repose him, and take all the rest that he might, because he would be fresh at that day of jousts.

So Sir Launcelot and Sir Lavaine departed, that no creature wist where he was become, but the noble men of his blood. And when he was come to the hermitage, wit ye well he had good cheer. And so daily Sir Launcelot would go to a well fast by the hermitage, and there he would lie down, and see the well spring and burble, and sometime he slept there. So at that time there was a lady dwelt in that forest, and she was a great huntress, and daily she used to hunt, and ever she bare her bow with her; and no men went never with her, but always women, and they were shooters, and could well kill a deer, both at the stalk and at the trest; and they daily bare bows and arrows, horns and wood-knives, and many good dogs they had, both for the string and for a bait. So it happed this lady the huntress had abated her dog for the bow at a barren hind, and so this barren hind took the flight over hedges and woods. And ever this lady and part of her women costed the hind, and checked it by the noise of the hounds, to have met with the hind at some water; and so it happed, the hind came to the well whereas Sir Launcelot was sleeping and slumbering. And so when the hind came to the well, for heat she went to soil, and there she lay a great while; and the dog came after, and umbecast about, for she had lost the very perfect feute of the hind. Right so came that lady the huntress, that knew by the dog that she had, that the hind was at the soil in that well; and there she came stiffly and found the hind, and she put a broad arrow in her bow, and shot at the hind, and over-shot the hind; and so by misfortune the arrow smote Sir Launcelot in the thick of the buttock, over the barbs. When Sir Launcelot felt himself so hurt, he hurled up woodly, and saw the lady that had smitten him. And when he saw she was a woman, he said thus: Lady or damosel, what that thou be, in an evil time bear ye a bow; the devil made you a shooter.

CHAPTER XXII

*How Launcelot after that he was hurt of a gentlewoman
came to an hermit, and of other matters.*

Now mercy, fair sir, said the lady, I am a gentlewoman that useth
here in this forest hunting, and God knoweth I saw ye not; but as
here was a barren hind at the soil in this well, and I weened to have
done well, but my hand swerved. Alas, said Sir Launcelot, ye have
mischieved me. And so the lady departed, and Sir Launcelot as he
might pulled out the arrow, and left that head still in his buttock, and
so he went weakly to the hermitage ever more bleeding as he went.
And when Sir Lavaine and the hermit espied that Sir Launcelot was
hurt, wit you well they were passing heavy, but Sir Lavaine wist not
how that he was hurt nor by whom. And then were they wroth out
of measure.

Then with great pain the hermit gat out the arrow's head out of Sir
Launcelot's buttock, and much of his blood he shed, and the wound
was passing sore, and unhappily smitten, for it was in such a place that
he might not sit in no saddle. Have mercy, Jesu, said Sir Launcelot, I
may call myself the most unhappiest man that liveth, for ever when I
would fainest have worship there befalleth me ever some unhappy
thing. Now so Jesu me help, said Sir Launcelot, and if no man would
but God, I shall be in the field upon Candlemas Day at the jousts,
whatsomever fall of it: so all that might be gotten to heal Sir
Launcelot was had.

So when the day was come Sir Launcelot let devise that he was
arrayed, and Sir Lavaine, and their horses, as though they had been
Saracens; and so they departed and came nigh to the field. The King
of Northgalis with an hundred knights with him, and the King of
Northumberland brought with him an hundred good knights, and
King Anguish of Ireland brought with him an hundred good knights
ready to joust, and Sir Galahad, the haut prince, brought with him an
hundred good knights, and the King with the Hundred Knights
brought with him as many, and all these were proved good knights.
Then came in King Arthur's party; and there came in the King of

Scots with an hundred knights, and King Uriens of Gore brought with him an hundred knights, and King Howel of Brittany brought with him an hundred knights, and Chaleins of Clarance brought with him an hundred knights, and King Arthur himself came into the field with two hundred knights, and the most part were knights of the Table Round, that were proved noble knights; and there were old knights set in scaffolds for to judge, with the queen, who did best.

CHAPTER XXIII

*How Sir Launcelot behaved him at the jousts,
and other men also.*

Then they blew to the field; and there the King of Northgalis encountered with the King of Scots, and there the King of Scots had a fall; and the King of Ireland smote down King Uriens; and the King of Northumberland smote down King Howel of Brittany; and Sir Galahad, the haut prince, smote down Chaleins of Clarance. And then King Arthur was wood wroth, and ran to the King with the Hundred Knights, and there King Arthur smote him down; and after with that same spear King Arthur smote down three other knights. And then when his spear was broken King Arthur did passingly well; and so therewithal came in Sir Gawaine and Sir Gaheris, Sir Agravaine and Sir Mordred, and there everych of them smote down a knight, and Sir Gawaine smote down four knights; and then there began a strong medley, for then there came in the knights of Launcelot's blood, and Sir Gareth and Sir Palomides with them, and many knights of the Table Round, and they began to hold the four kings and the mighty duke so hard that they were discomfit; but this Duke Galahad, the haut prince, was a noble knight, and by his mighty prowess of arms he held the knights of the Table Round strait enough.

All this doing saw Sir Launcelot, and then he came into the field with Sir Lavaine as it had been thunder. And then anon Sir Bors and the knights of his blood espied Sir Launcelot, and said to them all: I warn you beware of him with the sleeve of gold upon his head, for he is himself Sir Launcelot du Lake; and for great goodness Sir Bors warned Sir Gareth. I am well apaid, said Sir Gareth, that I may know him. But who is he, said they all, that rideth with him in the same array? That is the good and gentle knight Sir Lavaine, said Sir Bors. So Sir Launcelot encountered with Sir Gawaine, and there by force Sir Launcelot smote down Sir Gawaine and his horse to the earth, and so he smote down Sir Agravaine and Sir Gaheris, and also he smote down Sir Mordred, and all this was with one spear. Then Sir Lavaine met with Sir Palomides, and either met other so hard and so fiercely that both their horses fell to the earth. And then were they horsed again, and then met Sir Launcelot with Sir Palomides, and there Sir Palomides had a fall; and so Sir Launcelot or ever he stint, as fast as he might get spears, he smote down thirty knights, and the most part of them were knights of the Table Round; and ever the knights of his blood withdrew them, and made them ado in other places where Sir Launcelot came not.

And then King Arthur was wroth when he saw Sir Launcelot do such deeds; and then the king called unto him Sir Gawaine, Sir Mordred, Sir Kay, Sir Griflet, Sir Lucan the Butler, Sir Bedivere, Sir Palomides, Sir Safere, his brother; and so the king with these nine knights made them ready to set upon Sir Launcelot, and upon Sir Lavaine. All this espied Sir Bors and Sir Gareth. Now I dread me sore, said Sir Bors, that my lord, Sir Launcelot, will be hard matched. By my head, said Sir Gareth, I will ride unto my lord Sir Launcelot, for to help him, fall of him what fall may, for he is the same man that made me knight. Ye shall not so, said Sir Bors, by my counsel, unless that ye were disguised. Ye shall see me disguised, said Sir Gareth; and therewithal he espied a Welsh knight where he was to repose him, and he was sore hurt afore by Sir Gawaine, and to him Sir Gareth rode, and prayed him of his knighthood to lend him his shield for his. I will well, said the Welsh knight. And when Sir Gareth had his shield, the book saith it was green, with a maiden that seemed in it.

Then Sir Gareth came driving to Sir Launcelot all that he might and said: Knight, keep thyself, for yonder cometh King Arthur with nine noble knights with him to put you to a rebuke, and so I am come to bear you fellowship for old love ye have showed me. Gramercy, said Sir Launcelot. Sir, said Sir Gareth, encounter ye with Sir Gawaine, and I shall encounter with Sir Palomides; and let Sir Lavaine match with the noble King Arthur. And when we have delivered them, let us three hold us sadly together. Then came King Arthur with his nine knights with him, and Sir Launcelot encountered with Sir Gawaine, and gave him such a buffet that the arson of his saddle brast, and Sir Gawaine fell to the earth. Then Sir Gareth encountered with the good knight Sir Palomides, and he gave him such a buffet that both his horse and he dashed to the earth. Then encountered King Arthur with Sir Lavaine, and there either of them smote other to the earth, horse and all, that they lay a great while. Then Sir Launcelot smote down Sir Agravaine, and Sir Gaheris, and Sir Mordred; and Sir Gareth smote down Sir Kay, and Sir Safere, and Sir Griflet. And then Sir Lavaine was horsed again, and he smote down Sir Lucan the Butler and Sir Bedevere; and then there began great throng of good knights.

Then Sir Launcelot hurtled here and there, and raced and pulled off helms, so that at that time there might none sit him a buffet with spear nor with sword; and Sir Gareth did such deeds of arms that all men marvelled what knight he was with the green shield, for he smote down that day and pulled down mo than thirty knights. And, as the French book saith, Sir Launcelot marvelled, when he beheld Sir Gareth do such deeds, what knight he might be; and Sir Lavaine pulled down and smote down twenty knights. Also Sir Launcelot knew not Sir Gareth, for an Sir Tristram de Liones, outher Sir Lamorak de Galis had been alive, Sir Launcelot would have deemed he had been one of them twain. So ever as Sir Launcelot, Sir Gareth, Sir Lavaine fought, and on the one side Sir Bors, Sir Ector de Maris, Sir Lionel, Sir Lamorak de Galis, Sir Bleoberis, Sir Galihud, Sir Galihodin, Sir Pelleas, and with mo other of King Ban's blood fought upon another party, and held the King with the Hundred Knights and the King of Northumberland right strait.

CHAPTER XXIV

How King Arthur marvelled much of the jousting in the field, and how he rode and found Sir Launcelot.

So this tournament and this jousts dured long, till it was near night, for the knights of the Round Table relieved ever unto King Arthur; for the king was wroth out of measure that he and his knights might not prevail that day. Then Sir Gawaine said to the king: I marvel where all this day [be] Sir Bors de Ganis and his fellowship of Sir Launcelot's blood, I marvel all this day they be not about you: it is for some cause said Sir Gawaine. By my head, said Sir Kay, Sir Bors is yonder all this day upon the right hand of this field, and there he and his blood do more worshipfully than we do. It may well be, said Sir Gawaine, but I dread me ever of guile; for on pain of my life, said Sir Gawaine, this knight with the red sleeve of gold is himself Sir Launcelot, I see well by his riding and by his great strokes; and the other knight in the same colours is the good young knight, Sir Lavaine. Also that knight with the green shield is my brother, Sir Gareth, and yet he hath disguised himself, for no man shall never make him be against Sir Launcelot, because he made him knight. By my head, said Arthur, nephew, I believe you; therefore tell me now what is your best counsel. Sir, said Sir Gawaine, ye shall have my counsel: let blow unto lodging, for an he be Sir Launcelot du Lake, and my brother, Sir Gareth, with him, with the help of that good young knight, Sir Lavaine, trust me truly it will be no boot to strive with them but if we should fall ten or twelve upon one knight, and that were no worship, but shame. Ye say truth, said the king; and for to say sooth, said the king, it were shame to us so many as we be to set upon them any more; for wit ye well, said King Arthur, they be three good knights, and namely that knight with the sleeve of gold.

So then they blew unto lodging; but forthwithal King Arthur let send unto the four kings, and to the mighty duke, and prayed them that the knight with the sleeve of gold depart not from them, but that the king may speak with him. Then forthwithal King Arthur alighted and unarmed him, and took a little hackney and rode after Sir Launcelot, for ever he had a spy upon him. And so he found him among the four kings and the duke; and there the king prayed them all unto supper, and they said they would with good will. And when they were unarmed then King Arthur knew Sir Launcelot, Sir Lavaine, and Sir Gareth. Ah, Sir Launcelot, said King Arthur, this day ye have heated me and my knights.

So they yede unto Arthur's lodging all together, and there was a great feast and great revel, and the prize was given unto Sir Launcelot; and by heralds they named him that he had smitten down fifty knights, and Sir Gareth five-and-thirty, and Sir Lavaine four-and-twenty knights. Then Sir Launcelot told the king and the queen how the lady huntress shot him in the forest of Windsor, in the buttock, with an broad arrow, and how the wound thereof was that time six inches deep, and in like long. Also Arthur blamed Sir Gareth because he left his fellowship and held with Sir Launcelot. My lord, said Sir Gareth, he made me a knight, and when I saw him so hard bestead, methought it was my worship to help him, for I saw him do so much, and so many noble knights against him; and when I understood that he was Sir Launcelot du Lake, I shamed to see so many knights against him alone. Truly, said King Arthur unto Sir Gareth, ye say well, and worshipfully have ye done and to yourself great worship; and all the days of my life, said King Arthur unto Sir Gareth, wit you well I shall love you, and trust you the more better. For ever, said Arthur, it is a worshipful knight's deed to help another worshipful knight when he seeth him in a great danger, for ever a worshipful man will be loath to see a worshipful man shamed; and he that is of no worship, and fareth with cowardice, never shall he show gentleness, nor no manner of goodness where he seeth a man in any danger, for then ever will a coward show no mercy; and always a good man will do ever to another man as he would be done to himself. So then there were great feasts unto kings and dukes, and revel, game, and play, and all manner of noblesse was used; and he that was courteous, true, and faithful, to his friend was that time cherished.

CHAPTER XXV

How true love is likened to summer.

And thus it passed on from Candlemass until after Easter, that the month of May was come, when every lusty heart beginneth to blossom, and to bring forth fruit; for like as herbs and trees bring forth fruit and flourish in May, in like wise every lusty heart that is in any manner a lover, springeth and flourisheth in lusty deeds. For it giveth unto all lovers courage, that lusty month of May, in something to constrain him to some manner of thing more in that month than in any other month, for divers causes. For then all herbs and trees renew a man and woman, and likewise lovers call again to their mind old gentleness and old service, and many kind deeds that were forgotten by negligence. For like as winter rasure doth alway arase and deface green summer, so fareth it by unstable love in man and woman. For in many persons there is no stability; for we may see all day, for a little blast of winter's rasure, anon we shall deface and lay apart true love for little or nought, that cost much thing; this is no wisdom nor stability, but it is feebleness of nature and great disworship, whosomever useth this. Therefore, like as May month flowereth and flourisheth in many gardens, so in like wise let every man of worship flourish his heart in this world, first unto God, and next unto the joy of them that he promised his faith unto; for there was never worshipful man or worshipful woman, but they loved one better than another; and worship in arms may never be foiled, but first reserve the honour to God, and secondly the quarrel must come of thy lady: and such love I call virtuous love.

But nowadays men can not love seven night but they must have all their desires: that love may not endure by reason; for where they be soon accorded and hasty heat, soon it cooleth. Right so fareth love nowadays, soon hot soon cold: this is no stability. But the old love was not so; men and women could love together seven years, and no licours lusts were between them, and then was love, truth, and faithfulness: and lo, in like wise was used love in King Arthur's days. Wherefore I liken love nowadays unto summer and winter; for like as the one is hot and the other cold, so fareth love nowadays; therefore all ye that be lovers call unto your remembrance the month of May, like as did Queen Guenever, for whom I make here a little mention, that while she lived she was a true lover, and therefore she had a good end.

𝕰𝖝𝖕𝖑𝖎𝖈𝖎𝖙 𝖑𝖎𝖇𝖊𝖗 𝕺𝖈𝖙𝖔𝖉𝖊𝖈𝖎𝖒𝖚𝖘.

𝕬𝖓𝖉 𝖍𝖊𝖗𝖊 𝖋𝖔𝖑𝖑𝖔𝖜𝖊𝖙𝖍 𝖑𝖎𝖇𝖊𝖗 𝖝𝖎𝖝.

BOOK NINETEEN

CHAPTER I

*How Queen Guenever rode a-Maying with certain knights
of the Round Table and clad all in green.*

So it befell in the month of May, Queen Guenever called unto her
knights of the Table Round; and she gave them warning that early
upon the morrow she would ride a-Maying into woods and fields
beside Westminster. And I warn you that there be none of you but
that he be well horsed, and that ye all be clothed in green, outher in
silk outher in cloth; and I shall bring with me ten ladies, and every
knight shall have a lady behind him, and every knight shall have a
squire and two yeomen; and I will that ye all be well horsed. So they
made them ready in the freshest manner. And these were the names
of the knights: Sir Kay le Seneschal, Sir Agravaine, Sir Brandiles, Sir
Sagramore le Desirous, Sir Dodinas le Savage, Sir Ozanna le Cure
Hardy, Sir Ladinas of the Forest Savage, Sir Persant of Inde, Sir
Ironside, that was called the Knight of the Red Launds, and Sir
Pelleas, the lover; and these ten knights made them ready in the
freshest manner to ride with the queen. And so upon the morn they
took their horses with the queen, and rode a-Maying in woods and
meadows as it pleased them, in great joy and delights; for the queen
had cast to have been again with King Arthur at the furthest by ten of
the clock, and so was that time her purpose.

Then there was a knight that hight Meliagrance, and he was son
unto King Bagdemagus, and this knight had at that time a castle of
the gift of King Arthur within seven mile of Westminster. And this
knight, Sir Meliagrance, loved passing well Queen Guenever, and so
had he done long and many years. And the book saith he had lain in
await for to steal away the queen, but evermore he forbare for
because of Sir Launcelot; for in no wise he would meddle with the

queen an Sir Launcelot were in her company, outher else an he were near-hand her. And that time was such a custom, the queen rode never without a great fellowship of men of arms about her, and they were many good knights, and the most part were young men that would have worship; and they were called the Queen's Knights, and never in no battle, tournament, nor jousts, they bare none of them no manner of knowledging of their own arms, but plain white shields, and thereby they were called the Queen's Knights. And then when it happed any of them to be of great worship by his noble deeds, then at the next Feast of Pentecost, if there were any slain or dead, as there was none year that there failed but some were dead, then was there chosen in his stead that was dead the most men of worship, that were called the Queen's Knights. And thus they came up all first, or they were renowned men of worship, both Sir Launcelot and all the remnant of them.

But this knight, Sir Meliagrance, had espied the queen well and her purpose, and how Sir Launcelot was not with her, and how she had no men of arms with her but the ten noble knights all arrayed in green for Maying. Then he purveyed him a twenty men of arms and an hundred archers for to destroy the queen and her knights, for he thought that time was best season to take the queen.

CHAPTER II

How Sir Meliagrance took the queen and her knights, which were sore hurt in fighting.

So as the queen had Mayed and all her knights, all were bedashed with herbs, mosses and flowers, in the best manner and freshest. Right so came out of a wood Sir Meliagrance with an eight score men well harnessed, as they should fight in a battle of arrest, and bade the queen and her knights abide, for maugre their heads they should abide. Traitor knight, said Queen Guenever, what cast thou for to do? Wilt thou shame thyself? Bethink thee how thou art a king's son, and knight of the Table Round, and thou to be about to dishonour the noble king that made thee knight; thou shamest all knighthood and thyself, and me, I let thee wit, shalt thou never shame, for I had liefer cut mine own throat in twain rather than thou shouldest dishonour me. As for all this language, said Sir Meliagrance, be it as it be may, for wit you well, madam, I have loved you many a year, and never or now could I get you at such an advantage as I do now, and therefore I will take you as I find you.

Then spake all the ten noble knights at once and said: Sir Meliagrance, wit thou well ye are about to jeopard your worship to dishonour, and also ye cast to jeopard our persons howbeit we be unarmed. Ye have us at a great avail, for it seemeth by you that ye have laid watch upon us; but rather than ye should put the queen to a shame and us all, we had as lief to depart from our lives, for an if we other ways did, we were shamed for ever. Then said Sir Meliagrance: Dress you as well ye can, and keep the queen. Then the ten knights of the Table Round drew their swords, and the other let run at them with their spears, and the ten knights manly abode them, and smote away their spears that no spear did them none harm. Then they lashed together with swords, and anon Sir Kay, Sir Sagramore, Sir Agravaine, Sir Dodinas, Sir Ladinas, and Sir Ozanna were smitten to the earth with grimly wounds. Then Sir Brandiles, and Sir Persant, Sir Ironside, Sir Pelleas fought long, and they were sore wounded, for these ten knights, or ever they were laid to the ground, slew forty men of the boldest and the best of them.

So when the queen saw her knights thus dolefully wounded, and needs must be slain at the last, then for pity and sorrow she cried Sir Meliagrance: Slay not my noble knights, and I will go with thee upon this covenant, that thou save them, and suffer them not to be no more hurt, with this, that they be led with me wheresomever thou leadest me, for I will rather slay myself than I will go with thee, unless that these my noble knights may be in my presence. Madam, said Meliagrance, for your sake they shall be led with you into mine own castle, with that ye will be ruled, and ride with me. Then the queen prayed the four knights to leave their fighting, and she and they would not depart. Madam, said Sir Pelleas, we will do as ye do, for as for me I take no force of my life nor death. For as the French book saith, Sir Pelleas gave such buffets there that none armour might hold him.

CHAPTER III

How Sir Launcelot had word how the queen was taken, and how Sir Meliagrance laid a bushment for Launcelot.

Then by the queen's commandment they left battle, and dressed the wounded knights on horseback, some sitting, some overthwart their horses, that it was pity to behold them. And then Sir Meliagrance charged the queen and all her knights that none of all her fellowship should depart from her; for full sore he dread Sir Launcelot du Lake, lest he should have any knowledging. All this espied the queen, and privily she called unto her a child of her chamber that was swiftly horsed, to whom she said: Go thou, when thou seest thy time, and bear this ring unto Sir Launcelot du Lake, and pray him as he loveth me that he will see me and rescue me, if ever he will have joy of me; and spare not thy horse, said the queen, neither for water, neither for land. So the child espied his time, and lightly he took his horse with the spurs, and departed as fast as he might. And when Sir Meliagrance saw him so flee, he understood that it was by the queen's commandment for to warn Sir Launcelot. Then they that were best horsed chased him and shot at him, but from them all the child went suddenly. And then Sir Meliagrance said to the queen: Madam, ye are about to betray me, but I shall ordain for Sir Launcelot that he shall not come lightly at you. And then he rode with her, and they all, to his castle, in all the haste that they might. And by the way Sir Meliagrance laid in an embushment the best archers that he might get in his country, to the number of thirty, to await upon Sir Launcelot, charging them that if they saw such a manner of knight come by the way upon a white horse, that in any wise they slay his horse, but in no manner of wise have not ado with him bodily, for he is over-hardy to be overcome.

So this was done, and they were come to his castle, but in no wise the queen would never let none of the ten knights and her ladies out of her sight, but always they were in her presence; for the book saith, Sir Meliagrance durst make no masteries, for dread of Sir Launcelot, insomuch he deemed that he had warning. So when the child was departed from the fellowship of Sir Meliagrance, within a while he came to Westminster, and anon he found Sir Launcelot. And when he had told his message, and delivered him the queen's ring: Alas, said Sir Launcelot, now I am shamed for ever, unless that I may rescue that noble lady from dishonour. Then eagerly he asked his armour; and ever the child told Sir Launcelot how the ten knights fought marvellously, and how Sir Pelleas, and Sir Ironside, and Sir Brandiles, and Sir Persant of Inde, fought strongly, but namely Sir Pelleas, there might none withstand him; and how they all fought till at the last they were laid to the earth; and then the queen made appointment for to save their lives, and go with Sir Meliagrance.

Alas, said Sir Launcelot, that most noble lady, that she should be so destroyed; I had liefer, said Sir Launcelot, than all France, that I had been there well armed. So when Sir Launcelot was armed and upon his horse, he prayed the child of the queen's chamber to warn Sir Lavaine how suddenly he was departed, and for what cause. And pray him as he loveth me, that he will hie him after me, and that he stint not until he come to the castle where Sir Meliagrance abideth, or dwelleth; for there, said Sir Launcelot, he shall hear of me an I am a man living, and rescue the queen and the ten knights the which he traitorously hath taken, and that shall I prove upon his head, and all them that hold with him.

CHAPTER IV

How Sir Launcelot's horse was slain, and how Sir Launcelot rode in a cart for to rescue the queen.

Then Sir Launcelot rode as fast as he might, and the book saith he took the water at Westminster Bridge, and made his horse to swim over Thames unto Lambeth. And then within a while he came to the same place thereas the ten noble knights fought with Sir Meliagrance. And then Sir Launcelot followed the track until that he came to a wood, and there was a straight way, and there the thirty archers bade Sir Launcelot turn again, and follow no longer that track. What commandment have ye thereto, said Sir Launcelot, to cause me that am a knight of the Round Table to leave my right way? This way shalt thou leave, other-else thou shalt go it on thy foot, for wit thou well thy horse shall be slain. That is little mastery, said Sir Launcelot, to slay mine horse; but as for myself, when my horse is slain, I give right nought for you, not an ye were five hundred more. So then they shot Sir Launcelot's horse, and smote him with many arrows; and then Sir Launcelot avoided his horse, and went on foot; but there were so many ditches and hedges betwixt them and him that he might not meddle with none of them. Alas for shame, said Launcelot, that ever one knight should betray another knight; but it is an old saw, A good man is never in danger but when he is in the danger of a coward. Then Sir Launcelot went a while, and then he was foul cumbered of his armour, his shield, and his spear, and all that longed unto him. Wit ye well he was full sore annoyed, and full loath he was for to leave anything that longed unto him, for he dread sore the treason of Sir Meliagrance.

Then by fortune there came by him a chariot that came thither for to fetch wood. Say me, carter, said Sir Launcelot, what shall I give thee to suffer me to leap into thy chariot, and that thou bring me unto a castle within this two mile? Thou shalt not come within my chariot, said the carter, for I am sent for to fetch wood for my lord, Sir Meliagrance. With him would I speak. Thou shalt not go with me, said the carter. Then Sir Launcelot leapt to him, and gave him such a buffet that he fell to the earth stark dead. Then the other carter, his fellow, was afeard, and weened to have gone the same way; and then he cried: Fair lord, save my life, and I shall bring you where ye will. Then I charge thee, said Sir Launcelot, that thou drive me and this chariot even unto Sir Meliagrance's gate. Leap up into the chariot, said the carter, and ye shall be there anon. So the carter drove on a great wallop, and Sir Launcelot's horse followed the chariot, with more than a forty arrows broad and rough in him.

And more than an hour and an half Dame Guenever was awaiting in a bay window with her ladies, and espied an armed knight standing in a chariot. See, madam, said a lady, where rideth in a chariot a goodly armed knight; I suppose he rideth unto hanging. Where? said the queen. Then she espied by his shield that he was there himself, Sir Launcelot du Lake. And then she was ware where came his horse ever after that chariot, and ever he trod his guts and his paunch under his feet. Alas, said the queen, now I see well and prove, that well is him that hath a trusty friend. Ha, ha, most noble knight, said Queen

Guenever, I see well thou art hard bestead when thou ridest in a chariot. Then she rebuked that lady that likened Sir Launcelot to ride in a chariot to hanging. It was foul mouthed, said the queen, and evil likened, so for to liken the most noble knight of the world unto such a shameful death. O Jesu defend him and keep him, said the queen, from all mischievous end. By this was Sir Launcelot come to the gates of that castle, and there he descended down, and cried, that all the castle rang of it: Where art thou, false traitor, Sir Meliagrance, and knight of the Table Round? now come forth here, thou traitor knight, thou and thy fellowship with thee; for here I am, Sir Launcelot du Lake, that shall fight with you. And therewithal he bare the gate wide open upon the porter, and smote him under his ear with his gauntlet, that his neck brast a-sunder.

CHAPTER V

How Sir Meliagrance required forgiveness of the queen, and how she appeased Sir Launcelot; and other matters.

When Sir Meliagrance heard that Sir Launcelot was there he ran unto Queen Guenever, and fell upon his knee, and said: Mercy, madam, now I put me wholly into your grace. What aileth you now? said Queen Guenever; forsooth I might well wit some good knight would revenge me, though my lord Arthur wist not of this your work. Madam, said Sir Meliagrance, all this that is amiss on my part shall be amended right as yourself will devise, and wholly I put me in your grace. What would ye that I did? said the queen. I would no more, said Meliagrance, but that ye would take all in your own hands, and that ye will rule my lord Sir Launcelot; and such cheer as may be made him in this poor castle ye and he shall have until to-morn, and then may ye and all they return unto Westminster; and my body and all that I have I shall put in your rule. Ye say well, said the queen, and better is peace than ever war, and the less noise the more is my worship.

Then the queen and her ladies went down unto the knight, Sir Launcelot, that stood wroth out of measure in the inner court, to abide battle; and ever he bade: Thou traitor knight come forth. Then the queen came to him and said: Sir Launcelot, why be ye so moved? Ha, madam, said Sir Launcelot, why ask ye me that question? Meseemeth, said Sir Launcelot, ye ought to be more wroth than I am, for ye have the hurt and the dishonour, for wit ye well, madam, my hurt is but little for the killing of a mare's son, but the despite grieveth me much more than all my hurt. Truly, said the queen, ye say truth; but heartily I thank you, said the queen, but ye must come in with me peaceably, for all thing is put in my hand, and all that is evil shall be for the best, for the knight full sore repenteth him of the misadventure that is befallen him. Madam, said Sir Launcelot, sith it is so that ye been accorded with him, as for me I may not be again it, howbeit Sir Meliagrance hath done full shamefully to me, and cowardly. Ah madam, said Sir Launcelot, an I had wist ye would have been so soon accorded with him I would not have made such haste unto you. Why say ye so, said the queen, do ye forthink yourself of your good deeds? Wit you well, said the queen, I accorded never unto him for favour nor love that I had unto him, but for to lay down every shameful noise. Madam, said Sir Launcelot, ye understand full well I was never willing nor glad of shameful slander nor noise; and there is neither king, queen, nor knight, that beareth the life, except my lord King Arthur, and you, madam, should let me, but I should make Sir Meliagrance's heart full cold or ever I departed from hence. That wot I well, said the queen, but what will ye more? Ye shall have all thing ruled as ye list to have it. Madam, said Sir Launcelot, so ye be pleased I care not, as for my part ye shall soon please.

Right so the queen took Sir Launcelot by the bare hand, for he had put off his gauntlet, and so she went with him till her chamber; and then she commanded him to be unarmed. And then Sir Launcelot asked where were the ten knights that were wounded sore; so she showed them unto Sir Launcelot, and there they made great joy of the coming of him, and Sir Launcelot made great dole of their hurts, and bewailed them greatly. And there Sir Launcelot told them how cowardly and traitorly Meliagrance set archers to slay his horse, and how he was fain to put himself in a chariot. Thus they complained everych to other; and full fain they would have been revenged, but they peaced themselves because of the queen. Then, as the French book saith, Sir Launcelot was called many a day after le Chevaler du Chariot, and did many deeds, and great adventures he had. And so leave we of this tale le Chevaler du Chariot, and turn we to this tale.

So Sir Launcelot had great cheer with the queen, and then Sir Launcelot made a promise with the queen that the same night Sir Launcelot should come to a window outward toward a garden; and that window was y-barred with iron, and there Sir Launcelot promised to meet her when all folks were asleep. So then came Sir Lavaine driving to the gates, crying: Where is my lord, Sir Launcelot du Lake? Then was he sent for, and when Sir Lavaine saw Sir Launcelot, he said: My lord, I found well how ye were hard bestead, for I have found your horse that was slain with arrows. As for that, said Sir Launcelot, I pray you, Sir Lavaine, speak ye of other matters, and let ye this pass, and we shall right it another time when we best may.

CHAPTER VI

How Sir Launcelot came in the night to the queen and lay with her, and how Sir Meliagrance appeached the queen of treason.

Then the knights that were hurt were searched, and soft salves were laid to their wounds; and so it passed on till supper time, and all the cheer that might be made them there was done unto the queen and all her knights. Then when season was, they went unto their chambers, but in no wise the queen would not suffer the wounded knights to be from her, but that they were laid within draughts by her chamber, upon beds and pillows, that she herself might see to them, that they wanted nothing.

So when Sir Launcelot was in his chamber that was assigned unto him, he called unto him Sir Lavaine, and told him that night he must go speak with his lady, Dame Guenever. Sir, said Sir Lavaine, let me go with you an it please you, for I dread me sore of the treason of Sir Meliagrance. Nay, said Sir Launcelot, I thank you, but I will have nobody with me. Then Sir Launcelot took his sword in his hand, and privily went to a place where he had espied a ladder to-forehand, and that he took under his arm, and bare it through the garden, and set it up to the window, and there anon the queen was ready to meet him. And then they made either to other their complaints of many divers things, and then Sir Launcelot wished that he might have come into her. Wit ye well, said the queen, I would as fain as ye, that ye might come in to me. Would ye, madam, said Sir Launcelot, with your heart that I were with you? Yea, truly, said the queen. Now shall I prove my might, said Sir Launcelot, for your love; and then he set his hands upon the bars of iron, and he pulled at them with such a might that he brast them clean out of the stone walls, and therewithal one of the bars of iron cut the brawn of his hands throughout to the bone; and then he leapt into the chamber to the queen. Make ye no noise, said the queen, for my wounded knights lie here fast by me. So, to pass upon this tale, Sir Launcelot went unto bed with the queen, and he took no force of his hurt hand, but took his pleasaunce and his liking until it was in the dawning of the day; and wit ye well he slept not but watched, and when he saw his time that he might tarry no longer he took his leave and departed at the window, and put it together as well as he might again, and so departed unto his own chamber: and there he told Sir Lavaine how he was hurt. Then Sir Lavaine dressed his hand and staunched it, and put upon it a glove, that it should not be espied; and so the queen lay long in her bed until it was nine of the clock.

Then Sir Meliagrance went to the queen's chamber, and found her ladies there ready clothed. Jesu mercy, said Sir Meliagrance, what aileth you, madam, that ye sleep thus long? And right therewithal he opened the curtain for to behold her; and then was he ware where she lay, and all the sheet and pillow was bebled with the blood of Sir Launcelot and of his hurt hand. When Sir Meliagrance espied that blood, then he deemed in her that she was false to the king, and that some of the wounded knights had lain by her all that night. Ah, madam, said Sir Meliagrance, now I have found you a false traitress unto my lord Arthur; for now I prove well it was not for nought that ye laid these wounded knights within the bounds of your chamber; therefore I will call you of treason before my lord, King Arthur. And now I have proved you, madam, with a shameful deed; and that they be all false, or some of them, I will make good, for a wounded knight this night hath lain by you. That is false, said the queen, and that I will report me unto them all. Then when the ten knights heard Sir Meliagrance's words, they spake all in one voice and said to Sir Meliagrance: Thou sayest falsely, and wrongfully puttest upon us such a deed, and that we will make good any of us; choose which thou list of us when we are whole of our wounds. Ye shall not, said Sir Meliagrance, away with your proud language, for here ye may all see, said Sir Meliagrance, that by the queen this night a wounded knight hath lain. Then were they all ashamed when they saw that blood; and wit you well Sir Meliagrance was passing glad that he had the queen at such an advantage, for he deemed by that to hide his treason. So with this rumour came in Sir Launcelot, and found them all at a great array.

CHAPTER VII

How Sir Launcelot answered for the queen, and waged battle against Sir Meliagrance; and how Sir Launcelot was taken in a trap.

What array is this? said Sir Launcelot. Then Sir Meliagrance told them what he had found, and showed them the queen's bed. Truly, said Sir Launcelot, ye did not your part nor knightly, to touch a queen's bed while it was drawn, and she lying therein; for I dare say my lord Arthur himself would not have displayed her curtains, she being within her bed, unless that it had pleased him to have lain down by her; and therefore ye have done unworshipfully and shamefully to yourself. I wot not what ye mean, said Sir Meliagrance, but well I am sure there hath one of her wounded knights lain by her this night, and therefore I will prove with my hands that she is a traitress unto my lord Arthur. Beware what ye do, said Launcelot, for an ye say so, an ye will prove it, it will be taken at your hands.

My lord, Sir Launcelot, said Sir Meliagrance, I rede you beware what ye do; for though ye are never so good a knight, as ye wot well ye are renowned the best knight of the world, yet should ye be advised to do battle in a wrong quarrel, for God will have a stroke in every battle. As for that, said Sir Launcelot, God is to be dread; but as to that I say nay plainly, that this night there lay none of these ten wounded knights with my lady Queen Guenever, and that will I prove with my hands, that ye say untruly in that now. Hold, said Sir Meliagrance, here is my glove that she is traitress unto my lord, King Arthur, and that this night one of the wounded knights lay with her. And I receive your glove, said Sir Launcelot. And so they were sealed with their signets, and delivered unto the ten knights. At what day shall we do battle together? said Sir Launcelot. This day eight days, said Sir Meliagrance, in the field beside Westminster. I am agreed, said Sir Launcelot. But now, said Sir Meliagrance, sithen it is so that we must fight together, I pray you, as ye be a noble knight, await me with no treason, nor none villainy the meanwhile, nor none for you. So God me help, said Sir Launcelot, ye shall right well wit I was never of no such conditions, for I report me to all knights that ever have known me, I fared never with no treason, nor I loved never the fellowship of no man that fared with treason. Then let us go to dinner, said Meliagrance, and after dinner ye and the queen and ye may ride all to Westminster. I will well, said Sir Launcelot.

Then Sir Meliagrance said to Sir Launcelot: Pleaseth it you to see the estures of this castle? With a good will, said Sir Launcelot. And then they went together from chamber to chamber, for Sir Launcelot dread no perils; for ever a man of worship and of prowess dreadeth least always perils, for they ween every man be as they be; but ever he that fareth with treason putteth oft a man in great danger. So it befell upon Sir Launcelot that no peril dread, as he went with Sir Meliagrance he trod on a trap and the board rolled, and there Sir Launcelot fell down more than ten fathom into a cave full of straw; and then Sir Meliagrance departed and made no fare as that he nist where he was.

And when Sir Launcelot was thus missed they marvelled where he was become; and then the queen and many of them deemed that he was departed as he was wont to do, suddenly. For Sir Meliagrance made suddenly to put away aside Sir Lavaine's horse, that they might all understand that Sir Launcelot was departed suddenly. So it passed on till after dinner; and then Sir Lavaine would not stint until that he ordained litters for the wounded knights, that they might be laid in them; and so with the queen and them all, both ladies and gentlewomen and other, went unto Westminster; and there the knights told King Arthur how Meliagrance had appealed the queen of high treason, and how Sir Launcelot had received the glove of him: And this day eight days they shall do battle afore you. By my head, said King Arthur, I am afeard Sir Meliagrance hath taken upon him a great charge; but where is Sir Launcelot? said the king. Sir, said they all, we wot not where he is, but we deem he is ridden to some adventures, as he is ofttimes wont to do, for he hath Sir Lavaine's horse. Let him be, said the king, he will be founden, but if he be trapped with some treason.

CHAPTER VIII

*How Sir Launcelot was delivered out of prison by a lady, and
took a white courser and came for to keep his day.*

So leave we Sir Launcelot lying within that cave in great pain; and
every day there came a lady and brought him his meat and his drink,
and wooed him, to have lain by him; and ever the noble knight, Sir
Launcelot, said her nay. Sir Launcelot, said she, ye are not wise, for ye
may never out of this prison, but if ye have my help; and also your
lady, Queen Guenever, shall be brent in your default, unless that ye
be there at the day of battle. God defend, said Sir Launcelot, that she
should be brent in my default; and if it be so, said Sir Launcelot, that I
may not be there, it shall be well understanded, both at the king and
at the queen, and with all men of worship, that I am dead, sick,
outher in prison. For all men that know me will say for me that I am
in some evil case an I be not there that day; and well I wot there is
some good knight either of my blood, or some other that loveth me,
that will take my quarrel in hand; and therefore, said Sir Launcelot,
wit ye well ye shall not fear me; and if there were no more women in
all this land but ye, I will not have ado with you. Then art thou
shamed, said the lady, and destroyed for ever. As for world's shame,
Jesu defend me, and as for my distress, it is welcome whatsoever it be
that God sendeth me.

So she came to him the same day that the battle should be, and said:
Sir Launcelot, methinketh ye are too hardhearted, but wouldest thou
but kiss me once I should deliver thee, and thine armour, and the best
horse that is within Sir Meliagrance's stable. As for to kiss you, said Sir
Launcelot, I may do that and lose no worship; and wit ye well an I
understood there were any disworship for to kiss you I would not do
it. Then he kissed her, and then she gat him, and brought him to his
armour. And when he was armed, she brought him to a stable, where
stood twelve good coursers, and bade him choose the best. Then Sir
Launcelot looked upon a white courser the which liked him best; and
anon he commanded the keepers fast to saddle him with the best
saddle of war that there was; and so it was done as he bade. Then gat

he his spear in his hand, and his sword by his side, and commended the lady unto God, and said: Lady, for this good deed I shall do you service if ever it be in my power.

CHAPTER IX

How Sir Launcelot came the same time that Sir Meliagrance abode him in the field and dressed him to battle.

Now leave we Sir Launcelot wallop all that he might, and speak we of Queen Guenever that was brought to a fire to be brent; for Sir Meliagrance was sure, him thought, that Sir Launcelot should not be at that battle; therefore he ever cried upon King Arthur to do him justice, other-else bring forth Sir Launcelot du Lake. Then was the king and all the court full sore abashed and shamed that the queen should be brent in the default of Sir Launcelot. My lord Arthur, said Sir Lavaine, ye may understand that it is not well with my lord Sir Launcelot, for an he were alive, so he be not sick outher in prison, wit ye well he would be here; for never heard ye that ever he failed his part for whom he should do battle for. And therefore, said Sir Lavaine, my lord, King Arthur, I beseech you give me license to do battle here this day for my lord and master, and for to save my lady, the queen. Gramercy gentle Sir Lavaine, said King Arthur, for I dare say all that Sir Meliagrance putteth upon my lady the queen is wrong, for I have spoken with all the ten wounded knights, and there is not one of them, an he were whole and able to do battle, but he would prove upon Sir Meliagrance's body that it is false that he putteth upon my queen. So shall I, said Sir Lavaine, in the defence of my lord, Sir Launcelot, an ye will give me leave. Now I give you leave, said King Arthur, and do your best, for I dare well say there is some treason done to Sir Launcelot.

Then was Sir Lavaine armed and horsed, and suddenly at the lists' end he rode to perform this battle; and right as the heralds should cry: Lesses les aler, right so came in Sir Launcelot driving with all the force of his horse. And then Arthur cried: Ho! and Abide! Then was Sir Launcelot called on horseback to-fore King Arthur, and there he told openly to-fore the king and all, how Sir Meliagrance had served him first to last. And when the king, and the queen, and all the lords, knew of the treason of Sir Meliagrance they were all ashamed on his behalf. Then was Queen Guenever sent for, and set by the king in great trust of her champion. And then there was no more else to say, but Sir Launcelot and Sir Meliagrance dressed them unto battle, and took their spears; and so they came together as thunder, and there Sir Launcelot bare him down quite over his horse's croup. And then Sir Launcelot alighted and dressed his shield on his shoulder, with his sword in his hand, and Sir Meliagrance in the same wise dressed him unto him, and there they smote many great strokes together; and at the last Sir Launcelot smote him such a buffet upon the helmet that he fell on the one side to the earth. And then he cried upon him aloud: Most noble knight, Sir Launcelot du Lake, save my life, for I yield me unto you, and I require you, as ye be a knight and fellow of the Table Round, slay me not, for I yield me as overcome; and whether I shall live or die I put me in the king's hands and yours.

Then Sir Launcelot wist not what to do, for he had had liefer than all the good of the world he might have been revenged upon Sir Meliagrance; and Sir Launcelot looked up to the Queen Guenever, if he might espy by any sign or countenance what she would have done. And then the queen wagged her head upon Sir Launcelot, as though she would say: Slay him. Full well knew Sir Launcelot by the wagging of her head that she would have him dead; then Sir Launcelot bade him rise for shame and perform that battle to the utterance. Nay, said Sir Meliagrance, I will never arise until ye take me as yolden and recreant. I shall proffer you large proffers, said Sir Launcelot, that is for to say, I shall unarm my head and my left quarter of my body, all that may be unarmed, and let bind my left hand behind me, so that it shall not help me, and right so I shall do battle with you. Then Sir Meliagrance started up upon his legs, and said on high: My lord Arthur, take heed to this proffer, for I will take it, and let him be disarmed and bounden according to his proffer. What say ye, said King Arthur unto Sir Launcelot, will ye abide by your proffer? Yea, my lord, said Sir Launcelot, I will never go from that I have once said.

Then the knights parters of the field disarmed Sir Launcelot, first his head, and sithen his left arm, and his left side, and they bound his left arm behind his back, without shield or anything, and then they were put together. Wit you well there was many a lady and knight marvelled that Sir Launcelot would jeopardy himself in such wise. Then Sir Meliagrance came with his sword all on high, and Sir Launcelot showed him openly his bare head and the bare left side; and when he weened to have smitten him upon the bare head, then lightly he avoided the left leg and the left side, and put his right hand and his sword to that stroke, and so put it on side with great sleight; and then with great force Sir Launcelot smote him on the helmet such a buffet that the stroke carved the head in two parts. Then there was no more to do, but he was drawn out of the field. And at the great instance of the knights of the Table Round, the king suffered him to be interred, and the mention made upon him, who slew him, and for what cause he was slain; and then the king and the queen made more of Sir Launcelot du Lake, and more he was cherished, than ever he was aforehand.

CHAPTER X

How Sir Urre came into Arthur's court for to be healed of his wounds, and how King Arthur would begin to handle him.

Then as the French book maketh mention, there was a good knight in the land of Hungary, his name was Sir Urre, and he was an adventurous knight, and in all places where he might hear of any deeds of worship there would he be. So it happened in Spain there was an earl's son, his name was Alphegus, and at a great tournament in Spain this Sir Urre, knight of Hungary, and Sir Alphegus of Spain encountered together for very envy; and so either undertook other to the utterance. And by fortune Sir Urre slew Sir Alphegus, the earl's son of Spain, but this knight that was slain had given Sir Urre, or ever he was slain, seven great wounds, three on the head, and four on his body and upon his left hand. And this Sir Alphegus had a mother, the which was a great sorceress; and she, for the despite of her son's death, wrought by her subtle crafts that Sir Urre should never be whole, but ever his wounds should one time fester and another time bleed, so that he should never be whole until the best knight of the world had searched his wounds; and thus she made her avaunt, wherethrough it was known that Sir Urre should never be whole.

Then his mother let make an horse litter, and put him therein under two palfreys; and then she took Sir Urre's sister with him, a full fair damosel, whose name was Felelolie; and then she took a page with him to keep their horses, and so they led Sir Urre through many countries. For as the French book saith, she led him so seven year through all lands christened, and never she could find no knight that might ease her son. So she came into Scotland and into the lands of England, and by fortune she came nigh the feast of Pentecost until King Arthur's court, that at that time was holden at Carlisle. And when she came there, then she made it openly to be known how that she was come into that land for to heal her son.

Then King Arthur let call that lady, and asked her the cause why she brought that hurt knight into that land. My most noble king, said that lady, wit you well I brought him hither for to be healed of his wounds, that of all this seven year he might not be whole. And then she told the king where he was wounded, and of whom; and how his mother had discovered in her pride how she had wrought that by enchantment, so that he should never be whole until the best knight of the world had searched his wounds. And so I have passed through all the lands christened to have him healed, except this land. And if I fail to heal him here in this land, I will never take more pain upon me, and that is pity, for he was a good knight, and of great nobleness. What is his name? said Arthur. My good and gracious lord, she said, his name is Sir Urre of the Mount. In good time, said the king, and sith ye are come into this land, ye are right welcome; and wit you well here shall your son be healed, an ever any Christian man may heal him. And for to give all other men of worship courage, I myself will assay to handle your son, and so shall all the kings, dukes, and earls that be here present with me at this time; thereto will I command them, and well I wot they shall obey and do after my commandment. And wit you well, said King Arthur unto Urre's sister, I shall begin to handle him, and search unto my power, not presuming upon me that I am so worthy to heal your son by my deeds, but I will courage other men of worship to do as I will do. And then the king commanded all the kings, dukes, and earls, and all noble knights of the Round Table that were there that time present, to come into the meadow of Carlisle. And so at that time there were but an hundred and ten of the Round Table, for forty knights were that time away; and so here we must begin at King Arthur, as is kindly to begin at him that was the most man of worship that was christened at that time.

CHAPTER XI

How King Arthur handled Sir Urre, and after him many other knights of the Round Table.

Then King Arthur looked upon Sir Urre, and the king thought he was a full likely man when he was whole; and then King Arthur made him to be taken down off the litter and laid him upon the earth, and there was laid a cushion of gold that he should kneel upon. And then noble Arthur said: Fair knight, me repenteth of thy hurt, and for to courage all other noble knights I will pray thee softly to suffer me to handle your wounds. Most noble christened king, said Urre, do as ye list, for I am at the mercy of God, and at your commandment. So then Arthur softly handled him, and then some of his wounds renewed upon bleeding. Then the King Clarence of Northumberland searched, and it would not be. And then Sir Barant le Apres that was called the King with the Hundred Knights, he assayed and failed; and so did King Uriens of the land of Gore; so did King Anguish of Ireland; so did King Nentres of Garloth; so did King Carados of Scotland; so did the Duke Galahad, the haut prince; so did Constantine, that was Sir Carados' son of Cornwall; so did Duke Chaleins of Clarance; so did the Earl Ulbause; so did the Earl Lambaile; so did the Earl Aristause.

Then came in Sir Gawaine with his three sons. Sir Gingalin, Sir Florence, and Sir Lovel, these two were begotten upon Sir Brandiles' sister; and all they failed. Then came in Sir Agravaine, Sir Gaheris, Sir Mordred, and the good knight, Sir Gareth, that was of very knighthood worth all the brethren. So came knights of Launcelot's kin, but Sir Launcelot was not that time in the court, for he was that time upon his adventures. Then Sir Lionel, Sir Ector de Maris, Sir Bors de Ganis, Sir Blamore de Ganis, Sir Bleoberis de Ganis, Sir Gahalantine, Sir Galihodin, Sir Menaduke, Sir Villiars the Valiant, Sir Hebes le Renoumes. All these were of Sir Launcelot's kin, and all they failed. Then came in Sir Sagramore le Desirous, Sir Dodinas le Savage, Sir Dinadan, Sir Bruin le Noire, that Sir Kay named La Cote Male Taile, and Sir Kay le Seneschal, Sir Kay de Stranges, Sir Meliot de Logris, Sir Petipase of Winchelsea, Sir Galleron of Galway, Sir Melion of the Mountain, Sir Cardok, Sir Uwaine les Avoutres, and Sir Ozanna le Cure Hardy.

Then came in Sir Astamor, and Sir Gromere, Grummor's son, Sir Crosselm, Sir Servause le Breuse, that was called a passing strong knight, for as the book saith, the chief Lady of the Lake feasted Sir Launcelot and Servause le Breuse, and when she had feasted them both at sundry times she prayed them to give her a boon. And they granted it her. And then she prayed Sir Servause that he would promise her never to do battle against Sir Launcelot du Lake, and in the same wise she prayed Sir Launcelot never to do battle against Sir Servause, and so either promised her. For the French book saith, that Sir Servause had never courage nor lust to do battle against no man, but if it were against giants, and against dragons, and wild beasts. So we pass unto them that at the king's request made them all that were there at that high feast, as of the knights of the Table Round, for to search Sir Urre: to that intent the king did it, to wit which was the noblest knight among them.

Then came Sir Aglovale, Sir Durnore, Sir Tor, that was begotten upon Aries, the cowherd's wife, but he was begotten afore Aries wedded her, and King Pellinore begat them all, first Sir Tor, Sir Aglovale, Sir Durnore, Sir Lamorak, the most noblest knight one that ever was in Arthur's days as for a worldly knight, and Sir Percivale that was peerless except Sir Galahad in holy deeds, but they died in the quest of the Sangreal. Then came Sir Griflet le Fise de Dieu, Sir Lucan the Butler, Sir Bedevere his brother, Sir Brandiles, Sir Constantine, Sir Cador's son of Cornwall, that was king after Arthur's days, and Sir Clegis, Sir Sadok, Sir Dinas le Seneschal of Cornwall, Sir Fergus, Sir Driant, Sir Lambegus, Sir Clarrus of Cleremont, Sir Cloddrus, Sir Hectimere, Sir Edward of Carnarvon, Sir Dinas, Sir Priamus, that was christened by Sir Tristram the noble knight, and these three were brethren; Sir Hellaine le Blank that was son to Sir Bors, he begat him upon King Brandegoris' daughter, and Sir Brian de Listinoise; Sir Gautere, Sir Reynold, Sir Gillemere, were three brethren that Sir Launcelot won upon a bridge in Sir Kay's arms. Sir Guyart le Petite, Sir Bellangere le Beuse, that was son to the good knight, Sir Alisander le Orphelin, that was slain by the treason of King Mark. Also that traitor king slew the noble knight Sir Tristram, as he sat harping afore his lady La Beale Isoud, with a trenchant glaive, for whose death was much bewailing of every knight that ever were in Arthur's days; there was never none so bewailed as was Sir Tristram and Sir Lamorak, for they were traitorously slain, Sir Tristram by King Mark, and Sir Lamorak by Sir Gawaine and his brethren. And this Sir Bellangere revenged the death of his father Alisander, and Sir Tristram slew King Mark, and La Beale Isoud died swooning upon the corse of Sir Tristram, whereof was great pity. And all that were with King Mark that were consenting to the death of Sir Tristram were slain, as Sir Andred and many other.

Then came Sir Hebes, Sir Morganore, Sir Sentraile, Sir Suppinabilis, Sir Bellangere le Orgulous, that the good knight Sir Lamorak won in plain battle; Sir Nerovens and Sir Plenorius, two good knights that Sir Launcelot won; Sir Darras, Sir Harry le Fise Lake, Sir Erminide, brother to King Hermaunce, for whom Sir Palomides fought at the Red City with two brethren; and Sir Selises of the Dolorous Tower, Sir Edward of Orkney, Sir Ironside, that was called the noble Knight of the Red Launds that Sir Gareth won for the love of Dame Liones, Sir Arrok de Grevaunt, Sir Degrane Saunce Velany that fought with the giant of the black lowe, Sir Epinogris, that was the king's son of Northumberland. Sir Pelleas that loved the lady Ettard, and he had died for her love had not been one of the ladies of the lake, her name was Dame Nimue, and she wedded Sir Pelleas, and she saved him that he was never slain, and he was a full noble knight; and Sir Lamiel of Cardiff that was a great lover. Sir Plaine de Fors, Sir Melleaus de Lile, Sir Bohart le Cure Hardy that was King Arthur's son, Sir Mador de la Porte, Sir Colgrevance, Sir Hervise de la Forest Savage, Sir Marrok, the good knight that was betrayed with his wife, for she made him seven year a wer-wolf, Sir Persaunt, Sir Pertilope, his brother, that was called the Green Knight, and Sir Perimones, brother to them both, that was called the Red Knight, that Sir Gareth won when he was called Beaumains. All these hundred knights and ten searched Sir Urre's wounds by the commandment of King Arthur.

CHAPTER XII

*How Sir Launcelot was commanded by Arthur to handle his
wounds, and anon he was all whole, and how they thanked God.*

Mercy Jesu, said King Arthur, where is Sir Launcelot du Lake that he
is not here at this time? Thus, as they stood and spake of many things,
there was espied Sir Launcelot that came riding toward them, and
told the king. Peace, said the king, let no manner thing be said until
he be come to us. So when Sir Launcelot espied King Arthur, he
descended from his horse and came to the king, and saluted him and
them all. Anon as the maid, Sir Urre's sister, saw Sir Launcelot, she
ran to her brother thereas he lay in his litter, and said: Brother, here is
come a knight that my heart giveth greatly unto. Fair sister, said Sir
Urre, so doth my heart light against him, and certainly I hope now to
be healed, for my heart giveth unto him more than to all these that
have searched me.

Then said Arthur unto Sir Launcelot: Ye must do as we have done;
and told Sir Launcelot what they had done, and showed him them
all, that had searched him. Jesu defend me, said Sir Launcelot, when
so many kings and knights have assayed and failed, that I should
presume upon me to enchieve that all ye, my lords, might not
enchieve. Ye shall not choose, said King Arthur, for I will command
you for to do as we all have done. My most renowned lord, said Sir
Launcelot, ye know well I dare not nor may not disobey your
commandment, but an I might or durst, wit you well I would not
take upon me to touch that wounded knight in that intent that I
should pass all other knights; Jesu defend me from that shame. Ye
take it wrong, said King Arthur, ye shall not do it for no
presumption, but for to bear us fellowship, insomuch ye be a fellow
of the Table Round; and wit you well, said King Arthur, an ye
prevail not and heal him, I dare say there is no knight in this land may
heal him, and therefore I pray you, do as we have done.

And then all the kings and knights for the most part prayed Sir
Launcelot to search him; and then the wounded knight, Sir Urre, set
him up weakly, and prayed Sir Launcelot heartily, saying: Courteous

knight, I require thee for God's sake heal my wounds, for methinketh ever sithen ye came here my wounds grieve me not. Ah, my fair lord, said Sir Launcelot, Jesu would that I might help you; I shame me sore that I should be thus rebuked, for never was I able in worthiness to do so high a thing. Then Sir Launcelot kneeled down by the wounded knight saying: My lord Arthur, I must do your command-ment, the which is sore against my heart. And then he held up his hands, and looked into the east, saying secretly unto himself: Thou blessed Father, Son and Holy Ghost, I beseech thee of thy mercy, that my simple worship and honesty be saved, and thou blessed Trinity, thou mayst give power to heal this sick knight by thy great virtue and grace of thee, but, Good Lord, never of myself. And then Sir Launcelot prayed Sir Urre to let him see his head; and then devoutly kneeling he ransacked the three wounds, that they bled a little, and forthwith all the wounds fair healed, and seemed as they had been whole a seven year. And in likewise he searched his body of other three wounds, and they healed in likewise; and then the last of all he searched the which was in his hand, and anon it healed fair.

Then King Arthur and all the kings and knights kneeled down and gave thankings and lovings unto God and to His Blessed Mother. And ever Sir Launcelot wept as he had been a child that had been beaten. Then King Arthur let array priests and clerks in the most devoutest manner, to bring in Sir Urre within Carlisle, with singing and loving to God. And when this was done, the king let clothe him in the richest manner that could be thought; and then were there but few better made knights in all the court, for he was passingly well made and bigly; and Arthur asked Sir Urre how he felt himself. My good lord, he said, I felt myself never so lusty. Will ye joust and do deeds of arms? said King Arthur. Sir, said Urre, an I had all that longed unto jousts I would be soon ready.

CHAPTER XIII

How there was a party made of an hundred knights against
an hundred knights, and of other matters.

Then Arthur made a party of hundred knights to be against an hundred knights. And so upon the morn they jousted for a diamond, but there jousted none of the dangerous knights; and so for to shorten this tale, Sir Urre and Sir Lavaine jousted best that day, for there was none of them but he overthrew and pulled down thirty knights; and then by the assent of all the kings and lords, Sir Urre and Sir Lavaine were made knights of the Table Round. And Sir Lavaine cast his love unto Dame Felelolie, Sir Urre's sister, and then they were wedded together with great joy, and King Arthur gave to everych of them a barony of lands. And this Sir Urre would never go from Sir Launcelot, but he and Sir Lavaine awaited evermore upon him; and they were in all the court accounted for good knights, and full desirous in arms; and many noble deeds they did, for they would have no rest, but ever sought adventures.

Thus they lived in all that court with great noblesse and joy long time. But every night and day Sir Agravaine, Sir Gawaine's brother, awaited Queen Guenever and Sir Launcelot du Lake to put them to a rebuke and shame. And so I leave here of this tale, and overskip great books of Sir Launcelot du Lake, what great adventures he did when he was called Le Chevaler du Chariot. For as the French book saith, because of despite that knights and ladies called him the knight that rode in the chariot like as he were judged to the gallows, therefore in despite of all them that named him so, he was carried in a chariot a twelvemonth, for, but little after that he had slain Sir Meliagrance in the queen's quarrel, he never in a twelvemonth came on horseback. And as the French book saith, he did that twelvemonth more than forty battles. And because I have lost the very matter of Le Chevaler du Chariot, I depart from the tale of Sir Launcelot, and here I go unto the morte of King Arthur; and that caused Sir Agravaine.

Explicit liber xix.
And hereafter followeth the most piteous history of the
morte of King Arthur, the which is the twentieth book.

BOOK TWENTY

CHAPTER I

How Sir Agravaine and Sir Mordred were busy upon Sir Gawaine for to disclose the love between Sir Launcelot and Queen Guenever.

In May when every lusty heart flourisheth and bourgeoneth, for as the season is lusty to behold and comfortable, so man and woman rejoice and gladden of summer coming with his fresh flowers: for winter with his rough winds and blasts causeth a lusty man and woman to cower, and sit fast by the fire. So in this season, as in the month of May, it befell a great anger and unhap that stinted not till the flower of chivalry of all the world was destroyed and slain; and all was long upon two unhappy knights, the which were named Agravaine and Sir Mordred, that were brethren unto Sir Gawaine. For this Sir Agravaine and Sir Mordred had ever a privy hate unto the queen Dame Guenever and to Sir Launcelot, and daily and nightly they ever watched upon Sir Launcelot.

So it mishapped, Sir Gawaine and all his brethren were in King Arthur's chamber; and then Sir Agravaine said thus openly, and not in no counsel, that many knights might hear it: I marvel that we all be not ashamed both to see and to know how Sir Launcelot lieth daily and nightly by the queen, and all we know it so; and it is shamefully suffered of us all, that we all should suffer so noble a king as King Arthur is so to be shamed.

Then spake Sir Gawaine, and said: Brother Sir Agravaine, I pray you and charge you move no such matters no more afore me, for wit you well, said Sir Gawaine, I will not be of your counsel. So God me help, said Sir Gaheris and Sir Gareth, we will not be knowing, brother Agravaine, of your deeds. Then will I, said Sir Mordred. I lieve well that, said Sir Gawaine, for ever unto all unhappiness, brother Sir Mordred, thereto will ye grant; and I would that ye left all this, and made you not so busy, for I know, said Sir Gawaine, what will fall of it. Fall of it what fall may, said Sir Agravaine, I will disclose it to the king. Not by my counsel, said Sir Gawaine, for an there rise war and wrack betwixt Sir Launcelot and us, wit you well brother, there will many kings and great lords hold with Sir Launcelot. Also, brother Sir Agravaine, said Sir Gawaine, ye must remember how ofttimes Sir Launcelot hath rescued the king and the queen; and the best of us all had been full cold at the heart-root had not Sir Launcelot been better than we, and that hath he proved himself full oft. And as for my part, said Sir Gawaine, I will never be against Sir Launcelot for one day's deed, when he rescued me from King Carados of the Dolorous Tower, and slew him, and saved my life. Also, brother Sir Agravaine and Sir Mordred, in like wise Sir Launcelot rescued you both, and threescore and two, from Sir Turquin. Methinketh brother, such kind deeds and kindness should be remembered. Do as ye list, said Sir Agravaine, for I will lain it no longer. With these words came to them King Arthur. Now brother, stint your noise, said Sir Gawaine. We will not, said Sir Agravaine and Sir Mordred. Will ye so? said Sir Gawaine; then God speed you, for I will not hear your tales ne be of your counsel. No more will I, said Sir Gareth and Sir Gaheris, for we will never say evil by that man; for because, said Sir Gareth, Sir Launcelot made me knight, by no manner owe I to say ill of him: and therewithal they three departed, making great dole. Alas, said Sir Gawaine and Sir Gareth, now is this realm wholly mischieved, and the noble fellowship of the Round Table shall be disparpled: so they departed.

CHAPTER II

How Sir Agravaine disclosed their love to King Arthur, and how King Arthur gave them licence to take him.

And then Sir Arthur asked them what noise they made. My lord, said Agravaine, I shall tell you that I may keep no longer. Here is I, and my brother Sir Mordred, brake unto my brothers Sir Gawaine, Sir Gaheris, and to Sir Gareth, how this we know all, that Sir Launcelot holdeth your queen, and hath done long; and we be your sister's sons, and we may suffer it no longer, and all we wot that ye should be above Sir Launcelot; and ye are the king that made him knight, and therefore we will prove it, that he is a traitor to your person.

If it be so, said Sir Arthur, wit you well he is none other, but I would be loath to begin such a thing but I might have proofs upon it; for Sir Launcelot is an hardy knight, and all ye know he is the best knight among us all; and but if he be taken with the deed, he will fight with him that bringeth up the noise, and I know no knight that is able to match him. Therefore an it be sooth as ye say, I would he were taken with the deed. For as the French book saith, the king was full loath thereto, that any noise should be upon Sir Launcelot and his queen; for the king had a deeming, but he would not hear of it, for Sir Launcelot had done so much for him and the queen so many times, that wit ye well the king loved him passingly well. My lord, said Sir Agravaine, ye shall ride to-morn a-hunting, and doubt ye not Sir Launcelot will not go with you. Then when it draweth toward night, ye may send the queen word that ye will lie out all that night, and so may ye send for your cooks, and then upon pain of death we shall take him that night with the queen, and outher we shall bring him to you dead or quick. I will well, said the king; then I counsel you, said the king, take with you sure fellowship. Sir, said Agravaine, my brother, Sir Mordred, and I, will take with us twelve knights of the Round Table. Beware said King Arthur, for I warn you ye shall find him wight. Let us deal, said Sir Agravaine and Sir Mordred.

So on the morn King Arthur rode a-hunting, and sent word to the queen that he would be out all that night. Then Sir Agravaine and Sir Mordred gat to them twelve knights, and hid themself in a chamber in the Castle of Carlisle, and these were their names: Sir Colgrevance, Sir Mador de la Porte, Sir Gingaline, Sir Meliot de Logris, Sir Petipase of Winchelsea, Sir Galleron of Galway, Sir Melion of the Mountain, Sir Astamore, Sir Gromore Somir Joure, Sir Curselaine, Sir Florence, Sir Lovel. So these twelve knights were with Sir Mordred and Sir Agravaine, and all they were of Scotland, outher of Sir Gawaine's kin, either well-willers to his brethren.

So when the night came, Sir Launcelot told Sir Bors how he would go that night and speak with the queen. Sir, said Sir Bors, ye shall not go this night by my counsel. Why? said Sir Launcelot. Sir, said Sir Bors, I dread me ever of Sir Agravaine, that waiteth you daily to do you shame and us all; and never gave my heart against no going, that ever ye went to the queen, so much as now; for I mistrust that the king is out this night from the queen because peradventure he hath lain some watch for you and the queen, and therefore I dread me sore of treason. Have ye no dread, said Sir Launcelot, for I shall go and come again, and make no tarrying. Sir, said Sir Bors, that me repenteth, for I dread me sore that your going out this night shall wrath us all. Fair nephew, said Sir Launcelot, I marvel much why ye say thus, sithen the queen hath sent for me; and wit ye well I will not be so much a coward, but she shall understand I will see her good grace. God speed you well, said Sir Bors, and send you sound and safe again.

CHAPTER III

How Sir Launcelot was espied in the queen's chamber, and how Sir Agravaine and Sir Mordred came with twelve knights to slay him.

So Sir Launcelot departed, and took his sword under his arm, and so in his mantle that noble knight put himself in great jeopardy; and so he passed till he came to the queen's chamber, and then Sir Launcelot was lightly put into the chamber. And then, as the French book saith, the queen and Launcelot were together. And whether they were abed or at other manner of disports, me list not hereof make no mention, for love that time was not as is now-adays. But thus as they were together, there came Sir Agravaine and Sir Mordred, with twelve knights with them of the Round Table, and they said with crying voice: Traitor-knight, Sir Launcelot du Lake, now art thou taken. And thus they cried with a loud voice, that all the court might hear it; and they all fourteen were armed at all points as they should fight in a battle. Alas, said Queen Guenever, now are we mischieved both. Madam, said Sir Launcelot, is there here any armour within your chamber, that I might cover my poor body withal? An if there be any give it me, and I shall soon stint their malice, by the grace of God. Truly, said the queen, I have none armour, shield, sword, nor spear; wherefore I dread me sore our long love is come to a mischievous end, for I hear by their noise there be many noble knights, and well I wot they be surely armed; against them ye may make no resistance. Wherefore ye are likely to be slain, and then shall I be brent. For an ye might escape them, said the queen, I would not doubt but that ye would rescue me in what danger that ever I stood in. Alas, said Sir Launcelot, in all my life thus was I never bestead, that I should be thus shamefully slain for lack of mine armour.

But ever in one Sir Agravaine and Sir Mordred cried: Traitor-knight, come out of the queen's chamber, for wit thou well thou art so beset that thou shalt not escape. O Jesu mercy, said Sir Launcelot, this shameful cry and noise I may not suffer, for better were death at once than thus to endure this pain. Then he took the queen in his arms, and kissed her, and said: Most noble Christian queen, I beseech you as ye have been ever my special good lady, and I at all times your true poor knight unto my power, and as I never failed you in right nor in wrong sithen the first day King Arthur made me knight, that ye will pray for my soul if that I here be slain; for well I am assured that Sir Bors, my nephew, and all the remnant of my kin, with Sir Lavaine and Sir Urre, that they will not fail you to rescue you from the fire; and therefore, mine own lady, recomfort yourself, whatsomever come of me, that ye go with Sir Bors, my nephew, and Sir Urre, and they all will do you all the pleasure that they can or may, that ye shall live like a queen upon my lands. Nay, Launcelot, said the queen, wit thou well I will never live after thy days, but an thou be slain I will take my death as meekly for Jesu Christ's sake as ever did any Christian queen. Well, madam, said Launcelot, sith it is so that the day is come that our love must depart, wit you well I shall sell my life as dear as I may; and a thousandfold, said Sir Launcelot, I am more heavier for you than for myself. And now I had liefer than to be lord of all Christendom, that I had sure armour upon me, that men might speak of my deeds or ever I were slain. Truly, said the queen, I would an it might please God that they would take me and slay me, and suffer you to escape. That shall never be, said Sir Launcelot, God defend me from such a shame, but Jesu be Thou my shield and mine armour!

CHAPTER IV

How Sir Launcelot slew Sir Colgrevance, and armed him
in his harness, and after slew Sir Agravaine,
and twelve of his fellows.

And therewith Sir Launcelot wrapped his mantle about his arm well and surely; and by then they had gotten a great form out of the hall, and therewithal they rashed at the door. Fair lords, said Sir Launcelot, leave your noise and your rashing, and I shall set open this door, and then may ye do with me what it liketh you. Come off then, said they all, and do it, for it availeth thee not to strive against us all; and therefore let us into this chamber, and we shall save thy life until thou come to King Arthur. Then Launcelot unbarred the door, and with his left hand he held it open a little, so that but one man might come in at once; and so there came striding a good knight, a much man and large, and his name was Colgrevance of Gore, and he with a sword struck at Sir Launcelot mightily; and he put aside the stroke, and gave him such a buffet upon the helmet, that he fell grovelling dead within the chamber door. And then Sir Launcelot with great might drew that dead knight within the chamber door; and Sir Launcelot with help of the queen and her ladies was lightly armed in Sir Colgrevance's armour.

And ever stood Sir Agravaine and Sir Mordred crying: Traitor-knight, come out of the queen's chamber. Leave your noise, said Sir Launcelot unto Sir Agravaine, for wit you well, Sir Agravaine, ye shall not prison me this night; and therefore an ye do by my counsel, go ye all from this chamber door, and make not such crying and such manner of slander as ye do; for I promise you by my knighthood, an ye will depart and make no more noise, I shall as to-morn appear afore you all before the king, and then let it be seen which of you all, outher else ye all, that will accuse me of treason; and there I shall answer you as a knight should, that hither I came to the queen for no manner of mal engin, and that will I prove and make it good upon you with my hands. Fie on thee, traitor, said Sir Agravaine and Sir Mordred, we will have thee maugre thy head, and slay thee if we list;

for we let thee wit we have the choice of King Arthur to save thee or to slay thee. Ah sirs, said Sir Launcelot, is there none other grace with you? then keep yourself.

So then Sir Launcelot set all open the chamber door, and mightily and knightly he strode in amongst them; and anon at the first buffet he slew Sir Agravaine. And twelve of his fellows after, within a little while after, he laid them cold to the earth, for there was none of the twelve that might stand Sir Launcelot one buffet. Also Sir Launcelot wounded Sir Mordred, and he fled with all his might. And then Sir Launcelot returned again unto the queen, and said: Madam, now wit you well all our true love is brought to an end, for now will King Arthur ever be my foe; and therefore, madam, an it like you that I may have you with me, I shall save you from all manner adventures dangerous. That is not best, said the queen; meseemeth now ye have done so much harm, it will be best ye hold you still with this. And if ye see that as to-morn they will put me unto the death, then may ye rescue me as ye think best. I will well, said Sir Launcelot, for have ye no doubt, while I am living I shall rescue you. And then he kissed her, and either gave other a ring; and so there he left the queen, and went until his lodging.

CHAPTER V

How Sir Launcelot came to Sir Bors, and told him how
he had sped, and in what adventure he had been,
and how he had escaped.

When Sir Bors saw Sir Launcelot he was never so glad of his home-coming as he was then. Jesu mercy, said Sir Launcelot, why be ye all armed: what meaneth this? Sir, said Sir Bors, after ye were departed from us, we all that be of your blood and your well-willers were so dretched that some of us leapt out of our beds naked, and some in their dreams caught naked swords in their hands; therefore, said Sir Bors, we deem there is some great strife at hand; and then we all deemed that ye were betrapped with some treason, and therefore we made us thus ready, what need that ever ye were in.

My fair nephew, said Sir Launcelot unto Sir Bors, now shall ye wit all, that this night I was more harder bestead than ever I was in my life, and yet I escaped. And so he told them all how and in what manner, as ye have heard to-fore. And therefore, my fellows, said Sir Launcelot, I pray you all that ye will be of good heart in what need somever I stand, for now is war come to us all. Sir, said Bors, all is welcome that God sendeth us, and we have had much weal with you and much worship, and therefore we will take the woe with you as we have taken the weal. And therefore, they said all (there were many good knights), look ye take no discomfort, for there nis no bands of knights under heaven but we shall be able to grieve them as much as they may us. And therefore discomfort not yourself by no manner, and we shall gather together that we love, and that loveth us, and what that ye will have done shall be done. And therefore, Sir Launcelot, said they, we will take the woe with the weal. Grant mercy, said Sir Launcelot, of your good comfort, for in my great distress, my fair nephew, ye comfort me greatly, and much I am beholding unto you. But this, my fair nephew, I would that ye did in all haste that ye may, or it be forth days, that ye will look in their lodging that be lodged here nigh about the king, which will hold with me, and which will not, for now I would know which were my friends from my foes. Sir, said Sir Bors, I shall do my pain, and or it be seven of the clock I shall wit of such as ye have said before, who will hold with you.

Then Sir Bors called unto him Sir Lionel, Sir Ector de Maris, Sir Blamore de Ganis, Sir Bleoberis de Ganis, Sir Gahalantine, Sir Galihodin, Sir Galihud, Sir Menadeuke, Sir Villiers the Valiant, Sir Hebes le Renoumes, Sir Lavaine, Sir Urre of Hungary, Sir Nerounes, Sir Plenorius. These two knights Sir Launcelot made, and the one he won upon a bridge, and therefore they would never be against him. And Harry le Fise du Lake, and Sir Selises of the Dolorous Tower, and Sir Melias de Lile, and Sir Bellangere le Beuse, that was Sir Alisander's son Le Orphelin, because his mother was Alice le Beale Pellerin and she was kin unto Sir Launcelot, and he held with him. So there came Sir Palomides and Sir Safere, his brother, to hold with Sir Launcelot, and Sir Clegis of Sadok, and Sir Dinas, Sir Clarius of Cleremont. So these two-and-twenty knights drew them together, and by then they were armed on horseback, and promised Sir Launcelot to do what he would. Then there fell to them, what of North Wales and of Cornwall, for Sir Lamorak's sake and for Sir Tristram's sake, to the number of a fourscore knights.

My lords, said Sir Launcelot, wit you well, I have been ever since I came into this country well willed unto my lord, King Arthur, and unto my lady, Queen Guenever, unto my power; and this night because my lady the queen sent for me to speak with her, I suppose it was made by treason, howbeit I dare largely excuse her person, notwithstanding I was there by a forecast near slain, but as Jesu provided me I escaped all their malice and treason. And then that noble knight Sir Launcelot told them all how he was hard bestead in the queen's chamber, and how and in what manner he escaped from them. And therefore, said Sir Launcelot, wit you well, my fair lords, I am sure there nis but war unto me and mine. And for because I have slain this night these knights, I wot well, as is Sir Agravaine Sir Gawaine's brother, and at the least twelve of his fellows, for this cause now I am sure of mortal war, for these knights were sent and ordained by King Arthur to betray me. And therefore the king will in his heat and malice judge the queen to the fire, and that may I not suffer, that she should be brent for my sake; for an I may be heard and suffered and so taken, I will fight for the queen, that she is a true lady unto her lord; but the king in his heat I dread me will not take me as I ought to be taken.

CHAPTER VI

*Of the counsel and advice that was taken by Sir Launcelot
and his friends for to save the queen.*

My lord, Sir Launcelot, said Sir Bors, by mine advice ye shall take the woe with the weal, and take it in patience, and thank God of it. And sithen it is fallen as it is, I counsel you keep yourself, for an ye will yourself, there is no fellowship of knights christened that shall do you wrong. Also I will counsel you my lord, Sir Launcelot, that an my lady, Queen Guenever, be in distress, insomuch as she is in pain for your sake, that ye knightly rescue her; an ye did otherwise, all the world will speak of you shame to the world's end. Insomuch as ye were taken with her, whether ye did right or wrong, it is now your part to hold with the queen, that she be not slain and put to a mischievous death, for an she so die the shame shall be yours. Jesu defend me from shame, said Sir Launcelot, and keep and save my lady the queen from villainy and shameful death, and that she never be destroyed in my default; wherefore my fair lords, my kin, and my friends, said Sir Launcelot, what will ye do? Then they said all: We will do as ye will do. I put this to you, said Sir Launcelot, that if my lord Arthur by evil counsel will to-morn in his heat put my lady the queen to the fire there to be brent, now I pray you counsel me what is best to do. Then they said all at once with one voice: Sir, us thinketh best that ye knightly rescue the queen, insomuch as she shall be brent it is for your sake; and it is to suppose, an ye might be handled, ye should have the same death, or a more shamefuler death. And sir, we say all, that ye have many times rescued her from death for other men's quarrels, us seemeth it is more your worship that ye rescue the queen from this peril, insomuch she hath it for your sake.

Then Sir Launcelot stood still, and said: My fair lords, wit you well I would be loath to do that thing that should dishonour you or my blood, and wit you well I would be loath that my lady, the queen, should die a shameful death; but an it be so that ye will counsel me to rescue her, I must do much harm or I rescue her; and peradventure I shall there destroy some of my best friends, that should much repent me; and peradventure there be some, an they could well bring it about, or disobey my lord King Arthur, they would soon come to me, the which I were loath to hurt. And if so be that I rescue her, where shall I keep her? That shall be the least care of us all, said Sir Bors. How did the noble knight Sir Tristram, by your good will? kept not he with him La Beale Isoud near three year in Joyous Gard? the which was done by your alther device, and that same place is your own; and in likewise may ye do an ye list, and take the queen lightly away, if it so be the king will judge her to be brent; and in Joyous Gard ye may keep her long enough until the heat of the king be past. And then shall ye bring again the queen to the king with great worship; and then peradventure ye shall have thank for her bringing home, and love and thank where other shall have maugre.

That is hard to do, said Sir Launcelot, for by Sir Tristram I may have a warning, for when by means of treaties, Sir Tristram brought again La Beale Isoud unto King Mark from Joyous Gard, look what befell on the end, how shamefully that false traitor King Mark slew him as he sat harping afore his lady La Beale Isoud, with a grounden glaive he thrust him in behind to the heart. It grieveth me, said Sir

Launcelot, to speak of his death, for all the world may not find such a knight. All this is truth, said Sir Bors, but there is one thing shall courage you and us all, ye know well King Arthur and King Mark were never like of conditions, for there was never yet man could prove King Arthur untrue of his promise.

So to make short tale, they were all consented that for better outher for worse, if so were that the queen were on that morn brought to the fire, shortly they all would rescue her. And so by the advice of Sir Launcelot, they put them all in an embushment in a wood, as nigh Carlisle as they might, and there they abode still, to wit what the king would do.

CHAPTER VII

How Sir Mordred rode hastily to the king, to tell him of the affray and death of Sir Agravaine and the other knights.

Now turn we again unto Sir Mordred, that when he was escaped from the noble knight, Sir Launcelot, he anon gat his horse and mounted upon him, and rode unto King Arthur, sore wounded and smitten, and all forbled; and there he told the king all how it was, and how they were all slain save himself all only. Jesu mercy, how may this be? said the king; took ye him in the queen's chamber? Yea, so God me help, said Sir Mordred, there we found him unarmed, and there he slew Colgrevance, and armed him in his armour; and all this he told the king from the beginning to the ending. Jesu mercy, said the king, he is a marvellous knight of prowess. Alas, me sore repenteth, said the king, that ever Sir Launcelot should be against me. Now I am sure the noble fellowship of the Round Table is broken for ever, for with him will many a noble knight hold; and now it is fallen so, said the king, that I may not with my worship, but the queen must suffer the death. So then there was made great ordinance in this heat, that the queen must be judged to the death. And the law was such in those days that whatsomever they were, of what estate or degree, if they were found guilty of treason, there should be none other remedy but death; and outher the men or the taking with the deed should be causer of their hasty judgment. And right so was it ordained for Queen Guenever, because Sir Mordred was escaped sore wounded, and the death of thirteen knights of the Round Table. These proofs and experiences caused King Arthur to command the queen to the fire there to be brent.

Then spake Sir Gawaine, and said: My lord Arthur, I would counsel you not to be over-hasty, but that ye would put it in respite, this judgment of my lady the queen, for many causes. One it is, though it were so that Sir Launcelot were found in the queen's chamber, yet it might be so that he came thither for none evil; for ye know my lord, said Sir Gawaine, that the queen is much beholden unto Sir Launcelot, more than unto any other knight, for ofttimes he hath saved her life, and done battle for her when all the court refused the queen; and peradventure she sent for him for goodness and for none evil, to reward him for his good deeds that he had done to her in times past. And peradventure my lady, the queen, sent for him to that intent that Sir Launcelot should come to her good grace privily and secretly, weening to her that it was best so to do, in eschewing and dreading of slander; for ofttimes we do many things that we ween it be for the best, and yet peradventure it turneth to the worst. For I dare say, said Sir Gawaine, my lady, your queen, is to you both good and true; and as for Sir Launcelot, said Sir Gawaine, I dare say he will make it good upon any knight living that will put upon himself villainy or shame, and in like wise he will make good for my lady, Dame Guenever.

That I believe well, said King Arthur, but I will not that way with Sir Launcelot, for he trusteth so much upon his hands and his might that he doubteth no man; and therefore for my queen he shall never fight more, for she shall have the law. And if I may get Sir Launcelot, wit you well he shall have a shameful death. Jesu defend, said Sir Gawaine, that I may never see it. Why say ye so? said King Arthur; forsooth ye have no cause to love Sir Launcelot, for this night last past he slew your brother, Sir Agravaine, a full good knight, and almost he had slain your other brother, Sir Mordred, and also there he slew thirteen noble knights; and also, Sir Gawaine, remember ye he slew two sons of yours, Sir Florence and Sir Lovel. My lord, said Sir Gawaine, of all this I have knowledge, of whose deaths I repent me sore; but insomuch I gave them warning, and told my brethren and my sons aforehand what would fall in the end, insomuch they would not do by my counsel, I will not meddle me thereof, nor revenge me nothing of their deaths; for I told them it was no boot to strive with Sir Launcelot. Howbeit I am sorry of the death of my brethren and of my sons, for they are the causers of their own death; for ofttimes I warned my brother Sir Agravaine, and I told him the perils the which be now fallen.

CHAPTER VIII

How Sir Launcelot and his kinsmen rescued the queen from the fire, and how he slew many knights.

Then said the noble King Arthur to Sir Gawaine: Dear nephew, I pray you make you ready in your best armour, with your brethren, Sir Gaheris and Sir Gareth, to bring my queen to the fire, there to have her judgment and receive the death. Nay, my most noble lord, said Sir Gawaine, that will I never do; for wit you well I will never be in that place where so noble a queen as is my lady, Dame Guenever, shall take a shameful end. For wit you well, said Sir Gawaine, my heart will never serve me to see her die; and it shall never be said that ever I was of your counsel of her death.

Then said the king to Sir Gawaine: Suffer your brothers Sir Gaheris and Sir Gareth to be there. My lord, said Sir Gawaine, wit you well they will be loath to be there present, because of many adventures the which be like there to fall, but they are young and full unable to say you nay. Then spake Sir Gaheris, and the good knight Sir Gareth, unto Sir Arthur: Sir, ye may well command us to be there, but wit you well it shall be sore against our will; but an we be there by your strait commandment ye shall plainly hold us there excused: we will be there in peaceable wise, and bear none harness of war upon us. In the name of God, said the king, then make you ready, for she shall soon have her judgment anon. Alas, said Sir Gawaine, that ever I should endure to see this woful day. So Sir Gawaine turned him and wept heartily, and so he went into his chamber; and then the queen was led forth without Carlisle, and there she was despoiled into her smock. And so then her ghostly father was brought to her, to be shriven of her misdeeds. Then was there weeping, and wailing, and wringing of hands, of many lords and ladies, but there were but few in comparison that would bear any armour for to strength the death of the queen.

Then was there one that Sir Launcelot had sent unto that place for to espy what time the queen should go unto her death; and anon as he saw the queen despoiled into her smock, and so shriven, then he gave Sir Launcelot warning. Then was there but spurring and plucking up of horses, and right so they came to the fire. And who that stood against them, there were they slain; there might none withstand Sir Launcelot, so all that bare arms and withstood them, there were they slain, full many a noble knight. For there was slain Sir Belliance le Orgulous, Sir Segwarides, Sir Griflet, Sir Brandiles, Sir Aglovale, Sir Tor; Sir Gauter, Sir Gillimer, Sir Reynolds' three brethren; Sir Damas, Sir Priamus, Sir Kay the Stranger, Sir Driant, Sir Lambegus, Sir Herminde; Sir Pertilope, Sir Perimones, two brethren that were called the Green Knight and the Red Knight. And so in this rushing and hurling, as Sir Launcelot thrang here and there, it mishapped him to slay Gaheris and Sir Gareth, the noble knight, for they were unarmed and unware. For as the French book saith, Sir Launcelot smote Sir Gareth and Sir Gaheris upon the brain-pans, wherethrough they were slain in the field; howbeit in very truth Sir Launcelot saw them not, and so were they found dead among the thickest of the press.

Then when Sir Launcelot had thus done, and slain and put to flight all that would withstand him, then he rode straight unto Dame Guenever, and made a kirtle and a gown to be cast upon her; and then he made her to be set behind him, and prayed her to be of good cheer. Wit you well the queen was glad that she was escaped from the death. And then she thanked God and Sir Launcelot; and so he rode his way with the queen, as the French book saith, unto Joyous Gard, and there he kept her as a noble knight should do; and many great lords and some kings sent Sir Launcelot many good knights, and many noble knights drew unto Sir Launcelot. When this was known openly, that King Arthur and Sir Launcelot were at debate, many knights were glad of their debate, and many were full heavy of their debate.

CHAPTER IX

*Of the sorrow and lamentation of King Arthur for the
death of his nephews and other good knights,
and also for the queen, his wife.*

So turn we again unto King Arthur, that when it was told him how
and in what manner of wise the queen was taken away from the fire,
and when he heard of the death of his noble knights, and in especial
of Sir Gaheris and Sir Gareth's death, then the king swooned for pure
sorrow. And when he awoke of his swoon, then he said: Alas, that
ever I bare crown upon my head! for now have I lost the fairest
fellowship of noble knights that ever held Christian king together.
Alas, my good knights be slain away from me: now within these two
days I have lost forty knights, and also the noble fellowship of Sir
Launcelot and his blood, for now I may never hold them together no
more with my worship. Alas that ever this war began. Now fair
fellows, said the king, I charge you that no man tell Sir Gawaine of
the death of his two brethren; for I am sure, said the king, when Sir
Gawaine heareth tell that Sir Gareth is dead he will go nigh out of his
mind. Mercy Jesu, said the king, why slew he Sir Gareth and Sir
Gaheris, for I dare say as for Sir Gareth he loved Sir Launcelot above
all men earthly. That is truth, said some knights, but they were slain
in the hurtling as Sir Launcelot thrang in the thick of the press; and as
they were unarmed he smote them and wist not whom that he
smote, and so unhappily they were slain. The death of them, said
Arthur, will cause the greatest mortal war that ever was; I am sure,
wist Sir Gawaine that Sir Gareth were slain, I should never have rest
of him till I had destroyed Sir Launcelot's kin and himself both,
outher else he to destroy me. And therefore, said the king, wit you
well my heart was never so heavy as it is now, and much more I am
sorrier for my good knights' loss than for the loss of my fair queen; for
queens I might have enow, but such a fellowship of good knights
shall never be together in no company. And now I dare say, said King
Arthur, there was never Christian king held such a fellowship
together; and alas that ever Sir Launcelot and I should be at debate.

Ah Agravaine, Agravaine, said the king, Jesu forgive it thy soul, for thine evil will, that thou and thy brother Sir Mordred hadst unto Sir Launcelot, hath caused all this sorrow: and ever among these complaints the king wept and swooned.

Then there came one unto Sir Gawaine, and told him how the queen was led away with Sir Launcelot, and nigh a twenty-four knights slain. O Jesu defend my brethren, said Sir Gawaine, for full well wist I that Sir Launcelot would rescue her, outher else he would die in that field; and to say the truth he had not been a man of worship had he not rescued the queen that day, insomuch she should have been brent for his sake. And as in that, said Sir Gawaine, he hath done but knightly, and as I would have done myself an I had stood in like case. But where are my brethren? said Sir Gawaine, I marvel I hear not of them. Truly, said that man, Sir Gareth and Sir Gaheris be slain. Jesu defend, said Sir Gawaine, for all the world I would not that they were slain, and in especial my good brother, Sir Gareth. Sir, said the man, he is slain, and that is great pity. Who slew him? said Sir Gawaine. Sir, said the man, Launcelot slew them both. That may I not believe, said Sir Gawaine, that ever he slew my brother, Sir Gareth; for I dare say my brother Gareth loved him better than me, and all his brethren, and the king both. Also I dare say, an Sir Launcelot had desired my brother, Sir Gareth, with him he would have been with him against the king and us all, and therefore I may never believe that Sir Launcelot slew my brother. Sir, said this man, it is noised that he slew him.

CHAPTER X

How King Arthur at the request of Sir Gawaine concluded to make war against Sir Launcelot, and laid siege to his castle called Joyous Gard.

Alas, said Sir Gawaine, now is my joy gone. And then he fell down and swooned, and long he lay there as he had been dead. And then, when he arose of his swoon, he cried out sorrowfully, and said: Alas! And right so Sir Gawaine ran to the king, crying and weeping: O King Arthur, mine uncle, my good brother Sir Gareth is slain, and so is my brother Sir Gaheris, the which were two noble knights. Then the king wept, and he both; and so they fell a-swooning. And when they were revived then spake Sir Gawaine: Sir, I will go see my brother, Sir Gareth. Ye may not see him, said the king, for I caused him to be interred, and Sir Gaheris both; for I well understood that ye would make over-much sorrow, and the sight of Sir Gareth should have caused your double sorrow. Alas, my lord, said Sir Gawaine, how slew he my brother, Sir Gareth? Mine own good lord I pray you tell me. Truly, said the king, I shall tell you how it is told me, Sir Launcelot slew him and Sir Gaheris both. Alas, said Sir Gawaine, they bare none arms against him, neither of them both. I wot not how it was, said the king, but as it is said, Sir Launcelot slew them both in the thickest of the press and knew them not; and therefore let us shape a remedy for to revenge their deaths.

My king, my lord, and mine uncle, said Sir Gawaine, wit you well now I shall make you a promise that I shall hold by my knighthood, that from this day I shall never fail Sir Launcelot until the one of us have slain the other. And therefore I require you, my lord and king, dress you to the war, for wit you well I will be revenged upon Sir Launcelot; and therefore, as ye will have my service and my love, now haste you thereto, and assay your friends. For I promise unto God, said Sir Gawaine, for the death of my brother, Sir Gareth, I shall seek Sir Launcelot throughout seven kings' realms, but I shall slay him or else he shall slay me. Ye shall not need to seek him so far, said the king, for as I hear say, Sir Launcelot will abide me and you in the Joyous Gard; and much people draweth unto him, as I hear say. That may I believe, said Sir Gawaine; but my lord, he said, assay your friends, and I will assay mine. It shall be done, said the king, and as I suppose I shall be big enough to draw him out of the biggest tower of his castle.

So then the king sent letters and writs throughout all England, both in the length and the breadth, for to assummon all his knights. And so unto Arthur drew many knights, dukes, and earls, so that he had a great host. And when they were assembled, the king informed them how Sir Launcelot had bereft him his queen. Then the king and all his host made them ready to lay siege about Sir Launcelot, where he lay within Joyous Gard. Thereof heard Sir Launcelot, and purveyed him of many good knights, for with him held many knights; and some for his own sake, and some for the queen's sake. Thus they were on both parties well furnished and garnished of all manner of thing that longed to the war. But King Arthur's host was so big that Sir Launcelot would not abide him in the field, for he was full loath to do battle against the king; but Sir Launcelot drew him to his strong castle with all manner of victual, and as many noble men as he might suffice within the town and the castle. Then came King Arthur with Sir Gawaine with an huge host, and laid a siege all about Joyous Gard, both at the town and at the castle, and there they made strong war on both parties. But in no wise Sir Launcelot would ride out, nor go out of his castle, of long time; neither he would none of his good knights to issue out, neither none of the town nor of the castle, until fifteen weeks were past.

CHAPTER XI

Of the communication between King Arthur and Sir Launcelot, and how King Arthur reproved him.

Then it befell upon a day in harvest time, Sir Launcelot looked over the walls, and spake on high unto King Arthur and Sir Gawaine: My lords both, wit ye well all is in vain that ye make at this siege, for here win ye no worship but maugre and dishonour; for an it list me to come myself out and my good knights, I should full soon make an end of this war. Come forth, said Arthur unto Launcelot, an thou durst, and I promise thee I shall meet thee in midst of the field. God defend me, said Sir Launcelot, that ever I should encounter with the most noble king that made me knight. Fie upon thy fair language, said the king, for wit you well and trust it, I am thy mortal foe, and ever will to my death day; for thou hast slain my good knights, and full noble men of my blood, that I shall never recover again. Also thou hast lain by my queen, and holden her many winters, and sithen like a traitor taken her from me by force.

My most noble lord and king, said Sir Launcelot, ye may say what ye will, for ye wot well with yourself will I not strive; but thereas ye say I have slain your good knights, I wot well that I have done so, and that me sore repenteth; but I was enforced to do battle with them in saving of my life, or else I must have suffered them to have slain me.

And as for my lady, Queen Guenever, except your person of your highness, and my lord Sir Gawaine, there is no knight under heaven that dare make it good upon me, that ever I was a traitor unto your person. And where it please you to say that I have holden my lady your queen years and winters, unto that I shall ever make a large answer, and prove it upon any knight that beareth the life, except your person and Sir Gawaine, that my lady, Queen Guenever, is a true lady unto your person as any is living unto her lord, and that will I make good with my hands. Howbeit it hath liked her good grace to have me in chierté, and to cherish me more than any other knight; and unto my power I again have deserved her love, for ofttimes, my lord, ye have consented that she should be brent and destroyed, in your heat, and then it fortuned me to do battle for her, and or I departed from her adversary they confessed their untruth, and she full worshipfully excused. And at such times, my lord Arthur, said Sir Launcelot, ye loved me, and thanked me when I saved your queen from the fire; and then ye promised me for ever to be my good lord; and now methinketh ye reward me full ill for my good service. And my good lord, meseemeth I had lost a great part of my worship in my knighthood an I had suffered my lady, your queen, to have been brent, and insomuch she should have been brent for my sake. For sithen I have done battles for your queen in other quarrels than in mine own, meseemeth now I had more right to do battle for her in right quarrel. And therefore my good and gracious lord, said Sir Launcelot, take your queen unto your good grace, for she is both fair, true, and good.

Fie on thee, false recreant knight, said Sir Gawaine; I let thee wit my lord, mine uncle, King Arthur, shall have his queen and thee, maugre thy visage, and slay you both whether it please him. It may well be, said Sir Launcelot, but wit you well, my lord Sir Gawaine, an me list to come out of this castle ye should win me and the queen more harder than ever ye won a strong battle. Fie on thy proud words, said Sir Gawaine; as for my lady, the queen, I will never say of her shame. But thou, false and recreant knight, said Sir Gawaine, what cause hadst thou to slay my good brother Sir Gareth, that loved thee more than all my kin? Alas thou madest him knight thine own hands; why slew thou him that loved thee so well? For to excuse me, said Sir Launcelot, it helpeth me not, but by Jesu, and by the faith that I owe to the high order of knighthood, I should with as good will have slain my nephew, Sir Bors de Ganis, at that time. But alas that ever I was so unhappy, said Launcelot, that I had not seen Sir Gareth and Sir Gaheris.

Thou liest, recreant knight, said Sir Gawaine, thou slewest him in despite of me; and therefore, wit thou well I shall make war to thee, and all the while that I may live. That me repenteth, said Sir Launcelot; for well I understand it helpeth not to seek none accordment while ye, Sir Gawaine, are so mischievously set. And if ye were not, I would not doubt to have the good grace of my lord Arthur. I believe it well, false recreant knight, said Sir Gawaine; for thou hast many long days overled me and us all, and destroyed many of our good knights. Ye say as it pleaseth you, said Sir Launcelot; and yet may it never be said on me, and openly proved, that ever I by forecast of treason slew no good knight, as my lord, Sir Gawaine, ye have done; and so did I never, but in my defence that I was driven thereto, in saving of my life. Ah, false knight, said Sir Gawaine, that thou meanest by Sir Lamorak: wit thou well I slew him. Ye slew him not yourself, said Sir Launcelot; it had been overmuch on hand for you to have slain him, for he was one of the best knights christened of his age, and it was great pity of his death.

CHAPTER XII

How the cousins and kinsmen of Sir Launcelot excited him to go out to battle, and how they made them ready.

Well, well, said Sir Gawaine to Launcelot, sithen thou enbraidest me of Sir Lamorak, wit thou well I shall never leave thee till I have thee at such avail that thou shalt not escape my hands. I trust you well enough, said Sir Launcelot, an ye may get me I get but little mercy. But as the French book saith, the noble King Arthur would have taken his queen again, and have been accorded with Sir Launcelot, but Sir Gawaine would not suffer him by no manner of mean. And then Sir Gawaine made many men to blow upon Sir Launcelot; and all at once they called him false recreant knight.

Then when Sir Bors de Ganis, Sir Ector de Maris, and Sir Lionel, heard this outcry, they called to them Sir Palomides, Sir Safere's brother, and Sir Lavaine, with many more of their blood, and all they went unto Sir Launcelot, and said thus: My lord Sir Launcelot, wit ye well we have great scorn of the great rebukes that we heard Gawaine say to you; wherefore we pray you, and charge you as ye will have our service, keep us no longer within these walls; for wit you well plainly, we will ride into the field and do battle with them; for ye fare as a man that were afeard, and for all your fair speech it will not avail you. For wit you well Sir Gawaine will not suffer you to be accorded with King Arthur, and therefore fight for your life and your right, an ye dare. Alas, said Sir Launcelot, for to ride out of this castle, and to do battle, I am full loath.

Then Sir Launcelot spake on high unto Sir Arthur and Sir Gawaine: My lords, I require you and beseech you, sithen that I am thus required and conjured to ride into the field, that neither you, my lord King Arthur, nor you Sir Gawaine, come not into the field. What shall we do then? said Sir Gawaine, [N]is this the king's quarrel with thee to fight? and it is my quarrel to fight with thee, Sir Launcelot, because of the death of my brother Sir Gareth. Then must I needs unto battle, said Sir Launcelot. Now wit you well, my lord Arthur and Sir Gawaine, ye will repent it whensomever I do battle with you.

And so then they departed either from other; and then either party made them ready on the morn for to do battle, and great purveyance was made on both sides; and Sir Gawaine let purvey many knights for to wait upon Sir Launcelot, for to overset him and to slay him. And on the morn at underne Sir Arthur was ready in the field with three great hosts. And then Sir Launcelot's fellowship came out at three gates, in a full good array; and Sir Lionel came in the foremost battle, and Sir Launcelot came in the middle, and Sir Bors came out at the third gate. Thus they came in order and rule, as full noble knights; and always Sir Launcelot charged all his knights in any wise to save King Arthur and Sir Gawaine.

CHAPTER XIII

*How Sir Gawaine jousted and smote down Sir Lionel, and
how Sir Launcelot horsed King Arthur.*

Then came forth Sir Gawaine from the king's host, and he came
before and proffered to joust. And Sir Lionel was a fierce knight, and
lightly he encountered with Sir Gawaine; and there Sir Gawaine
smote Sir Lionel through-out the body, that he dashed to the earth
like as he had been dead; and then Sir Ector de Maris and other more
bare him into the castle. Then there began a great stour, and much
people was slain; and ever Sir Launcelot did what he might to save
the people on King Arthur's party, for Sir Palomides, and Sir Bors,
and Sir Safere, overthrew many knights, for they were deadly
knights. And Sir Blamore de Ganis, and Sir Bleoberis de Ganis, with
Sir Bellangere le Beuse, these six knights did much harm; and ever
King Arthur was nigh about Sir Launcelot to have slain him, and Sir
Launcelot suffered him, and would not strike again. So Sir Bors
encountered with King Arthur, and there with a spear Sir Bors smote
him down; and so he alighted and drew his sword, and said to Sir
Launcelot: Shall I make an end of this war? and that he meant to have
slain King Arthur. Not so hardy, said Sir Launcelot, upon pain of thy
head, that thou touch him no more, for I will never see that most
noble king that made me knight neither slain ne shamed. And
therewithal Sir Launcelot alighted off his horse and took up the king
and horsed him again, and said thus: My lord Arthur, for God's love
stint this strife, for ye get here no worship, and I would do mine
utterance, but always I forbear you, and ye nor none of yours
forbeareth me; my lord, remember what I have done in many places,
and now I am evil rewarded.

Then when King Arthur was on horseback, he looked upon Sir
Launcelot, and then the tears brast out of his eyen, thinking on the
great courtesy that was in Sir Launcelot more than in any other man;
and therewith the king rode his way, and might no longer behold
him, and said: Alas, that ever this war began. And then either parties
of the battles withdrew them to repose them, and buried the dead,

and to the wounded men they laid soft salves; and thus they endured that night till on the morn. And on the morn by underne they made them ready to do battle. And then Sir Bors led the forward.

So upon the morn there came Sir Gawaine as brim as any boar, with a great spear in his hand. And when Sir Bors saw him he thought to revenge his brother Sir Lionel of the despite that Sir Gawaine did him the other day. And so they that knew either other feutred their spears, and with all their mights of their horses and themselves, they met together so felonously that either bare other through, and so they fell both to the earth; and then the battles joined, and there was much slaughter on both parties. Then Sir Launcelot rescued Sir Bors, and sent him into the castle; but neither Sir Gawaine nor Sir Bors died not of their wounds, for they were all holpen. Then Sir Lavaine and Sir Urre prayed Sir Launcelot to do his pain, and fight as they had done; For we see ye forbear and spare, and that doth much harm; therefore we pray you spare not your enemies no more than they do you. Alas, said Sir Launcelot, I have no heart to fight against my lord Arthur, for ever meseemeth I do not as I ought to do. My lord, said Sir Palomides, though ye spare them all this day they will never con you thank; and if they may get you at avail ye are but dead. So then Sir Launcelot understood that they said him truth; and then he strained himself more than he did aforehand, and because his nephew Sir Bors was sore wounded. And then within a little while, by evensong time, Sir Launcelot and his party better stood, for their horses went in blood past the fetlocks, there was so much people slain. And then for pity Sir Launcelot withheld his knights, and suffered King Arthur's party for to withdraw them aside. And then Sir Launcelot's party withdrew them into his castle, and either parties buried the dead, and put salve unto the wounded men.

So when Sir Gawaine was hurt, they on King Arthur's party were not so orgulous as they were toforehand to do battle. Of this war was noised through all Christendom, and at the last it was noised afore the Pope; and he considering the great goodness of King Arthur, and of Sir Launcelot, that was called the most noblest knights of the world, wherefore the Pope called unto him a noble clerk that at that time was there present; the French book saith, it was the Bishop of Rochester; and the Pope gave him bulls under lead unto King Arthur of England, charging him upon pain of interdicting of all England, that he take his queen Dame Guenever unto him again, and accord with Sir Launcelot.

CHAPTER XIV

How the Pope sent down his bulls to make peace, and how
Sir Launcelot brought the queen to King Arthur.

So when this Bishop was come to Carlisle he showed the king these
bulls. And when the king understood these bulls he nist what to do:
full fain he would have been accorded with Sir Launcelot, but Sir
Gawaine would not suffer him; but as for to have the queen, thereto
he agreed. But in nowise Sir Gawaine would not suffer the king to
accord with Sir Launcelot; but as for the queen he consented. And
then the Bishop had of the king his great seal, and his assurance as he
was a true anointed king that Sir Launcelot should come safe, and go
safe, and that the queen should not be spoken unto of the king, nor
of none other, for no thing done afore time past; and of all these
appointments the Bishop brought with him sure assurance and
writing, to show Sir Launcelot.

So when the Bishop was come to Joyous Gard, there he showed
Sir Launcelot how the Pope had written to Arthur and unto him, and
there he told him the perils if he withheld the queen from the king. It
was never in my thought, said Launcelot, to withhold the queen
from my lord Arthur; but, insomuch she should have been dead for
my sake, meseemeth it was my part to save her life, and put her from
that danger, till better recover might come. And now I thank God,
said Sir Launcelot, that the Pope hath made her peace; for God
knoweth, said Sir Launcelot, I will be a thousandfold more gladder to
bring her again, than ever I was of her taking away; with this, I may
be sure to come safe and go safe, and that the queen shall have her
liberty as she had before; and never for no thing that hath been
surmised afore this time, she never from this day stand in no peril. For
else, said Sir Launcelot, I dare adventure me to keep her from an
harder shour than ever I kept her. It shall not need you, said the
Bishop, to dread so much; for wit you well, the Pope must be
obeyed, and it were not the Pope's worship nor my poor honesty to
wit you distressed, neither the queen, neither in peril, nor shamed.
And then he showed Sir Launcelot all his writing, both from the

Pope and from King Arthur. This is sure enough, said Sir Launcelot, for full well I dare trust my lord's own writing and his seal, for he was never shamed of his promise. Therefore, said Sir Launcelot unto the Bishop, ye shall ride unto the king afore, and recommend me unto his good grace, and let him have knowledging that this same day eight days, by the grace of God, I myself shall bring my lady, Queen Guenever, unto him. And then say ye unto my most redoubted king, that I will say largely for the queen, that I shall none except for dread nor fear, but the king himself, and my lord Sir Gawaine; and that is more for the king's love than for himself.

So the Bishop departed and came to the king at Carlisle, and told him all how Sir Launcelot answered him; and then the tears brast out of the king's eyen. Then Sir Launcelot purveyed him an hundred knights, and all were clothed in green velvet, and their horses trapped to their heels; and every knight held a branch of olive in his hand, in tokening of peace. And the queen had four-and-twenty gentlewomen following her in the same wise; and Sir Launcelot had twelve coursers following him, and on every courser sat a young gentleman, and all they were arrayed in green velvet, with sarps of gold about their quarters, and the horse trapped in the same wise down to the heels, with many ouches, y-set with stones and pearls in gold, to the number of a thousand. And she and Sir Launcelot were clothed in white cloth of gold tissue; and right so as ye have heard, as the French book maketh mention, he rode with the queen from Joyous Gard to Carlisle. And so Sir Launcelot rode throughout Carlisle, and so in the castle, that all men might behold; and wit you well there was many a weeping eye. And then Sir Launcelot himself alighted and avoided his horse, and took the queen, and so led her where King Arthur was in his seat: and Sir Gawaine sat afore him, and many other great lords. So when Sir Launcelot saw the king and Sir Gawaine, then he led the queen by the arm, and then he kneeled down, and the queen both. Wit you well then was there many bold knight there with King Arthur that wept as tenderly as though they had seen all their kin afore them. So the king sat still, and said no word. And when Sir Launcelot saw his countenance, he arose and pulled up the queen with him, and thus he spake full knightly.

CHAPTER XV

*Of the deliverance of the queen to the king by Sir Launcelot,
and what language Sir Gawaine had to Sir Launcelot.*

My most redoubted king, ye shall understand, by the Pope's
commandment and yours, I have brought to you my lady the queen,
as right requireth; and if there be any knight, of whatsomever degree
that he be, except your person, that will say or dare say but that she is
true and clean to you, I here myself, Sir Launcelot du Lake, will make
it good upon his body, that she is a true lady unto you; but liars ye
have listened, and that hath caused debate betwixt you and me. For
time hath been, my lord Arthur, that ye have been greatly pleased
with me when I did battle for my lady, your queen; and full well ye
know, my most noble king, that she hath been put to great wrong or
this time; and sithen it pleased you at many times that I should fight
for her, meseemeth, my good lord, I had more cause to rescue her
from the fire, insomuch she should have been brent for my sake. For
they that told you those tales were liars, and so it fell upon them; for
by likelihood had not the might of God been with me, I might never
have endured fourteen knights, and they armed and afore purposed,
and I unarmed and not purposed. For I was sent for unto my lady
your queen, I wot not for what cause; but I was not so soon within
the chamber door, but anon Sir Agravaine and Sir Mordred called me
traitor and recreant knight. They called thee right, said Sir Gawaine.
My lord Sir Gawaine, said Sir Launcelot, in their quarrel they proved
themselves not in the right. Well well, Sir Launcelot, said the king, I
have given thee no cause to do to me as thou hast done, for I have
worshipped thee and thine more than any of all my knights.

My good lord, said Sir Launcelot, so ye be not displeased, ye shall
understand I and mine have done you oft better service than any other
knights have done, in many divers places; and where ye have been full
hard bestead divers times, I have myself rescued you from many
dangers; and ever unto my power I was glad to please you, and my
lord Sir Gawaine; both in jousts, and tournaments, and in battles set,
both on horseback and on foot, I have often rescued you, and my lord

Sir Gawaine, and many mo of your knights in many divers places. For now I will make avaunt, said Sir Launcelot, I will that ye all wit that yet I found never no manner of knight but that I was overhard for him, an I had done my utterance, thanked be God; howbeit I have been matched with good knights, as Sir Tristram and Sir Lamorak, but ever I had a favour unto them and a deeming what they were. And I take God to record, said Sir Launcelot, I never was wroth nor greatly heavy with no good knight an I saw him busy about to win worship; and glad I was ever when I found any knight that might endure me on horseback and on foot: howbeit Sir Carados of the Dolorous Tower was a full noble knight and a passing strong man, and that wot ye, my lord Sir Gawaine; for he might well be called a noble knight when he by fine force pulled you out of your saddle, and bound you overthwart afore him to his saddle bow; and there, my lord Sir Gawaine, I rescued you, and slew him afore your sight. Also I found his brother Sir Turquin, in likewise leading Sir Gaheris, your brother, bounden afore him; and there I rescued your brother and slew that Turquin, and delivered three-score-and-four of my lord Arthur's knights out of his prison. And now I dare say, said Sir Launcelot, I met never with so strong knights, nor so well fighting, as was Sir Carados and Sir Turquin, for I fought with them to the uttermost. And therefore, said Sir Launcelot unto Sir Gawaine, meseemeth ye ought of right to remember this; for, an I might have your good will, I would trust to God to have my lord Arthur's good grace.

CHAPTER XVI

Of the communication between Sir Gawaine and Sir Launcelot, with much other language.

The king may do as he will, said Sir Gawaine, but wit thou well, Sir Launcelot, thou and I shall never be accorded while we live, for thou hast slain three of my brethren; and two of them ye slew traitorly and piteously, for they bare none harness against thee, nor none would bear. God would they had been armed, said Sir Launcelot, for then had they been alive. And wit ye well Sir Gawaine, as for Sir Gareth, I love none of my kinsmen so much as I did him; and ever while I live, said Sir Launcelot, I will bewail Sir Gareth's death, not all only for the great fear I have of you, but many causes cause me to be sorrowful. One is, for I made him knight; another is, I wot well he loved me above all other knights, and the third is, he was passing noble, true, courteous, and gentle, and well conditioned; the fourth is, I wist well, anon as I heard that Sir Gareth was dead, I should never after have your love, but everlasting war betwixt us; and also I wist well that ye would cause my noble lord Arthur for ever to be my mortal foe. And as Jesu be my help, said Sir Launcelot, I slew never Sir Gareth nor Sir Gaheris by my will; but alas that ever they were unarmed that unhappy day. But thus much I shall offer me, said Sir Launcelot, if it may please the king's good grace, and you, my lord Sir Gawaine, I shall first begin at Sandwich, and there I shall go in my shirt, barefoot; and at every ten miles' end I will found and gar make an house of religion, of what order that ye will assign me, with an whole convent, to sing and read, day and night, in especial for Sir Gareth's sake and Sir Gaheris. And this shall I perform from Sandwich unto Carlisle; and every house shall have sufficient livelihood. And this shall I perform while I have any livelihood in Christendom; and there nis none of all these religious places, but they shall be performed, furnished and garnished in all things as an holy place ought to be, I promise you faithfully. And this, Sir Gawaine, methinketh were more fairer, holier, and more better to their souls, than ye, my most noble king, and you, Sir Gawaine, to war upon me, for thereby shall ye get none avail.

Then all knights and ladies that were there wept as they were mad, and the tears fell on King Arthur's cheeks. Sir Launcelot, said Sir Gawaine, I have right well heard thy speech, and thy great proffers, but wit thou well, let the king do as it pleased him, I will never forgive my brothers' death, and in especial the death of my brother, Sir Gareth. And if mine uncle, King Arthur, will accord with thee, he shall lose my service, for wit thou well thou art both false to the king and to me. Sir, said Launcelot, he beareth not the life that may make that good; and if ye, Sir Gawaine, will charge me with so high a thing, ye must pardon me, for then needs must I answer you. Nay, said Sir Gawaine, we are past that at this time, and that caused the Pope, for he hath charged mine uncle, the king, that he shall take his queen again, and to accord with thee, Sir Launcelot, as for this season, and therefore thou shalt go safe as thou camest. But in this land thou shalt not abide past fifteen days, such summons I give thee: so the king and we were consented and accorded or thou camest. And else, said Sir Gawaine, wit thou well thou shouldst not have come here, but if it were maugre thy head. And if it were not for the Pope's commandment, said Sir Gawaine, I should do battle with mine own body against thy body, and prove it upon thee, that thou hast been both false unto mine uncle King Arthur, and to me both; and that shall I prove upon thy body, when thou art departed from hence, wheresomever I find thee.

CHAPTER XVII

How Sir Launcelot departed from the king and from Joyous Gard over seaward, and what knights went with him.

Then Sir Launcelot sighed, and therewith the tears fell on his cheeks, and then he said thus: Alas, most noble Christian realm, whom I have loved above all other realms, and in thee I have gotten a great part of my worship, and now I shall depart in this wise. Truly me repenteth that ever I came in this realm, that should be thus shamefully banished, undeserved and causeless; but fortune is so variant, and the wheel so moveable, there nis none constant abiding, and that may be proved by many old chronicles, of noble Ector, and Troilus, and Alisander, the mighty conqueror, and many mo other; when they were most in their royalty, they alighted lowest. And so fareth it by me, said Sir Launcelot, for in this realm I had worship, and by me and mine all the whole Round Table hath been increased more in worship, by me and mine blood, than by any other. And therefore wit thou well, Sir Gawaine, I may live upon my lands as well as any knight that here is. And if ye, most redoubted king, will come upon my lands with Sir Gawaine to war upon me, I must endure you as well as I may. But as to you, Sir Gawaine, if that ye come there, I pray you charge me not with treason nor felony, for an ye do, I must answer you. Do thou thy best, said Sir Gawaine; therefore hie thee fast that thou were gone, and wit thou well we shall soon come after, and break the strongest castle that thou hast, upon thy head. That shall not need, said Sir Launcelot, for an I were as orgulous set as ye are, wit you well I should meet you in midst of the field. Make thou no more language, said Sir Gawaine, but deliver the queen from thee, and pike thee lightly out of this court. Well, said Sir Launcelot, an I had wist of this short coming, I would have advised me twice or that I had come hither; for an the queen had been so dear to me as ye noise her, I durst have kept her from the fellowship of the best knights under heaven.

And then Sir Launcelot said unto Guenever, in hearing of the king and them all: Madam, now I must depart from you and this noble fellowship for ever; and sithen it is so, I beseech you to pray for me, and say me well; and if ye be hard bestead by any false tongues, lightly my lady send me word, and if any knight's hands may deliver you by battle, I shall deliver you. And therewithal Sir Launcelot kissed the queen; and then he said all openly: Now let see what he be in this place that dare say the queen is not true unto my lord Arthur, let see who will speak an he dare speak. And therewith he brought the queen to the king, and then Sir Launcelot took his leave and departed; and there was neither king, duke, nor earl, baron nor knight, lady nor gentlewoman, but all they wept as people out of their mind, except Sir Gawaine. And when the noble Sir Launcelot took his horse to ride out of Carlisle, there was sobbing and weeping for pure dole of his departing; and so he took his way unto Joyous Gard. And then ever after he called it the Dolorous Gard. And thus departed Sir Launcelot from the court for ever.

And so when he came to Joyous Gard he called his fellowship unto him, and asked them what they would do. Then they answered all wholly together with one voice, they would as he would do. My fair fellows, said Sir Launcelot, I must depart out of this most noble realm, and now I shall depart it grieveth me sore, for I shall depart with no worship, for a flemed man departed never out of a realm with no worship; and that is my heaviness, for ever I fear after my days that men shall chronicle upon me that I was flemed out of this land; and else, my fair lords, be ye sure, an I had not dread shame, my lady, Queen Guenever, and I should never have departed.

Then spake many noble knights, as Sir Palomides, Sir Safere his brother, and Sir Bellangere le Beuse, and Sir Urre, with Sir Lavaine, with many others: Sir, an ye be so disposed to abide in this land we will never fail you; and if ye list not to abide in this land there nis none of the good knights that here be will fail you, for many causes. One is, all we that be not of your blood shall never be welcome to the court. And sithen it liked us to take a part with you in your distress and heaviness in this realm, wit you well it shall like us as well to go in other countries with you, and there to take such part as ye do. My fair lords, said Sir Launcelot, I well understand you, and as I can, thank you: and ye shall understand, such livelihood as I am born unto I shall depart with you in this manner of wise; that is for to say, I shall depart all my livelihood and all my lands freely among you, and I myself will have as little as any of you, for have I sufficient that may long to my person, I will ask none other rich array; and I trust to God to maintain you on my lands as well as ever were maintained any knights. Then spake all the knights at once: He have shame that will leave you; for we all understand in this realm will be now no quiet, but ever strife and debate, now the fellowship of the Round Table is broken; for by the noble fellowship of the Round Table was King Arthur upborne, and by their noblesse the king and all his realm was in quiet and rest, and a great part they said all was because of your noblesse.

CHAPTER XVIII

How Sir Launcelot passed over the sea, and how he made great lords of the knights that went with him.

Truly, said Sir Launcelot, I thank you all of your good saying; howbeit, I wot well, in me was not all the stability of this realm, but in that I might I did my devoir; and well I am sure I knew many rebellions in my days that by me were peaced, and I trow we all shall hear of them in short space, and that me sore repenteth. For ever I dread me, said Sir Launcelot, that Sir Mordred will make trouble, for he is passing envious and applieth him to trouble. So they were accorded to go with Sir Launcelot to his lands; and to make short tale, they trussed, and paid all that would ask them; and wholly an hundred knights departed with Sir Launcelot at once, and made their avows they would never leave him for weal nor for woe.

And so they shipped at Cardiff, and sailed unto Benwick: some men call it Bayonne, and some men call it Beaune, where the wine of Beaune is. But to say the sooth, Sir Launcelot and his nephews were lords of all France, and of all the lands that longed unto France; he and his kindred rejoiced it all through Sir Launcelot's noble prowess. And then Sir Launcelot stuffed and furnished and garnished all his noble towns and castles. Then all the people of those lands came to Sir Launcelot on foot and hands. And so when he had stablished all these countries, he shortly called a parliament; and there he crowned Sir Lionel, King of France; and Sir Bors [he] crowned him king of all King Claudas' lands; and Sir Ector de Maris, that was Sir Launcelot's youngest brother, he crowned him King of Benwick, and king of all Guienne, that was Sir Launcelot's own land. And he made Sir Ector prince of them all, and thus he departed.

Then Sir Launcelot advanced all his noble knights, and first he advanced them of his blood; that was Sir Blamore, he made him Duke of Limosin in Guienne, and Sir Bleoberis he made him Duke of Poictiers, and Sir Gahalantine he made him Duke of Querne, and Sir Galihodin he made him Duke of Sentonge, and Sir Galihud he made him Earl of Perigot, and Sir Menadeuke he made him Earl of Roerge, and Sir Villiars the Valiant he made him Earl of Bearn, and Sir Hebes le Renoumes he made him Earl of Comange, and Sir Lavaine he made him Earl of Arminak, and Sir Urre he made him Earl of Estrake, and Sir Neroneus he made him Earl of Pardiak, and Sir Plenorius he made Earl of Foise, and Sir Selises of the Dolorous Tower he made him Earl of Masauke, and Sir Melias de Lile he made him Earl of Tursauk, and Sir Bellangere le Beuse he made Earl of the Launds, and Sir Palomides he made him Duke of the Provence, and Sir Safere he made him Duke of Landok, and Sir Clegis he gave him the Earldom of Agente, and Sir Sadok he gave the Earldom of Surlat, and Sir Dinas le Seneschal he made him Duke of Anjou, and Sir Clarrus he made him Duke of Normandy. Thus Sir Launcelot rewarded his noble knights and many more, that meseemeth it were too long to rehearse.

CHAPTER XIX

How King Arthur and Sir Gawaine made a great host ready to go over sea to make war on Sir Launcelot.

So leave we Sir Launcelot in his lands, and his noble knights with him, and return we again unto King Arthur and to Sir Gawaine, that made a great host ready, to the number of threescore thousand; and all thing was made ready for their shipping to pass over the sea, and so they shipped at Cardiff. And there King Arthur made Sir Mordred chief ruler of all England, and also he put Queen Guenever under his governance; because Sir Mordred was King Arthur's son, he gave him the rule of his land and of his wife; and so the king passed the sea and landed upon Sir Launcelot's lands, and there he brent and wasted, through the vengeance of Sir Gawaine, all that they might overrun.

When this word came to Sir Launcelot, that King Arthur and Sir Gawaine were landed upon his lands, and made a full great destruction and waste, then spake Sir Bors, and said: My lord Sir Launcelot, it is shame that we suffer them thus to ride over our lands, for wit you well, suffer ye them as long as ye will, they will do you no favour an they may handle you. Then said Sir Lionel that was wary and wise: My lord Sir Launcelot, I will give this counsel, let us keep our strong walled towns until they have hunger and cold, and blow on their nails; and then let us freshly set upon them, and shred them down as sheep in a field, that aliens may take example for ever how they land upon our lands.

Then spake King Bagdemagus to Sir Launcelot: Sir, your courtesy will shende us all, and thy courtesy hath waked all this sorrow; for an they thus over our lands ride, they shall by process bring us all to nought whilst we thus in holes us hide. Then said Sir Galihud unto Sir Launcelot: Sir, here be knights come of kings' blood, that will not long droop, and they are within these walls; therefore give us leave, like as we be knights, to meet them in the field, and we shall slay them, that they shall curse the time that ever they came into this country. Then spake seven brethren of North Wales, and they were seven noble knights; a man might seek in seven kings' lands or he might find such seven knights. Then they all said at once: Sir Launcelot, for Christ's sake let us out ride with Sir Galihud, for we be never wont to cower in castles nor in noble towns.

Then spake Sir Launcelot, that was master and governor of them all: My fair lords, wit you well I am full loath to ride out with my knights for shedding of Christian blood; and yet my lands I understand be full bare for to sustain any host awhile, for the mighty wars that whilom made King Claudas upon this country, upon my father King Ban, and on mine uncle King Bors; howbeit we will as at this time keep our strong walls, and I shall send a messenger unto my lord Arthur, a treaty for to take; for better is peace than always war.

So Sir Launcelot sent forth a damosel and a dwarf with her, requiring King Arthur to leave his warring upon his lands; and so she start upon a palfrey, and the dwarf ran by her side. And when she came to the pavilion of King Arthur, there she alighted; and there met her a gentle knight, Sir Lucan the Butler, and said: Fair damosel, come ye from Sir Launcelot du Lake? Yea sir, she said, therefore I come hither to speak with my lord the king. Alas, said Sir Lucan, my lord Arthur would love Launcelot, but Sir Gawaine will not suffer him. And then he said: I pray to God, damosel, ye may speed well, for all we that be about the king would Sir Launcelot did best of any knight living. And so with this Lucan led the damosel unto the king where he sat with Sir Gawaine, for to hear what she would say. So when she had told her tale, the water ran out of the king's eyen, and all the lords were full glad for to advise the king as to be accorded with Sir Launcelot, save all only Sir Gawaine, and he said: My lord mine uncle, what will ye do? Will ye now turn again, now ye are passed thus far upon this journey? all the world will speak of your villainy. Nay, said Arthur, wit thou well, Sir Gawaine, I will do as ye will advise me; and yet meseemeth, said Arthur, his fair proffers were not good to be refused; but sithen I am come so far upon this journey, I will that ye give the damosel her answer, for I may not speak to her for pity, for her proffers be so large.

CHAPTER XX

What message Sir Gawaine sent to Sir Launcelot; and how
King Arthur laid siege to Benwick, and other matters.

Then Sir Gawaine said to the damosel thus: Damosel, say ye to Sir
Launcelot that it is waste labour now to sue to mine uncle; for tell
him, an he would have made any labour for peace, he should have
made it or this time, for tell him now it is too late; and say that I, Sir
Gawaine, so send him word, that I promise him by the faith I owe
unto God and to knighthood, I shall never leave him till he have slain
me or I him. So the damosel wept and departed, and there were
many weeping eyen; and so Sir Lucan brought the damosel to her
palfrey, and so she came to Sir Launcelot where he was among all his
knights. And when Sir Launcelot had heard this answer, then the
tears ran down by his cheeks. And then his noble knights strode
about him, and said: Sir Launcelot, wherefore make ye such cheer,
think what ye are, and what men we are, and let us noble knights
match them in midst of the field. That may be lightly done, said Sir
Launcelot, but I was never so loath to do battle, and therefore I pray
you, fair sirs, as ye love me, be ruled as I will have you, for I will
always flee that noble king that made me knight. And when I may no
further, I must needs defend me, and that will be more worship for
me and us all than to compare with that noble king whom we have
all served. Then they held their language, and as that night they took
their rest.

And upon the morn early, in the dawning of the day, as knights
looked out, they saw the city of Benwick besieged round about; and
fast they began to set up ladders, and then they defied them out of the
town, and beat them from the walls wightly. Then came forth Sir
Gawaine well armed upon a stiff steed, and he came before the chief
gate, with his spear in his hand, crying: Sir Launcelot, where art thou?
is there none of you proud knights dare break a spear with me? Then
Sir Bors made him ready, and came forth out of the town, and there
Sir Gawaine encountered with Sir Bors. And at that time he smote
Sir Bors down from his horse, and almost he had slain him; and so Sir

Bors was rescued and borne into the town. Then came forth Sir
Lionel, brother to Sir Bors, and thought to revenge him; and either
feutred their spears, and ran together; and there they met spitefully,
but Sir Gawaine had such grace that he smote Sir Lionel down, and
wounded him there passing sore; and then Sir Lionel was rescued and
borne into the town. And this Sir Gawaine came every day, and he
failed not but that he smote down one knight or other.

So thus they endured half a year, and much slaughter was of people
on both parties. Then it befell upon a day, Sir Gawaine came afore
the gates armed at all pieces on a noble horse, with a great spear in his
hand; and then he cried with a loud voice: Where art thou now,
thou false traitor, Sir Launcelot? Why hidest thou thyself within holes
and walls like a coward? Look out now, thou false traitor knight, and
here I shall revenge upon thy body the death of my three brethren.
All this language heard Sir Launcelot every deal; and his kin and his
knights drew about him, and all they said at once to Sir Launcelot: Sir
Launcelot, now must ye defend you like a knight, or else ye be
shamed for ever; for, now ye be called upon treason, it is time for you
to stir, for ye have slept over-long and suffered over-much. So God
me help, said Sir Launcelot, I am right heavy of Sir Gawaine's words,
for now he charged me with a great charge; and therefore I wot it as
well as ye, that I must defend me, or else to be recreant.

Then Sir Launcelot bade saddle his strongest horse, and bade let
fetch his arms, and bring all unto the gate of the tower; and then Sir
Launcelot spake on high unto King Arthur, and said: My lord Arthur,
and noble king that made me knight, wit you well I am right heavy
for your sake, that ye thus sue upon me; and always I forbare you, for
an I would have been vengeable, I might have met you in midst of
the field, and there to have made your boldest knights full tame. And
now I have forborne half a year, and suffered you and Sir Gawaine to
do what ye would do; and now may I endure it no longer, for now
must I needs defend myself, insomuch Sir Gawaine hath appealed me
of treason; the which is greatly against my will that ever I should fight
against any of your blood, but now I may not forsake it, I am driven
thereto as a beast till a bay.

Then Sir Gawaine said: Sir Launcelot, an thou durst do battle, leave
thy babbling and come off, and let us ease our hearts. Then Sir
Launcelot armed him lightly, and mounted upon his horse, and either
of the knights gat great spears in their hands, and the host without

stood still all apart, and the noble knights came out of the city by a great number, insomuch that when Arthur saw the number of men and knights, he marvelled, and said to himself: Alas, that ever Sir Launcelot was against me, for now I see he hath forborne me. And so the covenant was made, there should no man nigh them, nor deal with them, till the one were dead or yelden.

<h2 style="text-align:center">CHAPTER XXI</h2>

How Sir Launcelot and Sir Gawaine did battle together, and how Sir Gawaine was overthrown and hurt.

Then Sir Gawaine and Sir Launcelot departed a great way asunder, and then they came together with all their horses' might as they might run, and either smote other in midst of their shields; but the knights were so strong, and their spears so big, that their horses might not endure their buffets, and so their horses fell to the earth; and then they avoided their horses, and dressed their shields afore them. Then they stood together and gave many sad strokes on divers places of their bodies, that the blood brast out on many sides and places. Then had Sir Gawaine such a grace and gift that an holy man had given to him, that every day in the year, from underne till high noon, his might increased those three hours as much as thrice his strength, and that caused Sir Gawaine to win great honour. And for his sake King Arthur made an ordinance, that all manner of battles for any quarrels that should be done afore King Arthur should begin at underne; and all was done for Sir Gawaine's love, that by likelihood, if Sir Gawaine were on the one part, he should have the better in battle while his strength endureth three hours; but there were but few knights that time living that knew this advantage that Sir Gawaine had, but King Arthur all only.

Thus Sir Launcelot fought with Sir Gawaine, and when Sir Launcelot felt his might evermore increase, Sir Launcelot wondered and dread him sore to be shamed. For as the French book saith, Sir Launcelot weened, when he felt Sir Gawaine double his strength, that he had been a fiend and none earthly man; wherefore Sir Launcelot traced and traversed, and covered himself with his shield, and kept his might and his braide during three hours; and that while Sir Gawaine gave him many sad brunts, and many sad strokes, that all the knights that beheld Sir Launcelot marvelled how that he might endure him; but full little understood they that travail that Sir Launcelot had for to endure him. And then when it was past noon Sir Gawaine had no more but his own might. When Sir Launcelot felt him so come down, then he stretched him up and stood near Sir Gawaine, and said thus: My lord Sir Gawaine, now I feel ye have done; now my lord Sir Gawaine, I must do my part, for many great and grievous strokes I have endured you this day with great pain.

Then Sir Launcelot doubled his strokes and gave Sir Gawaine such a buffet on the helmet that he fell down on his side, and Sir Launcelot withdrew him from him. Why withdrawest thou thee? said Sir Gawaine; now turn again, false traitor knight, and slay me, for an thou leave me thus, when I am whole I shall do battle with thee again. I shall endure you, Sir, by God's grace, but wit thou well, Sir Gawaine, I will never smite a felled knight. And so Sir Launcelot went into the city; and Sir Gawaine was borne into King Arthur's pavilion, and leeches were brought to him, and searched and salved with soft ointments. And then Sir Launcelot said: Now have good day, my lord the king, for wit you well ye win no worship at these walls; and if I would my knights outbring, there should many a man die. Therefore, my lord Arthur, remember you of old kindness; and however I fare, Jesu be your guide in all places.

CHAPTER XXII

Of the sorrow that King Arthur made for the war, and of another battle where also Sir Gawaine had the worse.

Alas, said the king, that ever this unhappy war was begun; for ever Sir Launcelot forbeareth me in all places, and in likewise my kin, and that is seen well this day by my nephew Sir Gawaine. Then King Arthur fell sick for sorrow of Sir Gawaine, that he was so sore hurt, and because of the war betwixt him and Sir Launcelot. So then they on King Arthur's part kept the siege with little war withoutforth; and they withinforth kept their walls, and defended them when need was.

Thus Sir Gawaine lay sick three weeks in his tents, with all manner of leechcraft that might be had. And as soon as Sir Gawaine might go and ride, he armed him at all points, and start upon a courser, and gat a spear in his hand, and so he came riding afore the chief gate of Benwick; and there he cried on height: Where art thou, Sir Launcelot? Come forth, thou false traitor knight and recreant, for I am here, Sir Gawaine, will prove this that I say on thee.

All this language Sir Launcelot heard, and then he said thus: Sir Gawaine, me repents of your foul saying, that ye will not cease of your language; for you wot well, Sir Gawaine, I know your might and all that ye may do; and well ye wot, Sir Gawaine, ye may not greatly hurt me. Come down, traitor knight, said he, and make it good the contrary with thy hands, for it mishapped me the last battle to be hurt of thy hands; therefore wit thou well I am come this day to make amends, for I ween this day to lay thee as low as thou laidest me. Jesu defend me, said Sir Launcelot, that ever I be so far in your danger as ye have been in mine, for then my days were done. But Sir Gawaine, said Sir Launcelot, ye shall not think that I tarry long, but sithen that ye so unknightly call me of treason, ye shall have both your hands full of me. And then Sir Launcelot armed him at all points, and mounted upon his horse, and gat a great spear in his hand, and rode out at the gate. And both the hosts were assembled, of them without and of them within, and stood in array full manly. And both parties were charged to hold them still, to see and behold the battle of these two noble knights. And then they laid their spears in their rests, and they came together as thunder, and Sir Gawaine brake his spear upon Sir Launcelot in a hundred pieces unto his hand; and Sir Launcelot smote him with a greater might, that Sir Gawaine's horse's feet raised, and so the horse and he fell to the earth. Then Sir Gawaine deliverly avoided his horse, and put his shield afore him, and eagerly drew his sword, and bade Sir Launcelot: Alight, traitor knight, for if this mare's son hath failed me, wit thou well a king's son and a queen's son shall not fail thee.

Then Sir Launcelot avoided his horse, and dressed his shield afore him, and drew his sword; and so stood they together and gave many sad strokes, that all men on both parties had thereof passing great wonder. But when Sir Launcelot felt Sir Gawaine's might so marvellously increase, he then withheld his courage and his wind, and kept himself wonder covert of his might; and under his shield he traced and traversed here and there, to break Sir Gawaine's strokes and his courage; and Sir Gawaine enforced himself with all his might and power to destroy Sir Launcelot; for as the French book saith, ever as Sir Gawaine's might increased, right so increased his wind and his evil will. Thus Sir Gawaine did great pain unto Sir Launcelot three hours, that he had right great pain for to defend him.

And when the three hours were passed, that Sir Launcelot felt that Sir Gawaine was come to his own proper strength, then Sir Launcelot said unto Sir Gawaine: Now have I proved you twice, that ye are a full dangerous knight, and a wonderful man of your might; and many wonderful deeds have ye done in your days, for by your might increasing you have deceived many a full noble and valiant knight; and, now I feel that ye have done your mighty deeds, now wit you well I must do my deeds. And then Sir Launcelot stood near Sir Gawaine, and then Sir Launcelot doubled his strokes; and Sir Gawaine defended him mightily, but nevertheless Sir Launcelot smote such a stroke upon Sir Gawaine's helm, and upon the old wound, that Sir Gawaine sinked down upon his one side in a swoon. And anon as he did awake he waved and foined at Sir Launcelot as he lay, and said: Traitor knight, wit thou well I am not yet slain, come thou near me and perform this battle unto the uttermost. I will no more do than I have done, said Sir Launcelot, for when I see you on foot I will do battle upon you all the while I see you stand on your feet; but for to smite a wounded man that may not stand, God defend me from such a shame. And then he turned him and went his way toward the city. And Sir Gawaine evermore calling him traitor knight, and said: Wit thou well Sir Launcelot, when I am whole I shall do battle with thee again, for I shall never leave thee till that one of us be slain. Thus as this siege endured, and as Sir Gawaine lay sick near a month; and when he was well recovered and ready within three days to do battle again with Sir Launcelot, right so came tidings unto Arthur from England that made King Arthur and all his host to remove.

Here followeth the xxi. book.

BOOK TWENTY-ONE

CHAPTER I

How Sir Mordred presumed and took on him to be King of England, and would have married the queen, his father's wife.

As Sir Mordred was ruler of all England, he did do make letters as though that they came from beyond the sea, and the letters specified that King Arthur was slain in battle with Sir Launcelot. Wherefore Sir Mordred made a parliament, and called the lords together, and there he made them to choose him king; and so was he crowned at Canterbury, and held a feast there fifteen days; and afterward he drew him unto Winchester, and there he took the Queen Guenever, and said plainly that he would wed her which was his uncle's wife and his father's wife. And so he made ready for the feast, and a day prefixed that they should be wedded; wherefore Queen Guenever was passing heavy. But she durst not discover her heart, but spake fair, and agreed to Sir Mordred's will. Then she desired of Sir Mordred for to go to London, to buy all manner of things that longed unto the wedding. And because of her fair speech Sir Mordred trusted her well enough, and gave her leave to go. And so when she came to London she took the Tower of London, and suddenly in all haste possible she stuffed it with all manner of victual, and well garnished it with men, and so kept it.

Then when Sir Mordred wist and understood how he was beguiled, he was passing wroth out of measure. And a short tale for to make, he went and laid a mighty siege about the Tower of London, and made many great assaults thereat, and threw many great engines unto them, and shot great guns. But all might not prevail Sir Mordred, for Queen Guenever would never for fair speech nor for foul, would never trust to come in his hands again.

Then came the Bishop of Canterbury, the which was a noble clerk and an holy man, and thus he said to Sir Mordred: Sir, what will ye do? will ye first displease God and sithen shame yourself, and all knighthood? Is not King Arthur your uncle, no farther but your mother's brother, and on her himself King Arthur begat you upon his own sister, therefore how may you wed your father's wife? Sir, said the noble clerk, leave this opinion or I shall curse you with book and bell and candle. Do thou thy worst, said Sir Mordred, wit thou well I shall defy thee. Sir, said the Bishop, and wit you well I shall not fear me to do that me ought to do. Also where ye noise where my lord Arthur is slain, and that is not so, and therefore ye will make a foul work in this land. Peace, thou false priest, said Sir Mordred, for an thou chafe me any more I shall make strike off thy head. So the Bishop departed and did the cursing in the most orgulist wise that might be done. And then Sir Mordred sought the Bishop of Canterbury, for to have slain him. Then the Bishop fled, and took part of his goods with him, and went nigh unto Glastonbury; and there he was as priest hermit in a chapel, and lived in poverty and in holy prayers, for well he understood that mischievous war was at hand.

Then Sir Mordred sought on Queen Guenever by letters and sonds, and by fair means and foul means, for to have her to come out of the Tower of London; but all this availed not, for she answered him shortly, openly and privily, that she had liefer slay herself than to be married with him. Then came word to Sir Mordred that King Arthur had araised the siege for Sir Launcelot, and he was coming homeward with a great host, to be avenged upon Sir Mordred; wherefore Sir Mordred made write writs to all the barony of this land, and much people drew to him. For then was the common voice among them that with Arthur was none other life but war and strife, and with Sir Mordred was great joy and bliss. Thus was Sir Arthur depraved, and evil said of. And many there were that King Arthur had made up of nought, and given them lands, might not then say him a good word. Lo ye all Englishmen, see ye not what a mischief here was! for he that was the most king and knight of the world, and most loved the fellowship of noble knights, and by him they were all upholden, now might not these Englishmen hold them content with him. Lo thus was the old custom and usage of this land; and also men say that we of this land have not yet lost nor forgotten that custom and usage. Alas, this is a great default of us Englishmen, for there may no thing please us no term. And so fared the people at that time, they were better pleased with Sir Mordred than they were with King Arthur; and much people drew unto Sir Mordred, and said they would abide with him for better and for worse. And so Sir Mordred drew with a great host to Dover, for there he heard say that Sir Arthur would arrive, and so he thought to beat his own father from his lands; and the most part of all England held with Sir Mordred, the people were so new-fangle.

CHAPTER II

How after that King Arthur had tidings, he returned and came to Dover, where Sir Mordred met him to let his landing; and of the death of Sir Gawaine.

And so as Sir Mordred was at Dover with his host, there came King Arthur with a great navy of ships, and galleys, and carracks. And there was Sir Mordred ready awaiting upon his landing, to let his own father to land upon the land that he was king over. Then there was launching of great boats and small, and full of noble men of arms; and there was much slaughter of gentle knights, and many a full bold baron was laid full low, on both parties. But King Arthur was so courageous that there might no manner of knights let him to land, and his knights fiercely followed him; and so they landed maugre Sir Mordred and all his power, and put Sir Mordred aback, that he fled and all his people.

So when this battle was done, King Arthur let bury his people that were dead. And then was noble Sir Gawaine found in a great boat, lying more than half dead. When Sir Arthur wist that Sir Gawaine was laid so low, he went unto him; and there the king made sorrow out of measure, and took Sir Gawaine in his arms, and thrice he there swooned. And then when he awaked, he said: Alas, Sir Gawaine, my sister's son, here now thou liest, the man in the world that I loved most; and now is my joy gone, for now, my nephew Sir Gawaine, I will discover me unto your person: in Sir Launcelot and you I most had my joy, and mine affiance, and now have I lost my joy of you both; wherefore all mine earthly joy is gone from me. Mine uncle King Arthur, said Sir Gawaine, wit you well my death-day is come, and all is through mine own hastiness and wilfulness; for I am smitten upon the old wound the which Sir Launcelot gave me, on the which I feel well I must die; and had Sir Launcelot been with you as he was, this unhappy war had never begun; and of all this am I causer, for Sir Launcelot and his blood, through their prowess, held all your cankered enemies in subjection and daunger. And now, said Sir Gawaine, ye shall miss Sir Launcelot. But alas, I would not accord with him, and therefore, said Sir Gawaine, I pray you, fair uncle, that I may have paper, pen, and ink, that I may write to Sir Launcelot a cedle with mine own hands.

And then when paper and ink was brought, then Gawaine was set up weakly by King Arthur, for he was shriven a little to-fore; and then he wrote thus, as the French book maketh mention: Unto Sir Launcelot, flower of all noble knights that ever I heard of or saw by my days, I, Sir Gawaine, King Lot's son of Orkney, sister's son unto the noble King Arthur, send thee greeting, and let thee have knowledge that the tenth day of May I was smitten upon the old wound that thou gavest me afore the city of Benwick, and through the same wound that thou gavest me I am come to my death-day. And I will that all the world wit, that I, Sir Gawaine, knight of the Table Round, sought my death, and not through thy deserving, but it was mine own seeking; wherefore I beseech thee, Sir Launcelot, to return again unto this realm, and see my tomb, and pray some prayer more or less for my soul. And this same day that I wrote this cedle, I was hurt to the death in the same wound, the which I had of thy hand, Sir Launcelot; for of a more nobler man might I not be slain. Also Sir Launcelot, for all the love that ever was betwixt us, make no tarrying, but come over the sea in all haste, that thou mayst with thy noble knights rescue that noble king that made thee knight, that is my lord Arthur; for he is full straitly bestead with a false traitor, that is my half-brother, Sir Mordred; and he hath let crown him king, and would have wedded my lady Queen Guenever, and so had he done had she not put herself in the Tower of London. And so the tenth day of May last past, my lord Arthur and we all landed upon them at Dover; and there we put that false traitor, Sir Mordred, to flight, and there it misfortuned me to be stricken upon thy stroke. And at the date of this letter was written, but two hours and a half afore my death, written with mine own hand, and so subscribed with part of my heart's blood. And I require thee, most famous knight of the world, that thou wilt see my tomb. And then Sir Gawaine wept, and King Arthur wept; and then they swooned both. And when they awaked both, the king made Sir Gawaine to receive his Saviour. And then Sir Gawaine prayed the king for to send for Sir Launcelot, and to cherish him above all other knights.

And so at the hour of noon Sir Gawaine yielded up the spirit; and then the king let inter him in a chapel within Dover Castle; and there yet all men may see the skull of him, and the same wound is seen that Sir Launcelot gave him in battle. Then was it told the king that Sir Mordred had pight a new field upon Barham Down. And upon the morn the king rode thither to him, and there was a great battle betwixt them, and much people was slain on both parties; but at the last Sir Arthur's party stood best, and Sir Mordred and his party fled unto Canterbury.

CHAPTER III

How after, Sir Gawaine's ghost appeared to King Arthur, and warned him that he should not fight that day.

And then the king let search all the towns for his knights that were slain, and interred them; and salved them with soft salves that so sore were wounded. Then much people drew unto King Arthur. And then they said that Sir Mordred warred upon King Arthur with wrong. And then King Arthur drew him with his host down by the seaside, westward toward Salisbury; and there was a day assigned betwixt King Arthur and Sir Mordred, that they should meet upon a down beside Salisbury, and not far from the seaside; and this day was assigned on a Monday after Trinity Sunday, whereof King Arthur was passing glad, that he might be avenged upon Sir Mordred. Then Sir Mordred araised much people about London, for they of Kent, Southsex, and Surrey, Estsex, and of Southfolk, and of Northfolk, held the most part with Sir Mordred; and many a full noble knight drew unto Sir Mordred and to the king: but they that loved Sir Launcelot drew unto Sir Mordred.

So upon Trinity Sunday at night, King Arthur dreamed a wonderful dream, and that was this: that him seemed he sat upon a chaflet in a chair, and the chair was fast to a wheel, and thereupon sat King Arthur in the richest cloth of gold that might be made; and the king thought there was under him, far from him, an hideous deep black water, and therein were all manner of serpents, and worms, and wild beasts, foul and horrible; and suddenly the king thought the wheel turned up-so-down, and he fell among the serpents, and every beast took him by a limb; and then the king cried as he lay in his bed and slept: Help. And then knights, squires, and yeomen, awaked the king; and then he was so amazed that he wist not where he was; and then he fell a-slumbering again, not sleeping nor thoroughly waking. So the king seemed verily that there came Sir Gawaine unto him with a number of fair ladies with him. And when King Arthur saw him, then he said: Welcome, my sister's son; I weened thou hadst been dead, and now I see thee alive, much am I beholding unto Almighty Jesu. O fair nephew and my sister's son, what be these ladies that hither be come with you? Sir, said Sir Gawaine, all these be ladies for whom I have foughten when I was man living, and all these are those that I did battle for in righteous quarrel; and God hath given them that grace at their great prayer, because I did battle for them, that they should bring me hither unto you: thus much hath God given me leave, for to warn you of your death; for an ye fight as to-morn with Sir Mordred, as ye both have assigned, doubt ye not ye must be slain, and the most part of your people on both parties. And for the great grace and goodness that almighty Jesu hath unto you, and for pity of you, and many more other good men there shall be slain, God hath sent me to you of his special grace, to give you warning that in no wise ye do battle as to-morn, but that ye take a treaty for a month day; and proffer you largely, so as to-morn to be put in a delay. For within a month shall come Sir Launcelot with all his noble knights, and rescue you worshipfully, and slay Sir Mordred, and all that ever will hold with him. Then Sir Gawaine and all the ladies vanished.

And anon the king called upon his knights, squires, and yeomen, and charged them wightly to fetch his noble lords and wise bishops unto him. And when they were come, the king told them his avision, what Sir Gawaine had told him, and warned him that if he fought on the morn he should be slain. Then the king commanded Sir Lucan the Butler, and his brother Sir Bedivere, with two bishops with them, and charged them in any wise, an they might Take a treaty for a month day with Sir Mordred, and spare not, proffer him lands and goods as much as ye think best. So then they departed, and came to Sir Mordred, where he had a grim host of an hundred thousand men. And there they entreated Sir Mordred long time; and at the last Sir Mordred was agreed for to have Cornwall and Kent, by Arthur's days: after, all England, after the days of King Arthur.

CHAPTER IV

*How by misadventure of an adder the battle began, where
Mordred was slain, and Arthur hurt to the death.*

Then were they condescended that King Arthur and Sir Mordred should meet betwixt both their hosts, and everych of them should bring fourteen persons; and they came with this word unto Arthur. Then said he: I am glad that this is done: and so he went into the field. And when Arthur should depart, he warned all his host that an they see any sword drawn: Look ye come on fiercely, and slay that traitor, Sir Mordred, for I in no wise trust him. In like wise Sir Mordred warned his host that: An ye see any sword drawn, look that ye come on fiercely, and so slay all that ever before you standeth; for in no wise I will not trust for this treaty, for I know well my father will be avenged on me. And so they met as their appointment was, and so they were agreed and accorded thoroughly; and wine was fetched, and they drank. Right soon came an adder out of a little heath bush, and it stung a knight on the foot. And when the knight felt him stung, he looked down and saw the adder, and then he drew his sword to slay the adder, and thought of none other harm. And when the host on both parties saw that sword drawn, then they blew beams, trumpets, and horns, and shouted grimly. And so both hosts dressed them together. And King Arthur took his horse, and said: Alas this unhappy day! and so rode to his party. And Sir Mordred in like wise. And never was there seen a more dolefuller battle in no Christian land; for there was but rushing and riding, foining and striking, and many a grim word was there spoken either to other, and many a deadly stroke. But ever King Arthur rode throughout the battle of Sir Mordred many times, and did full nobly as a noble king should, and at all times he fainted never; and Sir Mordred that day put him in devoir, and in great peril. And thus they fought all the long day, and never stinted till the noble knights were laid to the cold earth; and ever they fought still till it was near night, and by that time was there an hundred thousand laid dead upon the down. Then was Arthur wood wroth out of measure, when he saw his people so slain from him.

Then the king looked about him, and then was he ware, of all his host and of all his good knights, were left no more alive but two knights; that one was Sir Lucan the Butler, and his brother Sir Bedivere, and they were full sore wounded. Jesu mercy, said the king, where are all my noble knights become? Alas that ever I should see this doleful day, for now, said Arthur, I am come to mine end. But would to God that I wist where were that traitor Sir Mordred, that hath caused all this mischief. Then was King Arthur ware where Sir Mordred leaned upon his sword among a great heap of dead men. Now give me my spear, said Arthur unto Sir Lucan, for yonder I have espied the traitor that all this woe hath wrought. Sir, let him be, said Sir Lucan, for he is unhappy; and if ye pass this unhappy day ye shall be right well revenged upon him. Good lord, remember ye of your night's dream, and what the spirit of Sir Gawaine told you this night, yet God of his great goodness hath preserved you hitherto. Therefore, for God's sake, my lord, leave off by this, for blessed be God ye have won the field, for here we be three alive, and with Sir Mordred is none alive: and if you leave off now this wicked day of destiny is past. Tide me death, betide me life, saith the king, now I see him yonder alone he shall never escape mine hands, for at a better avail shall I never have him. God speed you well, said Sir Bedivere.

Then the king gat his spear in both his hands, and ran toward Sir Mordred, crying: Traitor, now is thy deathday come. And when Sir Mordred heard Sir Arthur, he ran until him with his sword drawn in his hand. And there King Arthur smote Sir Mordred under the shield, with a foin of his spear, throughout the body, more than a fathom. And when Sir Mordred felt that he had his death wound he thrust himself with the might that he had up to the bur of King Arthur's spear. And right so he smote his father Arthur, with his sword holden in both his hands, on the side of the head, that the sword pierced the helmet and the brain-pan, and therewithal Sir Mordred fell stark dead to the earth; and the noble Arthur fell in a swoon to the earth, and there he swooned ofttimes. And Sir Lucan the Butler and Sir Bedivere ofttimes heaved him up. And so weakly they led him betwixt them both, to a little chapel not far from the seaside. And when the king was there he thought him well eased.

Then heard they people cry in the field. Now go thou, Sir Lucan, said the king, and do me to wit what betokens that noise in the field. So Sir Lucan departed, for he was grievously wounded in many places. And so as he yede, he saw and hearkened by the moonlight, how that pillers and robbers were come into the field, to pill and to rob many a full noble knight of brooches, and beads, of many a good ring, and of many a rich jewel; and who that were not dead all out, there they slew them for their harness and their riches. When Sir Lucan understood this work, he came to the king as soon as he might, and told him all what he had heard and seen. Therefore by my rede, said Sir Lucan, it is best that we bring you to some town. I would it were so, said the king.

CHAPTER V

How King Arthur commanded to cast his sword Excalibur into the water, and how he was delivered to ladies in a barge.

But I may not stand, mine head works so. Ah Sir Launcelot, said King Arthur, this day have I sore missed thee: alas, that ever I was against thee, for now have I my death, whereof Sir Gawaine me warned in my dream. Then Sir Lucan took up the king the one part, and Sir Bedivere the other part, and in the lifting the king swooned; and Sir Lucan fell in a swoon with the lift, that the part of his guts fell out of his body, and therewith the noble knight's heart brast. And when the king awoke, he beheld Sir Lucan, how he lay foaming at the mouth, and part of his guts lay at his feet. Alas, said the king, this is to me a full heavy sight, to see this noble duke so die for my sake, for he would have holpen me, that had more need of help than I. Alas, he would not complain him, his heart was so set to help me: now Jesu have mercy upon his soul! Then Sir Bedivere wept for the death of his brother. Leave this mourning and weeping, said the king, for all this will not avail me, for wit thou well an I might live myself, the death of Sir Lucan would grieve me evermore; but my time hieth fast, said the king. Therefore, said Arthur unto Sir Bedivere, take thou Excalibur, my good sword, and go with it to yonder water side, and when thou comest there I charge thee throw my sword in that water, and come again and tell me what thou there seest. My lord, said Bedivere, your commandment shall be done, and lightly bring you word again.

So Sir Bedivere departed, and by the way he beheld that noble sword, that the pommel and the haft was all of precious stones; and then he said to himself: If I throw this rich sword in the water, thereof shall never come good, but harm and loss. And then Sir Bedivere hid Excalibur under a tree. And so, as soon as he might, he came again unto the king, and said he had been at the water, and had thrown the sword in the water. What saw thou there? said the king. Sir, he said, I saw nothing but waves and winds. That is untruly said of thee, said the king, therefore go thou lightly again, and do my commandment; as thou art to me lief and dear, spare not, but throw it in. Then Sir Bedivere returned again, and took the sword in his hand; and then him thought sin and shame to throw away that noble sword, and so eft he hid the sword, and returned again, and told to the king that he had been at the water, and done his commandment. What saw thou there? said the king. Sir, he said, I saw nothing but the waters wap and waves wan. Ah, traitor untrue, said King Arthur, now hast thou betrayed me twice. Who would have weened that, thou that hast been to me so lief and dear? and thou art named a noble knight, and would betray me for the richness of the sword. But now go again lightly, for thy long tarrying putteth me in great jeopardy of my life, for I have taken cold. And but if thou do now as I bid thee, if ever I may see thee, I shall slay thee with mine own hands; for thou wouldst for my rich sword see me dead.

Then Sir Bedivere departed, and went to the sword, and lightly took it up, and went to the water side; and there he bound the girdle about the hilts, and then he threw the sword as far into the water as he might; and there came an arm and an hand above the water and met it, and caught it, and so shook it thrice and brandished, and then vanished away the hand with the sword in the water. So Sir Bedivere came again to the king, and told him what he saw. Alas, said the king, help me hence, for I dread me I have tarried over long. Then Sir Bedivere took the king upon his back, and so went with him to that water side. And when they were at the water side, even fast by the bank hoved a little barge with many fair ladies in it, and among them all was a queen, and all they had black hoods, and all they wept and shrieked when they saw King Arthur. Now put me into the barge, said the king. And so he did softly; and there received him three queens with great mourning; and so they set them down, and in one of their laps King Arthur laid his head. And then that queen said: Ah, dear brother, why have ye tarried so long from me? alas, this wound on your head hath caught over-much cold. And so then they rowed from the land, and Sir Bedivere beheld all those ladies go from him. Then Sir Bedivere cried: Ah my lord Arthur, what shall become of me, now ye go from me and leave me here alone among mine enemies? Comfort thyself, said the king, and do as well as thou mayst, for in me is no trust for to trust in; for I will into the vale of Avilion to heal me of my grievous wound: and if thou hear never more of me, pray for my soul. But ever the queens and ladies wept and shrieked, that it was pity to hear. And as soon as Sir Bedivere had lost the sight of the barge, he wept and wailed, and so took the forest; and so he went all that night, and in the morning he was ware betwixt two holts hoar, of a chapel and an hermitage.

CHAPTER VI

How Sir Bedivere found him on the morrow dead in an hermitage, and how he abode there with the hermit.

Then was Sir Bedivere glad, and thither he went; and when he came into the chapel, he saw where lay an hermit grovelling on all four, there fast by a tomb was new graven. When the hermit saw Sir Bedivere he knew him well, for he was but little to-fore Bishop of Canterbury, that Sir Mordred flemed. Sir, said Bedivere, what man is there interred that ye pray so fast for? Fair son, said the hermit, I wot not verily, but by deeming. But this night, at midnight, here came a number of ladies, and brought hither a dead corpse, and prayed me to bury him; and here they offered an hundred tapers, and they gave me an hundred besants. Alas, said Sir Bedivere, that was my lord King Arthur, that here lieth buried in this chapel. Then Sir Bedivere swooned; and when he awoke he prayed the hermit he might abide with him still there, to live with fasting and prayers. For from hence will I never go, said Sir Bedivere, by my will, but all the days of my life here to pray for my lord Arthur. Ye are welcome to me, said the hermit, for I know ye better than ye ween that I do. Ye are the bold Bedivere, and the full noble duke, Sir Lucan the Butler, was your brother. Then Sir Bedivere told the hermit all as ye have heard to-fore. So there bode Sir Bedivere with the hermit that was to-fore Bishop of Canterbury, and there Sir Bedivere put upon him poor clothes, and served the hermit full lowly in fasting and in prayers.

Thus of Arthur I find never more written in books that be authorised, nor more of the very certainty of his death heard I never read, but thus was he led away in a ship wherein were three queens; that one was King Arthur's sister, Queen Morgan le Fay; the other was the Queen of Northgalis; the third was the Queen of the Waste Lands. Also there was Nimue, the chief lady of the lake, that had wedded Pelleas the good knight; and this lady had done much for King Arthur, for she would never suffer Sir Pelleas to be in no place where he should be in danger of his life; and so he lived to the uttermost of his days with her in great rest. More of the death of King Arthur could I never find, but that ladies brought him to his burials; and such one was buried there, that the hermit bare witness that sometime was Bishop of Canterbury, but yet the hermit knew not in certain that he was verily the body of King Arthur: for this tale Sir Bedivere, knight of the Table Round, made it to be written.

CHAPTER VII

Of the opinion of some men of the death of King Arthur; and how Queen Guenever made her a nun in Almesbury.

Yet some men say in many parts of England that King Arthur is not dead, but had by the will of our Lord Jesu into another place; and men say that he shall come again, and he shall win the holy cross. I will not say it shall be so, but rather I will say: here in this world he changed his life. But many men say that there is written upon his tomb this verse:

Hic jacet Arthurus, Rex quondam, Rexque futurus.

Thus leave I here Sir Bedivere with the hermit, that dwelled that time in a chapel beside Glastonbury, and there was his hermitage. And so they lived in their prayers, and fastings, and great abstinence. And when Queen Guenever understood that King Arthur was slain, and all the noble knights, Sir Mordred and all the remnant, then the queen stole away, and five ladies with her, and so she went to Almesbury; and there she let make herself a nun, and ware white clothes and black, and great penance she took, as ever did sinful lady in this land, and never creature could make her merry; but lived in fasting, prayers, and alms-deeds, that all manner of people marvelled how virtuously she was changed. Now leave we Queen Guenever in Almesbury, a nun in white clothes and black, and there she was Abbess and ruler as reason would; and turn we from her, and speak we of Sir Launcelot du Lake.

CHAPTER VIII

*How when Sir Launcelot heard of the death of
King Arthur, and of Sir Gawaine, and other matters,
he came into England.*

And when he heard in his country that Sir Mordred was crowned king in England, and made war against King Arthur, his own father, and would let him to land in his own land; also it was told Sir Launcelot how that Sir Mordred had laid siege about the Tower of London, because the queen would not wed him; then was Sir Launcelot wroth out of measure, and said to his kinsmen: Alas, that double traitor Sir Mordred, now me repenteth that ever he escaped my hands, for much shame hath he done unto my lord Arthur; for all I feel by the doleful letter that my lord Sir Gawaine sent me, on whose soul Jesu have mercy, that my lord Arthur is full hard bestead. Alas, said Sir Launcelot, that ever I should live to hear that most noble king that made me knight thus to be overset with his subject in his own realm. And this doleful letter that my lord, Sir Gawaine, hath sent me afore his death, praying me to see his tomb, wit you well his doleful words shall never go from mine heart, for he was a full noble knight as ever was born; and in an unhappy hour was I born that ever I should have that unhap to slay first Sir Gawaine, Sir Gaheris the good knight, and mine own friend Sir Gareth, that full noble knight. Alas, I may say I am unhappy, said Sir Launcelot, that ever I should do thus unhappily, and, alas, yet might I never have hap to slay that traitor, Sir Mordred.

Leave your complaints, said Sir Bors, and first revenge you of the death of Sir Gawaine; and it will be well done that ye see Sir Gawaine's tomb, and secondly that ye revenge my lord Arthur, and my lady, Queen Guenever. I thank you, said Sir Launcelot, for ever ye will my worship.

Then they made them ready in all the haste that might be, with ships and galleys, with Sir Launcelot and his host to pass into England. And so he passed over the sea till he came to Dover, and there he landed with seven kings, and the number was hideous to behold. Then Sir Launcelot spered of men of Dover where was King Arthur become. Then the people told him how that he was slain, and Sir Mordred and an hundred thousand died on a day; and how Sir Mordred gave King Arthur there the first battle at his landing, and there was good Sir Gawaine slain; and on the morn Sir Mordred fought with the king upon Barham Down, and there the king put Sir Mordred to the worse. Alas, said Sir Launcelot, this is the heaviest tidings that ever came to me. Now, fair sirs, said Sir Launcelot, show me the tomb of Sir Gawaine. And then certain people of the town brought him into the castle of Dover, and showed him the tomb. Then Sir Launcelot kneeled down and wept, and prayed heartily for his soul. And that night he made a dole, and all they that would come had as much flesh, fish, wine and ale, and every man and woman had twelve pence, come who would. Thus with his own hand dealt he this money, in a mourning gown; and ever he wept, and prayed them to pray for the soul of Sir Gawaine. And on the morn all the priests and clerks that might be gotten in the country were there, and sang mass of Requiem; and there offered first Sir Launcelot, and he offered an hundred pound; and then the seven kings offered forty pound apiece; and also there was a thousand knights, and each of them offered a pound; and the offering dured from morn till night, and Sir Launcelot lay two nights on his tomb in prayers and weeping.

Then on the third day Sir Launcelot called the kings, dukes, earls, barons, and knights, and said thus: My fair lords, I thank you all of your coming into this country with me, but we came too late, and that shall repent me while I live, but against death may no man rebel. But sithen it is so, said Sir Launcelot, I will myself ride and seek my lady, Queen Guenever, for as I hear say she hath had great pain and much disease; and I heard say that she is fled into the west. Therefore ye all shall abide me here, and but if I come again within fifteen days, then take your ships and your fellowship, and depart into your country, for I will do as I say to you.

CHAPTER IX

How Sir Launcelot departed to seek the Queen Guenever, and how he found her at Almesbury.

Then came Sir Bors de Ganis, and said: My lord Sir Launcelot, what think ye for to do, now to ride in this realm? wit ye well ye shall find few friends. Be as be may, said Sir Launcelot, keep you still here, for I will forth on my journey, and no man nor child shall go with me. So it was no boot to strive, but he departed and rode westerly, and there he sought a seven or eight days; and at the last he came to a nunnery, and then was Queen Guenever ware of Sir Launcelot as he walked in the cloister. And when she saw him there she swooned thrice, that all the ladies and gentlewomen had work enough to hold the queen up. So when she might speak, she called ladies and gentlewomen to her, and said: Ye marvel, fair ladies, why I make this fare. Truly, she said, it is for the sight of yonder knight that yonder standeth; wherefore I pray you all call him to me.

When Sir Launcelot was brought to her, then she said to all the ladies: Through this man and me hath all this war been wrought, and the death of the most noblest knights of the world; for through our love that we have loved together is my most noble lord slain. Therefore, Sir Launcelot, wit thou well I am set in such a plight to get my soul-heal; and yet I trust through God's grace that after my death to have a sight of the blessed face of Christ, and at domesday to sit on his right side, for as sinful as ever I was are saints in heaven. Therefore, Sir Launcelot, I require thee and beseech thee heartily, for all the love that ever was betwixt us, that thou never see me more in the visage; and I command thee, on God's behalf, that thou forsake my company, and to thy kingdom thou turn again, and keep well thy realm from war and wrack; for as well as I have loved thee, mine heart will not serve me to see thee, for through thee and me is the flower of kings and knights destroyed; therefore, Sir Launcelot, go to thy realm, and there take thee a wife, and live with her with joy and bliss; and I pray thee heartily, pray for me to our Lord that I may amend my misliving. Now, sweet madam, said Sir Launcelot, would ye that I should now return again unto my country, and there to wed a lady? Nay, madam, wit you well that shall I never do, for I shall never be so false to you of that I have promised; but the same destiny that ye have taken you to, I will take me unto, for to please Jesu, and ever for you I cast me specially to pray. If thou wilt do so, said the queen, hold thy promise, but I may never believe but that thou wilt turn to the world again. Well, madam, said he, ye say as pleaseth you, yet wist you me never false of my promise, and God defend but I should forsake the world as ye have done. For in the quest of the Sangreal I had forsaken the vanities of the world had not your lord been. And if I had done so at that time, with my heart, will, and thought, I had passed all the knights that were in the Sangreal except Sir Galahad, my son. And therefore, lady, sithen ye have taken you to perfection, I must needs take me to perfection, of right. For I take record of God, in you I have had mine earthly joy; and if I had found you now so disposed, I had cast me to have had you into mine own realm.

CHAPTER X

How Sir Launcelot came to the hermitage where the Archbishop of Canterbury was, and how he took the habit on him.

But sithen I find you thus disposed, I ensure you faithfully, I will ever take me to penance, and pray while my life lasteth, if I may find any hermit, either gray or white, that will receive me. Wherefore, madam, I pray you kiss me and never no more. Nay, said the queen, that shall I never do, but abstain you from such works: and they departed. But there was never so hard an hearted man but he would have wept to see the dolour that they made; for there was lamentation as they had been stung with spears; and many times they swooned, and the ladies bare the queen to her chamber.

And Sir Launcelot awoke, and went and took his horse, and rode all that day and all night in a forest, weeping. And at the last he was ware of an hermitage and a chapel stood betwixt two cliffs; and then he heard a little bell ring to mass, and thither he rode and alighted, and tied his horse to the gate, and heard mass. And he that sang mass was the Bishop of Canterbury. Both the Bishop and Sir Bedivere knew Sir Launcelot, and they spake together after mass. But when Sir Bedivere had told his tale all whole, Sir Launcelot's heart almost brast for sorrow, and Sir Launcelot threw his arms abroad, and said: Alas, who may trust this world. And then he kneeled down on his knee, and prayed the Bishop to shrive him and assoil him. And then he besought the Bishop that he might be his brother. Then the Bishop said: I will gladly; and there he put an habit upon Sir Launcelot, and there he served God day and night with prayers and fastings.

Thus the great host abode at Dover. And then Sir Lionel took fifteen lords with him, and rode to London to seek Sir Launcelot; and there Sir Lionel was slain and many of his lords. Then Sir Bors de Ganis made the great host for to go home again; and Sir Bors, Sir Ector de Maris, Sir Blamore, Sir Bleoberis, with more other of Sir Launcelot's kin, took on them to ride all England overthwart and endlong, to seek Sir Launcelot. So Sir Bors by fortune rode so long till he came to the same chapel where Sir Launcelot was; and so Sir Bors heard a little bell knell, that rang to mass; and there he alighted and heard mass. And when mass was done, the Bishop, Sir Launcelot, and Sir Bedivere, came to Sir Bors. And when Sir Bors saw Sir Launcelot in that manner clothing, then he prayed the Bishop that he might be in the same suit. And so there was an habit put upon him, and there he lived in prayers and fasting. And within half a year, there was come Sir Galihud, Sir Galihodin, Sir Blamore, Sir Bleoberis, Sir Villiars, Sir Clarras, and Sir Gahalantine. So all these seven noble knights there abode still. And when they saw Sir Launcelot had taken him to such perfection, they had no lust to depart, but took such an habit as he had.

Thus they endured in great penance six year; and then Sir Launcelot took the habit of priesthood of the Bishop, and a twelvemonth he sang mass. And there was none of these other knights but they read in books, and holp for to sing mass, and rang bells, and did bodily all manner of service. And so their horses went where they would, for they took no regard of no worldly riches. For when they saw Sir Launcelot endure such penance, in prayers, and fastings, they took no force what pain they endured, for to see the noblest knight of the world take such abstinence that he waxed full lean. And thus upon a night, there came a vision to Sir Launcelot, and charged him, in remission of his sins, to haste him unto Almesbury: And by then thou come there, thou shalt find Queen Guenever dead. And therefore take thy fellows with thee, and purvey them of an horse bier, and fetch thou the corpse of her, and bury her by her husband, the noble King Arthur. So this avision came to Sir Launcelot thrice in one night.

CHAPTER XI

How Sir Launcelot went with his seven fellows to Almesbury,
and found there Queen Guenever dead,
whom they brought to Glastonbury.

Then Sir Launcelot rose up or day, and told the hermit. It were well done, said the hermit, that ye made you ready, and that you disobey not the avision. Then Sir Launcelot took his eight fellows with him, and on foot they yede from Glastonbury to Almesbury, the which is little more than thirty mile. And thither they came within two days, for they were weak and feeble to go. And when Sir Launcelot was come to Almesbury within the nunnery, Queen Guenever died but half an hour afore. And the ladies told Sir Launcelot that Queen Guenever told them all or she passed, that Sir Launcelot had been priest near a twelvemonth, And hither he cometh as fast as he may to fetch my corpse; and beside my lord, King Arthur, he shall bury me. Wherefore the queen said in hearing of them all: I beseech Almighty God that I may never have power to see Sir Launcelot with my worldly eyen; and thus, said all the ladies, was ever her prayer these two days, till she was dead. Then Sir Launcelot saw her visage, but he wept not greatly, but sighed. And so he did all the observance of the service himself, both the dirige, and on the morn he sang mass. And there was ordained an horse bier; and so with an hundred torches ever brenning about the corpse of the queen, and ever Sir Launcelot with his eight fellows went about the horse bier, singing and reading many an holy orison, and frankincense upon the corpse incensed. Thus Sir Launcelot and his eight fellows went on foot from Almesbury unto Glastonbury.

And when they were come to the chapel and the hermitage, there she had a dirige, with great devotion. And on the morn the hermit that sometime was Bishop of Canterbury sang the mass of Requiem with great devotion. And Sir Launcelot was the first that offered, and then also his eight fellows. And then she was wrapped in cered cloth of Raines, from the top to the toe, in thirtyfold; and after she was put in a web of lead, and then in a coffin of marble. And when she was put in the earth Sir Launcelot swooned, and lay long still, while the hermit came and awaked him, and said: Ye be to blame, for ye displease God with such manner of sorrow-making. Truly, said Sir Launcelot, I trust I do not displease God, for He knoweth mine intent. For my sorrow was not, nor is not, for any rejoicing of sin, but my sorrow may never have end. For when I remember of her beauty, and of her noblesse, that was both with her king and with her, so when I saw his corpse and her corpse so lie together, truly mine heart would not serve to sustain my careful body. Also when I remember me how by my default, mine orgule and my pride, that they were both laid full low, that were peerless that ever was living of Christian people, wit you well, said Sir Launcelot, this remembered, of their kindness and mine unkindness, sank so to mine heart, that I might not sustain myself. So the French book maketh mention.

CHAPTER XII

*How Sir Launcelot began to sicken, and after died, whose
body was borne to Joyous Gard for to be buried.*

Then Sir Launcelot never after ate but little meat, ne drank, till he
was dead. For then he sickened more and more, and dried, and
dwined away. For the Bishop nor none of his fellows might not make
him to eat, and little he drank, that he was waxen by a cubit shorter
than he was, that the people could not know him. For evermore, day
and night, he prayed, but sometime he slumbered a broken sleep;
ever he was lying grovelling on the tomb of King Arthur and Queen
Guenever. And there was no comfort that the Bishop, nor Sir Bors,
nor none of his fellows, could make him, it availed not. So within six
weeks after, Sir Launcelot fell sick, and lay in his bed; and then he
sent for the Bishop that there was hermit, and all his true fellows.
Then Sir Launcelot said with dreary steven: Sir Bishop, I pray you
give to me all my rites that longeth to a Christian man. It shall not
need you, said the hermit and all his fellows, it is but heaviness of
your blood, ye shall be well mended by the grace of God to-morn.
My fair lords, said Sir Launcelot, wit you well my careful body will
into the earth, I have warning more than now I will say; therefore
give me my rites. So when he was houseled and anealed, and had all
that a Christian man ought to have, he prayed the Bishop that his
fellows might bear his body to Joyous Gard. Some men say it was
Alnwick, and some men say it was Bamborough. Howbeit, said Sir
Launcelot, me repenteth sore, but I made mine avow sometime, that
in Joyous Gard I would be buried. And because of breaking of mine
avow, I pray you all, lead me thither. Then there was weeping and
wringing of hands among his fellows.

So at a season of the night they all went to their beds, for they all
lay in one chamber. And so after midnight, against day, the Bishop
[that] then was hermit, as he lay in his bed asleep, he fell upon a great
laughter. And therewith all the fellowship awoke, and came to the
Bishop, and asked him what he ailed. Ah Jesu mercy, said the Bishop,
why did ye awake me? I was never in all my life so merry and so well

at ease. Wherefore? said Sir Bors. Truly, said the Bishop, here was Sir Launcelot with me with mo angels than ever I saw men in one day. And I saw the angels heave up Sir Launcelot unto heaven, and the gates of heaven opened against him. It is but dretching of swevens, said Sir Bors, for I doubt not Sir Launcelot aileth nothing but good. It may well be, said the Bishop; go ye to his bed, and then shall ye prove the sooth. So when Sir Bors and his fellows came to his bed they found him stark dead, and he lay as he had smiled, and the sweetest savour about him that ever they felt.

Then was there weeping and wringing of hands, and the greatest dole they made that ever made men. And on the morn the Bishop did his mass of Requiem; and after, the Bishop and all the nine knights put Sir Launcelot in the same horse bier that Queen Guenever was laid in to-fore that she was buried. And so the Bishop and they all together went with the body of Sir Launcelot daily, till they came to Joyous Gard; and ever they had an hundred torches brenning about him. And so within fifteen days they came to Joyous Gard. And there they laid his corpse in the body of the quire, and sang and read many psalters and prayers over him and about him. And ever his visage was laid open and naked, that all folks might behold him. For such was the custom in those days, that all men of worship should so lie with open visage till that they were buried. And right thus as they were at their service, there came Sir Ector de Maris, that had seven years sought all England, Scotland, and Wales, seeking his brother, Sir Launcelot.

CHAPTER XIII

How Sir Ector found Sir Launcelot his brother dead,
and how Constantine reigned next after Arthur;
and of the end of this book.

And when Sir Ector heard such noise and light in the quire of Joyous Gard, he alighted and put his horse from him, and came into the quire, and there he saw men sing and weep. And all they knew Sir Ector, but he knew not them. Then went Sir Bors unto Sir Ector, and told him how there lay his brother, Sir Launcelot, dead; and then

Sir Ector threw his shield, sword, and helm from him. And when he beheld Sir Launcelot's visage, he fell down in a swoon. And when he waked it were hard any tongue to tell the doleful complaints that he made for his brother. Ah Launcelot, he said, thou were head of all Christian knights, and now I dare say, said Sir Ector, thou Sir Launcelot, there thou liest, that thou were never matched of earthly knight's hand. And thou were the courteoust knight that ever bare shield. And thou were the truest friend to thy lover that ever bestrad horse. And thou were the truest lover of a sinful man that ever loved woman. And thou were the kindest man that ever struck with sword. And thou were the goodliest person that ever came among press of knights. And thou was the meekest man and the gentlest that ever ate in hall among ladies. And thou were the sternest knight to thy mortal foe that ever put spear in the rest. Then there was weeping and dolour out of measure.

Thus they kept Sir Launcelot's corpse aloft fifteen days, and then they buried it with great devotion. And then at leisure they went all with the Bishop of Canterbury to his hermitage, and there they were together more than a month. Then Sir Constantine, that was Sir Cador's son of Cornwall, was chosen king of England. And he was a full noble knight, and worshipfully he ruled this realm. And then this King Constantine sent for the Bishop of Canterbury, for he heard say where he was. And so he was restored unto his Bishopric, and left that hermitage. And Sir Bedivere was there ever still hermit to his life's end. Then Sir Bors de Ganis, Sir Ector de Maris, Sir Gahalantine, Sir Galihud, Sir Galihodin, Sir Blamore, Sir Bleoberis, Sir Villiars le Valiant, Sir Clarrus of Clermont, all these knights drew them to their countries. Howbeit King Constantine would have had them with him, but they would not abide in this realm. And there they all lived in their countries as holy men. And some English books make mention that they went never out of England after the death of Sir Launcelot, but that was but favour of makers. For the French book maketh mention, and is authorised, that Sir Bors, Sir Ector, Sir Blamore, and Sir Bleoberis, went into the Holy Land thereas Jesu Christ was quick and dead, and anon as they had stablished their lands. For the book saith, so Sir Launcelot commanded them for to do, or ever he passed out of this world. And these four knights did many battles upon the miscreants or Turks. And there they died upon a Good Friday for God's sake.

Here is the end of the book of King Arthur, and of his
noble knights of the Round Table, that when they were
whole together there was ever an hundred and forty.
And here is the end of the death of Arthur. I pray you
all, gentlemen and gentlewomen that readeth this book
of Arthur and his knights, from the beginning to the
ending, pray for me while I am alive, that God send me
good deliverance, and when I am dead, I pray you all
pray for my soul. For this book was ended the ninth
year of the reign of King Edward the Fourth,
by Sir Thomas Maleore, knight, as Jesu help him for
his great might, as he is the servant of
Jesu both day and night.

Thus endeth this noble and joyous book entitled
Le Morte Darthur. Notwithstanding it treateth of the
birth, life, and acts of the said King Arthur, of his
noble knights of the Round Table, their marvellous
enquests and adventures, the achieving of the Sangreal,
and in the end the dolourous death and departing out of
this world of them all. Which book was reduced into
English by Sir Thomas Malory, knight, as afore is
said, and by me divided into twenty-one books,
chaptered and enprinted, and finished in
the abbey, Westminster, the last day of July
the year of our Lord mcccclxxxv.

Caxton me fieri fecit.

GLOSSARY

Abashed, abased, lowered
Abashed, astounded
Abate, depress, calm
Abought, paid for
Abraid, started up
Accompted, counted
Accorded, agreed
Accordment, agreement
Acquit, repay
Actually, actively
Adoubted, afraid
Advision, vision
Afeard, afraid
Afterdeal, disadvantage
Againsay, retract
Aknown, known, informed of
Aligement, alleviation
Allegeance, alleviation
Allow, approve
Almeries, chests
Alther, *gen. pl.,* of all
Amounted, mounted
Anealed, anointed
Anguishly, in pain
Anon, at once
Apaid, contented, repaid
Apair, weaken
Apparelled, fitted up
Appeach, impeach
Appealed, challenged, accused

Appertices, displays
Araged, enraged, confused
Araised, raised
Arase, obliterate
Areared, reared
Armyvestal, martial
Array, plight, state of affairs
Arrayed, situated
Arretted, reckoned, counted
Arson, saddle-bow
Askance, casually
Aspies, enquiries
Assoiled, absolved
Assotted, infatuated
Assummon, summon
Astonied, amazed, stunned
At, of, by
At-after, after
Attaint, overcome
Aumbries, chests
Avail (at), at an advantage
Avaled, lowered
Avaunt, boast
Aventred, couched
Avised, be advised, take thought
Avision, vision
Avoid, quit
Avoided, got clear off
Avow, vow
Await of (in), in watch for

Awayward, away
Awk, sideways

Bachelors, probationers for
  knighthood
Bain, bath
Barbican, gate-tower
Barget, little ship
Battle, division of an army
Bawdy, dirty
Beams, trumpets
Be-closed, enclosed
Become, *pp.*, befallen, gone to
Bedashed, splashed
Behests, promises
Behight, promised
Beholden (beholding) to, obliged
  to
Behote, promise
Benome, deprived of, taken away
  from
Besants, gold coins
Beseek, beseech
Beseen, appointed, arrayed
Beskift, shove off
Bestead, beset
Betaken, entrusted
Betaught, entrusted, recommended
Betid, happened
Betook, committed, entrusted
Bevered, quivered
Board, *sb.*, deck
Bobaunce, boasting, pride
Boishe, bush, branch of a tree
Boistous, rough
Bole, trunk of a tree
Boot, remedy
Borrow out, redeem
Borrows, pledges

Bote, remedy
Bound, ready
Bourded, jested
Bourder, jester
Braced, embraced
Brachet, little hound
Braide, quick movement
Brast, burst, break
Breaths, breathing holes
Brenning, burning
Brent, burnt
Brief, shorten
Brim, fierce, furious
Brised, broke
Broached, pierced
Broaches, spits
Brunt, blow, attack
Bur, hand-guard of a spear
Burble, bubble
Burbling, bubbling
Burgenetts, buds, blossoms
Bushment, ambush
By and by, immediately
Bywaryed, expended, bestowed

Canel bone, collar bone
Cankered, inveterate
Cantel, slice, strip
Careful, sorrowful, full of troubles
Cast (of bread), loaves baked at the
  same time
Cast, *ref. v.*, propose
Cedle, schedule, note
Cere, wax over, embalm
Certes, certainly
Chafe, heat, decompose;
  chafed, heated
Chaflet, platform, scaffold
Champaign, open country

Chariot (Fr. *charette*), cart

Cheer, countenance, entertainment

Chierté, dearness

Child, shield

Clatter, talk confusedly

Cleight, clutched

Cleped, called

Clipping, embracing

Cog, small boat

Cognisance, badge, mark of
distinction

Coif, head-piece

Comfort, strengthen, help

Cominal, common

Complished, complete

Con, know, be able to;
con thank, be grateful

Conserve, preserve

Conversant, abiding in

Cording, agreement

Coronal, circlet

Cost, side

Costed, kept up with

Couched, lay

Courage, encourage

Courtelage, courtyard

Covert, sheltered

Covetise, covetousness

Covin, deceit

Cream, oil

Credence, faith

Croup, crupper

Curteist, most courteous

Daffish, foolish

Danger (in), under obligation to, in
the power of

Dawed, revived

Deadly, mortal, human,

Deal, part, portion

Debate, quarrel, strife

Debonair, courteous

Deceivable, deceitful

Defaded, faded

Default, fault

Defend, forbid;
defended, forbade

Defoiled, trodden down, fouled,
deflowered

Degree (win the), rank, superiority

Delibered, determined

Deliverly, adroitly

Departed, divided

Departition, departure

Dere, harm

Descrive, describe

Despoiled, stripped

Detrenched, cut to pieces

Devised, looked carefully at

Devoir, duty, service

Did off, doffed

Dight, prepared

Dindled, trembled

Dirige, dirge

Disadventure, misfortune

Discover, reveal

Disherited, disinherited

Disparpled, scattered

Dispenses, expenses

Disperplyd, scattered

Dispoiled, stripped

Distained, sullied, dishonoured

Disworship, shame

Dole, gift of alms

Dole, sorrow

Domineth, dominates, rules

Don, gift

Doted, foolish

Doubted, redoubtable

Draughts, privities, secret interviews, recesses

Drenched, drowned

Dress, make ready

Dressed up, raised

Dretched, troubled in sleep

Dretching, being troubled in sleep

Dromounds, war vessels

Dure, endure, last

Duresse, bondage, hardship

Dwined, dwindled

Eased, entertained

Eft, after, again

Eftures, passages

Embattled, ranged for battle

Embushed, concealed in the woods

Eme, uncle

Empoison, poison

Emprised, undertook

Enbraid

Enchafe, heat; *enchafed*, heated

Enchieve, achieve

Endlong, alongside of

Enewed, painted

Enforce, constrain

Engine, device

Enow, enough

Enquest, enterprise

Ensured, assured

Entermete, intermeddle

Errant, wandering

Estates, ranks

Estures, kitchens

Even hand, at an equality

Evenlong, along

Everych, each, every one

Fain, glad, gladly

Faiter, vagabond

Fare, *sb.*, ado, commotion

Faren, *pp.*, treated

Faute, *v.*, lack; *fauted*, lacked

Fealty, oath of fidelity

Fear, frighten

Felonously, fiercely, violently

Feute, trace, track

Feuter, set in rest, couch

Feutred, set in socket

Fiaunce, affiance, promise

Flang, flung

Flatling, prostrate

Fleet, float

Flemed, put to flight

Flittered, fluttered

Foiled, defeated, shamed

Foined, thrust

Foining, thrusting

Foins, thrusts

Foot-hot, hastily

For-bled, spent with bleeding

Force (no), no concern

Fordeal, advantage

Fordo, destroy

Forecast, preconcerted plot

For-fared, worsted

Forfend, forbid

Forfoughten, weary with fighting

Forhewn, hewn to pieces

Forjousted, tired with jousting

Forthinketh, repents

Fortuned, happened

Forward, vanguard

Forwounded, sorely wounded

Free, noble

Froward, away from

Gad, wedge or spike of iron

Gainest, readiest

Gar, cause

Gart, compelled

Gentily, like a gentleman

Gerfalcon, a fine hawk

Germane, closely allied

Gest, deed, story

Gisarm, halberd, battle-axe

Glaive, sword

Glasting, barking

Glatisant, barking, yelping

Gobbets, lumps

Grame, anger, wrath

Graithed, made ready

Gree, degree, superiority

Greed, *pp.*, pleased, content

Greese, grease

Greses, steps

Grimly, ugly

Grovelling, on his face

Guerdonless, without reward

Guise, fashion

Habergeon, hauberk with leggings attached

Hair, a hair-shirt

Hale and how, a sailor's cry

Halp, helped

Halsed, embraced

Halsing, embracing

Handfast, betrothed

Handle, get their hands on

Handsel, earnest-money, payment

Hangers, testicles

Harbingers, messengers sent to prepare lodgings

Harness, armour

Hart of greese, fat deer

Hauberk, coat of mail

Haunt, resort to, use frequently

Haut, high, noble

Hauteyn, haughty

Heavy, sad

Hete, command

Hide, skin

Hied, hurried

High (on), aloud

Higher hand, the uppermost

Hight, called

Hilled, covered, concealed

Holden, held

Holp, helped

Holts, woods

Hough-bone, back part of knee-joint

Houseled, given the Eucharist

Hoved, hovered, waited about

Hurled, dashed, staggered

Hurtle, dash

Incontinent, forthwith

Ind, dark blue

Infellowship, join in fellowship

In like, alike

Inly, completely, thoroughly

Intermit, interpose

Japer, jester

Japes, jests

Jesseraunt, a short cuirass

Keep, *sb.*, care

Keep, *v.*, care, reck

Kemps, champions

Kind, nature

Kindly, natural

Knights parters, marshals

Know, acknowledge

Knowledging, acknowledgment, confession

Lain, conceal

Langering, sauntering

Lapped, took in her lap

Large, generous

Largeness, liberality

Laton, latten, brass

Laund, waste plain

Layne, conceal

Lazar-cot, leper-house

Learn, teach

Lears, cheeks

Leaved, leafy

Lecher, fornicator

Leech, physician

Leman, lover

Lesses les aler, laisser les aller

Let, caused to

Let, hinder

Lewdest, most ignorant

Licours, lecherous

Lief, dear

Liefer, more gladly

Lieve, believe

Limb-meal, limb from limb

List, desire, pleasure

Lithe, joint

Longing unto, belonging to

Long on (upon), because of

Loos, praise

Lotless, without a share

Loveday, day for settling disputes

Loving, praising

Lunes, leashes, strings

Lusk, lubber

Lusts, inclinations

Maims, wounds

Makeless, matchless

Makers, authors, poets

Mal-ease, discomfort

Mal engine, evil design

Mal-fortune, ill-luck, mishap

Marches, borders

Mass-penny, offering at mass for the dead

Mastery, feat of strength

Matchecold, machicolated, with holes for defence

Maugre, *sb. and prep.*, despite

Measle, disease

Medled, mingled

Medley, melée, general encounter

Meeked, abased

Meiny, retinue

Mickle, much

Minever, ermine

Mischieved, hurt

Mischievous, painful

Miscomfort, discomfort

Miscreature, unbeliever

Missay, revile

Mister, need

Mo, more

More and less, rich and poor

Mote, may, might, must

Motes, notes on a horn

Mountenance, amount of, extent

Much, great

Myster, *see* Mister

Naked, unarmed

Namely, especially

Ne, nor

Near-hand, nearly

Needly, needs, on your own compulsion

Nere, were (it) not

Nesh, soft, tender

Nigh-hand, nearly

Nill, will not

Nilt, will not

Nis (ne is), is not

Nist (ne wist), knew not

Noblesse, nobleness

Nobley, nobility, splendour

Noised, reported

Nold, would not

Noseling, on his nose

Not for then, nevertheless

Notoyrly, notoriously

Noyous, hurtful

Obeissance, obedience

Or, before

Orgule, haughtiness

Orgulist, haughtiest

Orgulité, pride, arrogance

Orgulous, proud

Other, or

Ouches, jewels

Ought, owned

Outcept, except

Outher, or

Out-taken, except

Over-evening, last night

Overget, overtake

Overhylled, covered

Over-led, domineered over

Overlong, the length of

Overslip, v., pass

Overthwart, adj., cross

Overthwart, sb., mischance

Overthwart and endlong, by the
    breadth and length, from side to
    side and end to end

Painture, painting

Paitrelles, breastplate of a horse

Paltocks, short coats

Parage, descent

Pareil, like

Passing, surpassingly

Paynim, pagan

Pensel, pennon

Perclos, partition

Perdy, par Dieu

Perigot, falcon

Perish, destroy

Peron, tombstone

Pight, pitched

Pike, steal away

Piked, stole

Pillers, plunderers

Pilling, plundering

Pleasaunce, pleasure

Plenour, complete

Plump, sb., cluster

Pointling, aiming

Pont, bridge

Port, gate

Posseded, possessed

Potestate, governor

Precessours, predecessors

Press, throng

Pretendeth, belongs to

Pricker, hard rider

Pricking, spurring

Prime, a.m.

Prise, capture

Puissance, power

Purfle, trimming

Purfled, embroidered

Purvey, provide

Quarrels, arrowheads

Questing, barking

Quick, alive

Quit, repaid;
  acquitted, behaved

Quite, re[pay

Raced (rased), tore

Rack (of bulls), herd

Raines, a town in Brittany famous
  for its cloth

Ramping, raging

Range, rank, station

Ransacked, searched

Rashed, fell headlong

Rashing, rushing

Rasing, rushing

Rasure, erasure, scraping away

Raundon, impetuosity

Rear, raise

Rechate, note of recall

Recomforted, comforted, cheered

Recounter, rencontre, encounter

Recover, rescue

Rede, advise;
  sb., counsel

Redounded, glanced back

Religion, religious order

Reneye, deny

Report, refer

Resemblaunt, semblance

Retrayed, drew back

Rightwise, rightly

Rivage, shore

Romed, roared

Roted, practised

Rought, recked, cared

Rove, cleft

Rownsepyk, a branch

Sacring, consecrating

Sad, serious

Sadly, heartily, earnestly

Salle, room

Samite, silk stuff with gold or silver
  threads

Sangreal, Holy Grail

Sarps, girdles

Saw, proverb

Scathes, harms, hurts

Scripture, writing

Search, probe wounds

Selar, canopy

Semblable, like

Semblant, semblance

Sendal, fine cloth

Sennight, week

Servage, slavery

Sewe, follow

Sewer, officer who set on dishes
  and tasted them

Shaft-mon, handbreadth

Shaw, thicket

Sheef, thrust

Sheer-Thursday, Thursday in Holy
  Week

Shend, harm

Shend, put to shame or confusion

Shende, see Shend

Shenship, disgrace

Shent, undone, blamed, harmed

Shour, attack

Shrew, rascal

Shrewd, knavish

Sib, akin to

Sideling, sideways

Siege, seat

Signified, likened

Siker, sure

Sikerness, assurance

Sith, since

Sithen, afterwards, since

Skift, change, changed

Slade, valley

Slake, glen

Sodden, boiled

Soil (to go to), hunting term for taking the water

Sonds, messages

Sort, company

Sperd, bolted

Spere, ask, inquire

Sperhawk, sparrowhawk

Sprent, sprinkled

Stale, station

Stark, thoroughly

Stead, place

Stert, started, rose quickly

Steven, appointment; *steven set*, appointment made

Steven, voice

Stigh, path

Stilly, silently

Stint, cut short, cease, stop

Stint, fixed revenue

Stonied, astonished; became confused

Stour, battle

Strain, race, descent

Strait, narrow

Straked, blew a horn

Strength stand up for, compel

Sue, pursue

Surcingles, saddle girths

Swallow, gulf

Swang, swung

Sweven, dream

Swough, sound of wind

Talent, desire

Tallages, taxes

Tallies, taxes

Tamed, crushed

Tatches, qualities

Taught, showed the way

Tene, sorrow

Term, period of time

Thilk, that same

Tho, then

Thrang, pushed

Thrulled, pushed

Till, to

To-brast, burst

To-fore, before

To-morn, tomorrow

Took, gave

To-rove, broke up

To-shivered, broken to pieces

Traced, advanced and retreated

Trains, devices, wiles

Trasing, pressing forward

Travers (met at), came across

Traverse, slantwise

Traversed, moved sideways

Tray, grief

Treatise, treaty

Tree, timber

Trenchant, cutting, sharp

Trest, hunting term

Truage, tribute

Trussed, packed

Trussed, picked up

Ubblie, wafer, Host

Umbecast, cast

Umberere, the part of the helmet which shaded the eyes

Umbre, shade

Unavised, thoughtlessly

Uncouth, strange

Underne, a.m. to noon

Ungoodly, rudely

Unhappy, unlucky

Unhilled, uncovered

Unnethe, scarcely

Unsicker, unstable

Unwimpled, uncovered

Unwrast, untwisted, unbound

Upright, flat on the back

Up-so-down, upside down

Ure, usage

Utas, octave of a festival

Utterance, uttermost

Varlet, servant

Venery, hunting

Ventails, breathing holes

Villein, man of low birth

Visors, the perforated parts of helmets

Voided, slipped away from

Wagging, shaking

Wait, watch

Wallop, gallop

Wanhope, despair

Wap, ripple

Ware, aware

Warison, reward

Warn, forbid, refuse

Weeds, garments

Weltered, rolled about

Wend, thought

Wer-wolf, a man turned into a wolf by magic

Where, whereas

Wide-where, over wide space

Wield, possess, have power over

Wield himself, come to himself

Wight, brave, strong

Wightly, swiftly

Wildsome, desolate

Wimpled, with the head covered

Win, make way

Wite, blame

Within-forth, on the inside

Without-forth, on the outside

Wittiest, cleverest

Wittily, cleverly

Witting, knowledge

Wold or nold, would or would not

Wonder, *adj.*, wondrous

Wonder, *adv.*, wondrously

Wonderly, wonderfully

Wood, mad

Woodness, madness

Wood shaw, thicket of the wood

Worship, honour

Worshipped, caused to be honoured

Worts, roots

Wot, know

Wrack, destruction

Wroken, wreaked

Wrothe, twisted

Yede, ran, went

Yelden, yielded

Yerde, stick, stem

Yode, went

Yolden, yielded

Y-wis, certainly

INDEX